Blind

Kisscut

Karin Slaughter

arrow books

This edition published by Arrow Books in 2007

Copyright © Karin Slaughter 2007

Karin Slaughter has asserted her right under the
Copyright, Designs and Patents Act, 1988 to be identified
as the author of this work

Blindsighted copyright © Karin Slaughter 2001
Kisscut © Karin Slaughter 2002

Arrow Books
The Random House Group Limited
20 Vauxhall Bridge Road, London SW1V 2SA

www.randomhouse.co.uk

Addresses for companies within The Random House Group Limited
can be found at:
www.randomhouse.co.uk/offices.htm

The Random House Group Limited Reg. No. 954009

A CIP catalogue record for this book
is available from the British Library

ISBN 9780099521891

The Random House Group Limited makes every effort to ensure
that the papers used in its books are made from trees that
have been legally sourced from well-managed and credibly
certified forests. Our paper procurement policy can be found at:
www.randomhouse.co.uk/paper.htm

Typeset by Deltatype Ltd, Birkenhead, Merseyside

Printed and bound in Great Britain by
Cox & Wyman Ltd, Reading, Berkshire

Karin Slaughter grew up in a small south Georgia town and has been writing short stories and novels since she was a child. She is also the author of the bestselling novels *Kisscut*, *A Faint Cold Fear*, *Indelible*, *Faithless* and *Triptych*, a stand-alone novel set in the same world as the Grant County series. Karin also contributed to and edited *Like a Charm*. Her forthcoming novel is *Skin Privilege*.

'Don't read this alone. Don't read this after dark. But do read it'   *Mirror*

'This gripping debut novel, filled with unremittingly graphic forensic details, is likely to have Patricia Cornwell and Kathy Reichs glancing nervously in their rearview mirrors because rookie Karin Slaughter is off the starting grid as quickly as Michael Schumacher and is closing on them fast'   *Irish Independent*

'Chilling but thrilling'   *OK!*

'Wildly readable ... [Slaughter] has been compared to Thomas Harris and Patricia Cornwell, and for once the hype is justified ... deftly crafted, damnably suspenseful and, in the end, deadly serious. Slaughter's plotting is brilliant, her suspense relentless'   *Washington Post*

'Slaughter . . . brings the story to a shattering climax'   *Sunday Telegraph*

'Pacy and intriguing . . . Karin Slaughter builds up the urgency to fever pitch'   *Punch*

'*Blindsighted* is a debut novel of rare quality that grips like a vice from the first page. It's hard to believe this is Karin Slaughter's first outing, so mature is the prose, so taut the suspense, so extreme the engagement with the reader. Against the backdrop of a small Southern town, a terrible drama is played out that will affect Slaughter's readers as much as it affects her characters. A lot of writers are going to read this and weep'
Val McDermid, author of *Killing the Shadows*

'Unsparing, exciting, genuinely alarming . . . excellent handling of densely woven plot, rich in interactions, well characterised and as subtle as it is shrewd . . . A formidable debut'   *Literary Review*

'An extraordinary debut . . . Slaughter has created a ferociously taut and terrifying story which is, at the same time, compassionate and real. I defy anyone to read it in more than three sittings'
Denise Mina, author of *Exile*

For my daddy, who taught me to love the South, and for Billie Bennett, who encouraged me to write about it

Blindsighted

MONDAY

ONE

Sara Linton leaned back in her chair, mumbling a soft 'Yes, Mama' into the telephone. She wondered briefly if there would ever come a point in time when she would be too old to be taken over her mother's knee.

'Yes, Mama,' Sara repeated, tapping her pen on the desk. She felt heat coming off her cheeks, and an overwhelming sense of embarrassment took hold.

A soft knock came at the office door, followed by a tentative 'Dr. Linton?'

Sara suppressed her relief. 'I need to go,' she said to her mother, who shot off one last admonishment before hanging up the phone.

Nelly Morgan slid open the door, giving Sara a hard look. As office manager for the Heartsdale Children's Clinic, Nelly was the closest thing Sara had to a secretary. Nelly had been running the place for as long as Sara could remember, even as far back as when Sara was herself a patient here.

Nelly said, 'Your cheeks are on fire.'

'I just got yelled at by my mother.'

Nelly raised an eyebrow. 'I assume with good reason.'

'Well,' Sara said, hoping that would end it.

'The labs on Jimmy Powell came in,' Nelly said, still eyeing Sara. 'And the mail,' she added, dropping a stack of letters on top of the inbasket. The plastic bowed under the added weight.

Sara sighed as she read over the fax. On a good day, she diagnosed earaches and sore throats. Today, she would have to tell the parents of a twelve-year-old boy that he had acute myeloblastic leukemia.

'Not good,' Nelly guessed. She had worked at the clinic long enough to know how to read a lab report.

'No,' Sara agreed, rubbing her eyes. 'Not good at all.' She sat back in her chair, asking, 'The Powells are at Disney World, right?'

'For his birthday,' Nelly said. 'They should be back tonight.'

Sara felt a sadness come over her. She had never gotten used to delivering this kind of news.

Nelly offered, 'I can schedule them for first thing in the morning.'

'Thanks,' Sara answered, tucking the report into Jimmy Powell's chart. She glanced at the clock on the wall as she did this and let out an audible gasp. 'Is that right?' she asked, checking the time against her watch. 'I was supposed to meet Tessa at lunch fifteen minutes ago.'

Nelly checked her own watch. 'This late in the day? It's closer to suppertime.'

'It was the only time I could make it,' Sara said, gathering charts together. She bumped the in-box and papers fell onto the floor in a heap, cracking the plastic tray.

'Crap,' Sara hissed.

Nelly started to help, but Sara stopped her. Aside from the fact that Sara did not like other people cleaning up her messes, if Nelly somehow managed to get down on her knees, it was doubtful she would be able to get back up without considerable assistance.

4

'I've got it,' Sara told her, scooping up the whole pile and dropping it on her desk. 'Was there anything else?'

Nelly flashed a smile. 'Chief Tolliver's holding on line three.'

Sara sat back on her heels, a feeling of dread washing over her. She did double duty as the town's pediatrician and coroner. Jeffrey Tolliver, her ex-husband, was the chief of police. There were only two reasons for him to be calling Sara in the middle of the day, neither of them particularly pleasant.

Sara stood and picked up the phone, giving him the benefit of the doubt. 'Somebody better be dead.'

Jeffrey's voice was garbled, and she assumed he was using his cellular phone. 'Sorry to disappoint you,' he said, then, 'I've been on hold for ten minutes. What if this had been an emergency?'

Sara started shoving papers into her briefcase. It was an unwritten clinic policy to make Jeffrey jump through hoops of fire before he could speak to Sara on the telephone. She was actually surprised that Nelly remembered to tell Sara he was on the phone.

She glanced at the door, mumbling, 'I knew I should've just left.'

'What?' he asked, his voice echoing slightly on the cellular.

'I said you always send someone if it's an emergency,' she lied. 'Where are you?'

'At the college,' he answered. 'I'm waiting for the deputy dogs.'

He was using their term for the campus security at Grant Tech, the state university at the center of town.

She asked, 'What is it?'

'I just wanted to see how you were doing.'

'Fine,' she snapped, pulling the papers back out of her briefcase, wondering why she had put them there in the first place. She flipped through some charts, shoving them into the side pocket.

She said, 'I'm late for lunch with Tess. What did you need?'

He seemed taken aback by her curt tone. 'You just looked distracted yesterday,' he said. 'In church.'

'I wasn't distracted,' she mumbled, flipping through the mail. She stopped at the sight of a postcard, her whole body going rigid. The front of the card showed a picture of Emory University in Atlanta, Sara's alma mater. Neatly typed on the back beside her address at the children's clinic were the words, 'Why hast thou forsaken me?'

'Sara?'

A cold sweat came over her. 'I need to go.'

'Sara, I –'

She hung up the phone before Jeffrey could finish his sentence, shoving three more charts into her briefcase along with the postcard. She slipped out the side door without anyone seeing her.

Sunlight beamed down on Sara as she walked into the street. There was a chill in the air that had not been there this morning, and the dark clouds promised rain later on tonight.

A red Thunderbird passed, a small arm hanging out the window.

'Hey, Dr. Linton,' a child called.

Sara waved, calling 'Hey' back as she crossed the street. Sara switched the briefcase from one hand to the other as she cut across the lawn in front of the college. She took a right onto the sidewalk, heading toward Main Street, and was at the diner in less than five minutes.

Tessa was sitting in a booth on the far wall of the

empty diner, eating a hamburger. She did not look pleased.

'Sorry I'm late,' Sara offered, walking toward her sister. She tried a smile, but Tessa did not respond in kind.

'You said two. It's nearly two-thirty.'

'I had paperwork,' Sara explained, tucking her briefcase into the booth. Tessa was a plumber, like their father. While clogged drains were no laughing matter, very seldom did Linton and Daughters get the kind of emergency phone calls that Sara did on a daily basis. Her family could not grasp what a busy day was like for Sara and were constantly irritated by her lateness.

'I called the morgue at two,' Tessa informed her, nibbling a french fry. 'You weren't there.'

Sara sat down with a groan, running her fingers through her hair. 'I dropped back by the clinic and Mama called and the time got away from me.' She stopped, saying what she always said. 'I'm sorry. I should have called.' When Tessa did not respond, Sara continued, 'You can keep being mad at me for the rest of lunch or you can drop it and I'll buy you a slice of chocolate cream pie.'

'Red velvet,' Tessa countered.

'Deal,' Sara returned, feeling an inordinate sense of relief. It was bad enough having her mother mad at her.

'Speaking of calls,' Tessa began, and Sara knew where she was going even before she asked the question. 'Hear from Jeffrey?'

Sara raised up, tucking her hand into her front pocket. She pulled out two five-dollar bills. 'He called before I left the clinic.'

Tessa barked a laugh that filled the restaurant. 'What did he say?'

7

'I cut him off before he could say anything,' Sara answered, handing her sister the money.

Tessa tucked the fives into the back pocket of her blue jeans. 'So, Mama called? She was pretty pissed at you.'

'I'm pretty pissed at me, too,' Sara said. After being divorced for two years, she still could not let go of her ex-husband. Sara vacillated between hating Jeffrey Tolliver and hating herself because of this. She wanted just one day to go by without thinking about him, without having him in her life. Yesterday, much like today, had not been that day.

Easter Sunday was important to her mother. While Sara was not particularly religious, putting on panty hose one Sunday out of the year was a small price to pay for Cathy Linton's happiness. Sara had not planned on Jeffrey being at church. She had caught him out of the corner of her eye just after the first hymn. He was sitting three rows behind and to the right of her, and they seemed to notice each other at the same time. Sara had forced herself to look away first.

Sitting there in church, staring at the preacher without hearing a word the man was saying, Sara had felt Jeffrey's gaze on the back of her neck. There was a heat from the intensity of his stare that caused a warm flush to come over her. Despite the fact that she was sitting in church with her mother on one side of her and Tessa and her father on the other, Sara had felt her body responding to the look Jeffrey had given her. There was something about this time of year that turned her into a completely different person.

She was actually fidgeting in her seat, thinking about Jeffrey touching her, the way his hands felt on her skin, when Cathy Linton jabbed her elbow into Sara's ribs. Her mother's expression said she knew exactly what was going through Sara's mind at that moment and did

8

not like it one bit. Cathy had crossed her arms angrily, her posture indicating she was resigning herself to the fact that Sara would go to hell for thinking about sex at the Primitive Baptist on Easter Sunday.

There was a prayer, then another hymn. After what seemed like an appropriate amount of time, Sara glanced over her shoulder to find Jeffrey again, only to see him with his head bent down to his chest as he slept. This was the problem with Jeffrey Tolliver, the idea of him was much better than the reality.

Tessa tapped her fingers on the table for Sara's attention. 'Sara?'

Sara put her hand to her chest, conscious that her heart was pounding the same way it had yesterday morning in church. 'What?'

Tessa gave her a knowing look, but thankfully did not pursue it. 'What did Jeb say?'

'What do you mean?'

'I saw you talking to him after the service,' Tessa said. 'What did he say?'

Sara debated whether or not to lie. Finally, she answered, 'He asked me out for lunch today, but I told him I was seeing you.'

'You could've cancelled.'

Sara shrugged. 'We're going out Wednesday night.'

Tessa did everything but clap her hands together.

'God,' Sara groaned. 'What was I thinking?'

'Not about Jeffrey for a change,' Tessa answered. 'Right?'

Sara took the menu from behind the napkin holder, though she hardly needed to look at it. She or some member of her family had eaten at the Grant Filling Station at least once a week since Sara was three years old, and the only change to the menu in all that time had been when Pete Wayne, the owner, had added peanut brittle to the dessert menu in honor of then president Jimmy Carter.

Tessa reached across the table, gently pushing down the menu. 'You okay?'

'It's that time of year again,' Sara said, rummaging around in her briefcase. She found the postcard and held it up.

Tessa did not take the card, so Sara read aloud from the back, 'Why hast thou forsaken me?' She put the card down on the table between them, waiting for Tessa's response.

'From the Bible?' Tessa asked, though surely she knew.

Sara looked out the window, trying to compose herself. Suddenly, she stood up from the table, saying, 'I need to go wash my hands.'

'Sara?'

She waved off Tessa's concern, walking to the back of the diner, trying to hold herself together until she reached the bathroom. The door to the women's room had stuck in the frame since the beginning of time, so Sara gave the handle a hard yank. Inside, the small black-and-white tiled bathroom was cool and almost comforting. She leaned back against the wall, hands to her face, trying to wipe out the last few hours of her day. Jimmy Powell's lab results still haunted her. Twelve years ago, while working her medical internship at Atlanta's Grady Hospital, Sara had grown familiar with, if not accustomed to, death. Grady had the best ER in the Southeast, and Sara had seen her share of difficult traumas, from a kid who had swallowed a pack of razor blades to a teenage girl who had been given a clothes hanger abortion. These were horrible cases, but not altogether unexpected in such a large city.

Cases like Jimmy Powell's coming through the children's clinic hit Sara with the force of a wrecking ball. This would be one of the rare cases when Sara's two jobs would converge. Jimmy Powell, who liked to watch college basketball and held one of the largest collections of Hot Wheels Sara had personally ever seen, would more than likely be dead within the next year.

Sara clipped her hair back into a loose ponytail as she waited for the sink to fill with cold water. She leaned over the sink, pausing at the sickly sweet smell coming from the basin. Pete had probably dumped vinegar down the drain to keep it from smelling sour. It was an old plumber's trick, but Sara hated the smell of vinegar.

She held her breath as she leaned back over, splashing her face with water, trying to wake up. A glance back at the mirror showed nothing had improved, but a wet spot from the water was just below the neckline of her shirt.

'Great,' Sara mumbled.

She dried her hands on her pants as she walked toward the stalls. After seeing the contents of the toilet, she moved to the next stall, the handicap stall, and opened the door.

'Oh,' Sara breathed, stepping back quickly, only stopping when the sink basin pressed against the back of her legs. She put her hands behind her, bracing herself on the counter. A metallic taste came to her mouth, and Sara forced herself to take in gulps of air so that she wouldn't pass out. She dropped her head down, closing her eyes, counting out a full five seconds before she looked up again.

Sibyl Adams, a professor at the college, sat on the toilet. Her head was tilted back against the tiled wall, her eyes closed. Her pants were pulled down around her ankles, legs splayed wide open. She had been stabbed in the abdomen. Blood filled the toilet between her legs, dripping onto the tiled floor.

Sara forced herself to move into the stall, crouching in front of the young woman. Sibyl's shirt was pulled up, and Sara could see a large vertical cut down her abdomen, bisecting her navel and stopping at the pubic bone. Another cut, much deeper, slashed horizontally under her breasts. This was the source of most of the blood, and it still dripped in a steady stream down the body. Sara put her hand to the wound, trying to halt the bleeding, but blood seeped between her fingers as if she were squeezing a sponge.

Sara wiped her hands on the front of her shirt, then tilted Sibyl's head forward. A small moan escaped from the woman's lips, but Sara could not tell if this was a simple release of air from a corpse or the plea of a living woman. 'Sibyl?' Sara whispered, barely able to manage the word. Fear sat in the back of her throat like a summer cold.

'Sibyl?' she repeated, using her thumb to press open Sibyl's eyelid. The woman's skin was hot to the touch, as if she had been out in the sun too long. A large bruise covered the right side of her face. Sara could see the impression of a fist under the eye. Bone moved under Sara's hand when she touched the bruise, clicking like two marbles rubbing together.

Sara's hand shook as she pressed her fingers against Sibyl's carotid artery. A fluttering rose against her fingertips, but Sara wasn't sure if it was the tremor in her own hands or life that she was feeling. Sara closed her eyes, concentrating, trying to separate the two sensations.

Without warning, the body jerked violently, pitching forward and slamming Sara onto the floor. Blood spread out around both of them, and Sara instinctively clawed to get out from under the convulsing woman. With her feet and hands she groped for some kind of purchase on the slick bathroom floor. Finally, Sara managed to slide out from underneath her. She turned Sibyl over, cradling her head, trying to help her through the convulsions. Suddenly, the jerking stopped. Sara put her ear to Sibyl's mouth, trying to make out breathing sounds. There were none.

Sitting up on her knees, Sara started compressions, trying to push life back into Sibyl's heart. Sara pinched the younger woman's nose, breathing air into her mouth. Sibyl's chest rose briefly, but nothing more. Sara tried again, gagging as blood coughed up into her mouth. She spat several times to clear her mouth, prepared to continue, but she could tell it was too late. Sibyl's eyes rolled back into her head and her breath hissed out with a low shudder. A trickle of urine came from between her legs.

She was dead.

TWO

Grant County was named for the good Grant, not Ulysses, but Lemuel Pratt Grant, a railroad builder who in the mid-1800s extended the Atlanta line deep into South Georgia and to the sea. It was on Grant's rails that trains carted cotton and other commodities all across Georgia. This rail line had put cities like Heartsdale, Madison, and Avondale on the map, and there were more than a few Georgia towns named after the man. At the start of the Civil War, Colonel Grant also developed a defense plan should Atlanta ever come under siege; unfortunately, he was better with railroad lines than front lines.

During the Depression, the citizens of Avondale, Heartsdale, and Madison decided to combine their police and fire departments as well as their schools. This helped economize on much needed services and helped persuade the railroads to keep the Grant line open; the county was much larger as a whole than as individual cities. In 1928, an army base was built in Madison, bringing families from all over the nation to tiny Grant County. A few years later, Avondale became a stopping point for railroad maintenance on the Atlanta-Savannah line. A few more years passed, and Grant College sprang up in Heartsdale. For nearly sixty years, the county prospered, until base closings, consolidations, and Reaganomics trickled down, crushing the economies of Madison and Avondale within three years of each other. But for the college, which in 1946 became a technological university specializing in agri-business, Heartsdale would have followed the same downward trend as its sister cities.

As it was, the college was the lifeblood of the city, and police chief Jeffrey Tolliver's first directive from Heartsdale's mayor was to keep the college happy if he wanted to keep his job. Jeffrey was doing just that, meeting with the campus police, discussing a plan of action for a recent outbreak of bicycle thefts, when his cell phone rang. At first, he did not recognize Sara's voice and thought the call was some kind of prank. In the eight years he had known her, Sara had never sounded so desperate. Her voice trembled as she said three words he had never expected to come from her mouth: I need you.

Jeffrey took a left outside the college gates and drove his Lincoln Town Car up Main Street toward the diner. Spring was very early this year, and already the dogwood trees lining the street were blooming, weaving a white curtain over the road. The women from the garden club had planted tulips in little planters lining the sidewalks, and a couple of kids from the high school were out sweeping the street instead of spending a week in afterschool detention. The owner of the dress shop had put a rack of clothes on the sidewalk, and the hardware store had set up an outdoor gazebo display complete with porch swing. Jeffrey knew the scene would be a sharp contrast to the one waiting for him at the diner.

He rolled down the window, letting fresh air into the stuffy car. His tie felt tight against his throat, and he found himself taking it off without thinking. In his mind, he kept playing Sara's phone call over and over in his head, trying to get more from it than the obvious facts. Sibyl Adams had been stabbed and killed at the diner.

Twenty years as a cop had not prepared Jeffrey for this kind of news. Half of his career had been spent in Birmingham, Alabama, where murder seldom surprised. Not a week went by when he wasn't called out to investigate at least one homicide, usually a product of Birmingham's extreme poverty: drug transactions gone wrong, domestic disputes where guns were too readily available. If Sara's call had come from Madison or even Avondale, Jeffrey would not have been surprised. Drugs and gang violence were fast becoming a problem in the outlying towns. Heartsdale was the jewel of the three cities. In ten years, the only suspicious fatality in Heartsdale involved an old woman who had a heart attack when she caught her grandson stealing her television.

'Chief?'

Jeffrey reached down, picking up his radio. 'Yeah?'

Marla Simms, the receptionist at the station house, said, 'I've taken care of that thing you wanted.'

'Good,' he answered, then, 'Radio silence until further notice.'

Marla was quiet, not asking the obvious question. Grant was still a small town, and even in the station house there were people who would talk. Jeffrey wanted to keep a lid on this as long as possible.

'Copy?' Jeffrey asked.

Finally, she answered, 'Yes, sir.'

Jeffrey tucked his cell phone into his coat pocket as he got out of the car. Frank Wallace, his senior detective on the squad, was already standing sentry outside the diner.

'Anyone in or out?' Jeffrey asked.

He shook his head. 'Brad's on the back door,' he said. 'The alarm's disconnected. I gotta think the perp used it for his in and out.'

Jeffrey looked back at the street. Betty Reynolds, the owner of the five-and-dime, was out sweeping the sidewalk, casting suspicious glances at the diner. People would start walking over soon, if not out of curiosity, then for supper.

Jeffrey turned back to Frank. 'Nobody saw anything?'

'Not a thing,' Frank confirmed. 'She walked here from her house. Pete says she comes here every Monday after the lunch rush.'

Jeffrey managed a tight nod, walking into the diner. The Grant Filling Station was central to Main Street. With its big red booths and speckled white countertops, chrome rails and straw dispensers, it looked much as it probably had the day Pete's dad opened for business. Even the solid white linoleum tiles on the floor, so worn in spots the black adhesive showed through, were original to the restaurant. Jeffrey had eaten lunch here almost every day for the last ten years. The diner had been a source of comfort, something familiar after working with the dregs of humanity. He looked around the open room, knowing it would never be the same for him again.

Tessa Linton sat at the counter, her head in her hands. Pete Wayne sat opposite her, staring blindly out the window. Except for the day the space shuttle *Challenger* had exploded, this was the first time Jeffrey had ever seen him not wearing his paper hat inside the diner. Still, Pete's hair was bunched up into a point at the top, making his face look longer than it already was.

'Tess?' Jeffrey asked, putting his hand on her shoulder. She leaned into him, crying. Jeffrey smoothed her hair, giving Pete a nod.

Pete Wayne was normally a cheerful man, but his expression today was one of absolute shock. He barely acknowledged Jeffrey, continuing to stare out the windows lining the front of the restaurant, his lips moving slightly, no sound coming out.

A few moments of silence passed, then Tessa sat up. She fumbled with the napkin dispenser until Jeffrey offered his handkerchief. He waited until she had blown her nose to ask, 'Where's Sara?'

Tessa folded the handkerchief. 'She's still in the bathroom. I don't know –' Tessa's voice caught. 'There was so much blood. She wouldn't let me go in.'

He nodded, stroking her hair back off her face. Sara was very protective of her little sister, and this instinct had transferred to Jeffrey during their marriage. Even after the divorce, Jeffrey still felt in some way that Tessa and the Lintons were his family.

'You okay?' he asked.

She nodded. 'Go ahead. She needs you.'

Jeffrey tried not to react to this. If not for the fact that Sara was the county coroner, he would never see her. It said a lot about their relationship that somebody had to die in order for her to be in the same room with him.

Walking to the back of the diner, Jeffrey felt a sense of dread overcome him. He knew that something violent had happened. He knew that Sibyl Adams had been killed. Other than that, he had no idea what to expect when he tugged open the door to the women's bathroom. What he saw literally took his breath away.

Sara sat in the middle of the room, Sibyl Adams's head in her lap. Blood was everywhere, covering the body, covering Sara, whose shirt and pants were soaked down the front, as if someone had taken a hose and sprayed her. Bloody shoe and hand prints marked the floor as if a great struggle had occurred.

Jeffrey stood in the doorway, taking all this in, trying to catch his breath.

'Shut the door,' Sara whispered, her hand resting on Sibyl's forehead. He did as he was told, walking around the periphery of the room. His mouth opened, but nothing would come out. There were the obvious questions to ask, but part of Jeffrey did not want to know the answers. Part of him wanted to take Sara out of this room, put her in his car, and drive until neither one of them could remember the way this tiny bathroom looked and smelled. There was the taste of violence in the air, morbid and sticky in the back of his throat. He felt dirty just standing there.

'She looks like Lena,' he finally said, referring to Sibyl Adams's twin sister, a detective on his force. 'For just a second I thought . . .' He shook his head, unable to continue.

'Lena's hair is longer.'

'Yeah,' he said, unable to take his eyes off the victim. Jeffrey had seen a lot of horrible things in his time, but he had never personally known a victim of violent crime. Not that he knew Sibyl Adams well, but in a town as small as Heartsdale, everyone was your neighbor.

Sara cleared her throat. 'Did you tell Lena yet?'

Her question fell on him like an anvil. Two weeks into his job as police chief, he had hired Lena Adams out of the academy in Macon. Those early years, she was like Jeffrey, an outsider. Eight years later he had promoted her to detective. At thirty-three, she was the youngest detective and only woman on the senior squad. And now her sister had been murdered in their own backyard, little more than two hundred yards from the police station. He felt a sense of personal responsibility that was almost suffocating.

'Jeffrey?'

Jeffrey took a deep breath, letting it go slowly. 'She's taking some evidence to Macon,' he finally answered. 'I called the highway patrol and asked them to bring her back here.'

Sara was looking at him. Her eyes were rimmed with red, but she hadn't been crying. Jeffrey was glad of this one thing, because he had never seen Sara cry. He thought if he saw her crying that something in him would give.

'Did you know she was blind?' she asked.

Jeffrey leaned against the wall. He had somehow forgotten that detail.

'She didn't even see it coming,' Sara whispered. She bent her head down, looking at Sibyl. As usual, Jeffrey couldn't imagine what Sara was thinking. He decided to wait for her to talk. Obviously, she needed a few moments to collect her thoughts.

He tucked his hands into his pockets, taking in the space. There were two stalls with wooden doors across from a sink that was so old the fixtures for hot and cold were on opposite sides of the basin. Over this was a gold speckled mirror that was worn through at the edges. All told, the room was not more than twenty feet square, but the tiny black and white tiles on the floor made it seem even smaller. The dark blood pooling around the body didn't help matters. Claustrophobia had never been a problem for Jeffrey, but Sara's silence was like a fourth presence in the room. He looked up at the white ceiling, trying to get some distance.

Finally Sara spoke. Her voice was stronger, more confident. 'She was on the toilet when I found her.'

For lack of anything better to do, Jeffrey took out a small spiralbound notebook. He grabbed a pen from his breast pocket and started to write as Sara narrated the events that had led up to this moment. Her voice became monotone as she described Sibyl's death in clinical detail.

'Then I asked Tess to bring my cell phone.' Sara stopped speaking, and Jeffrey answered her question before she could get it out.

'She's okay,' he provided. 'I called Eddie on the way here.'

'Did you tell him what happened?'

Jeffrey tried to smile. Sara's father was not one of his biggest fans. 'I was lucky he didn't hang up on me.'

Sara did not so much as smile, but her eyes finally met Jeffrey's. There was a softness there that he had not seen in ages. 'I need to do the prelim, then we can take her to the morgue.'

Jeffrey tucked the pad into his coat pocket as Sara gently slid Sibyl's head to the floor. She sat back on her heels, wiping her hands on the back of her pants.

She said, 'I want to have her cleaned up before Lena sees her.'

Jeffrey nodded. 'She's at least two hours away. That should give us time to process the scene.' He indicated the stall door. The lock was busted off. 'Was the lock that way when you found her?'

'The lock's been that way since I was seven,' Sara said, pointing to her briefcase beside the door. 'Hand me a pair of gloves.'

Jeffrey opened the case, trying not to touch the blood on the handles. He pulled out a pair of latex gloves from an inside pocket. When he turned around, Sara was standing at the foot of the body. Her expression had changed, and despite the blood staining the front of her clothes, she seemed to be back in control.

Still, he had to ask, 'Are you sure you want to do this? We can call somebody from Atlanta.'

Sara shook her head as she slipped on the gloves with practiced efficiency. 'I don't want a stranger touching her.'

Jeffrey understood what she meant. This was a county matter. County people would take care of her.

Sara tucked her hands into her hips as she walked around the body. He knew she was trying to get some perspective on the scene, to take herself out of the equation. Jeffrey found himself studying his ex-wife as she did this. Sara was a tall woman, an inch shy of six feet, with deep green eyes and dark red hair. He was letting his mind wander, remembering how good it felt to be with her, when the sharp tone of her voice brought him back to reality.

'Jeffrey?' Sara snapped, giving him a hard look.

He stared back at her, aware that his mind had wandered off to what seemed like a safer place.

She held his gaze a second longer, then turned toward the stall. Jeffrey took another pair of gloves out of her briefcase and slipped them on as she talked.

'Like I said,' Sara began, 'she was on the toilet when I found her. We struggled to the floor, I rolled her on her back.'

Sara lifted Sibyl's hands, checking under her fingernails. 'There's nothing here. I imagine she was taken by surprise, didn't know what was going on until it was too late.'

'You think it was quick?'

'Not too quick. Whatever he did, it looks planned to me. The scene was very clean until I came along. She would've bled out on the toilet if I hadn't had to use the rest room.' Sara looked away. 'Or maybe not, if I hadn't been late getting here.'

Jeffrey tried to comfort her. 'You can't know that.'

She shrugged this off. 'There's some bruising on her wrists where her arms hit the handicap bars. Also' – she opened Sibyl's legs slightly – 'see here on her legs?'

Jeffrey followed her directions. The skin on the inside of both knees was scratched away. 'What's that?' he asked.

'The toilet seat,' she said. 'The bottom edge is pretty sharp. I imagine she squeezed her legs together as she struggled. You can see some of the skin caught on the seat.'

Jeffrey glanced at the toilet, then looked back at Sara. 'Think he pushed her back on the toilet, then stabbed her?'

Sara didn't answer him. Instead, she pointed to Sibyl's bare torso. 'The incision isn't deep until the middle of the cross,' she explained, pressing into the abdomen, opening up the wound so that he could see. 'I'd guess it was a double-edged blade. You can see the Y shape on either side of the puncture.' Sara easily slipped her index finger inside the wound. The skin made a sucking noise as she did this, and Jeffrey gritted his teeth, looking away. When he turned back, Sara was giving him a questioning look.

She asked, 'Are you okay?'

He nodded, afraid to open his mouth.

She moved her finger around inside the hole in Sibyl Adams's chest. Blood seeped out from the wound. 'I'd say it's at least a four-inch blade,' she concluded, keeping her eyes on him. 'Is this bothering you?'

He shook his head, even though the sound was making his stomach turn.

Sara slipped her finger out, continuing, 'It was a very

sharp blade. There's no hesitation around the incision, so like I said, he knew what he was doing when he started.'

'What was he doing?'

Her tone was very matter-of-fact. 'He was carving her stomach. His strokes were very assured, one down, one across, then a thrust into the upper torso. That was the death blow, I would imagine. Cause will probably be exsanguination.'

'She bled to death?'

Sara shrugged. 'Best guess right now, yeah. She bled to death. It probably took about ten minutes. The convulsions were from shock.'

Jeffrey couldn't suppress the shudder that came. He indicated the wound. 'It's a cross, right?'

Sara studied the cuts. 'I'd say so. I mean, it can't really be anything else, can it?'

'Do you think this is some kind of religious statement?'

'Who can tell with rape?' she said, stopping at the look on his face. 'What?'

'She was raped?' he said, glancing at Sibyl Adams, checking for obvious signs of damage. There was no bruising on her thighs or scrapes around the pelvic area. 'Did you find anything?'

Sara was quiet. Finally she said, 'No. I mean, I don't know.'

'What did you find?'

'Nothing.' She snapped off her gloves. 'Just what I told you. I can finish this back at the morgue.'

'I don't –'

'I'll call Carlos to come get her,' she said, referring to her assistant at the morgue. 'Meet me back there when you're finished here, okay?' When he didn't answer, she

24

said, 'I don't know about the rape, Jeff. Really. It was just a guess.'

Jeffrey didn't know what to say. One thing he knew about his ex-wife was she did not make guesses in the field. 'Sara?' he asked. Then, 'Are you all right?'

Sara gave a mirthless laugh. 'Am I all right?' she repeated. 'Jesus, Jeffrey, what a stupid question.' She walked over to the door, but didn't open it. When she spoke, her words came out clear and succinct. 'You have to find the person who did this,' she said.

'I know.'

'No, Jeffrey.' Sara turned around, giving him a piercing look. 'This is a ritualistic attack, not a one-off. Look at her body. Look at the way she was left here.' Sara paused, then continued, 'Whoever killed Sibyl Adams planned it out carefully. He knew where to find her. He followed her into the bathroom. This is a methodical murder by someone who wants to make a statement.'

He felt light-headed as he realized that what she was saying was the truth. He had seen this kind of murder before. He knew exactly what she was talking about. This was not the work of an amateur. Whoever had done this was probably working his way up to something much more dramatic at this very moment.

Sara still did not seem to think he understood. 'Do you think he'll stop with one?'

Jeffrey did not hesitate this time. 'No.'

THREE

Lena Adams frowned, flashing her headlights at the blue Honda Civic in front of her. The posted speed limit on this particular stretch of Georgia I-20 was sixty-five, but like most rural Georgians, Lena saw the signs as little more than a suggestion for tourists on their way to and from Florida. Case in point, the Civic's tags were from Ohio.

'Come on,' she groaned, checking her speedometer. She was boxed in by an eighteen-wheeler on her right and the Civic-driving Yankee in front, who was obviously determined to keep her just above the speed limit. For a second, Lena wished she had taken one of Grant County's cruisers. Not only was it a smoother ride than her Celica, there was the added pleasure of scaring the crap out of speeders.

Miraculously, the eighteen-wheeler slowed, letting the Civic pull over. Lena gave a cheery wave as the driver flipped her off. She hoped he had learned his lesson. Driving through the South was Darwinism at its best.

The Celica climbed up to eighty-five as she sped out of the Macon city limits. Lena took a cassette tape out of its case. Sibyl had made her some driving music for the trip back. Lena slid the tape into the radio and smiled when the music started, recognizing the opening to Joan Jett's 'Bad Reputation.' The song had been the sisters' anthem during high school, and they had spent many a night speeding through back roads, singing 'I don't give a damn about my bad reputation' at the top of their lungs. Thanks to an errant uncle, the girls were considered trash without the benefit of being particularly poor or, courtesy of their half Spanish mother, all that white.

Running evidence up to the GBI lab in Macon was little more than courier work in the big scheme of things, but Lena was glad to have the assignment. Jeffrey had said she could take the day to cool down, his euphemism for getting her temper under control. Frank Wallace and Lena were butting heads over the same problem that had haunted their partnership from the beginning. At fifty-eight years old, Frank wasn't thrilled to have women on the force, let alone one as a partner. He was constantly leaving Lena out of investigations, while she was constantly trying to force herself back in. Something would have to give. As Frank was two years from retirement, Lena knew she would not be the one to bend first.

In truth, Frank was not a bad guy. Other than suffering from the kind of crankiness brought on by old age, he seemed to make an effort. On a good day, she could understand that his overbearing attitude came from a deeper place than his ego. He was the kind of man who opened doors for women and took his hat off indoors. Frank was even a Mason at the local lodge. He was not the kind of guy who would let his female partner lead an interrogation, let alone take point on a house raid. On a bad day, Lena wanted to lock him in his garage with the car running.

Jeffrey was right about the trip cooling her down. Lena made good time to Macon, shaving a full thirty minutes off the drive courtesy of the Celica's V-6. She liked her boss, who was the exact opposite of Frank Wallace. Frank was all gut instinct, while Jeffrey was more cerebral. Jeffrey was also the kind of man who was comfortable around women and did not mind when they voiced their opinions. The fact that he had from day one groomed Lena for her job as detective was not lost on her. Jeffrey did not promote her to meet some county quota or make himself look better than his predecessor; this was Grant County, after all, a town that had not even been on the maps until fifty years ago. Jeffrey had given Lena the job because he respected her work and her mind. The fact that she was a woman had nothing to do with it.

'Shit,' Lena hissed, catching the flash of blue lights behind her. She slowed the car, pulling over as the Civic passed her. The Yankee beeped his horn and waved. It was Lena's turn to give the Ohioan a one-finger salute.

The Georgia highway patrolman took his time getting out of his car. Lena turned to her purse in the backseat, rummaging around for her badge. When she turned back around, she was surprised to see the cop standing just to the rear of her vehicle. His hand was on his weapon, and she kicked herself for not waiting for him to come to the car. He probably thought she was looking for a gun.

Lena dropped the badge in her lap and held her hands in the air, offering, 'Sorry,' out the open window.

The cop took a tentative step forward, his square jaw working as he came up to the car. He took off his sunglasses and gave her a close look.

'Listen,' she said, hands still raised. 'I'm on the job.'

He interrupted her. 'Are you Detective Salena Adams?'

She lowered her hands, giving the patrolman a questioning look. He was kind of short, but his upper body was muscled in that way short men have of overcompensating for what they lacked in height. His arms were so thick they wouldn't rest flat to his sides. The buttons of his uniform were pulled tight against his chest.

'It's Lena,' she offered, glancing at his name tag. 'Do I know you?'

'No, ma'am,' he returned, slipping on his sunglasses. 'We got a call from your chief. I'm supposed to escort you back to Grant County.'

'I'm sorry?' Lena asked, sure she hadn't heard correctly. 'My chief? Jeffrey Tolliver?'

He gave a curt nod. 'Yes, ma'am.' Before she could ask him any further questions, he was walking back to his car. Lena waited for the patrolman to pull back onto the road, then started off after him. He sped up quickly, edging up to ninety within minutes. They passed the blue Civic, but Lena did not pay much attention. All she could think was, What did I do this time?

FOUR

Though the Heartsdale Medical Center anchored the end of Main Street, it was not capable of looking nearly as important as its name would imply. Just two stories tall, the small hospital was equipped to do little more than handle whatever scrapes and upset stomachs couldn't wait for doctors' hours. There was a larger hospital about thirty minutes away in Augusta that handled the serious cases. If not for the county morgue being housed in the basement, the medical center would have been torn down to make way for student housing a long time ago.

Like the rest of the town, the hospital had been built during the town's upswing in the 1930s. The main floors had been renovated since then, but the morgue was obviously not important to the hospital board. The walls were lined with light blue tile that was so old it was coming back into style. The floors were a mixed check pattern of green and tan linoleum. The ceiling overhead had seen its share of water damage, but most of it had been patched. The equipment was dated but functional.

Sara's office was in the back, separated from the rest of the morgue by a large glass window. She sat behind her desk, looking out the window, trying to collect her thoughts. She concentrated on the white noise of the morgue: the air compressor on the freezer, the swish-

swish of the water hose as Carlos washed down the floor. Since they were below ground, the walls of the morgue absorbed rather than deflected the sounds, and Sara felt oddly comforted by the familiar hums and swishes. The shrill ring of the phone interrupted the silence.

'Sara Linton,' she said, expecting Jeffrey. Instead, it was her father.

'Hey, baby.'

Sara smiled, feeling a lightness overcome her at the sound of Eddie Linton's voice. 'Hey, Daddy.'

'I've got a joke for you.'

'Yeah?' She tried to keep her tone light, knowing humor was her father's way of dealing with stress. 'What's that?'

'A pediatrician, a lawyer, and a priest were on the *Titanic* when it started to go down,' he began. 'The pediatrician says, 'Save the children.' The lawyer says, 'Fuck the children!' And the priest says, 'Do we have time?''

Sara laughed, more for her father's benefit than anything else. He was quiet, waiting for her to talk. She asked, 'How's Tessie?'

'Taking a nap,' he reported. 'How about you?'

'Oh, I'm okay.' Sara started drawing circles on her desk calendar. She wasn't normally a doodler, but she needed something to do with her hands. Part of her wanted to check her briefcase, to see if Tessa had thought to put the postcard in there. Part of her did not want to know where it was.

Eddie interrupted her thoughts. 'Mom says you have to come to breakfast tomorrow.'

'Yeah?' Sara asked, drawing squares over the circles.

His voice took on a singsong quality. 'Waffles and grits and toast and bacon.'

'Hey,' Jeffrey said.

Sara jerked her head up, dropping the pen. 'You scared me,' she said, then, to her father, 'Daddy, Jeffrey's here –'

Eddie Linton made a series of unintelligible noises. In his opinion, there was nothing wrong with Jeffrey Tolliver that a solid brick to the head would not fix.

'All right,' Sara said into the phone, giving Jeffrey a tight smile. He was looking at the etched sign on the glass, where her father had slapped a piece of masking tape over the last name TOLLIVER and written in LINTON with a black marker. Since Jeffrey had cheated on Sara with the only sign maker in town, it was doubtful that the lettering would be more professionally fixed anytime soon.

'Daddy,' Sara interrupted, 'I'll see you in the morning.' She hung up the phone before he could get another word in.

Jeffrey asked, 'Let me guess, he sends his love.'

Sara ignored the question, not wanting to get into a personal conversation with Jeffrey. This was how he sucked her back in, making her think that he was a normal person capable of being honest and supportive when in actuality the minute Jeffrey felt like he was back in Sara's good graces he'd probably run for cover. Or, under the covers, to be more exact.

He said, 'How's Tessa doing?'

'Fine,' Sara said, taking her glasses out of their case. She slid them on, asking, 'Where's Lena?'

He glanced at the clock on the wall. 'About an hour away. Frank's going to page me when she's ten minutes out.'

Sara stood, adjusting the waist of her scrubs. She had showered in the hospital lounge, storing her bloodied clothes in an evidence bag in case they were needed for trial.

She asked, 'Have you thought about what you're going to tell her?'

He shook his head no. 'I'm hoping we can get something concrete before I talk to her. Lena's a cop. She's going to want answers.'

Sara leaned over the desk, knocking on the glass. Carlos looked up. 'You can go now,' she said. Then, explaining to Jeffrey, 'He's going to run blood and urine up to the crime lab. They're going to put it through tonight.'

'Good.'

Sara sat back in her chair. 'Did you get anything from the bathroom?'

'We found her cane and glasses behind the toilet. They were wiped clean.'

'What about the stall door?'

'Nothing,' he said. 'I mean, not nothing, but every woman in town's been in and out of that place. Last count Matt had over fifty different prints.' He took some Polaroids out of his pocket and tossed them onto the desk. There were close-ups of the body lying on the floor alongside pictures of Sara's bloody shoe and hand prints.

Sara picked up one of these, saying, 'I guess it didn't help matters that I contaminated the scene.'

'It's not like you had a choice.'

She kept her thoughts to herself, putting the pictures in logical sequence.

He repeated her earlier evaluation. 'Whoever did this knew what he was doing. He knew she would go to the restaurant alone. He knew she couldn't see. He knew the place would be deserted that time of day.'

'You think he was waiting for her?'

Jeffrey gave a shrug. 'Seems that way. He probably came in and out the back door. Pete had disconnected the alarm so they could leave it open to air the place out.'

'Yeah,' she said, remembering the back door to the diner was propped open more times than not.

'So, we're looking for someone who knew her activities, right? Somebody who was familiar with the layout of the diner.'

Sara did not want to answer this question, which implied that the killer was someone living in Grant, someone who knew the people and places the way only a resident could. Instead, she stood and walked back to the metal filing cabinet on the other side of her desk. She took out a fresh lab coat and slipped it on, saying, 'I've already taken X rays and checked her clothing. Other than that, she's ready.'

Jeffrey turned, staring out at the table in the center of the morgue. Sara looked, too, thinking that Sibyl Adams was a lot smaller in death than she seemed in life. Even Sara couldn't get used to the way death reduced people.

Jeffrey asked, 'Did you know her well?'

Sara mulled over his question. Finally she said, 'I guess. We both did career day at the middle school last year. Then, you know, I ran into her at the library sometimes.'

'The library?' Jeffrey asked. 'I thought she was blind.'

'They have books on tape there, I guess.' She stopped in front of him, crossing her arms. 'Listen, I have to tell you this. Lena and I kind of had a fight a few weeks back.'

Obviously, he was surprised. Sara was surprised, too. There were not a lot of people in town she did not get along with. But Lena Adams was certainly one of them.

Sara explained, 'She called Nick Shelton at the GBI asking for a tox report on a case.'

Jeffrey shook his head side to side, not understanding. 'Why?'

Sara shrugged. She still didn't know why Lena had tried to go over her head, especially considering it was well known that Sara had a very good working relationship with Nick Shelton, the Georgia Bureau of Investigation's field agent for Grant County.

'And?' Jeffrey prompted.

'I don't know what Lena thought she could accomplish by calling Nick directly. We had it out. No blood was shed, but I wouldn't say we parted on friendly terms.'

Jeffrey shrugged, as if to say, What can you do? Lena had made a career out of ticking people off. Back when Sara and Jeffrey were married, Jeffrey had often voiced his concern over Lena's impetuous behavior.

'If she was' – he stopped, then – 'if she was raped, Sara. I don't know.'

'Let's get started,' Sara answered quickly, walking past him into the morgue. She stood in front of the supply cabinet, looking for a surgical gown. She paused, her hands on the doors as she played back their conversation in her mind, wondering how it had turned from a forensic evaluation into a discussion about Jeffrey's potential outrage had Sibyl Adams not just been killed but raped as well.

'Sara?' he asked. 'What's wrong?'

Sara felt her anger spark at his stupid question. 'What's wrong?' She found the gown and slammed the doors shut. The metal frame rattled from the force. Sara turned, ripping the sterile pack open. 'What's wrong is I'm tired of you asking me what's wrong when it's

35

pretty damn obvious what's wrong.' She paused, snapping out the gown. 'Think about it, Jeffrey. A woman literally died in my arms today. Not just a stranger, someone I knew. I should be at home right now taking a long shower or walking the dogs and instead I've got to go in there and cut her up, worse than she already is, so I can tell you whether or not you need to start pulling in all the perverts in town.'

Her hands shook with anger as she tried to get into the gown. The sleeve was just out of her reach, and she was turning to get a better angle when Jeffrey moved to help her.

Her tone was nasty when she snapped, 'I've got it.'

He held his hands up, palms toward her as if in surrender. 'Sorry.'

Sara fumbled with the ties on the gown, ending up knotting the strings together. 'Shit,' she hissed, trying to work them back out.

Jeffrey offered, 'I could get Brad to go walk the dogs.'

Sara dropped her hands, giving up. 'That's not the point, Jeffrey.'

'I know it's not,' he returned, approaching her the way he might a rabid dog. He took the strings and she looked down, watching him work out the knot. Sara let her gaze travel to the top of his head, noting a few grey strands in with the black. She wanted to will into him the ability to comfort her instead of trying to make a joke of everything. She wanted for him to magically develop the capacity for empathy. After ten years, she should have known better.

He loosened the knot with a smile, as if with this simple act he had just made everything better. He said, 'There.'

Sara took over, tying the strings together in a bow.

He put his hand under her chin. 'You're okay,' he said, not a question this time.

'Yeah,' she agreed, stepping away. 'I'm okay.' She pulled out a pair of latex gloves, turning to the task at hand. 'Let's just get the prelim over with before Lena gets back.'

Sara walked over to the porcelain autopsy table bolted to the floor in the middle of the room. Curved with high sides, the white table hugged Sibyl's small body. Carlos had placed her head on a black rubber block and draped a white sheet over her. Except for the black bruise over her eye, she could be sleeping.

'Lord,' Sara muttered as she folded back the sheet. Taking the body out of the kill zone had intensified the damage. Under the bright lights of the morgue, every aspect of the wound stood out. The incisions were long and sharp across the abdomen, forming an almost perfect cross. The skin puckered in places, drawing her attention away from the deep gouge at the intersection of the cross. Postmortem, wounds took on a dark, almost black, appearance. The rifts in Sibyl Adams's skin gaped open like tiny wet mouths.

'She didn't have a lot of body fat,' Sara explained. She indicated the belly, where the incision opened wider just above the navel. The cut there was deeper, and the skin was pulled apart like a tight shirt that had popped a button. 'There's fecal matter in the lower abdomen where the intestines were breached by the blade. I don't know if it was this deep on purpose or if the depth was accidental. It looks stretched.'

She indicated the edges of the wound. 'You can see the striation here at the tip of the wound. Maybe he moved the knife around. Twisted it. Also . . . ' She paused, figuring things out as she went along. 'There are traces of excrement on her hands as well as the bars in

37

the stall, so I have to think she was cut, she put her hands to her belly, then she wrapped her hands around the bars for some reason.'

She looked up at Jeffrey to see how he was holding up. He seemed rooted to the floor, transfixed by Sibyl's body. Sara knew from her own experience that the mind could play tricks, smoothing out the sharp lines of violence. Even for Sara, seeing Sibyl again was perhaps worse than seeing her the first time.

Sara put her hands on the body, surprised that it was still warm. The temperature in the morgue was always low, even during the summer, because the room was underground. Sibyl should have been a lot cooler by now.

'Sara?' Jeffrey asked.

'Nothing,' she answered, not prepared to make guesses. She pressed around the wound in the center of the cross. 'It was a double-edged knife,' she began. 'Which helps you out some. Most stabbings are serrated hunting knives, right?'

'Yeah.'

She pointed to a tan-looking mark around the center wound. Cleaning the body, Sara had been able to see a lot more than her initial exam in the bathroom had revealed. 'This is from the cross guard, so he put it all the way in. I imagine I'll see some chipping on the spine when I open her up. I felt some irregularities when I put my finger in. There's probably some chipped bone still in there.'

Jeffrey nodded for her to continue.

'If we're lucky, we'll get some kind of impression from the blade. If not that, then maybe something from the cross guard bruising. I can remove and fix the skin after Lena sees her.'

She pointed to the puncture wound at the center of

38

the cross. 'This was a hard stab, so I would imagine the killer did it from a superior position. See the way the wound is angled at about a forty-five?' She studied the incision, trying to make sense of it. 'I would almost say that the belly stab is different from the chest wound. It doesn't make sense.'

'Why is that?'

'The punctures have a different pattern.'

'Like how?'

'I can't tell,' she answered truthfully. She let this drop for the moment, concentrating on the stab wound at the center of the cross. 'So he's probably standing in front of her, legs bent at the knee, and he takes the knife back to his side' – she demonstrated, pulling her hand back – 'then rams it into her chest.'

'He uses two knives to do this?'

'I can't tell,' Sara admitted, going back to the belly wound. Something wasn't adding up.

Jeffrey scratched his chin, looking at the chest wound. He asked, 'Why not stab her in the heart?'

'Well, for one, the heart isn't at the center of the chest, which is where you would have to stab in order to hit the center of the cross. So, there's an aesthetic quality to his choice. For another, there's rib and cartilage surrounding the heart. He would have to stab her repeatedly to break through. That would mess up the appearance of the cross, right?' Sara paused. 'There would be a great amount of blood if the heart was punctured. It would come out at a considerable velocity. Maybe he wanted to avoid that.' She shrugged, looking up at Jeffrey. 'I suppose he could have gone under the rib cage and up if he wanted to get to the heart, but that would have been a crapshoot at best.'

'You're saying the attacker had some kind of medical knowledge?'

Sara asked, 'Do you know where the heart is?'

He put his hand over the left side of his chest.

'Right. You also know your ribs don't meet all the way in the center.'

He tapped his hand against the center of his chest. 'What's this?'

'Sternum,' she answered. 'The cut's lower, though. It's in the xiphoid process. I can't say if that's blind luck or calculated.'

'Meaning?'

'Meaning, if you're hell-bent on carving a cross on somebody's abdomen and putting a knife through the center, this is the best place to stab somebody if you want the knife to go through. There are three parts to the sternum,' she said, using her own chest to illustrate. 'The manubrium, which is the upper part, the body, which is the main part, then the xiphoid process. Of those three, the xiphoid is the softest. Especially in someone this age. She's what, early thirties?'

'Thirty-three.'

'Tessa's age,' Sara mumbled, and for a second she flashed on her sister. She shook this from her mind, focusing back on the body. 'The xiphoid process calcifies as you age. The cartilage gets harder. So, if I was going to stab someone in the chest, this is where I'd make my X.'

'Maybe he didn't want to cut her breasts?'

Sara considered this. 'This seems more personal than that.' She tried to find the words. 'I don't know, I would think that he would want to cut her breasts. Know what I mean?'

'Especially if it's sexually motivated,' he offered. 'I mean, rape is generally about power, right? It's about being angry at women, wanting to control them. Why would he cut her there instead of in a place that makes her a woman?'

'Rape is also about penetration,' Sara countered. 'This certainly qualifies. It's a strong cut, nearly clean through. I don't think –' She stopped, staring at the wound, a new idea forming in her mind. 'Jesus,' she mumbled.

'What is it?' Jeffrey asked.

She could not speak for a few seconds. Her throat felt as if it was closing in on her.

'Sara?'

A beeping filled the morgue. Jeffrey checked his pager. 'That can't be Lena,' he said. 'Mind if I use the phone?'

'Sure.' Sara crossed her arms, feeling the need to protect herself from her own thoughts. She waited until Jeffrey was sitting behind her desk before she continued the examination.

Sara reached above her head, turning the light so that she could get a better look at the pelvic area. Adjusting the metal speculum, she mumbled a prayer to herself, to God, to anybody who would listen, to no avail. By the time Jeffrey returned, she was sure.

'Well?' he asked.

Sara's hands shook as she peeled off her gloves. 'She was sexually assaulted early on in the attack.' She paused, dropping the soiled gloves on the table, imagining in her mind Sibyl Adams sitting on the toilet, putting her hands to the open wound in her abdomen, then bracing herself against the bars on either side of the stall, completely blind to what was happening to her.

He waited a few beats before prompting, 'And?'

Sara put her hands on the edges of the table. 'There was fecal matter in her vagina.'

Jeffrey did not seem to follow. 'She was sodomized first?'

'There's no sign of anal penetration.'

'But you found fecal matter,' he said, still not getting it.

'Deep in her vagina,' Sara said, not wanting to spell it out, knowing she would have to. She heard an uncharacteristic waver in her voice when she said, 'The incision in her belly was deep on purpose, Jeffrey.' She stopped, searching for words to describe the horror she had found.

'He raped her,' Jeffrey said, not a question. 'There was vaginal penetration.'

'Yes,' Sara answered, still searching for a way to clarify. Finally she said, 'There was vaginal penetration after he raped the wound.'

FIVE

Night had come quickly, the temperature dropping along with the sun. Jeffrey was crossing the street just as Lena pulled into the parking lot of the station house. She was out of her car before he reached her.

'What's going on?' she demanded, but he could tell she already knew something was wrong. 'Is it my uncle?' she asked, rubbing her arms to fight the chill. She was wearing a thin T-shirt and jeans, not her usual work attire, but the trip to Macon was a casual one.

Jeffrey took off his jacket, giving it to her. The weight of what Sara had told him sat on his chest like a heavy stone. If Jeffrey had anything to do with it, Lena would never know exactly what had happened to Sibyl Adams. She would never know what that animal had done to her sister.

'Let's go inside,' he said, putting his hand under her elbow.

'I don't want to go inside,' she answered, jerking her arm away. His coat fell between them.

Jeffrey leaned down, retrieving his jacket. When he looked up, Lena had her hands on her hips. As long as he had known her, Lena Adams had sported a chip on her shoulder the size of Everest. Somewhere in the back of his mind, Jeffrey had been thinking she would need a shoulder to cry on or words of comfort. He could not accept that there wasn't a soft side to Lena, maybe because she was a woman. Maybe because just a few minutes earlier he had seen her sister lying ripped apart in the morgue. He should have remembered that Lena Adams was harder than that. He should have anticipated the anger.

Jeffrey slipped his jacket back on. 'I don't want to do this outside.'

'What are you going to say?' she demanded. 'You're going to say he was driving, right? And that he swerved off the road, right?' She ticked off the progression on her fingertips, giving him nearly verbatim the police handbook procedure for informing someone that a family member had died. Build up to it, the manual said. Don't spring it on them suddenly. Let the family member/loved one get used to the idea.

Lena counted it off, her voice getting louder with each sentence. 'Was he hit by another car? Huh? And they took him to the hospital? And they tried to save him, but they couldn't. They did everything they could, huh?'

'Lena –'

She walked back toward her car, then turned around. 'Where's my sister? Did you already tell her?'

Jeffrey took a breath, releasing it slowly.

'Look at that,' Lena hissed, turning toward the station house, waving her hand in the air. Marla Simms was looking out one of the front windows. 'Come on out, Marla,' Lena yelled.

'Come on,' Jeffrey said, trying to stop her.

She stepped away from him. 'Where is my sister?'

His mouth did not want to move. Through sheer force of will, he managed, 'She was in the diner.'

Lena turned, walking down the street toward the diner.

Jeffrey continued, 'She went to the bathroom.'

44

Lena stopped in her tracks.

'There was someone in there. He stabbed her in the chest.' Jeffrey waited for her to turn around, but she still did not. Lena's shoulders were straight, her posture a study in stillness. He continued, 'Dr. Linton was having lunch with her sister. She went into the bathroom and found her.'

Lena turned slowly, her lips slightly parted.

'Sara tried to save her.'

Lena looked him straight in the eye. He forced himself not to look away.

'She's dead.'

The words hung in the air like moths around a streetlamp.

Lena's hand went to her mouth. She walked in an almost drunken half circle, then turned back to Jeffrey. Her eyes bored into his, a question there. Was this some kind of joke? Was he capable of being this cruel?

'She's dead,' he repeated.

Her breathing came in short staccatos. He could almost see her mind kicking into action as she absorbed the information. Lena walked toward the station house, then stopped. She turned to Jeffrey, mouth open, but said nothing. Without warning, she took off toward the diner.

'Lena!' Jeffrey called, running after her. She was fast for her size, and his dress shoes were no match for her sneakers pounding down the pavement. He tucked his arms in, pumping, pushing himself to catch her before she reached the diner.

He called her name again as she neared the diner, but she blew past it, taking a right turn toward the medical center.

'No,' Jeffrey groaned, pushing himself harder. She was going to the morgue. He called her name again, but

Lena did not look back as she crossed onto the hospital's drive. She slammed her body into the sliding doors, popping them out of their frames, sounding the emergency alarm.

Jeffrey was seconds behind her. He rounded the corner to the stairs, hearing Lena's tennis shoes slapping against the rubber treads. A boom echoed up the narrow stairwell as she opened the door to the morgue.

Jeffrey stopped on the fourth step from the bottom. He heard Sara's surprised 'Lena' followed by a pained groan.

He forced himself to take the last few steps down, made himself walk into the morgue.

Lena was bent over her sister, holding her hand. Sara had obviously tried to cover the worst of the damage with the sheet, but most of Sibyl's upper torso still showed.

Lena stood beside her sister, her breath coming in short pants, her whole body shaking as if from some bone-chilling cold.

Sara cut Jeffrey in two with a look. All he could do was hold his hands out. He had tried to stop her.

'What time was it?' Lena asked through chattering teeth. 'What time did she die?'

'Around two-thirty,' Sara answered. Blood was on her gloves, and she tucked them under her arms as if to hide it.

'She feels so warm.'

'I know.'

Lena lowered her voice. 'I was in Macon, Sibby,' she told her sister, stroking back her hair. Jeffrey was glad to see Sara had taken the time to comb some of the blood out.

Silence filled the morgue. It was eerie seeing Lena standing beside the dead woman. Sibyl was her identical twin, alike in every way. They were both petite women, about five four and little more than one hundred twenty pounds. Their skin had the same olive tone. Lena's dark brown hair was longer than her sister's, Sibyl's curlier. The sisters' faces were a study in contrast, one flat and emotionless, the other filled with grief.

Sara turned slightly to the side, removing her gloves. She suggested, 'Let's go upstairs, okay?'

'You were there,' Lena said, her voice low. 'What did you do to help her?'

Sara looked down at her hands. 'I did what I could do.'

Lena stroked the side of her sister's face, her tone a little sharper when she asked, 'What exactly was it that you could do?'

Jeffrey stepped forward, but Sara gave him a sharp look to stop him, as if to say his time to help the situation had come and gone about ten minutes ago.

'It was very fast,' Sara told Lena, obviously with some reluctance. 'She started to go into convulsions.'

Lena laid Sibyl's hand down on the table. She pulled the sheet up, tucking it under her sister's chin as she spoke. 'You're a pediatrician, right? What exactly did you do to help my sister?' She locked eyes with Sara. 'Why didn't you call a real doctor?'

Sara gave a short incredulous laugh. She inhaled deeply before answering, 'Lena, I think you should let Jeffrey take you home now.'

'I don't want to go home,' Lena answered, her tone calm, almost conversational. 'Did you call an ambulance? Did you call your boyfriend?' A tilt of her head indicated Jeffrey.

Sara's hands went behind her back. She seemed to be physically restraining herself. 'We're not going to have this conversation now. You're too upset.'

'I'm too upset,' Lena repeated, clenching her hands. 'You think I'm upset?' she said, her voice louder this time. 'You think I'm too fucking upset to talk to you about why you fucking couldn't help my sister?'

As quickly as she had taken off in the parking lot, Lena was in Sara's face.

'You're a doctor!' Lena screamed. 'How can she die with a fucking doctor in the room?'

Sara did not answer. She looked off to the side.

'You can't even look at me,' Lena said. 'Can you?'

Sara's focus did not change.

'You let my sister die and you can't even fucking look at me.'

'Lena,' Jeffrey said, finally stepping in. He put his hand on her arm, trying to get her to back off.

'Let me go,' she screamed, punching him with her fists. She started to pummel his chest, but he grabbed her hands, holding them tight. She still fought him, screaming, spitting, kicking. Holding her hands was like grabbing a live wire. He kept a firm hand, taking the abuse, letting her get it all out until she crumpled into a ball on the floor. Jeffrey sat beside her, holding her while she sobbed. When he thought to look, Sara was nowhere to be found.

Jeffrey pulled a handkerchief out of his desk with one hand, holding the phone to his ear with the other. He put the cloth to his mouth, dabbing at the blood as a metallic version of Sara's voice asked him to wait for the beep.

'Hey,' he said, taking away the cloth. 'You there?' He waited a few seconds. 'I want to make sure you're okay, Sara.' More seconds passed. 'If you don't pick up, I'm going to come over.' He expected to get a response to this, but nothing came. He heard the machine run out and hung up the phone.

Frank knocked on his office door. 'The kid's in the bathroom,' he said, meaning Lena. Jeffrey knew Lena hated to be called a kid, but this was the only way Frank Wallace could think to show his partner that he cared.

Frank said, 'She's got a mean right, huh?'

'Yeah.' Jeffrey folded the handkerchief for a fresh corner. 'She know I'm waiting for her?'

Frank offered, 'I'll make sure she doesn't make any detours.'

'Good,' Jeffrey said, then, 'Thanks.'

He saw Lena walking through the squad room, her chin tilted up defiantly. When she got to his office, she took her time shutting the door, then slumped into one of the two chairs across from him. She had the look of a teenager who had been called into the principal's office.

'I'm sorry I hit you,' she mumbled.

'Yeah,' Jeffrey returned, holding up the handkerchief. 'I got worse at the Auburn-Alabama game.' She did not respond, so he added, 'And I was in the stands at the time.'

Lena propped her elbow on the armrest and leaned her head into her hand. 'What leads do you have?' she asked. 'Any suspects?'

'We're running the computer right now,' he said. 'We should have a list in the morning.'

She put her hand over her eyes. He folded the handkerchief, waiting for her to speak.

She whispered, 'She was raped?'

'Yes.'

'How badly?'

'I don't know.'

'She was cut,' Lena said. 'This is some Jesus freak?'

49

His answer was the truth. 'I don't know.'

'You don't seem to know a hell of a lot,' she finally said.

'You're right,' he agreed. 'I need to ask you some questions.'

Lena did not look up, but he saw her give a slight nod.

'Was she seeing anybody?'

Finally she looked up. 'No.'

'Any old boyfriends?'

Something flickered in her eyes, and her answer didn't come as quickly as the last. 'No.'

'You sure about that?'

'Yes, I'm sure.'

'Not even somebody from a few years back? Sibyl moved here, what, about six years ago?'

'That's right,' Lena said, her voice hostile again. 'She took a job at the college so she could be near me.'

'Was she living with someone?'

'What does that mean?'

Jeffrey dropped the handkerchief. 'It means what it means, Lena. She was blind. I'm assuming she needed help getting around. Was she living with someone?'

Lena pursed her lips, as if debating whether or not to answer. 'She was sharing a house on Cooper with Nan Thomas.'

'The librarian?' This would explain why Sara had seen her at the library.

Lena mumbled, 'I guess I have to tell Nan about this, too.'

Jeffrey assumed Nan Thomas already knew. Secrets did not stay kept for very long in Grant. Still, he offered, 'I can tell her.'

'No,' she said, giving him a scathing look. 'I think it would be better coming from someone who knows her.'

The implication was clear to Jeffrey, but he chose not to confront her. Lena was looking for another fight, that much was obvious. 'I'm sure she's probably already heard something. She won't know the details.'

'She won't know about the rape, you mean?' Lena's leg bobbed up and down in a nervous twitch. 'I guess I shouldn't tell her about the cross?'

'Probably not,' he answered. 'We need to keep some of the details close in case somebody confesses.'

'I'd like to handle a false confession,' Lena mumbled, her leg still shaking.

'You shouldn't be alone tonight,' he told her. 'You want me to call your uncle?' He reached for the phone, but she stopped him with a no.

'I'm fine,' she said, standing. 'I guess I'll see you tomorrow.'

Jeffrey stood, too, glad to conclude this. 'I'll call you as soon as we have something.'

She gave him a funny look. 'What time's the briefing?'

He saw where she was going with this. 'I'm not going to let you work on this case, Lena. You have to know that.'

'You don't understand,' she said. 'If you don't let me work on this, then you're going to have another stiff for your girlfriend down at the morgue.'

SIX

Lena banged her fist on the front door of her sister's house. She was about to go back to her car and get her spare set of keys when Nan Thomas opened the door.

Nan was shorter than Lena and about ten pounds heavier. Her short mousy brown hair and thick glasses made her resemble the prototypical librarian that she was.

Nan's eyes were swollen and puffy, fresh tears still streaking down her cheeks. She held a balled-up piece of tissue in her hand.

Lena said, 'I guess you heard.'

Nan turned, walking back into the house, leaving the door open for Lena. The two women had never gotten along. Except for the fact that Nan Thomas was Sibyl's lover, Lena would not have said two words to her.

The house was a bungalow built in the 1920s. Much of the original architecture had been left in place, from the hardwood floors to the simple molding lining the doorways. The front door opened into a large living room with a fireplace at one end and the dining room at the other. Off this was the kitchen. Two small bedrooms and a bath finished the simple plan.

Lena walked purposefully down the hallway. She opened the first door on the right, entering the bedroom that had been turned into Sibyl's study. The room was neat and orderly, mostly by necessity. Sibyl was blind, things had to be put in their place or she would not be able to find them. Braille books were stacked neatly on the shelves. Magazines, also in Braille, were lined up on the coffee table in front of an old futon. A computer sat on the desk lining the far wall. Lena was turning it on when Nan walked into the room.

'What do you think you're doing?'

'I need to go through her things.'

'Why?' Nan asked, going over to the desk. She put her hand over the keyboard, as if she could stop Lena.

'I need to see if anything was strange, if anyone was following her.'

'You think you'll find it in here?' Nan demanded, picking up the keyboard. 'She only used this for school. You don't even understand the voice recognition software.'

Lena grabbed the keyboard back. 'I'll figure it out.'

'No, you won't,' Nan countered. 'This is my house, too.'

Lena put her hands on her hips, walking toward the center of the room. She spotted a stack of papers beside an old Braille typewriter. Lena picked them up, turning to Nan. 'What's this?'

Nan ran over, grabbing the papers. 'It's her diary.'

'Can you read it?'

'It's her personal diary,' Nan repeated, aghast. 'These are her private thoughts.'

Lena chewed her bottom lip, trying for a softer tactic. That she had never liked Nan Thomas was not exactly a secret in this house. 'You can read Braille, right?'

'Some.'

'You need to tell me what this says, Nan. Somebody killed her.' Lena tapped the pages. 'Maybe she was being followed. Maybe she was scared of something and didn't want to tell us.'

Nan turned away, her head tilted down toward the pages. She ran her fingers along the top line of dots, but Lena could tell she wasn't reading it. For some reason, Lena got the impression she was touching the pages because Sibyl had, as if she could absorb some sense of Sibyl rather than just words.

Nan said, 'She always went to the diner on Mondays. It was her time out to do something on her own.'

'I know.'

'We were supposed to make burritos tonight.' Nan stacked the papers against the desk. 'Do what you need to do,' she said. 'I'll be in the living room.'

Lena waited for her to leave, then continued the task at hand. Nan was right about the computer. Lena did not know how to use the software, and Sibyl had only used it for school. Sibyl dictated into the computer what she needed, and her teaching assistant made sure copies were made.

The second bedroom was slightly larger than the first. Lena stood in the doorway, taking in the neatly made bed. A stuffed Pooh bear was tucked between the pillows. Pooh was old, balding in places. Sibyl had rarely been without him throughout her childhood, and throwing him away had seemed like heresy. Lena leaned against the door, getting a mental flash of Sibyl as a child, standing with the Pooh bear. Lena closed her eyes, letting the memory overwhelm her. There wasn't much Lena wanted to remember about her childhood, but a particular day stuck out. A few months after the accident that had blinded Sibyl, they were in the backyard, Lena pushing her sister on the swing. Sibyl held Pooh tight to her chest, her head thrown back as she felt the breeze, a huge smile on her face as she relished this simple pleasure. There was such a trust there, Sibyl getting on the swing, trusting Lena not to push her too hard or too high. Lena had felt a responsibility. Her chest swelled from it, and she kept pushing Sibyl until her arms had ached.

Lena rubbed her eyes, shutting the bedroom door. She went into the bathroom and opened the medicine cabinet. Other than Sibyl's usual vitamins and herbs, the cabinet was empty. Lena opened the closet, rummaging past the toilet paper and tampons, hair gel and hand towels. What she was looking for, Lena did not know. Sibyl didn't hide things. She would be the last person to be able to find them if she did.

'Sibby,' Lena breathed, turning back to the mirror on the medicine cabinet. Seeing Sibyl, not herself. Lena spoke to her reflection, whispering, 'Tell me something. Please.'

She closed her eyes, trying to navigate the space as Sibyl would. The room was small, and Lena could touch both walls with her hands as she stood in the center. She opened her eyes with a weary sigh. There was nothing there.

Back in the living room, Nan Thomas sat on the couch. She held Sibyl's diary in her lap, not looking up when Lena came in. 'I read the last few days' worth of stuff,' she said, her tone flat. 'Nothing out of place. She was worried about a kid at school who was flunking.'

'A guy?'

Nan shook her head. 'Female. A freshman.'

Lena leaned her hand against the wall. 'Did you have any workmen in or out in the last month?'

'No.'

'Same mailman delivering to the house? No UPS or FedEx?'

'Nobody new. This is Grant County, Lee.'

Lena bristled at the familiar name. She tried to bite

back her anger. 'She didn't say she felt like she was being followed or anything?'

'No, not at all. She was perfectly normal.' Nan clutched the papers to her chest. 'Her classes were fine. We were fine.' A slight smile came to her lips. 'We were supposed to take a day trip to Eufalla this weekend.'

Lena took her car keys out of her pocket. 'Right,' she quipped. 'I guess if anything comes up you should call me.'

'Lee –'

Lena held up her hand. 'Don't.'

Nan acknowledged the warning with a frown. 'I'll call you if I think of anything.'

By midnight, Lena was finishing off her third bottle of Rolling Rock, driving across the Grant County line outside of Madison. She contemplated throwing the empty out the car window but stopped herself at the last minute. She laughed at her twisted sense of morality; she would drive under the influence but she would not litter. The line had to be drawn somewhere.

Angela Norton, Lena's mother, grew up watching her brother Hank dig himself deeper and deeper into a bottomless pit of alcohol and drug abuse. Hank had told Lena that her mother had been adamantly against alcohol. When Angela married Calvin Adams, her only rule of the house was that he not go out drinking with his fellow policemen. Cal was known to slip out now and then, but for the most part, he honored his wife's wishes. Three months into his marriage, he was making a routine traffic stop along a dirt road outside of Reece, Georgia, when the driver pulled a gun on him. Shot twice in the head, Calvin Adams died before his body hit the ground.

At twenty-three, Angela was hardly prepared to be a

widow. When she passed out at her husband's funeral, her family chalked it up to nerves. Four weeks of morning sickness later, a doctor finally gave her the diagnosis. She was pregnant.

As her condition progressed, Angela became more despondent. She wasn't a happy woman to begin with. Life in Reece was not easy, and the Norton family had seen its share of hardship. Hank Norton was known for his volatile temper and was considered to be the kind of mean chunk you didn't want to run into in a dark alley. At her older brother's knee, Angela had learned not to put up much of a fight. Two weeks after giving birth to twin baby girls, Angela Adams succumbed to an infection. She was twenty-four years old. Hank Norton was the only relative willing to take in her two girls.

To hear Hank tell the story, Sibyl and Lena had turned his life around. The day he took them home was the day he stopped abusing his body. He claimed to have found God through their presence and to this day said he could recall minute by minute what it was like to hold Lena and Sibyl for the first time.

In truth, Hank only stopped shooting up speed when the girls came to live with him. He did not stop drinking until much later. The girls were eight when it happened. A bad day at work had sent Hank on a binge. When he ran out of liquor, he decided to drive instead of walk to the store. His car didn't even make it to the street. Sibyl and Lena were playing ball out in the front yard. Lena still didn't know what had been going through Sibyl's mind as she chased the ball into the driveway. The car had struck her from the side, the steel bumper slamming into her temple as she bent to retrieve the ball.

County services had been called in, but nothing came of the investigation. The closest hospital was a forty-minute drive from Reece. Hank had plenty of time to sober up and give a convincing story. Lena could still recall being in the car with him, watching his mouth work as he figured out the story in his mind. At the time, eight-year-old Lena was not quite sure what had happened, and when the police interviewed her she had supported Hank's story.

Sometimes Lena still had dreams about the accident, and in these dreams Sibyl's body bounced against the ground much as the ball had. That Hank had allegedly not touched another drop of alcohol since then was of no conscquence to Lena. The damage had been done.

Lena opened another bottle of beer, removing both hands from the wheel to twist off the cap. She took a long pull, grimacing at the taste. Alcohol had never appealed to her. Lena hated being out of control, hated the dizzy sensation and the numbness. Getting drunk was something for the weak, a crutch for people who were not strong enough to live their own lives, to stand on their own two feet. Drinking was running away from something. Lena took another swig of beer, thinking there was no better time than the present for all of these things.

The Celica fishtailed as she took the turn off the exit too hard. Lena corrected the wheel with one hand, holding tight to the bottle with the other. A hard right at the top of the exit took her to the Reece Stop 'n' Save. The store inside was dark. Like most businesses in town, the gas station closed at ten. Though, if memory served, a walk around the building would reveal a group of teenagers drinking, smoking cigarettes, and doing things their parents did not want to know about. Lena and Sibyl had walked to this store many a dark night, sneaking out of the house under Hank's none-too-watchful eye.

Scooping up the empty bottles, Lena got out of the

car. She stumbled, her foot catching on the door. A bottle slipped out of her hands and busted on the concrete. Cursing, she kicked the shards away from her tires, walking toward the trash can. Lena stared at her reflection in the store's plate glass windows as she tossed her empties. For a second, it was like looking at Sibyl. She reached over to the glass, touching her lips, her eyes.

'Jesus.' Lena sighed. This was one of the many reasons she did not like to drink. She was turning into a basket case.

Music blared from the bar across the street. Hank considered it a test of will that he owned a bar but never imbibed. The Hut looked like its name, with a southern twist. The roof was thatched only until it mattered, then a rusted tin lined the pitched surface. Tiki torches with orange and red lightbulbs instead of flames stood on either side of the entrance, and the door was painted to look like it had been fashioned from grass. Paint peeled from the walls, but for the most part you could still make out the bamboo design.

Drunk as she was, Lena had the sense to look both ways before she crossed the street. Her feet were about ten seconds behind her body, and she held her hands out to her sides for balance as she walked across the gravel parking lot. Of the fifty or so vehicles in the lot, about forty were pickup trucks. This being the new South, instead of gun racks they sported chrome runners and gold striping along their sides. The other cars were Jeeps and four-wheel drives. Nascar numbers were painted onto the back windshields. Hank's cream-colored L983 Mercedes was the only sedan in the lot.

The Hut reeked of cigarette smoke, and Lena had to take a few shallow breaths so she wouldn't choke. Her eyes burned as she walked over to the bar. Not much had changed in the last twenty or so years. The floor was still sticky from beer and crunchy from peanut shells. To the left were booths that probably had more DNA material in them than the FBI lab at Quantico. To the right was a long bar fashioned from fifty-gallon barrels and heart of pine. A stage was on the far wall, the rest rooms for men and women on either side. In the middle of the bar was what Hank called a dance floor. Most nights, it was packed back to front with men and women in various stages of drunken arousal. The Hut was a two-thirty bar, meaning everybody looked good at two-thirty in the morning.

Hank was nowhere to be seen, but Lena knew he wouldn't be far on amateur night. Every other Monday, patrons of the Hut were invited to stand onstage and embarrass themselves in front of the rest of the town. Lena shuddered as she thought about it. Reece made Heartsdale look like a bustling metropolis. Except for the tire factory, most of the men in this room would have left a long time ago. As it was, they were content to drink themselves to death and pretend they were happy.

Lena slid onto the first vacant stool she could find. The country song on the jukebox had a pounding bass, and she leaned her elbows on the bar, cupping her hands over her ears so that she could hear herself think.

She felt a bump on her arm and looked up in time to see *Websters* definition of a hick sitting down beside her. His face was sunburned from his neck to about an inch from his hairline where he had obviously been working outside wearing a baseball hat. His shirt was starched within an inch of its life, and the cuffs were tight around his thick wrists. The jukebox stopped abruptly, and Lena worked her jaw, trying to make her ears pop so she didn't feel like she was in a tunnel.

Her gentleman neighbor bumped her arm again, smiling, saying, 'Hey, lady.'

Lena rolled her eyes, catching the bartender's eye. 'JD on the rocks,' she ordered.

'That'n's on me,' the man said, slapping down a ten-dollar bill. When he spoke, his words slurred together like a wrecked train, and Lena realized he was a lot drunker than she planned ever to be.

The man gave her a sloppy smile. 'You know, sugar, I'd love to get biblical with you.'

She leaned over, close to his ear. 'If I ever find out you have, I'll cut your balls off with my car keys.'

He opened his mouth to reply but was jerked off the barstool before he could get a word out. Hank stood there with the man's shirt collar in his hand, then shoved him into the crowd. The look he fixed Lena with was just as hard as the one she imagined was on her own face.

Lena had never liked her uncle. Unlike Sibyl, she wasn't the forgiving type. Even when Lena drove Sibyl to Reece for visits, Lena spent most of her time in the car or sitting on the front porch steps, keys in her hand, ready to go as soon as Sibyl walked out the front door.

Despite the fact that Hank Norton had injected speed into his veins for the better part of his twenties and thirties, he was not an idiot. Lena showing up on Hank's proverbial doorstep in the middle of the night could only mean one thing.

Their eyes were still locked as music started to blare again, shaking the walls, sending a vibration from the floor up the barstool. She saw rather than heard what Hank was asking when he said, 'Where's Sibyl?'

Tucked behind the bar, more like an outhouse than a place of business, Hank's office was a small wooden box with a tin roof. A lightbulb hung from a frayed electrical wire that had probably been installed by the WPA. Posters from beer and liquor companies served as wallpaper. White cartons filled with liquor were stacked against the back wall, leaving about ten square feet for a desk with two chairs on either side. Surrounding these were piles of boxes stuffed with receipts that Hank had accumulated from running the bar over the years. A stream running behind the shack kept mold and moisture in the air. Lena imagined Hank liked working in this dark, dank place, passing his days in an environment more suitable for a tongue.

'I see you've redecorated,' Lena said, setting her glass on top of one of the boxes. She could not tell if she wasn't drunk anymore or if she was too drunk to notice.

Hank gave the glass a cursory glance, then looked back at Lena. 'You don't drink.'

She held up the glass in a toast. 'To the late bloomer.'

Hank sat back in his office chair, his hands clasped in front of his stomach. He was tall and skinny, with skin that tended to flake in the winter. Despite the fact that his father was Spanish, Hank's appearance more closely resembled his mother's, a pasty woman who was as sour as her complexion. In her mind, Lena had always thought it appropriate that Hank bore a close resemblance to an albino snake.

He asked, 'What brings you to these parts?'

'Just dropping by,' she managed around the glass. The whiskey was bitter in her mouth. She kept an eye on Hank as she finished the drink and banged the empty glass back down on the box. Lena did not know what was stopping her. For years she had waited to get the upper hand with Hank Norton. This was her time to hurt him as much as he had hurt Sibyl.

'You started snortin' coke, too, or have you been crying?'

Lena wiped her mouth with the back of her hand. 'What do you think?'

Hank stared at her, working his hands back and forth. This was more than a nervous habit, Lena knew. Speed injected into the veins of his hands had given Hank arthritis at an early age. Since most of the veins in his arms had calcified from the powdered additive used to cut the drug, there wasn't much circulation there, either. His hands were cold as ice most days and a constant source of pain.

The rubbing stopped abruptly. 'Let's get it over with, Lee. I've got the show to put on.'

Lena tried to open her mouth, but nothing came out. Part of her was angered by his flippant attitude, which had marked their relationship from the very beginning. Part of her did not know how to tell him. As much as Lena hated her uncle, he was a human being. Hank had doted on Sibyl. In high school, Lena could not take her sister everywhere, and Sibyl had spent a lot of time home with Hank. There was an undeniable bond there, and as much as Lena wanted to hurt her uncle, she felt herself holding back. Lena had loved Sibyl, Sibyl had loved Hank.

Hank picked up a ballpoint pen, turning it head over end on the desk several times before he finally asked, 'What's wrong, Lee? Need some money?'

If only it were that simple, Lena thought.

'Car broke down?'

She shook her head slowly side to side.

'It's Sibyl,' he stated, his voice catching in his throat.

When Lena did not answer, he nodded slowly to himself, putting his hands together, as if to pray. 'She's sick?' he asked, his voice indicating he expected the worst. With this one sentence, he showed more emotion than Lena had ever seen him express in a lifetime of knowing her uncle. She looked at him closely as if for the first time. His pale skin was blotched with those red dots pasty men get on their faces as they age. His hair, silver for as long as she could recall, was dulled with yellow under the sixty-watt bulb. His Hawaiian shirt was rumpled, which was not his style, and his hands tremored slightly as he fidgeted with them.

Lena did it the same way Jeffrey Tolliver had. 'She went to the diner in the middle of town,' she began. 'You know the one across from the dress shop?'

A slight nod was all he gave.

'She walked there from the house,' Lena continued. 'She did it every week, just to be able to do something on her own.'

Hank clasped his hands together in front of his face, touching the sides of his index fingers to his forehead.

'So, uhm.' Lena picked up the glass, needing something to do. She sucked what little liquor was left off the ice cubes, then continued. 'She went to the bathroom, and somebody killed her.'

There was little sound in the tiny office. Grasshoppers chirped outside. Gurgling came from the stream. A distant throbbing came from the bar.

Without preamble, Hank turned around, picking through the boxes, asking, 'What've you had to drink tonight?'

Lena was surprised by his question, though she shouldn't have been. Despite his AA brainwashing, Hank Norton was a master at avoiding the unpleasant. His need to escape was what had brought Hank to drugs and alcohol in the first place. 'Beer in the car,' she said, playing along, glad for once that he did not want the gory details. 'JD here.'

He paused, his hand around a bottle of Jack Daniel's. 'Beer before liquor, never sicker,' he warned, his voice catching on the last part.

Lena held out her glass, rattling the ice for attention. She watched Hank as he poured the drink, not surprised when he licked his lips.

'How's work treating you?' Hank asked, his voice tinny in the shack. His lower lip trembled slightly. His expression was one of total grief, in direct opposition to the words coming from his mouth. He said, 'Doing okay?'

Lena nodded. She felt as if she was smack in the middle of a car accident. She finally understood the meaning of the word *surreal*. Nothing seemed concrete in this tiny space. The glass in her hand felt dull. Hank was miles away. She was in a dream.

Lena tried to snap herself out of it, downing her drink quickly. The alcohol hit the back of her throat like fire, burning and solid, as if she had swallowed hot asphalt.

Hank watched the glass, not Lena, as she did this.

This was all she needed. She said, 'Sibyl's dead, Hank.'

Tears came to his eyes without warning, and all that Lena could think was that he looked so very, very old. It was like watching a flower wilt. He took out his handkerchief and wiped his nose.

Lena repeated the words much as Jeffrey Tolliver had earlier this evening. 'She's dead.'

His voice wavered as he asked, 'Are you sure?'

Lena nodded quickly up and down. 'I saw her.' Then, 'Somebody cut her up pretty bad.'

His mouth opened and closed like a fish's. He kept his eyes even with Lena's the way he used to do when he was trying to catch her in a lie. He finally looked away, mumbling, 'That doesn't make sense.'

She could have reached out and patted his old hand, maybe tried to comfort him, but she didn't. Lena felt frozen in her chair. Instead of thinking of Sibyl, which had been her mind's initial reaction, she concentrated on Hank, on his wet lips, his eyes, the hairs growing out of his nose.

'Oh, Sibby.' He sighed, wiping his eyes. Lena watched his Adam's apple bob as he swallowed. He reached for the bottle, resting his hand on the neck. Without asking, he unscrewed the cap and poured Lena another drink. This time, the dark liquid nearly touched the rim.

More time passed, then Hank blew his nose loudly, patting at his eyes with the handkerchief. 'I can't see anyone trying to kill her.' His hands shook even more as he folded the handkerchief over and over. 'Doesn't make sense,' he mumbled. 'You, I could understand.'

'Thanks a lot.'

This was sufficient enough to spark Hank's irritation. 'I mean because of the job you do. Now get that damn chip off your shoulder.'

Lena did not comment. This was a familiar order.

He put his palms down on the desk, fixing Lena with a stare. 'Where were you when this happened?'

Lena tossed back the drink, not feeling the burn so much this time. When she returned the glass to the desk, Hank was still staring at her.

She mumbled, 'Macon.'

'Was it some sort of hate crime, then?'

Lena reached over, picking up the bottle. 'I don't know. Maybe.' The whiskey gurgled in the bottle as she poured. 'Maybe he picked her because she was gay. Maybe he picked her because she was blind.' Lena gave a sideways glance, catching his pained reaction to this. She decided to expound upon her speculation. 'Rapists tend to pick women they think they can control, Hank. She was an easy target.'

'So, this all comes back to me?'

'I didn't say that.'

He grabbed the bottle. 'Right,' he snapped, dropping the half empty bottle back into its box. His tone was angry now, back to the nuts and bolts. Like Lena, Hank was never comfortable with the emotional side of things. Sibyl had often said the main reason Hank and Lena never got along was that they were too much alike. Sitting there with Hank, absorbing his grief and anger as it filled the tiny shed, Lena realized that Sibyl was right. She was looking at herself in twenty years, and there was nothing she could do to stop it.

Hank asked, 'Have you talked to Nan?'

'Yeah.'

'We've got to plan the service,' he said, picking up the pen and drawing a box on his desk calendar. At the top he wrote the word FUNERAL in all caps. 'Is there somebody in Grant you think would do a good job?' He waited for her response, then added, 'I mean, most of her friends were there.'

'What?' Lena asked, the glass paused at her lips. 'What are you talking about?'

'Lee, we've got to make arrangements. We've got to take care of Sibby.'

Lena finished the drink. When she looked at Hank, his features were blurred. As a matter of fact, the whole room was blurred. She had the sensation of being on a roller coaster, and her stomach reacted accordingly. Lena put her hand to her mouth, fighting the urge to be sick.

Hank had probably seen her expression many times before, most likely in the mirror. He was beside her,

holding a trash can under her chin, just as she lost the
battle.

TUESDAY

SEVEN

Sara leaned over the kitchen sink in her parents' house, using her father's wrench to loosen the faucet. She had spent most of the evening in the morgue performing Sibyl Adams's autopsy. Going back to a dark house, sleeping alone, had not been something she wanted to do. Add to that Jeffrey's last threat on her answering machine to come by her house, and Sara did not really have a choice as to where she slept last night. Except for sneaking in to pick up the dogs, she had not even bothered to change out of her scrubs.

She wiped sweat from her forehead, glancing at the clock on the coffeemaker. It was six-thirty in the morning and she had slept all of two hours. Every time she closed her eyes, she thought of Sibyl Adams sitting on the toilet, blind to what was happening to her, feeling everything her attacker was doing.

On the plus side, short of some type of family catastrophe, there was no way in hell today could possibly be as bad as yesterday.

Cathy Linton walked into the kitchen, opened a cabinet, and took down a coffee cup before she noticed her oldest daughter standing beside her. 'What are you doing?'

Sara slid a new washer over the threaded bolt. 'The faucet was leaking.'

'Two plumbers in the family,' Cathy complained,

pouring herself a cup of coffee, 'and my daughter the doctor ends up fixing the leaky faucet.'

Sara smiled, putting her shoulder behind the wrench. The Lintons were a plumbing family, and Sara had spent most of her summers during school working alongside her father, snaking drains and welding pipe. Sometimes she thought the only reason she had finished high school a year early and worked through summers getting her undergrad degree was so she would not have to poke around spider-infested crawl spaces with her father. Not that she didn't love her father, but, unlike Tessa, Sara's fear of spiders could not be overcome.

Cathy slid onto the kitchen stool. 'Did you sleep here last night?'

'Yeah,' Sara answered, washing her hands. She turned off the faucet, smiling when it didn't leak. The sense of accomplishment lifted some of the weight off her shoulders.

Cathy smiled her approval. 'If that medical thing doesn't work out, at least you'll have plumbing to fall back on.'

'You know, that's what Daddy told me when he drove me to college the first day.'

'I know,' Cathy said. 'I could have killed him.' She took a sip of coffee, eyeing Sara over the rim of the cup. 'Why didn't you go home?'

'I worked late and I just wanted to come here. Is that okay?'

'Of course it's okay,' Cathy said, tossing Sara a towel. 'Don't be ridiculous.'

Sara dried her hands. 'I hope I didn't wake you up when I came in.'

'Not me,' Cathy answered. 'Why didn't you sleep with Tess?'

Sara made herself busy straightening the towel on the

rack. Tessa lived in a two-bedroom apartment over the garage. In the last few years, there had been nights when Sara had not wanted to sleep alone in her own house. She generally stayed with her sister rather than risk waking her father, who invariably wanted to discuss at great length what was troubling her.

Sara answered, 'I didn't want to bother her.'

'Oh, bullshit.' Cathy laughed. 'Good Lord, Sara, nearly a quarter of a million dollars to that college and they didn't teach you to lie better than that?'

Sara took down her favorite mug and poured herself some coffee. 'Maybe you should've sent me to law school instead.'

Cathy crossed her legs, frowning. She was a small woman who kept herself trim by doing yoga. Her blond hair and blue eyes had skipped over Sara and been passed on to Tessa. Except for their matching temperaments, anyone would be hard-pressed to tell that Cathy and Sara were mother and daughter.

'Well?' Cathy prompted.

Sara couldn't keep the smile off of her lips. 'Let's just say Tess was a little busy when I walked in and leave it at that.'

'Busy by herself?'

'No.' Sara barked an uncomfortable laugh, feeling her cheeks turn red. 'God, Mother.'

After a few moments, Cathy lowered her voice, asking, 'Was it Devon Lockwood?'

'Devon?' Sara was surprised by the name. She hadn't been able to see exactly who Tessa was wrangling around with in bed, but Devon Lockwood, the new plumber's helper Eddie Linton had hired two weeks ago, was the last name she was expecting to come up.

Cathy shushed her. 'Your father will hear.'

'Hear what?' Eddie asked, shuffling into the kitchen.

His eyes lit up when he saw Sara. 'There's my baby,' he said, kissing her cheek with a loud smack. 'Was that you I heard coming in this morning?'

'That was me,' Sara confessed.

'I got some paint chips in the garage,' he offered. 'Maybe we can go look at them after we eat, pick a pretty color for your room.'

Sara sipped her coffee. 'I'm not moving back in, Dad.'

He jabbed a finger at the cup. 'That'll stunt your growth.'

'I should be so lucky,' Sara grumbled. Since the ninth grade, she had been the tallest member of her immediate family, just inching past her father by a hair.

Sara slid onto the stool her mother vacated. She watched her parents as they went through their morning routine, her father walking around the kitchen, getting in her mother's way until Cathy pushed him into a chair. Her father smoothed his hair back as he leaned over the morning paper. His salt-and-pepper hair stuck out in three different directions, much like his eyebrows. The T-shirt he was wearing was so old and worn holes were breaking through over his shoulder blades. The pattern on his pajama pants had faded out over five years ago, and his bedroom slippers were falling apart at the heels. That she had inherited her mother's cynicism and her father's sense of dress was something Sara would never forgive them for.

Eddie said, 'I see the *Observer's* milking this thing for every penny.'

Sara glanced at the headline of Grant's local paper. It read: 'College Professor Slain in Grisly Attack.'

'What's it say?' Sara asked before she could stop herself.

He traced his finger down the page as he read. ' "Sibyl Adams, a professor at GIT, was savagely beaten

74

to death yesterday at the Grant Filling Station. Local police are baffled. Police Chief Jeffrey Tolliver" ' – Eddie stopped, muttering, 'the bastard' under his breath – ' ' "reports they are exploring every possible lead in order to bring the young professor's murderer to justice." '

'She wasn't beaten to death,' Sara said, knowing that the punch to Sibyl Adams's face had not killed her. Sara gave an involuntary shudder as she recalled the physical findings during the autopsy.

Eddie seemed to notice her reaction. He said, 'Was anything else done to her?'

Sara was surprised her father had asked this. Normally, her family went out of their way not to ask questions about that side of Sara's life. She had felt from the beginning that they were all more than a little uncomfortable with her part-time job.

Sara asked, 'Like what?' before she got her father's meaning. Cathy looked up from mixing the pancake batter, a look of trepidation on her face.

Tessa burst into the kitchen, popping the swinging door on its hinge, obviously expecting to find Sara alone. Her mouth opened in a perfect o.

Cathy, standing at the stove making pancakes, tossed over her shoulder, 'Good morning, sunshine.'

Tessa kept her head down, making a beeline for the coffee.

'Sleep well?' Eddie asked.

'Like a baby,' Tessa returned, kissing the top of his head.

Cathy waved her spatula in Sara's direction. 'You could learn from your sister.'

Tessa had the common sense to ignore this comment. She opened the French door leading to the deck and jerked her head outside, indicating Sara should follow.

Sara did as she was told, holding her breath until the door was closed firmly behind her. She whispered, 'Devon Lockwood?'

'I still haven't told them about your date with Jeb,' Tessa countered.

Sara pressed her lips together, silently agreeing to the truce.

Tessa tucked one of her legs underneath her as she sat on the porch swing. 'What were you doing out so late?'

'I was at the morgue,' Sara answered, sitting beside her sister. She rubbed her arms, fighting the early morning chill. Sara was still in her scrubs and a thin white T-shirt, hardly enough for the temperature. 'I needed to check some things. Lena –' She stopped herself, not sure she could tell Tessa what had happened with Lena Adams in the morgue last night. The accusations still stung, even though Sara knew it was Lena's grief talking.

She said, 'I wanted to get it over with, you know?'

All mirth had left Tessa's features. 'Did you find anything?'

'I faxed a report to Jeffrey. I think it's going to help him get some solid leads.' She stopped, making sure she had Tessa's attention. 'Listen, Tessie. Be careful, okay? I mean, keep the doors locked. Don't go out alone. That kind of thing.'

'Yeah.' Tessa squeezed her hand. 'Okay. Sure.'

'I mean –' Sara stopped, not wanting to terrify her sister, but not wanting to put her in danger either. 'You're both the same age. You and Sibyl. Do you see what I'm getting at?'

'Yeah,' Tessa answered, but it was obvious she did not want to talk about it. Sara couldn't blame her sister. Knowing in intimate detail what had happened to Sibyl Adams, Sara was finding it hard to get through the day.

'I put the postcard –' Tessa began, but Sara stopped her.

'I found it in my briefcase,' she said. 'Thanks.'

'Yeah,' Tessa said, a stillness to her voice.

Sara stared out at the lake, not thinking about the postcard, not thinking about Sibyl Adams or Jeffrey or anything. There was something so peaceful about the water that for the first time in weeks, Sara felt herself relax. If she squinted her eyes, she could see the dock at the back of her own house. It had a covered boathouse, a small floating barnlike structure, like most of the docks on the lake.

She imagined herself sitting in one of the deck chairs, sipping a margarita, reading a trashy novel. Why she pictured herself doing this, Sara did not know. She seldom had time to sit lately, she did not like the taste of alcohol, and at the end of the day she was nearly cross-eyed from reading patient charts, pediatric journals, and forensic field manuals.

Tessa interrupted her thoughts. 'I guess you didn't get much sleep last night?'

Sara shook her head as she leaned against her sister's shoulder.

'How was it being around Jeffrey yesterday?'

'I wish I could take a pill and forget all about him.'

Tessa raised her arm, putting it around Sara's shoulders. 'Is that why you couldn't sleep?'

Sara sighed, closing her eyes. 'I don't know. I was just thinking about Sibyl. About Jeffrey.'

'Two years is a long time to carry a torch for somebody,' Tessa said. 'If you really want to get over him, then you need to start dating.' She stopped Sara's protest. 'I mean real dates, where you don't drop the guy as soon as he gets close.'

Sara sat up, pulling her knees to her chest. She knew

what her sister was suggesting. 'I'm not like you. I can't just sleep around.' Tessa didn't take offense at this. Sara had not expected her to. That Tessa Linton enjoyed an active sex life was pretty much known to everyone in town but their father.

'I was just sixteen when Steve and I got together,' Sara began, referring to her first serious boyfriend. 'Then, well, you know what happened in Atlanta.' Tessa nodded. 'Jeffrey made me like sex. I mean, for the first time in my life, I felt like a complete person.' She clenched her fists, as if she could hold on to that feeling. 'You have no idea what that meant to me, to be suddenly awake after all those years of focusing on school and work and not seeing anybody or having any kind of life.'

Tessa was quiet, letting Sara talk.

'I remember our first date,' she continued. 'He was driving me back to the house in the rain and he stopped the car all of a sudden. I thought it was a joke, because we'd both been talking about how much we liked to walk in the rain just a few minutes earlier. But he left the lights on and he got out of the car.' Sara closed her eyes, seeing Jeffrey standing in the rain, his coat collar turned up to the cold. 'There was a cat in the road. It had been hit, and it was obviously dead.'

Tessa was silent, waiting. 'And?' she prompted.

'And he picked it up and moved it out of the road so that no one else would hit it.'

Tessa couldn't hide her shock. 'He picked it up?'

'Yeah.' Sara smiled fondly at the memory. 'He didn't want anyone else to hit it.'

'He touched a dead cat?'

Sara laughed at her reaction. 'I never told you that before?'

'I think I'd remember.'

Sara sat back in the swing, using her foot to keep it steady. 'The thing was, at dinner he told me how much he hates cats. And here he was, stopping in the middle of the road in the dark, in the rain, to move the cat out of the road so that no one else would hit it.'

Tessa could not mask her distaste. 'Then he got back in the car with dead-cat hands?'

'I drove, because he didn't want to touch anything.'

Tessa wrinkled her nose. 'Is this the part where it gets romantic, because I'm feeling slightly sick to my stomach.'

Sara gave her a sideways glance. 'I drove him back to the house, and of course he had to come in to wash his hands.' Sara laughed. 'His hair was all wet from the rain and he kept his hands up like he was a surgeon who didn't want to mess up his scrub.' Sara held her arms in the air, palms facing back, to illustrate.

'And?'

'And I took him into the kitchen to wash his hands because that's where the antibacterial soap is, and he couldn't squeeze the bottle without contaminating it, so I squeezed it for him.' She sighed heavily. 'And he was leaning over the sink washing his hands, then I was lathering up his hands for him, and they felt so strong and warm and he's always so goddamn sure of himself that he just looked up and kissed me right on the lips, without any hesitation, like he knew all along that while I was touching his hands all I could think about was how it would feel to have his hands on me, touching me.'

Tessa waited until she was finished, then said, 'Except for the dead cat part, that's the most romantic story I've ever heard.'

'Well.' Sara stood, walking over to the deck railing.

'I'm sure he makes all his girlfriends feel special. That's one thing he's very good at, I guess.'

'Sara, you'll never understand that sex is different for some people. Sometimes it's just fucking.' She paused. 'Sometimes it's just a way to get some attention.'

'He certainly got my attention.'

'He still loves you.'

Sara turned, sitting on the railing. 'He only wants me back because he lost me.'

'If you were really serious about getting him out of your life,' Tessa began, 'then you would quit your job with the county.'

Sara opened her mouth to respond, but she could not think of how to tell her sister that some days her county work was the only thing that kept her sane. There were only so many sore throats and earaches Sara could take before her mind started to go numb. To give up her job as coroner would be giving up a part of her life that she really enjoyed, despite the macabre aspects.

Knowing Tessa could never understand this, Sara said, 'I don't know what I'm going to do.'

There was no response. Tessa was looking back at the house. Sara followed her gaze through the kitchen window. Jeffrey Tolliver was standing by the stove, talking to her mother.

The Linton home was a split level that had been constantly renovated throughout its forty-year life. When Cathy took an interest in painting, a studio with a half bath was added on to the back. When Sara became obsessed with school, a study with a half bath was built into the attic. When Tessa became interested in boys, the basement was renovated in such a way that Eddie could get from anywhere in the house to the basement in three seconds flat. A stairway was at either end of the room and the closest bathroom was one floor up.

The basement had not changed much since Tessa moved away for college. The carpet was avocado green and the sectional sofa a dark rust. A combination Ping-Pong/pool table dominated the center of the room. Sara had broken her hand once, diving for a Ping-Pong ball and slamming into the console television instead.

Sara's two dogs, Billy and Bob, were on the couch when Sara and Jeffrey walked down the stairs. She clapped her hands, trying to get them to move. The greyhounds did not budge until Jeffrey gave a low whistle. Their tails wagged as he walked over to pet them.

Jeffrey didn't mince words as he scratched Bob's belly. 'I tried to call you all night. Where were you?'

Sara didn't feel he was entitled to that kind of information. She asked, 'Did you get anything on Sibyl yet?'

He shook his head. 'According to Lena, she wasn't seeing anybody. That rules out an angry boyfriend.'

'Anybody in her past?'

'Nobody,' he answered. 'I guess I'll ask her roommate some questions today. She was living with Nan Thomas. You know, the librarian?'

'Yeah,' Sara said, feeling things starting to click in her head. 'Did you get my report yet?'

He shook his head, not understanding. 'What?'

'That's where I was last night, doing the autopsy.'

'What?' he repeated. 'You can't do an autopsy without someone present.'

'I know that, Jeffrey,' Sara snapped back, crossing her arms. One person questioning her competency in the last twelve hours was quite enough. She said, 'That's why I called Brad Stephens.'

'Brad Stephens?' He turned his back to her, muttering something under his breath as he stroked underneath Billy's chin.

'What did you say?'

'I said you're acting strange lately.' He turned, facing her. 'You performed the autopsy in the middle of the night?'

'I'm sorry you find that strange, but I have two jobs to do, not just what I do for you.' He tried to stop her but she continued. 'In case you've forgotten, I have a full patient load at the clinic in addition to what I do at the morgue. Patients, by the way' – she checked her watch, not really noting the time – 'that I have to start seeing in a few minutes.' She tucked her hands into her hips. 'Was there a reason you came by?

'To check on you,' he said. 'Obviously you're all right. I guess that should come as no surprise to me. You're always all right.'

'That's right.'

'Sara Linton, stronger than steel.'

Sara gave what she hoped was a condescending look. They had played out this scene so many times around the time of their divorce that she could recite both sides of the argument by heart. Sara was too independent. Jeffrey was too demanding.

She said, 'I have to go.'

'Wait a minute,' he said. 'The report?'

'I faxed it to you.'

It was his turn to put his hands on his hips. 'Yeah, I got that. You think you found something?'

'Yes,' she answered, then, 'No.' She crossed her arms defensively. She hated when he downshifted from an argument into something to do with work. It was a cheap trick, and it always caught her off guard. She recovered somewhat, saying, 'I need to hear back on the

82

blood this morning. Nick Shelton is supposed to call me at nine, then I can tell you something.' She added, 'I wrote this on the cover page for my report.'

'Why did you rush the blood?' he asked.

'Gut feeling,' Sara answered. That was all she was prepared to give him at this moment. Sara did not like to go on half pieces of information. She was a doctor, not a fortune-teller. Jeffrey knew this.

'Take me through it,' he said.

Sara folded her arms, not wanting to do this. She glanced back up the stairs to make sure no one was listening. 'You read the report,' she said.

'Please,' he said. 'I want to hear it from you.'

Sara leaned against the wall. She closed her eyes for a brief second, not to help her recall the facts, but to give herself some distance from what she knew.

She began, 'She was attacked on the toilet. She was probably easily subdued because of her blindness and the surprise element. I think he cut her early on, lifting her shirt, making the cross with his knife. The cut to her belly came early. It's not deep enough for full penetration. I think he inserted his penis more to defile her than anything else. He then raped her vaginally, which would explain the excrement I found there. I'm not sure if he climaxed. I don't imagine climax would be the issue for him.'

'You think it's more about defiling her?'

She shrugged. Many rapists had some sort of sexual dysfunction. She didn't see why it would be any different with this one. The gut rape practically pointed it out.

She said, 'Maybe it's the thrill of doing it in a semipublic place. Even though the lunch rush was over, someone could have come in and caught him.'

He scratched his chin, obviously letting himself absorb this.

'Anything else?'

'Can you clear some time to come by?' he asked. 'I can set up a briefing at nine-thirty.'

'A full briefing?'

He shook his head. 'I don't want anybody to know about that,' he ordered, and for the first time in a long while, she was in complete agreement with him.

She said, 'That's fine.'

'Can you come in around nine-thirty?' he repeated.

Sara ran through her morning. Jimmy Powell's parents would be in her office at eight. Going from one horrible meeting to another would probably make her day easier. What's more, she knew that the sooner she briefed the detectives on Sibyl Adams's autopsy results, the sooner they could go out and find the man who had killed her.

'Yeah,' she said, walking toward the stairs. 'I'll be there.'

'Wait a minute,' he said. 'Lena's going to be there, too.'

Sara turned around, shaking her head. 'No way. I'm not going to give a blow-by-blow of Sibyl's death in front of her sister.'

'She has to be there, Sara. Trust me on this.' He must have gathered her thoughts from the look she gave him. He said, 'She wants the details. It's how she deals with things. She's a cop.'

'It's not going to be good for her.'

'She's made her decision,' he repeated. 'She'll get the facts one way or another, Sara. It's better she gets the truth from us than read whatever lies they put in the paper.' He paused, probably seeing he still had not changed her mind. 'If it was Tessa, you would want to know what happened.'

'Jeffrey,' Sara said, feeling herself relent despite her better judgment. 'She doesn't need to remember her sister this way.'

He shrugged. 'Maybe she does.'

At a quarter till eight in the morning, Grant County was just waking up. A sudden overnight rain had washed the pollen out of the streets, and though it was still cool out, Sara drove her BMW Z3 with the top down. The car had been purchased during a post-divorce crisis when Sara had needed something to make herself feel better. It had worked for about two weeks, then the stares and the comments about the flashy car had made her feel a bit ridiculous. This was not the kind of car to drive in a small town, especially since Sara was a doctor, and not just a doctor but a pediatrician. Had she not been born and raised in Grant, Sara suspected she would have been forced to sell the car or lose half her patients at the clinic. As it was, she had to put up with the constant comments from her mother about how ridiculous it was for a person who barely managed to coordinate her wardrobe to drive a flashy sports car.

Sara tossed a wave to Steve Mann, the owner of the hardware store, as she drove toward the clinic. He waved back, a surprised smile on his face. Steve was married with three kids now, but Sara knew he still had a crush on her in that way that first loves tend to hold on. As her first real boyfriend, Sara had a fondness for him, but nothing more than that. She remembered those awkward moments she spent as a teenager, being groped in the back of Steve's car. How she was too embarrassed to look him in the eye the day after they had first had sex.

Steve was the kind of guy who was happy to set his roots down in Grant, who cheerfully went from being the star quarterback at Robert E. Lee High School to working with his father in the hardware store. At that age, Sara had wanted nothing more than to get out of Grant, to go to Atlanta and live a life that was more exciting, more challenging, than what her home town could offer. How she ended up back here was as much a mystery to Sara as anyone else.

She kept her eyes straight ahead as she passed the diner, not wanting to be reminded of yesterday afternoon. She was so intent on avoiding that side of the street that she nearly ran into Jeb McGuire as he walked in front of the pharmacy.

Sara pulled alongside him, apologizing, 'I'm sorry.'

Jeb laughed good-naturedly as he jogged over to her car. 'Trying to get out of our date tomorrow?'

'Of course not,' Sara managed, forcing a smile onto her face. With all that had happened yesterday, she had completely forgotten about agreeing to go out with him. She had dated Jeb off and on when he first moved to Grant eleven years ago and bought the town's pharmacy. Nothing serious had ever developed between them, and things had pretty much cooled between them by the time Jeffrey came along. Why she had agreed to start dating him again after all this time, Sara could not say.

Jeb pushed his hair back off his forehead. He was a lanky man with a runner's build. Tessa had once compared his body to Sara's greyhounds. He was good-looking, though, and certainly did not have to look far to find a woman who would go out with him.

He leaned on Sara's car, asking, 'Have you thought about what you want for dinner?'

Sara gave a shrug. 'I can't decide,' she lied. 'Surprise me.'

Jeb raised an eyebrow. Cathy Linton was right. She was a horrible liar.

'I know you got caught up in all that yesterday,' he began, waving toward the diner. 'I totally understand if you want to cancel.'

Sara felt her heart flip at the offer. Jeb McGuire was a nice man. As the town's pharmacist, he engendered a certain amount of trust and respect from the people he served. On top of that, he was pretty good-looking. The only problem was he was too nice, too agreeable. They had never argued because he was too laid back to care. If anything, this made Sara think of him more as she would a brother rather than a potential lover.

'I don't want to cancel,' she said, and oddly enough, she didn't. Maybe it would be good for her to get out more. Maybe Tessa was right. Maybe it was time.

Jeb's face lit up. 'If it's not too cool, I can bring my boat and take you out on the lake.'

She gave him a teasing look. 'I thought you weren't going to get one until next year?'

'Patience has never been a strong suit,' he answered, though the fact that he was talking to Sara proved that point to the contrary. He jabbed his thumb toward the pharmacy, indicating he needed to go. 'I'll see you around six, okay?'

'Six,' Sara confirmed, feeling some of his excitement rub off on her. She put the car in gear as he trotted over to the pharmacy. Marty Ringo, the woman who did checkout at the pharmacy, was standing at the entrance, and he put his arm around her shoulder as he unlocked the door.

Sara coasted into the clinic's parking lot. The Hearts-dale Children's Clinic was rectangular in shape with an octagonal room made of glass brick swelling out at the front. This was the waiting area for patients. Fortunately, Dr. Barney, who had designed the building himself, was a better doctor than he was an architect. The front room had a southern exposure, and the glass bricks turned the place into an oven in the summer and a freezer in the winter. Patients had been known to have their fevers break while waiting to see a doctor.

The waiting room was cool and empty when Sara opened the door. She looked around the dark room, thinking not for the first time that she should redecorate. Chairs that could hardly be called anything but utilitarian were set out for patients and their parents. Sara and Tessa had spent many a day sitting in those chairs, Cathy beside them, waiting for their names to be called. In the corner was a play area with three tables so children who felt like it could draw or read while they waited. Issues of *Highlights* sat beside *People* magazine and *House & Garden*. Crayons were stacked neatly in their trays, paper beside them.

Looking back, Sara wondered if she had decided in this room to become a doctor. Unlike Tessa, the prospect of going to Dr. Barney never frightened Sara, probably because Sara was rarely sick as a child. She liked the part when they were called back and got to go into the places that only the doctors were allowed to go. In seventh grade, when Sara had shown an interest in science, Eddie had found a biology professor at the college who needed his main water line replaced. The professor tutored Sara in exchange for the work. Two years later, a chemistry professor needed his whole house replumbed, and Sara was performing experiments alongside college students.

The lights came on and Sara blinked to adjust her

eyes. Nelly opened the door separating the exam rooms from the waiting room.

'Good morning, Dr. Linton,' Nelly said, handing Sara a stack of pink messages, taking Sara's briefcase. 'I got your message this morning about the meeting at the station. I've already moved around your appointments. You don't mind working a little late?'

Sara shook her head, going through the messages.

'The Powells will be here in about five minutes, and there's a fax on your desk.'

Sara looked up to thank her, but she was already off, probably running down Elliot Felteau's schedule. Sara had hired Elliot straight out of his residency at Augusta Hospital. He was eager to learn what he could and eventually buy a partnership in the practice. While Sara wasn't sure how she felt about having a partner, she also knew Elliot was at least ten years away from being in a position to make an offer.

Molly Stoddard, Sara's nurse, met her in the hallway. 'Ninety-five percent blast on the Powell kid,' she said, citing the lab results.

Sara nodded. 'They'll be here any minute.'

Molly offered Sara a smile that said she did not envy Sara the task ahead of her. The Powells were good people. They had divorced a couple of years ago but shown surprising solidarity where their children were concerned.

Sara said, 'Can you pull a phone number for me? I want to send them to a man I know at Emory. He's doing some interesting trials with early stage AML.'

Sara gave the name as she slid open her office door. Nelly had put Sara's briefcase by her chair and a cup of coffee on her desk. Beside this was the fax she had mentioned. It was the GBI report on Sibyl Adams's blood work. Nick had scribbled an apology at the top, saying he would be in meetings most of the day and knew Sara would want to know the results as soon as possible. Sara read the report twice, feeling a cold ache in her stomach as she digested it.

She sat back in her chair, looking around her office. Her first month on the job had been hectic, but nothing like Grady. Maybe three months passed before Sara got used to the slower pace. Earaches and sore throats were plentiful, but not many kids came in with critical cases. Those went to the hospital over in Augusta.

Darryl Harp's mother was the first parent to give Sara a picture of her child. More parents followed suit, and pretty soon she started taping them to the walls of her office. Twelve years had passed since that first picture, and photographs of kids wallpapered her office wall and spilled into the bathroom. She could glance at any one of them and remember the kid's name and most of the time his or her medical history. Already she was seeing them come back to the clinic as young adults, telling them at nineteen years old they should probably consider seeing a general practitioner. Some of them actually cried. Sara had gotten choked up on a couple of occasions. Since she wasn't able to have children, she often found she developed strong attachments to her patients.

Sara opened her briefcase to find a chart, stopping at the sight of the postcard she had gotten in the mail. She stared at the photograph of Emory University's entrance gates. Sara remembered the day the acceptance letter had come from Emory. She had been offered scholarships to schools up north with more recognizable names, but Emory had always been a dream of hers. Real medicine took place there, and Sara could not imagine herself living anywhere else but the South.

She flipped the card over, tracing her finger along the

neatly typed address. Every year since Sara had left Atlanta, around the middle of April, she got a postcard like this one. Last year's had been from The World of Coke, the message stating, 'He's got the whole world in His hands.'

She started when Nelly's voice came through the speaker on the phone.

'Dr. Linton?' Nelly said. 'The Powells are here.'

Sara let her finger rest just above the red reply button. She dropped the card back in her briefcase, saying, 'I'll be right out to get them.'

EIGHT

When Sibyl and Lena were in the seventh grade, an older boy named Boyd Little thought it was funny to sneak up on Sibyl and snap his fingers in her ear. Lena followed him off the school bus one day and jumped on his back. Lena was small and quick, but Boyd was one year older and about fifty pounds heavier. He beat her to a pulp before the bus driver could break them up.

Keeping this episode in mind, Lena Adams could honestly say that she had never felt so physically ravaged as she did the morning after her sister's death. She finally understood why they called it 'hung over' because her entire body felt hung over her bones, and it took a good half hour under a hot shower before she could stand up straight. Her head felt ready to crack open from the stress in her brain. No amount of toothpaste could take the horrendous taste out of her mouth, and her stomach felt as if someone had wrapped it tightly into a ball and tied a couple of strings of dental floss around it.

She sat at the back of the briefing room of the station house, willing herself not to throw up again. Not that there was much left she could vomit. Her insides felt so vacant that her stomach was actually concave.

Jeffrey walked over to her, offering a cup of coffee. 'Drink some of this,' he ordered.

She didn't argue. At the house this morning, Hank

had told her the same thing. She had been too embarrassed to take anything from him, let alone advice, so she had suggested a different place for him to put the coffee.

As soon as she put the cup down, Jeffrey said, 'It's not too late, Lena.'

'I want to be here,' she countered. 'I have to know.'

He held her gaze for what seemed like an eternity. Despite the fact that any source of light was like needles in her eyes, she was not the first to break contact. Lena waited until he had left the room to sit back in her chair. She leaned the bottom of the cup on her knee as she closed her eyes.

Lena did not remember how she got home last night. The thirtyminute trip from Reece was still a blur. She did know that Hank had driven her car, because when she got into it this morning to drive to the station, the seat was pushed all the way back and the mirror was adjusted at an odd angle. The last thing Lena remembered was looking at her reflection in the plate glass window of the Stop 'n' Save. The next memory was the blaring ring of the telephone when Jeffrey had called to tell her about the briefing, practically begging her not to come. Everything else was lost to her.

Getting dressed this morning had been the hardest part. After the long shower, Lena wanted nothing more than to crawl back into bed, tucked into a ball. She would have been perfectly happy doing this for the rest of the day, but she couldn't give in to that weakness. Last night had been a mistake, but a necessary one. Obviously, she had needed to let herself go, to grieve as much as she could without falling apart.

This morning was a different story. Lena had forced herself to put on slacks and a nice jacket, the kind of outfit she wore every day on the job. Strapping on her holster, checking her gun, Lena had felt herself slipping back into being a cop instead of the victim's sister. Still, her head ached and her thoughts seemed to be stuck like glue on the inside of her brain. With an unprecedented sympathy, she understood how alcoholics got started. Somewhere in the back of her mind, she couldn't help thinking that a stiff drink would do her a world of good.

The door to the briefing room squeaked open, and Lena looked up in time to see Sara Linton standing in the hallway, her back to Lena. Sara was saying something to Jeffrey, and it did not look polite. Lena felt a pang of guilt for the way she treated Sara the night before. Despite what Lena had said, she knew that Sara was a good doctor. From all accounts, Linton had given up a very promising career in Atlanta to come back to Grant. She was owed an apology, something Lena did not even want to think about at this point in time. If records had been kept on the matter, Lena's outburst-to-apology ratio would be heavily weighted in the outburst department.

'Lena,' Sara said. 'Come on back with me.'

Lena blinked, wondering when Sara had crossed the room. She was standing at the door to the supply closet.

Lena scooted up in her chair to stand, forgetting about the coffee. Some of it spilled on her pants, but she didn't care. She set the cup on the floor and followed Sara's orders. The supply closet was large enough to be called a room, but the sign on the door had given it this designation years ago, and nobody had bothered to make a clarification. Among other things stored here were evidence, dummies for the CPR classes the police gave in the fall, and the emergency supply kit.

'Here,' Sara said, pulling up a chair. 'Sit.'

Again, Lena did as she was told. She watched as Sara rolled out a tank of oxygen.

Sara hooked up a mask to the tank, saying, 'Your head is hurting because the alcohol depletes oxygen in your blood.' She flexed the rubber band around the mask, holding it out to Lena. 'Take slow, deep breaths and it should start to feel better.'

Lena took the mask, not actually trusting Sara, but at this point she would have sucked the ass end of a skunk if someone had told her it would make her head stop pounding.

After a few more breaths, Sara asked, 'Better?'

Lena nodded, because it was better. She wasn't feeling up to her usual self, but at least she could open her eyes all the way.

'Lena,' Sara said, taking the mask back. 'I wanted to ask you about something I found.'

'Yeah?' Lena said, feeling put on her guard. She was expecting Sara to try to talk her out of being here during the briefing, so when the other woman spoke, Lena was surprised.

'When I was examining Sibyl,' Sara began, storing the tank back against the wall, 'I found some physical evidence that I wasn't exactly expecting.'

'Like what?' Lena asked, her mind starting to work again.

'I don't think it has a bearing on the case, but I have to tell Jeffrey what I found. It's not up to me to make that kind of decision.'

Despite the fact that Sara had helped her headache, Lena did not have patience for her games. 'What are you talking about?'

'I'm talking about the fact that your sister's hymen was intact up until the rape.'

Lena felt her stomach drop. She should have thought

of this, but too much had happened in the last twenty-four hours for Lena to come to logical conclusions. Now the whole world would know her sister was gay.

'I don't care, Lena,' Sara said. 'Really. However she wanted to live her life is fine with me.'

'What the hell does that mean?'

'It means what it means,' Sara answered, obviously thinking that was enough. When Lena did not respond, she added, 'Lena, I know about Nan Thomas. I put two and two together.'

Lena leaned her head back against the wall, closing her eyes. 'I guess you're giving me a heads up, huh? For telling everybody else my sister was gay?'

Sara was quiet, then, 'I hadn't planned on putting that in my briefing.'

'I'll tell him,' Lena decided, opening her eyes. 'Can you give me a minute?'

'Sure.'

Lena waited until Sara had left the room, then put her head into her hands. She wanted to cry, but no tears would come. Her body was so dehydrated she was amazed she still had spit in her mouth. She took a deep breath to brace herself and stood.

Frank Wallace and Matt Hogan were in the briefing room when she came out of the supply closet. Frank gave her a nod, but Matt made himself busy putting cream in his coffee. Both detectives were in their fifties, both from a very different time than the one Lena had grown up in. Like the rest of the detectives on the senior squad, they operated by the old rules of the police fraternity, where justice at any cost was right. The force was their family, and anything that happened to one of their officers affected them as it would a brother. If Grant was a close-knit community, the detectives were even closer. As a matter of fact, Lena knew that every one of her fellow detectives were members at the local lodge. Except for the simple matter of her not having a penis, she imagined she would have been invited to join a long time ago, if not out of respect, then obligation.

She wondered what these two old men would think knowing they were working a case to find out who had raped a lesbian. Once, a long time ago, Lena had actually heard Matt start a sentence with the words, 'Back when the Klan was doing some good . . . ' Would they be as vigilant if they knew about Sibyl, or would their anger dissipate? Lena did not want to find out the hard way.

Jeffrey was reading a report when she knocked on his open office door.

'Sara get you straightened out?' he asked.

She did not like the way he phrased his question, but Lena said yes anyway as she closed the door.

Jeffrey was obviously surprised to see her close the door. He set aside the report and waited for her to sit down before asking, 'What's up?'

Lena felt the best thing to do was blurt it out. 'My sister was a lesbian.'

Her words hung in the air over their heads like cartoons. Lena fought the urge to give a nervous laugh. She had never spoken them out loud before. Sibyl's sexuality was something Lena was not comfortable talking about, even with her sister. When Sibyl moved in with Nan Thomas a short year after moving to Grant, Lena had not pushed for details. She honestly had not wanted to know them.

'Well,' Jeffrey said, his voice indicating surprise, 'thank you for telling me that.'

'Do you think it impacts the investigation?' Lena asked, wondering if this was all for nothing.

'I don't know,' he answered, and she felt he was

telling the truth. 'Has anyone been sending her threatening mail? Making disparaging remarks?'

Lena wondered about this, too. Nan had said nothing new had happened in the last few weeks, but she also knew Lena was not open to discussing anything that might bring up the fact that Nan was fucking her sister. 'I guess you should talk to Nan.'

'Nan Thomas?'

'Yeah,' Lena said. 'They lived together. The address is on Cooper. Maybe we could go after the briefing?'

'Later today,' he said. 'Around four?'

Lena nodded her agreement. She couldn't stop herself from asking, 'Are you going to tell the guys?'

He seemed surprised by her question. After giving her a long look, he said, 'I don't think it's necessary at this stage. We'll talk to Nan tonight and go from there.'

Lena felt an inordinate amount of relief.

Jeffrey glanced at his watch. 'We'd better get to the briefing.'

NINE

Jeffrey stood at the front of the briefing room, waiting for Lena to come out of the bathroom. After their discussion, she had asked for a few minutes. He hoped she took the time to get herself together. Despite her temper, Lena Adams was a smart woman and a good cop. He hated to see her going through this alone. Jeffrey also knew that she would not have it any other way.

Sara sat in the front row, her legs crossed. She was wearing an olive-colored linen dress that fell to just above her ankles. Two slits came up either side of her legs, stopping just below her knees. Her red hair was pulled up into a ponytail behind her neck, like she had worn it to church on Sunday. Jeffrey remembered the expression on her face when she had noticed him sitting in the pew behind her and wondered if there would ever be a time in his life again when Sara was actually pleased to see him. He had stared at his hands the entire service, biding his time until he could slip out without causing too much commotion.

Sara Linton was what Jeffrey's father liked to call a tall drink of water. Jeffrey had been attracted to Sara because of her strong will, her fierce independence. He liked her aloofness and the way she talked down to his football buddies. He liked the way her mind worked and the fact that he could talk about every aspect of his job and know she would understand. He liked that she couldn't cook and that she could sleep through a hurricane. He liked that she was a horrible house cleaner and that her feet were so big she could wear his shoes. What he really liked was that she knew all these things about herself and was actually proud of them.

Of course, her independence had a downside. Even after six years of marriage, he wasn't sure he knew one damn thing about her. Sara was so good at projecting a strong facade that after a while he wondered if she even needed him. Between her family, the clinic, and the morgue, there did not seem to be a whole lot of time left for Jeffrey.

While he knew cheating on Sara was not the best way to go about changing things, he did know that at that point in time, something had to give in their marriage. He wanted to see her hurt. He wanted to see her fight for him and their relationship. That the first would happen and not the latter still kept his mind spinning. At times, Jeffrey was almost angry with Sara that something so meaningless, something so stupid as a mindless sexual indiscretion, had broken up their marriage.

Jeffrey leaned against the podium, his hands clasped in front of him. He pushed Sara from his mind and concentrated on the task at hand. On the card table beside him was a sixteen-page list of names and addresses. All convicted sexual offenders living in or moving to the state of Georgia were required to register their name and address with the Georgia Bureau of Investigation's Crime Information Center. Jeffrey had spent last night and most of the morning compiling this information on the sixty-seven Grant residents who had registered since the law was passed in 1996. Going through their crimes was a daunting task, not least of all because he knew that sexual predators were like cockroaches. For every one you saw, there were twenty more hiding behind the walls.

He did not let his mind dwell on this as he waited to start the meeting. The briefing room was hardly filled to capacity. Frank Wallace, Matt Hogan, and five other detectives were part of the senior squad. Jeffrey and Lena rounded out this number to nine. Of the nine, only Jeffrey and Frank had worked in municipalities larger than Grant. Sibyl Adams's killer certainly seemed to have better odds.

Brad Stephens, a junior patrolman who despite his youth and lack of rank knew how to keep his mouth shut, stood just beside the door in case anyone tried to come in. Brad was a kind of mascot around the squad, and the fact that he still had most of his baby fat gave him a round, cartoonish appearance. His thin blond hair always looked as if someone had just rubbed a balloon against it. His mother often brought his lunch to the station. He was a good kid, though. Brad had still been in high school when he contacted Jeffrey about being on the force. Like most of his younger cops, he came from Grant; his people were here. He had a vested interest in keeping the streets safe.

Jeffrey cleared his throat for attention as Brad opened the door for Lena. If anyone was surprised to see her there, they didn't say. She took a chair in the back, her arms crossed over her chest, her eyes still red either from her recent binge or from crying or from both.

'Thank you for coming on such short notice,' Jeffrey began. He gave Brad a nod, indicating that he should start circulating the five packets Jeffrey had put together earlier.

'Let me preface this by saying anything said in this room today should be treated as highly confidential information. What you hear today is not for general consumption and any leaks could greatly impede our case.' He waited as Brad finished his rounds.

'I'm sure all of you know by now that Sibyl Adams was killed yesterday at the Filling Station.' Nods came from the men who were not going through the copies. What he said next made them all look up. 'She was raped before she was killed.'

There seemed to be a rise in the temperature of the room as he let this set in. These men were from different times. Women were as mysterious to them as the origins of the planet. Sibyl's rape would galvanize them into action like nothing else.

Jeffrey held up his copy of the list as Brad passed out the packets according to the names Jeffrey had written on the outside. Jeffrey said, 'I pulled this list of offenders off the computer this morning. I've sectioned them off to the usual teams, with the exception of Frank and Lena.' He saw her mouth open to complain, but continued. 'Brad will be working with you, Lena. Frank is with me.'

Lena sat back in a defiant posture. Brad was hardly on her level, and her look said she knew exactly what he was doing. She would also realize as soon as she interviewed the third or fourth man on her list that Jeffrey was keeping her on a tight leash. Rapists tended to attack women in their own ethnic and age group. Lena and Brad would be interviewing every minority over the age of fifty with a sexual assault on his record.

'Dr. Linton will give you the rundown on the specifics.' He paused, then, 'My first guess would be that the attacker has some kind of religious leaning, maybe a fanatic. I don't want that to be the focus of your questioning, but keep it in the back of your mind.' He stacked the papers on the podium. 'If somebody comes up that we should look at, I want a call on my radio. I don't want any suspect falling down in custody or accidentally getting his head blown off.'

Jeffrey studiously avoided meeting Sara's eyes as he said this last part. Jeffrey was a cop, he knew how things worked in the street. He knew that every man in this room had something to prove where Sibyl Adams was concerned. He also knew how easy it was to slip over that line between legal justice and human justice when you were out in the field, facing down the kind of animal who could rape a blind woman and carve a cross onto her abdomen.

'That clear?' he asked, not expecting an answer and not getting one. 'I'll turn this over to Dr. Linton, then.'

He walked to the back of the room, standing behind and to the right of Lena as Sara took the podium. She walked over to the chalkboard, reached up, and pulled down the white projection screen. Most of the men in this room had seen her in diapers, and the fact that they all had their notebooks out said volumes about Sara's professional abilities.

She gave Brad Stephens a nod and the room went dark.

The green opaque projector whirred to life, sending a flash of bright light onto the screen. Sara moved a photograph onto the bed and slid it under the glass.

'Sibyl Adams was found by me in the women's bathroom of the Filling Station around two-thirty yesterday afternoon,' she said, focusing the projector's lens.

There was movement in the room as a Polaroid of Sibyl Adams lying partially nude on the bathroom floor came into view. Jeffrey found himself staring at the hole in her chest, wondering what kind of man could do the things that had been done to that poor young woman.

He did not want to think about Sibyl Adams, blind, sitting on that toilet while her attacker slit her open for his own sick reasons. He did not want to think about what was going through her mind as her abdomen was being raped.

Sara continued. 'She was sitting on the toilet when I opened the door.

'Her arms and legs were splayed open and the cut you see here' – she indicated the screen – 'was bleeding profusely.'

Jeffrey leaned over slightly, trying to see what Lena's reaction to this was. She stood stock still, her spine a perfect right angle to the floor. He understood why she needed to do this, but he could not grasp how she was doing it. If someone in his family had gone through this, if Sara had been ravaged like this, Jeffrey knew in his heart that he would not want to know. He could not know.

Sara stood at the front of the room, her arms crossed over her chest. 'She started to seize shortly after I established that she had a pulse. We fell to the ground. I tried to control the seizures, but she expired several seconds later.'

Sara jerked the projector's drawer out to replace the photo with another. The machine was a dinosaur, borrowed from the high school. It wasn't as if Sara could send the crime photos down to the Jiffy Photo for enlargements.

The next picture that came on-screen was a close up of Sibyl Adams's head and neck. 'The bruise under her eye came from a superior position, probably early on in the assault to discourage a struggle. A knife was held at her throat, very sharp, measuring about six inches. I'd say this was a boning knife, probably common to any kitchen. You can see a slight cut here.' She traced her finger on the screen, along the middle of Sibyl's neck. 'It didn't draw blood, but enough pressure was used to score the skin.' She looked up, catching Jeffrey's eye. 'I would imagine the knife was used to keep her from calling out while he raped her.'

She continued. 'There is a small bite mark on her left shoulder.' The picture of this came up. 'Bite marks are common with rape. This one shows the impression of the upper teeth only. I found nothing distinctive in the pattern, but I've sent the . . . ' Sara paused, probably remembering Lena was in the room. 'The impression was sent to the FBI lab for cross matching. If a known offender on file matches the impression, then we could assume that he's the perpetrator in this crime. However,' she warned, 'as we all know, the FBI won't consider this a high-priority case, so I don't think we can hang our hats on this piece of evidence. A more likely scenario would be to use the impression as validation after the fact. That is to say, find a solid suspect and nail him with the dental impression.'

Next, the screen showed a photograph of the inner sides of Sibyl's legs. 'You can see scrapes here at the knee where she gripped her legs around the toilet bowl during the assault.' Another picture came, this one of Sibyl's bottom. 'There are irregular bruises and scrapes on the buttocks, again from friction against the toilet seat.

'Her wrists,' Sara said, putting in another photo, 'show bruising from the handicap bars on the stall. Two fingernails were broken in the process of gripping the bars, probably to lift herself up and away from her assailant.'

Sara slid in the next photograph. 'This is a close-up of the incisions to her abdomen,' she narrated. 'The first cut was made from just below the collarbone all the way to the pelvic bone. The second cut was made from right to left.' She paused. 'I would guess from the irregular depth of the second cut that this was a backhanded movement by a lefthanded assailant. The cut is deeper as it moves to her right side.'

The next Polaroid was a close-up of Sibyl's chest. Sara was quiet for a few beats, probably thinking the same thing Jeffrey was thinking. Up close, he could see where the puncture wound had been stretched. Not for the first time, he felt his stomach roll at the thought of what was done to this poor woman. He hoped to God she had not been conscious of what was happening to her.

Sara said, 'This is the final cut. It's a puncture wound through the sternum. It goes straight through to her spine. I would guess this was the source of most of the blood.' Sara turned to Brad. 'Lights?'

She walked toward her briefcase, saying, 'The symbol on her chest seems to be a cross. The assailant used a condom during the rape, which as we know is pretty common with the advent of DNA testing. Black lighting revealed no sperm or fluids. Blood on the scene appears to be only from the victim.' She took a sheet of paper out of her briefcase. 'Our friends at the Georgia Bureau of Investigation were nice enough to pull some strings last night. They worked up the blood analysis for me.'

She put on her copper-rimmed glasses and began reading, 'High concentrations of hyoscyamine, atrosin and belladonnine as well as traces of scopolamine were found in her central blood and urine.' She looked up. 'This would suggest that Sibyl Adams ingested a lethal dose of belladonna, which belongs in the deadly nightshade plant family.'

Jeffrey glanced at Lena. She remained quiet, her eyes on Sara.

'An overdose of belladonna can mimic a complete shutdown of the parasympathetic nervous system. Sibyl Adams was blind, but her pupils were dilated from the drug. The bronchioles in her lungs were swollen. Her core body temperature was still high, which is what made me wonder about her blood in the first place.' She turned to Jeffrey, answering the question he had asked this morning. 'During the post, her skin was still warm to the touch. There were no environmental factors that would cause this. I knew it had to be something in the blood.'

She continued. 'Belladonna can be broken down for medical applications, but it's also used as a recreational drug.'

'You think the perp gave it to her?' Jeffrey asked. 'Or is this the kind of thing she would take on her own?'

Sara seemed to consider this. 'Sibyl Adams was a chemist. She certainly wouldn't take such a volatile drug, then run out for lunch. This is a very strong hallucinogen. It affects the heart, breathing, and circulation.'

'Nightshade grows all over town,' Frank pointed out.

'It's pretty common,' Sara agreed, looking back at her notes. 'The plant isn't easy to process. Ingestion is going to be the key component here. According to Nick, the easiest and most popular way to take belladonna is to soak the seeds in hot water. Just this morning I found three recipes on the Internet for preparing belladonna as a tea.'

Lena offered, 'She liked to drink hot tea.'

'There you go,' Sara said. 'The seeds are highly soluble. I imagine within minutes of drinking it she would have started experiencing elevated blood pressure, heart palpitations, dry mouth, and extreme nervousness. I would also guess this led her to the bathroom, where her rapist was waiting for her.'

Frank turned to Jeffrey. 'We need to talk to Pete Wayne. He served her lunch. He gave her the tea.'

'No way,' Matt countered. 'Pete's lived in town all his life. This isn't the kind of thing he'd do.' Then, as if this was the most important thing in Pete's favor, Matt added, 'He's in the lodge.'

Murmurs came from the other men. Someone, Jeffrey wasn't sure who, said, 'What about Pete's colored man?'

Jeffrey felt a trickle of sweat run down his back. He could see where this was going already. He held his hands up for silence. 'Frank and I will talk to Pete. You guys have your assignment. I want reports back at the end of the day.'

Matt seemed about to say something, but Jeffrey stopped him. 'We're not helping Sibyl Adams by sitting in this room pulling theories out of our asses.' He paused, then indicated the packets Brad had handed out. 'Knock on every goddamn door in town if you have to, but I want an accounting for every man on those lists.'

As Jeffrey and Frank walked to the diner, the words 'Frank's colored man' sat in the back of Jeffrey's mind like a piece of hot coal. The vernacular was familiar from his childhood, but he had not heard it used in at least thirty years. It amazed Jeffrey to see that such overt racism still existed. It also scared him that he had heard it in his own squad room. Jeffrey had worked in Grant for ten years, but he was still an outsider. Even his southern roots didn't pay his dues into the good old boy club. Coming from Alabama didn't help matters. A typical prayer among southern states was 'Thank God for Alabama,' meaning, thank God we're not as bad off as they are. This was part of the reason he was keeping Frank Wallace close at hand. Frank was a part of these men. He was in the club.

Frank shucked off his coat, folding it across his arm as he walked. He was tall and thin like a reed with a face rendered unreadable from years of being a cop.

Frank said, 'This black guy, Will Harris. I got called in a few years back on a domestic dispute. He popped his wife.'

Jeffrey stopped. 'Yeah?'

Frank stopped alongside him. 'Yeah,' he said. 'Beat her pretty bad. Busted her lip. When I got there, she was on the floor. She was wearing this cotton bag-looking kind of dress.' He shrugged. 'Anyway, it was torn.'

'You think he raped her?'

Frank shrugged. 'She wouldn't press charges.'

Jeffrey started walking again. 'Anybody else know about this?'

'Matt,' Frank said. 'He was my partner then.'

Jeffrey felt a sense of dread as he opened the door to the diner.

'We're closed,' Pete called from the back.

Jeffrey said, 'It's Jeffrey, Pete.'

He came out of the storeroom, wiping his hands on his apron. 'Hey, Jeffrey,' he said, nodding. Then, 'Frank.'

'We should be finished up in here this afternoon, Pete,' Jeffrey said. 'You'll be able to open tomorrow.'

'Closing for the rest of the week,' Pete said as he retied his apron strings. 'Don't seem right to be open what with Sibyl and all.' He indicated the row of stools in front of the bar. 'Get y'all some coffee?'

'That'd be great,' Jeffrey said, taking the first stool. Frank followed suit, sitting down beside him.

Jeffrey watched Pete walk around the counter and take out three thick ceramic mugs. The coffee steamed as he poured it into the cups.

Pete asked, 'You got anything yet?'

Jeffrey took one of the mugs. 'Can you run through what happened yesterday? I mean, from the point Sibyl Adams came into the restaurant?'

Pete leaned back against the grill. 'I guess she came in about one-thirty,' he said. 'She always came in after the lunch rush. I guess she didn't want to be poking around with her cane in front of all those people. I mean, we knew she was blind, sure, but she didn't like drawing attention to it. You could see that. She was kind of nervous in crowds.'

Jeffrey took out his notebook, though he didn't really need to take notes. What he did know was that Pete seemed to know a lot about Sibyl Adams. 'She come in here a lot?'

'Every Monday like clockwork.' He squinted his eyes, thinking. 'I guess for the last five years or so. She came in sometimes late at night with other teachers or Nan from the library. I think they rented a house over on Cooper.'

Jeffrey nodded.

'But that was only occasionally. Mostly it was Mondays, always by herself. She walked here, ordered her lunch, then was out by around two usually.' He rubbed his chin, a sad look coming over his face. 'She always left a nice tip. I didn't think anything about it when I saw her table empty. I guess I just thought she had gone while I wasn't looking.'

Jeffrey asked, 'What'd she order?'

'Same thing as always,' Pete said. 'The number three.'

Jeffrey knew this was the waffle platter with eggs, bacon, and a side of grits.

'Only,' Pete clarified, 'she didn't eat meat, so I always left off the bacon. And she didn't drink coffee, so I gave her some hot tea.'

Jeffrey wrote this down. 'What kind of tea?'

He rooted around behind the counter and pulled out a box of generic brand tea bags. 'I picked it up for her at the grocery store. She didn't drink caffeine.' He gave a small laugh. 'I liked to make her comfortable, you know? She didn't get out much. She used to say to me that she liked coming here, that she felt comfortable.' He fiddled with the box of tea.

'What about the cup she used?' Jeffrey asked.

'I don't know about that. They all look the same.' He walked to the end of the counter and pulled out a large metal drawer. Jeffrey leaned over to look inside. The drawer was actually a large dishwasher filled with cups and plates.

Jeffrey asked, 'Those from yesterday?'

Pete nodded. 'I can't begin to guess which one was hers. I started the washer before she was –' He stopped, looking down at his hands. 'My dad, he always told me to take care of the customers and they'd take care of you.' He looked up, tears in his eyes. 'She was a nice girl, you know? Why would anybody want to hurt her?'

'I don't know, Pete,' Jeffrey said. 'Mind if we take this?' He pointed to the box of tea.

Pete shrugged. 'Sure, nobody else drank it.' The laugh came again. 'I tried it once just to see. Tasted like brown water.'

Frank pulled a tea bag out of the box. Each bag was wrapped and sealed in a paper envelope. He asked, 'Was old Will working here yesterday?'

Pete seemed taken aback by the question. 'Sure, he's

worked lunch every day for the last fifty years. Comes in about eleven, leaves by two or so.' He studied Jeffrey. 'He does odd jobs for people around town after he leaves here. Mostly yard work, some light carpentry.'

'He buses tables here?' Jeffrey asked, though he had eaten enough lunches in the diner to know what Will Harris did.

'Sure,' Pete said. 'Buses tables, mops the floors, takes people their food.' He gave Jeffrey a curious look. 'Why?'

'No reason,' Jeffrey answered. Leaning over, he shook the man's hand, saying, 'Thanks, Pete. We'll let you know if we need anything else.'

TEN

Lena traced her finger along the street map in her lap. 'Left here,' she told Brad.

He did as he was told, steering the cruiser onto Baker Street. Brad was okay, but he tended to take people at face value, which is why back at the station when Lena said she had to go to the bathroom, then headed the exact opposite direction of the women's room, he hadn't said anything. A joke around the station house was to hide Brad's patrolman's hat from him. At Christmas, they had stuck it on top of one of the reindeer on display in front of city hall. A month ago, Lena had spotted the hat on top of the statue of Robert E. Lee in front of the high school.

Lena knew Jeffrey partnering her with Brad Stephens was his way of keeping her at the periphery of the investigation. If she had to guess, she would say that every man on their list was either dead or too old to stand up without help.

'The next right,' she said, folding the map. She had sneaked into Marla's office and looked up Will Harris's address in the phone book during her alleged trip to the bathroom. Jeffrey would interview Pete first. Lena wanted a crack at Will Harris before her chief could get to him.

'Right here,' Lena said, indicating he could pull over. 'You can stay here.'

Brad slowed the car, putting his fingers to his mouth. 'What's the address?'

'Four-thirty-one,' she said, spotting the mailbox. She slipped off her seat belt and opened her door before the car came to a complete stop. She was walking up the driveway by the time Brad caught up with her.

'What are you doing?' he asked, trotting alongside her like a puppy. 'Lena?'

She stopped, putting her hand in her pocket. 'Listen, Brad, just go back to the car.' She was two ranks above him. Technically, Brad was supposed to follow her orders. This thought seemed to cross his mind, but he shook his head no.

He said, 'This is Will Harris's place, isn't it?'

Lena turned her back to him, continuing up the driveway.

Will Harris's house was small, probably little more than two rooms and a bath. The clapboard was painted bright white and the lawn was neatly tended. There was a well-tended look to the place that set Lena on edge. She could not think that the person who lived in this house could do such a thing to her sister.

Lena knocked on the screen door. She could hear a television inside, and distant movement. Through the screen mesh, she could see a man struggling to get out of his chair. He was wearing a white undershirt and white pajama pants. A puzzled expression was on his face.

Unlike most people who worked in town, Lena wasn't a regular at the diner. Somewhere in the back of her mind Lena had considered the diner Sibyl's territory and hadn't wanted to intrude. Lena had never really met Will Harris. She had been expecting someone younger. Someone more menacing. Will Harris was an old man.

When he finally reached the door and saw Lena, his lips parted in surprise. Neither spoke for a moment, then Will finally said, 'You must be her sister.'

Lena stared at the old man. She knew in her gut that Will Harris had not killed her sister, but there was still the possibility that he knew who had.

She said, 'Yes, sir. Do you mind if I come in?'

The hinge on the screen door screeched as it opened. He stepped aside, holding the door open for Lena.

'You gotta excuse my appearance,' he said, indicating his pajamas. 'I wasn't exactly expecting visitors.'

'That's okay,' Lena offered, glancing around the small room. The living room and kitchen space were blended, a couch delineating the two. There was a square hallway off the left through which Lena could see a bathroom. She guessed the bedroom was on the other side of the wall. Like the outside of the house, everything was neat and tidy, well cared for despite its age. A television dominated the living room. Surrounding the set were wall-to-wall bookcases packed with videos.

'I like to watch a lot of movies,' Will said.

Lena smiled. 'Obviously.'

'Mostly, I like the old black and white ones,' the old man started, then turned his head toward the large picture window lining the front of the room. 'Lord a'mighty,' he mumbled. 'I seem to be real popular today.'

Lena suppressed a groan as Jeffrey Tolliver walked up the driveway. Either Brad had told on her or Pete Wayne had fingered Will.

'Morning, sir,' Will said, opening the screen door for Jeffrey.

Jeffrey gave him a nod, then shot Lena the kind of look that made her palms sweat.

Will seemed to sense the tension in the room. 'I can go in the back if you need.'

Jeffrey turned to the old man and shook his hand. 'No need, Will,' he said. 'I just need to ask you a few questions.'

Will indicated the couch with a sweep of his hand. 'Mind if I get me some more coffee?'

'No, sir,' Jeffrey answered, walking past Lena toward the couch. He fixed her with the same hard look, but Lena sat beside him anyway.

Will shuffled back to his chair, groaning as he sat. His knees popped and he smiled apologetically, explaining, 'Spend most of my days on my knees in the yard.'

Jeffrey took out his notebook. Lena could almost feel the anger coming off of him. 'Will, I've got to ask you some questions.'

'Yes, sir?'

'You know what happened at the diner yesterday?'

Will placed his coffee cup down on a small side table. 'That girl never hurt nobody,' he said. 'What was done to her –' He stopped, looking at Lena. 'My heart goes out to you and your family, sweetheart. It really does.'

Lena cleared her throat. 'Thank you.'

Jeffrey had obviously been expecting a different response from her. His look changed, but she couldn't make out what he was thinking. He turned back to Will. 'You were at the diner until what time yesterday?'

'Oh, around one-thirty or a little before two, I think. I saw your sister,' he told Lena, 'just as I was leaving.'

Jeffrey waited a few beats, then said, 'You're sure about that?'

'Oh, yes, sir,' Will returned. 'I had to go pick up my auntie at the church. They get out of choir practice at two-fifteen sharp. She don't like to wait.'

Lena asked, 'Where does she sing?'

'The AME over in Madison,' he answered. 'You ever been there?'

She shook her head, doing the math in her head. Even if Will Harris had been a viable suspect, there was no way he could have killed Sibyl, then made it to Madison in time to pick up his aunt. A quick phone call would give Will Harris an airtight alibi.

'Will,' Jeffrey began, 'I hate to ask you about this, but my man Frank says there was some problem a while back.'

Will's face dropped. He had been looking at Lena up until this point, but now he stared at the carpet. 'Yes, sir, that's right.' He looked over Jeffrey's shoulder as he spoke. 'My wife, Eileen. I used to go at her something bad. I guess it was before your time we got into a scuffle. Maybe eighteen, nineteen years ago.' He shrugged. 'She left me after that. I guess I let the drink lead me down the wrong path, but I'm a good Christian man now. I don't go in for all that. I don't see my son much, but I see my daughter often as I can. She lives in Savannah now.' His smile came back. 'I got two grandbabies.'

Jeffrey tapped his pen on the notebook. Lena could see over his shoulder that he had not written anything. He asked, 'Did you ever take Sibyl her meals? In the diner, I mean.'

If he was surprised by the question, Will didn't let it register. 'I guess I did. Most days I help Pete out with things like that. His daddy kept a woman around to wait tables when he was running the place, but Pete,' he said, chuckling, 'old Pete, he can hold on to a dollar.' Will waved his hand, dismissing the trouble. 'It don't hurt me none to fetch some ketchup or make sure somebody gets their coffee.'

Jeffrey asked, 'Did you serve Sibyl tea?'

'Sometimes. Is there a problem?'

Jeffrey closed his notebook. 'Not at all,' he said. 'Did you see anyone suspicious hanging around the diner yesterday?'

'Lord God,' Will breathed. 'I surely would've told you by now. It was just me and Pete there, and all the regulars for lunch.'

'Thank you for your time.' Jeffrey stood and Lena followed suit. Will shook first Jeffrey's, then Lena's hand.

He held on to hers a little longer, saying, 'God bless you, girl. You take care now.'

'Goddammit, Lena,' Jeffrey cursed, slamming his notebook into the dashboard of the car. The pages fluttered out, and Lena held her hands up in front of her to keep from getting whacked in the head. 'What the hell were you thinking?'

Lena picked up the notebook off the floor. 'I wasn't thinking,' she answered.

'No fucking joke,' he snapped, grabbing the notebook.

His jaw was a tight line as he backed the car out of Will Harris's driveway. Frank had gone back to the station with Brad while Lena had been practically thrown into Jeffrey's car. He bumped the gear on the steering wheel column and the car jerked into drive.

'Why can't I trust you?' he demanded. 'Why can't I trust you to do one thing I tell you to do?' He did not wait for her answer. 'I sent you out with Brad to do something, Lena. I gave you a job on this investigation because you asked me, not because I thought you were in any position to do it. And what's my reward for this? I've got Frank and Brad seeing you go behind my back like some teenager sneaking out of the house. Are you a fucking cop or are you a fucking kid?' He slammed on the brakes, and Lena felt her seat belt cutting into her chest. They were stopped in the middle of the road, but Jeffrey did not seem to notice.

'Look at me,' he said, turning to her. Lena did as she was told, trying to keep the fear out of her eyes. Jeffrey had been mad at her plenty of times, but never like this. If she had been right about Will Harris, Lena might have a leg to stand on; as it was, she was screwed.

'You have got to get your head on straight. Do you hear me?'

She gave a sharp nod.

'I can't have you going around behind my back. What if he had done something to you?' He let that sink in. 'What if Will Harris is the man who killed your sister? What if he opened his door, saw you, and freaked out?' Jeffrey slammed his fist into the steering wheel, hissing another curse. 'You have got to do what I say, Lena. Is that clear? From now on.' He jabbed his finger in her face. 'If I tell you to interview every ant on the playground, you bring me back signed depositions on each one. Is that clear?'

She managed to nod again. 'Yeah.'

Jeffrey wasn't satisfied. 'Is that clear, Detective?'

'Yes, sir,' Lena repeated.

Jeffrey put the car back into gear. The tires caught as he accelerated, leaving a good deal of rubber on the road. Both hands gripped the wheel so hard that his knuckles were white. Lena kept quiet, hoping his anger would pass. He had every right to be pissed, but she did not know what to say. An apology seemed as useless as treating a toothache with honey.

Jeffrey rolled his window down, loosening his tie. Suddenly, he said, 'I don't think Will did it.'

Lena nodded her head up and down, afraid to open her mouth.

'Even if he did have this episode in his past,' Jeffrey began, anger coming back into his voice, 'Frank failed to mention that this thing with his wife was twenty years ago.'

Lena was silent.

'Anyway' – Jeffrey waved this off – 'even if he had it in him, he's at least sixty, maybe seventy years old. He couldn't even get into his chair, let alone overpower a healthy thirty-three-year-old woman.'

Jeffrey continued, 'So that leaves us with Pete in the diner, right?' He didn't wait for her answer; he was obviously just thinking aloud. 'Only I called Tessa on the way over here. She got there a little before two o'clock. Will was gone, and Pete was the only one there. She said Pete stayed behind the cash register until she placed her order, then he grilled her burger.' Jeffrey shook his head. 'He might've slipped into the back, but when? When did he have time? That'd take, what? Ten, fifteen minutes? Plus the planning. How did he know it would work out?' Again these questions seemed rhetorical. 'And we all know Pete. I mean, Jesus, this isn't the kind of thing a first timer would pull.'

He was silent, obviously still thinking, and Lena left him alone. She stared out the window, processing what Jeffrey had said about Pete Wayne and Will Harris. An hour ago these two men had looked like good suspects to her. Now there was nobody. Jeffrey was right to be angry at her. She could have been out with Brad, tracking down the men on their list, maybe finding the man who had killed Sibyl.

Lena's eyes focused on the houses they were driving by. At the turn, she checked the street sign, noting that they were on Cooper.

Jeffrey asked, 'You think Nan will be home?'

Lena shrugged.

The smile he gave her said he was trying. 'You can talk now, you know.'

Her lips came up, but she couldn't quite return the smile. 'Thanks.' Then, 'I'm sorry about –'

He held up his hand to stop her. 'You're a good cop, Lena. You're a damn good cop.' He pulled the car to the curb in front of Nan and Sibyl's house. 'You just need to start listening.'

'I know.'

'No, you don't,' he said, but he did not seem angry anymore. 'Your whole life has turned upside down and you don't even know it yet.'

She started to speak then stopped.

Jeffrey said, 'I understand needing to work on this, needing to keep your mind occupied, but you've got to trust me on this, Lena. If you ever cross that line with me again, I will bust you so low you'll be fetching coffee for Brad Stephens. Is that clear?'

She managed to nod her head.

'Okay,' he said, opening the car door. 'Let's go.'

Lena took her time taking off her seat belt. She got out of the car, adjusting her gun and holster as she walked toward the house. By the time she reached the front door, Nan had already let Jeffrey in.

'Hey,' Lena offered.

'Hey,' Nan resumed. She was holding a ball of tissue in her hand, the same as she had been last night. Her eyes were puffy and her nose was bright red.

'Hey,' Hank said.

Lena stopped. 'What are you doing here?'

Hank shrugged, rubbing his hands together. He was wearing a sleeveless T-shirt, and the needle tracks up his arms were on full display. Lena felt a rush of embarrassment. She had only seen Hank in Reece, where everybody knew about his past. She had seen the scars so many times that she had almost blocked them out. Now she was seeing them through Jeffrey's eyes for the first time, and she wanted to run from the room.

Hank seemed to be waiting for Lena to say something. She stumbled, managing an introduction. 'This is Hank Norton, my uncle,' she said. 'Jeffrey Tolliver, chief of police.'

Hank held out his hand, and Lena cringed to see the raised scars on his forearms. Some of them were half an inch long in places where he had jabbed the needle into his skin, looking for a good vein.

Hank said, 'How d'you do, sir.'

Jeffrey took the offered hand, giving it a firm shake. 'I'm sorry we had to meet under these circumstances.'

Hank clasped his hands in front of him. 'Thank you for that.'

They were all silent, then Jeffrey said, 'I guess you know why we're here.'

'About Sibyl,' Nan answered, her voice a few octaves lower, probably from crying all night.

'Right,' Jeffrey said, indicating the sofa. He waited for Nan to sit, then took the space beside her. Lena was surprised when he took Nan's hand and said, 'I'm so sorry for your loss, Nan.'

Tears welled into Nan's eyes. She actually smiled. 'Thank you.'

'We're doing everything we can to find out who did this,' he continued. 'I want you to know if there's anything else you need we're here for you.'

She whispered another thank-you, looking down, picking at a string on her sweat pants.

Jeffrey asked, 'Was anybody angry at you or Sibyl, do you know?'

'No,' Nan answered. 'I told Lena last night. Everything's been the same as usual lately.'

'I know that Sibyl and you chose to live kind of quietly,' Jeffrey said.

Lena got his meaning. He was being a lot more subtle than she had been last night.

'Yeah,' Nan agreed. 'We like it here. We're both small-town people.'

Jeffrey asked, 'You can't think of anybody who might have figured something out?'

Nan shook her head. She looked down, her lips trembling. There was nothing else she could tell him.

'Okay,' he said, standing. He put his hand on Nan's shoulder, indicating she should stay seated. 'I'll let myself out.' He reached into his pocket and brought out a card. Lena watched as he cupped it in one hand and wrote on the back. 'This is my home number,' he said. 'Call me if you think of anything.'

'Thank you,' Nan said, taking the card.

Jeffrey turned to Hank. 'Do you mind giving Lena a ride home?'

Lena felt dumbstruck. She couldn't stay here.

Hank was obviously taken aback as well. 'No,' he mumbled. 'That's fine.'

'Good.' He patted Nan on the shoulder, then said to Lena, 'You and Nan can take tonight to put together a list of the people Sibyl worked with.' Jeffrey gave Lena a knowing smile. 'Be at the station at seven tomorrow morning. We'll go over to the college before classes start.'

Lena didn't understand. 'Am I back with Brad?'

He shook his head. 'You're with me.'

WEDNESDAY

ELEVEN

Ben Walker, the chief of police before Jeffrey, had kept his office in the back of the station, just off the briefing room. A desk the size of an upended commercial refrigerator was in the center of the room with a row of uncomfortable chairs in front of it. Every morning, the men on the senior squad were called into Ben's office to hear their assignments for the day, then they left and the chief shut his door. What Ben did from this time until five o'clock, when he could be seen scooting down the street to the diner for his supper, was a mystery.

Jeffrey's first task when he took over Ben's job was to move his office to the front of the squad room. Using a skill saw, Jeffrey cut a hole in the Sheetrock and installed a glass picture window so that he could sit at his desk and see his men and, more important, so that his men could see him. There were blinds on the window, but he never closed them, and for the most part, his office door was always open.

Two days after Sibyl Adams's body had been found, Jeffrey sat in his office, reading a report that Marla had just handed him. Nick Shelton at the GBI had been kind enough to rush through the analysis on the box of tea. Results: it was tea.

Jeffrey scratched his chin, looking around his office. It was a small room, but he had built a set of bookshelves into one of the walls in order to keep things neat. Field manuals and statistical reports were stacked alongside marksman trophies he had won at the Birmingham competitions and a signed team football from when he had played at Auburn. Not that he really played. Jeffrey had spent most of his time on the bench, watching the other players build careers for themselves.

A photograph of his mother was tucked into the far corner of the shelf. She was wearing a pink blouse and holding a small wrist corsage in her hands. The photo was taken at Jeffrey's high school graduation. He had caught his mother giving one of her rare smiles in front of the camera. Her eyes were lit up, probably with the possibilities she saw in front of her son. That he had dropped out of Auburn a year from graduation and taken a job on the Birmingham police force was something she still had not forgiven her only child for.

Marla tapped on his office door, holding a cup of coffee in one hand and a doughnut in the other. On Jeffrey's first day, she told him that she had never fetched coffee for Ben Walker and she wasn't about to fetch it for him. Jeffrey had laughed; the thought had never occurred to him. Marla had been bringing him his coffee ever since.

'The doughnut's for me,' she said, handing him the paper cup. 'Nick Shelton's on line three.'

'Thank you,' he said, waiting for her to leave. Jeffrey sat back in his chair as he picked up the phone. 'Nick?'

Nick's southern drawl came across the line. 'How are you?'

'Not so great,' Jeffrey answered.

'I hear you,' Nick returned. Then, 'Got my report?'

'On the tea?' Jeffrey picked up the sheet of paper, looking over the analysis. For such a simple beverage, a lot of chemicals went into processing tea. 'It's just cheap store-bought tea, right?'

'You got it,' Nick said. 'Listen, I tried to call Sara this morning, but I couldn't find her.'

'That so?'

Nick gave a low chuckle. 'You're never gonna forgive me for asking her out that time, are you, buddy?'

Jeffrey smiled. 'Nope.'

'One of my drug people here at the lab is hot on this belladonna. Not many cases come in, and he volunteered to give you guys a face-to-face rundown.'

'That'd be an awfully big help,' Jeffrey said. He saw Lena through the glass window and waved her in.

'Sara talking to you this week?' Nick didn't wait for an answer. 'My guy is gonna want to talk to her about how the victim presented.'

Jeffrey bit back the cutting remark that wanted to come, forcing some cheerfulness into his voice as he said, 'How about around ten?'

Jeffrey was noting the meeting on his calendar when Lena walked in. As soon as he looked up, she began speaking.

'He doesn't do drugs anymore.'

'What?'

'At least I don't think so.'

Jeffrey shook his head, not understanding. 'What are you talking about?'

She lowered her voice, saying, 'My uncle Hank.' She held her forearms out to him.

'Oh.' Jeffrey finally got it. He had not been sure if Hank Norton was a past drug addict or had been in a disfiguring fire, his arms were so scarred. 'Yeah, I saw they were old.'

She said, 'He was a speed freak, okay?'

Her tone was hostile. Jeffrey gathered she had been stewing on this since he had left her at Nan Thomas's house. So, this made two things she was ashamed of, her sister's homosexuality and her uncle's past drug problem. Jeffrey wondered if there was anything in Lena's life other than her job that gave Lena pleasure.

'What?' Lena demanded.

'Nothing,' Jeffrey said, standing. He took his suit coat off the peg behind his door and ushered Lena out of the office. 'You got the list?'

She seemed irritated that he did not want to chastise her for her uncle's old drug habit.

She handed him a sheet of notebook paper. 'This is what Nan and I came up with last night. It's a list of people who worked with Sibyl, who might have talked to her before she . . . ' Lena did not finish the sentence.

Jeffrey glanced down. There were six names. One had a star drawn beside it. Lena seemed to anticipate his question.

She said, 'Richard Carter is her GTA. Graduate teaching assistant. She had a nine o'clock class at the school. Other than Pete, he's probably the last person who saw her alive.'

'That name sounds familiar for some reason,' Jeffrey said, slipping on his coat. 'He's the only student on the list?'

'Yes,' Lena answered. 'Plus, he's kind of weird.'

'Meaning?'

'I don't know.' She shrugged. 'I've never liked him.'

Jeffrey held his tongue, thinking that Lena did not like a lot of people. That was hardly a good reason to look at someone for murder.

He said, 'Let's start with Carter first, then we'll talk to the dean.' At the entrance, he held the door open for her. 'The mayor will have a heart attack if we don't go through the proper protocols with the professors. Students are fair game.'

The Grant Institute of Technology's campus consisted of a student center, four classroom buildings, the administrative building, and an agricultural wing that had been donated by a very grateful seed manufacturer. Lush grounds surrounded the university on one side, with the lake backing up to the other. Student housing was within walking distance of all the buildings, and bicycles were the most common mode of campus transportation.

Jeffrey followed Lena to the third floor of the science classroom building. She had obviously met her sister's assistant before, because Richard Carter's face soured when he recognized Lena at the door. He was a short, balding man who wore heavy black glasses and an ill-fitting lab coat over a bright yellow dress shirt. He had that anal-retentive air about him that most of the college people had. The Grant Institute of Technology was a school for geeks, plain and simple. English classes were mandatory but not exactly difficult. The school was geared more toward turning out patents than socially evolved men and women. That was the biggest problem Jeffrey had with the school. Most of the professors and all of the students had their heads so far up their asses they couldn't see the world in front of them.

'Sibyl was a brilliant scientist,' Richard said, leaning over a microscope. He mumbled something, then looked back up, directing his words to Lena. 'She had an amazing memory.'

'She had to,' Lena said, taking out her notebook. Jeffrey wondered not for the first time if he should let Lena ride along with him. More than anything, he wanted her underfoot. After yesterday, he did not know if he could trust her to do what he told her to do. It was better to keep her close by and safe than let her go off on her own.

'Her work,' Richard began. 'I can't describe how meticulous she was, how exacting. It's very rare to see such a high standard of attention in this field anymore. She was my mentor.'

'Right,' Lena said.

Richard gave her a sour, disapproving look, asking, 'When's the funeral?'

Lena seemed taken aback by the question. 'She's being cremated,' she said. 'That's what she wanted.'

Richard clasped his hands in front of his belly. The same disapproving look was on his face. It was almost condescending, but not quite. For just a moment, Jeffrey caught something behind his expression. Richard turned, though, and Jeffrey was not sure if he had been reading too much into things.

Lena began, 'There's a wake, I guess you'd call it, tonight.' She scribbled on her pad, then ripped the sheet off. 'It's at Brock's Funeral Home on King Street at five.'

Richard glanced down his nose at the paper before folding it neatly in two, then again, then tucking it into the pocket of his lab coat. He sniffed, using the back of his hand to wipe his nose. Jeffrey could not tell if he had a cold or was trying not to cry.

Lena asked, 'So, was there anyone strange hanging around the lab or Sibyl's office?'

Richard shook his head. 'Just the usual weirdos.' He laughed, then stopped abruptly. 'I guess that's not altogether appropriate.'

'No,' Lena said. 'It's not.'

Jeffrey cleared his throat, getting the young man's attention. 'When was the last time you saw her, Richard?'

'After her morning class,' he said. 'She wasn't feeling well. I think I caught her cold.' He took out a tissue as if to support this. 'She was such a wonderful person. I really can't tell you how lucky I was that she took me under her wing.'

'What did you do after she left school?' Jeffrey asked.

He shrugged. 'Probably went to the library.'

'Probably?' Jeffrey asked, not liking his casual tone.

Richard seemed to pick up on Jeffrey's irritation. 'I was at the library,' he amended. 'Sibyl asked me to look up some references.'

Lena took over, asking, 'Was there anyone acting strange around her? Maybe dropping by more than usual?'

Richard shook his head side to side again, his lips pursed. 'Not really. We're more than halfway through the term. Sibyl teaches upper level classes, so most of her students have been here for a couple of years at least.'

'No new faces in the crowd?' Jeffrey asked.

Again Richard shook his head. He reminded Jeffrey of one of those bobbing dogs some people put on their dashboards.

Richard said, 'We're a small community here. Somebody acting strange would stick out.'

Jeffrey was about to ask another question when Kevin Blake, the dean of the college, walked into the room. He did not look happy.

'Chief Tolliver,' Blake said. 'I assume you're here about the missing student.'

Julia Matthews was a twenty-three-year-old junior majoring in physical science. She had been missing for two days, according to her dorm mate.

Jeffrey walked around the young women's dorm

room. There were posters on the wall with encouraging statements about success and victory. On the bedside table was a photograph of the missing girl standing beside a man and a woman who were obviously her parents. Julia Matthews was an attractive girl in a plain, wholesome way. In the photograph, her dark hair was pulled into pigtails on either side of her head. She had a snaggled front tooth, but other than that, she looked like the perfect girl next door. As a matter of fact, she looked very much like Sibyl Adams.

'They're out of town,' Jenny Price, the missing girl's dorm mate, supplied. She stood in the doorway wringing her hands as she watched Jeffrey and Lena search the room.

She continued. 'It's their twentieth wedding anniversary. They went on a cruise to the Bahamas.'

'She's very pretty,' Lena said, obviously trying to calm the girl. Jeffrey wondered if Lena noticed the similarity between Julia Matthews and her sister. They both had olive-colored skin and dark hair. They both looked to be about the same age, though Sibyl was in fact ten years older. Jeffrey felt uncomfortable and set the picture down as he realized that both women resembled Lena as well.

Lena turned her attention to Jenny, asking, 'When did you first notice she was missing?'

'When I got back from class yesterday, I guess,' Jenny answered. A slight redness came to her cheeks. 'She's been gone overnight before, right?'

'Sure,' Lena supplied.

'I thought maybe she was out with Ryan. That's her old boyfriend?' She paused. 'They broke up about a month ago. I saw them at the library together a couple of days ago, around nine o'clock at night. That was the last time I saw her.'

Lena picked up on the boyfriend, saying, 'It's pretty stressful trying to have a relationship when you've got classes and work to do.'

Jenny gave her a weak smile. 'Yeah. Ryan's in the agricultural school. His workload isn't nearly as heavy as Julia's.' She rolled her eyes. 'As long as his plants don't die, he gets an A. Meanwhile we're studying all night, trying to get lab time.'

'I remember what it was like,' Lena said, though she had never been to college. The easy way lies came to her both alarmed and impressed Jeffrey. She was one of the best interviewers he had ever seen.

Jenny smiled and her shoulders relaxed. Lena's lie had done the trick. 'You know how it is, then. It's hard to make time to breathe, let alone have a boyfriend.'

Lena asked, 'They broke up because she didn't have enough time for him?'

Jenny nodded. 'He's her first boyfriend ever. Julia was really upset.' She gave Jeffrey a nervous glance. 'She really fell hard for him, you know? She was sick, like, with grief, when they broke up. She wouldn't even get out of bed.'

Lena lowered her voice, as if to leave Jeffrey out. 'I guess when you saw them in the library, they weren't exactly studying.'

Jenny glanced at Jeffrey. 'No.' She laughed nervously.

Lena walked over, blocking his view of the girl. Jeffrey took the hint. He turned his back to the two women, pretending to take an interest in the contents of Julia's desk.

Lena's voice dropped to a conversational tone. 'What do you think about Ryan?'

'You mean, do I like him?'

'Yeah,' Lena answered. 'I mean, not like like him. I mean, does he seem like a nice guy?'

The girl was quiet for a while. Jeffrey picked up a science book and thumbed through the pages.

Finally, Jenny said, 'Well, he was kind of selfish, you know? And he didn't like it when she couldn't see him.'

'Kind of controlling?'

'Yeah, I guess,' the girl answered. 'She's from the sticks, okay? Ryan kind of takes advantage of that. Julia doesn't know a lot about the world. She thinks he does.'

'Does he?'

'God, no.' Jenny laughed. 'I mean, he's not a bad guy –'

'Of course not.'

'He's just . . . ' She paused. 'He doesn't like for her to talk to other people, okay? He's, like, scared that she'll see there are better guys out there. At least, that's what I think. Julia's kind of been sheltered all her life. She doesn't know to look out for guys like that.' Again she paused. 'He's not a bad guy, he's just needy, you know? He has to know where she's going, who she'll be with, when she'll be back. He doesn't like for her to have any time to herself at all.'

Lena's voice was still low. 'He never hit her, did he?'

'No, not like that.' Again the girl was silent. Then, 'He just yelled at her a lot. Sometimes when I would come back from study group, I would listen at the door, you know?'

'Yeah,' Lena said. 'To make sure.'

'Right,' Jenny agreed, a nervous giggle escaping. 'Well, one time, I heard him in here and he was being so mean to her. Just saying nasty things.'

'Nasty like what?'

'Like that she was bad,' Jenny said. 'Like that she was going to hell for being so bad.'

Lena took her time asking the next question. 'He's a religious guy?'

Jenny made a derisive sound. 'When it's convenient. He knows that Julia is. She's really into church and all. I mean, she was back home. She doesn't go much here, but she's always talking about being in the choir and being a good Christian and that kind of thing.'

'But Ryan's not religious?'

'Only when he thinks he can work her with something. Like he says he's real religious, but he's got all kinds of body piercings, and he's always wearing black and he –' She stopped speaking.

Lena lowered her voice. 'What?' she asked then, even lower. 'I won't tell anybody.'

Jenny whispered something, but Jeffrey couldn't make out what she was saying.

'Oh,' Lena said as if she had heard it all. 'Guys are so stupid.'

Jenny laughed. 'She believed him.'

Lena chuckled with her, then asked, 'What did Julia do that was so bad, do you think? I mean, to get Ryan upset at her like that?'

'Nothing,' Jenny answered vehemently. 'That's what I asked her later. She wouldn't tell me. She just lay in bed all day, not saying anything.'

'This was around the time they broke up?'

'Yeah,' Jenny confirmed. 'Last month, like I said.' There was worry in her voice when she asked, 'You don't think he has anything to do with her being missing, do you?'

'No,' Lena said. 'I wouldn't worry about that.'

Jeffrey turned around, asking, 'What's Ryan's last name?'

'Gordon,' the girl supplied. 'Do you think Julia's in trouble?'

Jeffrey considered her question. He could tell her not to worry, but that might give the girl a false sense of security. He settled for, 'I don't know, Jenny. We'll do everything we can to find her.'

A quick visit to the registrar's office revealed that Ryan Gordon was study hall monitor this time of day. The agricultural wing was on the outskirts of the campus, and Jeffrey felt his anxiety build with every step they took across the campus. He sensed the tension coming from Lena as well. Two days had passed with no solid leads. They could very well be about to meet the man who had killed Sibyl Adams.

Granted, Jeffrey was not prepared to be Ryan Gordon's best friend, but there was something about the kid that set Jeffrey against him the minute they met. He had his eyebrow and both ears pierced as well as a ring hanging out from the septum in the middle of his nose. The ring looked black and crusty, more like something you would put in an ox rather than in a human nose. Jenny's description of Ryan Gordon had not been kind, but in retrospect, Jeffrey thought she had been generous. Ryan looked filthy. His face was an oily mix of acne and healing scabs. His hair looked like it had not been washed in days. His black jeans and shirt were rumpled. There was an odd odor coming off him.

Julia Matthews was, by all accounts, a very attractive young woman. How someone like Ryan Gordon had managed to snag her was a mystery to Jeffrey. This said a lot about the type of kid Gordon was, if he could manage to control someone who could quite clearly do a hell of a lot better than him.

Jeffrey noticed the kind part of Lena that had earlier worked Jenny Price was long gone by the time they reached the study hall classroom. She walked purposefully into the room, ignoring the curious glances coming from the other students, mostly male, as she made a beeline for the kid sitting behind the desk in front of the class.

'Ryan Gordon?' she asked, leaning over the desk. Her jacket pulled back, and Jeffrey saw the kid's eyes gave her gun a sharp glance. His lips stayed pressed into a tight, surly line, though, and when he answered, Jeffrey felt the urge to smack him.

Gordon said, 'What's it to you, bitch?'

Jeffrey grabbed the kid up by his collar and duck-walked him out of the room. Even as he did this, Jeffrey was certain there would be an angry message from the mayor before he got back to the office.

Outside the study room, he pushed Gordon into the wall. Jeffrey took out his handkerchief, wiping the grease off his hand. 'They got showers in your dorm?' he asked.

Gordon's voice was just as whiny as Jeffrey had expected. 'This is police brutality.'

To Jeffrey's surprise, Lena gave Gordon an open-palmed slap.

Gordon rubbed his cheek, his mouth turned down at the corners. He seemed to size Lena up. Jeffrey found the look he gave her almost comical. Ryan Gordon was thin as a rail, about Lena's height if not her weight. She had attitude on him in spades. Jeffrey had no doubt that Lena would rip his throat open with her bare teeth if Gordon tried to push her.

Gordon seemed to understand this. He took on a passive posture, his voice a nasally whine, perhaps from the ring in his nose, which bobbed when he spoke. 'What do you want from me, man?'

He held his arms up defensively as Lena's hand reached out to his chest.

She said, 'Put your hands down, you pussy.' She

reached down into his shirt and pulled up the cross hanging on a chain around his neck.

'Nice necklace,' she said.

Jeffrey asked, 'Where were you Monday afternoon?'

Gordon looked from Lena to Jeffrey. 'What?'

'Where were you Monday afternoon?' Jeffrey repeated.

'I don't know, man,' he whined. 'Sleeping, probably.' He sniffed, rubbing his nose. Jeffrey fought the urge to cringe as the ring in his nose moved back and forth.

'Up against the wall,' Lena ordered, pushing him around. Gordon started to protest, but a look from Lena stopped him. He spread his arms and legs out, assuming the position.

Lena patted him down, asking, 'I'm not going to find any needles, am I? Nothing that would hurt me?'

Gordon groaned, 'No,' as she reached into his front pocket.

Lena smiled, pulling out a bag of white powder. 'This isn't sugar, is it?' she asked Jeffrey.

He took the bag, surprised that she had found it. This would certainly explain Gordon's appearance. Drug addicts weren't the most conscientious groomers in the world. For the first time that morning, Jeffrey was glad to have Lena around. He would never have thought to frisk the boy.

Gordon glanced over his shoulder, looking at the bag. 'These aren't my pants.'

'Right,' Lena snapped. Spinning Gordon around, she asked, 'When was the last time you saw Julia Matthews?'

Gordon's face registered his thoughts. He obviously knew where this was leading. The powder was the least of his problems. 'We broke up a month ago.'

'That doesn't answer the question,' Lena said. She

repeated, 'When was the last time you saw Julia Matthews?'

Gordon crossed his arms in front of his chest. Jeffrey realized instantly that he had mishandled this whole thing. Nerves and excitement had gotten the better of him. In his mind, Jeffrey said the words that Gordon spoke aloud.

'I want to talk to a lawyer.'

Jeffrey propped his feet on the table in front of his chair. They were in the interview room, waiting for Ryan Gordon to be processed. Unfortunately, Gordon had kept his mouth closed tighter than a steel trap from the minute Lena read him his rights. Luckily, Gordon's roommate at the dorms had been more than happy to allow a search. This had yielded nothing more suspicious than a pack of rolling papers and a mirror with a razor blade lying on top of it. Jeffrey wasn't sure, but judging from the roommate, the drug paraphernalia could have belonged to either boy. A search of the lab where Gordon worked did not add any additional clues to the pot. The best-case scenario was Julia Matthews had realized what an asshole her boyfriend was and split.

'We fucked up,' Jeffrey said, resting his hand on a copy of the *Grant County Observer*.

Lena nodded. 'Yeah.'

He took a deep breath and let it go. 'I suppose a kid like that would've lawyered up anyway.'

'I don't know,' Lena answered. 'Maybe he watches too much TV.'

Jeffrey should have expected this. Any idiot with a television knew to ask for a lawyer when the cops showed up at your door.

'I could have been a little softer,' she countered.

'Obviously, if he's our guy, he wouldn't exactly be happy to have a woman pushing him around.' She gave a humorless laugh. 'Especially me, looking just like her.'

'Maybe that'll work some in our favor,' he offered. 'What about I leave you two alone here while we wait for Buddy Conford?'

'He got Buddy?' Lena asked, her tone indicating her displeasure. There were a handful of lawyers in Grant who took on public defender work for a reduced fee. Of them all, Buddy Conford was the most tenacious.

'He's on the rotation this month,' Jeffrey said. 'You think Gordon's stupid enough to talk?'

'He's never been arrested before. He doesn't strike me as particularly savvy.'

Jeffrey was silent, waiting for her to continue.

'He's probably pretty pissed at me for slapping him,' she said, and he could see her working out an approach in her mind. 'Why don't you help me set it up? Tell me not to talk to him.'

Jeffrey nodded. 'It might work.'

'Couldn't hurt.'

Jeffrey was silent, staring at the table. Finally he tapped his finger on the front page of the paper. A picture of Sibyl Adams took up most of the space above the fold. 'I guess you saw this?'

She nodded, not looking at the photo.

Jeffrey turned the paper over. 'It doesn't say she was raped, but they hint at it. I told them she was beaten, but she wasn't.'

'I know,' she mumbled. 'I read it.'

'Frank and the guys,' Jeffrey began, 'they haven't found anything solid from the known offender list. There were a couple Frank wanted to look at seriously, but nothing panned out. They both had alibis.'

Lena stared at her hands.

Jeffrey said, 'You can leave after this. I know you probably need to get some things together for tonight.'

Her acquiescence surprised him. 'Thank you.'

A knock came at the door, then Brad Stephens poked his head in. 'I've got your guy out here.'

Jeffrey stood, saying, 'Bring him in.'

Ryan Gordon looked even more puny in the orange jailhouse jumper than he had in his black jeans and shirt. His feet shuffled in the matching orange slippers, and his hair was still wet from the hosing down Jeffrey had ordered. Gordon's hands were cuffed behind his back, and Brad handed Jeffrey the key before leaving.

'Where's my lawyer?' Gordon demanded.

'He should be here in about fifteen minutes,' Jeffrey answered, pushing the kid down into a chair. He unlocked the handcuffs, but before Gordon could move his arms he had cuffed him back through the rungs of the chair.

'That's too tight,' Gordon whined, pushing his chest out to exaggerate his discomfort. He pulled at the chair, but his hands stayed tight behind him.

'Live with it,' Jeffrey muttered, then said to Lena, 'I'm going to leave you in here with him. Don't let him say anything off-the-record, do you hear me?'

Lena cast her eyes down. 'Yes, sir.'

'I mean it, Detective.' He gave her what he hoped was a stern look, then walked out of the room. Jeffrey took the next door down, entering the observation room. He stood with his arms crossed, watching Gordon and Lena through the one-way glass.

The interview room was relatively small with painted cement blocks for walls. A table was bolted to the center of the floor with three chairs spread around it. Two on one side, one on the other. Jeffrey watched Lena pick up the newspaper. She propped her feet up on the table, leaning the chair back a little as she opened the *Grant County Observer* to an inside page. Jeffrey heard the speaker next to him crackle as she folded the paper along the seam.

Gordon said, 'I want some water.'

'Don't talk,' Lena ordered, her voice so low Jeffrey had to turn up the speaker on the wall to hear her.

'Why? You gonna get in trouble?'

Lena kept her nose in the paper.

'You should get in trouble,' Gordon said, leaning over as much as he could in the chair. 'I'm gonna tell my lawyer you slapped me.'

Lena snorted a laugh. 'What do you weigh, one fifty? You're about five six?' She put the paper down, giving him a soft, innocent expression. Her voice was high-pitched and girlish. 'I would never hit a suspect in custody, Your Honor. He's so big and strong, I'd be afraid for my life.'

Gordon's eyes narrowed to slits. 'You think you're pretty funny.'

'Yeah,' Lena said, returning to the paper. 'I really do.'

Gordon took a minute or two to refigure his approach. He pointed to the newspaper. 'You're that dyke's sister.'

Lena's voice was still light, though Jeffrey knew she must have wanted to climb over the table and kill him. She said, 'That's right.'

'She got killed,' he said. 'Everybody on campus knew she was a dyke.'

'She certainly was.'

Gordon licked his lips. 'Fucking dyke.'

'Yep.' Lena turned the page, looking as if she was bored.

'Dyke,' he repeated. 'Fucking clit licker.' He paused,

waiting for a reaction, obviously irritated that there was none. He said, 'Gash grinder.'

Lena gave a bored sigh. 'Bushwhacker, eats at the Y, dials O on her friend's little pink telephone.' She paused, looking at him over the paper, asking, 'Leaving any out?'

While Jeffrey felt an appreciation for Lena's technique, he said a small prayer of thanks that she had not chosen a life of crime.

Gordon said, 'That's what you've got me in here for, right? You think I raped her?'

Lena kept the paper up, but Jeffrey knew her heartbeat was probably going as fast as his. Gordon could be guessing, or he could be looking for a way to confess.

Lena asked, 'Did you rape her?'

'Maybe,' Gordon said. He started rocking the chair back and forth, like a little boy craving attention. 'Maybe I fucked her. You wanna know about it?'

'Sure,' Lena said. She put the paper down, crossing her arms. 'Why don't you tell me all about it?'

Gordon leaned toward her. 'She was in the bathroom, right?'

'You tell me.'

'She was washing her hands, and I went in and fucked her up the ass. She liked it so much she died on the spot.'

Lena gave a heavy sigh. 'That's the best you can do?'

He seemed insulted. 'No.'

'Why don't you tell me what you did to Julia Matthews?'

He sat back in the chair, leaning on his hands. 'I didn't do anything to her.'

'Where is she then?'

He shrugged. 'Probably dead.'

'Why do you say that?'

He leaned forward, his chest pressed into the table. 'She's tried to kill herself before.'

Lena did not skip a beat. 'Yeah, I know. Slit her wrists.'

'That's right.' Gordon nodded, though Jeffrey could see the surprise in his face. Jeffrey was surprised, too, though it made perfect sense. Women were far more likely to choose slitting their wrists over the many other methods of suicide. Lena had made a calculated guess.

Lena summarized, 'She slit her wrists last month.'

He cocked his head, giving her a strange look. 'How'd you know that?'

Lena sighed again, picking the paper back up. She opened it with a snap, then started to read.

Gordon started rocking his chair back and forth again.

Lena did not look up from the paper. 'Where is she, Ryan?'

'I don't know.'

'Did you rape her?'

'I didn't have to rape her. She was a damn lapdog.'

'You let her go down on you?'

'That's right.'

'That the only way you could get it up, Ryan?'

'Shit.' He dropped the chair. 'You're not supposed to be talking to me anyway.'

'Why?'

' 'Cause this is off-the-record. I can say anything I want and it doesn't matter.'

'What do you want to say?'

His lips twitched. He leaned over further. From Jeffrey's perspective, he thought that with Gordon's hands cuffed behind him, the kid almost looked hogtied.

Gordon whispered, 'Maybe I want to talk about your sister some more.'

Lena ignored him.

'Maybe I wanna talk about how I beat her to death.'

'You don't look like the type of guy who knows how to use a hammer.'

He seemed taken aback by this. 'I am,' he assured her. 'I beat her in the head, then I fucked her with the hammer.'

Lena folded the paper to a new page. 'Where'd you leave the hammer?'

He looked smug. 'Wouldn't you like to know?'

'What was Julia up to, Ryan?' Lena asked casually. 'She screwing around on you? Maybe she found a real man.'

'Fuck that, bitch,' Gordon snapped. 'I am a real man.'

'Right.'

'Take off these cuffs and I'll show you.'

'I bet you will,' Lena said, her tone indicating she was not in the least bit threatened. 'Why did she run around on you?'

'She didn't,' he said. 'That bitch Jenny Price tell you that? She doesn't know anything about it.'

'About how Julia wanted to leave you? About how you followed her around all the time, wouldn't leave her alone?'

'Is that what this is about?' Gordon asked. 'That why you got me freaking chained up?'

'We've got you chained up for the coke in your pocket.'

He snorted. 'It wasn't mine.'

'Not your pants, right?'

He slammed his chest into the table, his face a mask of anger. 'Listen, bitch –'

Lena stood in front of him, leaning over the table, her face in his. 'Where is she?'

Spit came from his mouth. 'Fuck you.'

In one quick motion, Lena grabbed the ring hanging down from his nose.

'Ow, shit,' Gordon screamed as he leaned over, his chest slamming into the table, his arms sticking up behind his back. 'Help!' he screamed. The glass in front of Jeffrey shook from the noise.

Lena whispered, 'Where is she?'

'I saw her a couple of days ago,' he managed through gritted teeth. 'Jesus, please let go.'

'Where is she?'

'I don't know,' he yelled. 'Please, I don't know! You're gonna pull it out.'

Lena released the ring, wiping her hand on her pants. 'You stupid little twit.'

Ryan wiggled his nose, probably making sure it was still there. 'You hurt me,' he whined. 'That hurt.'

'You want me to hurt you some more?' Lena offered, resting her hand on her gun.

Gordon tucked his head into his chest, mumbling, 'She tried to kill herself because I left her. She loved me that much.'

'I think she didn't have a clue,' Lena countered. 'I think she was pretty much fresh off the truck and you took advantage of her.' She stood up, leaning halfway over the table. 'What's more, I don't think you have the balls to kill a fly, let alone a living person, and if I ever' – Lena slammed her hands into the table, her anger bursting like a grenade, 'if I ever hear you say anything else about my sister, Ryan, anything at all, I will kill you. Trust me on this, I know I have it in me. I don't doubt that for a second.'

Gordon's mouth moved wordlessly.

Jeffrey was so engrossed in the interview that he didn't notice the knock at the door.

'Jeffrey?' Marla said, poking her head into the observation room. 'We got a situation at Will Harris's place.'

'Will Harris?' Jeffrey asked, thinking that was the last name he had expected to hear today. 'What happened?'

Marla stepped into the room, lowering her voice. 'Somebody threw a rock in the front window of his house.'

Frank Wallace and Matt Hogan were standing on Will Harris's front lawn when Jeffrey pulled up. He wondered how long they had been there. Wondered, too, if they knew who had done this. Matt Hogan did not have qualms about hiding his prejudices. Frank, on the other hand, Jeffrey was not sure about. What he did know was Frank had been in on the interview of Pete Wayne yesterday. Jeffrey felt his tension build as he parked the car. He did not like being in a position where he could not trust his own men.

'What the hell happened?' Jeffrey asked, getting out of the car. 'Who did this?'

Frank said, 'He got home about half an hour ago. Said he was working at old Miss Betty's house, aerating her yard. Came home and saw this.'

'It was a rock?'

'Brick, actually,' Frank said. 'Same kind you see everywhere. Had a note around it.'

'What'd it say?'

Frank looked down at the ground, then back up. 'Will's got it.'

Jeffrey looked at the picture window, which had a large hole in it. The two windows on either side were untouched, but the glass in the center would cost a small fortune to replace. 'Where is he?' Jeffrey asked.

Matt nodded toward the front door. He had the same smug look Jeffrey had seen on Ryan Gordon a few minutes ago.

Matt said, 'In the house.'

Jeffrey started toward the door, then stopped himself. He reached into his wallet and pulled out a twenty. 'Go buy some plywood,' he said. 'Bring it back here as soon as possible.'

Matt's jaw set, but Jeffrey levered him with a hard stare. 'You got something you want to say to me, Matt?'

Frank interjected, 'We'll see if we can get some glass on order while we're there.'

'Yeah,' Matt grumbled, walking toward the car.

Frank started to follow, but Jeffrey stopped him. He asked, 'You got any idea who might have done this?'

Frank stared down at his feet for a few seconds. 'Matt was with me all morning, if that's what you're getting at.'

'It was.'

Frank looked back up. 'I'll tell you what, Chief, I find out who did, I'll take care of it.'

He did not wait around for Jeffrey's opinion on this. He turned, walking back toward Matt's car. Jeffrey waited for them to drive off before walking up the drive to Will Harris's house.

Jeffrey gave the screen door a gentle knock before letting himself in. Will Harris was sitting in his chair, a glass of iced tea beside him. He stood when Jeffrey entered the room.

'I didn't mean to bring you out here,' Will said. 'I was just reporting it. My neighbor got me kind of scared.'

'Which one?' Jeffrey asked.

'Mrs. Barr across the way.' He pointed out the window. 'She's an older woman, scares real easy. She said she didn't see anything. Your people already asked her.' He walked back to his chair and picked up a piece of white paper, which he offered to Jeffrey. 'I got kind of scared, too, when I saw this.'

Jeffrey took the paper, tasting bile in the back of his throat as he read the threatening words typed onto the white sheet of paper. The note said: 'Watch your back, nigger.'

Jeffrey folded the paper, tucking it into his pocket. He put his hands on his hips, looking around the room. 'Nice place you got here.'

'Thank you,' Will returned.

Jeffrey turned toward the front windows. He did not have a good feeling about this. Will Harris's life was in danger simply because Jeffrey had talked to him the other day. He asked, 'You mind if I sleep on your couch tonight?'

Will seemed surprised. 'You think that's necessary?'

Jeffrey shrugged. 'Better safe than sorry, don't you think?'

TWELVE

Lena sat at the kitchen table in her house, staring at the salt and pepper shakers. She tried to get her head around what had happened today. She was certain that Ryan Gordon's only crime was being an asshole. If Julia Matthews was smart, she had headed back home or was lying low for a while, probably trying to get away from her boyfriend. This left the reason Jeffrey and Lena had gone to the college wide open. There were still no suspects for her sister's murder.

With each minute that passed, with each hour that went by with no solid lead toward finding the man who had killed her sister, Lena felt herself getting more and more angry. Sibyl had always warned Lena that anger was a dangerous thing, that she should allow other emotions to come through. Right now, Lena could not imagine herself ever being happy again, or even sad. She was numbed by the loss, and anger was the only thing that made her feel like she was still alive. She was embracing her anger, letting it grow inside of her like a cancer, so that she would not break down into a powerless child. She needed her anger to get her through this. After Sibyl's killer was caught, after Julia Matthews was found, Lena would let herself grieve.

'Sibby.' Lena sighed, putting her hands over her eyes. Even during the interview with Gordon, images of Sibyl had started to seep into Lena's mind. The harder she fought them off, the stronger they were.

They came in flashes, these memories. One minute, she was sitting across from Gordon, listening to his pathetic posturing, the next she was twelve years old, at the beach, leading Sibyl down to the ocean so they could play in the water. Early on after the accident that had blinded Sibyl, Lena had become her sister's eyes; through Lena, Sibyl was sighted again. To this day, Lena thought this trick was what made her a good detective. She paid attention to detail. She listened to her gut instinct. Right now, her gut was telling her any more time focusing on Gordon was wasted.

'Hey there,' Hank said, taking a Coke out of the refrigerator. He held up a bottle for Lena, but she shook her head.

Lena asked, 'Where did those come from?'

'I went to the store,' he said. 'How'd it go today?'

Lena didn't answer his question. 'Why did you go to the store?'

'You didn't have anything to eat,' he said. 'I'm surprised you haven't wasted away.'

'I don't need you to go to the store for me,' Lena countered. 'When are you going back to Reece?'

He seemed pained by her question. 'In a couple of days, I guess. I can stay with Nan if you don't want me here.'

'You can stay here.'

'It's no trouble, Lee. She's already offered her sofa.'

'You don't need to stay with her,' Lena snapped. 'Okay? Just drop it. If it's only a few days, that's fine.'

'I could stay in a hotel.'

'Hank,' Lena said, aware her voice was louder than it needed to be. 'Just drop it, okay? I've had a really hard day.'

Hank fiddled with his bottle of Coke. 'Wanna talk about it?'

Lena bit back the 'Not with you' that was on the tip of her tongue. 'No,' she said.

He took a swig of Coke, staring somewhere over her shoulder.

'There are no leads,' Lena said. 'Other than the list.' Hank look puzzled, and she explained, 'We've got this list of everybody who moved to Grant in the last six years who's a sexual predator.'

'They keep a list of that?'

'Thank God they do,' Lena said, heading off any civil liberties arguments he wanted to start. As an ex-addict, Hank tended to side with personal privacy over common sense. Lena was in no mood for a discussion about how ex-cons had paid their dues.

'So,' Hank said, 'you've got this list?'

'We've all got lists,' Lena clarified. 'We're knocking on doors, trying to see if anybody matches up.'

'To?'

She stared at him, trying to decide whether or not to go on. 'Someone with a violent sexual assault in their background. Someone who's white, between the ages of twenty-eight and thirty-five. Someone who thinks of himself as a religious person. Someone who might have seen Sibyl around. Whoever attacked her knew her routines, so this person had to be someone who knew her by sight or in passing.'

'That sounds like a pretty narrow margin.'

'There are nearly a hundred people on the list.'

He gave a low whistle. 'In Grant?' He shook his head side to side, not quite buying this.

'That's just the last six years, Hank. I guess if we go through these without finding anyone, we'll go back even further. Maybe ten or fifteen years.'

Hank pushed his hair back off his forehead, giving Lena a good look at his forearms. She pointed to his bare arms. 'I want you to keep your coat on tonight.'

Hank looked down at the old track marks. 'If you want me to, okay.'

'Cops will be there. Friends of mine. People I work with. They see those tracks and they're gonna know.'

He looked down at his arms. 'I don't think you'd have to be a cop to know what these are.'

'Don't embarrass me, Hank. It's bad enough I had to tell my boss you're a junkie.'

'I'm sorry about that.'

'Yeah, well,' Lena said, not knowing what else to offer. She was tempted to look him over, to pick at him until he exploded and she got a good fight out of him.

Instead, she turned in her chair, looking away from him. 'I'm not in the mood for a heart-to-heart.'

'Well, I'm sorry to hear that,' Hank said, but he did not get up. 'We need to talk about what to do with your sister's ashes.'

Lena held her hand up to stop him. 'I can't do that right now.'

'I've been talking to Nan –'

She interrupted him. 'I don't care what Nan has to say about this.'

'She was her lover, Lee. They had a life together.'

'So did we,' Lena snapped. 'She was my sister, Han. For God's sake, I'm not going to let Nan Thomas have her.'

'Nan seems like a real nice person.'

'I'm sure she is.'

Hank fiddled with the bottle. 'We can't leave her out of this just because you're uncomfortable with it, Lee.' He paused, then, 'They were in love with each other. I don't know why you have a problem accepting that.'

'Accepting it?' Lena laughed. 'How could I not accept it? They lived together. They took vacations together.' She remembered Gordon's earlier comment. 'Evidently the whole fucking college knew about it,' she said. 'It's not like I had a choice.'

Hank sat back with a sigh. 'I don't know, baby. Were you jealous of her?'

Lena cocked her head. 'Of who?'

'Nan.'

She laughed. 'That's the stupidest thing I've ever heard you say.' She added, 'And we both know I've heard you say some really stupid shit.'

Hank shrugged. 'You had Sibby to yourself for a long time. I can see where her meeting somebody, getting involved with someone, might make it difficult for her to be there for you.'

Lena felt her mouth open in shock. The fight she was hoping for seconds ago was now blowing up in her face. 'You think I was jealous of Nan Thomas because she was fucking my sister?'

He flinched at her words. 'You think that's all they were about?'

'I don't know what they were about, Hank,' Lena said. 'We didn't talk about that part of her life, okay?'

'I know that.'

'Then why did you bring it up?'

He did not answer. 'You're not the only one who lost her.'

'When did you hear me say that I was?' Lena snapped, standing.

'It just seems that way,' Hank said. 'Listen, Lee, maybe you need to talk to somebody about this.'

'I'm talking to you about it right now.'

'Not me.' Hank frowned. 'What about that boy you were seeing? Is he still around?'

She laughed. 'Greg and I split up a year ago, and even if we hadn't, I don't think I'd be crying on his shoulder.'

'I didn't say you would be.'

'Good.'

'I know you better than that.'

'You don't know a goddamn thing about me,' she snapped. Lena left the room, her fists clenching as she took the steps upstairs two at a time, slamming her bedroom door behind her.

Her closet was filled mostly with suits and slacks, but Lena found a black dress tucked in the back. She pulled out the ironing board, stepping back, but not in time to miss the iron slipping off the shelf and smashing into her toe.

'Damnit,' Lena hissed, grabbing her foot. She sat down on the bed, rubbing her toes. This was Hank's fault, getting her worked up this way. He was always doing this kind of thing, always pushing his damn AA philosophies about closure and sharing onto Lena. If he wanted to live his life that way, if he needed to live his life that way so that he did not end up shooting himself full of dope or drinking himself to death, that was fine, but he had no right to try to push that onto Lena.

As for his armchair diagnosis of Lena being jealous of Nan, that was just ridiculous. Her entire life, Lena had worked to help Sibyl become independent. It was Lena who had read reports aloud so that Sibyl did not have to wait for Braille translations. It was Lena who listened to Sibyl practice her oral exams and Lena who helped Sibyl with experiments. All that had been for Sibyl, to help her go out on her own, to get a job, to make a life for herself.

Lena opened the ironing board and placed the dress on it. She smoothed the material, remembering the last time she had worn this dress. Sibyl had asked Lena to take her to a faculty party at the college. Lena was surprised but had agreed to go. There was a clear line between college people and town folks, and she had felt uncomfortable in that crowd, surrounded by people who had completed not only college but also gone on to get higher degrees. Lena was not a country bumpkin, but she remembered feeling like she stuck out like a sore thumb.

Sibyl, on the other hand, had been in her element. Lena could remember seeing her at the center of a crowd, talking to a group of professors who seemed to be really interested in what she was saying. No one was staring at her the way people did when the girls were growing up. No one was making fun of her or making snide comments about the fact that she could not see. For the first time in her life, Lena had realized that Sibyl did not need her.

Nan Thomas had nothing to do with this revelation. Hank was wrong about that. Sibyl had been independent from day one. She knew how to take care of herself. She knew how to get around. She may have been blind, but in some ways she was sighted. In some ways, Sibyl could read people better than someone who could see because she listened to what they were saying. She heard the change of cadence in their voices when they were lying or the tremor when they were upset. She had understood Lena like no one else in her life.

Hank knocked at the door. 'Lee?'

Lena wiped her nose, realizing that she had been crying. She did not open the door. 'What?'

His voice was muffled, but she could hear him loud and clear. He said, 'I'm sorry I said that, honey.'

Lena took a deep breath, then let it go. 'It's okay.'

'I'm just worried about you.'

'I'm okay,' Lena said, turning on the iron. 'Give me ten minutes and I'll be ready to go.'

She watched the door, saw the doorknob turn slightly, then turn back as it was released. She heard his footsteps as he walked down the hall.

The Brock Funeral Home was packed to the gills with Sibyl's friends and colleagues. After ten minutes of shaking hands and accepting condolences from people she had never met in her life, Lena had a tight knot developing in her stomach. She felt like she might explode from standing still for too long. She did not want to be here, sharing her grief with strangers. The room seemed to be closing in on her, and though the air-conditioning was low enough to keep some people in their coats, Lena was sweating.

'Hey,' Frank said, cupping her elbow in his hand.

Lena was surprised at the gesture but did not pull away. She felt overwhelmed with relief to talk to someone familiar.

'You hear what happened?' Frank asked, shooting Hank a sideways look. Lena felt a blush of embarrassment at the look, knowing that Frank had pegged her uncle for a punk. Cops could smell it from a mile away.

'No,' Lena said, escorting Frank to the side of the room.

'Will Harris,' he began in a low tone. 'Somebody threw a rock through his front window.'

'Why?' Lena asked, already guessing the answer.

Frank shrugged. 'I don't know.' He looked over his shoulder. 'I mean, Matt.' Again the shrug came. 'He was with me all day. I don't know.'

Lena pulled him into the hallway so they would not have to whisper. 'You think Matt did something?'

'Matt or Pete Wayne,' he said. 'I mean, they're the only two I can think of.'

'Maybe somebody in the lodge?'

Frank bristled, like she knew he would. She might as well have accused the pope of fiddling with a ten-year-old.

Lena asked, 'What about Brad?'

Frank gave her a look.

'Yeah,' Lena said. 'I know what you mean.' She could not say without a shadow of a doubt that Brad Stephens might not like Will Harris, but she knew that Brad would cut off his own arm before he broke the law. Once Brad had backtracked three miles just to pick up some trash that had accidentally blown out of his car window.

'I was thinking of talking to Pete later on,' Frank said.

Without thinking, Lena checked the time. It was a little after five-thirty. Pete would probably be home.

'Can we take your car?' she asked, thinking she could leave hers for Hank to take home.

Frank looked back into the parlor. 'You wanna leave your sister's wake?' he asked, not hiding his shock.

Lena stared at the floor, knowing she should feel ashamed at the very least. The fact was, she had to get out of this room with these strangers before grief took hold and she became too paralyzed to do anything but sit in her room crying.

Frank said, 'Meet me around the side in ten minutes.'

Lena walked back into the room, looking for Hank. He was standing by Nan Thomas, his arm around her shoulder. She felt herself bristle, seeing them together like that. He certainly had no problem comforting a complete stranger, no matter that his own flesh and blood was not ten feet away from him, alone.

Lena went back into the hallway to get her coat. She was slipping it on when she felt someone helping her. She was surprised to see Richard Carter behind her.

'I wanted to tell you,' he said, his tone hushed, 'that I'm sorry about your sister.'

'Thanks,' she managed. 'I appreciate that.'

'Have you found anything about that other girl?'

'Matthews?' she asked before she could catch herself. Lena had grown up in a small town, but she was still amazed at how quickly word got around.

'That Gordon,' Richard said, giving a dramatic shudder. 'He's not a very nice boy.'

'Yeah,' Lena mumbled, trying to move him along. 'Listen, thanks for coming tonight.'

His smile was slight. He realized she was moving him along, but obviously he did not want to make it easy for her. He said, 'I really enjoyed working with your sister. She was very good to me.'

Lena shifted from one foot to another, not wanting to give him the impression that she was looking for a long conversation. She knew Frank well enough to know he wouldn't wait for very long.

'She enjoyed working with you, too, Richard,' Lena offered.

'Did she say that?' he asked, obviously pleased. 'I mean, I know she respected my work, but did she say that?'

'Yes,' Lena said. 'All the time.' She picked out Hank in the crowd. He still had his arm around Nan. She pointed them out to Richard. 'Ask my uncle. He was just talking about it the other day.'

'Really?' Richard said, putting his hands up to his mouth.

'Yes,' Lena answered, taking her car keys out of her coat pocket. 'Listen, can you give these to my uncle?'

He stared at the keys without taking them. This was one of the reasons Sibyl had gotten along so well with Richard, she wasn't able to see the condescending looks he gave. In fact, Sibyl seemed to have the patience of Job where Richard Carter was concerned. Lena knew for a fact that Sibyl had helped him get out of academic probation on more than one occasion.

'Richard?' she asked, dangling the keys.

'Sure,' he finally said, holding out his hand.

Lena dropped the keys onto his palm. She waited until he had taken a few steps away, then scooted out the side door. Frank was waiting in his car, the lights out.

'Sorry I'm late,' Lena said, getting in. She wrinkled her nose when she smelled smoke. Technically, Frank was not allowed to smoke around her when they were on the job, but she kept her mouth shut since he was doing her a favor letting her ride along.

'Those college people,' Frank said. He took a drag on the cigarette, then chucked it out the window. 'Sorry,' he offered.

'It's okay,' Lena said. She felt odd being dressed up and in Frank's car. For some reason, she was reminded of her first date. Lena was strictly a jeans and T-shirt girl, so putting on a dress was a big deal. She felt awkward wearing heels and hose, and never knew how to sit or where to put her hands. She missed her holster.

'About your sister,' Frank began.

Lena let him off the hook. 'Yeah, thanks,' she said.

Night had fallen while Lena was in the funeral home, and the farther away from town they got, the farther away from streetlights and people, the darker it got in the car.

'This thing at old Will's house,' Frank began, breaking the silence. 'I don't know about that, Lena.'

'You think Pete had a hand in it?'

'I don't know,' Frank repeated. 'Will worked for his daddy, maybe twenty years before Pete came along. That's something you shouldn't forget.' He reached for a cigarette, then stopped himself. 'I just don't know.'

Lena waited, but there was nothing more. She kept her hands in her lap, staring ahead as Frank drove out of town. They crossed the city line and were well into Madison before Frank slowed his car, taking a hard right onto a dead-end street.

Pete Wayne's brick ranch house was modest, much like the man. His car, a 1996 Dodge with red tape where the taillights used to be, was parked in the driveway at an angle.

Frank pulled the car up to the curb and cut the headlights. He gave a nervous laugh. 'You all dressed up like that, I feel like I should get your door for you.'

'Don't you dare,' Lena countered, grabbing the handle in case he was serious.

'Hold on,' Frank said, putting his hand on Lena's arm. She thought he was pushing the joke, but something about his tone made her look up. Pete was coming out of his house, a baseball bat in his hand.

Frank said, 'Stay here.'

'The hell I will,' Lena said, opening her door before he could stop her. The dome light came on in the car, and Pete Wayne looked up.

Frank said, 'Good going, kid.'

Lena bit back her anger over the nickname. She walked up the driveway behind Frank, feeling stupid in the high heels and long dress.

Pete watched them coming, keeping the bat at his side. 'Frank?' he asked. 'What's up?'

'Mind if we come in for a second?' Frank asked, adding, 'Brother.'

Pete gave a nervous sideways look to Lena. She knew these lodge people had their own special code of language. What exactly Frank meant by calling Pete his brother, she had no idea. For all she knew, Frank was telling Pete to hit Lena with the bat.

Pete said, 'I was just going out.'

'I see that,' Frank said, eyeing the bat. 'Little late for practice, ain't it?'

Pete handled the bat nervously. 'I was just putting it into the van. Got a little nervous about what happened at the diner,' he said. 'Thought I'd keep it behind the bar.'

'Let's go inside,' Frank said, not giving Pete a chance to respond. He walked up the front steps and stood at the front door, waiting for Pete to catch up, hovering over the other man as he fumbled with his keys in the lock.

Lena followed them. By the time they reached the kitchen, Pete was noticeably on guard. His hand was wrapped so tightly around the bat that his knuckles had turned white.

'What's the problem here?' Pete asked, directing his question toward Frank.

'Will Harris had a problem this afternoon,' Frank said. 'Somebody threw a rock into his front window.'

'That's too bad,' Pete answered, his voice flat.

'I gotta say, Pete,' Frank said, 'I think you did it.'

Pete laughed uncomfortably. 'You think I got time to run down and toss a brick through that boy's window? I've got a business to run. I don't have time to take a crap most days, let alone take a trip.'

Lena said, 'What makes you think it was a brick?'

Pete swallowed hard. 'Just a guess.'

Frank grabbed the bat out of his hand. 'Will's worked for your family for nearly fifty years.'

'I know that,' Pete said, taking a step back.

'There were times when your daddy had to pay him with food instead of money because he couldn't afford help otherwise.' Frank weighted the bat in his hand. 'You remember that, Pete? You remember when the base closed and y'all almost went under?'

Pete's face flushed. ''Course I remember that.'

'Let me tell you something, boy,' Frank said, putting the tip of the bat squarely against Pete's chest. 'You listen to me good when I tell you this. Will Harris didn't touch that girl.'

'You know that for a fact?' Pete countered.

Lena put her hand on the bat, bringing it down. She stepped in front of Pete, looking him in the eye. She said, 'I do.'

Pete broke eye contact first. His eyes went to the floor, and his posture took on a nervous stance. He shook his head, letting out a heavy breath. When he looked up, it was Frank he spoke to. 'We've gotta talk.'

THIRTEEN

Eddie Linton had purchased acreage around the lake when he first started making money from his plumbing business. He also owned six houses near the college that he rented out to students, as well as an apartment complex over in Madison that he was always threatening to sell. When Sara moved back to Grant from Atlanta, she had refused to live in her parents' house. Something about moving back home, living in her old room, smacked of defeat to Sara, and at the time she was feeling beaten down enough without the constant reminder that she did not even have a space of her own.

She had rented one of her father's houses her first year back, then started working weekends at the hospital in Augusta in order to save up a down payment for her own place. She had fallen in love with her house the first time the realtor showed her through. Built in a shotgun style, the house's front door lined up directly with the back door. Off to the sides of the long hallway were two bedrooms, a bathroom, and a small den on the right, with the living room, dining room, another bathroom and kitchen on the left. Of course, she would have bought the house if it had been a shack, because the view to the lake was phenomenal from the deck off the back. Her bedroom took full advantage of this, a large picture window flanked by three windows that opened out on either side.

On days like today, she could see clear across, nearly to the university. Some days, when the weather was right, Sara took her boat into the school dock and walked to work.

Sara opened the window in her bedroom so she could hear Jeb's boat when he got to the dock. Last night had seen another soft rain, and a cool breeze was coming off the lake. She studied her appearance in the mirror on the back of the door. She had chosen a wraparound skirt with a small floral print and a tight black Lycra shirt that fell just below her navel. Already, she had put her hair up, then let it back down. She was in the process of pinning it back up when she heard a boat at the dock. She slipped on her sandals and grabbed two glasses and a bottle of wine before walking out the back door.

'Ahoy,' Jeb said, tossing her a rope. He tucked his hands into his orange life vest, affecting what Sara supposed he thought was a jaunty sailor look.

'Ahoy yourself,' Sara answered, kneeling by the bollard. She put the wine and glasses down on the dock as she tied off the line. 'Still haven't learned to swim, have you?'

'Both my parents were terrified of the water,' he explained. 'They never got around to it. And it's not like I grew up near water.'

'Good point,' she said. Having grown up on a lake, swimming came second nature to Sara. She could not imagine not knowing how. 'You should learn,' she said. 'Especially since you're boating.'

'Don't need to know how,' Jeb said, patting the boat as he would a dog. 'I can walk on water with this baby.'

She stood up, admiring the boat. 'Nice.'

'Real babe magnet,' he joked, unhooking the vest. She knew he was teasing, but the boat, painted a deep metallic black, was sleek and sexy, with a dangerous look about it. Unlike Jeb McGuire in his bulky orange life jacket.

Jeb said, 'I'll tell you what, Sara, if you ever looked at me the way you're looking at my boat right now, I'd have to marry you.'

She laughed at herself, saying, 'It's a very pretty boat.'

He pulled out a picnic basket and said, 'I'd offer to take you for a ride, but it's a bit nippy on the water.'

'We can sit here,' she said, indicating the chairs and table on the edge of the dock. 'Do I need to get silverware or anything?'

Jeb smiled. 'I know you better than that, Sara Linton.' He opened the picnic basket and took out silverware and napkins. He had also had the foresight to bring plates and glasses. Sara tried not to lick her lips when he pulled out fried chicken, mashed potatoes, peas, corn, and biscuits.

'Are you trying to seduce me?' she asked.

Jeb stopped, his hand on a tub of gravy. 'Is it working?'

The dogs barked, and all Sara could think was Thank God for small favors. She turned back to the house, saying, 'They never bark. I'll just go check.'

'You want me to come, too?'

Sara was about to tell him no but changed her mind. She had not been making that part up about the dogs. Billy and Bob had barked exactly twice since she had rescued them from the racing track in Ebro; once when Sara had accidentally stepped on Bob's tail, and once when a bird had flown down the chimney into the living room.

She felt Jeb's hand at her back as they walked up the yard toward the house. The sun was just dipping down over the roofline, and she shielded her eyes with her hand, recognizing Brad Stephens standing at the edge of the driveway.

'Hey, Brad,' Jeb said.

The patrolman gave a curt nod to Jeb, but his eyes were on Sara.

'Brad?' she asked.

'Ma'am.' Brad took off his hat. 'The chief's been shot.'

Sara had never really pushed the Z3 Roadster. Even when she drove it back from Atlanta, the speedometer had stayed at a steady seventy-five the entire way. She was doing ninety as she drove the back route to the Grant Medical Center. The ten-minute drive seemed to take hours, and by the time Sara made the turn into the hospital, her palms were sweating on the wheel.

She pulled into a handicap space at the side of the building so she would not block the ambulance doors. Sara was running by the time she reached the emergency room.

'What happened?' she asked Lena Adams, who was standing in front of the admitting desk. Lena opened her mouth to answer, but Sara ran past her into the hallway. She checked each room as she went by, finally finding Jeffrey in the third exam room.

Ellen Bray did not seem surprised to see Sara in the room. The nurse was putting a blood pressure cuff around his arm when Sara walked in.

Sara put her hand on Jeffrey's forehead. His eyes opened slightly, but he did not seem to register her presence.

'What happened?' she asked.

Ellen handed Sara the chart, saying, 'Buckshot to his leg. Nothing serious or they would've taken him to Augusta.'

Sara glanced down at the chart. Her eyes wouldn't focus. She couldn't even make out the columns.

'Sara?' Ellen said, her voice filled with compassion. She had worked in the Augusta emergency room most of her career. She was in semiretirement now, supplementing her pension by working nights at the Grant Medical Center. Sara had worked with her years ago, and the two women had a solid professional relationship built on mutual respect.

Ellen said, 'He's fine, really. The Demerol should knock him out soon. Most of his pain is coming from Hare digging around in his leg.'

'Hare?' Sara asked, feeling a little relief for the first time in the last twenty minutes. Her cousin Hareton was a general practitioner who sometimes filled in at the hospital. 'Is he here?'

Ellen nodded, pumping the cuff's bladder. She held up her finger for silence.

Jeffrey stirred, then slowly opened his eyes. When he recognized Sara, a slight smile crept across his lips.

Ellen released the blood pressure cuff, saying, 'One-forty-five over ninety-two.'

Sara frowned, looking back at Jeffrey's chart. The words finally started to make sense.

'I'll go fetch Dr. Earnshaw,' Ellen said.

'Thanks,' Sara said, flipping the chart open. 'When did you start on Coreg?' she asked. 'How long have you had high blood pressure?'

Jeffrey smiled slyly. 'Since you walked into the room.'

Sara skimmed the chart. 'Fifty milligrams a day. You just switched from captopril? Why did you stop?' She got the answer in the chart. ' "Nonproductive cough prompted change," ' she read aloud.

Hare walked into the room, saying, 'That's common with ACE inhibitors.'

Sara ignored her cousin as he put his arm around her shoulders.

She asked Jeffrey, 'Who are you seeing for this?'

'Lindley,' Jeffrey answered.

'Did you tell him about your father?' Sara snapped the chart closed. 'I can't believe he didn't give you an inhaler. What's your cholesterol like?'

'Sara.' Hare snatched the chart from her hands. 'Shut up.'

Jeffrey laughed. 'Thank you.'

Sara crossed her arms, anger welling up. She had been so worried on the drive over, expecting the worst, and now that she was here, Jeffrey was fine. She was inordinately relieved that he was okay, but for some reason she was feeling tricked by her emotions.

'Lookit,' Hare said, popping an X ray into the lightbox mounted on the wall. He gasped audibly, saying, 'Oh my God, that's the worst I've ever seen.'

Sara cut him with a look, turning the X ray right side up.

'Oh, thank God.' Hare sighed dramatically. When he saw she wasn't enjoying his sideshow, he frowned. The thing that made Sara both love and hate her cousin was he seldom took things very seriously.

Hare said, 'Missed his artery, missed his bone. Cut right through here on the inside.' He gave her a reassuring smile. 'Nothing bad at all.'

Sara ignored the evaluation, leaning closer to double-check Hare's findings. Aside from the fact that her relationship with her cousin had always been riddled with fierce competition, she wanted to make sure for herself that nothing had been missed.

'Let's turn you over on your left side,' Hare suggested to Jeffrey, waiting for Sara to help. Sara kept Jeffrey's injured right leg stable as they turned him, offering,

'This should help bring your blood pressure down a little. Are you due for your medication tonight?'

Jeffrey supplied, 'I'm late on a few doses.'

'Late?' Sara felt her own blood pressure rise. 'Are you an idiot?'

'I ran out,' Jeffrey mumbled.

'Ran out? You're within walking distance of the pharmacy.' She leveled a deep frown at Jeffrey. 'What were you thinking?'

'Sara?' Jeffrey interrupted. 'Did you come all the way over here to yell at me?'

She did not have an answer.

Hare suggested, 'Maybe she can give you a second opinion on whether or not you should go home tonight?'

'Ah.' Jeffrey's eyes crinkled with a smile. 'Well, since you're giving a second opinion, Dr. Linton, I've been experiencing some tenderness in my groin. Do you mind taking a look?'

Sara offered a tight smile. 'I could do a rectal exam.'

'It's about time you got your turn.'

'Je-e-sus,' Hare groaned. 'I'm gonna leave you two lovebirds alone.'

'Thanks, Hare,' Jeffrey called. Hare tossed a wave over his shoulder as he left the room.

'So,' Sara began, crossing her arms.

Jeffrey raised an eyebrow. 'So?'

'What happened? Did her husband come home?'

Jeffrey laughed, but there was a strained look in his eyes. 'Close the door.'

Sara did as she was told. 'What happened?' she repeated.

Jeffrey put his hand to his eyes. 'I don't know. It was so fast.'

Sara took a step closer, taking his hand despite her better judgment.

'Will Harris's house was vandalized today.'

'Will from the diner?' Sara asked. 'For God's sake, why?'

He shrugged. 'I guess some people got it into their heads that he was involved with what happened to Sibyl Adams.'

'He wasn't even there when it happened,' Sara answered, not understanding. 'Why would anyone think that?'

'I don't know, Sara.' He sighed, dropping his hand. 'I knew something bad would happen. Too many people are jumping to conclusions. Too many people are pushing this thing out of hand.'

'Like who?'

'I don't know,' he managed. 'I was staying at Will's house to make sure he was safe. We were watching a movie when I heard something outside.' He shook his head, as if he still could not believe what had happened. 'I got up off the couch to see what was going on, and one of the side windows just exploded like that.' He snapped his fingers. 'Next thing I know, I'm on the floor, my leg's on fire. Thank God Will was sitting in his chair or he would've been hit, too.'

'Who did it?'

'I don't know,' he answered, but she could tell from the set of his jaw that he had a good guess.

She was about to question him further when he reached his hand out, resting it on her hip. 'You look beautiful.'

Sara felt a small jolt of electricity as his thumb slipped under her shirt, stroking her side. His fingers slipped under the back of her shirt. They were warm against her skin.

'I had a date,' she said, feeling a rush of guilt for leaving Jeb at her house. He had been very understanding, as usual, but she still felt bad about abandoning him.

Jeffrey watched her through half-closed eyes. He either did not believe her about the date or he would not accept that it could have been anything serious. 'I love it when your hair is down,' he said. 'Did you know that?'

'Yeah,' she said, putting her hand over his, stopping him, breaking the spell. 'Why didn't you tell me you have high blood pressure?'

Jeffrey let his arm drop. 'I didn't want to give you one more fault to add to your list.' His smile was a little forced and incongruous with the glassy look in his eyes. Like Sara, he seldom took anything stronger than aspirin, and the Demerol seemed to be working fast.

'Give me your hand,' Jeffrey said. She shook her head, but he persisted, holding his hand out to her. 'Hold my hand.'

'Why should I?'

'Because you could've seen me at the morgue tonight instead of the hospital.'

Sara bit her lip, fighting back the tears that wanted to come. 'You're okay now,' she said, putting her hand to his cheek. 'Go to sleep.'

He closed his eyes. She could tell that he was fighting to stay awake for her benefit.

'I don't want to go to sleep,' he said, then fell asleep.

Sara stared at him, watching his chest rise and fall with each breath. She reached out, smoothing his hair back off his forehead, leaving her hand there for a few seconds before putting her palm to his cheek. His beard was coming in, a speckled black against his face and neck. She brushed her fingers lightly along the stubble, smiling at the memories that came. Sleeping, he reminded her of the Jeffrey she had fallen in love with: the man who listened to her talk about her day, the man who opened doors for her and killed spiders and changed the batteries in the smoke detectors. Sara finally took his hand and kissed it before leaving the room.

She took her time walking back up the hallway toward the nurses' station, feeling an overwhelming sense of exhaustion. The clock on the wall showed she had been here an hour, and Sara realized with a start that she was back on hospital time, where eight hours went by like eight seconds.

'He asleep?' Ellen asked.

Sara leaned her elbows on the counter of the admitting desk. 'Yeah,' she answered. 'He'll be okay.'

Ellen smiled. 'Sure he will.'

'There you are,' Hare said, rubbing Sara's shoulders. 'How's it feel to be in a real hospital with the big doctors?'

Sara exchanged a look with Ellen. 'You'll have to excuse my cousin, Ellen. What he lacks in hair and height he makes up for by being an asshole.'

'Ow.' Hare winced, pressing his thumbs into Sara's shoulders. 'Want to fill in for me while I run out for a bite to eat?'

'What've we got?' Sara asked, thinking that going home right now probably was not the best thing for her.

Ellen gave a small smile. 'We've got a frequent flier getting fluorescent light therapy in two.'

Sara laughed out loud. In the obscure language of hospital lingo, Ellen had just informed her that the patient in room two was a hypochondriac who had been left to stare at the overhead lights until he felt better.

'Microdeckia,' Hare concluded. The patient was not playing with a full deck.

'What else?'

'Some kid from the college sleeping off a long one,' Ellen said.

Sara turned to Hare. 'I don't know if I can take these complicated cases.

He chucked her under her chin. 'There's a girl.'

'I guess I should go move my car,' Sara said, remembering she had parked in the handicap spot. As every cop in town knew the car she drove, Sara doubted she was likely to get a ticket. Still, she wanted to walk outside for some fresh air, take some time to collect her thoughts, before she went back in to check on Jeffrey.

'How is he?' Lena asked as soon as Sara walked into the waiting room. Sara looked around, surprised to see the room was empty but for Lena.

'We kept it off the radio,' Lena provided. 'This kind of thing . . . ' She let her voice trail off.

'This kind of thing what?' Sara prompted. 'Am I missing something here, Lena?'

Lena looked away nervously.

'You know who did it, huh?' Sara asked.

Lena shook her head. 'I'm not sure.'

'That's where Frank is? Taking care of business?'

She shrugged. 'I don't know. He dropped me off here.'

'Pretty easy not to know what's going on when you don't bother to ask,' Sara snapped. 'I guess the fact that Jeffrey could've died tonight is lost on you.'

'I know that.'

'Yeah?' Sara demanded. 'Who was watching his back, Lena?'

Lena started to answer, but she turned away before saying anything.

Sara slammed the emergency room doors open with her hands, feeling anger well up. She knew exactly what was going on here. Frank knew who was responsible for shooting Jeffrey, but he was keeping his mouth closed out of some obscure sense of loyalty, probably to Matt Hogan. What was going through Lena's mind, Sara could not begin to guess. After everything Jeffrey had done for her, to have Lena turn her back on him like this was inexcusable.

Sara took a deep breath, trying to calm herself as she walked around to the side of the hospital. Jeffrey could have been killed. The glass could have sliced through his femoral artery and he could have bled to death. For that matter, the original shot could have gone into his chest instead of through the window. Sara wondered what Frank and Lena would be doing now if Jeffrey had died. Probably drawing straws to see who got his desk.

'Oh, God.' Sara stopped short at the sight of her car. Lying on the hood of Sara's car was a nude young woman with her arms spread out. She was on her back, her feet crossed at the ankle in an almost casual pose. Sara's first instinct was to look up to see if the woman had jumped from one of the windows. There were no windows on this side of the two-story building, though, and the hood of the car showed no signs of impact.

Sara took three quick steps to the car, checking the woman's pulse. A fast, hard beat came under Sara's fingers, and she muttered a small prayer before running back into the hospital.

'Lena!'

Lena jumped up, fists clenched, as if she expected Sara to come over and start a fight.

'Get a stretcher,' Sara ordered. When Lena did not move, Sara yelled, 'Now!'

Sara jogged back to the woman, half expecting her to

be gone. Everything was moving in slow time for Sara, even the wind in her hair.

'Ma'am?' Sara called to the woman, raising her voice loud enough to be heard across town. The woman did not respond. 'Ma'am?' Sara tried again. Still nothing.

Sara assessed the body, seeing no immediate signs of trauma. The skin was pink and ruddy, very hot to the touch despite the night cold. With her arms out and feet crossed as they were, the woman could've been sleeping. In the bright light, Sara could make out crusted blood around the palms of the woman's hands. Sara lifted one of the hands to examine it, and the arm moved awkwardly to the side. There was an obvious dislocation at the shoulder.

Sara looked back at the woman's face and was startled to notice that a silver piece of duct tape had been wrapped around her mouth. Sara couldn't remember if the tape had been there before she had gone back into the hospital. Surely she would've noticed it before. Something like a taped mouth wasn't easily overlooked, especially when the tape was at least two inches across by four inches long and dark silver. For just a brief second, Sara felt paralyzed, but Lena Adams's voice brought her back to reality.

'It's Julia Matthews,' Lena said, but her voice sounded far away to Sara.

'Sara?' Hare asked, walking quickly over to the car. His mouth dropped open at the sight of the nude woman.

'Okay, okay,' Sara mumbled, trying to get herself calm. She shot Hare a look of sheer panic, which he returned in kind. Hare was used to an occasional overdose or heart attack, nothing like this.

As if to remind them both of where they were, the woman's body began to convulse.

'She's going to be sick,' Sara said, picking at the edge of the tape. Without pausing, she ripped off the tape. In one swift motion, she rolled the woman onto her side and held her head down as she vomited in fits and starts. A sour smell came, almost like bad cider or beer, and Sara had to turn away to take a breath.

'It's okay,' Sara whispered. She stroked the woman's dirty brown hair back behind her ear, remembering that she had done the same thing for Sibyl just two days ago. The vomiting stopped abruptly, and Sara gently rolled her back over, keeping her head steady.

Hare's tone was urgent. 'She's not breathing.'

Sara cleared the woman's mouth with her finger, surprised to feel some resistance. After a few seconds of digging, she pulled out a folded driver's license, which she handed to a surprised Lena Adams.

'Breathing's back,' Hare said, relief flooding his voice.

Sara rubbed her fingers clean on her skirt, wishing she'd had on a pair of gloves before she had stuck her fingers into the woman's mouth.

Ellen jogged to the car, her jaw set as she angled a long stretcher in front of her. Without words, she stepped to the woman's feet, waiting for Sara's signal.

Sara counted to three, then they both moved the woman onto the bed. Sara felt a sick taste in her mouth as they did this, and for a few seconds she saw herself on the bed instead of the woman. Sara's mouth went dry and she felt a numbness overcome her.

'Ready,' Hare said, strapping the woman to the bed.

Sara trotted beside the gurney, holding on to the young woman's hand. The time it took them to get back into the hospital was interminable. The bed seemed to be rolling through glue as they entered the first trauma room. The woman made small murmurs of pain with each jolt of the bed. Briefly, Sara latched on to the woman's fear.

Twelve years had passed since Sara had practiced emergency medicine and she needed to concentrate on the tasks at hand. In her head, Sara went over what she'd learned her first day in the ER. As if to prompt Sara, the woman started wheezing, then gasping for air. The first priority was to establish an airway.

'Jesus,' Sara hissed as she opened the woman's mouth. Under the bright lights of the exam room, Sara could see that her top front teeth had been knocked out, obviously within the last few days. Again, Sara felt herself freezing up. She tried to shake this off. Sara had to think of this woman as a patient or they would both be in trouble.

In seconds Sara had intubated the woman, careful with the tape so as not to do further damage to the skin around the mouth. Sara fought the urge to cringe as the ventilator kicked in. The sound almost sickened her.

'She's got good sounds,' Hare reported, handing Sara a stethoscope.

'Sara?' Ellen said. 'I can't get a peripheral.'

'She's dehydrated,' Sara reported as she tried to find a vein on the woman's other arm. 'We should drop a central anyway.' Sara held her hand out for the needle, but one was not immediately placed in her hand.

'I'll get it from two,' Ellen said, then left the room.

Sara turned back to the young woman on the bed. There did not seem to be any bruises or cuts on her body other than the marks on her hands and feet. Her skin was warm to the touch, which could point to any number of things. Sara did not want to jump to conclusions, but already the similarities between Sibyl Adams and the woman in front of her were going through her mind. They were both petite women. They both had dark brown hair.

Sara checked the woman's pupils. 'Dilated,' she said, because the last time she'd done something like this, the rule had been to call out your findings. She exhaled slowly, noticing for the first time that Hare and Lena were in the room.

'What's her name?' Sara asked.

'Julia Matthews,' Lena provided. 'We were looking for her at the school. She's been missing for a couple of days.'

Hare glanced at the monitor. 'Pulse ox is falling.'

Sara checked the ventilator. 'FiO2 is thirty percent. Bump it up a little.'

'What's that smell?' Lena interrupted.

Sara sniffed the woman's body. 'Clorox?' she asked.

Lena caught another whiff. 'Bleach,' she confirmed.

Hare nodded as well.

Sara examined the woman's skin carefully. There were lines of superficial scrapes all along the body. Sara noticed for the first time that the woman's pubic hair had been shaved off. From the lack of growth, Sara guessed she had been shaved in the last day or so.

Sara said, 'She's been scrubbed clean.'

She smelled the woman's mouth but did not pick up the strong scent that usually comes from ingesting bleach. Sara had seen some rawness in the back of the throat when she'd tubed the woman, but nothing out of the ordinary. Obviously the woman had been given a drug similar to if not actually belladonna. Her skin was so hot to the touch that Sara could feel it through her gloves.

Ellen entered the room. Sara watched the nurse as she opened the central line kit on one of the trays. Ellen's hands didn't seem as steady as they usually did. This scared Sara more than anything else.

Sara held her breath as she jabbed the three-inch needle into the woman's jugular. The needle, called an introducer, would act as a funnel for three separate IV ports. When they found out what kind of drug the woman had been given, Sara would use one of the extra ports to help counteract the effects.

Ellen stood back from the patient, waiting for Sara's orders.

Sara rattled off the tests as she flushed the ports with heparin solution to keep them from clotting. 'Blood gases, tox screen, LFT, CBC, chem twenty-seven. Go ahead and pull for a coag panel while you're at it.' Sara paused. 'Dip her urine stat. I want to know what's going on before I do anything else. Something's keeping her knocked out. I think I know what it is, but I need to be sure before we start treatment.'

'All right,' Ellen answered.

Sara checked for positive blood return, then flushed the lines again. 'Normal saline, wide open.'

Ellen did as she was told, adjusting the IV.

'Do you have a portable X ray? I'll need to make sure I did this right' Sara said, indicating the internal jugular line. 'Plus I need a chest, a flat of the abdomen, and a look at her shoulder.'

Ellen said, 'I'll get it from down the hall after I draw the blood work.'

'Also, check for GHB, roofies.' Sara spoke as she secured the dressing around the needle. 'We'll need to do a rape kit.'

'Rape?' Lena questioned, stepping forward.

'Yes,' Sara answered, her tone sharp. 'Why else would someone do this to her?'

Lena's mouth worked, but no answer came. She had obviously kept this case separate from her sister's up until that point. Lena's eyes locked on to the young woman, and she stood at the foot of the bed, her body ramrod straight. Sara was reminded of the night Lena had come to the morgue to see Sibyl Adams. The young detective's mouth was set in that same angry line.

'She seems stable,' Ellen offered, more to herself than anyone else.

Sara watched as the nurse used a small syringe to draw blood from the radial artery. Sara rubbed her own wrist, knowing how painful the procedure could be. She leaned against the bed, her hands on Julia Matthews's arm, trying to somehow convey that she was safe now.

Hare brought her back with a gentle 'Sara?'

'Hm?' Sara was startled. They were all looking at her. She turned to Lena. 'Can you help Ellen with the portable?' she asked, trying to use a firm voice.

'Yeah,' Lena returned, giving Sara an odd look.

Ellen filled the last syringe. 'It's down the hall,' she told Lena.

Sara heard them leave, but she kept her eyes on Julia Matthews. Sara's vision tunneled, and for the second time she felt herself on the gurney, saw a doctor leaning over her, taking her pulse, checking her vitals.

'Sara?' Hare was looking at the woman's hands, and Sara was reminded of the marks she had first seen in the parking lot.

Both palms were punctured through the center. Sara glanced down at the woman's feet, noting that they, too, had been punctured in the same way. She bent to examine the wounds, which were clotting rapidly. Specks of rust added color to the dried black blood.

'The palm has been pierced through,' Sara offered. She looked under the woman's fingernails, recognizing thin slivers of wood pressed under the nails. 'Wood,' she reported, wondering why someone would take the time to scrub the victim down with bleach in order to remove physical traces, yet leave slivers of wood under the nails. It did not make sense. And then to leave her arranged on the car in such a way.

Sara worked all of this out in her head, and her stomach responded to the obvious conclusion with a slight pitch. She closed her eyes, picturing the woman as she had been when Sara first found her: legs crossed at the ankles, arms at ninety-degree angles from the body.

The woman had been crucified.

'Those are puncture wounds, right?' Hare said.

Sara nodded, not taking her eyes off the woman. Her body was well nourished and her skin had been taken care of. There were no needle marks to indicate prolonged drug use. Sara stopped in her tracks, realizing she'd assessed the woman as if she was at the morgue rather than the hospital. As if sensing this, the heart monitor went into failure, the shrill scream of the machine putting Sara on alert.

'No,' Sara hissed as she leaned over the woman, starting compressions. 'Hare, bag her.'

He fumbled around in the drawers for the bag. Within seconds, he was squeezing air into the woman's lungs. 'She's in V-tach,' he warned.

'Slow,' Sara said, wincing as she felt one of the patient's ribs crack under her hands. She kept her eyes on Hare, willing him to cooperate. 'One, two, squeeze. Quick and hard. Keep it calm.'

'Okay, okay,' Hare mumbled, concentrating on squeezing the bag.

Despite the great press given CPR, it was merely a stopgap measure. CPR was the act of physically forcing the heart to circulate blood into the brain, and very rarely could this be done manually as efficiently as a healthy heart performing the task on its own. If Sara stopped, so would the heart. It was a time-buying procedure until something else could be done.

Lena, obviously alerted by the shrieking monitor, ran back into the room. 'What happened?'

'She crashed,' Sara said, feeling a slight sense of relief as she spotted Ellen in the hallway. 'Amp of Epi,' she ordered.

Sara watched impatiently as Ellen popped open a box of Epi and put the syringe together.

'Jeesh.' Lena cringed as Sara administered the drug straight into the woman's heart.

Hare's voice rose a few octaves. 'She's in V-fib.'

With one hand Ellen took the paddles off the cart behind her, charging the defibrillator with the other.

'Two hundred,' Sara ordered. The woman's body jumped into the air as Sara electrocuted her. Sara watched the monitor, frowning when there was no corresponding reaction. Sara shocked her two more times with the same response. 'Lidocaine,' she ordered just as Ellen popped another box.

Sara administered the drug, keeping an eye on the monitor.

'Flat line,' Hare reported.

'Again.' Sara reached for the paddles. 'Three hundred,' she ordered.

Again, she shocked the woman. Again, there was no response. Sara felt a cold sweat come over her. 'Epi.'

The sound of the box popping open was like a needle in Sara's ear. She took the syringe, pushing the Adrenalin directly into the woman's heart one more time. They all waited.

'Flat line,' Hare reported.

'Let's go to three-sixty.'

For the fifth time, a charge went through the woman's body with no response.

'Goddamnit, goddamnit,' Sara muttered, resuming compressions. 'Time?' she called.

Hare glanced at the clock. 'Twelve minutes.'

It had seemed like two seconds to Sara.

Lena must have sensed from Hare's tone of voice where he was going with this. She whispered under her breath, 'Don't let her die. Please, don't let her die.'

'She's in prolonged asystole, Sara,' Hare said. He was telling her that it was too late. It was time to stop, time to let go.

Sara narrowed her eyes at him. She turned to Ellen. 'I'm going to crack her chest.'

Hare shook his head, saying, 'Sara, we don't have the capabilities here.'

Sara ignored him. She felt down the woman's ribs, cringing as she made contact with the one she had broken. When Sara's fingers reached the bottom of the diaphragm, she took a scalpel and sliced a six-inch opening into the upper abdomen. She slipped her hand into the incision, reaching under the rib cage and into the woman's chest.

She kept her eyes closed, blocking out the hospital as she massaged the woman's heart. The monitor showed false hope as Sara squeezed, manually circulating the woman's blood. A tingling came to her fingers, and in her ears she could hear a slight piercing tone. Nothing else mattered as she waited for the heart to respond. It was like squeezing a small balloon filled with warm water. Only this balloon was life.

Sara stopped. She counted to five seconds, eight, then up to twelve, before being rewarded with spontaneous beeps from the heart monitor.

Hare asked, 'Is that her or you?'

'Her,' Sara offered, letting her hand slip out. 'Start a lidocaine drip.'

'Jesus Christ,' Lena muttered, hand to her own chest. 'I can't believe you just did that.'

Sara snapped off her gloves, not answering.

The room was quiet but for the beeps of the heart monitor and the in and out of the ventilator.

'So,' Sara said. 'We'll do a darkfield for syphilis and a gram stain for gonorrhea.' Sara felt her face flush over this. 'I'm sure a condom was used, but make a note to follow up in a few days for pregnancy.' Sara was conscious of a waver in her voice that she hoped Ellen and Lena did not pick up. Hare was another matter. She could hear what he was thinking without even looking at him.

He seemed to sense her nervousness and tried to make light of it. 'Good God, Sara. That's the sloppiest incision I've ever seen.'

Sara licked her lips, willing her own heart to calm. 'I was trying not to upstage you.'

'Prima donna,' Hare offered, wiping perspiration from his forehead with a pad of surgical gauze. 'Jesus Christ.' He laughed uncomfortably.

'We don't see much of this around here,' Ellen said as she packed surgical towels into the incision to control the bleeding until it was closed. 'I can call Larry Headley over in Augusta. He lives about fifteen minutes from here.'

'I would appreciate that,' Sara said, taking another pair of gloves from the box on the wall.

'You okay?' Hare asked, his tone casual. His eyes showed his concern.

'Fine,' Sara answered, checking the IV. She told Lena, 'I guess you can find Frank?'

Lena had the decency to look embarrassed. 'I'll go see.' She left the room, her head down.

Sara waited until she was gone, then asked Hare, 'Can you take a look at her hands?'

Hare was silent as he examined the woman's palms, feeling the bone structure. After a few minutes, he said, 'This is interesting.'

Sara asked, 'What's that?'

'Missed all the bones,' Hare answered, rotating the wrist. When he got to the shoulder, he stopped. 'Dislocated,' he said.

Sara crossed her arms, suddenly cold. 'From trying to get away?'

Hare frowned. 'Do you realize how much force it would take to dislocate your shoulder blade?' He shook his head, unable to accept it. 'You'd pass out from the pain before you'd –'

'Do you realize how terrifying it is to be raped?' Sara's gaze bored right into him.

Pain registered in his expression. 'I'm sorry, honey. Are you okay?'

Tears stung the back of her eyes, and Sara had to fight to keep her voice even. 'Check her hips, please. I want you to do a full report.'

He did as he was told, giving Sara a curt nod after the examination. 'I'm thinking there's some ligature damage in the hip, here. I need to do this when she's awake; it's fairly subjective.'

Sara asked, 'Can you tell anything else?'

'All the bones in her hands and feet were missed. Her feet were speared between the second and third cuneiforms and the navicular. That's very precise. Whoever did it knew what he was doing.' He paused, looking down at the floor to regain his composure. 'I don't see why someone would do this.'

'Look at this,' Sara said, pointing to the skin around the woman's ankles. They both had angry black bruises around their circumference. 'Obviously there was a secondary restraint to hold the feet down.' Sara picked up the woman's hand, noticing a fresh scar at the wrist. The other had the same mark. Julia Matthews had attempted suicide at some point during the last month. The scar was a white line slashing vertically across her small wrist. A dark bruise put the old wound in stark relief.

Sara did not bring this to Hare's attention. Instead, she offered, 'It looks to me like a band was used, probably leather.'

'I'm not following.'

'The piercing was symbolic.'

'Of?'

'Crucifixion, I would imagine.' Sara put the woman's hand back by her side.

Sara rubbed her arms, fighting the chill in the room. She walked over, opening drawers, looking for a sheet to cover the young woman. 'If I had to guess, I would say that the hands and feet were nailed back from the body.'

'Crucifixion?' Hare dismissed this. 'That's not how Jesus was crucified. The feet would be together.'

Sara snapped, 'Nobody wanted to rape Jesus, Hare. Of course her legs were spread apart.'

Hare's Adam's apple bobbed as he swallowed this. 'Is this what you do at the morgue?'

She shrugged, looking for a sheet.

'Christ, you've got more balls than I do,' Hare said, breathing heavily.

Sara tucked the sheet around the young woman, trying to comfort her. 'I don't know about that,' she said.

Hare asked, 'What about her mouth?'

'Her front teeth were knocked out, I imagine to facilitate fellatio.'

His voice rose in shock. 'What?'

'It's more common than you think,' Sara told him. 'The Clorox removes trace evidence. I imagine he shaved her so we couldn't do a comb for his pubic hair. Even during normal sex, hairs are torn out. He could have shaved her for the sexual thrill, though. A lot of attackers like to think of their victims as children. Shaving the pubic hair would fuel that fantasy.'

Hare shook his head, overcome with the nastiness of the crime. 'What kind of animal would do this?'

Sara stroked back the woman's hair. 'A methodical one.'

'Do you think she knew him?'

'No,' Sara answered, never more sure of anything in her life. She walked over to the counter where Lena had left the evidence bag. 'Why did he give us her driver's license? He doesn't care if we know who she is.'

Hare's tone was incredulous. 'How can you be so sure?'

'He left –' Sara tried to catch her breath. 'He left her in front of the hospital where anybody could've seen him dump her.' She put her hand over her eyes for just a second, wishing that she could hide. She had to get out of this room. That much she was certain of.

Hare seemed to be trying to read her expression. His face, normally open and kind, took on a stern look. 'She was raped in a hospital.'

'Outside a hospital.'

'Her mouth was taped shut.'

'I know that.'

'By someone who obviously has some kind of religious fixation.'

'Right.'
'Sara –'
She held up her hand for silence as Lena returned.
Lena said, 'Frank's on his way.'

THURSDAY

FOURTEEN

Jeffrey blinked his eyes several times, forcing himself not to go back to sleep. For a few seconds, he did not know where he was, but a quick glance around the room reminded him of what had happened last night. He looked over at the window, his eyes taking their time coming into focus. He saw Sara.

He leaned his head back into the pillow, letting out a long sigh. 'Remember when I used to brush your hair?'

'Sir?'

Jeffrey opened his eyes. 'Lena?'

She seemed embarrassed as she walked over to the bed. 'Yeah.'

'I thought you were . . . ' He waved this off. 'Never mind.'

Jeffrey forced himself to sit up in bed, despite the pain shooting through his right leg. He felt stiff and drugged, but he knew if he did not stay upright, the rest of the day would be blown.

'Hand me my pants,' he said.

'They had to throw them away,' she reminded him. 'Remember what happened?'

Jeffrey grumbled an answer as he put his feet on the floor. Standing hurt like a hot knife in his leg, but he could live with the pain. 'Can you find me some pants?' he asked.

Lena left the room and Jeffrey leaned against the wall

so that he wouldn't sit back down. He tried to remember what had happened the night before. Part of him didn't want to deal with it. There was enough on his plate trying to find out who had killed Sibyl Adams.

'How are these?' Lena asked, tossing him a pair of scrubs.

'Great,' Jeffrey said, waiting for her to turn around. He slipped them on, suppressing a groan as he lifted his leg. 'We've got a full day ahead of us,' he said. 'Nick Shelton is coming in at ten with one of his drug guys. We'll get a rundown on the belladonna. We've got that punk, what's his name, Gordon?' He tied the string in the pants. 'I want to go at him again, see if he can remember anything about when he last saw Julia Matthews.' He leaned his hand against the table. 'I don't think he knows where she is, but maybe he saw something.'

Lena turned around without being told. 'We found Julia Matthews.'

'What?' he asked. 'When?'

'She showed up at the hospital last night,' Lena answered. There was something about her voice that sent a sense of dread coursing through his veins.

He sat back down on the bed without even thinking about it.

Lena closed the door and narrated last night's events for him. By the time she was finished, Jeffrey was pacing the room in an awkward gait.

'She just showed up on Sara's car?' he asked.

Lena nodded.

'Where is it now?' he asked. 'The car, I mean?

'Frank had it impounded,' Lena said, a defensive tone to her voice.

'Where is Frank?' Jeffrey asked, leaning his hand on the bed railing.

Lena was silent, then, 'I don't know.'

He gave her a hard look, thinking she knew exactly where Frank was but wouldn't say.

She said, 'He put Brad on guard upstairs.'

'Gordon's still in jail, right?'

'Yeah, that was the first thing I checked. He was in jail all night. There's no way he could've put her on Sara's car.'

Jeffrey hit the bed with his fist. He knew last night he shouldn't have taken that Demerol. This was the middle of a case, not a holiday.

'Hand me my jacket.' Jeffrey held his hand out, taking the jacket from Lena. He limped out of the room, Lena on his heels. The elevator was slow in coming, but neither of them spoke.

'She's been sleeping all night,' Lena said.

'Right.' Jeffrey jabbed at the button. The elevator bell dinged several seconds later, and they rode up together, still in silence.

Lena began, 'About last night. The shooting.'

Jeffrey waved her off, stepping out of the elevator. 'We'll deal with that later, Lena.'

'It's just –'

He held his hand up. 'You have no idea how little that matters to me right now,' he said, using the railing lining the hallway to work his way toward Brad.

'Hey, Chief,' Brad said, standing up from his chair.

'Nobody in?' Jeffrey asked, motioning for him to sit down.

'Not since Dr. Linton around two this morning,' he answered.

Jeffrey said, 'Good,' leaning his hand on Brad's shoulder as he opened the door.

Julia Matthews was awake. She stared blindly out the window, not moving when they came in.

'Miss Matthews?' he said, leaning his hand against the railing of her bed.

She continued to stare, not answering.

Lena said, 'She hasn't spoken since Sara took the tube out.'

He looked out the window, wondering what held her attention. Dawn had broken about thirty minutes ago, but other than the clouds there wasn't anything remarkable to see out the window.

Jeffrey repeated, 'Miss Matthews?'

Tears streamed down her face, but still she said nothing. He left the room, using Lena's arm to lean on.

As soon as they were outside the room, Lena provided, 'She hasn't said anything all night.'

'Not one word?'

She shook her head. 'We got an emergency number from the college and found an aunt. She's tracking down the parents. They're flying into Atlanta on the first available flight.'

'When's that?' Jeffrey asked, checking his watch.

'Around three today.'

'Frank and I will pick them up,' he said, turning to Brad Stephens. 'Brad, you've been on all night?'

'Yes, sir.'

'Lena will relieve you in a couple of hours.' He looked at Lena, daring her to protest. When nothing came, he said, 'Take me home, then back to the station. You can walk to the hospital from there.'

Jeffrey stared straight ahead as Lena drove to his house, trying to work his mind around what had happened last night. He felt a tension in his neck that even a handful of aspirin couldn't tame. He still could not shake the lethargy from being drugged last night, and his brain was getting sidetracked left and right, even as he came to accept that all this had happened three doors down from where he lay sleeping like a baby. Thank God Sara had been there or he would have two victims instead of one on his hands.

Julia Matthews proved that the killer was escalating. He had gone from a quick assault and murder in the bathroom to keeping a girl for a few days so that he could take his time with her. Jeffrey had seen this kind of behavior over and over again. Serial rapists learned from their mistakes. Their lives were spent figuring out the best way to obtain their objectives, and this rapist, this murderer, was honing his skills even now as Jeffrey and Lena talked about how to catch him.

He had Lena repeat her story about Julia Matthews, trying to see if it was any different in the telling, trying to pull out additional clues. There were none. Lena was very good at reporting things as she saw them, and nothing new came with the second telling.

Jeffrey asked, 'What happened after?'

'After Sara left?'

He nodded.

'Dr. Headley came from Augusta. He closed her up.'

Jeffrey became aware of the fact that throughout Lena's narration of events of the night before, she was using 'her' instead of the woman's name. It was common in law enforcement to look at the criminal rather than the victim, and Jeffrey always felt that this was the quickest way to lose sight of why they did the job in the first place. He didn't want Lena to do this, especially considering what had happened to her sister.

There was something different about Lena today. Whether it was a higher level of tension or anger, he could not say. Her body seemed to vibrate with it, and his main goal was to get her back to the hospital, where she could sit and decompress. He knew Lena would not leave her guard at Julia Matthews's bedside. The hospital was the only place to trust her to stay. There was, of course, the added bonus of knowing that if Lena did finally have some sort of nervous breakdown, she was in the right place. For now, he needed to use her. He needed her to be his eyes and ears for what happened last night.

He said, 'Tell me what Julia looked like.'

Lena tapped the horn, shooing a squirrel out of the road. 'Well, she looked normal.' Lena paused. 'I mean, I thought it was an OD or something from the way she looked. I never would've pegged her for a rape.'

'What convinced you otherwise?'

Lena's jaw worked again. 'Dr. Linton, I suppose. She pointed out the holes in her hands and feet. I must've been blind, I don't know. The bleach smell and all of that gave it away.'

'All of what?'

'Just, you know, physical signs that something wasn't right.' Lena paused again. Her tone took a defensive ring. 'She had her mouth taped shut, with her driver's license shoved down her throat. I suppose she looked raped, but I wasn't seeing it. I don't know why. I would've figured it out; I'm not stupid. It's just that she looked so normal, you know? Not like a rape victim.'

He was surprised by this last part. 'What does a rape victim look like?'

Lena shrugged. 'Like my sister, I guess,' she mumbled. 'Like somebody who can't really take care of themselves.'

Jeffrey had been expecting a physical description, some comment on the state of Julia Matthews's body. He said, 'I don't follow you.'

'Never mind.'

'No,' Jeffrey said. 'Tell me.'

Lena seemed to think over how to phrase her words, then, 'I guess I can understand with Sibyl, because she was blind.' She stopped. 'I mean there's this whole thing about women asking for it and all. I don't think Sibyl was like that, but I know rapists. I've talked to them, I've busted them. I know how they think. They don't pick somebody who they think is going to put up a fight.'

'You think so?'

Lena shrugged. 'I guess you can go into all that feminist bullshit about how women should be able to do whatever they want to do and men should just get used to it, but . . .' Lena paused again. 'It's like this,' she said. 'If I parked my car in the middle of Atlanta with the windows rolled down and the keys in the ignition, whose fault is it when somebody steals it?'

Jeffrey didn't quite get her logic.

'There are sexual predators out there,' Lena continued. 'Everybody knows there are some sick people, usually men, who prey on women. And they're not picking the ones who look like they can take care of themselves. They're picking the ones who won't, or can't, put up a fight. They're picking the quiet ones like Julia Matthews. Or the handicapped ones.' Lena added, 'Like my sister.'

Jeffrey stared at her, not sure he bought her logic. Lena surprised him sometimes, but what she had just said blew him out of the water. He would expect this kind of talk from someone like Matt Hogan, but never from a woman. Not even Lena.

He leaned his head against the headrest, quiet for a few beats. After a while, he asked, 'Run down the case for me. Julia Matthews. Give me the physicals.'

Lena took her time answering. 'Her front teeth were knocked out. Her ankles had been bound. Her pubic hair had been shaved off.' Lena paused. 'Then, you know, he'd cleaned her out on the inside.'

'Bleach?'

Lena nodded. 'Mouth, too.'

Jeffrey watched her closely. 'What else?'

'There was no bruising on her.' Lena indicated her lap. 'No defensive wounds or marks on her hands, other than the holes in her palms and the bruises from the straps.'

Jeffrey considered this. Julia Matthews had probably been drugged the entire time, though that didn't make sense to him either. Rape was a crime of violence, and most rapists got off more from causing women pain, controlling them, than actually having sex with them.

Jeffrey said, 'Tell me what else. What did Julia look like when you found her?'

'She looked like a normal person,' Lena answered. 'I told you that.'

'Naked?'

'Yeah, naked. She was totally naked, and she was laid out like, with her hands straight out. Her feet were crossed at the ankles. Right across the hood of the car.'

'Do you think she was placed like that for a reason?'

Lena answered, 'I dunno. Everybody knows Dr. Linton. Everybody knows what car she drives. It's the only one in town.'

Jeffrey felt his stomach lurch. This was not the response he had been fishing for. He'd meant for Lena to specifically address the positioning of the body, to draw the same conclusion he had, which was that the woman was displayed in a crucifixion pose. He had assumed Sara's car was chosen because it had been parked closest to the hospital where someone would see it. The possibility that this action was directed toward Sara was chilling.

Jeffrey dismissed these thoughts for the moment, quizzing Lena. 'What do we know about our rapist?'

Lena thought out her answer. 'Okay, he's white because rapists tend to rape within their own ethnic group. He's super-retentive, because she was scrubbed thoroughly with bleach; bleach means he's up on his forensics, because that's the best way to dispose of physical evidence. He's probably an older man, has his own house, because he obviously nailed her to some floor or wall or whatever, and it's not like you can do that in an apartment building, so he must be established in town. He's probably not married, because he'd have a lot of explaining to do if his wife came home and found a woman nailed down in the basement.'

'Why do you say basement?'

Lena shrugged again. 'I don't imagine he can keep her out in the open.'

'Even if he lives alone?'

'Not unless he's sure nobody's gonna drop by.'

'So, he's a loner?'

'Well, maybe. But, then, how did he meet her?'

'Good point,' Jeffrey said. 'Did Sara send blood for the tox screen?'

'Yeah,' Lena said. 'She drove it over to Augusta. At least, that's where she said she was going. She said she knew what she was looking for.'

Jeffrey pointed to a side street. 'There.'

Lena made a sharp turn. 'Are we gonna cut Gordon loose today?' she asked.

'I don't think so,' Jeffrey said. 'We can use the drug charge to get his cooperation on who Julia's been hanging around with. From what Jenny Price said, he kept her on a tight leash. He'd be the most likely person to notice who was new in her life.'

'Yeah,' Lena agreed.

'Up here on the right,' he instructed, sitting up. 'You want to come in?'

Lena sat behind the wheel. 'I'll stay here, thanks.'

Jeffrey sat back in his seat. 'There's something else you're not telling me, isn't there?'

She took a deep breath, then let it go. 'I feel like I let you down.'

'About last night?' he asked, then: 'Me getting shot?'

She said, 'There's things you don't know.'

Jeffrey put his hand on the door handle. 'Is Frank taking care of it?'

She nodded.

'Could you have stopped what happened?'

She shrugged, her shoulders going up to her ears. 'I don't know if I can stop anything anymore.'

'Good thing that's not your job,' he said. He wanted to say more to her, to take some of her load, but Jeffrey knew from experience that Lena would have to work this out for herself. She had spent the last thirty-three years building a fortress around herself. He wasn't about to break through it in three days.

Instead, he said, 'Lena, my number one focus right now is to find out who killed your sister and who raped Julia Matthews. This' – he indicated his leg — 'I can deal with when it's over. I think we both know where to start looking. It's not like they're all gonna leave town.'

He pushed the door open and physically lifted his injured leg out with his hand. 'Jesus Christ,' he groaned, feeling an intense protest from his knee. His leg had gotten stiff from sitting in the car for so long. By the time Jeffrey stood up from the car, a line of perspiration beaded over his lip.

Pain shot through his leg as he walked toward his house. His house keys were on the same ring as the car keys, so he walked to the back of the house, entering through the kitchen. For the last two years, Jeffrey had been remodeling the house himself. His latest project was the kitchen, and he had gutted the back wall of the house one three-day weekend, planning to have it built back in time to return to work. A shooting had cut his plans short, and he had ended up buying plastic strips from a freezer supply house in Birmingham and nailing them up over the naked two-by-fours. The plastic kept the rain and wind out, but meanwhile he still had a big hole at the back of his house.

In the living room, Jeffrey picked up the phone and dialed Sara's number, hoping he could catch her before she left for work. Her machine picked up, so he dialed the Linton house.

Eddie Linton answered the phone on the third ring. 'Linton and Daughters.'

Jeffrey tried to remain pleasant. 'Hey, Eddie, it's Jeffrey.'

The phone clattered as it was dropped onto the floor. Jeffrey could hear dishes and pans in the background, then muffled conversation. A few seconds later Sara picked up the phone.

'Jeff?'

'Yeah,' he answered. He could hear her opening the door onto the deck. The Lintons were the only people he knew who didn't have a cordless phone in their house. There was an extension in the bedroom and one in the kitchen. If not for the ten-foot cord the girls had put on the kitchen phone when they were back in high school, privacy would not have been possible.

He heard the door close, then Sara said, 'Sorry.'

'How're you doing?'

She skipped an answer, saying, 'I'm not the one who got shot last night.'

Jeffrey paused, wondering about the sharp tone to her

voice. 'I heard about what happened with Julia Matthews.'

'Right,' Sara said. 'I ran the blood in Augusta. Belladonna has two specific markers.'

He cut short a chemistry lesson. 'You found both of them?'

'Yes,' she answered.

'So, we're looking for the same guy on both.'

Her voice was clipped. 'Looks that way.'

A few seconds passed, then Jeffrey said, 'Nick has this guy who's kind of a specialist on belladonna poisoning. He's bringing him by at ten. Can you make it?'

'I can pop over between patients, but I can't stay long,' Sara offered. There was a change in her voice, something softer, when she said, 'I need to go now, okay?'

'I want to go over what happened last night.'

'Later, okay?' She didn't give him time to answer. The phone clicked in his ear.

Jeffrey let out a sigh as he limped toward the bathroom. On the way, he looked out the window, checking on Lena. She was still in the car, both hands gripping the wheel. It seemed like every woman in his life had something they were hiding today.

After a hot shower and shave, Jeffrey felt considerably better. His leg was still stiff, but the more he moved it the less it hurt. There was something to be said for staying mobile. The drive to the station was tense and quiet, the only noise in the car being the sound of Lena's teeth gritting. Jeffrey was glad to see the back of her as she walked toward the hospital.

Marla met him at the front door, her hands clasped in front of her chest. 'I'm so glad you're okay,' she said, taking his arm, leading him back toward his office. He put a stop to her fussing when she opened the door for him.

'I've got it,' Jeffrey said. 'Where's Frank?'

Marla's face fell. If Grant was a small place, its police force was even smaller. Rumors traveled faster within the ranks than a bolt of lightning through a steel rod.

Marla said, 'I think he's in the back.'

'Go fetch him for me, will you?' Jeffrey asked, making his way toward his office.

Jeffrey sat in his chair with a groan. He knew he was tempting fate with his leg, keeping it still for a while, but he did not have a choice. His men needed to know he was back on the job, ready to work.

Frank rapped his knuckles on the door and Jeffrey nodded him in.

Frank asked, 'How you doing?'

Jeffrey made sure he had the other man's attention. 'I'm not gonna get shot at anymore, am I?'

Frank had the decency to look down at his shoes. 'No, sir.'

'What about Will Harris?'

Frank rubbed his chin. 'I hear he's going to Savannah.'

'That right?'

'Yeah,' Frank answered. 'Pete gave him a bonus. Will bought himself a bus ticket.' Frank shrugged. 'Said he was gonna spend a couple of weeks with his daughter.'

'What about his house?'

'Some fellas at the lodge volunteered to take care of the window.'

'Good,' Jeffrey said. 'Sara's gonna want her car back. Did you find anything?'

Frank took a plastic evidence bag out of his pocket and set it down on the desk.

'What's this?' Jeffrey asked, but it was a stupid question. There was a Ruger .357 Magnum in the bag.

'It was under her seat,' Frank said.

'Sara's seat?' he asked, still not getting it. The gun was a man stopper, the caliber enough to blow a hole into someone's chest. 'In her car? This is hers?'

Frank shrugged. 'She doesn't have a permit for it.'

Jeffrey stared at the gun as if it could talk to him. Sara certainly wasn't against private citizens having weapons, but he knew for a fact that she wasn't exactly comfortable around guns, especially the kind that could shoot the lock off a barn door. He slipped the gun out of the bag, checking it.

'Serial numbers were filed off,' Frank said.

'Yeah,' Jeffrey answered. He could see that. 'Was it loaded?'

'Yep.' Frank was obviously impressed with the weapon. 'Ruger security six, stainless steel. That's a custom handle, too.'

Jeffrey dropped the gun into his desk drawer, then looked back at Frank. 'Anything on the sex offender lists yet?'

Frank seemed disappointed that the discussion about Sara's gun was over. He answered, 'Not really. Most of 'em have some kind of alibi. The ones who don't aren't really what we're looking for.'

'We've got a meeting at ten with Nick Shelton. He's got a specialist on belladonna. Maybe we can give the guys something more to look for after that.'

Frank took a seat. 'I got that nightshade in my own backyard.'

'Me, too,' Jeffrey said, then, 'I want to head over to the hospital after the meeting, see if Julia Matthews feels like talking.' He paused, thinking about the young girl. 'Her parents will be in around three. I want to be at the airport to meet them. You're riding shotgun with me today.' If Frank found Jeffrey's word choice funny, he did not comment.

FIFTEEN

Sara left the clinic at quarter till ten so that she could go by the pharmacy before she saw Jeffrey. There was a chill in the air and the clouds promised more rain. She tucked her hands into her pockets as she walked down the street, keeping her eyes on the sidewalk in front of her, hoping her posture and her pace would make her seem unapproachable. She needn't have bothered, though. Since Sibyl's death downtown had taken on an eerie quiet. It was as if the whole town had died with her. Sara knew how they felt.

All night, Sara had lain awake in bed, going over each step she had taken with Julia Matthews. No matter what she did, Sara kept seeing the girl laid out on her car, her hands and feet pierced, her eyes glazed as she stared without seeing the night sky. Sara never wanted to go through anything like that again.

The bell over the pharmacy door jingled as Sara walked in, breaking her out of her solitude.

'Hey, Dr. Linton,' Marty Ringo called from behind the checkout counter. Her head was bent down, reading a magazine. Marty was a plump woman with an unfortunate mole growing just above her right eyebrow. Black hairs shot out from it like bristles on a brush. Working in the pharmacy, she knew the latest gossip about anyone and everyone in town. Marty would be certain to mention to whoever wandered into the store next that Sara Linton made a special trip to see Jeb today.

Marty smiled slyly. 'You looking for Jeb?'

'Yes,' Sara answered.

'Heard about last night,' Marty said, obviously fishing for information. 'That's a college girl, huh?'

Sara nodded, because that much could be found from the paper.

Marty's voice lowered. 'Heard she was messed with.'

'Mmm,' Sara answered, looking around the store. 'Is he here?' she asked.

'They both looked alike, too.'

'What's that?' Sara asked, suddenly paying attention.

'Both them girls,' Marty said. 'You think there's some kind of connection?'

Sara cut the conversation short. 'I really need to talk to Jeb.'

'He's out back.' Marty pointed toward the pharmacy, a hurt expression on her face.

Sara thanked Marty with a forced smile as she made her way toward the back of the store. Sara had always liked being in the pharmacy. She had bought her first tube of mascara here. On weekends, her father used to drive them to the store for candy. Not much had changed since Jeb bought the place. The soda counter, which was more for show than for serving drinks, still shone from polish. Contraceptives were still kept behind the counter. The narrow aisles up and down the length of the store were still labeled with signs made from marker and poster board.

Sara peered over the pharmacy counter but didn't see Jeb. She noticed the back door was open, and with a look over her shoulder, she walked behind the counter.

'Jeb?' she called. There was no response, and Sara walked to the open door. Jeb was standing to the side, his back to Sara. She tapped him on the shoulder and he jumped.

'God,' he yelled, turning around quickly. The fear on his face was replaced by pleasure when he saw Sara.

He laughed. 'You scared the crap out of me.'

'I'm sorry,' Sara apologized, but the truth was she was glad he could get worked up over something. 'What were you doing?'

He pointed to a row of bushes lining the long parking lot behind the buildings. 'See in that bush?'

Sara shook her head, not seeing anything but bushes. Then, 'Oh,' as she saw a small bird nest.

'Finches,' Jeb said. 'I put a feeder out there last year, but some kids from the school took it away.'

Sara turned toward him. 'About last night,' she began.

He waved her off. 'Please, Sara, believe me, I understand. You were with Jeffrey a long time.'

'Thank you,' she said, meaning it.

Jeb looked back into the pharmacy, lowering his voice. 'I'm sorry about what happened, too. You know, with the girl.' He shook his head slowly side to side. 'It's just hard to think about things like that happening in your own town.'

'I know,' Sara answered, not really wanting to get into it.

'I guess I can forgive you, skipping out on our date to save somebody's life.' He put his hand over the right side of his chest. 'Did you really put your hand on her heart?'

Sara moved his hand to the left side. 'Yes.'

'Good Lord,' Jeb breathed. 'How did it feel?'

Sara gave him the truth. 'Scary,' she said. 'Very scary.'

His voice was filled with admiration when he said,

'You are a remarkable woman, Sara. Do you know that?'

She felt silly being praised. 'I'll give you a rain check if you want,' she offered, trying to move him off the topic of Julia Matthews. 'For our date, I mean.'

He smiled, genuinely pleased. 'That'd be great.'

A breeze came and Sara rubbed her arms. 'It's getting cold again.'

'Here.' He led her back inside, shutting the door behind them. 'You doing anything this weekend?'

'I don't know,' Sara said. Then, 'Listen, I came to see if Jeffrey picked up his medication.'

'Well.' Jeb clasped his hands together. 'I guess that means you're busy this weekend.'

'No, it doesn't.' Sara paused, then said, 'It's just complicated.'

'Yeah.' He forced a smile. 'No problem. I'll check his script.'

She couldn't stand to see the disappointment on his face. She turned the Medic Alert display to give herself something to do. Bookmarks with religious sayings were alongside diabetes bracelets.

Jeb opened a large drawer under the counter and pulled out an orange pill bottle. He double-checked the label, then said, 'He called it in but didn't pick it up yet.'

'Thanks,' Sara managed, taking the bottle. She held it in her hand, staring at Jeb. She spoke before she could back out of it. 'Why don't you call me?' she asked. 'About this weekend.'

'Yeah, I will.'

She reached out with her free hand, smoothing the lapel of his lab coat. 'I mean it, Jeb. Call me.'

He was quiet for a few seconds, then suddenly he

leaned down, kissing her lightly on the lips. 'I'll call you tomorrow.'

'Great,' Sara said. She realized she was gripping the pill bottle so tightly that the top was about to pop off. She had kissed Jeb before. It was really no big deal. Something in the back of her mind was scared that Marty would see, though. Something in her mind was scared that news of the kiss would get back to Jeffrey.

'I can give you a bag for that,' Jeb offered, pointing to the bottle.

'No,' Sara mumbled, tucking the bottle into her jacket pocket.

She murmured a thanks and was out the door before Marty could look up from her magazine.

Jeffrey and Nick Shelton were out in the hall when Sara got to the station. Nick stood with his hands tucked into the back pockets of his jeans, his regulation GBI dark blue dress shirt tight across his chest. His nonregulation beard and mustache were trimmed neatly to his face, and his equally forbidden gold rope chain was hanging from his neck. At just under five feet six inches, he was short enough for Sara to rest her chin on the top of his head. This had not prevented him from asking her out a number of times.

'Hey, girl,' Nick said, putting his arm around her waist.

Jeffrey had about as much to worry about competition-wise from Nick Shelton as he did from a reindeer, but he still seemed to bristle at the familiar way Nick held her. Sara thought Nick was overly solicitous for this very reason.

'Why don't we start the meeting?' Jeffrey grumbled. 'Sara has to get back to work.'

Sara caught up with Jeffrey as they walked down the

hallway toward the back. She tucked the pill bottle into his coat pocket.

'What's this?' he asked, taking it out. Then, 'Oh.'

'Oh,' Sara repeated, opening the door.

Frank Wallace and a reedy-looking young man in khakis and a shirt like Nick's were sitting in the briefing room when they entered. Frank stood, shaking Nick's hand. He gave Sara a firm nod, which she did not return. Something told Sara that Frank had a hand in what happened last night, and she did not like it.

'This is Mark Webster,' Nick said, indicating the other man. He was a boy, really, hardly older than twenty-one. He had that still-wet-behind-the-ears look about him, and a piece of his hair stuck out in the back in a classic cowlick.

'Nice to meet you,' Sara said, shaking his hand. It was like squeezing a fish, but if Nick had brought Mark Webster all the way down here from Macon, he couldn't be as goofy as he looked.

Frank said, 'Why don't you tell them what you were telling me?'

The boy cleared his throat and actually tugged at his collar. He addressed his words toward Sara. 'I was saying it's interesting your twist picked belladonna for his drug of choice. It's very unusual. I've only seen three cases in my work, and most of those were rule-outs, stupid kids who thought they'd have some fun.'

Sara nodded her head, knowing that 'rule-outs' meant ruling out foul play in a death. As a coroner as well as a pediatrician, she was especially careful when young children came into the morgue with cause of death unknown.

Mark leaned against the table, addressing his remarks to the rest of the group. 'Belladonna is in the deadly nightshade family. During the Middle Ages, women chewed small quantities of the seeds in order to dilate their pupils. A woman with dilated eyes was considered more attractive, and that's where they got the name "belladonna." It means "beautiful woman." '

Sara supplied, 'Both victims had extremely dilated pupils.'

'Even a slight dose would cause this,' Mark answered. He picked up a white Tyvek envelope and pulled out some photographs, which he handed to Jeffrey to circulate.

Mark said, 'Belladonna is bell shaped, usually purple, and smells kind of funny. It's not something you'd keep around in your yard if you had kids or small animals. Whoever is growing it probably has a fence around it, maybe three feet tall at the least, in order to keep from poisoning everybody around.'

'Does it need any specific kind of soil or feed?' Jeffrey asked, passing the photo to Frank.

'It's a weed. It can grow practically anywhere. That's what makes it so popular. The only thing is, it's a bad drug.' Mark paused at this. 'The high is prolonged, lasts about three to four hours, depending on how much you take. Users report very real hallucinations. A lot of times they'll actually think it happened, if they can remember it.'

Sara asked, 'It causes amnesia?'

'Oh yes, ma'am, selective amnesia, which means they only remember bits and pieces. Like she might remember it was a man that took her, but she won't remember what he looked like even if she was staring him in the face. Or she might say he was purple with green eyes.' He paused. 'It's a hallucinogen, but not like your typical PCP or LSD. Users report that there's no discerning between the hallucination and the real thing. With, say, angel dust, ecstasy, what have you, you know you're hallucinating. Belladonna makes everything seem real. If I gave you a cup of Datura, when you came around you might swear to me you had a conversation with a coatrack. I could hook you up to a lie detector and you'd come out as telling the truth. It takes things that are there in reality and puts a twist on them.'

'Tea?' Jeffrey ased, giving Sara a look.

'Yes, sir. Kids've been boiling it in tea to drink.' He clasped his hands behind him. 'I've got to tell you, though, it's dangerous stuff. Real easy to OD on.'

Sara asked, 'How else can you ingest it?

'If you've got the patience,' Mark answered, 'you can soak the leaves in alcohol for a couple of days, then evaporate it. It's still a crapshoot, though, because the consistency isn't guaranteed, even with people who grow it for medical purposes.'

'What medical purposes?' Jeffrey asked.

'Well, you know when you go to the eye doctor and he dilates your eyes? It's a belladonna compound. Very diluted, but it's belladonna. You couldn't take a couple of bottles of the eyedrops and kill somebody, for instance. At this low level of concentration, the worst you could do is give them a really bad headache and killer constipation. It's at the pure level that you have to be careful.'

Frank bumped her arm, handing her the photograph. Sara looked down at the plant. It looked pretty much like every plant she had ever seen. Sara was a doctor, not a horticulturist. She couldn't even grow a Chia Pet.

Without warning, her mind was racing again, thinking back to when she first found Julia Matthews on her car. She was trying to remember if the duct tape had been there. With sudden clarity, Sara remembered that it had. She could see the tape on the woman's mouth.

She could see Julia Matthews's body crucified on the hood of the car.

'Sara?' Jeffrey asked.

'Hm?' Sara looked up. Everyone was staring at her, as if they were anticipating a response to something. 'I'm sorry,' she apologized. 'What was it you asked?'

Mark answered, 'I asked if you noticed anything strange about the victims. Were they unable to speak? Did they have a blank stare?'

Sara handed back the photo. 'Sibyl Adams was blind,' she provided. 'So of course her stare was blank. Julia Matthews . . . ' She paused, trying to force the image from her mind. 'Her eyes were glazed. I imagine it was from being gorked out on this drug more than anything else.'

Jeffrey gave her a funny look. 'Mark mentioned something about belladonna interfering with vision.'

'There's a sort of blindsightedness,' Mark said in a tone that implied he was repeating himself. 'According to user reports, you can see, but your mind can't make out what it is you're seeing. Like I could show you an apple or an orange, and you would be aware that you were seeing something round, maybe textured, but your brain wouldn't recognize what it is.'

'I know what blindsightedness is,' Sara returned, realizing too late that her tone was condescending. She tried to cover for this by saying, 'Do you think Sibyl Adams experienced this? Maybe that's why she didn't scream out?'

Mark looked at the other men. Obviously, this was another thing he had covered while Sara was zoning out. 'There's been reported loss of voice from the drug. Nothing physically happens in the voice box. There's no physical restraint or damage caused by the drug. I think it's more to do with something happening in the language center of the brain. It has to be similar to whatever causes the sight recognition problems.'

'Makes sense,' Sara agreed.

Mark continued. 'Some signs that it's been ingested would be cotton mouth, dilated pupils, high body temperature, elevated heart rate, and difficulty breathing.'

'Both victims experienced all of those symptoms,' Sara provided. 'What kind of dose would bring this about?'

'It's pretty potent stuff. Just one bag of tea can send somebody loopy, especially if they're not recreational drug users. The berries aren't that bad on a scale of things, but anything from the root or the leaf is going to be dangerous, unless you know exactly what you're doing. And then there's no guarantee.'

'The first victim was a vegetarian,' Sara said.

'She was a chemist, too, right?' Mark asked. 'I can think of a million different drugs to fool around with other than belladonna. I don't think anybody who took the time to research it would take that kind of risk. It's Russian roulette, especially if you're dealing with the root. That's the deadliest part. Just a little bit too much from the root and you're gone. There's no known antidote.'

'I didn't see any signs of drug use in Julia Matthews.' She said to Jeffrey, 'I suppose you're going to interview her after this?'

He nodded, then asked Mark, 'Anything else?'

Mark brushed his fingers through his hair. 'After the drug, there's noted constipation, still the cotton mouth, sometimes hallucinations. It's interesting to know that the drug was used in a sex crime, ironic even.'

'How's that?' Jeffrey asked.

'During the Middle Ages, the drug was sometimes

inserted with a vaginal applicator so that the rush would come sooner. There are even some people who think the whole myth of witches flying on broomsticks comes from the image of a woman inserting the drug with a wooden applicator.' He smiled. 'But then we'd have to get into a protracted discussion on deity worshipping and the rise of Christianity in European cultures.'

Mark seemed to sense he had lost his audience. 'People in drug communities who know about belladonna tend to stay away from it.' He looked at Sara. 'If you'll excuse the language, ma'am?'

Sara shrugged. Between the clinic and her father, she had pretty much heard it all.

Mark still blushed when he said, 'It's a total mind fuck.' He offered Sara a smile in apology. 'The number one memory, even among users with amnesia, is flying. They really believe they're flying, and they can't understand, even after they come down, that they haven't actually flown.'

Jeffrey crossed his arms. 'That might explain why she keeps staring out the window.'

'Has she said anything yet?' Sara asked.

He shook his head. 'Nothing.' Then, 'We're going to the hospital next if you want to see her.'

Sara looked at her watch, pretending to consider this. There was no way in hell she was going to see Julia Matthews again. It was too much to even think about. 'I've got patients,' she said.

Jeffrey indicated his office. 'Sara, mind if I talk to you for a second?'

Sara felt the urge to bolt, but she fought it. 'Is this about my car?'

'No.' Jeffrey waited until she was in his office, then shut the door. Sara sat on the edge of his desk, trying for a casual pose. 'I had to take my boat in to work this morning,' Sara said. 'Do you know how cold it is on the lake?'

He ignored this, getting straight to the point. 'Found your gun.'

'Oh,' Sara answered, trying to think of what to say. Of all the things she had been expecting him to say, this was the last one. The Ruger had been in her car for so long that she had forgotten about it. 'Am I under arrest?'

'Where did you get it?'

'It was a gift.'

Jeffrey gave her a hard look. 'What, somebody gave you a three-fifty-seven with the serial numbers filed off for your birthday?'

Sara shrugged this off. 'I've had it for years, Jeffrey.'

'When did you buy that car, Sara? Couple of years ago?'

'I moved it from the old one when I bought it.'

He stared at her, not speaking. Sara could tell that he was mad, but she did not know what to say. She tried, 'I've never used it.'

'That makes me feel good, Sara,' he snapped. 'You've got a gun in your car capable of literally taking somebody's head off and you don't know how to use it?' He paused, obviously trying to understand. 'What're you gonna do if someone comes after you, huh?'

Sara knew the answer to this, but she did not say.

Jeffrey asked, 'Why do you have it in the first place?'

Sara studied her ex-husband, trying to figure out the best way to get out of this office without having another fight. She was tired and she was upset. This wasn't the time to go a few rounds with Jeffrey. Sara just did not have the fight in her at the moment.

'I just had it,' she answered.

'You don't just have this kind of gun,' he said.

'I need to get back to the clinic.' She stood, but he was blocking her exit.

'Sara, what the hell is going on?'

'What do you mean?'

His eyes narrowed, but he did not answer. He moved aside, opening the door for her.

Sara thought for a second that it was a trick. 'That's it?' she asked.

He stepped aside. 'It's not like I can beat it out of you.'

She put her hand to his chest, feeling guilty. 'Jeffrey.'

He looked out into the squad room, 'I need to go over to the hospital,' he said, obviously dismissing her.

SIXTEEN

Lena leaned her head into her hand, trying to close her eyes for just a minute of rest. She had been sitting in a chair outside Julia Matthews's room for over an hour, and the last few days were finally catching up with her. She was tired and about to start her period. Despite this, her pants were loose on her hips from not eating. When she snapped her paddle holster on over her belt this morning, it was loose against her hip. As the day wore on, it started to rub, chafing her side.

Lena knew she needed to eat, needed to get back to living her life instead of just dragging along through every day like she was living on borrowed time. For now, she could not imagine doing that. She didn't want to get up in the morning and go for a run, like she had every morning for the last fifteen years. She did not want to go down to the Krispy Kreme and get coffee with Frank and the other detectives. She did not want to go to pack her lunch or go out to dinner. Every time she looked at food, she felt sick. All she could think was that Sibyl would never eat again. Lena was walking around while Sibyl was dead. Lena was breathing while Sibyl was not. Nothing made sense. Nothing would ever be the same again.

Lena took a deep breath and let it go, looking up and down the hallway. Julia Matthews was the only patient in the hospital today, which made Lena's job easy.

Except for a nurse who had been floated down on loan from Augusta, it was just Lena and Julia on this floor.

She stood, trying to walk some sense into her brain. She was feeling punch-drunk, and Lena could not think of anything to fight this other than to remain in motion. Her body ached from restless sleep, and she was still unable to get the image of Sibyl in the morgue out of her mind. Part of Lena was glad that there was another victim, though. Part of Lena wanted to go into Julia Matthews's room and shake her, to beg her to speak, to tell them who had done this to her, who had killed Sibyl, but Lena knew this would get them nowhere.

The few times Lena had gone into the room to check on the girl, she had been silent, not answering even the most innocuous questions from Lena. Did she want another pillow? Was there anyone she wanted Lena to call for her?

Thirsty, the girl had pointed to the pitcher on the hospital table rather than asked for water. Her eyes still had a haunted look about them, too, caused by the fact that the drug was still in her system. Her pupils were wide open, and she had the look of someone who was blind – blind like Sibyl had been. Only Julia Matthews would recover from this. Julia Matthews would see again. She would get better. She would go back to school and make friends, maybe meet a husband one day and have kids. Memories of what had happened would always be in the back of Julia Matthews's mind, but at least she would have a life. At least she would have a future. Lena knew that part of her resented Matthews for this. Lena knew, too, that she would trade Julia Matthews's life for Sibyl's on a second's notice.

The elevator dinged open, and Lena put her hand to her gun without thinking. Jeffrey and Nick Shelton walked into the hallway, followed by Frank and a skinny-looking kid who looked like he had just come from his high school graduation. She dropped her hand, walking to meet them, thinking she'd be damned if all those men were going to go into the small hospital room containing a woman who had just been raped. Especially Opie.

'How's she doing?' Jeffrey asked.

Lena skipped the question. 'You're not all going in there, are you?'

The look on Jeffrey's face said he had planned just this.

'She's still not talking,' Lena said, trying to help him save face. 'She hasn't said anything.'

'Maybe just you and I should go in,' he finally decided. 'Sorry, Mark.'

The young man did not seem to mind. 'Hey, I'm just glad this got me out of the office for a day.'

Lena thought it was pretty shitty of him to say this within walking distance of a woman who had arguably been to hell and back, but Jeffrey caught her arm before she could say anything. He led her up the hallway, talking as they walked.

'She's stable?' he asked. 'Her medical condition?'

'Yeah.'

Jeffrey stopped at the door to the room, his hand on the handle but not opening it. 'How about you? You're doing okay?'

'Sure.'

'I have a feeling her parents are going to want to move her to Augusta. How do you feel about going with her?'

Lena's first impulse was to protest, but she nodded an uncharacteristic acquiescence. It might do her some good to get out of town. Hank would be going back to

Reece in a day or two. Maybe she would feel differently when she had the house back to herself.

'I'll let you start,' Jeffrey said. 'If she looks like she'll be more comfortable with just you, then I'll step out.'

'Right,' Lena said, knowing this was standard procedure. Generally, the last thing a woman who had been raped wanted to do was talk to a man about it. As the only female detective on the squad, this job had fallen to Lena a couple of times before. She had even gone to Macon once to help interview a young girl there who had been brutally beaten and raped by her next-door neighbor. Still, even though Lena had been at the hospital all day with Julia, something about actually talking to the girl, interviewing her, made Lena feel sick to her stomach. It was too close to home.

'You ready?' Jeffrey asked, his hand on the door.

'Yeah.'

Jeffrey opened the door, letting Lena go in ahead of him. Julia Matthews was asleep, but she woke at the noise. Lena didn't imagine the young girl would have a good night's sleep for a long while, if ever.

'Want some water?' Lena asked, walking to the far side of the bed, picking up the pitcher. She filled the girl's glass, then turned the straw so she could drink.

Jeffrey stood with his back close to the door, obviously wanting to give the young girl space. He said, 'I'm Chief Tolliver, Julia. Do you remember me from this morning?'

She gave a slow nod.

'You've ingested a drug called belladonna. Do you know what that is?'

She shook her head side to side.

'It causes you to lose your voice sometimes. Do you think you can speak?'

The girl opened her mouth, and a scratchy sound

came out. She moved her lips, obviously trying to form words.

Jeffrey gave an encouraging smile. 'Want to try to tell me your name?'

She opened her mouth again, her voice raspy and small. 'Julia.'

'Good,' Jeffrey said. 'This is Lena Adams. You know her, right?'

Julia nodded, her eyes finding Lena.

'She's going to ask you some questions, okay?'

Lena tried not to hide her surprise. She wasn't sure she could tell Julia Matthews the time of day, let alone question the young woman. Lena fell back on her training, starting with what she knew.

'Julia?' Lena pulled a chair up to the young woman's bed. 'We need to know if you can tell us anything about what was done to you.'

Julia closed her eyes. Her lips quivered, but she did not answer.

'Did you know him, sweetie?'

She shook her head.

'Was it someone from one of your classes? Had you seen him around school?'

Julia's eyes closed. Tears came a few seconds later. She finally said, 'No.'

Lena put her hand on the girl's arm. It was thin and frail, much as Sibyl's had seemed in the morgue. She tried not to think about her sister when she said, 'Let's talk about his hair. Can you tell me what color it was?'

Again she shook her head.

'Any tattoos or marks that might help us identify him?'

'No.'

Lena said, 'I know this is hard, honey, but we have to

find out what happened. We need to get this guy off the street so he can't hurt anyone else.'

Julia kept her eyes closed. The room was intolerably quiet, so much so that Lena felt the urge to do something loud. The silence was making her nervous for some reason.

Without warning, Julia finally spoke. Her voice was husky. 'He tricked me.'

Lena pressed her lips together, letting the girl have her time.

'He tricked me,' Julia repeated, squeezing her eyes shut even tighter. 'I was at the library.'

Lena thought about Ryan Gordon. Her heart thumped in her chest. Had she been wrong about him? Was he capable of doing something like this? Maybe Julia had escaped while he was in jail.

'I had a test,' Julia continued, 'and I stayed late to study.' Her breathing became labored at the memory.

'Let's take some deep breaths,' Lena said, then she breathed in and out, in and out, with Julia. 'That's good, honey. Just keep calm.'

She started to cry in earnest now. 'Ryan was there,' she said.

Lena allowed herself to look at Jeffrey. He was focused on Matthews, his brow furrowed. She could almost read his thoughts.

'At the library?' Lena asked, trying not to sound too pushy.

Julia nodded, then reached out for her glass of water.

'Here,' Lena said, helping her lean up so that she could drink.

The girl took several swallows, then let her head drop back down. She stared out the window again, her mind obviously taking time to recover. Lena tried not to tap her foot. She wanted to reach over the bed and force the girl to talk. She could not understand how Julia Matthews could be so passive in her interrogation. If Lena were in that bed, she would be spitting out every detail she had. Lena would be pushing whoever would listen to find the man who did this. Her hands would be itching to rip his heart out of his chest. How Julia Matthews could just lie there, she did not know.

Lena counted to twenty, forcing herself to give the woman some time. She had counted in the Ryan Gordon interview; it was an old trick of hers and the only way she could make herself at least appear patient. When she reached fifty, Lena asked, 'Ryan was there?'

Julia nodded.

'In the library?'

She nodded again.

Lena reached over, putting her hand on Julia's arm again. She would have held her hand if it had not been wrapped in tight bandages. She kept her tone even, putting in just a little bit of pressure, as she said, 'You saw Ryan at the library. Then what happened?'

Julia responded to the pressure. 'We talked a little while, then I had to go back to the dorm.'

'Were you mad at him?'

Julia's eyes found Lena's. Something passed between them, an unvoiced message. Lena knew then that Ryan had some kind of control over Julia, but that she wanted to break it. Lena also knew that as much of a bastard as Ryan Gordon was, he had not been the man to do this to his girlfriend.

Lena asked, 'Did you argue?'

'We kind of made up, though.'

'Kind of, but not really?' Lena clarified, sensing what had happened in the library that night. She could see Ryan Gordon trying to push Julia into making some kind of commitment to him. She could also see that

Julia's eyes had finally been opened as to what kind of person her ex-boyfriend was. Julia had finally seen him for what he was. But someone else more evil than Ryan Gordon could ever hope to be had been waiting for her.

Lena asked, 'So you left the library, then what?'

'There was a man,' she said. 'On the way to the dorm.'

'Which way did you walk?'

'The back way, around the agri-building.'

'By the lake?'

She shook her head. 'The other side.'

Lena waited for her to continue.

'I ran into him, and he dropped his books, and I dropped mine.' Her voice trailed off, but her breathing became loud in the small room. She was nearly panting.

'Did you see his face then?'

'I don't remember. He gave me a shot.'

Lena felt her eyebrows furrow. 'Like a shot with a syringe?'

'I felt it. I didn't see it.'

'Where did you feel it?'

She put her hand to her left hip.

'He was behind you when you felt it?' Lena asked, thinking this would make the killer left-handed, just like Sibyl's attacker.

'Yeah.'

'So he took you then?' Lena asked. 'He ran into you, then you felt the shot, then he took you somewhere?'

'Yes.'

'In his car?'

'I don't remember,' she said. 'The next thing I knew, I was in a basement.' She put her hands over her face, crying in earnest. Her body started to shake with grief.

'It's okay,' Lena said, putting her hand over the other

woman's. 'Do you want to stop now? You're in charge of this.'

The room was quiet again but for Julia's breathing. When she did speak again, her voice was a hoarse, almost imperceptible whisper. 'He raped me.'

Lena felt a lump in her throat. She knew this already, of course, but the way Julia said the word stripped Lena of every defense she had. Lena felt raw and exposed. She did not want Jeffrey in the room. For some reason, he seemed to sense this. When she looked up at him, he nodded toward the door. Lena mouthed a yes, and he left without a sound.

'Do you know what happened next?' Lena asked.

Julia moved her head, trying to find Jeffrey.

'He's gone,' Lena said, giving her voice an assured tone that she did not feel. 'It's just us, Julia. It's just you and me, and we've got all day if you need it. All week, all year.' She paused, lest the girl take that as encouragement to stop the interview. 'Just keep in mind that the sooner we get the details, the sooner we can stop him. You don't want him to do this to another girl, do you?'

She took the question hard, as Lena expected she would. Lena knew she had to be a little tough or the girl would simply shut up, keeping the details to herself.

Julia sobbed, the noise filling the room, ringing in Lena's ears.

Julia said, 'I don't want this to happen to anyone else.'

'Me, either,' Lena answered. 'You have to tell me what he did to you.' She paused, then, 'Did you see his face at any time?'

'No,' she answered. 'I mean, I did, but I couldn't tell. I couldn't make the connection. It was so dark all the time. There was no light at all.'

'Are you sure it was a basement?'

'It smelled,' she said. 'Musty, and I could hear water dripping.'

'Water?' Lena asked. 'Like dripping from a faucet, or maybe from the lake?'

'A faucet,' Julia said. 'More like a faucet. It sounded . . . ' She closed her eyes, and for a few seconds she seemed to let herself go back to that place. 'Like a metallic clinking.' She mimicked the sound, 'Clink, clink, clink, over and over. It never stopped.' She put her hands over her ears, as if to stop the noise.

'Let's go back to the college,' Lena said. 'You felt the shot in your hip, then what? Do you know what kind of car he was driving?'

Julia shook her head again in an exaggerated sweep left to right. 'I don't remember. I was picking up my books, and then the next thing I knew, I was, I was . . . ' Her voice trailed off.

'In the basement?' Lena provided. 'Do you remember anything about where you were?'

'It was dark.'

'You couldn't make anything out?'

'I couldn't open my eyes. They wouldn't open.' Her voice so soft that Lena had to strain to hear. 'I was flying.'

'Flying?'

'I kept floating up, like I was on water. I could hear the waves from the ocean.'

Lena took a deep breath, then let it out slowly. 'Did he have you on your back?'

Julia's face crumpled at this, and she shook with sobs.

'Honey,' Lena prompted. 'Was he white? Black? Could you tell?'

She shook her head again. 'I couldn't open my eyes. He talked to me. His voice.' Her lips were trembling, and her face had turned an alarming shade of red. The tears came in earnest now, marking a continual stream down her face. 'He said he loved me.' She gasped for air as the panic took hold. 'He kept kissing me. His tongue.' She stopped, sobbing.

Lena took a deep breath, trying to calm herself down. She was pushing too hard. Lena counted to a slow one hundred, then said, 'The holes in your hands. We know he put something in your hands and feet.'

Julia looked at the bandages, as if seeing them for the first time. 'Yes,' she said. 'I woke up, and my hands were nailed down. I could see the nail go through, but it didn't hurt.'

'You were on the floor?'

'I think so. I felt' – she seemed to look for a word – 'I felt suspended. I was flying. How did he make me fly? Was I flying?'

Lena cleared her throat. 'No,' she answered. Then began, 'Julia, can you think of anybody new in your life, maybe someone on campus or in town, who was making you uncomfortable? Maybe you felt like you were being watched?'

'I'm still being watched,' she said, looking out the window.

'I'm watching you,' Lena said, turning the girl's face back toward her. 'I'm watching you, Julia. Nobody is going to hurt you again. Do you understand that? Nobody.'

'I don't feel safe,' she said, her face crumpling as she started to cry again. 'He can see me. I know he can see me.'

'It's just you and me here,' Lena assured her. When she spoke, it was like talking to Sibyl, assuring Sibyl that she would be taken care of. 'When you go to

Augusta, I'll be with you. I'm not going to let you out of my sight. Do you understand that?'

Julia seemed to be more frightened despite Lena's words. Her voice was raspy when she asked, 'Why am I going to Augusta?'

'I don't know that for sure,' Lena answered, reaching for the water pitcher. 'Don't worry about that right now.'

'Who's going to send me to Augusta?' Julia asked, her lips trembling.

'Drink some more water,' Lena told her, holding the cup up to her lips. 'Your parents are going to be here soon. Don't worry about anything but taking care of yourself and getting better.'

The girl choked, and water spilled down her neck and onto the bed. Her eyes opened wide in panic. 'Why are you moving me?' she asked. 'What's going to happen?'

'We won't move you if you don't want,' Lena said. 'I'll talk to your parents.'

'My parents?'

'They should be here soon,' Lena assured her. 'It's okay.'

'Do they know?' Julia asked, her voice raised. 'Did you tell them what happened to me?'

'I don't know,' Lena answered. 'I'm not sure if they know any of the details.'

'You can't tell my daddy,' the girl sobbed. 'Nobody can tell my father, okay? He can't know what happened.'

'You didn't do anything,' Lena said. 'Julia, your dad's not going to blame you for this.'

Julia was quiet. After a while, she looked back out the window, tears streaming down her cheeks.

'It's okay,' Lena soothed, taking a tissue out of the box on the table. She reached over the girl, blotting the water off the pillow. The last thing this girl needed to think about was how her father would react to what had happened to her. Lena had worked with rape victims before. She knew how the blame worked. Very seldom did a victim blame anyone but herself.

There was a strange noise Lena found vaguely familiar. Too late she realized it was her gun.

'Move away,' Julia whispered. She held the gun awkwardly in her bandaged hands. It tilted toward Lena, then back toward Julia as she tried to get a better grip on the weapon. Lena looked toward the door, thinking to call for Jeffrey, but Julia warned her, 'Don't.'

Lena held her hands out to her sides, but did not back up.

Lena said, 'Give me the gun.'

'You don't understand,' the girl said, tears welling into her eyes. 'You don't understand what he did to me, how he –' She stopped, choking on a sob. She did not have a good grip on the gun, but the barrel was pointed toward Lena and her finger was on the trigger. Lena felt a cold sweat overcome her, and she honestly could not recall if the safety was on or off. What she did know was that a round was already chambered. Once the safety was off, a tap on the trigger would fire the weapon.

Lena tried to keep her voice calm. 'What, sweetheart? What don't I understand?'

Julia tilted the gun back toward her own head. She fumbled, almost dropping it, before letting the barrel rest on her chin.

'Don't do that,' Lena begged. 'Please give me the gun. There's a bullet in the chamber.'

'I know about guns.'

'Julia, please,' Lena said, knowing she needed to keep the girl talking. 'Listen to me.'

A slight smile came to her lips. 'My daddy used to take me hunting with him. He used to let me help him clean the rifles.'

'Julia –'

'When I was there.' She choked back a sob. 'When I was with him.'

'The man? The man who abducted you?'

'You don't know what he did,' she said, her voice tight in her throat. 'The things he did to me. I can't tell you.'

'I'm so sorry,' Lena said. She wanted to move forward, but there was a look to Julia Matthews's eyes that kept her rooted to the floor. Charging the girl was not an option.

Lena said, 'I won't let him hurt you again, Julia. I promise.'

'You don't understand,' the girl sobbed, sliding the gun up to the cleft of her chin. She could barely grip the weapon, but Lena knew this wouldn't matter at such a close range.

'Honey, please don't,' Lena said, her eyes going to the door. Jeffrey was on the other side, maybe she could alert him somehow without letting Julia know.

'Don't,' Julia said, as if reading Lena's mind.

'You don't have to do this,' Lena said. She tried to make her voice firmer, but the truth was Lena had only read about this kind of situation in procedural manuals. She had never talked someone out of suicide.

Julia said, 'The way he touched me. The way he kissed me.' Her voice broke. 'You just don't know.'

'What?' Lena asked, slowly moving her hand toward the gun. 'What don't I know?'

'He –' She stopped, a guttural sound coming from her throat. 'He made love to me.'

'He –'

'He made love to me,' she repeated, a whisper that echoed in the room. 'Do you know what that means?' she asked. 'He kept saying he didn't want to hurt me. He wanted to make love to me. He did.'

Lena felt her mouth open, but there was nothing she could say. She couldn't be hearing what she thought she was hearing. 'What are you saying?' she asked, aware of the sharpness in her tone. 'What do you mean?'

'He made love to me,' Julia repeated. 'The way he touched me.'

Lena shook her head, as if to rid this from her mind. She could not keep the incredulity out of her tone when she asked, 'Are you saying you enjoyed it?'

A snapping sound came as Julia disengaged the safety. Lena felt too stunned to move but somehow managed to reach Julia seconds before the girl pulled the trigger. Lena looked down in time to see Julia Matthews's head explode beneath her.

The water from the shower came like needles against Lena's skin. She was aware of the burning, but it was not uncomfortable. She was numb to all sensations, numb from the inside out. Her knees gave, and Lena let herself slide down into the tub. She pulled her knees to her chest, closing her eyes as the water beat down on her breasts and face. She bent her head forward, feeling like a rag doll. The water pummeled the top of her head, bruised the back of her neck, but she did not care. Her body did not belong to her anymore. She was empty. She could not think of one thing that had meaning in her life, not her job, not Jeffrey, not Hank Norton, and certainly not herself.

Julia Matthews was dead, just like Sibyl. Lena had failed them both.

The water started to run cold, the spray pricking against her skin. Lena turned off the shower and dried herself with a towel, feeling as if she was just going through the motions. Her body still felt dirty despite the fact that this was her second shower in the last five hours. There was a strange taste in her mouth, too. Lena wasn't sure if it was her imagination or if something had gone into her mouth when Julia had pulled the trigger.

She shuddered thinking about this.

'Lee?' Hank called from outside the bathroom door.

'I'll be down in a minute,' Lena answered, putting paste on her toothbrush. She looked at herself in the mirror as she tried to scrub the taste out of her mouth. The resemblance to Sibyl was gone today. There was nothing left of her sister.

Lena went down to the kitchen in her robe and bedroom slippers. Outside the kitchen door, she put her hand to the wall, feeling lightheaded and sick to her stomach. She was forcing her body to move, otherwise she would go to sleep and never wake up. Her body ached to give in to that, ached to cut off, but Lena knew that as soon as her head hit the pillow she would be wide awake, her mind playing back the sight of Julia Matthews just before she killed herself. The girl had been looking at Lena when she pulled the trigger. Their eyes had locked, and Lena did not need to see the gun to know that death was on the younger woman's mind.

Hank was at the kitchen table, drinking a Coke. He stood when she entered the room. Lena felt a flush of shame and couldn't look him in the eye. She had been strong in the car as Frank drove her back to the house. She had not said a word to her partner, or commented on the fact that despite her efforts to clean herself at the hospital, she had grey matter and blood sticking to her like hot wax. There were pieces of bone in her breast pocket, and she could feel blood dripping down her face and neck, even though she had wiped it all off at the hospital. It was not until she had the front door closed behind her that Lena let herself go. That Hank had been there, that she had let him hold her in his arms while she sobbed, was something that still brought a sense of shame to her. She did not know herself anymore. She did not know who this weak person was.

Lena glanced out the window, noting, 'It's dark out.'

'You slept awhile,' Hank said, going to the stove. 'You want some tea?'

'Yeah,' Lena said, though she had not slept at all. Closing her eyes only brought her closer to what had happened. If she never slept again, Lena would be fine.

'Your boss called to check on you,' Hank said.

'Oh,' Lena answered, sitting at the table, her leg tucked underneath her. She wondered what was going through Jeffrey's mind. He had been out in the hallway, waiting for Lena to call him in, when the gun went off. Lena remembered the expression of absolute shock on his face when he burst through the doorway. Lena had stood there, still leaning over Julia, flesh and bone dripping from her chest and face. Jeffrey had forced her out of this position, patting his hands down Lena's body, checking to make sure she had not been shot in the process.

Lena had stood mute while he did this, unable to take her eyes off what was left of Julia Matthews's face. The young girl had put the gun under her chin, blowing out the back of her head. The wall behind and over the bed was splattered. A bullet hole was three feet down from the ceiling. Jeffrey had forced Lena to stay in that room, drilling her for every bit of information she had gotten from Julia Matthews, questioning every detail of Lena's narrative as Lena stood there, her lip trembling uncontrollably, unable to follow the words coming out of her own mouth.

Lena put her head in her hands. She listened as Hank filled the kettle, heard the click as the electric starter on the gas stove kicked in.

Hank sat in front of her, his hands crossed in front of him. 'You okay?' he asked.

'I don't know,' she answered, her own voice sounding far away. The gun had gone off close to her ear. The ringing had stopped a while ago, but sounds still came like a dull ache.

'You know what I was thinking?' Hank asked, sitting back in his chair. 'Remember that time you fell off the front porch?'

Lena stared at him, not understanding where he was going with this. 'Yeah?'

'Well.' He shrugged, smiling for some reason. 'Sibyl pushed you.'

Lena wasn't sure she had heard him right. 'What?'

He assured Lena, 'She pushed you. I saw her.'

'She pushed me off the porch?' Lena shook her head. 'She was trying to keep me from falling.'

'She was blind, Lee, how did she know you were falling?'

Lena's mouth worked. He had a point. 'I had to get sixteen stitches in my leg.'

'I know.'

'She pushed me?' Lena questioned, her voice raised a few octaves. 'Why did she push me?'

'I don't know. Maybe she was just kidding.' Hank chuckled. 'You let out such a holler I thought the neighbors were gonna come.'

'I doubt the neighbors would've come if they'd heard a twenty-one gun salute,' Lena commented. Hank Norton's neighbors had learned early on to expect all kinds of commotion coming from his house night and day.

'Remember that time at the beach?' Hank began.

Lena stared at him, trying to figure out why he was bringing this up. 'What time?'

'When you couldn't find your kickboard?'

'The red one?' Lena asked. Then, 'Don't tell me, she pushed it off the balcony.'

He chuckled. 'Nope. She lost it in the pool.'

'How can you lose a kickboard in the pool?'

He waved this off. 'I guess some kid took it. The point was, it was yours. You told her not to take it and she did, and she lost it.'

Despite herself, Lena felt some of the weight on her shoulders lifting. 'Why are you telling me this?' she asked.

Again, he gave a small shrug. 'I don't know. I was just thinking about her this morning. Remember that shirt she used to wear? The one with the green stripes?'

Lena nodded.

'She still had it.'

'No,' Lena said, surprised. They had fought over that shirt during high school until Hank had settled it with a coin toss. 'Why did she keep it?'

'It was hers,' Hank said.

Lena stared at her uncle, not sure what to say.

He stood up, taking a mug from the cabinet. 'You want some time to yourself, or do you want me around?'

Lena considered his question. She needed to be alone, to get some sense of herself back, and she could not do that around Hank of all people. 'Are you going back to Reece?'

'I thought I'd stay at Nan's tonight and help her sort through some things.'

Lena felt a slight panic. 'She's not throwing things away, is she?'

'No, of course not. She's just going through things, getting her clothes together.' Hank leaned against the counter, his arms crossed. 'She shouldn't have to do that alone.'

Lena stared at her hands. There was something under her fingernails. She couldn't tell if it was dirt or blood. She put her finger in her mouth, using her bottom teeth to clean it.

Hank watched this. He said, 'You could come by later if you felt like it.' Lena shook her head, biting the nail. She would tear it off to the quick before she let the blood stay there. 'I have to get up early for work tomorrow,' she lied.

'But if you change your mind?'

'Maybe,' she mumbled around her finger. She tasted blood, surprised to see that it was her own. The cuticle had come away on the nail. A bright red dot radiated from the spot.

Hank stood, staring, then grabbed his coat off the back of his chair. They had been through this kind of thing before, though admittedly never on this scale. It was an old, familiar dance, and they both knew the moves. Hank took one step forward, Lena took two steps back. Now wasn't the time to change any of this.

He said, 'You can call me if you need me. You know that, right?'

'Mm-hm,' she mumbled, pressing her lips together. She was going to cry again, and Lena thought that a part of her would die if she broke down in front of Hank again.

He seemed to sense this because he put his hand on her shoulder, then kissed the top of her head.

Lena kept her head down, waiting for the click as the front door closed. She gave a long sigh as Hank's car backed out of the driveway.

The kettle was steaming, but the whistle had not started yet. Lena did not particularly like tea, but she rummaged around in the cabinets anyway, looking for the bags. She found a box of Tummy Mint just as a knock came at the back door.

She expected to see Hank, so Lena was surprised when she opened the door.

'Oh, hi,' she said, rubbing her ear as a shrill noise came. She realized the teakettle was whistling and said, 'Hold on a second.'

She was turning off the burner when she felt a presence behind her, then a sharp sting came to her left thigh.

SEVENTEEN

Sara stood in front of the body of Julia Matthews with her arms crossed over her chest. She stared at the girl, trying to assess her with a clinical eye, trying to separate the girl whose life Sara had saved from the dead woman on the table. The incision Sara had made to access Julia's heart was not yet healed, the black sutures still thick with dried blood. A small hole was at the base of the woman's chin. Burns around the entrance wound revealed the barrel of the gun was pressed into the chin when it was fired. A gaping hole at the back of the girl's head revealed the exit wound. Bone hung from the open skull, like macabre ornaments on a bloody Christmas tree. The smell of gunpowder was in the air.

Julia Matthews's body lay on the porcelain autopsy table much as Sibyl Adams's had a few days ago. At the head of the table was a faucet with a black rubber hose attached. Hanging over this was an organ scale much like the scales grocers use to weigh fruit and vegetables. Beside the table were the tools of autopsy: a scalpel, a sixteen-inch-long surgically sharpened bread knife, a pair of equally sharpened scissors, a pair of forceps, or 'pickups,' a Stryker saw to cut bone, and a set of longhandled pruning shears one would normally find in a garage by the lawn mower. Cathy Linton had a similar set for herself, and whenever Sara saw her mother pruning azaleas she always thought about using the shears at the morgue to cut away the rib cage.

Sara mindlessly followed the various steps for preparing the body of Julia Matthews for autopsy. Her thoughts were elsewhere, back to the night before, when Julia Matthews was on Sara's car; back to when the girl was alive and had a chance.

Sara had never minded performing autopsies before, never been disturbed by death. Opening a body was like opening a book; there were many things which could be learned from tissue and organ. In death, the body was available for thorough evaluation. Part of the reason Sara had taken the job as medical examiner for Grant County was that she had become bored with her practice at the clinic. The coroner's job presented a challenge, an opportunity to learn a new skill and to help people. Though the thought of cutting up Julia Matthews, exposing her body to more abuse, cut through Sara like a knife.

Again, Sara looked at what was left of Julia Matthews's head. Gunshots to the head were notoriously unpredictable. Most times the victim ended up comatose, a vegetable who, through the miracles of modern science, quietly lived out the rest of the life they did not want in the first place. Julia Matthews had done a better job than most when she put the gun under her chin and pulled the trigger. The bullet had entered her skull at an upward trajectory, breaking the spheroid, plowing along the lateral cerebral fissure, then busting out through the occipital bone. The back of the head was gone, affording a straight view into the brain case. Unlike in her earlier suicide attempt witnessed by the scarring on her wrists, Julia Matthews had meant to end her life. Unquestionably, the girl had known what she was doing.

Sara felt sick to her stomach. She wanted to shake the girl back to life, to demand she go on living, to ask her how she could have gone through everything that had happened to her in the last few days only to end up taking her life. It seemed that the very horrors Julia Matthews had survived had also ended up killing her.

'You okay?' Jeffrey asked, giving her a concerned look.

'Yeah,' Sara managed, wondering if she really was. She felt raw, like a wound that would not scab. Sara knew that if Jeffrey made a pass at her, she would take him up on the offer. All she could think of was how good it would feel to let him take her into his arms, to feel his lips kissing hers, his tongue in her mouth. Her body ached for him now in a way she had not ached for him in years. She did not particularly want sex, she just wanted the assurance of his presence. She wanted to feel protected. She wanted to belong to him. Sara had learned a long time ago that sex was the only way Jeffrey knew how to give her these things.

From across the table, Jeffrey asked, 'Sara?'

She opened her mouth, thinking to proposition him, but stopped herself. So much had happened in the last few years. So much had changed. The man she wanted did not really exist anymore. Sara wasn't sure if he ever had.

She cleared her throat. 'Yeah?'

'You want to hold off on this?' he asked.

'No,' Sara answered in a clipped tone, inwardly berating herself for thinking she needed Jeffrey. The truth was she didn't. She had gotten this far without him. She could certainly go further.

She tapped her foot on the remote for the Dictaphone, stating, 'This is the unembalmed body of a thin but well-built, well-nourished young adult white female weighing' – Sara looked at the chalkboard over Jeffrey's shoulder where she had made notations – 'one hundred and twelve pounds and having a length of sixty-four inches.' She tapped the recorder off, taking a deep breath to clear her mind. Sara was having trouble breathing.

'Sara?'

She tapped the recorder back on, shaking her head at him. The sympathy she had so wanted a few minutes ago now irritated her. She felt exposed.

She dictated, 'The appearance of the decedent is consistent with the stated age of twenty-two. The body has been refrigerated for a period of no less than three hours and is cool to the touch.' Sara stopped, clearing her throat. 'Rigor mortis is formed and fixed in the upper and lower extremities, and patches of livor mortis are seen posteriorly on the trunk and extremities, except in areas of pressure.'

And on it went, this clinical description of a woman who only hours ago had been battered but alive, who weeks ago had been content if not happy. Sara cataloged the exterior appearance of Julia Matthews, imagining in her mind what the woman must have gone through. Was she awake when her teeth were pulled out so that her attacker could rape her face? Was she conscious when her rectum was being ripped open? Did the drugs block the sensations when she was nailed to the floor? An autopsy could only reveal the physical damage; the girl's state of mind, her level of consciousness, would remain a mystery. No one would know what was going through her mind as she was assaulted. No one would ever see exactly what this girl had seen. Sara could only guess, and she did not like the images such guessing brought to mind. Again, she saw herself on the hospital gurney. Again, she saw herself being examined.

Sara forced herself to look up from the body, feeling shaky and out of place. Jeffrey was staring at her, a strange look on his face. 'What?' she asked.

He shook his head, still keeping his eyes on her.

'I wish,' Sara began, then stopped, clearing the lump in her throat. 'I wish you wouldn't look at me like that, okay?' She waited, but he did not acknowledge her request.

He asked, 'How am I looking at you?'

'Predatorily,' she answered, but that wasn't quite right. He was looking at her the way she wanted him to look at her. There was a sense of responsibility to his expression, like he wanted nothing more than to take charge of things, to make things better. She hated herself for wanting this.

'It's unintentional,' he said.

She snapped off her gloves. 'Okay.'

'I'm worried about you, Sara. I want you to talk to me about what's going on.'

Sara walked toward the supply cabinet, not wanting to have this conversation over the body of Julia Matthews. 'You don't get to do that anymore. Remember why?'

If she had slapped him, his expression would have been the same. 'I never stopped caring about you.'

She swallowed hard, trying not to let this get to her. 'Thanks.'

'Sometimes,' he began, 'when I wake up in the morning, I forget that you're not there. I forget that I lost you.'

'Kind of like when you forgot you were married to me?'

He walked toward her, but she stepped back until she

was a few inches from the cabinet. He stood in front of her, his hands on her arms. 'I still love you.'

'That's not enough.'

He stepped closer to her. 'What is?'

'Jeffrey,' she said. 'Please.'

He finally backed away, his tone sharp as he asked, 'What do you think?' He was referring to the body. 'Do you think you'll find anything?'

Sara crossed her arms, feeling the need to protect herself. 'I think she died with her secrets.'

Jeffrey gave her a strange look, probably because Sara wasn't one to buy into melodrama. She made a conscious effort to act more like herself, to be more clinical about the situation, but even the thought of doing this was too emotionally taxing.

Sara kept her hand steady as she made the standard Y-incision across the chest. The sound as she skinned back the flesh cut through her thoughts. She tried to talk over them. 'How are her parents holding up?'

Jeffrey said, 'You can't imagine how horrible it was telling them she'd been raped. And then, this.' He indicated the body. 'You can't imagine.'

Sara's mind wandered again. She saw her own father standing over a hospital bed, her mother embracing him from behind. She closed her eyes for a few seconds, willing this image from her mind. She would not be able to do this if she kept putting herself in Julia Matthews's place.

'Sara?' Jeffrey asked.

Sara looked up, surprised to realize that she had stopped the autopsy. She was standing in front of the body, arms crossed in front of her. Jeffrey waited patiently, not asking her the obvious question.

Sara picked up the scalpel and went to work, dictating, 'The body is opened with the usual Y-incision and the organs of the thoracic and abdominal cavities are in their normal anatomic positions.'

Jeffrey started talking again as soon as she stopped. Thankfully, he chose a different topic this time. He said, 'I don't know what I'm going to do about Lena.'

'What's that?' Sara asked, glad for the sound of his voice.

'She's not holding up well,' he said. 'I told her to take a couple of days off.'

'Do you think she will?'

'I think she actually might.'

Sara picked up the scissors, cutting the pericardial sac with quick snips. 'So, then, what's the problem?'

'She's at the edge. I can sense that. I just don't know what to do.' He indicated Julia Matthews. 'I don't want her to end up doing something like this.'

Sara scrutinized him over the rim of her glasses. She did not know whether or not he was using dime store psychology, hiding his concern for Sara by pretending a concern for Lena, or if he really was looking for advice on how to handle Lena.

She gave him an answer that would suit either scenario. 'Lena Adams?' She shook her head no, certain of this one thing. 'She's a fighter. People like Lena don't kill themselves. They kill other people, but they don't kill themselves.'

'I know,' Jeffrey answered. He was quiet then as Sara clamped off and removed the stomach.

'This won't be pleasant,' she warned, placing the stomach in a stainless steel bowl. Jeffrey had been through plenty of autopsies before, but there was nothing so pungent as the odors of the digestive tract.

'Hey.' Sara stopped, surprised at what she saw. 'Look at this.'

'What is it?'

She stood to the side so that he could see the contents of the stomach. The digestive juices were black and soupy, so she used a strainer to scoop out the contents.

'What is it?' he repeated.

'I don't know. Maybe seeds of some sort,' Sara told him, using a pair of pickups to remove one. 'I think we should call Mark Webster.'

'Here,' he offered, holding out an evidence bag.

She dropped the seed into the bag, asking, 'You think he wants to get caught?'

'They all want to get caught, don't they?' he countered. 'Look at where he left them. Both in semipublic places, both displayed. He's getting off on the risk as much as anything else.'

'Yeah,' she agreed, willing herself not to say more. She did not want to go into the gritty details of the case. She wanted to do her job and get out of here, away from Jeffrey.

Jeffrey didn't seem to want to comply. He asked, 'The seeds are potent, right?'

Sara nodded.

'So, you think he kept her out of it while he was raping her?'

'I couldn't begin to guess,' she answered truthfully.

He paused, as if he did not know how to phrase his next sentence.

'What?' she prompted.

'Lena,' he said. 'I mean, Julia told Lena that she enjoyed it.'

Sara felt her brow furrow. 'What?'

'Not exactly that she enjoyed it, but that he made love to her.'

'He pulled her teeth out and ripped her rectum open. How could anyone call what he did to her making love?'

He shrugged, as if the answer was lost on him, but said, 'Maybe he kept her so drugged up that she didn't feel it. Maybe she didn't know what was going on until after.'

Sara considered this. 'It's possible,' she said, uncomfortable with the scenario.

'It's what she said, anyway,' he answered.

The room was quiet but for the compressor on the freezer cycling down. Sara went back to the autopsy, using clamps to section off the small and large intestines. They were limp in her hands, like wet spaghetti, as she lifted them out of the body. Julia Matthews had not eaten anything of substance during the last few days of her life. Her digestive system was relatively empty.

'Let's see,' Sara said, placing the intestines on the grocer's scale to weigh them. A metallic clink came, like a penny being dropped into a tin cup.

'What's that?' Jeffrey asked.

Sara did not answer him. She picked the intestines back up, then dropped them again. The same noise came, a tinny vibration through the scale. 'Something's in there,' Sara mumbled, walking over to the light box mounted on the wall. She used her elbow to turn on the light, illuminating Julia Matthews's X rays. Her pelvic series was in the center.

'See anything?' Jeffrey asked.

'Whatever it is, it's in the large intestines,' Sara answered, staring at what looked like a splinter in the bottom half of the rectum. She had not noticed the sliver before or had assumed it was a problem with the film. The portable X ray in the morgue was old and not known for its reliability.

Sara studied the film for another few seconds, then walked back to the scale. She separated the terminal ileum at the ileocecal valve and carried the large intestines to the foot of the table. After using the faucet to clean off the blood, she squeezed her fingers down from the base of the sigmoid colon, searching for the object that had made the noise. She found a hard lump about five inches into the rectum.

'Hand me the scalpel,' she ordered, holding out her hand. Jeffrey did as he was told, watching her work.

Sara made a small incision, releasing a foul odor into the room. Jeffrey stepped back, but Sara did not have that luxury. She used the pickups to remove an object that was approximately a half inch long. A rinse under the faucet revealed that it was a small key.

'A handcuff key?' Jeffrey asked, leaning over for a better look.

'Yes,' Sara answered, feeling a little light-headed. 'It was forced up into the rectum from the anus.'

'Why?'

'I guess so that we would find it,' Sara answered. 'Could you get an evidence bag?'

Jeffrey did as he was told, opening the bag so that she could drop the key in. 'Do you think we'll find anything on it?'

'Bacteria,' she answered. 'If you mean fingerprints, I seriously doubt it.' She pressed her lips together, thinking this through. 'Turn the lights off for a second.'

'What are you thinking?'

Sara walked toward the light box, using her elbow to turn it off. 'I'm thinking he put the key up there relatively early in the game. I'm thinking the edge is sharp. Maybe it tore the condom.'

Jeffrey walked over to the light switch as Sara peeled off her gloves. She picked up the black light, which would highlight traces of seminal fluid.

'Ready?' he asked.

'Yeah,' she said, and the lights went out.

Sara blinked several times, letting her eyes adjust to the unnatural light. Slowly, she cast the black light along the incision she had made in the rectum. 'Hold this,' she said, giving Jeffrey the light. She slipped on a fresh pair of gloves and with the scalpel opened the incision farther. A small pocket of purple showed in the opening.

Jeffrey gave a small sigh, as if he had been holding his breath. 'Is it enough for a DNA comparison?'

Sara stared at the purplish glowing matter. 'I think so.'

Sara tiptoed through her sister's apartment, peeking around the bedroom door to make sure Tessa was still alone.

'Tessie?' she whispered, shaking her slightly.

'What?' Tessa grumbled, rolling over. 'What time is it?'

Sara looked at the clock on the bedside table. 'About two in the morning.'

'What?' Tessa repeated, rubbing her eyes. 'What's wrong?'

Sara said, 'Scoot over.'

Tessa did as she was told, holding up the sheet for Sara. 'What's wrong?'

Sara did not answer. She pulled the comforter up under her chin.

'Is something wrong?' Tessa repeated.

'Nothing's wrong.'

'Is that girl really dead?'

Sara closed her eyes. 'Yes.'

Tessa sat up in bed, turning on the light. 'We've got to talk, Sara.'

Sara rolled over, her back to her sister. 'I don't want to talk.'

'I don't care,' Tessa answered, pulling the covers away from Sara. 'Sit up.'

'Don't order me around,' Sara countered, feeling annoyed. She had come here to feel safe so that she could sleep, not to be pushed around by her kid sister.

'Sara,' Tessa began. 'You have got to tell Jeffrey what happened.'

Sara sat up, angry that this was starting again. 'No,' she answered, her lips a tight line.

'Sara,' Tessa said, her voice firm. 'Hare told me about that girl. He told me about the tape on her mouth and about the way she was put on your car.'

'He shouldn't talk about that kind of stuff with you.'

'He wasn't telling it as a point of interest,' Tessa said. She got out of bed, obviously angry.

'What are you so pissed at me about?' Sara demanded, standing, too. They faced each other on opposite sides of the room, the bed between them.

Sara put her hands on her hips. 'It's not my fault, okay? I did everything I could do to help that girl, and if she couldn't live with it, then that's her choice.'

'Great choice, huh? I guess it's better to put a bullet in your brain than to keep it in all the time.'

'What the fuck does that mean?'

'You know what it means,' Tessa snapped back. 'You need to tell Jeffrey, Sara.'

'I won't.'

Tessa seemed to size her up. She crossed her arms over her chest, threatening, 'If you don't, I will.'

'What?' Sara gasped. If Tessa had punched her, Sara would have felt less shock. Her mouth opened in surprise. 'You wouldn't.'

'Yes, I would,' Tessa answered, her mind obviously made up. 'If I don't, then Mom will.'

'You and Mom hatched this little plan together?' Sara

gave a humorless laugh. 'I suppose Dad's in on it, too?' She threw her hands up into the air. 'My whole family's ganging up on me.'

'We're not ganging up on you,' Tessa countered. 'We're trying to help you.'

'What happened to me,' Sara began, her words clipped and precise, 'has nothing to do with what happened to Sibyl Adams and Julia Matthews.' She leaned across the bed, giving Tessa a look of warning. They could both play at this game.

'That's not your decision to make,' Tessa countered.

Sara felt her anger boiling over at the threat. 'You want me to tell you how they're different, Tessie? You want to know the things I know about these cases?' She did not give her sister time to answer. 'For one, nobody carved a cross on my chest and left me to bleed out in the toilet.' She paused, knowing the impact her words would have. If Tessa wanted to push Sara, Sara knew how to push back.

Sara continued, 'For another, no one knocked out my front teeth so they could sodomize my face.'

Tessa's hand went to her mouth. 'Oh, God.'

'Nobody nailed my hands and feet to the floor so he could fuck me.'

'No,' Tessa breathed, tears coming to her eyes.

Sara could not stop herself, even though her words were obviously acid in Tessa's ears. 'Nobody scrubbed out my mouth with Clorox. Nobody shaved my pubic hair so there wouldn't be any trace evidence.' She paused for breath. 'Nobody stabbed a hole in my gut so he could –' Sara forced herself to stop, knowing she was going too far. Still, a small sob escaped from Tessa's mouth as she made the connection. Her eyes had been on Sara's the entire time, and the look of horror on her face sent waves of guilt through Sara.

Sara whispered, 'I'm sorry, Tessie. I'm so sorry.'

Tessa's hand slowly fell from her mouth. She said, 'Jeffrey is a policeman.'

Sara put her hand to her chest. 'I know that.'

'You're so beautiful,' Tessa said. 'And you're smart and you're funny and you're tall.'

Sara laughed so that she wouldn't cry.

'And this time twelve years ago, you were raped,' Tessa finished.

'I know that.'

'He sends you postcards every year, Sara. He knows where you live.'

'I know that.'

'Sara,' Tessa began, a begging quality to her voice. 'You have to tell Jeffrey.'

'I can't.'

Tessa stood firm. 'You don't have a choice.'

FRIDAY

EIGHTEEN

Jeffrey slipped on a pair of underwear and limped toward the kitchen. His knee was still stiff from the buckshot, and his stomach had been upset since he walked into Julia Matthews's room. He was worried about Lena. He was worried about Sara. He was worried about his town.

Brad Stephens had taken the DNA sample to Macon a few hours ago. It would take at least a week to get something back, perhaps another week to get time on the FBI DNA database to cross-check for known offenders. As with most police work, this was a waiting game. Meanwhile, there was no telling what the perpetrator was up to. For all Jeffrey knew, he could be stalking his next victim at this very moment. He could be raping his next victim at this very moment, doing things to her that only an animal would think to do.

Jeffrey opened the refrigerator, taking out the milk. On the way to get a glass, he flicked the overhead light switch, but nothing happened. He mumbled a curse toward himself as he took a glass out of the cabinet. He had disconnected the kitchen lights a couple of weeks ago when a new fixture he had ordered arrived in the mail. A call had come from the station just as he was stripping the wires, and the chandelier sat upended in its box, waiting for Jeffrey to find the time to hang it. At this rate, Jeffrey would be eating by the light from the refrigerator for the next few years.

He finished his milk and limped over to the sink to rinse the glass. He wanted to call Sara, to check on her, but knew better than that. She was blocking him out for her own reasons. He didn't really have a leg to stand on since the divorce. Maybe she was with Jeb tonight. He had heard through Marla who had been talking to Marty Ringo that Sara and Jeb were seeing each other again. He vaguely remembered Sara saying something about a date at the hospital the other night, but his mind could not connect her words. Since the memory had come after Marla had deigned to mention the gossip to him, he could not rely on it.

Jeffrey groaned as he sat back down on the bar stool in front of the kitchen island. He had built the island months ago. He had actually built it twice, because he had not been pleased with the way it had looked the first time. Jeffrey was above all things a perfectionist, and he hated when things weren't symmetrical. Since he lived in an old house, this meant that he was constantly having to adjust and readjust, because there wasn't a wall in the house that was straight.

A slight breeze stirred the thick plastic strips lining the back wall of the kitchen. He was vacillating between French doors and a wall of windows, or extending the kitchen out about ten feet into the backyard. Some kind of breakfast nook would be nice, a place to sit in the mornings and look out at the birds in the backyard. What he really wanted was to put a large deck out there with a hot tub or maybe one of those fancy outdoor barbecues. Whatever he did, he wanted to keep the house open. Jeffrey liked the way the light came in during the day through the semitransparent strips. He liked being able to see into the backyard, especially at times like right now, when he saw someone walking back there.

Jeffrey stood, grabbing a bat out of the laundry room. He slid through a crack in the plastic strips, tiptoeing across the lawn. The grass was wet from a slight mist in the night air, and Jeffrey shivered from the chill, hoping to God he did not get shot again, especially since he was dressed only in a pair of underwear. The thought occurred to him that whoever was lurking in the backyard might collapse from laughter rather than fear at seeing Jeffrey standing in the yard, naked but for his green boxers, holding a bat over his head.

He heard a familiar noise. It was a lapping, licking sound, the kind a dog made while grooming. He squinted in the moonlight, making out three figures by the side of the house. Two of them were short enough to be dogs. One of them was tall enough to only be Sara. She was looking into his bedroom window.

Jeffrey let the bat hang down as he tiptoed up behind her. He wasn't worried about Billy or Bob, as the two greyhounds were the laziest animals he had ever seen. True to form, they barely moved as he sneaked up behind her.

'Sara?'

'Oh, Jesus.' Sara jumped, tripping over the nearest dog. Jeffrey reached forward, catching her before she fell on her backside.

Jeffrey laughed, giving Bob a pat on the head. 'Peeping Tom?' he asked.

'You asshole,' Sara hissed, slapping her hands into his chest. 'You scared the shit out of me.'

'What?' Jeffrey asked innocently. 'I'm not the one sneaking around your house.'

'Like you haven't before.'

'That's me,' Jeffrey pointed out. 'Not you.' He leaned

against the bat. Now that his adrenaline had stopped pumping, the dull ache had come back to his leg. 'You want to explain why you're looking in my window in the middle of the night?'

'I didn't want to wake you up if you were asleep.'

'I was in the kitchen.'

'In the dark?' Sara crossed her arms, levering him with a nasty look. 'Alone?'

'Come on in,' Jeffrey offered, not waiting for her to respond. He kept his pace slow as he walked back toward the kitchen, glad when he heard Sara's footsteps behind him. She was wearing a pair of faded blue jeans with an equally old white button-down shirt.

'You walk the dogs over here?'

'I borrowed Tessa's car,' Sara said, scratching Bob on the head.

'Good thinking, bringing your attack dogs.'

'I'm glad you weren't looking to kill me.'

'What makes you think I wasn't?' Jeffrey asked, using the bat to hold the plastic aside so that she could get into the house.

Sara looked at the plastic, then at him. 'I love what you've done to the place.'

'It needs a woman's touch,' Jeffrey suggested.

'I'm sure there are plenty of volunteers.'

He suppressed a groan as he headed back into the kitchen. 'Power's out in here,' he offered, lighting a candle by the stove.

'Ha-ha,' Sara said, trying the light switch nearest her. She walked across the room, trying the other switch as Jeffrey lit another candle. 'What's the deal?'

'Old house.' He shrugged, not wanting to confess his laziness. 'Brad took the sample to Macon.'

'A couple of weeks, huh?'

'Yeah,' he nodded. 'Do you think he's a cop?'

'Brad?'

'No, the perpetrator. Do you think he's a cop? Maybe that's why he left the handcuff key in . . . there.' He paused. 'You know, as a clue.'

'Maybe he uses handcuffs to restrain them,' Sara said. 'Maybe he's into S&M. Maybe his mama used to cuff him to the bed when he was a little boy.'

He was puzzled by her flippant tone but knew better than to comment on it.

Out of the blue, Sara said, 'I want a screwdriver.'

Jeffrey frowned at this, but he walked over to his toolbox and rummaged around. 'Phillips?'

'No, a drink,' Sara answered. She opened the freezer door, taking out the vodka.

'I don't think I've got orange juice,' he said as she opened the other door.

'This'll do,' she said, holding out the cranberry juice. She rummaged in the cabinets for a glass, then poured what looked like a very stiff drink.

Jeffrey watched all this, concerned. Sara seldom drank, and when she did a glass of wine could turn her tipsy. He had never seen her drink anything stronger than a margarita their entire marriage.

Sara shuddered as she swallowed the drink. 'How much was I supposed to put?' she asked.

'Probably a third of what you poured,' he answered, taking the drink from her. He took a small sip, nearly gagging from the taste. 'Jesus Christ,' he managed around a cough. 'Are you trying to kill yourself?'

'Me and Julia Matthews,' she tossed back. 'Do you have anything sweet?'

Jeffrey opened his mouth to ask her what the hell she meant by that comment, but Sara was already rummaging through the cabinets.

He offered, 'There's some pudding in the fridge. Bottom shelf in the back.'

'Fat free?' she asked.

'Nope.'

'Good,' Sara said, bending at the waist to find the pudding.

Jeffrey crossed his arms, watching her. He wanted to ask her what she was doing in his kitchen in the middle of the morning. He wanted to ask her what had been going on lately, why she was acting so odd.

'Jeff?' Sara asked, rooting through the fridge.

'Hmm?'

'Are you looking at my ass?'

Jeffrey smiled. He hadn't been, but he answered, 'Yeah.'

Sara stood, holding the pudding cup in the air like a trophy. 'Last one.'

'Yep.'

Sara pulled the top off the pudding as she scooted onto the counter. 'This is getting to be a bad thing.'

'You think?'

'Well.' She shrugged, licking the pudding off the top. 'College girls being raped, killing themselves. That's not what we're all about, is it?'

Again, Jeffrey was surprised by her cavalier attitude. This wasn't like Sara, but lately he wasn't sure exactly how she was.

'I guess not,' he said.

'You tell her parents?'

Jeffrey answered, 'Frank picked them up at the airport.' He paused, then said, 'Her father.' He stopped again. The sight of Jon Matthews's anguished face was not something Jeffrey would soon forget.

'Father took it hard, huh?' Sara said. 'Daddies don't like to know their little girls have been messed with.'

'I guess not,' Jeffrey answered, wondering at her choice of words.

'You would guess right.'

'Yeah,' Jeffrey said. 'He took it really hard.'

Something flashed in Sara's eyes, but she looked down before he could tell what was going on. She took a long drink from her glass, spilling some down the front of her shirt. She actually giggled.

Despite his better judgment, Jeffrey asked, 'What's wrong with you, Sara?'

She pointed at his waist. 'When'd you start wearing those?' she asked.

Jeffrey looked down. Since the only thing he was wearing were his green boxers, he assumed that's what she meant. He looked back at her, shrugging. 'A while ago.'

'Less than two years,' she noted, licking more pudding.

'Yeah,' he offered, walking over to her, arms out from his sides, showing off his underwear. 'You like 'em?'

She clapped her hands.

'What're you doing here, Sara?'

She stared at him for a few seconds, then put the pudding down beside her. She leaned back, her heels lightly hitting the bottom cabinets. 'I was thinking the other day about that time I was on the dock. Do you remember?'

He shook his head, because they had spent practically every free second of every summer on the dock.

'I had just gone for a swim, and I was sitting on the dock, brushing my hair. And you came up and you took the brush and you started to brush it for me.'

He nodded, remembering that was the very thing he

had been thinking about when he woke up in the hospital this morning. 'I remember.'

'You brushed my hair for at least an hour. Do you remember that?'

He smiled.

'You just brushed my hair, and then we got ready for dinner. Remember?'

He nodded again.

'What did I do wrong?' she asked, and the look in her eyes almost killed him. 'Was it sex?'

He shook his head. Sex with Sara had been the most fulfilling experience of his adult life. 'Of course not,' he said.

'Did you want me to cook you dinner? Or be there more when you got home?'

He tried to laugh. 'You did cook me dinner, remember? I was sick for three days.'

'I'm being serious, Jeff. I want to know what I did wrong.'

'It wasn't you,' he answered, knowing the excuse was trite even as he finished the sentence. 'It was me.'

Sara sighed heavily. She reached for the glass, finishing the drink in one gulp.

'I was stupid,' he continued, knowing he should just shut up. 'I was scared because I loved you so much.' He paused, wanting to say this the right way. 'I didn't think you needed me as much as I needed you.'

She levered him with a gaze. 'Do you still want me to need you?'

He was surprised to feel her hand on his chest, her fingers lightly stroking his hair. He closed his eyes as she traced her fingers up to his lips.

She said, 'Right now, I really need you.'

He opened his eyes. For just a split second, he thought she was joking. 'What did you say?'

'You don't want it now that you have it?' Sara asked, still touching his lips.

He licked the tip of her finger with his tongue.

Sara smiled, her eyes narrowing, as if to read his mind. 'Are you going to answer me?'

'Yeah,' he said, not even remembering the question. Then, 'Yes. Yes, I still want you.'

She started kissing his neck, her tongue making light strokes along his skin. He put his hands around her waist, pulling her closer to the edge of the counter. She wrapped her legs around his waist.

'Sara.' He sighed, trying to kiss her mouth, but she pulled away, instead letting her lips travel down his chest. 'Sara,' he repeated. 'Let me make love to you.'

She looked back at him, a sly smile on her face. 'I don't want to make love.'

His mouth opened, but he did not know how to respond. Finally he managed, 'What does that mean?'

'It means . . . ' she began, then took his hand and held it up to her mouth. He watched as she traced the tip of his index finger with her tongue. Slowly, she took his finger into her mouth and sucked it. After what seemed not nearly enough time, she took it out, smiling playfully. 'Well?'

Jeffrey leaned in to kiss her, but she slid off the counter before he could. He moaned as Sara took her time kissing her way down his chest, nipping the band of his underwear with her teeth. With difficulty, he knelt on the floor in front of her, again trying to kiss her mouth. Again, she pulled away.

'I want to kiss you,' he said, surprised at the begging tone to his voice.

She shook her head, unbuttoning her shirt. 'I can think of some other things you can do with your mouth.'

'Sara –'

She shook her head. 'Don't talk, Jeffrey.'

He thought it was odd that she had said this, because the best part of sex with Sara was the talking. He put his hands to either side of her face. 'Come here,' he said.

'What?'

'What's wrong with you?'

'Nothing.'

'I don't believe you.' He waited for her to answer his question, but she just stared at him.

He asked, 'Why won't you let me kiss you?'

'I just don't feel like kissing.' Her smile was not as sly. 'On the mouth.'

'What's wrong?' he repeated.

She narrowed her eyes at him as a warning.

'Answer me,' he repeated.

Sara kept her eyes on him as she let her hand travel down past the waist of his shorts. She pressed her hand against him, as if to make sure he got her meaning. 'I don't want to talk to you.'

He stopped her hand with his own. 'Look at me.'

She shook her head, and when he made her look up she closed her eyes.

He whispered, 'What's wrong with you?'

Sara didn't answer. She kissed him full on the mouth, her tongue forcing its way past his teeth. It was a sloppy kiss, far from what he was used to with Sara, but there was an underlying passion that would have buckled his knees had he been standing.

She stopped suddenly, dropping her head to his chest. He tried to make her look back up at him, but she wouldn't.

He asked, 'Sara?'

He felt her arms go around him again, but in a very

different way from before. There was a desperate quality to her tightening hold, as if she were drowning.

'Just hold me,' she begged. 'Please just hold me.'

Jeffrey woke with a start. He reached out, knowing even as he did that Sara would not be there beside him. He vaguely recalled her sneaking out some time ago, but Jeffrey had been too tired to move, let alone stop her. He turned over, pressing his face into the pillow she had used. He could smell lavender from her shampoo and a slight trace of the perfume she wore. Jeffrey held the pillow, rolling over onto his back. He stared at the ceiling, trying to remember what had happened last night. He still could not get his head around it. He had carried Sara to bed. She had cried softly on his shoulder. He had been so afraid of what was behind her tears that he had not questioned her anymore.

Jeffrey sat up, scratching his chest. He could not stay in bed all day. There was still the list of convicted sexual offenders to complete. He still needed to interview Ryan Gordon and whoever had been at the library with Julia Matthews the last night she had been seen before the abduction. He also needed to see Sara, to make sure she was okay.

He stretched, touching the top of the door jamb as he walked into the bathroom. He stopped in front of the toilet. There was a stack of papers on the sink basin. A silver sliding clip was across the top pages, binding together what looked to be about two hundred sheets of paper. The pages looked dog-eared and yellowed, as if someone had paged through them a number of times. It was, Jeffrey recognized, a trial transcript.

He looked around the bathroom, as if the transcript fairy who had left it might still be around. The only person who had been in the house was Sara, and he could not think why she would leave something like this. He read the title page, noting the date was from twelve years ago. The case was the *State of Georgia v. Jack Allen Wright.*

A yellow Post-it note was sticking out from one of the pages. He flipped the transcript open, stopping at what he saw. Sara's name was listed at the top of the page. Another name, Ruth Jones, probably the district attorney who had prosecuted the case, was listed as the questioner.

Jeffrey sat on the toilet and began to read Ruth Jones's examination of Sara Linton.

Q. Dr. Linton, could you please tell us in your own words the events which took place on the twenty-third day of April, this time last year?

A. I was working at Grady Hospital where I was a pediatric resident. I had a difficult day and decided to go for a drive in my car between shifts.

Q. Was there anything unusual you noticed at this time?

A. When I got to my car, the word cunt had been scraped into the passenger's side door. I thought perhaps this was the work of a vandal, so I used some duct tape I kept in the trunk to cover it.

Q. Then what did you do?

A. I went back into the hospital for my shift.

Q. Would you like a drink of water?

A. No, thank you. I went to the rest room, and while I was washing my hands at the sink, Jack Wright came in.

Q. The defendant?

A. That's correct. He came in. He was carrying a mop and wearing grey coveralls. I knew he was the janitor. He apologized for not knocking, said he'd come back later to clean, then left the bathroom.

Q. Then what happened?

A. I went into the stall to use the bathroom. The defendant, Jack Wright, jumped down from the ceiling. It was a drop ceiling. He handcuffed my hands to the handicapped railing, then taped my mouth shut with silver duct tape.

Q. Are you sure this was the defendant?

A. Yes. He had on a red ski mask, but I recognized his eyes. He has very distinctive blue eyes. I remember thinking before that with his long blond hair, beard, and blue eyes he looked like Bible pictures of Jesus. I am certain that it was Jack Wright who attacked me.

Q. Is there any other distinguishing mark that leads you to believe it was the defendant who raped you?

A. I saw a tattoo on his arm of Jesus nailed to the cross with the words JESUS above it and SAVES below it. I recognized this tattoo as belonging to Jack Wright, a janitor at the hospital. I had seen him several times before in the hallway, but we had never spoken to each other.

Q. What happened next, Dr. Linton?

A. Jack Wright pulled me down off the toilet. My ankles were pinned by my pants. They were on the floor. My pants. Around my ankles.

Q. Please, take your time, Dr. Linton.

A. I was pulled forward, but my arms were back behind me like this. He kept me pulled forward by putting one arm around my waist. He held a long knife, approximately six inches, to my face. He cut my lip to warn me, I suppose.

Q. Then what did the defendant do?

A. He put his penis in me and raped me.

Q. Dr. Linton, could you tell us what, if anything, the defendant said during the time he raped you?

A. He kept referring to me as 'cunt.'

Q. Could you tell us what happened next?

A. He tried several times to bring himself to ejaculation, but was unsuccessful. He pulled his penis out of me and brought himself to climax [mumbled]

Q. Could you repeat that?

A. He brought himself to climax on my face and chest.

Q. Could you tell us what happened then?

A. He cursed me again, then stabbed me with his knife. In the left side, here.

Q. Then what happened?

A. I tasted something in my mouth. I choked. It was vinegar.

Q. He poured vinegar into your mouth?

A. Yes, he had a small vial, like a perfume sample would come in. He tilted it into my mouth and said, 'It is finished.'

Q. Does this phrase have any particular significance to you, Dr. Linton?

A. It's from John, in the King James version of the Bible. 'It is finished.' According to John, these are the last words Jesus says as he's dying on the cross. He calls for something to drink, and they give him vinegar. He drinks the vinegar, then, to quote the verse, he gives up the ghost. He dies.

Q. This is from the crucifixion?

A. Yes.

Q. Jesus says, 'It is finished.'

A. Yes.

Q. His arms pinned back like this?

A. Yes.

Q. A sword is stabbed into his side?

A. Yes.

Q. Was anything else said?

A. No. Jack Wright said this, then left the bathroom.

Q. Dr. Linton, do you have any idea how long you were left in the bathroom?

A. No.

Q. Were you still handcuffed?

A. Yes. I was still handcuffed and I was on my knees looking down at the floor. I was unable to right myself, to sit back.

Q. Then what happened?

A. One of the nurses came in. She saw the blood on the floor and started to scream. A few seconds later, Dr. Lange, my supervisor, came into the room. I'd lost a great deal of blood, and I was still handcuffed. They started to help me, but they couldn't do much with the cuffs on. Jack Wright had rigged the lock so that they would not open. He had shoved something into the lock, a toothpick or something. A locksmith had to be called to cut them off. I passed out during this time. The position of my body was such that blood continued to pool from the stab wound. I lost a great deal of blood during this time from the stab wound.

Q. Dr. Linton, take your time. Would you like to take a short break?

A. No, I want to continue.

Q. Could you tell me what happened subsequent to the rape?

A. I became pregnant from this contact, and subsequently developed an ectopic pregnancy, which is to say that an egg was implanted in my fallopian

275

tube. There was a rupture which caused bleeding into my abdomen.

Q. What effect, if any, has this had on you?

A. A partial hysterectomy was performed wherein my reproductive organs were removed. I can no longer have children.

Q. Dr. Linton?

A. I would like to take a recess.

Jeffrey sat in his bathroom, staring at the pages of the transcript. He read through them again, then once more, sobs echoing in the bathroom as he cried for the Sara he had never known.

NINETEEN

Lena lifted her head slowly, trying to get some sense of where she was. All she saw was darkness. She held her hand inches from her face, unable to make out her palm and fingers. The last thing she remembered was sitting in her kitchen talking to Hank. After that, she drew a complete blank. It was as if she blinked one second and the next was transported to this spot. Wherever this spot was.

She groaned, moving to her side so that she could sit up. With sudden clarity, she realized that she was naked. The floor underneath her was rough against her skin. She could feel the grain in the wooden planks. Her heart started pounding for some reason, but her mind would not tell her why. Lena reached in front of her, feeling more rough wood, but it was vertical, a wall.

Pressing her hands into the wall, she managed to stand. In the back of her mind, she could make out a noise, but it was unfamiliar to her. Everything seemed disjointed and out of place. She felt physically as if she did not belong here. Lena found she was leaning her head against the wall, the wood pressing into the skin of her forehead. The noise was a staccato in her periphery, pounding, then nothing, pounding, then nothing, like a hammer on a piece of steel. Like a blacksmith fashioning a horseshoe.

Clink, clink, clink.

Where had she heard that before?

Lena's heart stopped as she finally made the connection. In the darkness, she could see Julia Matthews's lips moving, voicing the noise.

Clink, clink, clink.

The sound was dripping water.

TWENTY

Jeffrey stood behind the one-way glass, looking into the interview room. Ryan Gordon sat at the table, his skinny arms crossed over his concave chest. Buddy Conford sat beside him, his hands clasped in front of him on the table. Buddy was a fighter. At the age of seventeen, he had lost his right leg from the knee down in a car accident. At the age of twenty-six, he had lost his left eye from cancer. At thirty-nine, a dissatisfied client had attempted to pay Buddy off with two bullets. Buddy had lost a kidney and suffered a collapsed lung, but was back in the courtroom two weeks later. Jeffrey was hoping Buddy's sense of right and wrong would help move things along today. Jeffrey had downloaded a picture of Jack Allen Wright from the state database this morning. Jeffrey would have a lot stronger leg to stand on in Atlanta if he had a positive ID.

Jeffrey had never considered himself an emotional man, but there was an ache in his chest that would not go away. He wanted to talk to Sara so badly, but he was terrified that he would say the wrong thing. Driving in to work, he had gone over and over in his mind what he would say to her, even talking out loud to see how his words sounded. Nothing would come out right, and Jeffrey ended up sitting in his office for ten minutes with his hand on the phone before he could coax up enough courage to dial Sara's number at the clinic.

After telling Nelly Morgan that it wasn't an emergency but he would like to talk to Sara anyway, he got a snippy 'She's with a patient,' followed by a slam of the phone. This brought Jeffrey an enormous sense of relief, then a feeling of disgust at his own cowardice.

He knew that he needed to be strong for her, but Jeffrey felt too blindsided to be capable of anything but sobbing like a child every time he thought about what had happened to Sara. Part of him was hurt that she had not trusted him enough to tell him what had happened to her in Atlanta. Another part of him was angry that she had flat out lied to him about everything. The scar on her side had been explained away as the result of an appendectomy, though, in retrospect, Jeffrey remembered the scar was jagged and vertical, nothing like a surgeon's clean incision.

That she could not have children was something he had never pushed her on, because obviously it was a sensitive topic. He was comfortable leaving her at peace with that, assuming that it was some medical condition or that perhaps, like some women, she just was not meant to carry a child. He was supposed to be a cop, a detective, and he had taken everything she said at face value because Sara was the type of woman who told the truth about things. Or at least he had thought she was.

'Chief?' Marla said, knocking on the door. 'Guy called from Atlanta and said to tell you everything's set up. Wouldn't leave a name. That mean anything to you?'

'Yes,' Jeffrey said, checking the folder he held in his hand to make sure the printout was still there. He stared at the picture again, even though he had practically memorized the blurred photo. He brushed past Marla into the hallway. 'I'm leaving for Atlanta after this. I don't know when I'll be back. Frank will be in charge.'

Jeffrey didn't give her time to respond. He opened the door to the interview room and walked in.

Buddy took on a righteous tone. 'We've been here ten minutes.'

'And we're only going to be here another ten more if your client decides to cooperate,' Jeffrey said, taking the chair across from Buddy.

The only thing Jeffrey knew with any certainty was that he wanted to kill Jack Allen Wright. He had never been a violent man off the football field, but Jeffrey wanted so badly to kill the man who had raped Sara that his teeth ached.

'We ready to start?' Buddy asked, tapping his hand on the table.

Jeffrey glanced out the small window in the door. 'We need to wait for Frank,' he said, wondering where the man was. Jeffrey hoped he was checking on Lena.

The door opened and Frank entered the room. He looked as if he hadn't slept all night. His shirt was untucked at the side, and a coffee stain was on his tie. Jeffrey gave a pointed glance at his watch.

'Sorry,' Frank said, taking the chair beside Jeffrey.

'Right,' Jeffrey said. 'We've got some questions we need to ask Gordon. In exchange for his being forthcoming, we'll drop the pending charges on the drug bust.'

'Fuck that,' Gordon snarled. 'I told you those weren't my pants.'

Jeffrey exchanged a look with Buddy. 'I don't have time for this. We'll just send him up to the Atlanta pen and cut our losses.'

'What kind of questions?' Buddy asked.

Jeffrey dropped the bomb. Buddy had been expecting a simple plead on yet another drug charge against one of the kids from the college. Jeffrey kept his tone even when he said, 'About the death of Sibyl Adams and the rape of Julia Matthews.'

Buddy seemed to register a little shock. His face turned white, making his black eye patch stand out even more against his pale face. He asked Gordon, 'Do you know anything about this?'

Frank answered for him. 'He was the last person to see Julia Matthews in the library. He was her boy-friend.'

Gordon piped up, 'I told you, they weren't my pants. Get me the fuck out of here.'

Buddy gave Gordon the eye. 'You'd best be telling them what happened or you're gonna be writing your mama letters from jail.'

Gordon crossed his arms, obviously angry. 'You're supposed to be my lawyer.'

'You're supposed to be a human being,' Buddy countered, picking up his briefcase. 'Those girls were beaten and killed, son. You're looking at walking on a felony possession by simply doing what you should be doing in the first place. If you got a problem with that, you need to get yourself another lawyer.'

Buddy stood, but Gordon stopped him. 'She was in the library, okay?' Buddy sat back down, but he kept his briefcase in his lap.

'On campus?' Frank asked.

'Yeah, on campus,' Gordon snapped. 'I just ran into her, okay?'

'Okay,' Jeffrey answered.

'So, I started talking to her, you know. She wanted me back. I could tell that.'

Jeffrey nodded, though he imagined Julia Matthews had been very upset to see Gordon in the library.

'Anyway, we talked, got a little lip action going, if

you know what I mean.' He nudged Buddy, who moved away. 'Made some plans to see each other later on.'

'Then what?' Jeffrey asked.

'Then, you know, she left. That's what I'm saying, she just left. Got her books and all, said she would meet me later, then she was out of there.'

Frank asked, 'Did you see anyone following her? Anyone suspicious?'

'Naw,' he answered. 'She was alone. I would've noticed if anyone was watching her, you know? She was my girl. I kept an eye on her.'

Jeffrey said, 'You can't think of anyone she might know, not just a stranger, who was making her uncomfortable? Maybe she was dating somebody after y'all broke up?'

Gordon gave him the same look he would give a stupid dog. 'She wasn't seeing anybody. She was in love with me.'

'You don't remember seeing any strange cars on campus?' Jeffrey asked. 'Or vans?'

Gordon shook his head. 'I didn't see anything, okay?'

Frank asked, 'Let's go back to the meeting. You were supposed to see her later on?'

Gordon supplied, 'She was supposed to meet me behind the agri-building at ten.'

'She didn't show up?' Frank said.

'No,' Gordon answered. 'I waited around, you know. Then, I got kind of pissed off and I went to find her. I went to her room to see what was up, and she wasn't there.'

Jeffrey cleared his throat. 'Was Jenny Price there?'

'That whore?' Gordon waved this off. 'She was probably out fucking half the science team.'

Jeffrey felt himself bristle over this. He had a problem with men who saw all women as whores, not least because this attitude usually went hand in hand with violence toward women. 'So, Jenny wasn't there,' Jeffrey summarized. 'Then what did you do?'

'I went back to my dorm.' He shrugged. 'I went to bed.'

Jeffrey sat back in his seat, crossing his arms over his chest. 'What aren't you telling us, Ryan?' he asked. 'Because the way I'm looking at it, the "forthcoming" part of our deal isn't being met here. The way I'm looking at it, that orange jumper you're wearing is gonna be on your back for the next ten years.'

Gordon stared at Jeffrey with what Jeffrey assumed the young punk thought was a menacing look. 'I told you everything.'

'No,' Jeffrey said. 'You didn't. You're leaving something out that's pretty important, and I swear to God we're not gonna leave this room until you tell me what you know.'

Gordon turned shifty-eyed. 'I don't know anything.'

Buddy leaned over and whispered something that made Gordon's eyes go as round as two walnuts. Whatever the attorney had said to his client, it worked.

Gordon said, 'I followed her out of the library.'

'Yeah?' Jeffrey encouraged.

'She met up with this guy, okay?' Gordon fiddled with his hands in front of him. Jeffrey wanted to reach over and throttle the punk. 'I tried to catch up with them, but they were fast.'

'Fast meaning how?' Jeffrey asked. 'Was she walking with him?'

'No,' Gordon said. 'He was carrying her.'

Jeffrey felt a knot in the pit of his stomach. 'And you didn't think this was suspicious, her being carried off by a guy?'

Gordon's shoulders went up to his ears. 'I was mad, okay? I was mad at her.'

'You knew she wouldn't meet you later on,' Jeffrey began, 'so you followed her.'

He gave a slight shrug that could have been a yes or no.

'And you saw this guy carrying her off?' Jeffrey continued.

'Yeah.'

Frank asked, 'What did he look like?'

'Tall, I guess,' Gordon said. 'I couldn't see his face, if that's what you mean.'

'White? Black?' Jeffrey quizzed.

'Yeah, white,' Gordon supplied. 'White and tall. He was wearing dark clothes, all black. I couldn't really see them except that she was wearing this white shirt, right? It kind of caught the light, so she showed up, but not him.'

Frank said, 'Did you follow them?'

Gordon shook his head.

Frank was silent, his jaw taut with anger. 'You know she's dead now, don't you?'

Gordon looked down at the table. 'Yeah, I know that.'

Jeffrey opened the file and showed Gordon the printout. He had used a black marker to cross out Wright's name, but the rest of the statistics were left uncovered. 'This the guy?'

Gordon glanced down. 'No.'

'Look at the fucking photograph,' Jeffrey ordered, his tone so loud that Frank started beside him.

Gordon did as he was told, putting his face so close to the printout that his nose almost touched it. 'I don't know, man,' he said. 'It was dark. I couldn't see his face.' His eyes scanned down the vitals on Wright. 'He was tall like this. About this build. It could've been him, I guess.' He gave a casual shrug. 'I mean, Jesus, I wasn't paying attention to him. I was watching her.'

The drive to Atlanta was long and tedious, with nothing but the occasional patch of trees with the requisite kudzu to break the monotony. He tried twice to call Sara at home and leave some kind of message, but her machine wouldn't pick up, even after twenty rings. Jeffrey felt a rush of relief followed by an overwhelming shame. The closer he got to the city, the more he convinced himself that he was doing the right thing. He could call Sara when he knew something. Maybe he could call her with the news that Jack Allen Wright had met with an unfortunate accident involving Jeffrey's gun and Wright's chest.

Even going eighty, it took Jeffrey four hours before he got off 20 and onto the downtown connector. He passed Grady Hospital a little ways past the split, and felt tears wanting to come again. The building was a monster looming over the interstate in what Atlanta traffic reporters called the Grady Curve. Grady was one of the largest hospitals in the world. Sara had told him that during any given year the emergency clinics saw over two hundred thousand patients. A recent four-hundred million-dollar renovation made the hospital look like part of the set for a Batman movie. In typical City of Atlanta politics, the renovation had been the subject of an explosive investigation, kickbacks and payoffs reaching as far up as city hall.

Jeffrey took the downtown exit, then drove by the capitol. His friend on the Atlanta force had been shot on the job and taken a guard's position at the courthouse rather than early retirement. A call back in Grant had scheduled a meeting for one o'clock. It was quarter till by the time Jeffrey found a parking space in the crowded capitol section of downtown.

Keith Ross was waiting outside the courts building when Jeffrey walked up. In one hand, he held a large file folder; in the other, a plain white mailing envelope.

'Ain't seen you in a coon's age,' Keith said, giving Jeffrey's hand a firm shake.

'Good to see you, too, Keith,' Jeffrey returned, trying to force a lightness into his voice that he did not feel. The ride up to Atlanta had done nothing but get Jeffrey more wound up. Even the brisk walk from the parking garage to the courts building had not alleviated his tension.

'I can only let you have these for a second,' Keith said, obviously sensing Jeffrey's need to move this along. 'I got it from a buddy of mine over at records.'

Jeffrey took the folder, but he did not open it. He knew what he would find inside: pictures of Sara, witness testimony, detailed descriptions of exactly what had happened in that bathroom.

'Let's go inside,' Keith said, ushering Jeffrey into the building.

Jeffrey flashed his badge at the door, bypassing the security check. Keith led him into a small office to the side of the entrance. A desk surrounded by television monitors filled the room. A kid wearing thick glasses and a police uniform looked up with surprise as they entered.

Keith took a twenty-dollar bill out of his pocket. 'Go buy yourself some candy,' he said.

The kid took the money and left without another word.

'Devotion to the job,' Keith commented wryly. 'You gotta wonder what they're doing on the force.'

'Yeah,' Jeffrey mumbled, not wanting to have a

protracted conversation about the quality of police recruits.

'I'll leave you to it,' Keith said. 'Ten minutes, okay?'

'Okay,' Jeffrey answered, waiting for the door to close.

The file was coded and dated with some obscure notations that only a city employee could figure out. Jeffrey rubbed his hand down the front of the folder, as if he could absorb the information without actually having to see it. When that did not work, he took a deep breath and opened the folder.

Pictures of Sara after the rape greeted him. Close-ups of her hands and feet, the stab wound in her side, and her battered female parts spilled out onto the desk in full color. He actually gasped at the sight of them. His chest felt tight and a stabbing pain ran down his arm. Jeffrey thought for just a second that he was having a heart attack, but a few deep breaths helped clear his mind. He realized that his eyes had been closed, and he opened them, not looking at the pictures of Sara as he turned them facedown.

Jeffrey loosened his tie, trying to push the images from his mind. He thumbed through the other photographs, finding a picture of Sara's car. It was a silver BMW 320 with black bumpers and a blue stripe down the sides. Carved into the door, probably with a key, was the word CUNT just as Sara had said in her trial testimony. Pictures showed a before and after of the door, with and without the silver duct tape. Jeffrey got a flash of Sara kneeling in front of the door, taping over the damage, probably thinking in her mind that she would get her uncle Al to repair the damage when she was back in Grant next.

Jeffrey checked his watch, noting five minutes had passed. He found Keith in one of the security cameras, his hands tucked into his pockets as he shot the shit with the guards at the door.

Thumbing through the back of the file, he found the arrest report on Jack Allen Wright. Wright had been arrested twice before on suspicion but never charged. In the first incident, a young woman about the age Sara had been when she was attacked had dropped the charges and moved out of town. In the other case, the young woman had taken her own life. Jeffrey rubbed his eyes, thinking about Julia Matthews.

A knock came at the door, then Keith said, 'I gotta call time, Jeffrey.'

'Yeah,' Jeffrey said, closing the file. He didn't want to hold it in his hands anymore. He held it out to Keith without looking at the other man.

'This help you any?'

Jeffrey gave a nod, straightening his tie. 'Some,' he said. 'Were you able to find out where this guy is?'

'Just down the street,' Keith answered. 'Working at the Bank Building.'

'That's what, ten minutes from the university? Another five from Grady?'

'You got it.'

'What's he do?'

'He's a janitor, like he was at Grady,' Keith said. He had obviously looked at the file before giving it to Jeffrey. 'All those college girls, and he's ten minutes from them.'

'Do the campus police know?'

'They do now,' Keith provided, giving Jeffrey a knowing look. 'Not that he's much of a threat anymore.'

'What does that mean?' Jeffrey asked.

'Part of his parole,' Keith said, indicating the file. 'You didn't get to that? He's taking Depo.'

Jeffrey felt an uneasiness spread over him like warm water. Depoprovera was the latest trend in treating sexual offenders. Normally used in women as part of a hormone replacement therapy, a high enough dosage could curb a man's sexual appetite. When the drug was used on sexual predators, it was referred to as chemical castration. Jeffrey knew the drug only worked as long as the perpetrator took it. It was more like a tranquilizer than a cure.

Jeffrey indicated the folder. He could not say Sara's name in this room. 'He raped someone else after this?'

'He raped two someone elses after this,' Keith answered. 'There was this Linton girl. He stabbed her, right? Attempted murder, six years. Got early parole for good behavior, went on the Depo, went off the Depo, went out and raped three more women. They caught him on one, other girl wouldn't testify, put him back in jail for three years, now he's out on parole with the Depo administered under close supervision.'

'He's raped six girls and he's only served ten years?'

'They only nailed him on three, and except for her' – he indicated Sara's file – 'the other IDs were pretty shaky. He wore a mask. You know how it gets with those girls on the stand. They get all nervous and before you know it opposing counsel has them wondering if they were even raped in the first place, let alone who did it.'

Jeffrey held his tongue, but Keith seemed to read his mind.

'Hey,' Keith said, 'I'd been working those cases, the bastard would've been sent to the chair. Know what I mean?'

'Yeah,' Jeffrey said, thinking this boasting wasn't getting them anywhere. 'Is he ready for his third strike?' he asked. Georgia, like many states, had enacted a 'third strike' law some time ago, meaning that a convict's third felony offence, no matter how innocuous, would send him or her back to jail, conceivably for the rest of his or her life.

'Sounds like it,' Keith answered.

'Who's his PO?'

'Already took care of that one,' Keith said. 'Wright's on a bracelet. PO says he's clean going back the last two years. Also says he'd pretty much cut off his head before going back to jail.'

Jeffrey nodded at this. Jack Wright was forced to wear a monitoring bracelet as a condition of his parole. If he left his designated roaming area or missed his curfew, an alarm would go off at the monitoring station. In the City of Atlanta, most parole officers were stationed at police precincts around town so they could snatch up violators on a moment's notice. It was a good system, and despite the fact that Atlanta was such a large city, not many parolees slipped through the cracks.

'Also,' Keith said, 'I walked on down to the Bank Building.' He shrugged apologetically, recognizing he had overstepped the line. This was Jeffrey's case, but Keith was probably bored out of his mind from checking purses for handguns all day.

'No,' Jeffrey said. 'That's fine. What'd you get?'

'Got a peek at his time cards. He was punched in every morning at seven, then out to lunch at noon, back at noon-thirty, then out at five.'

'Somebody could've punched it for him.'

Keith shrugged. 'Supervisor didn't eyeball him, but she says there would've been complaints from the offices if he hadn't been on the job. Evidently, those professional types like to have their cans taken care of bright and early.'

Jeffrey pointed to the white mailing envelope Keith held in his hand. 'What's that?'

'Registration,' Keith said, handing him the envelope. 'He drives a blue Chevy Nova.'

Jeffrey slit the envelope open with his thumb. Inside was a photocopy of Jack Allen Wright's vehicle registration. An address was under his name. 'Current?' Jeffrey asked.

'Yeah,' Keith answered. 'Only, you understand you didn't get it from me.'

Jeffrey knew what he meant. Atlanta's chief of police ran her department by its short hairs. Jeffrey knew her reputation and admired her work, but he also knew that if she thought some hick cop from Grant County was stepping on her toes, the next thing Jeffrey would feel would be a three-inch stiletto parked firmly on the back of his neck.

'You get what you need from Wright,' Keith said, 'then call in APD.' He handed Jeffrey a business card with Atlanta's rising phoenix in the center of it. Jeffrey turned it over, seeing a name and number scribbled on the back.

Keith said, 'This is his PO. She's a good gal, but she'll want something solid to explain why you just happen to be in Wright's face.'

'You know her?'

'Know of her,' Keith said. 'Real ball breaker, so watch yourself. You call her in to snatch up her boy and she thinks you're looking at her funny, she'll make sure you never see him again.'

Jeffrey said, 'I'll try to be a gentleman.'

Keith offered, 'Ashton is just off the interstate. Let me give you directions.'

TWENTY-ONE

Nick Shelton's voice boomed across the telephone line. 'Hey, lady.'

'Hey, Nick,' Sara returned, closing a chart on her desk. She had been at the clinic since eight that morning and seen patients right up until four o'clock. Sara felt as if she had been running in quicksand all day. There was a slight ache in her head and her stomach was queasy from drinking a little too much the night before, not to mention her uneasiness over the emotional drama that had unfolded. As the day wore on, Sara began to feel more drained. At lunch, Molly had commented that Sara looked as if she should be the patient today instead of the doctor.

'I showed Mark those seeds,' Nick said. 'He says they're belladonna all right, only it's the berries, not the seeds.'

'I guess that's good to know,' Sara managed. 'He's certain?'

'One hundred percent,' Nick returned. 'He says it's kind of funny they ate the berries. Remember, those are the least poisonous. Maybe your guy down there gives them the berries to keep them a little jazzed, then doesn't give them the final dose until he turns 'em loose.'

'That makes sense,' Sara said, not even wanting to think about it. She did not want to be a doctor today.

She did not want to be a coroner. She wanted to be in bed with some tea and mindless television. As a matter of fact, that was exactly what she was going to do as soon as she finished updating the last chart from today. Thankfully, Nelly had booked tomorrow for Sara's day off. She would take the weekend to decompress. Monday, Sara would be back to her old self.

Sara asked, 'Anything on the semen sample?'

'We're having some problems with that, considering where you found it. I think we'll be able to get something out of it, though.'

'That's good news, I guess.'

Nick said, 'You gonna tell Jeffrey about the berries, or should I call him?'

Sara felt her stomach drop at the mention of Jeffrey's name.

'Sara?' Nick asked.

'Yeah,' Sara answered. 'I'll talk to him about it as soon as I get off work.'

Sara hung up the phone after the appropriate good-byes, then sat in her office, rubbing the small of her back. She reviewed the next chart at a glance, updating a change in medication as well as a follow-up visit for lab results. By the time she had finished with the last chart, it was five-thirty.

Sara crammed a couple of files into her briefcase, knowing she would have some time over the weekend where guilt would set in and she would want to do some work. Dictation was something she could do at home with a small tape recorder. There was a transcription place in Macon that would type up the notes for her and have them back in a couple of days.

She buttoned her jacket as she crossed the street, heading downtown. She took the sidewalk opposite the pharmacy, not wanting to run into Jeb. Sara kept her head down, passing the hardware store and the dress shop, not wanting to invite conversation. That she stopped in front of the police station was something of a surprise. Her mind was working without her knowing, and with each step she got more and more angry with Jeffrey for not calling. She had arguably left her soul laid out on his bathroom sink, and he had not even had the decency to call her.

Sara walked into the station house, managing a smile for Marla. 'Is Jeffrey in?'

Marla frowned. 'I don't think so,' she said. 'He checked out about noon or so. You might ask Frank.'

'He's in the back?' Sara indicated the door with her briefcase.

'I think,' Marla answered, returning to the task before her.

Sara glanced down as she passed the older woman. Marla was working on a crossword puzzle.

The back room was empty, the ten or so desks normally occupied by the senior detective vacant for the time being. Sara assumed they were out working down Jeffrey's list or grabbing dinner. She kept her head up, strolling into Jeffrey's office. Of course he wasn't there.

Sara stood in the small office, resting her briefcase on his desk. She had been in this room so many times she couldn't begin to count them. Always, she had felt safe here. Even after the divorce, Sara had felt that in this one area, Jeffrey was trustworthy. As a policeman, he had always done the right thing. He had done everything in his power to make sure the people he served were protected.

When Sara first moved back to Grant twelve years ago, no amount of reassurances from her father and her family could convince her that she was safe. Sara had known that as soon as she walked into the pawnshop, news would spread that she had purchased a weapon. What's more, she knew that in order to register a gun, she would have to go to the police station. Ben Walker, the chief of police before Jeffrey, played poker with Eddie Linton every Friday night. There had been no way for Sara to buy it without alerting everyone who knew her.

Around that time, a gang banger had come into the Augusta hospital with his arm nearly torn off by a bullet. Sara had worked on the kid and saved his arm. He was only fourteen, and when his mother came in, she had started beating him on his head with her purse. Sara had left the room, but a few moments later, the mother had found her. The woman had given Sara her son's weapon and asked Sara to take care of it. If Sara had been a Christian woman, she would have called the event a miracle.

The gun, Sara knew, was now in Jeffrey's desk drawer. She checked over her shoulder before sliding it open, taking out the bag with the Ruger in it. She tucked it in her briefcase and was out the door within a few minutes.

Sara kept her head up as she walked toward the college. Her boat was docked in front of the boathouse, and she tossed her briefcase in with one hand while untying the line with another. Her parents had given her the boat as a housewarming present, and it was an old but sturdy vessel.

The engine was strong, and Sara had skied behind it many times, her father at the wheel, holding back on the throttle for fear of jerking her arms off.

After checking that she was not being watched, Sara slipped the gun out of her briefcase and locked it in the watertight glove box in front of the passenger's seat, plastic bag and all. She stepped her leg outside the boat, using her foot to push away from the dock. The engine sputtered when she turned the key. Technically, she should have had the motor checked before using the boat again after not using it all winter, but she did not really have a choice, since the techs would not be finished with her car until Monday. Asking her father for a lift would have invited too much conversation, and Jeffrey was not an option.

After emitting a cloud of nasty-looking blue smoke, the engine caught, and Sara pulled away from the dock, allowing a small smile. She had felt like a criminal leaving with the gun in her briefcase, but she was feeling safer. Whatever Jeffrey thought when he saw the gun was gone was not really Sara's concern.

By the time she reached the center of the lake, the boat was skipping across the water. Cold wind cut through her face, and she put her glasses on to protect her eyes. Though the sun was beating down, the water was cool from the recent rains that had fallen on Grant County. It looked ready to storm again tonight, but probably well after the sun went down.

Sara zipped her jacket closed to fight the cold. Still, by the time she could see the back of her house, her nose was running and her cheeks felt as if she had put her face into a bucket of cold ice water. Cutting a hard left, she steered away from a group of rocks under the water. There had been a sign marking the spot at one time, but it had rotted away years ago. With the recent rains, the lake was high, but Sara did not want to risk it.

She had docked into the boathouse and was using the electric winch to pull the boat out of the water when her mother appeared from the back of the house.

'Shit,' Sara mumbled, pressing the red button to stop the winch.

'I called the clinic,' Cathy said. 'Nelly said you were taking tomorrow off.'

'That's right,' Sara answered, pulling the chains to lower the door behind the boat.

'Your sister told me about your argument last night.'

Sara jerked the chain tight, sending a clattering through the metal structure. 'If you're here to threaten me, the damage has been done.'

'Meaning?'

Sara walked past her mother, stepping off the dock. 'Meaning he knows,' she said, tucking her hands into her hips, waiting for her mother to follow.

'What did he say?'

'I can't talk about it,' Sara answered, turning toward the house. Her mother followed her up the lawn but was thankfully silent.

Sara unlocked the back door, leaving it open for her mother as she went into the kitchen. She realized too late that the house was a mess.

Cathy said, 'Really, Sara, you can make time to clean.'

'I've been very busy at work.'

'That's not an excuse,' Cathy lectured. 'Just say to yourself, "I'm going to do one load of laundry every other day. I'm going to make sure I put things back where I found them." Pretty soon you're organized.'

Sara ignored the familiar advice as she walked into the living room. She pressed the scroll on the caller ID unit, but no calls had been logged.

'Power went off,' her mother said, pressing the buttons on the stove to set the time. 'These storms are playing havoc with the cable. Your father almost had a heart attack last night when he turned on *Jeopardy!* and got nothing but fuzz.'

Sara felt some relief from this. Maybe Jeffrey had

called. Stranger things had happened. She walked over to the sink, filling the teakettle with water. 'Do you want some tea?'

Cathy shook her head.

'Me, either,' Sara mumbled, leaving the kettle in the sink. She walked to the back of the house, taking off her shirt, then her skirt as she walked into the bedroom. Cathy followed her, keeping a trained mother's eye on her daughter.

'Are you fighting with Jeffrey again?'

Sara slipped a T-shirt over her head. 'I'm always fighting with Jeffrey, Mother. It's what we do.'

'When you're not busy squirming in your seat over him in church.'

Sara bit her lip, feeling her cheeks turn red.

Cathy asked, 'What happened this time?'

'God, Mama, I really don't want to talk about it.'

'Then tell me about this thing with Jeb McGuire.'

'There's no "thing." Really.' Sara slipped on a pair of sweatpants.

Cathy sat on the bed, smoothing the sheet out with the flat of her hand. 'That's good. He's not really your type.'

Sara laughed. 'What's my type?'

'Someone who can stand up to you.'

'Maybe I like Jeb,' Sara countered, aware there was a petulant tone to her voice. 'Maybe I like the fact that he's predictable and nice and calm. God knows he's waited long enough to go out with me. Maybe I should start seeing him.'

Cathy said, 'You're not as angry with Jeffrey as you think.'

'Oh, really?'

'You're just hurt, and that's making you feel angry. You so seldom open yourself up to other people,' Cathy continued. Sara noticed that her mother's voice was soothing yet firm, as if she were coaxing a dangerous animal out of its hole. 'I remember when you were little. You were always so careful about who you let be your friend.'

Sara sat on the bed so she could put on her socks. She said, 'I had lots of friends.'

'Oh, you were popular, but you only let a few people in.' She stroked Sara's hair back behind her ear. 'And after what happened in Atlanta –'

Sara put her hand over her eyes. Tears came, and she mumbled, 'Mama, I really can't talk about that right now. Okay? Please, not now.'

'All right,' Cathy relented, putting her arm around Sara's shoulder. She pulled Sara's head to her chest. 'Shh,' Cathy hushed, stroking Sara's hair. 'It's okay.'

'I just . . .' Sara shook her head, unable to continue. She had forgotten how good it felt to be comforted by her mother. The last few days she had been so intent upon pushing Jeffrey away that she had managed to distance herself from her family as well.

Cathy pressed her lips to the crown of Sara's head, saying, 'There was an indiscretion between your father and me.'

Sara was so surprised that she stopped crying. 'Daddy cheated on you?'

'Of course not.' Cathy frowned. A few seconds passed before she provided, 'It was the other way around.'

Sara felt like an echo. 'You cheated on Daddy?'

'It was never consummated, but in my heart I felt that it was.'

'What does that mean?' Sara shook her head, thinking this sounded like one of Jeffrey's excuses: flimsy. 'No, never mind.' She wiped her eyes with the back of her hands, thinking she did not really want to hear this. Her parents' marriage was the pedestal upon which Sara had placed all her ideas about relationships and love.

Cathy seemed intent on telling her story. 'I told your father that I wanted to leave him for another man.'

Sara felt silly with her mouth hanging open, but there wasn't much she could do about it. She finally managed, 'Who?'

'Just a man. He was stable, had a job over at one of the plants. Very calm. Very serious. Very different from your father.'

'What happened?'

'I told your father that I wanted to leave him.'

'And?'

'He cried and I cried. We were separated for about six months. In the end we decided to stay together.'

'Who was the other man?'

'It doesn't matter now.'

'Is he still in town?'

Cathy shook her head. 'Doesn't matter. He's not in my life anymore, and I'm with your father.'

Sara concentrated on her breathing for a while. She finally managed to ask, 'When did this happen?'

'Before you and Tessie were born.'

Sara swallowed past the lump in her throat. 'What happened?'

'What's that?'

Sara slipped a sock on. It was like pulling teeth getting the story from her mother. She prompted, 'To change your mind? What made you want to stay with Daddy?'

'Oh, about a million things,' Cathy answered, a sly smile at her lips. 'I think I just got a little distracted by this other man and I didn't realize how important your father was to me.' She sighed heavily. 'I remember waking up one morning in my old room at Mama's and all I could think was that Eddie should've been there with me. I wanted him so badly.' Cathy frowned at Sara's reaction to this. 'Don't go getting your color up, there are other ways to want someone.'

Sara cringed at the scolding, slipping on her other sock. 'So you called him up?'

'I went over to the house and I sat on the front porch and practically begged him to take me back. No, on second thought, I did beg. I told him that if we were both going to be miserable without each other, we might as well be miserable together and that I was so sorry and I'd never take him for granted again as long as I lived.'

'Take him for granted?'

Cathy put her hand on Sara's arm. 'That's the part that hurts, isn't it? The part where you feel like you don't matter to him as much as you used to.'

Sara nodded, trying to remember to breathe. Her mother had hit the nail on the head. She prompted, 'What did Daddy do when you said this?'

'Told me to get up off the porch and come in for some breakfast.' Cathy put her hand to her chest, patting it. 'I don't know how Eddie found it in his heart to forgive me, he's such a proud man, but I'm thankful he did. It made me love him even more to know that he could forgive me for something so horrible like that; that I could hurt him to the core and he could still love me. I think starting out like that made the marriage stronger.' The smile intensified. 'Of course, then, I did have a secret weapon.'

'What's that?'

'You.'

'Me?'

Cathy stroked Sara's cheek. 'I was seeing your father again, but it was so strained. Nothing was like it was before. Then I got pregnant with you, and life just took over. I think having you between us made your father see the big picture. Next thing Tessie was here, then you were both in school, then you were both grown and off to college.' She smiled. 'It just takes time. Love and time. And having a little redheaded hellion to chase after is a good distraction.'

'Well, I'm not going to get pregnant,' Sara countered, conscious of the edge to her tone.

Cathy seemed to think out her answer. 'Sometimes it takes thinking you've lost something to realize the real value of it,' she said. 'Don't tell Tessie.'

Sara nodded her agreement. She stood, tucking her T-shirt into her pants. 'I told him, Mama,' she said. 'I left the transcript for him.'

Cathy asked, 'The trial transcript?'

'Yeah,' Sara said, leaning against the chest of drawers. 'I know he's read it. I left it in the bathroom for him.'

'And?'

'And,' Sara said, 'he hasn't even called. He hasn't said anything to me all day.'

'Well,' Cathy said, her mind obviously made up. 'Fuck him, then. He's trash.'

TWENTY-TWO

Jeffrey found 633 Ashton Street easily enough. The house was dilapidated, no more than a square made of cinder blocks. The windows seemed to be an afterthought, none of them the same size. A ceramic fireplace was on the front porch, stacks of papers and magazines piled to the side of it, probably to use for kindling.

He took a look around the house, trying to act casually. Wearing a suit and tie, driving the white Town Car, it wasn't like Jeffrey fit in with the surroundings. Ashton Street, at least the part Jack Wright lived on, was run-down and seedy. Most of the houses in the vicinity were boarded up, yellow posters warning they were condemned. Kids played in the packed dirt yards of these houses, their parents nowhere to be seen. There was a smell to the place, not exactly sewage but something in that same family. Jeffrey was reminded of driving past the city dump on the outskirts of Madison. On a good day, even when you were downwind, the smell of decomposing trash still reached your nose. Even with the windows up and the air on.

Jeffrey took a few breaths, trying to get used to the smell as he approached the house. The door had a heavy mesh screen over it with a padlock securing it to the frame. The actual door had three dead bolts and one lock that looked like it required a puzzle piece to open it rather than a key. Jack Wright had been in prison a great deal of his life. This was obviously a man who wanted his privacy. Jeffrey took a look around before walking over to one of the windows. It, too, had a wire mesh and a heavy lock, but the casing was old and easily broken. A couple of firm pushes dislodged the entire frame. Jeffrey glanced around before removing the window, casing and all, and slipping into the house.

The living room was dark and dingy, with trash and papers stacked around the room. There was an orange couch on the floor with dark stains dripping down. Jeffrey could not tell if it was from tobacco juice or some kind of body fluid. What he did know was an overpowering odor of sweat mixed with Lysol permeated the room.

Edging the top of the living room walls like a decorative border were all kinds of crucifixes. They varied in size from something you would get out of a candy vending machine to some that were at least ten inches long. They were nailed into the wall, edge to edge, tight up against one another in one continuous band. Continuing the Jesus theme, posters on the wall that looked like they had been taken from a Sunday school room showed Jesus and the disciples. In one, He was holding a lamb. In another, He was holding out his hands, showing the wounds in His palms.

Jeffrey felt his heart rate quicken at the sight of this. He reached to his gun, taking the strap off his holster as he walked toward the front of the house to make sure no one was coming up the drive.

In the kitchen, plates were stacked in the sink, crusted and foul-looking. The floor was sticky, and the whole room felt wet from something other than water. The bedroom was the same way, a musky odor clinging like a wet washrag against Jeffrey's face. On the wall over the stained mattress was a large poster of Jesus Christ, a halo behind His head. Like the poster in the living room, Jesus held His palms out to show the wounds on His hands. The crucifixion motif continued around the periphery of the bedroom, but these were larger crosses. Standing on the bed, Jeffrey could see that someone, probably Wright, had used red paint to exaggerate Jesus' wounds, dripping the blood down the torso, enhancing the crown of thorns resting on his head. Black Xs were across the eyes on every Jesus Jeffrey could see. It was as if Wright had wanted to stop His eyes from watching him. What Wright was doing that he felt needed to be hidden was the question Jeffrey needed to answer.

Jeffrey stepped off the bed. He looked through some of the magazines, taking the time to put on a pair of latex gloves from his pockets before touching anything. The magazines were mostly older editions of *People* and *Life*. The bedroom closet was stacked floor to ceiling with pornography. *Busty Babes* sat beside *Righteous Redheads*. Jeffrey thought of Sara and a lump came to his throat.

Using his foot, Jeffrey kicked the mattress up. A Sig Sauer nine millimeter was resting on the boxspring. The weapon looked new and well cared for. In a neighborhood like this one, only an idiot would go to sleep without a gun handy. Jeffrey smiled as he pushed the mattress back. This could help him out later on.

Opening the dresser, Jeffrey did not know what he expected to find. More porn, maybe. Another gun, or some kind of makeshift weapon. Instead, the top two drawers were filled with women's underwear. Not just underwear, the silky, sexy kind that Jeffrey liked to see Sara in. There were teddies and thongs, French-cut panties with bows at the hips. And they were all extremely large; large enough to fit a man.

Jeffrey resisted the urge to shudder. He took out a pen to go through the contents of the drawers, not wanting to get stuck with a needle or anything sharp, not wanting to get a venereal disease. Jeffrey was about to close one of the drawers when something changed his mind. He was missing something. Moving aside a pair of dark green lace panties, he saw what he was looking for. The newspaper lining the bottom of the drawers was from the special Sunday section of the *Grant County Observer*. He had recognized the masthead.

Pushing aside the clothes, Jeffrey took out the sheet of newspaper. The front page showed a slow news day. A picture of the mayor holding a pig in his arms beamed back at Jeffrey. The date put the paper at more than a year old. He opened the other drawers, looking for more *Observers*. He found a few, but most of them carried innocuous stories. Jeffrey found it interesting that Jack Wright subscribed to the *Grant County Observer*.

He went back into the living room, checking out the stacks of papers on the floor with renewed interest. Brenda Collins, one of Wright's other victims after Sara, had been from Tennessee, Jeffrey remembered. A copy of the *Monthly Vols,* a newsletter for University of Tennessee graduates, was tucked in with some newspapers from Alexander City, Alabama. In the next stack, Jeffrey found more out-of-state papers, all from small towns. Beside these were postcards, all from Atlanta, all showing different scenes around town. The backs were blank, waiting to be filled in. Jeffrey could not imagine what a man like Wright would be doing with the postcards. He did not strike Jeffrey as the type of person to have friends.

Jeffrey turned around, making sure he had not missed anything in the cramped room. There was a television set tucked into the old fireplace. It looked fairly new, the kind you could buy on the street for fifty bucks if you did not ask too many questions about where it had come from. On top of the set was a cable converter box.

He walked back toward the front window to leave but stopped when he saw something under the couch. He used his foot to tilt the couch over, sending cockroaches scurrying across the floor. A small black keyboard was on the floor.

The converter box was actually a receiver for the keyboard. Jeffrey turned the set on, pressing the buttons on the keyboard until the receiver logged on to the Internet. He sat on the edge of the upturned couch as he waited for the system to make a connection. At the station, Brad Stephens was the computer person, but Jeffrey had learned enough from watching the young patrolman to know how to navigate his way around.

Wright's E-mail was easy enough to access. Aside from an offer from a Chevy parts dealership and the requisite hot young teens looking for college money, the kind of E-mail that everyone in the world got, there was a long letter from a woman who appeared to be Wright's mother. Another E-mail had a photo attachment of a young woman posed with her legs wide open. The sender's E-mail address was a series of random numbers. Probably, he was a prison buddy of Wright's. Still, Jeffrey wrote down the address on a scrap piece of paper he had in his pocket.

Using the arrow keys, Jeffrey went to the bookmarks section. In addition to various porn and violence sites, Jeffrey found a link for the *Grant Observer* on-line. He could not have been more shocked. There, on the television screen, was today's front page announcing the suicide of Julia Matthews last night. Jeffrey punched the down arrow, skimming the article again. He went into the archives and performed a search for Sibyl Adams. Seconds later, an article on career day from last year came on-screen. A search for Julia Matthews brought up today's front page, but nothing else. Over sixty articles came up when he typed in Sara's name.

Jeffrey logged off and turned the couch right side up. Outside, he pressed the window back into the hole he had made. It did not want to stay, so he was forced to drag one of the chairs over to prop it in. From his car, it didn't look like the window had been tampered with, but Jack Wright would know as soon as he walked on his front porch that someone had been in his house. As security conscious as the man seemed to be, this would probably be a good way to push his buttons.

The streetlight over Jeffrey's car came on as he got in. Even on this hellhole of a street, the sunset dipping into the Atlanta skyline was something to behold. Jeffrey imagined but for the sun setting and rising, the people on this block wouldn't feel human.

He waited for three and a half hours before the blue Chevy Nova pulled into the driveway. The car was old and dirty, flakes of rust showing through at the trunk and taillights. Wright had obviously tried to make a few repairs. Silver duct tape crisscrossed the tail end, and on one side of the bumper was a decal that said GOD IS MY COPILOT. On the other side was a zebra-striped sticker that said I'M GOING WILD AT THE ATLANTA ZOO.

Jack Wright had been in the system long enough to know what a cop looks like. He gave Jeffrey a wary glance as he stepped out of the Nova. Wright was a pudgy man with a receding hairline. His shirt was off, and Jeffrey could see he had what could only be described as breasts. Jeffrey guessed this was from the Depo. One of the main reasons rapists and pedophiles tended to go off the drug was the nasty side effect that caused some of them to put on weight and take on womanly attributes.

Wright nodded to Jeffrey as Jeffrey made his way up the driveway. As neglected as this area of town was, all the streetlights were in working order. The house was lit like it was broad daylight.

When Wright spoke, his voice was high-pitched, another side effect of the Depo. He asked, 'You looking for me?'

'That's right,' Jeffrey answered, stopping in front of the man who had raped and stabbed Sara Linton.

'Well, damn,' Wright said, pursing his lips. 'I guess some girl done got snatched up, huh? Y'all always come knocking on my door when some young thing goes missing.'

'Let's go into the house,' Jeffrey said.

'I don't think so,' Wright countered, leaning back against the car. 'She a pretty girl, the one missing?' He paused, as if he expected an answer. He licked his tongue slowly along his lips. 'I only pick the pretty ones.'

'It's an older case,' Jeffrey said, trying not to let himself get baited.

'Amy? Is it my sweet little Amy?'

Jeffrey stared. He recognized the name from the case file. Amy Baxter had taken her life after being raped by Jack Wright. She was a nurse who had moved to Atlanta from Alexander City.

'No, not Amy,' Wright said, putting his hand to his chin as if in thought. 'Was it that sweet little –' He stopped himself, looking over at Jeffrey's car. 'Grant County, huh? Why didn't you say so?' He smiled, showing one of his chipped front teeth. 'How's my little Sara doing?'

Jeffrey took a step toward the man, but Wright did not take the intimidation.

Wright said, 'Go on and hit me. I like it rough.'

Jeffrey stepped back, willing himself not to punch the man.

Suddenly, Wright scooped his breasts into his hands. 'You like these, daddy?' He smiled at the look of disgust that must have been on Jeffrey's face. 'I take the Depo, but you know that already, don't you, honey? You know what it does to me, too, don't you?' He lowered his voice. 'Makes me like a girl. Gives the boys the best of both worlds.'

'Stop it,' Jeffrey said, glancing around. Wright's neighbors had come out to see the show.

'I got balls the size of marbles,' Wright said, putting his hands to the waist of his blue jeans. 'You wanna see 'em?'

Jeffrey lowered his voice to a grumble. 'Not unless you want to take the word "chemical" out of your castration.'

Wright chuckled. 'You're a big, strong man, you know that?' he asked. 'You supposed to be taking care of my Sara?'

Jeffrey could do nothing but swallow.

'They all wanna know why I picked 'em. Why me? Why me?" he trilled, his voice higher. 'Her, I wanted to see was she a real redhead.'

Jeffrey stood there, unable to move.

'I guess you know she is, huh? I can tell by looking in your eyes.' Wright crossed his arms over his chest, his eyes on Jeffrey's. 'Now, she's got some great tits. I loved sucking them.' He licked his lips. 'I wish you could've seen the fear on her face. I could tell she wasn't used to it. Hadn't had herself a real man yet, know what I mean?'

Jeffrey put his hand around the man's neck, backing him into the car. The action was so fast Jeffrey wasn't even sure what he was doing until he felt Jack Wright's long fingernails digging into the skin on the back of his hand.

Jeffrey forced himself to take his hand away. Wright sputtered, coughing, trying to catch his breath. Jeffrey walked a tight circle, checking on the neighbors. None of them had moved. They all seemed entranced by the show.

'You think you can scare me?' Wright said, his voice raspy. 'I had bigger than you, two at a time, in prison.'

'Where were you last Monday?' Jeffrey asked.

'I was at work, brother. Check with my PO.'

'Maybe I will.'

'She made a spot check on me around' – Wright pretended to think this through – 'I'd say around two, two-thirty. That the time you looking for?'

Jeffrey did not answer. Sibyl Adams's time of death had been printed in the *Observer*.

'I was sweeping and mopping and taking out the trash,' Wright continued.

Jeffrey indicated the tattoo. 'I see you're a religious man.'

Wright looked at his arm. 'That's what caught me up with Sara.'

'You like to keep up with your girls, huh?' Jeffrey asked. 'Maybe look through the newspapers? Maybe keep up with them on the Internet?'

Wright looked nervous for the first time. 'You been in my house?'

'I like what you did with the walls,' he said. 'All those little Jesuses. Their eyes just follow you when you walk around the room.'

Wright's face changed. He showed Jeffrey the side

that only a handful of unfortunate women had ever seen as he screamed, 'That is my personal property. You don't belong in there.'

'I was in there,' Jeffrey said, able to be calm now that Wright was not. 'I went through everything.'

'You bastard,' Wright yelled, throwing a punch. Jeffrey sidestepped, twisting the man's arm behind him. Wright pitched forward, falling face first into the ground. Jeffrey was on top of him, his knee pressed into the man's back.

'What do you know?' Jeffrey demanded.

'Let me go,' Wright begged. 'Please, let me go.'

Jeffrey took out his handcuffs and forced Wright into them. The clicking sound of the locks sent the man into hyperventilation.

'I just read about it,' Wright said. 'Please, please, let me go.'

Jeffrey leaned down, whispering in the man's ear. 'You're going back to jail.'

'Don't send me back,' Wright begged. 'Please.'

Jeffrey reached down, tugging the ankle bracelet. Knowing how the City of Atlanta worked, this would be faster than dialing 911. When the bracelet would not budge, Jeffrey used the heel of his shoe to bust it.

'You can't do that,' Wright screamed. 'You can't do that. They saw you.'

Jeffrey looked up, remembering the neighbors. He watched wordlessly as they all turned their backs, disappearing into their houses.

'Oh, God, please don't send me back,' Wright begged. 'Please, I'll do anything.'

'They're not going to like that nine mill under your mattress, either, Jack.'

'Oh, God,' the man sobbed, shaking.

Jeffrey leaned against the Nova, taking out the

business card Keith had given him earlier. The name on the card was Mary Ann Moon. Jeffrey glanced at his watch. At ten till eight on a Friday night, he doubted very seriously that she would be happy to see him.

TWENTY-THREE

Lena closed her eyes as the sun beat down on her face. The water was warm and inviting, a slight breeze crossing her body as each wave gently rolled under her. She could not remember the last time she had been to the ocean, but the vacation was well earned to say the least.

'Look,' Sibyl said, pointing above them.

Lena followed her sister's finger, spotting a seagull in the ocean sky. She found herself concentrating on the clouds instead. They looked like cotton balls against a baby blue backdrop.

'Did you want this back?' Sibyl asked, handing Lena a red kickboard. Lena laughed. 'Hank told me you lost it.'

Sibyl smiled. 'I put it where he couldn't see it.'

With sudden clarity, Lena realized it was Hank and not Sibyl who had been blinded. She could not understand how she had gotten the two confused, but there was Hank on the beach, dark glasses covering his eyes. He sat back, propped up on his hands, letting the sun hit him square on the chest. He looked more tan than Lena had ever seen him. As a matter of fact, all the times they had gone to the beach before, Hank had stayed in the hotel room instead of going out on the beach with the girls. What he did in there all day, Lena did not know. Sometimes Sibyl would join him to take some time out from the sun, but Lena loved being on the beach. She loved playing in the water or looking for impromptu volleyball games she could flirt her way into.

That was how Lena had met Greg Mitchell, her last boyfriend of any consequence. Greg was playing volleyball with a group of his friends. He was about twenty-eight years old, but his friends were much younger and more interested in looking at girls than actually playing the game. Lena had walked over, knowing she was being sized up, rated like a side of meat, by the young men, and asked to join the game. Greg had thrown the ball at her straight from his chest and Lena had caught it the same way.

After a while, the younger men trailed off in search of alcohol or women or both. Lena and Greg played for what seemed like hours. If he had been expecting Lena to throw the games in honor of his masculinity, he had another thing coming. She had beaten him so badly that by the end of the third game, he had forfeited, offering to buy her dinner as her prize.

He took her to some cheap Mexican place that would have made Lena's grandfather keel over had he not already been dead. They drank sugary sweet margaritas, then they danced, then Lena gave Greg a sly smile instead of a good night kiss. The next day he was back in front of her hotel, this time with a surfboard. She had always wanted to learn how to surf, and she took up his offer for lessons without having to be asked twice.

Now, she could feel the surfboard underneath her, the waves sending her body up into the air, then down. Greg's hand was at the small of her back, then lower, then lower, until he was cupping her ass in his hand. She turned over slowly, letting him see and feel her naked body. The sun beat down, making her skin feel warm and alive.

He poured suntan oil in his hands, then started rubbing her feet. His hands encircled her ankles, pushing her legs far apart. They were still floating on the ocean but the water was somehow firm, holding her body up for Greg. His hands worked their way up her thighs, stroking, touching, moving past her intimate parts until his palms were cupping her breasts. He used his tongue, kissing then biting her nipples, her breasts, working his way up to her mouth. Greg's kisses were forceful and rough, like Lena had never known from him. She felt herself responding to him in ways she could not have imagined.

The pressure of his body on top of hers was alarmingly sensual. His hands were calloused, his touch rough, as he did with her what he wanted. For the first time in her life, Lena was not in control. For the first time in her life, Lena was completely helpless under this one man. She felt an emptiness that could only be filled by him. Anything he wanted, she would do. Any wish he uttered, she would fulfill.

His mouth moved down her body, his tongue exploring between her legs, his teeth rough against her. She tried to reach her hands to him, to pull him closer, but she found herself immobilized. Suddenly, he was on top of her, pushing her hands away from her body, out to the side as if to pin her back as he entered her. There was a wave of pleasure that seemed to last for hours, then sudden, excruciating release. Her whole body opened to him, her back arching, wanting to weld her flesh into his.

Then, it was over. Lena felt her body letting go, her mind coming back into focus. She rolled her head side to side, revering in the aftermath. She licked her lips, opening her eyes to just a slit as she looked into the dark room. A clinking sound came from far away. Another more immediate sound came from all around, an irregular ticktock, like a clock, only with water. She found that she could no longer remember the word for water pouring out of the clouds.

Lena tried to move, but her hands seemed unwilling. She glanced out, seeing the tips of her fingers, even though there was no light to show them. Something was around her wrists, something tight and unrelenting. Her mind made the connection to move her fingers, and she felt the rough surface of wood against the back of her hand. Likewise, something encircled her ankles, holding her feet to the floor. She could not move her legs or arms. She was literally splayed to the floor. Her body seemed to come alive with this one realization: she was trapped.

Lena was back in the dark room, back where she had been taken hours ago; or was it days? Weeks? The clinking was there, the slow beat of water torture pounding into her brain. The room had no windows and no light. There was only Lena and whatever was holding her to the floor.

A light came suddenly, a blinding light that burned her eyes. Lena tried to pull away from the restraints again, but she was helpless. Someone was there; someone she knew who should be helping her but was not. She writhed against the bonds, twisting her body, trying to free herself, to no avail. Her mouth opened, but no words would come. She forced the words through her mind – Help me, please – but was not rewarded with the sound of her own voice.

She turned her head to the side, blinking her eyes, trying to look past the light, just as a minute pressure came against the palm of her hand. The sensation was dull, but Lena could see from the light that the tip of a long nail was pressed into the palm of her hand. Also in the light, a hammer was raised.

Lena closed her eyes, not feeling the pain.

She was back at the beach, only not in the water. This time she was flying.

TWENTY-FOUR

Mary Ann Moon was not a pleasant woman. There was a set to her mouth that said 'don't fuck with me' before Jeffrey even had the opportunity to introduce himself. She had taken one look at Wright's broken monitoring bracelet and directed her comments to Jeffrey.

'Do you know how much those things cost?'

It had gone downhill from there.

Jeffrey's biggest problem with Moon, as she liked to be called, was the language barrier. Moon was from somewhere up east, the kind of place where consonants took on a life of their own. In addition to this, she spoke loudly and abruptly, two things that were considered very rude to southern ears. On the elevator ride up from central processing to the interview rooms, she stood too close to him, her mouth set in a fixed line of disapproval, her arms crossed low over her waist. Moon was about forty years old, but it was the hard kind of forty that too much smoking and drinking can do to a person. She had dark blond hair with light strands of grey mixed in. Her lips had wrinkles spreading out from them in deep rays.

Her nasal tone and the fact that she spoke sixty miles an hour gave Jeffrey the impression that he was talking to a French horn. Every response Jeffrey gave her was slow in coming because he had to wait for his brain to translate her words. He could tell early on that Moon took this slowness for stupidity, but there really wasn't anything he could do about it.

She said something to him over her shoulder as they walked through the precinct. He slowed it down, realizing she had said, 'Tell me about your case, Chief.'

He gave her a quick rundown of what had happened since Sibyl Adams had been found, leaving out his connection to Sara. He could tell the story wasn't progressing quickly enough, because Moon kept interrupting him with questions he was about to answer if she would give him a second to finish his sentence.

'I take it you went into my boy's house?' she said. 'You see all that Jesus shit?' She rolled her eyes. 'That nine mill didn't walk in under your pant leg, did it, Sheriff Taylor?'

Jeffrey gave her what he hoped was a threatening look. She responded with an outburst of laughter that pierced his eardrum. 'That name sounds familiar.'

'What's that?'

'Lipton. Tolliver, too.' She put her tiny hands on her slim hips. 'I'm very good about notification, Chief. I've called Sara maybe a handful of times to let her know where Jack Allen Wright is. It's my job to do victim notification on an annual basis. Her case was ten years ago?'

'Twelve.'

'So, that's at least twelve times I've talked to her.'

He came clean, knowing he was busted. 'Sara is my ex-wife. She was one of Wright's first victims.'

'They let you work the case knowing your connection?'

'I'm in charge of the case, Ms. Moon,' he answered.

She gave him a steady look that probably worked on her parolees, but did nothing but irritate Jeffrey. He was about two feet taller than Mary Ann Moon and not

321

about to be intimidated by this little ball of Yankee hate.

'Wright's a Depo freak. You know what I mean by that?'

'He obviously likes taking it.'

'This goes way back to his early days, right after Sara. You've seen pictures of him?'

Jeffrey shook his head.

'Follow me,' Moon said.

He did as he was told, trying not to step on her heels. She was fast about everything but walking, and his stride was more than double hers. She stopped in front of a small office that was jam-packed with file storage boxes. She stepped over a pile of manuals, pulling a file off her desk.

'This place is a mess,' she said, as if the fact had nothing to do with her. 'Here.'

Jeffrey opened the file, seeing a younger, slimmer, less womanly photograph of Jack Allen Wright clipped to the top page. He had more hair on his head, and his face was lean. His body was cut the way men who spend three hours a day lifting weights get, and his eyes were a piercing blue. Jeffrey remembered Wright's rheumy eyes from before. He also remembered that part of Sara's ID had come from his clear blue eyes. Every aspect of Wright's appearance had been altered since he had assaulted Sara. This was the man Jeffrey had been expecting when he searched Wright's house. This was the man who had raped Sara, who had robbed her of her ability to give Jeffrey a child.

Moon shuffled through the file. 'This is his release photo,' she said, sliding out another photograph.

Jeffrey nodded, seeing the man he knew as Wright.

'He served hard time, you know that?'

Jeffrey nodded again.

'Lots of men try to fight. Some of them just give in.'

'You're breaking my heart,' Jeffrey mumbled. 'He have many visitors in prison?'

'Just his mother.'

Jeffrey closed the file and handed it back to her. 'What about when he got out of jail? He obviously went off the Depo, right? He raped again.'

'He says he didn't, but there's no way in hell he'd be able to get it up on the dosage he was supposed to be taking.'

'Who was supervising it?'

'He was under his own supervision.' She stopped him before he could say anything. 'Listen, I know it's not perfect, but we have to trust them sometimes. Sometimes we're wrong. We were wrong with Wright.' She threw the folder back on her desk. 'He goes to the clinic now and gets his Depo injected once a week. It's all nice and clean. The bracelet you were kind enough to destroy kept him under close supervision. He was in line.'

'He hasn't left the city?'

'No,' she answered. 'I did a spot check on him last Monday at work. He was at the Bank Building.'

'Nice of you to put him near all those college girls.'

'You're crossing a line,' she warned.

He held up his hands, palms out.

'Write down whatever questions you want asked,' she said. 'I'll talk to Wright.'

'I need to work off his answers.'

'Technically, I don't even have to let you in here. You should be glad I'm not kicking your ass all the way back to Mayberry.'

He literally bit his tongue so he would not snap back at her. She was right. He could call some friends of his on the APD tomorrow morning so he would get better treatment, but for right now, Mary Ann Moon was in charge.

Jeffrey said, 'Can you give me a minute?' He indicated the desk. 'I need to check in with my people.'

'I can't make long-distance calls.'

He held up his cell phone. 'It's more privacy that I was looking for.'

She nodded, turning around.

'Thanks,' Jeffrey offered, but she did not answer in kind. He waited until she was down the hallway, then closed the door. After stepping over a group of boxes, he sat at her desk. The chair was low to the ground, and his knees felt like they were about to touch his ears. Jeffrey looked at his watch before dialing Sara's number. She was an early-to-bed kind of person, but he needed to talk to her. He felt a wave of excitement wash over him as the phone rang.

She answered the phone on the fourth ring, her voice heavy with sleep. 'Hello?'

He realized he had been holding his breath. 'Sara?'

She was silent, and for a moment he thought she had hung up the phone. He heard her moving, sheets rustling; she was in bed. He could hear rain falling outside, and a distant thunder rumbled over the phone. Jeffrey had a flash of a night they had shared a long time ago. Sara never liked storms, and she had awakened him, wanting Jeffrey to take her mind off the thunder and lightning.

'What do you want?' she asked.

He searched for something to say, knowing suddenly that he had waited too long to get in touch with her. He could tell from the tone of her voice that something had changed in their relationship. He was not altogether sure how or why.

'I tried to call before,' he said, feeling like he was lying even though he was not. 'At the clinic,' he said.

'That so?'

'I talked to Nelly,' he said.

'Did you tell her it was important?'

Jeffrey felt his stomach drop. He didn't answer.

Sara gave what he thought was a laugh.

He said, 'I didn't want to talk to you until I had something.'

'Something on what?'

'I'm in Atlanta.'

She was silent, then, 'Let me guess, 633 Ashton Street.'

'Earlier,' he answered. 'I'm at APD headquarters now. We've got him in an interview room.'

'Jack?' she asked.

Something about her familiar use of his name set Jeffrey's teeth on edge.

'Moon called me when his monitor went off,' Sara provided in a dull tone. 'I had a feeling that's where you were.'

'I wanted to talk to him about what's going on before I called in the cavalry.'

She sighed heavily. 'Good for you.'

The line was quiet again, and Jeffrey was again lost for words. Sara interrupted the silence.

She asked, 'Is that why you called me? To tell me that you arrested him?'

'To see if you were okay.'

She gave a small laugh. 'Oh, yeah. I'm just peachy, Jeff. Thanks for calling.'

'Sara?' he asked, scared she would hang up. 'I tried to call before.'

'Evidently not that hard,' she said.

Jeffrey could feel her anger coming across the phone.

'I wanted to have something to tell you when I called. Something concrete.'

She stopped him, her tone terse and low. 'You didn't know what to say, so instead of walking two blocks to the clinic or making sure you got through to me, you scooted off to Atlanta to see Jack face-to-face.' She paused. 'Tell me how it felt to see him, Jeff.'

He could not answer her.

'What'd you do, beat him up?' Her tone turned accusatory. 'Twelve years ago, I could've used that. Right now I just wanted you to be there for me. To support me.'

'I'm trying to support you, Sara,' Jeffrey countered, feeling blindsided. 'What do you think I'm doing up here? I'm trying to find out if this guy is still out there raping women.'

'Moon says he hasn't left town in the last two years.'

'Maybe Wright's involved in what's going on in Grant. Did you think of that?'

'No, actually,' she answered glibly. 'All I could think was I showed you that transcript this morning, I bared my soul to you, and your response was to get out of town.'

'I wanted –'

'You wanted to get away from me. You didn't know how to deal with it, so you left. I guess it's not as tricky as letting me come home and catch you with another woman in our bed, but it sends the same kind of message, doesn't it?'

He shook his head, not understanding how it had come to this. 'How is it the same? I'm trying to help you.'

Her voice changed then, and she didn't seem angry so much as deeply hurt. She had talked to him like this only once before, right after she had caught him cheating. He had felt then as he felt now, like a selfish asshole.

She said, 'How are you helping me in Atlanta? How does it help me having you four hours away? Do you know how I felt all day, jumping every time the phone rang, hoping it was you?' She answered for him. 'I felt like an idiot. Do you know how hard it was for me to show you that? To let you know what had happened to me?'

'I didn't –'

'I'm nearly forty years old, Jeffrey. I choose to be a good daughter to my parents and a supportive sister to Tessa. I chose to push myself so I could graduate at the top of my class from one of the finest universities in America. I chose to be a pediatrician so I could help kids. I chose to move back to Grant so I could be close to my family. I chose to be your wife for six years because I loved you so much, Jeffrey. I loved you so much.' She stopped, and he could tell that she was crying. 'I didn't choose to be raped.'

He tried to speak, but she wouldn't let him.

'What happened to me took fifteen minutes. Fifteen minutes and all of that was wiped out. None of it matters when you take those fifteen minutes into account.'

'That's not true.'

'It's not?' she asked. 'Then why didn't you call me this morning?'

'I tried to –'

'You didn't call me because you see me as a victim now. You see me the same way you see Julia Matthews and Sibyl Adams.'

'I don't, Sara,' he countered, shocked that she would accuse him of such a thing. 'I don't see –'

'I sat there in that hospital bathroom on my knees for

327

two hours before they cut me loose. I nearly bled to death,' she said. 'When he was done with me, there was nothing left. Nothing at all. I had to rebuild my life. I had to accept that because of that bastard I would never have children. Not that I ever wanted to think about having sex again. Not that I thought any man would want to touch me after what he did to me.' She stopped, and he wanted so badly to say something to her, but the words would not come.

Her voice was low when she said, 'You said I never opened up to you? Well, this is why. I tell you my deepest, darkest secret and what do you do? You run off to Atlanta to confront the man who did it instead of talking to me. Instead of comforting me.'

'I thought you'd want me to do something.'

'I did want you to do something,' she answered, her tone filled with sadness. 'I did.'

The phone clicked in his ear as she hung up. He dialed her number again, but the line was busy. He kept hitting 'send' on the phone, trying the line five more times, but Sara had taken her phone off the hook.

Jeffrey stood behind the one-way glass in the observation room, playing back his conversation with Sara in his mind. An overwhelming sadness enveloped him. He knew that she was right about calling. He should have insisted Nelly put him through. He should have gone to the clinic and told her that he still loved her, that she was still the most important woman in his life. He should have gotten on his knees and begged her to come back to him. He shouldn't have left her. Again.

Jeffrey thought of how Lena had used the term victim a few days ago, describing targets of sexual predators. She had put a spin on the word, saying it the same way she would say 'weak' or 'stupid.' Jeffrey had not liked that classification from Lena, and he certainly did not like hearing it from Sara. He probably knew Sara better than any other man in her life, and Jeffrey knew that Sara was not a victim of anything but her own damning self-judgment. He did not see her as a victim in that context. If anything, he saw her as a survivor. Jeffrey was hurt to his very core that Sara would think so little of him.

Moon interrupted his thoughts, asking, 'About ready to start?'

'Yeah,' Jeffrey answered, blocking Sara from his mind. No matter what she had said, Wright was still a viable lead to what was going on in Grant County. Jeffrey was already in Atlanta. There was no reason to go back until he had gotten everything he needed from the man. Jeffrey clenched his jaw, forcing himself to concentrate on the task at hand as he stared through the glass.

Moon entered the room loudly, banging the door closed behind her, raking a chair out from the table, the legs screeching against the tiled floor. For all the APD's money and special funding, the city's interview rooms were not nearly as clean as the ones in Grant County. The room Jack Allen Wright sat in was dingy and dirty. The cement walls were unpainted and gray. There was a gloominess to the room that would encourage anyone to confess just to get out of the place. Jeffrey took this all in as he watched Mary Ann Moon work Wright. She was not nearly as good as Lena Adams, but there was no denying Moon had a rapport with the rapist. She talked to him like a big sister.

She asked, 'That old redneck didn't fool with you, did he?'

Jeffrey knew she was trying to bridge some trust with Wright, but he did not appreciate the characterization, mostly because he guessed Mary Ann Moon thought it was an accurate one.

'He busted my bracelet,' Wright said. 'I didn't do that.'

'Jack.' Moon sighed, sitting across from him at the table. 'I know that, okay? We need to find out how that gun got under your mattress. That's a clear violation and you're on your third strike. Right?'

Wright glanced at the mirror, probably knowing full well that Jeffrey was behind it. 'I don't know how it got there.'

'Guess he put your fingerprints on it, too?' Moon asked, crossing her arms.

Wright seemed to think this over. Jeffrey knew that gun belonged to Wright, but he also knew that there was no way in hell Moon would have been able to run the gun through forensics this quickly and get any kind of ID on the prints.

'I was scared,' Wright finally answered. 'My neighbors know, all right? They know what I am.'

'What are you?'

'They know about my girls.'

Moon stood from the chair. She turned her back to Wright, looking out the window. A mesh just like the ones at Wright's house covered the frame. Jeffrey was startled to realize that the man had made his own home resemble a prison.

'Tell me about your girls,' Moon said. 'I'm talking about Sara.'

Jeffrey felt his hands clench at Sara's name.

Wright sat back, licking his lips. 'There was a tight pussy.' He smirked. 'She was good to me.'

Moon's voice was bored. She had been doing this long enough not to be shocked. She asked, 'She was?'

'She was so sweet.'

330

Moon turned around, leaning her back against the mesh. 'You know what's going on where she lives. I take it you know what's been happening to the girls.'

'I only know what I read in the papers,' Wright said, offering a shrug. 'You ain't gonna send me up on that gun, are you, boss? I had to protect myself. I was scared for my life.'

'Let's talk about Grant County,' Moon offered. 'Then we'll talk about the gun.'

Wright picked at his face, gauging her. 'You're being straight with me?'

'Of course I am, Jack. When have I not been straight with you?'

Wright seemed to weigh his options. As far as Jeffrey could see, it was a no-brainer: jail or cooperation. Still, he imagined Wright wanted some semblance of control in his life.

'That thing that was done to her car,' Wright said.

'What's that?' Moon asked.

'That word on her car,' Wright clarified. 'I didn't do that.'

'You didn't?'

'I told my lawyer, but he said it didn't matter.'

'It matters now, Jack,' Moon said, just the right amount of insistence in her voice.

'I wouldn't write that on somebody's car.'

'Cunt?' she asked. 'That's what you called her in the bathroom.'

'That was different,' he said. 'That was the heat of the moment.'

Moon did not respond to this. 'Who wrote it?'

'That, I don't know,' Wright answered. 'I was in the hospital all day, working. I didn't know what kind of car she drove. Could've guessed it, though. She had that attitude, you know? Like she was better than everybody else.'

'We're not going to get into that, Jack.'

'I know,' he said, looking down. 'I'm sorry.'

'Who do you think wrote that on her car?' Moon asked. 'Somebody at the hospital?'

'Somebody who knew her, knew what she drove.'

'Maybe a doctor?'

'I don't know.' He shrugged. 'Maybe.'

'You being straight with me?'

He seemed startled by her question. 'Hell, yeah, I am.'

'So, you think somebody at the hospital might have written that on her car. Why?'

'Maybe she pissed them off?'

'She piss a lot of people off?'

'No.' He shook his head vehemently. 'Sara was good to people. She always talked to everybody.' He seemed to not remember his earlier comments about how conceited Sara was. Wright continued, 'She always said hey to me in the hall. You know, not like "How you doing" or anything like that but, "Hey, I know you're there." Most people, they see you but they don't. Know what I mean?'

'Sara's a nice girl,' Moon said, keeping him on track. 'Who would do that to her car?'

'Maybe somebody was pissed at her about something?'

Jeffrey put his hand to the glass, feeling the hair on the back of his neck rise. Moon picked up on this as well.

She asked, 'About what?'

'I don't know,' Wright answered. 'I'm just saying I never wrote that on her car.'

'You're sure about that.'

Wright swallowed hard. 'You said you'd trade the gun for this, right?'

Moon gave him a nasty look. 'Don't question me, Jack. I told you up front that was the deal. What have you got for us?'

Wright glanced toward the mirror. 'That's all I have, that I didn't do that to her car.'

'Who did, then?'

Wright shrugged. 'I told you I don't know.'

'You think the same guy who scratched her car is doing this stuff in Grant County?'

He shrugged again. 'I'm not a detective. I'm just telling you what I know.'

Moon crossed her arms over her chest. 'We're gonna keep you in lockup over the weekend. When we talk on Monday, you see if you've got an idea who this person might be.'

Tears came to Wright's eyes. 'I'm telling you the truth.'

'We'll see if it's the same truth on Monday morning.'

'Don't send me back in there, please.'

'It's just holding, Jack,' Moon offered. 'I'll make sure you get your own cell.'

'Just let me go home.'

'I don't think so,' Moon countered. 'We'll let you stew for a day. Give you some time to get your priorities straight.'

'They are straight. I promise.'

Moon did not wait for more. She left Wright in the room, his head in his hands, crying.

SATURDAY

TWENTY-FIVE

Sara woke with a start, not certain where she was for a brief, panicked second. She looked around her bedroom, keeping her eyes on solid things, comforting things. The old chest of drawers that had belonged to her grandmother, the mirror she had found in a yard sale, the armoire that had been so wide her father had helped her take the hinges off the bedroom door so they could squeeze it in.

She sat up in bed, looking out the bank of windows at the lake. The water was rough from last night's storm, and choppy waves rode across the surface. Outside, the sky was a warm gray, blocking the sun, keeping the fog down low to the ground. The house was cold, and Sara imagined that outside was even colder. She took the quilt from the bed with her as she walked to the bathroom, wrinkling her nose as her feet padded across the cold floor.

In the kitchen, she started the coffeemaker, standing in front of the unit as she waited for enough to fill a cup. She went back to the bedroom, slipping on a pair of spandex running shorts, then an old pair of sweatpants. The phone was still off the hook from Jeffrey's call last night, and Sara replaced the receiver. The phone rang almost immediately.

Sara took a deep breath, then answered, 'Hello?'

'Hey, baby,' Eddie Linton said. 'Where you been?'

337

'I accidentally knocked the phone off the hook,' Sara lied.

Her father either did not catch the lie or was letting it pass. He said, 'We've got breakfast cooking here. Wanna come?'

'No, thanks,' Sara answered, her stomach protesting even as she did. 'I'm about to go for a run.'

'Maybe come by after?'

'Maybe,' Sara answered, walking toward the desk in the hallway. She opened the top drawer and pulled out twelve postcards. Twelve years since the rape, one postcard for every year. There was always a Bible verse along with her address typed across the back.

'Baby?' Eddie said.

'Yeah, Pop,' Sara answered, keying into what he was saying. She slid the cards back into the drawer, using her hip to shut it.

They made small talk about the storm, Eddie telling her that a tree limb had missed the Linton house by a couple of yards, and Sara offering to come by later and help clean up. As he talked, Sara flashed back to the time just after she was raped. She was in the hospital bed, the ventilator hissing in and out, the heart monitor assuring her that she had not died, though Sara remembered that she had not found that reminder in the least bit comforting.

She had been asleep, and when she woke, Eddie was there, holding her hand in both of his. She had never seen her father cry before, but he was then, small, pathetic sobs escaping from his lips. Cathy was behind him, her arms around his waist, her head resting on his back. Sara had felt out of place there and she had briefly wondered what had upset them until she remembered what had happened to her.

After a week in the hospital, Eddie had driven her

back to Grant. Sara had kept her head on his shoulder the entire way, sitting in the front seat of his old truck, tucked between her mother and father, much as she had been before Tessa was born. Her mother sang an off-key hymn Sara had never heard before. Something about salvation. Something about redemption. Something about love.

'Baby?'

'Yeah, Daddy,' Sara answered, wiping a tear from her eye. 'I'll drop by later, okay?' She blew a kiss to the phone. 'I love you.'

He answered in kind, but she could hear the concern in his voice. Sara kept her hand on the receiver, willing him not to be upset. The hardest part about recovering from what Jack Allen Wright had done to her was knowing that her father knew every single detail of the rape. She had felt so exposed to him for such a long time that the nature of their relationship had changed. Gone was the Sara he played pickup games with. Gone were the jokes about Eddie wishing she had become a gynecologist, at least, so that he could say both his girls were in plumbing. He did not see her as his invulnerable Sara anymore. He saw her as someone he needed to protect. As a matter of fact, he saw her the same way Jeffrey did now.

Sara tugged the laces on her tennis shoes, tightening them too much and not caring. She had heard pity in Jeffrey's voice last night. Instantly, she had known that things had irrevocably changed. He would only see her as a victim from now on. Sara had fought too hard to overcome that feeling only to let herself give in to it now.

Slipping on a light jacket, Sara left the house. She jogged down the driveway to the street, taking a left away from her parents' house. Sara did not like to jog on the street; she had seen too many injured knees blown from the constant impact. When she worked out, she used the treadmills at the Grant YMCA or swam in the pool there. In the summertime, she took early morning swims in the lake to clear her mind and get her focus back for the day ahead. Today, she wanted to push herself to the limit, damn the consequences to her joints. Sara had always been a physical person, and sweating brought her center back.

About two miles from her house, she took a side trail off the main road so that she could run along the lake. The terrain was rough in spots, but the view was spectacular. The sun was finally winning its battle with the dark clouds overhead when she realized she was at Jeb McGuire's house. She had stopped to look at the sleek black boat moored at his dock before she made the connection as to where she was. Sara cupped her hand over her eyes, staring at the back of Jeb's house.

He lived in the old Tanner place, which had just recently come on the market. Lake people were hesitant to give up their land, but the Tanner children, who had moved away from Grant years ago, were more than happy to take the money and run when their father finally succumbed to emphysema. Russell Tanner had been a nice man, but he had his quirks, like most old people. Jeb had delivered Russell's medications to him personally, something that probably helped Jeb get into the house cheap after the old man died.

Sara walked up the steep lawn toward the house. Jeb had gutted the place a week after moving in, replacing the old crank windows with double-paned ones, having the asbestos shingles removed from the roof and sideboards. The house had been a dark grey for as long as Sara remembered, but Jeb had painted over this in a cheery yellow. The color was too bright for Sara, but it suited Jeb.

'Sara?' Jeb asked, coming out of the house. He had a tool belt on with a shingle hammer hanging from the strap on the side.

'Hey,' she called, walking toward him. The closer she got to the house, the more aware she became of a dripping sound. 'What's that noise?' she asked.

Jeb pointed to a gutter hanging off the roofline. 'I'm just now getting to it,' he explained, walking toward her. He rested his hand on the hammer. 'I've been so busy at work, I haven't had time to breathe.'

She nodded, understanding the dilemma. 'Can I give you a hand?'

'That's okay,' Jeb returned, picking up a six-foot ladder. He carried it over to the hanging gutter as he talked. 'Hear that thumping? Damn thing's draining so slow, it hits the base of the downspout like a jackhammer.'

She heard the noise more clearly as she followed him toward the house. It was an annoying, constant thump, like a faucet dripping into a cast-iron sink. She asked, 'What happened?'

'Old wood, I guess,' he said, turning the ladder right side up. 'This house is a money pit, I hate to say. I get the roof fixed and the gutters fall off. I seal the deck and the footings start to sink.'

Sara looked under the deck, noting the standing water. 'Is your basement flooded?'

'Thank God I don't have one or it'd be high tide down there,' Jeb said, reaching into one of the leather pouches on his belt. He took out a gutter nail with one hand and fumbled for the hammer with the other.

Sara stared at the nail, making a connection. 'Can I see that?'

He gave her a funny look, then answered, 'Sure.'

She took the nail, testing its weight in her hand. At twelve inches, it was certainly long enough for the job of tacking up a gutter, but could someone have also used this type of nail to secure Julia Matthews to the floor?

'Sara?' Jeb asked. His hand was out for the nail. 'I've got some more in the storage shed,' he said, indicating the metal shed. 'If you want to keep one.'

'No,' she answered, handing him the nail. She needed to get back to her house and call Frank Wallace about this. Jeffrey was probably still in Atlanta, but certainly someone would need to track down who had bought this type of nail recently. It was a good lead.

She asked, 'Did you get this at the hardware store?'

'Yeah,' he answered, giving her a curious look. 'Why?'

Sara smiled, trying to put his mind at ease. He probably thought it was odd that she was so interested in the gutter nail. It wasn't like she could tell him why. Sara's dating pool was small enough without taking Jeb McGuire out of the picture by suggesting his gutter nails would be a good way to pin a woman to the floor so she could be raped.

She watched him secure the drooping gutter to the house. Sara found herself thinking about Jeffrey and Jack Wright in the same room together. Moon had said that Wright had let himself go in prison, that the chiseled threat to his body had been replaced by soft fat, but Sara still saw him as she had that day twelve years ago. His skin was tight to his bones, his veins sticking out along his arms. His expression was a carved study in hatred, his teeth gritting in a menacing smile as he raped her.

Sara gave an involuntary shudder. Her life for the last

twelve years had been spent blocking Wright out of her mind, and having him back now, in whatever form, be it through Jeffrey or a stupid postcard, was making her feel violated all over again. She hated Jeffrey for that, mostly because he was the only one who could suffer any impact from her hatred.

'Hold on,' Jeb said, snapping her out of her reflection. Jeb cupped his hand to his ear, listening. The thumping noise was still there as water dripped into the downspout.

'This is going to drive me crazy,' he said, over the thump, thump, thump of the water.

'I can see that,' she said, thinking that five minutes of the dripping sound was already giving her a headache.

Jeb came down off the ladder, tucking the hammer back into his belt. 'Is something wrong?'

'No,' she answered. 'Just thinking.'

'About what?'

She took a deep breath, then said, 'About our rain check.' She looked up at the sky. 'Why don't you come over to the house around two for a late lunch? I'll get some takeout from the deli in Madison.'

He smiled, an unexpected nervous edge to his voice. 'Yeah,' he answered. 'That sounds great.'

TWENTY-SIX

Jeffrey tried to keep his focus on driving, but there was too much going on in his mind to concentrate. He had not slept all night, and exhaustion was taking over his body. Even after pulling over to the side of the road for a thirty-minute nap, he still did not feel like his head was on straight. Too much was happening. Too many things were pulling him in different directions at the same time.

Mary Ann Moon had promised to subpoena the employment records from Grady Hospital dating back to the time Sara had worked there. Jeffrey prayed that the woman was as good as her word. She had estimated that the records would be available for Jeffrey's perusal sometime Sunday afternoon. Jeffrey's only hope was that a name from the hospital would sound familiar. Sara had never mentioned anyone from Grant working with her back in those days, but he still needed to ask her. Three calls to her house had gotten him her machine. He knew better than to leave a message for her to call. The tone of her voice last night had been enough to convince him that she would probably never talk to him again.

Jeffrey pulled the Town Car into the station parking lot. He needed to go home to shower and change, but he also had to show his face at work.

His trip to Atlanta had taken more time than

planned, and Jeffrey had missed the early morning briefing.

Frank Wallace was walking out the front door as Jeffrey put the car in park. Frank tossed a wave before walking around the car and getting in.

Frank said, 'The kid's missing.'

'Lena?'

Frank gave a nod as Jeffrey put the car in gear.

Jeffrey asked, 'What happened?'

'Her uncle Hank called at the station looking for her. He said the last he saw of her she was in the kitchen right after that Matthews went south.'

'That was two days ago,' Jeffrey countered. 'How the hell did this happen?'

'I left a message on her machine. I figured she was lying low. Didn't you give her time off ?'

'Yeah,' Jeffrey answered, feeling guilt wash over him. 'Hank's at her house?'

Frank gave another nod, slipping on his seat belt as Jeffrey pushed the car past eighty. Tension filled the car as they drove toward Lena's house. When they got there, Hank Norton was sitting on the front porch waiting.

Hank jogged to the car. 'Her bed hasn't been slept in,' he said as a greeting. 'I was at Nan Thomas's house. Neither one of us had heard from her. We assumed she was with you.'

'She wasn't,' Jeffrey said, offering the obvious. He walked into Lena's house, scanning the front room for clues. The house had two stories, like most homes in the neighborhood. The kitchen, dining room, and living room were on the main level with two bedrooms and a bath upstairs.

Jeffrey took the steps two at a time, his leg protesting at the movement. He walked into what he assumed was

Lena's bedroom, searching for anything that might make sense of all of this. A hot pain was at the back of his eyes and everything he looked at had a tinge of red to it. Going through her drawers, moving clothes around in her closet, he had no idea what he expected to find. He found nothing.

Downstairs in the kitchen, Hank Norton was talking to Frank, his words a hot staccato of blame and denial. 'She was supposed to be working with you,' Hank said. 'You're her partner.'

Jeffrey got a brief flash of Lena in her uncle's voice. He was angry, accusatory. There was the same underlying hostility he had always heard in Lena's tone.

Jeffrey took the heat off of Frank, saying, 'I gave her time off, Mr. Norton. We assumed she would be at home.'

'Girl blows her head off right under my niece and you just assume she's gonna be okay?' he hissed. 'Jesus Christ, that's the end of your responsibility, giving her the day off?'

'That's not what I meant, Mr. Norton.'

'For fuck sakes, stop calling me Mr. Norton,' he screamed, throwing his hands into the air.

Jeffrey waited for the man to say more, but he turned suddenly, walking out of the kitchen. He slammed the back door behind him.

Frank spoke slowly, visibly upset. 'I should've checked on her.'

'I should have,' Jeffrey said. 'She's my responsibility.'

'She's everybody's responsibility,' Frank countered. He started searching the kitchen, opening and closing drawers, going through cabinets. Frank obviously wasn't really paying attention to what he was doing. He slammed the cabinet doors, more to work out his anger than to look for anything concrete. Jeffrey watched this for a while, then walked toward the window. He saw Lena's black Celica in the driveway.

Jeffrey said, 'Car's still here.'

Frank slammed a drawer closed. 'I saw that.'

'I'll go check it out,' Jeffrey offered. He walked out the back door, passing Hank Norton, who was sitting on the steps leading into the backyard. He was smoking a cigarette, his movements awkward and angry.

Jeffrey asked him, 'Has the car been here all the time you were gone?'

'How the fuck would I know that?' Norton snapped.

Jeffrey let this slide. He walked to the car, noting the lock was down on both doors. The tires on the passenger's side looked fine and the hood of the car felt cool as he walked around it.

'Chief?' Frank called from the kitchen door. Hank Norton stood as Jeffrey walked back toward the house.

'What is it?' Norton asked. 'Did you find something?'

Jeffrey walked back into the kitchen, spotting instantly what Frank had found. The word CUNT had been carved on the inside door of the cabinet over the stove.

'I don't give a good goddamn about subpoenas,' Jeffrey told Mary Ann Moon as he sped toward the college. He held the phone in one hand and drove with the other.

'One of my detectives is missing right now, and the only lead I've got is this list.' He took a breath, trying to calm himself. 'I have got to get access to those employment records.'

Moon was diplomatic. 'Chief, we have to go through protocol here. This isn't Grant County. We step on somebody's toes and it's not like we can make nice at the next church social.'

'Do you know what this guy's been doing to women

here?' he asked. 'Are you willing to take responsibility for my detective being raped right now? Because I guarantee you that's what's happening to her.' He held his breath for a moment, trying not to let that image sink in.

When she did not respond, he said, 'Someone carved something on a cabinet in her kitchen.' He paused, letting her absorb that. 'Do you want to take a guess as to what that word is, Ms. Moon?'

Moon was silent, obviously thinking. 'I can probably talk to a girl I know in records over there. Twelve years is a long time. I can't make guarantees they'll keep something like that handy. It's probably on microfiche at the state records building.'

He gave her his cell phone number before ringing off.

'What's the dorm number?' Frank asked as they drove through the gates of the college.

Jeffrey took out his notepad, flipping back a few pages. 'Twelve,' he said. 'She's in Jefferson Hall.'

The Town Car fishtailed as he stopped in front of the dormitory. Jeffrey was out the door and up the steps in a flash. He pounded his fist on the door to number twelve, throwing it open when there was no answer.

'Oh, Jesus,' Jenny Price said, grabbing a sheet to cover herself. A boy Jeffrey had never seen before jumped up from the bed, slipping on his pants in one practiced movement.

'Get out,' Jeffrey told him, walking toward Julia Matthews's side of the room. Nothing had been moved since he had been here last time. Jeffrey did not imagine Matthews's parents felt much like going through their dead daughter's things.

Jenny Price was dressed, more bold than she had been the day before. 'What are you doing here?' she demanded.

Jeffrey ignored her question, searching through clothes and books.

Jenny repeated the question, this time to Frank.

'Police business,' he mumbled from the hallway.

Jeffrey turned the room upside down in seconds. There had not been much to begin with, and as with the search before, nothing new turned up. He stopped, looking around the room, trying to find what he was missing. He was turning to search the closet again when he noticed a stack of books by the door. A thin film of mud covered the spines. They had not been there the first time Jeffrey had searched the room. He would have remembered them.

He asked, 'What are those?'

Jenny followed his gaze. 'The campus police brought those by,' she explained. 'They were Julia's.'

Jeffrey clenched his fist, wanting to pound something. 'They brought them by here?' he asked, wondering why he was surprised. Grant Tech's campus security force was comprised of mostly middle-aged deputy dogs who hadn't a brain between them.

The girl explained, 'They found them outside the library.'

Jeffrey forced his hands to unclench, bending at the knee to examine the books. He thought about putting gloves on before touching them, but it was not as if a chain of custody had been maintained.

The Biology of Microorganisms was on top of the stack, flecks of mud scattered along the front cover. Jeffrey picked up the book, thumbing through the pages. On page twenty-three, he found what he was looking for. The word CUNT was printed in bold red marker across the page.

'Oh my God,' Jenny breathed, hand to her mouth.

Jeffrey left Frank to seal off the room. Instead of

driving to the science lab where Sibyl worked, he jogged across the campus, going the opposite direction he had gone with Lena just a few days ago. Again, he took the stairs two at a time; again, he did not bother to wait for an answer to his knock outside Sibyl Adams's lab.

'Oh,' Richard Carter said, looking up from a notebook. 'What can I do for you?'

Jeffrey leaned his hand on the closest desk, trying to catch his breath. 'Was there anything,' he began, 'unusual the day Sibyl Adams was killed?'

Carter's face took on an exasperated expression. Jeffrey wanted to smack it off him, but he refrained.

Carter said in a self-righteous tone, 'I told you before, there was nothing out of the ordinary. She's dead, Chief Tolliver, don't you think that I'd mention something unusual?'

'Maybe a word was written on something,' Jeffrey suggested, not wanting to give too much away. It was amazing what people thought they remembered if you asked them the right way. 'Did you see something written on one of her notebooks? Maybe she had something she kept close by that someone tampered with?'

Carter's face fell. Obviously, he remembered something. 'Now that you mention it,' he began, 'just before her early class on Monday, I saw something written on the chalkboard.' He crossed his arms over his large chest. 'Kids think it's funny to pull those kinds of pranks. She was blind, so she couldn't really see what they were doing.'

'What did they do?'

'Well, someone, I don't know who, wrote the word cunt on the blackboard.'

'This was Monday morning?'

'Yes.'

350

'Before she died?'

He had the decency to look away before answering, 'Yes.'

Jeffrey stared at the top of Richard's head for a moment, fighting the urge to pummel him. He said, 'If you had told me this last Monday, do you realize Julia Matthews might be alive?'

Richard Carter did not have an answer for that.

Jeffrey left, slamming the door behind him. He was making his way down the steps when his cell phone rang. He answered on the first ring. 'Tolliver.'

Mary Ann Moon got right to the point. 'I'm in the records department right now, looking at the list. It's everybody who worked on the first-floor emergency department, from the doctors to the custodians.'

'Go ahead,' Jeffrey said, closing his eyes, blocking out her Yankee twang as she called out the first, middle, and last names of the men who had worked with Sara. It took her a full five minutes to read them all. After the last one, Jeffrey was silent.

Moon asked, 'Anybody on there sound familiar?'

'No,' Jeffrey responded. 'Fax the list to my office if you don't mind.' He gave her the number, feeling as if he had been punched in the stomach. His mind conjured the image of Lena again, nailed to a basement floor, terrified.

Moon prompted, 'Chief?'

'I'll have some of my guys cross-reference it with voter polls and the phone book.' He paused, debating whether or not to go on. Finally, good breeding won out. 'Thank you,' he said. 'For looking that list up.'

Moon did not give him her customary abrupt good-bye. She said, 'I'm sorry the names didn't ring any bells.'

'Yeah,' he answered, checking his watch. 'Listen, I

can be back in Atlanta in around four hours. Do you think I can get some time alone with Wright?'

There was another hesitation, then, 'He was attacked this morning.'

'What?'

'Seems the guards at the lockup didn't think he deserved his own cell.'

'You promised to keep him out of the general population.'

'I know that,' she snapped. 'It's not like I can control what happens when he goes back inside. You of all people should know those good old boys operate by their own rules.'

Considering Jeffrey's behavior yesterday with Jack Wright, he was in no position to defend himself.

'He'll be out of it for a while,' Moon said. 'They cut him up pretty bad.'

He muttered a curse under his breath. 'He didn't give you anything after I left?'

'No.'

'Is he sure it's somebody who worked in the hospital?'

'No, as a matter of fact.'

'It's somebody who saw her at the hospital,' Jeffrey said. 'Who would see her at the hospital without working there?' He put his free hand over his eyes, trying to think. 'Can you pull patient files from there?'

'Like charts?' She sounded dubious. 'That's probably pushing it.'

'Just names,' he said. 'Just that day. April twenty-third.'

'I know the day.'

'Can you?'

She obviously had covered the mouthpiece on the phone, but he could still hear her talking to someone.

After a few beats, she was back on the line. 'Give me an hour, hour and a half.'

Jeffrey suppressed the groan that wanted to come. An hour was a lifetime. Instead, he said, 'I'll be here.'

TWENTY-SEVEN

Lena heard a door open somewhere. She lay there on the floor, waiting for him, because that's all she could do. When Jeffrey had told her Sibyl was dead, Lena's main focus had been on finding out who had killed Sibyl, on bringing him to justice. She had wanted nothing more than to find the bastard and send him to the chair. Those thoughts had so obsessed her from day one that she had not had time to stop and grieve. Not one day had been spent mourning the loss of her sister. Not one hour had gone by where she had stopped and taken the time to reflect on her loss.

Now, trapped in this house, nailed to the floor, Lena had no choice but to think about it. All of her time was devoted to memories of Sibyl. Even when she was drugged, a sponge held over her mouth, bittertasting water hitting the back of her throat until she was forced to swallow, Lena mourned Sibyl. There were days at school that were so real Lena could feel the grain of the pencil she held in her hand. Sitting with Sibyl in the back of classrooms, she could smell the ink from the ditto machine. There were car rides and vacations, senior pictures and field trips. She was reliving them all, Sibyl by her side, every one of them as if she was actually there in the moment.

The light came again as he entered the room. Her eyes were so dilated she could not see anything but shadows, but he still used the light to block her vision. The pain was so intense she was forced to close her eyes. Why he did this, she couldn't guess. Lena knew who her captor was. Even if she had not recognized his voice, the things he said could only come from the town's pharmacist.

Jeb sat at her feet, resting the light on the floor. The room was completely dark except for this small ray of light. Lena found it somewhat comforting to be able to see something after being in darkness for so long.

Jeb asked, 'Are you feeling better?'

'Yes,' Lena answered, not remembering if she had felt worse before. He was injecting her with something every four hours or so. She guessed from the way her muscles relaxed shortly after that it was some kind of pain medication. The drug was potent enough to keep her from hurting, but not enough to knock her out. He only knocked her out at night, then with whatever he was putting in the water. He held a wet sponge over her mouth, forcing her to swallow the bitter-tasting water. She prayed to God it was not belladonna she was ingesting. Lena had seen Julia Matthews with her own eyes. She knew how lethal the drug was. What's more, Lena doubted Sara Linton would be around to save her. Not that Lena was sure she wanted to be saved. In the back of her mind, Lena was coming to the conclusion that the best thing that could happen to her was for her to die here.

'I've tried to stop that dripping,' Jeb said, as if to apologize. 'I don't know what the problem is.'

Lena licked her lips, holding her tongue.

'Sara came by,' he said. 'You know, she really has no idea who I am.'

Again, Lena was silent. There was a lonely quality to his voice that she did not want to respond to. It was as if he wanted comfort.

'Do you want to know what I did to your sister?' he asked.

'Yes,' Lena answered before she could stop herself.

'She had a sore throat,' he began, taking off his shirt. Out of the corner of her eye, Lena watched him as he continued to undress himself. His tone was casual, the same one he used when recommending an over-the-counter cough medicine or a particular brand of vitamin.

He said, 'She didn't like to take any medication, even aspirin. She asked me if I knew of a good herbal cough remedy.' He was completely naked now, and he moved closer to Lena. She tried to jerk away as he lay down beside her, but it was useless. Her hands and feet were securely nailed to the floor. The secondary restraints all but paralyzed her.

Jeb continued, 'Sara told me she would be going to the diner at two. I knew Sibyl would be there. I used to watch her walk by every Monday on her way to eat lunch. She was very pretty, Lena. But not like you. She didn't have your spirit.'

Lena jerked as his hand came out to stroke her stomach. His fingers played lightly on her skin, sending a tremor of fear through her body.

He rested his head on her shoulder, watching his hand as he spoke. 'I knew Sara was going to be there, that Sara could save her, but of course that's not how it worked out, was it? Sara was late. She was late, and she let your sister die.'

Lena's body shook uncontrollably. He had kept her drugged during the past assaults, making them somewhat bearable. If he raped her now, like this, she wouldn't survive it. Lena remembered Julia Matthews's last words. She had said that Jeb made love to her; that was what had killed Julia. Lena knew if he made it gentle, if he was soft with her rather than savage, if he kissed her and caressed her as a lover, she would never be able to go back from this point. No matter what he did to her, if she lived beyond tomorrow, if she survived this ordeal, part of her would already be dead.

Jeb leaned over, tracing his tongue along her lower abdomen, into her navel. He gave a pleased laugh. 'You're so sweet, Lena,' he whispered, tracing his tongue up to her nipple. He sucked her breast gently, using his palm to attend to her other breast. His body was pressed into hers, and she could feel the hardness of him against her leg.

Lena's mouth trembled as she asked, 'Tell me about Sibyl.'

He used his fingers to gently squeeze her nipple. In another setting, under different circumstances, it would be almost playful. There was a hushed lover's tone to his voice that sent a wave of repulsion screaming down her spine.

Jeb said, 'I walked around the back of the buildings and hid in the toilet. I knew the tea would make her have to use the bathroom, so . . .' He ran his fingers down her stomach, stopping just above her pubic area. 'I locked myself in the other stall. It happened very fast. I should have guessed she was a virgin.' He gave the kind of satisfied sigh a dog would give after a large meal. 'She was so warm and wet when I was inside of her.'

Lena shuddered as his finger probed between her legs. He massaged her, his eyes locked onto hers to see her reaction. The direct stimulation caused her body to react in ways contrary to the terror she was feeling. He leaned over, kissing the side of her breasts. 'God, you've got a beautiful body,' he moaned, holding his finger up to her lips, pressing her mouth open. She tasted herself as he slid his finger deeper; in and out, in and out.

He said, 'Julia was pretty, too, but not like you.' He put his hand back between her legs, pressing his finger deep inside her. She felt herself being stretched as he slipped in another finger.

'I could give you something,' he said. 'Something to dilate you. I could get my whole fist inside of you.'

A sob filled the room: Lena's. She had never heard such grief in her life. The sound itself was more frightening than what Jeb was doing to her. Her entire body moved up and down as he fucked her, the chains from her restraints raking against the floor, the back of her head rubbing against the hard wood.

He slipped his fingers out and lay beside her, his body pressed into her side. She could feel every part of him, tell how excited this was making him. There was a sexual odor in the room that made it difficult for her to breathe. He was doing something, she could not tell what.

He put his lips close to her ear, whispering, ' "Behold, I give unto you power to tread on serpents and scorpions, and over all the power of the enemy; and nothing shall by any means hurt you." '

Lena's teeth started to chatter. She felt a pinch at her thigh and knew he had given her another injection.

' "For a small moment have I forsaken thee; but with great mercies I shall gather thee." '

'Please,' Lena cried, 'please don't do this.'

'Julia, Sara could save. Not your sister,' Jeb said. He sat up, crossing his legs again. He stroked himself as he spoke, his tone almost conversational. 'I don't know if she'll be able to save you, Lena. Do you?'

Lena could not look away from him. Even as he picked his pants off the floor and pulled something from

358

the back pocket, her eyes stayed on his. He held up a pair of pliers in her line of vision. They were large, about ten inches long, and the stainless steel gleamed in the light.

'I've got a late lunch,' he said, 'then I've got to run into town and take care of some paperwork. The bleeding should be stopped by then. I've mixed a blood-clotting compound with the Percodan. I also added a little something for the nausea. It's going to hurt a little. I won't lie to you.'

Lena rolled her head side to side, not understanding. She felt the drugs kicking in. Her body felt like it was melting to the floor.

'Blood is a great lubricant. Did you know that?'

Lena held her breath, not knowing what was coming, but sensing the danger.

His penis brushed against her chest as he straddled her body. He steadied her head with a strong hand, forcing her mouth open by pressing his fingers into her jaw. Her vision blurred, then doubled as he reached the pliers into her mouth.

TWENTY-EIGHT

Sara pulled back on the throttle as she neared the dock. Jeb was already there, taking off his orange life vest, looking just as goofy as he had before. Like Sara, he was wearing a heavy sweater and a pair of jeans. Last night's storm had dropped the temperature considerably, and she could not guess why anyone would get out on the lake today unless they absolutely had to.

'Let me help you,' he offered, reaching out toward her boat. He grabbed one of the lines and walked along the deck, pulling the boat toward the winch.

'Just tie it here,' Sara said, stepping out of the boat. 'I've got to go back over to my parents' house later.'

'Nothing wrong, I hope?'

'No,' Sara answered, tying the other line. She glanced at Jeb's rope, noting the girlie knot he had used looping it around the bollard. The boat would probably be loose inside of ten minutes, but Sara did not have the heart to give him a rope-tying lesson.

She reached into the boat, taking out two plastic grocery bags. 'I had to borrow my sister's car to go to the store,' she explained. 'My car's still impounded.'

'From the –' He stopped, looking somewhere over Sara's shoulder.

'Yeah,' she answered, walking along the dock. 'Did you get your gutter fixed?'

He was shaking his head as he caught up with her, taking the bags. 'I don't know what the problem is.'

'Have you thought about putting a sponge or something in the bottom of the spout?' she suggested. 'Maybe that'll help dampen the noise.'

'That's a great idea,' he said. They had reached the house, and she opened the back door for him.

He gave her a concerned look as he placed the bags on the counter alongside his boat keys. 'You really should lock your door, Sara.'

'I was just gone for a few minutes.'

'I know,' Jeb said. 'But, you never know. Especially with what's been going on lately. You know, with those girls.'

Sara sighed. He had a point. She just could not reconcile what was happening in town with her own home. It was as if Sara was somehow protected by the old 'lightning never strikes twice' rule. Of course, Jeb was right. She would need to be more careful.

She asked, 'How's the boat doing?' as she walked toward the answering machine. The message light was not blinking, but a scroll through the caller ID showed that Jeffrey had called three times in the last hour. Whatever he wanted to say, Sara wasn't listening. She was actually thinking about quitting at the coroner's office. There had to be a better way to get Jeffrey out of her life. She needed to focus on the present instead of wishing for the past. Truth be told, the past was not as great as she had made it out to be.

'Sara?' Jeb asked, holding out a glass of wine.

'Oh.' Sara took the glass, thinking it was a little early for her to be drinking alcohol.

Jeb held up his glass. 'Cheers.'

'Cheers,' Sara returned, tilting the glass. She gagged

at the taste. 'Oh, God,' she said, putting her hand to her mouth. The sharp taste sat on her tongue like a wet rag.

'What's wrong?'

'Ugh,' Sara groaned, holding her head under the kitchen faucet. She washed her mouth out several times before turning back to Jeb. 'It turned. The wine turned.'

He waved the glass under his nose, frowning. 'It smells like vinegar.'

'Yes,' she said, taking another swig of water.

'Gosh, I'm sorry. I guess I kept it a little too long.'

The phone rang as she turned off the faucet. Sara gave an apologetic smile to Jeb as she crossed the room, checking the caller ID. It was Jeffrey again. She did not pick up the phone.

'This is Sara,' her voice said from the answering machine. She was trying to remember which button to press when the beep came, then Jeffrey.

'Sara,' Jeffrey said, 'I'm getting patient records to go over from Grady so we –'

Sara pulled the power cord out of the back of the machine, cutting Jeffrey off in midsentence. She turned back to Jeb with what she hoped was an apologetic smile. 'Sorry,' she said.

'Is something wrong?' he asked. 'Didn't you use to work at Grady?'

'In another lifetime,' she answered, taking the phone off the hook. She listened for the dial tone, then rested the receiver on the table.

'Oh,' Jeb said.

She smiled at the quizzical look he gave her, fighting the urge to spit out the taste in her mouth. She walked over to the counter and started unpacking the bags. 'I got deli meats at the grocery store instead,' she offered. 'Roast beef, chicken, turkey, potato salad.' She stopped at the look he was giving her. 'What?'

He shook his head. 'You're so pretty.'

Sara felt herself blush at the compliment. 'Thanks,' she managed, taking out a loaf of bread. 'Do you want mayonnaise?'

He gave her a nod, still smiling. His expression was almost worshipful. It was making her uncomfortable.

To interrupt the moment, she suggested, 'Why don't you put on some music?'

Following her directions he turned toward the stereo. Sara finished making the sandwiches as he trailed his finger down her CD collection.

Jeb said, 'We've got the same taste in music.'

Sara suppressed a 'Great' as she took plates out of the cabinet. She was halving the sandwiches when the music came on. It was an old Robert Palmer CD she had not heard in ages.

'Great sound system,' Jeb said. 'Is that surround sound?'

'Yeah,' Sara answered. The speaker system was something Jeffrey had installed so that music could be heard throughout the house. There was even a speaker in the bathroom. They had taken baths at night sometimes, candles around the tub, something soft playing on the stereo.

'Sara?'

'Sorry,' she said, realizing she had zoned out.

Sara put down the plates on the kitchen table, setting them across from each other. She waited for Jeb to come back, then sat down, her leg tucked underneath her. 'I haven't heard this in a long time.'

'It's pretty old,' he said, taking a bite of his sandwich. 'My sister used to listen to this all the time.' He smiled. '*Sneakin' Sally Through the Alley*. That was her name, Sally.'

Sara licked some mayonnaise off her finger, hoping

the taste would mask the wine. 'I didn't know you had a sister.'

He sat up in his chair, taking his wallet out of his back pocket. 'She died a while ago,' he said, thumbing through the pictures in the front. He slid a photo from one of the plastic sleeves, holding it out to Sara. 'Just one of those things.'

Sara thought that was an odd thing to say about the death of his sister. Still, she took the picture, which showed a young girl in a cheerleading outfit. She held her pom-poms out from her sides. A smile was on her face. The girl looked just like Jeb. 'She was very pretty,' Sara said, handing him back the photograph. 'How old was she?'

'She had just turned thirteen,' he answered, looking at the picture for a few beats. He slipped it into its plastic sleeve, then tucked the wallet in his back pocket. 'She was a surprise baby for my parents. I was fifteen when she was born. My father had just gotten his first church.'

'He was a minister?' Sara asked, wondering how she could have dated Jeb before and not known this. She could have sworn he had once told her that his father was an electrician.

'He was a Baptist preacher,' Jeb clarified. 'He was a firm believer in the power of the Lord to heal what ails you. I'm glad he had his faith to get him through, but . . .' Jeb shrugged. 'Some things you just can't let go of. Some things you can't forget.'

'I'm sorry for your loss,' Sara answered, knowing what he meant about not being able to let go. She looked down at her sandwich, thinking it was probably not appropriate to take a bite at this moment. Her stomach growled to spur her on, but she ignored it.

'It was a long time ago,' Jeb finally answered. 'I was

just thinking about her today, with all that's been going on.'

Sara did not know what to say. She was tired of death. She did not want to comfort him. This date had been made to take her mind off what had been happening lately, not remind her of it.

She stood from the table, offering, 'Did you want something else to drink?' Sara walked over to the refrigerator as she talked. 'I've got Cokes, some Kool-Aid, orange juice.' She opened the door and the sucking sound reminded her of something. She just could not put her finger on it. Suddenly it hit her. Rubber stripping on the doors to the ER at Grady had made the exact same sucking noise when they opened. She had never made the connection before, but there it was.

Jeb said, 'Coke's fine.'

Sara reached into the fridge, shuffling around for the sodas. She stopped, her hand resting on the trademark red can. She felt a lightheadedness, as if she had too much air in her lungs. She closed her eyes, trying to keep her sense of balance. Sara was back in the ER. The doors opened with that sucking sound. A young girl was wheeled in on a gurney. Stats were called out by the EMT, IVs were started, the girl was intubated. She was in shock, her pupils blown, her body warm to the touch. Her temperature was called out, one hundred three. Her blood pressure was through the roof. She was bleeding profusely from between her legs.

Sara ran the case, trying to stop the bleeding. The girl started to convulse, jerking out the IVs, kicking over the supply tray at her feet. Sara leaned over her, trying to stop the girl from doing any further damage. The seizing stopped abruptly, and Sara thought she might have died. Her pulse was strong. Her reflexes were weak but registering.

A pelvic examination revealed the girl had recently had an abortion, though not one that had been given by a qualified physician. Her uterus was a mess, the walls of her vagina scraped and shredded. Sara repaired what she could, but the damage was done. Whatever healing she would do was left up to the girl.

Sara went to her car to change her shirt before talking to the girl's parents. She found them in the waiting area and told them the prognosis. She used the right phrases, like 'guarded optimism' and 'critical, but stable.' Only the girl did not make it through the next three hours. She had another seizure, effectively frying her brain.

At that point in her career, the thirteen-year-old girl was the youngest patient Sara had ever lost. The other patients who had died under Sara's care had been older, or sicker, and it was sad to lose them, but their deaths had not been so unexpected. Sara was shocked by the tragedy as she made her way toward the waiting area. The girl's parents seemed just as shocked. They had no idea their daughter had been pregnant. To their knowledge, she had never had a boyfriend. They couldn't understand how their daughter could be pregnant, let alone dead.

'My baby,' the father whispered. He repeated the phrase over and over, his voice quiet with grief. 'She was my baby.'

'You must be wrong,' the mother said. Rummaging around in her purse, she pulled out a wallet. Before Sara could stop her, a photograph was found, a school picture of the young girl in a cheerleading uniform. Sara did not want to look at the picture, but there was no consoling the woman until she did. Sara glanced down quickly, then looked a second, more careful time. The photograph showed a young girl in a cheerleading outfit. She held her pom-poms out from her sides. A smile was on her face. The expression was a sharp contrast to the one on the lifeless girl lying on the gurney, waiting to be moved to the morgue.

The father had reached out, taking Sara's hands. He bent his head down and mumbled a prayer that seemed to last a long time, asking for forgiveness, restating his belief in God. Sara was by no means a religious person, but there was something about his prayer that moved her. To be able to find such comfort in the face of such a horrible loss was amazing to her.

After the prayer, Sara had gone to her car to collect her thoughts, to maybe take a drive around the block and work her mind around this tragic, unnecessary death. That was when she had found the damage done to her car. That was when she had gone back into the bathroom. That was when Jack Allen Wright had raped her.

The picture Jeb had just shown her was the same picture she had seen twelve years ago in the waiting room.

'Sara?'

The song changed on the stereo. Sara felt her stomach drop as the words 'Hey, hey, Julia' came from the speakers.

'Something wrong?' Jeb asked, then quoted the words from the song. ' "You're acting so peculiar." '

Sara stood, holding up a can as she closed the refrigerator. 'This is the last Coke,' she said, edging toward the garage door. 'I've got some outside.'

'That's okay.' He shrugged. 'I'm fine with just water.' He had put his sandwich down and was staring at her.

Sara popped the top on the Coke. Her hands were shaking slightly, but she didn't think Jeb noticed. She brought the can to her mouth, sipping enough to let some of the Coke spill onto her sweater.

'Oh,' she said, trying to act surprised. 'Let me go change. I'll be right back.'

Sara returned the smile he gave her, her lips trembling as she did so. She forced herself to move, walking down the hall slowly so as not to raise the alarm. Inside her room, she snatched up the phone, glancing out the bank of windows, surprised to see the bright sunlight pouring in. It was so incongruous with the terror she felt. Sara dialed Jeffrey's number, but there were no corresponding beeps when she pressed the buttons. She stared at the phone, willing it to work.

'You took it off the hook,' Jeb said. 'Remember?'

Sara jumped up from her bed. 'I was just calling my dad. He's coming by in a few minutes.'

Jeb stood in the doorway, leaning against the jamb. 'I thought you said you were going by their house later.'

'That's right,' Sara answered, backing toward the other side of the room. This put the bed between them, but Sara was trapped, her back to the window. 'He's coming to get me.'

'You think so?' Jeb asked. He was smiling the same way he always did, a lopsided half grin that you would find on a child. There was something so casual about him, something so nonthreatening, that Sara wondered for half a second if she had drawn the wrong conclusion. A glance down at his hand snapped her out of it. He was holding a long boning knife at his side.

'What gave it away?' he asked. 'The vinegar, wasn't it? I had a bear of a time getting it in through the cork. Thank God for cardiac syringes.'

Sara put her hand behind her, feeling the cold glass of the window under her palm. 'You left them for me,' she said, going through the last few days in her mind. Jeb had known about her lunch with Tessa. Jeb had known she was at the hospital the night Jeffrey was shot.

'That's why Sibyl was in the bathroom. That's why Julia was on my car. You wanted me to save them.'

He smiled, nodding slowly. There was a sadness around his eyes, as if he regretted that the game was over. 'I wanted to give you that opportunity.'

'Is that why you showed me her picture?' she asked. 'To see if I would remember her?'

'I'm surprised you did.'

'Why?' Sara asked. 'Do you think I could forget something like that? She was a baby.'

He shrugged.

'Did you do that to her?' Sara asked, recalling the brutality of the home abortion. Derrick Lange, her supervisor, had guessed a clothes hanger had been used.

She said, 'Were you the one who did it?'

'How did you know?' Jeb asked, a defensive edge to his tone. 'Did she tell you?'

There was something more to what he was saying, a more sinister secret behind his words. When Sara spoke, she knew the answer before she even finished her sentence. Taking into account what she had seen Jeb was capable of, it made perfect sense.

She asked, 'You raped your sister, didn't you?'

'I loved my sister,' he countered, the defensive tone still there.

'She was just a child.'

'She came to me,' he said, as if this was some kind of excuse. 'She wanted to be with me.'

'She was thirteen years old.'

' "If a man shall take his sister, his father's daughter, and see her nakedness and she see his nakedness, it is a wicked thing." ' His smile seemed to say he was pleased with himself. 'Just call me wicked.'

'She was your sister.'

'We are all God's children, are we not? We share the same parents.'

'Can you quote a verse to justify rape? Can you quote a verse to justify murder?'

'The good thing about the Bible, Sara, is that it's open to interpretation. God gives us signs, opportunities, and we either follow them or we don't. We can choose what happens to us that way. We don't like to think about it, but we are the captains of our own destinies. We make the decisions that direct the course of our lives.' He stared at her, not speaking for a few beats. 'I would have thought you learned that lesson twelve years ago.'

Sara felt the earth shift under her feet as a thought came to her. 'Was it you? In the bathroom?'

'Lord, no,' Jeb said, waving this off. 'That was Jack Wright. He beat me to it, I guess. Gave me a good idea, though.' Jeb leaned against the door jamb, the same pleased smile twisting his lips. 'We're both men of faith, you see. We both let the Spirit guide us.'

'The only thing you both are is animals.'

'I guess I owe him for bringing us together,' Jeb said. 'What he did for you has served as an example for me, Sara. I want to thank you for that. On behalf of the many women who have come since then, and I do mean come in the biblical sense, I offer a sincere thank-you.'

'Oh, God,' Sara breathed, putting her hand to her mouth. She had seen what he had done to his sister, to Sibyl Adams, and to Julia Matthews. To think that this had all started when Jack Wright had attacked her made Sara's stomach turn. 'You monster,' she hissed. 'You murderer.'

He straightened, his expression suddenly changed by rage. Jeb went from being a quiet, unassuming pharmacist to the man who had raped and killed at least two

370

women. Anger radiated from his posture. 'You let her die. You killed her.'

'She was dead before she got to me,' Sara countered, trying to keep her voice steady. 'She lost too much blood.'

'That's not true.'

'You didn't get it all out,' she said. 'She was rotting from the inside.'

'You're lying.'

Sara shook her head. She moved her hand behind her, looking for the lock on the window. 'You killed her.'

'That's not true,' he repeated, though she could tell from the change in his voice that part of him believed her.

Sara found the lock, tried to twist it open. It wouldn't budge. 'Sibyl died because of you, too.'

'She was fine when I left her.'

'She had a heart attack,' Sara told him, pressing against the lock. 'She died from an overdose. She had a seizure, just like your sister.'

His voice was frighteningly loud in the bedroom, and the glass behind Sara shook when he yelled, 'That is not true.'

Sara gave up on the lock as he took a step toward her. He still held the knife down at his side, but the threat was there. 'I wonder if your cunt's still as sweet as it was for Jack,' he mumbled. 'I remember sitting through your trial, listening to the details. I wanted to take notes, but I found after the first day that I didn't need to.' He reached into his back pocket, taking out a pair of handcuffs. 'You still got that key I left for you?'

She stopped him with her words. 'I won't go through this again,' she said with conviction. 'You'll have to kill me first.'

He looked down at the floor, his shoulders relaxed.

She felt a brief moment of relief until he looked back up at her. There was a smile at his lips when he said, 'What makes you think it matters to me if you're dead or not?'

'You gonna cut a hole in my belly?'

He was so shocked that he dropped the handcuffs on the floor. 'What?' he whispered.

'You didn't sodomize her.'

She could see a bead of sweat roll down the side of his head as he asked, 'Who?'

'Sibyl,' Sara provided. 'How else could shit get inside her vagina?'

'That's disgusting.'

'Is it?' Sara asked. 'Did you bite her while you fucked the hole in her belly?'

He shook his head vehemently side to side. 'I didn't do that.'

'Your teeth marks are on her shoulder, Jeb.'

'They are not.'

'I saw them,' Sara countered. 'I saw everything you did to them. I saw how you hurt all of them.'

'They weren't hurting,' he insisted. 'They didn't hurt at all.'

Sara walked toward him until she was standing with her knees against the bed. He stood on the other side, watching her, a stricken look on his face. 'They suffered, Jeb. Both of them suffered, just like your sister. Just like Sally.'

'I never hurt them like that,' he whispered. 'I never hurt them. You're the one who let them die.'

'You raped a thirteen-year-old child, a blind woman, and an emotionally unstable twenty-two-year-old. Is that what gets you off, Jeb? Attacking helpless women? Controlling them?'

His jaw clenched. 'You're just going to make it harder for yourself.'

'Fuck you, you sick bastard.'

'No,' he said. 'It'll be the other way around.'

'Come on,' Sara taunted, clenching her fists. 'I dare you to try.'

Jeb lunged toward her, but Sara was already moving. She ran full force toward the picture window, tucking her head as she broke out the glass. Pain flooded her senses, shards of glass cutting into her body. She landed in the backyard, tucking as she rolled a few feet down the hill.

Sara stood quickly, not looking over her shoulder as she ran toward the lake. Her arm was cut across the bicep and a gash was in her forehead, but these were the least of her concerns. By the time she got to the dock, Jeb was close behind her. She dove into the cold water without thinking, swimming under the water until she could no longer breathe. Finally, she surfaced ten yards from the dock. Sara saw Jeb jump into her boat, too late remembering she had left the key in the ignition.

Sara dove under the water, pushing herself, swimming as far as she could before surfacing. When she looked back around, she could see the boat coming toward her. She dove down, touching the bottom of the lake as the boat sped over her. Sara turned underwater, heading toward the rock field lining the far side of the lake. The area was no more than twenty feet away, but Sara felt her arms tiring as she swam. The coldness of the water hit her like a slap in the face, and she realized that the low temperature would slow her down.

She surfaced, looking around for the boat. Again, Jeb came at her full throttle. Again, she ducked under the water. She came up just in time to see the boat skimming toward the submerged rocks. The nose of the boat hit the first one head-on, popping up, flipping the boat over. Sara watched as Jeb was thrown from the boat. He flew through the air, splashing into the water. His hands clawed helplessly as he tried to keep himself from drowning. Mouth open, eyes wide with terror, he flailed as he was pulled down below the surface. She waited, holding her breath, but he did not come back up.

Jeb had been thrown about ten feet from the boat, away from the rock field. Sara knew the only way she would make it to the shore was to swim through the rocks. She could tread water for only so long before the cold enveloped her. The distance to the dock was too great. She would never make it. The safest route to the shore would take Sara past the overturned boat.

What she really wanted to do was stay where she was, but Sara knew the cold water was luring her into a sense of complacency. The lake's temperature wasn't down to freezing, but it was cold enough to bring on moderate hypothermia if she stayed in too long.

She swam a slow crawl to conserve body heat, her head just above the water as she made her way through the field. Her breath was a cloud in front of her, but she tried to think of something warm; sitting in front of a fire, roasting marshmallows. The hot tub at the YMCA. The steam room. The warm quilt on her bed.

Altering her course, she went around the far side of the boat, away from where Jeb had gone down. She had seen too many movies. She was terrified he would come from the deep, grabbing her leg, pulling her down. As she passed the boat, she could see a large hole in the front where the rock had torn through the bow. It was overturned, the belly up to the sky. Jeb was on the other side, holding on to the torn bow. His lips were dark blue, a stark contrast against his white face. He was shivering uncontrollably, his breath coming out in sharp puffs of white. He had been struggling, wasting his energy trying to keep his head above water. The cold was probably lowering his core temperature with every passing minute.

Sara kept swimming, moving more slowly. Jeb's breathing and her hands pushing through the water were the only sounds on the still lake.

'I c-c-can't swim,' he said.

'That's too bad,' Sara answered, her voice tight in her throat. She felt as if she was circling a wounded but dangerous animal.

'You can't leave me here,' he managed around chattering teeth.

She started to sidestroke, turning in the water so as not to put her back to him. 'Yes, I can.'

'You're a doctor.'

'Yes, I am,' she said, continuing to move away from him.

'You'll never find Lena.'

Sara felt a weight drop onto her. She treaded water, keeping her eyes on Jeb. 'What about Lena?'

'I tot-took her,' he said. 'She's somewhere safe.'

'I don't believe you.'

He gave what she assumed was a shrug.

'Where's somewhere safe?' Sara demanded. 'What did you do to her?'

'I left her for you, Sara,' he said, his voice catching as his body started shaking. From the recesses of her mind, Sara recalled that the second stage of hypothermia was marked by uncontrollable shaking and irrational thought.

He said, 'I left her somewhere.'

Sara moved slightly closer, not trusting him. 'Where did you leave her?'

'You non-need to save her,' he mumbled, closing his eyes. His face dipped down, his mouth dropping below the waterline. He snorted as water went up his nose, his grip on the boat tightening. There was a cracking sound as the boat moved against the rock.

Sara felt a sudden rush of heat through her body. 'Where is she, Jeb?' When he didn't answer, she told him, 'You can die out here. The water's cold enough. Your heart will slow down until it stops. I'd give you twenty minutes, tops,' she said, knowing it would be more like a few hours. 'I'll let you die,' Sara warned, never more certain of anything in her life. 'Tell me where she is.'

'I'll tell you on th-th-the shore,' he mumbled.

'Tell me now,' she said. 'I know you wouldn't leave her somewhere to die alone.'

'I wouldn't,' he said, a spark of understanding in his eyes. 'I wouldn't leave her alone, Sara. I wouldn't let her die alone.'

Sara moved her arms out to her side, trying to keep her body moving so that she would not freeze. 'Where is she, Jeb?'

He shook so hard the boat shuddered in the water, sending small wakes toward Sara. He whispered, 'You need to save her, Sara. You need to save her.'

'Tell me or I'll let you die, Jeb, I swear to God, I'll let you drown out here.'

His eyes seemed to cloud and a slight smile came to his blue lips. He whispered, '"It is finished,"' as his head dropped again, but this time he didn't stop it. Sara watched as he let go of the boat, his head slipping under water.

'No,' Sara screamed, lunging toward him. She grabbed the back of his shirt, trying to pull him up. Instinctively, he started to fight her, pulling her down instead of letting her pull him up. They struggled this way, Jeb grabbing her pants, her sweater, trying to use her as a ladder to climb back up for air. His fingernails raked across the cut in her arm, and Sara reflexively pulled away. Jeb was pushed back from her, the tips of his fingers brushing across the front of her sweater as he tried to find purchase.

Sara was pulled down as he climbed up. There was a solid thud as his head slammed against the boat. His mouth opened in surprise, then he slipped soundlessly back under the water. Behind him, a streak of bright red blood marked the bow of the boat. Sara tried to ignore the pressure in her lungs as she reached toward him, trying to pull him back up. There was just enough sunlight for her to see him sinking to the bottom. His mouth was open, his hands stretched out to her.

She surfaced, gasping for air, then ducked her head back underwater. She did this several times, searching for Jeb. When she finally found him, he was resting against a large boulder, his arms held out in front of him, eyes open as he stared at her. Sara put her hand to his wrist, checking to see if he was alive. She went up for air, treading water, her arms out to the side. Her teeth were chattering, but she counted out loud.

'One-one thousand,' she said through clicking teeth. 'Two-one thousand.' Sara continued counting, furiously treading water. She was reminded of old games of Marco Polo, where either she or Tessa would tread water, their eyes closed, as they counted out the requisite number before searching each other out.

At fifty, she took a deep breath, then dove back down. Jeb was still there, his head back. She closed his eyes, then scooped him up under his arms. On the surface, she crooked her arm around his neck, using her other arm to swim. Holding him this way, she started toward the shore.

After what seemed like hours but was only a minute

at most, Sara stopped, treading water so that she could catch her breath. The shore seemed farther away than it had before. Her legs felt disconnected from her body, even as she willed them to tread water. Jeb was literally deadweight, pulling her down. Her head dipped just below the surface, but she stopped herself, coughing out the lake, trying to clear her mind. It was so cold, and she felt so sleepy. She blinked her eyes, trying not to keep them closed too long. A small period of rest would be good. She would rest here, then drag him back to the shore.

Sara leaned her head back, trying to float on her back. Jeb made this impossible, and again she started to dip below the water. She would have to let Jeb go. Sara realized that. She just could not force herself to do it. Even as the weight of his body started to pull her down again, Sara could not let go.

A hand grabbed her, then an arm was around her waist. Sara was too weak to struggle, her brain too frozen to make sense of what was happening. For a split second she thought it was Jeb, but the force pulling her up to the surface was too strong. Her grip around Jeb loosened, and she opened her eyes, watching his body float back down to the bottom of the lake.

Her head broke the surface and her mouth opened wide as she gasped for air. Her lungs ached with each breath, her nose ran. Sara started to cough the kind of wracking coughs that could stop the heart. Water came out of her mouth, then bile, as she choked on the fresh air. She felt someone beating on her back, knocking the water out of her. Her head tilted down into the water again, but she was jerked back by her hair.

'Sara,' Jeffrey said, one hand around her jaw, the other holding her up by the arm. 'Look at me,' he demanded. 'Sara.'

Her body went limp, and she was conscious of the fact that Jeffrey was pulling her back toward the shore. His arm was hooked across her body, under her arms, as he did an awkward one-handed backstroke.

Sara put her hands over Jeffrey's arm, leaned her head against his chest, and let him take her home.

TWENTY-NINE

Lena wanted Jeb. She wanted him to take the pain away from her. She wanted him to send her back to that place where Sibyl and their mother and father were. She wanted to be with her family. She did not care what price she had to pay; she wanted to be with them.

Blood trickled down the back of her throat in a steady stream, causing her to cough occasionally. He had been right about the throbbing pain in her mouth, but the Percodan made it bearable. She trusted Jeb that the bleeding would stop soon. She knew he was not finished with her yet. He would not let her choke to death on her own blood after all the trouble he had gone through to keep her here. Lena knew he had something more spectacular in mind for her.

When her mind wandered, she imagined herself being left in front of Nan Thomas's house. For some reason, this pleased her. Hank would see what had been done to Lena. He would know what had been done to Sibyl. He would see what Sibyl had not been able to see. It seemed fitting.

A familiar noise came from downstairs, footsteps across the hard wooden floor. The steps were muffled as he walked across the carpet. Lena assumed this was in the living room. She did not know the layout of the house, but by listening to the distinct noises, making the connection between the hollow taps of his shoes on the floor as he walked around the house and the dull thud as he took off his shoes to come see her, she could generally tell where he was.

Only, this time there seemed to be a second set of footsteps.

'Lena?' She could barely make out his voice, but she knew instinctively that it was Jeffrey Tolliver. For just a second, she wondered what he was doing there.

Her mouth opened, but she did not say anything. She was upstairs in the attic. Maybe he would not think to look here. Maybe he would leave her alone. She could die here and no one would ever know what had been done to her.

'Lena?' another voice called. It was Sara Linton.

Her mouth was still open, but she could not speak.

For what seemed like hours, they walked around downstairs. She heard the heavy scrapes and bangs as furniture was moved around, closets searched. The muffled sounds of their voices sounded like a disjointed harmony to her ears. She actually smiled, thinking they sounded like they were banging pots and pans together. It wasn't like Jeb could have hid her in the kitchen.

This thought struck her as funny. She started to laugh, an uncontrollable reaction that shook her chest, making her cough. Soon, she was laughing so hard that tears came to her eyes. Then, she was sobbing, her chest tightening with pain as her mind let her see everything that had happened to her in the last week. She saw Sibyl on the slab in the morgue. She saw Hank mourning the loss of his niece. She saw Nan Thomas, eyes red-rimmed and stricken. She saw Jeb on top of her, making love to her.

Her fingers curled in around the long nails securing her to the floor, her entire body seizing up at the knowledge of the physical assaults against her.

'Lena?' Jeffrey called, his voice stronger than it had been before. 'Lena?'

She heard him moving closer, heard knocking in quick staccato, then a pause, then more knocking.

Sara said, 'It's a false panel.'

More knocking came, then the sound of their footsteps on the attic stairs. The door burst open, light cutting through the darkness. Lena squeezed her eyes shut, feeling like needles were pressing into her eyeballs.

'Oh my God,' Sara gasped. Then, 'Get some towels. Sheets. Anything.'

Lena slit her eyes open as Sara knelt in front of her. There was a coldness coming off Sara's body, and she was wet.

'It's okay,' Sara whispered, her hand on Lena's forehead. 'You're going to be okay.'

Lena opened her eyes more, letting her pupils adjust to the light. She looked back at the door, searching for Jeb.

'He's dead,' Sara said. 'He can't hurt you –' She stopped, but Lena knew what she was going to say. She heard the last word to Sara's sentence in her mind if not her ears. He can't hurt you anymore, she had started to say.

Lena allowed herself to look up at Sara. Something flashed in Sara's eyes, and Lena knew that Sara somehow understood. Jeb was part of Lena now. He would be hurting her every day for the rest of her life.

SUNDAY

THIRTY

Jeffrey drove back from the hospital in Augusta feeling like a soldier returning from war. Lena would physically recover from her wounds, but he had no idea if she would ever recover from the emotional damage Jeb McGuire had wrought. Like Julia Matthews, Lena was not talking to anybody, not even her uncle Hank. Jeffrey did not know what to do for her, other than give her time.

Mary Ann Moon had called him exactly an hour and twenty minutes after they had talked. Sara's patient's name had been Sally Lee McGuire. Moon had taken the time to key the surname into a general search of the hospital staff. With a specific name, it only took a few seconds for Jeremy 'Jeb' McGuire's name to come up. He was doing his internship at the pharmacy on Grady's third floor when Sara worked there. Sara would have no cause to meet him, but Jeb could have certainly made it a point to meet her.

Jeffrey would never forget the look on Lena's face when he busted down the attic door. In his mind, he recalled the photographs of Sara whenever he thought of Lena lying there, nailed to Jeb's attic floor. The room had been designed to be a dark box. Dull black paint covered everything, including the panels of plywood nailed over the windows. Chains through eye hooks had been screwed to the floor, and two sets of nail holes at both the top and bottom of the restraints showed where the victims had been crucified.

In the car, Jeffrey rubbed his eyes, trying not to think about everything he had seen since Sibyl Adams had been murdered. As he crossed the Grant County line, all he could think was that everything was different now. He would never look at the people in town, the people who were his friends and neighbors, with the same trusting eyes as he had this time last Sunday. He felt shell-shocked.

Turning into Sara's driveway, Jeffrey was aware that her house, too, looked different to him. This was where Sara had fought Jeb. This was where Jeb had drowned. They had pulled his body out of the lake, but the memory of him would never be gone.

Jeffrey sat in his car, staring at the house. Sara had told him she needed time, but he wasn't about to give it to her. He needed to explain what had been going through his mind. He needed to reassure himself as well as her that there was no way in hell he was going to stay out of her life.

The front door was open, but Jeffrey gave a knock before walking in. He could hear Paul Simon singing 'Have a Good Time' on the stereo. The house was turned upside down. Boxes lined the hallway and books were off the shelves. He found Sara in the kitchen, holding a wrench. Dressed in a white sleeveless T-shirt and a pair of ratty grey sweatpants, he thought that she had never looked more beautiful in her life. She was looking down the drain when he knocked on the door jamb.

She turned, obviously not surprised to see him. 'Is this your idea of giving me some time?' she asked.

He shrugged, tucking his hands into his pockets. She had a bright green Band-Aid covering the cut on her forehead and a white bandage around her arm where the glass had gone deep enough for sutures. How she had managed to survive what she did was a miracle to Jeffrey. Her strength of spirit amazed him.

The next song came on the stereo, 'Fifty Ways to Leave Your Lover.' Jeffrey tried to joke with her, saying, 'It's our song.'

Sara gave him a wary look before fumbling for the remote. Abruptly, the music stopped, the silence replacing the song filling the house. They both seemed to take a few seconds to adjust to the change.

She said, 'What're you doing here?'

Jeffrey opened his mouth, thinking that he should say something romantic, something to sweep her off her feet. He wanted to tell her that she was the most beautiful woman he had ever known, that he had never really known what it meant to be in love until he had met her. None of these things came, though, so he offered her information instead.

'I found the transcripts from your trial, Wright's trial, in Jeb's house.'

She crossed her arms. 'That so?'

'He had newspaper clippings, photographs. That kind of thing.' He stopped, then, 'I guess Jeb moved here to be close to you.'

She gave a condescending, 'You think?'

He ignored the warning behind her tone. 'There are some other attacks over in Pike County,' Jeffrey continued. He couldn't stop himself, even though he could tell from her expression that he should just shut the hell up, that she did not want to know these things. The problem was that it was much easier to tell Sara the facts than for Jeffrey to come up with something on his own.

He continued. 'The sheriff over there has four cases

he's trying to tie to Jeb. We'll need to get some samples for the lab so he can do a crosscheck with the DNA samples they took at the scene. Plus what we have from Julia Matthews.' He cleared his throat. 'His body's over at the morgue.'

'I'm not doing it,' Sara answered.

'We can get somebody from Augusta.'

'No,' Sara corrected. 'You don't understand. I'm going to hand in my resignation tomorrow.'

He could not think of anything to say but 'Why?'

'Because I can't do this anymore,' she said, indicating the space between them. 'I can't keep this up, Jeffrey. This is why we divorced.'

'We divorced because I made a stupid mistake.'

'No,' she said, stopping him. 'We're not going to have this same argument over and over again. This is why I'm resigning. I can't keep putting myself through this. I can't let you hang around the periphery of my life. I have to get on with it.'

'I love you,' he said, as if that made any difference. 'I know I'm not good enough for you. I know I can't begin to understand you and I do the wrong things and I say the wrong things and I should've been here with you instead of going to Atlanta after you told me about – after I read about – what happened.' He paused, then, 'I know all that. And I still can't stop loving you.' She did not answer, so he said, 'Sara, I can't not be with you. I need you.'

'Which me do you need?' she asked. 'The one from before or the one who was raped?'

'They're both the same person,' he countered. 'I need them both. I love them both.' He stared at her, trying to find the right thing to say. 'I don't want to be without you.'

'You don't have a choice.'

'Yes, I do,' he answered. 'I don't care what you say, Sara. I don't care if you resign or you move out of town or you change your name, I'm still going to find you.'

'Like Jeb?'

Her words cut deep. Of all the things she could have said, this was the cruelest. She seemed to realize this, because she apologized quickly. 'That wasn't fair,' she said. 'I'm sorry.'

'Is that what you think? That I'm like him?'

'No.' She shook her head side to side. 'I know you're not like him.'

He looked at the floor, still feeling wounded by her words. She could have screamed that she hated him and caused less pain.

'Jeff,' she said, walking toward him. She put her hand to his cheek and he took it, kissing the palm.

He said, 'I don't want to lose you, Sara.'

'You already have.'

'No,' he said, not accepting this. 'I haven't. I know I haven't because you wouldn't be standing here right now. You would be back over there, telling me to leave.'

Sara did not contradict him, but she walked away, back toward the sink. 'I've got work to do,' she mumbled, picking up the wrench.

'Are you moving?'

'Cleaning,' she said. 'I started last night. I don't know where anything is. I had to sleep on the sofa because so much shit's on my bed.'

He tried to lighten things up. 'At the very least, you'll make your mama happy.'

She gave a humorless laugh, kneeling down in front of the sink. She covered the drain pipe with a towel, then locked the wrench over it. Putting her shoulder into it, she pushed the wrench. Jeffrey could tell it wouldn't budge.

'Let me help,' he offered, taking off his coat. Before she could stop him, he was kneeling beside her, pushing the wrench. The pipe was old, and the fitting would not budge. He gave up, saying, 'You'll probably have to cut it off.'

'No I won't,' she countered, gently pushing him out of the way. She braced her foot on the cabinet behind her and pushed with all of her might. The wrench turned slowly, Sara moving forward with it.

She flashed a smile of accomplishment. 'See?'

'You're amazing,' Jeffrey said, meaning it. He sat back on his heels, watching her take the pipe apart. 'Is there anything you can't do?'

'A long list of things,' she mumbled.

He ignored this, asking, 'Was it clogged?'

'I dropped something down it,' she answered, digging around the P trap with her finger. She pulled something out, cupping it in her palm before he could see it.

'What?' he asked, reaching toward her hand.

She shook her head, keeping her hand fisted.

He smiled, more curious than ever. 'What is it?' he repeated.

She sat up on her knees, holding her hands behind her back. Her brow furrowed in concentration for a moment, then she held her hands in front of her, fisted.

She said, 'Pick one.'

He did as he was told, tapping her right hand.

She said, 'Pick another one.'

He laughed, tapping her left hand.

Sara rolled her wrist, opening her fingers. A small gold band was in the palm of her hand. The last time he had seen the ring, Sara had been tugging it off her finger so she could throw it in his face.

Jeffrey was so surprised to see the ring he did not know what to say. 'You told me you threw that away.'

'I'm a better liar than you think.'

He gave her a knowing look, taking the wedding band from her. 'What are you still doing with it?'

'It's like a bad penny,' she said. 'Keeps turning up.'

He took this as an invitation, asking, 'What are you doing tomorrow night?'

She sat back on her heels, sighing. 'I don't know. Probably catching up at work.'

'Then what?'

'Home, I guess. Why?'

He slipped the ring in his pocket. 'I could bring dinner by.'

She shook her head. 'Jeffrey –'

'The Tasty Pig,' he tempted, knowing this was one of Sara's favorite places to eat. He took her hands in his, offering, 'Brunswick stew, barbecued ribs, pork sandwiches, beer baked beans.'

She stared at him, not answering. Finally she said, 'You know this won't work.'

'What have we got to lose?'

She seemed to think this over. He waited, trying to be patient. Sara let go of his hands, then used his shoulder to help her stand.

Jeffrey stood as well, watching her sort through one of many junk drawers. He opened his mouth to speak to her but knew there was nothing he could say. The one thing he knew about Sara Linton was that when she had made up her mind, there was no going back.

He stood behind her, kissing her bare shoulder. There should be a better way to say good-bye, but he could not think of one. Jeffrey had never been good at words. He was better at action. Most of the time, anyway.

He was walking down the hall when Sara called to him.

'Bring silverware,' she said.

He turned around, sure he had not heard right.

Her head was still bent down as she rummaged through the drawer. 'Tomorrow night,' she clarified. 'I can't remember where I put the forks.'

ACKNOWLEDGMENTS

Victoria Sanders, my agent, served as my anchor throughout this entire process. I do not know how I could have done any of this without her. My editor, Meaghan Dowling, was instrumental in helping me define this book and has my heartfelt gratitude for making me rise to the challenge. Captain Jo Ann Cain, chief of detectives for the city of Forest Park, Georgia, kindly shared her war stories. The Mitchell Cary family answered all of my plumbing questions and gave me some interesting ideas. Michael A. Rolnick, M.D., and Carol Barbier Rolnick lent Sara some credibility. Tamara Kennedy gave great advice early on. Any mistakes made in the above areas of expertise are entirely my own.

Fellow authors Ellen Conford, Jane Haddam, Eileen Moushey, and Katy Munger have my thanks; they each know why. Steve Hogan waded through my neuroses on a daily basis, and for that he should get some kind of medal. Readers Chris Cash, Cecile Dozier, Melanie Hammet, Judy Jordan, and Leigh Vanderels were invaluable. Greg Pappas, patron saint of signage, made things very easy. B.A. offered good advice and a quiet place to write. S.S. was my rock in a hard place. Lastly, thanks to D.A. – you are more myself than I am.

Kisscut

For Doris Smart,
who loved Auburn football
and reading – in that order

SATURDAY

ONE

'Dancing Queen,' Sara Linton mumbled with the music as she made her way around the skating rink. 'Young and sweet, only seventeen.'

She heard a furious clicking of wheels to her left and turned just in time to catch a small child before he crashed into her.

'Justin?' she asked, recognizing the seven year old. She held him up by the back of his shirt as his ankles wobbled over his in-line skates.

'Hey, Dr. Linton,' Justin managed around gasps for breath. His helmet was too big for his head, and he pushed it back several times as he tried to look up at her.

Sara returned his smile, trying not to laugh. 'Hello, Justin.'

'I guess you like this music, huh? My mom likes it, too.' He stared at her openly, his lips slightly parted. Like most of Sara's patients, Justin seemed a bit shocked to see her outside of the clinic. Sometimes she wondered if they thought she lived in the basement there, waiting for them to get colds or fevers so she could see them.

'Anyway,' Justin pushed back his helmet again, knocking himself in the nose with his elbow pad, 'I saw you singing it.'

'Here,' Sara offered, leaning down to adjust the chin

3

strap. The music in the rink was so loud that Sara could feel the bass vibrating through the plastic buckle as she tightened it under his chin.

'Thanks,' Justin yelled, then for some reason he put both his hands on top of the helmet, as if to rest them. The motion threw him off balance, and he stumbled, clamping on to Sara's leg.

Sara grabbed his shirt again and led them both over to the safety railing lining the rink. After trying on a pair of in-line skates herself, Sara had asked for the old four-wheel kind, not wanting to fall on her ass in front of half the town.

'Wow.' Justin giggled, throwing his arms over the railing for support. He was looking down at her skates. 'Your feet are so huge!'

Sara looked down at her skates, feeling a flush of embarrassment. She had been teased about her large feet since she was seven years old. After nearly thirty years of hearing it, Sara still felt the urge to hide under the bed with a bowl of chocolate-fudge ice cream.

'You're wearing boy's skates!' Justin screeched, letting go of the rail so that he could point at her black skates. Sara caught him just before he hit the ground.

'Sweetie,' Sara whispered politely into his ear. 'Remember this when you're due for your booster shots.'

Justin managed a smile for his pediatrician. 'I think my mom wants me,' he mumbled, edging along the rail, hand over hand, casting a wary eye over his shoulder to make sure Sara was not following him.

She crossed her arms, leaning against the railing as she watched him go. Sara loved kids, a characteristic most pediatricians shared, but there was something to be said for not spending her Saturday night surrounded by them.

'That your date?' Tessa asked, coming to a stop beside her.

Sara gave her sister a hard look. 'Remind me how I got roped into this.'

Tessa tried to smile. 'Because you love me?'

'Right,' Sara returned caustically. Across the rink, Sara picked out Devon Lockwood, Tessa's latest boyfriend, who also worked in the Linton family's plumbing business. Devon was leading his nephew around the kiddy rink while his brother watched.

'His mother hates me,' Tessa mumbled. 'She gives me nasty looks every time I get near him.'

'Daddy's the same way about us,' Sara reminded her.

Devon noticed them staring and waved.

'He's good with children,' Sara noted, returning his wave.

'He's good with his hands,' Tessa said in a low voice, almost to herself. She turned back to Sara. 'Speaking of which, where's Jeffrey?'

Sara looked back at the front entrance, wondering that herself. Wondering, too, why she cared whether or not her ex-husband showed up. 'I don't know,' she answered. 'When did this place get so packed?'

'It's Saturday night and football season hasn't started; what else are people going to do?' Tessa asked, but did not let Sara change the subject. 'Where's Jeffrey?'

'Maybe he won't come.'

Tessa smiled in a way that let Sara know she was holding back a snide comment.

'Go ahead and say it.'

'I wasn't going to say anything,' Tessa said, and Sara could not tell if she was lying or not.

'We're just dating.' Sara paused, wondering whom

she was trying to convince, Tessa or herself. She added, 'It's not even serious.'

'I know.'

'We've barely even kissed.'

Tessa held up her palms in resignation. 'I know,' she repeated, a smirk on her lips.

'Just a few dates. That's all.'

'You don't have to convince me.'

Sara groaned as she leaned back against the railing. She felt stupid, like a teenager instead of a grown woman. She had divorced Jeffrey two years ago after catching him with the woman who owned the sign shop in town. Why she had started seeing him again was as much a mystery to Sara as it was to her family.

A ballad came on, and the lights dimmed. Sara watched the mirrored ball drop down from the ceiling, scattering little squares of light all over the rink.

'I need to go to the bathroom,' Sara told her sister. 'Will you keep an eye out for Jeff?'

Tessa glanced over Sara's shoulder. 'Somebody just went in.'

'There are two stalls now.' Sara turned toward the women's rest room just in time to see a large teenage girl go in. Sara recognized the girl as Jenny Weaver, one of her patients. She waved, but the girl didn't see her.

Tessa muttered, 'Hope you can wait.'

Sara frowned, watching another teenager she did not recognize follow Jenny into the rest room. At this rate, Sara would go into renal failure before Jeffrey arrived.

Tessa tilted her head toward the front door. 'Speaking of tall, dark, and handsome.'

Sara felt a foolish smile come to her lips as she watched Jeffrey make his way toward the rink. He was still dressed for work in a charcoal-gray suit with a burgundy tie. As chief of police for Grant County, he knew most of the people in the room. He glanced around, looking for Sara, she supposed, stopping here and there to shake hands. She refused to do anything that would get his attention as he walked through the crowd. At this point in their relationship, Sara was content to let Jeffrey do all of the work.

Sara had met Jeffrey on one of her earlier cases as town coroner. She had taken the helm of the medical examiner's office as a way to earn extra money to buy out her retiring partner at the Heartsdale Children's Clinic. Even though she had paid off Dr. Barney years ago, Sara still kept the job. She liked the challenge of pathology. Twelve years ago, Sara had done her residency in the emergency room of Atlanta's Grady Hospital. Going from such a fast-paced, life-and-death job to tummy aches and sinus infections at the clinic had been a shock to her system. The coroner's job was a challenge that helped keep her mind sharp.

Jeffrey finally caught sight of her. He stopped in the middle of shaking Betty Reynolds's hand, the corners of his mouth rising slowly, then dipping into a frown as he was pulled back into conversation with the owner of the town's five-and-dime.

Sara could guess what Betty was talking about. The store had been broken into twice in the last three months. Betty's posture was adversarial, and even though Jeffrey's attention was obviously elsewhere, she continued to speak to him.

Finally, Jeffrey nodded, giving Betty a pat on the back as he shook her hand, probably making an appointment to talk with her tomorrow. He extricated himself, then walked toward Sara, a sly smile on his face.

'Hey,' Jeffrey said. Before she could stop herself,

Sara was shaking his hand the way almost everyone else in the rink had.

'Hello, Jeffrey,' Tessa interrupted, her tone uncharacteristically sharp. It was usually Eddie, their father, who was rude to Jeffrey.

Jeffrey gave a puzzled smile. 'Hey, Tessie.'

'Uh-huh,' Tessa mumbled, pushing off from the rail. She skated away, tossing Sara a knowing look over her shoulder.

Jeffrey asked, 'What was that about?'

Sara pulled back her hand, but Jeffrey held on to her fingers just long enough to let her know it was his choice to release her. He was so damn sure of himself. More than anything else, this quality appealed to Sara at a very base level.

She crossed her arms, saying, 'You're late.'

'I had trouble getting away.'

'Is her husband out of town?'

He gave her the same look he gave witnesses he knew were lying. 'I was talking to Frank,' he said, naming the lead detective on the Grant County squad. 'I told him that he's in charge tonight. I don't want anything to interrupt us.'

'Interrupt what?'

The same smile tugged at the corner of his lips. 'Oh, I thought I'd seduce you tonight.'

She laughed, backing up as he leaned in to kiss her.

'Kissing usually works better when the lips touch,' he suggested.

'Not in front of half my practice,' she countered.

'Come here, then.'

Despite her better judgment, Sara ducked under the railing and took his hand. He rolled her into the back of the rink by the bathroom, tucking them into a corner and out of sight.

'This better?' he asked.

'Yeah,' Sara answered, looking down at Jeffrey, because with the skates on she was a couple inches taller. 'Much better. I really need to use the bathroom.'

She started to move, but he stopped her, putting his hands on her waist.

'Jeff,' she said, aware her tone was far from threatening.

'You are so beautiful, Sara.'

She rolled her eyes like a teenager.

He laughed, trying, 'I thought about kissing you all last night.'

'Yeah?'

'I miss the way you taste.'

She tried to sound bored. 'It's still Colgate.'

'That's not the taste I was talking about.'

Her mouth opened in surprise, and he smiled, obviously pleased with her reaction. Sara felt something stir deep inside her and was about to say something – she had no idea what – when his pager went off.

He kept staring at her as if he didn't hear the beeping.

Sara cleared her throat, asking, 'Shouldn't you answer that?'

He finally looked down at the pager clipped to his belt, muttering, 'Shit,' at what he saw.

'What?'

'Break-in,' he answered curtly.

'I thought Frank was on call.'

'He is for the little things. I've got to use the pay phone.'

'Where's your cell phone?'

'Dead battery.' Jeffrey seemed to get his irritation under control enough to offer her a reassuring smile. 'Nothing is going to ruin tonight, Sara.' He put his hand to her cheek. 'Nothing is more important to me than tonight.'

'Got a hot date after our dinner?' she teased. 'Because we can cancel if you need to.'

He narrowed his eyes at her before turning away.

Sara watched him go, letting a 'Jesus Christ' hiss out between her lips as she leaned back against the wall. She could not believe that in less than three minutes he had managed to turn her into a blithering idiot.

She jumped as the bathroom door banged shut. Jenny Weaver stood there, looking out at the rink as if she was contemplating something. The teenager's skin looked pasty next to the black long sleeved T-shirt she was wearing. She held a dark red backpack in her hand, which she swung over her shoulder as Sara rolled toward her. The bag brushed against Sara's chest in a wide arc.

'Whoa,' Sara said, backing up.

Jenny blinked, recognizing her pediatrician. She mumbled a soft, 'Sorry,' averting her eyes.

'It's okay,' Sara returned, thinking to start a conversation; the girl seemed troubled. 'How about you?' Sara asked. 'Are you okay?'

'Yes, ma'am,' Jenny said, clutching the bag to her chest.

Before Sara could say anything else, Jenny walked away.

Sara watched the teenager retreat into a crowd of kids near the video game room. The light from the screens gave Jenny's body a green cast as she disappeared into the corner. Sara sensed something was wrong, but it wasn't like she could chase the girl down and demand to know what was going on. At that age, everything was a drama. Knowing teenage girls, there was probably a boy involved.

The lights came up as the ballad ended, and another old rock song blared over the speakers, the bass resonating in Sara's chest. She watched the skaters in the rink pick up the tempo, wondering if she had ever been that agile. While Skatie's had changed ownership several times since Sara was a teenager, it was still the hot spot for Grant County's teens. Sara had spent many a weekend night in the back of this very building, necking with Steve Mann, her first serious boyfriend. Their relationship had not been so much passionate as an alliance, both of them united in one cause: to get out of Grant. Steve's father had been struck down by a heart attack their senior year and Steve had been running the family hardware store ever since. Now he was married with kids. Sara had escaped to Atlanta, but returned a few years later.

And here she was tonight, back at Skatie's, necking with Jeffrey Tolliver. Or at least trying to.

Sara shrugged it off as she turned toward the bathroom. She put her hand on the doorknob, then jerked it back as she felt something sticky. The light was still low in this part of the rink, and Sara had to hold her hand close to her face in order to see what was on it. She caught the scent before she recognized the texture. She looked down at her shirt where Jenny Weaver's backpack had brushed against her.

A narrow streak of blood arced across her chest.

TWO

Jeffrey tried not to rip the pay phone off the wall, but that was exactly what his hands were itching to do. He took a calming breath, dialed the number to the station, and patiently waited through the rings.

Marla Simms, his secretary and the station's part-time dispatcher, answered, 'Good evening, Grant County Police Department, could you hold please?' then clicked him onto hold without waiting for an answer.

He took another deep breath, trying not to let his irritation get the best of him. Jeffrey thought about Sara back in the skating rink, probably talking herself out of their date tonight. Every step he took toward her, Sara took two steps back. He understood her reasons, but that did not mean he had to like them.

Jeffrey leaned against the wall, feeling the sweat start to drip down his back. August was coming on full force, making the record-breaking highs Georgia had seen in June and July look like winter weather. Some days, going outside, he felt as if he was breathing through a wet washrag. He loosened his tie and undid the top button of his shirt to let some air in.

A short bark of laughter came from the front of the building, and Jeffrey peered around the corner, to get a clear view of the parking lot. There was a small group of boys hanging out beside a beat-up old Camaro, passing a cigarette between them. The pay phone was to the side of the building, so Jeffrey was shadowed by the bright green-and-yellow canopy. He thought he caught a whiff of pot, but wasn't sure. The kids had the stance of boys up to no good. Jeffrey recognized this not just because he was a cop but because he had hung out with a similar group at that age.

He was debating whether or not to approach them when Marla clicked onto the line.

'Good evening, Grant County Police Department, thanks for holding. Can I help you?'

'Marla, it's Jeffrey.'

'Oh, hey, Chief,' she said. 'Sorry to bother you. It was a false alarm down at one of the stores.'

'Which one?' he asked, remembering the earful he had just gotten from Betty Reynolds, who owned the five-and-dime downtown.

'Cleaners,' she said. 'Old man Burgess accidentally set it off.'

Jeffrey wondered at Marla, who was well into her seventies, calling Bill Burgess an old man, but he let that slide. He asked, 'Anything else?'

'There was something at the diner Brad called in, but they didn't find anything.'

'What'd he call in?'

'Just said he thought he saw something, is all. You know how Brad is, calls in his own shadow.' She gave a small chuckle. Brad was somewhat of a mascot around the station house, a twenty-one-year-old man whose round face and wispy blond hair made him look more like a boy. It was a joke among the senior squad to steal Brad's hat and hide it around various landmarks in town. Jeffrey had seen it resting on top of the statue of General Lee in front of the high school just last week.

Jeffrey thought of Sara. 'Frank is in charge tonight. Don't page me unless someone's dead.'

'Two birds with one stone,' Marla chuckled again. 'The coroner and the chief in one call.'

He tried to remind himself that he had moved from Birmingham to Grant because he wanted to be in a small town where everyone knew their neighbor. Everyone knowing his own personal business was one of the few tradeoffs. Jeffrey was about to say something innocuous to Marla, but stopped when he heard a loud shriek from the parking lot.

He leaned around the corner to take a look just as a girl's voice yelled, 'Fuck you, you fucking bastard.'

Marla said, 'Chief?'

'Hold on,' he whispered, feeling his gut clench at the anger in the girl's voice. He knew from experience that a ticked-off young girl was the worst thing to have to deal with in a parking lot on a Saturday night. Boys he could handle, it was all a pissing contest and, for the most part, any young man wanted to be stopped from getting into an actual fight. Young girls tended to take a lot to get riled up and a hell of a lot more to get calmed back down. An angry teenage girl was something to fear, especially when she had a gun in her hand.

'I'm going to kill you, you fucking bastard,' she yelled at one of the boys. His friends quickly peeled off into a semicircle, and the young man stood alone, the gun pointed at his chest. The girl was no more than four feet away from her target, and as Jeffrey watched, she took a step closer, narrowing the gap.

'Shit,' Jeffrey hissed, then, remembering he had the phone in his hand, he ordered, 'Get Frank and Matt over to Skatie's right now.'

'They're over in Madison.'

'Lena and Brad, then,' he said. 'Silent approach. There's a girl with a gun in the front parking lot.'

Jeffrey slipped the phone back into its cradle, feeling his body tense. His throat was tight, and his carotid artery felt like a pulsating snake inside his throat. A thousand things went through his mind in the course of a few seconds, but he pushed these thoughts away as he took off his suit jacket and slid his paddle holster behind his back. Jeffrey held his arms out to the side as he walked into the parking lot. The young girl glanced his way as he came into her line of sight, but she still kept the gun leveled at the boy. The muzzle was pointing down toward the boy's gut and as Jeffrey drew closer he could see that her hand was shaking. Thankfully, her finger was not yet tucked around the trigger.

Jeffrey positioned himself so that he was parallel to the building. The girl's back was to the rink, the parking lot and highway in front of her. He hoped that Lena had the sense to make Brad come in from the side of the building. There was no telling what the girl would do if she felt crowded. One stupid mistake could end up killing a lot of people.

When Jeffrey was about twenty feet from the scene, he said, 'Hey,' loudly enough to get everyone's attention.

The girl startled, even though she had noticed his approach. Her finger slipped around the trigger. The weapon was a Beretta .32, a so-called mousegun, which was certainly not a man-stopper but could do plenty of damage up close. She had eight chances to kill somebody with that gun. If she was a good shot, and even a monkey would be at such close range, she was holding eight lives in the palm of her hand.

'Y'all get back,' Jeffrey told the young men standing

around. There was some hesitation before this sunk in, and the group finally moved toward the front of the parking lot. The smell of pot was pungent even at this distance, and Jeffrey could tell from the way the intended victim was swaying that he had smoked a great deal before the girl had surprised him.

'Go away,' the girl ordered Jeffrey. She was dressed in black, the sleeves of her T-shirt pushed up past her elbows, probably to fight the heat. She was barely a teenager, and her voice was soft, but she managed to project it well.

She repeated her order. 'I said go away.'

Jeffrey stood his ground, and she turned her gaze back to the boy and said, 'I'm gonna kill him.'

Jeffrey held his hands out, asking, 'Why?'

She seemed surprised by his question, which was why he had asked it. People with guns don't tend to do a lot of thinking when they're holding them. The nose of the gun tilted down slightly as she addressed Jeffrey.

'To stop him,' she said.

'Stop him from what?'

She seemed to mull this over in her mind. 'That's nobody's business.'

'No?' Jeffrey asked, taking a step closer, then another. He stopped at around fifteen feet from the girl, close enough to see what was going on, but not enough to threaten her.

'No, sir,' the girl answered, and her good manners put him a little more at ease. Girls who said 'sir' did not shoot people.

'Listen,' Jeffrey began, trying to think of something to say. 'Do you know who I am?'

'Yes, sir,' she answered. 'You're Chief Tolliver.'

'That's right,' he told her. 'What do I call you? What's your name?'

She ignored the question, but the boy stirred, as if his pot-altered brain had just clicked in to what was going on. He said, 'Jenny. It's Jenny.'

'Jenny?' Jeffrey asked her. 'That's a pretty name.'

'Yeah, w-well,' Jenny stammered, obviously taken aback. She recovered quickly, though, saying, 'Please just be quiet. I don't want to talk to you.'

'Maybe you do,' Jeffrey said. 'Seems to me like you've got a lot on your mind here.'

She seemed to debate this, then raised the gun back to the boy's chest. Her hand still shook. 'Go away or I'll kill him.'

'With that gun?' Jeffrey asked. 'Do you know what it's like to kill someone with a gun? Do you know what that feels like?' He watched her digest this, knowing immediately that she did not have it in her.

Jenny was a large girl, probably fifty pounds overweight. Dressed totally in black, she had the appearance of one of those girls who blends in with the scenery as a way of life. The boy she was aiming the gun at was a good-looking kid, probably the object of an unrequited crush. In Jeffrey's day, she would have left a nasty note in his locker. Today, she was pointing a gun.

'Jenny,' Jeffrey began, wondering if the gun was even loaded. 'Let's work this out. This guy's not worth getting into trouble over.'

'Go away,' Jenny repeated, though her voice was not as firm. She used her free hand to wipe her face. He realized that she was crying.

'Jenny, I don't think –' He stopped as she disengaged the safety. The metallic click was like a knife in his ear. He reached around to his back, putting his hand on his weapon but not drawing.

Jeffrey tried to keep his voice calm and reasonable.

'What's happening here, Jenny? Why don't we talk this through? It can't be that bad.'

She wiped her face again. 'Yes, sir,' she said. 'It is.'

Her voice was so cold that Jeffrey felt a chill on his neck. He suppressed a shiver as he slid his gun out of its holster. Jeffrey hated guns because, as a cop, he saw what kind of damage they could do. Carrying one was something he did because he had to, not because he wanted to. In his twenty years on the police force, Jeffrey had drawn his weapon on a suspect only a handful of times. Of those times, he had fired it twice, but never directly at a human being.

'Jenny,' he tried, putting some authority in his voice. 'Look at me.'

She kept her gaze on the boy in front of her for what seemed like forever. Jeffrey was silent, letting her have her sense of control. Slowly, she let her eyes turn toward Jeffrey. She let her gaze settle low, until she found the nine millimeter he held at his side.

She licked her lips nervously, obviously assessing the threat. The same dead tone rang in his ears when she said, 'Shoot me.'

He thought he had heard wrong. This was far from the answer he had been expecting.

She repeated, 'Shoot me now or I'm gonna shoot him.' With that, she lifted the Beretta toward the boy's head. Jeffrey watched as she spread her feet apart to a shoulder-width stance and cupped the butt of the gun with her free hand. Her posture was that of a young woman who knew how to hold a weapon. Her hands were steady now, and she kept her eyes locked on the boy's.

The boy whined, 'Oh, shit,' and there was a spattering sound on the asphalt as he urinated.

Jeffrey raised his gun as she fired, but her shot went

wide over the boy's head, splitting pieces of the plastic sign and canopy off the building.

'What was that?' Jeffrey hissed, knowing that the only reason Jenny was still standing was that his gut had stopped his own finger from pulling the trigger. She had hit the center of the dot on the 'i' in Skatie's. Jeffrey doubted most of his cops on the force could shoot with that much precision, under this much pressure.

'It was a warning,' Jenny said, though he had not expected her to answer. 'Shoot me,' the girl repeated. 'Shoot me or I swear to God I'm gonna blow his brains out right here.' She licked her lips again. 'I can do it. I know how to use this.' She jerked the gun slightly, indicating what she meant. 'You know I can do it,' she said, again taking a wide stance to counteract the Beretta's recoil. She turned the muzzle slightly and blasted out the apostrophe on the sign. People in the parking lot might have scattered or yelled, but Jeffrey did not notice. All he could see was the smoke coming off the muzzle of her gun.

When he could breathe again, Jeffrey said, 'There's a big difference between a sign and a human being.'

She mumbled, and he strained to hear her say, 'He's not a human being.'

Jeffrey caught movement out of the corner of his eye. He recognized Sara instantly. She had taken off her skates and her white socks stood stark against the black asphalt.

'Honey?' Sara called, her voice pitched up in fear. 'Jenny?' she said.

'Go away,' Jenny snapped, but her tone was petulant, more like the child she was than the monster she had been just a few seconds earlier. 'Please.'

'She's okay,' Sara said. 'I just found her inside, and she's fine.'

19

The gun faltered, then Jenny's resolve seemed to kick in as she raised it back, pointing the weapon squarely between the boy's eyes. The same dead voice came back with her resolve, and she said, 'You're lying.'

Jeffrey took one look at Sara and knew that the girl was right. Sara was not a practiced liar, so she was easy to read. Discounting that, even from this distance Jeffrey could see the blood covering the front of Sara's shirt and jeans. Someone inside the rink had obviously been injured and was possibly, probably, dead. He looked back at Jenny, finally able to reconcile the soft, little girl's face with the threat that she had become.

With a start, he realized that the safety was still engaged on his gun. He clicked it off, giving Sara a look of warning to stay back.

'Jenny?' Sara's throat made a visible swallow. Jeffrey did not recognize the singsong voice she used; she had never talked down to children. Obviously, whatever violence Jenny had wreaked inside the rink had altered Sara. Jeffrey did not know what to make of it. There hadn't been any gunfire in the rink, and Buell Parker, the rink's rent-a-cop, had said everything was fine when Jeffrey had checked in with him. Where was Buell, Jeffrey wondered. Was he inside, securing a crime scene, not letting anyone out? What had Jenny done inside the rink? Jeffrey would have given anything at that moment in time to pause the scene in front of him and find out exactly what had happened.

Jeffrey chambered a round into the nine-mil. Sara's head snapped around at the sound, and she held her hand out to him, palm down, as if to say, No, calm down. Don't do this. He looked past her shoulder at the rink entrance. He expected to see a group of spectators with their noses pressed to the glass, but the doorway was empty. What had happened inside that was more interesting than the scene playing out in front of him?

Sara tried again, saying, 'She's fine, Jenny. Come see.'

'Dr. Linton,' Jenny said, her voice wavering, 'please don't talk to me.'

'Sweetie,' Sara answered, her tone as shaky as Jenny's. 'Look at me. Please just look at me.' When the girl did not respond, Sara said, 'She's fine. I promise you she's fine.'

'You're lying,' Jenny answered. 'You're all liars.' She turned her attention back to the boy. 'And you're the worst liar of all,' she told him. 'You're going to burn in hell for what you did, you bastard.'

The boy spoke in a fit of rage, spittle flying from his mouth. 'I'll see you there, bitch.'

Jenny's voice took on a calmness. Something seemed to pass between her and the boy, and when she answered, her voice was childlike. 'I know you will.'

Out of the corner of his eye, Jeffrey saw Sara step forward. He watched as Jenny sighted down the barrel of the short-nosed gun, lining it up to the boy's head. The girl stood there, stock-still, waiting. Her hands did not shake, her lip did not tremble, and her hand did not falter. She seemed more resigned to the task in front of her than Jeffrey did.

'Jenny . . . ,' Jeffrey began, trying to see some way out of this. He was not going to shoot a little girl. There was no way he could shoot this kid.

Jenny looked over her shoulder and Jeffrey followed her gaze. A police car had finally pulled up, and Lena Adams and Brad stepped out, weapons drawn. They were in a textbook triangle formation, with Jeffrey at the top.

'Shoot me,' Jenny said, keeping her gun steady on the boy.

'Stand down,' Jeffrey told the officers. Brad followed orders, but he saw Lena hesitate. He gave her a hard look, about to repeat his order, but finally she lowered her weapon.

'I'll do it,' Jenny mumbled. She stood impossibly still, making Jeffrey wonder what was inside the girl that she could approach this situation with such resignation.

Jenny cleared her throat and said, 'I'll do it. I've done it before.'

Jeffrey looked to Sara for confirmation, but her attention was focused on the little girl with the gun.

'I've done it before,' Jenny repeated. 'Shoot me, or I'll kill him and then shoot myself anyway.'

For the first time that night, Jeffrey assessed his shot. He tried to force his brain to accept that she represented a clear danger to the boy in front of her, no matter what her age was. If he hit her in the leg or shoulder, she would have enough time to pull the trigger. Even if Jeffrey went for her torso, there was still the chance that she would squeeze off a shot before she went down. At the level Jenny was pointing the gun, the boy would be dead before she hit the ground.

'Men are so weak,' Jenny hissed, sighting the weapon. 'You never do the right thing. You say you will, but you never do.'

'Jenny . . . ,' Sara pleaded.

'I'll give you to five,' Jenny told him. 'One.'

Jeffrey swallowed hard. His heart was pounding so loudly in his ears that he saw rather than heard the girl as she counted.

'Two.'

'Jenny, please.' Sara clasped her hands in front of

her as if in prayer. They were dark, almost black with blood.

'Three.'

Jeffrey took aim. She wouldn't do this. There was no way she would do this. She could not have been more than thirteen. Thirteen-year-old girls did not shoot people. This was suicide.

'Four.'

Jeffrey watched the young woman's finger tighten on the trigger, watched the muscles along her forearm work in slow motion as she moved to tighten her finger.

'Five!' she screamed, the veins in her neck standing out. She ordered, 'Shoot me, goddamn it!' as she braced herself for the Beretta's recoil. He saw her arm tense and her wrist lock. Time moved so slowly that he could see her muscles engaging along her forearm as her finger tightened on the trigger.

She gave him one last chance, yelling, 'Shoot me!'

And he did.

THREE

At twenty-eight weeks old, Jenny Weaver's child might have been viable outside the womb had its mother not tried to flush it down the toilet. The fetus was well-developed and well-nourished. The brain stem was intact and, with medical intervention, the lungs would have matured over time. The hands would have learned to grasp, the feet to flex, the eyes to blink. Eventually, the mouth would have learned to speak of something other than the horrors it spoke of to Sara now. The lungs had taken breath, the mouth gasped for life. And then it had been killed.

For the past three-and-a-half hours, Sara had tried to reassemble the baby from the parts Jenny Weaver had left in the bathroom and in the red book bag they found in the trash by the video game room. Using tiny sutures instead of the usual baseball stitches, Sara had sewn the paper-thin flesh back together into the semblance of a child. Her hands shook, and Sara had redone some of the knots because her fingers were not nimble enough on the first try.

Still, it was not enough. Working on the child, tying the tiny sutures, was like pulling a thread on a sweater. For every area repaired, there was another that could not be concealed. There was no disguising the trauma the child had been through. In the end, Sara had finally accepted that her self-appointed task was an exercise in futility. The baby would go to the grave looking much the way she had looked the last time her mother had seen her.

Sara took a deep breath, reviewing her report again before signing off on her findings. She had not waited for Jeffrey or Frank to begin the autopsy. There had been no witnesses to the cutting and dissecting and reassembling Sara had performed. She had excluded them on purpose, because she did not think she could do this job while other people watched.

A large window separated Sara's office from the outer morgue, and she sat back in her chair, staring at the black body bag resting on the autopsy table. Her mind wandered, and she saw an alternative to the death she had been assessing. Sara saw a life of laughing and crying and loving and being loved, and then she saw the truth: Jenny's baby would never have had these things. Jenny herself had barely had these things.

Since an ectopic pregnancy several years ago, Sara had been unable to have children. This had been hard news to bear at the time, but over the years the loss had dulled itself with other things, and Sara had learned to stop wanting what she knew she would never have. Yet there was something about the unwanted child on the table, the child whose own mother had taken her life, that stirred up these emotions in Sara again.

Sara's job was taking care of children. She held them in her arms, cradled them, and cooed at them the way she would never be able to with her own child. Sitting in the morgue, staring at the black bag, that longing to carry a baby came back with startling clarity, and with it came an emptiness that made her chest feel hollow.

There were footsteps on the stairs, and Sara sat up,

wiping her eyes, trying to collect herself. She pushed her palms against the top of her desk and forced herself to stand as Jeffrey walked into the morgue. Sara was looking for her glasses, trying to compose herself, when she noticed that Jeffrey had not come directly into her office, as he normally did. Through the glass, she could see that he had stopped in front of the black bag. If he saw Sara, Jeffrey did not acknowledge her. Instead, he leaned over the table, his hands behind his back. Sara wondered what he was thinking, wondered if he was considering the life the baby could have had. Wondered, too, if Jeffrey was considering the fact that Sara could never give him children.

Sara cleared her throat as she walked into the room, holding the autopsy report to her chest. She slid the chart onto the edge of the table and stood across from Jeffrey, the baby between them. The bag was too large for the baby and it gaped open around the body like a blanket because Sara had not had the emotional strength to zip the child into more darkness and place her on a shelf in the freezer.

There was nothing she could think to say, so Sara was quiet. She tucked her hand into the pocket of her lab coat, surprised to find her glasses there. She was putting them on when Jeffrey finally spoke.

'So,' he said, his voice gravelly and low as if he had not used it much lately. 'This is what happens when you try to flush a baby down the toilet.'

She felt her heart stop at his callousness, and did not know how to respond to it. She slipped off her glasses and rubbed the lenses with the tail of her shirt to give herself something to do.

Jeffrey took a deep breath and let it go slowly. She leaned in closer, thinking she smelled alcohol, knowing this could not be the case because Jeffrey seldom drank more than the occasional beer while watching Saturday college football.

'Tiny feet,' he mumbled, his eyes still on the body. 'Are they always that small?'

Again, Sara did not answer. She looked at the feet, the ten toes, the wrinkled skin on the soles. These were the kind of feet a mother would kiss. These toes were the kind of toes a mother would count each day the way a gardener counts blooms on a rose bush.

Sara bit her lip, trying not to let herself go again. The emptiness in her chest was almost overwhelming, and she put her hand over her heart without thinking.

When Sara was finally able to look up, Jeffrey was staring at her. His eyes were bloodshot, tiny red lines shooting out from his irises. He seemed to be having trouble holding himself up. She did not know if this was from alcohol or grief.

'I thought you didn't drink,' she said, aware there was an accusatory tone to her voice.

'I thought I didn't shoot children, either,' he said, staring somewhere over her shoulder.

Sara wanted to help him, but she felt paralyzed by her own grief.

'Frank,' Jeffrey said. 'He gave me a shot of whiskey.'

'Did it help?'

His eyes watered, and she watched him fighting this. His jaw worked and he gave a humorless smile.

'Jeffrey –'

He shook off her concern, asking, 'Did you find anything?'

'No.'

'I don't –' He stopped, looking down, but not at the child. His eyes were focused on the tiled floor. 'I don't know how to behave,' he finally said. 'I don't know what I should be doing.'

Something in his tone cut Sara deep down. To see him broken like this hurt her more than the pain she was experiencing herself. She walked around the table and put her hand on his shoulder, but he would not turn toward her.

He asked, 'Did you think she was going to shoot him?'

Sara felt a lump in her throat, because she had not let herself consider this question up until now. Jenny's back had been to Sara. Only Jeffrey, Lena, and Brad had a clear view of the scene.

'Sara?'

The way Jeffrey was looking at her, Sara knew that now was not the time for equivocation.

'Yes,' she answered, making her voice firm. 'It was a clean shot, Jeffrey. You had to take it.'

Jeffrey walked away from her. He turned and leaned his back against the wall, asking, 'Mark is probably the father, right?' He rested his head against the wall. 'The boy she was going to shoot?'

Sara put her hands in her pockets, made her feet stay flat on the ground so that she would not walk over to him. She said, 'It would make sense.'

'His parents won't let us interview him until tomorrow. Did you know that?'

She shook her head slowly side to side. Mark wasn't under suspicion for anything. It wasn't as if Jeffrey could arrest the kid for having a gun pointed at his chest.

'They say he's been through enough.' Jeffrey let his head drop down. 'What would make her do something like that? What has she been through that would make her think . . . ?' His voice trailed off as he looked back up at Sara. 'She was one of yours, right?'

'They moved here about three years ago.' Sara paused, trying to shift gears. She knew that it would help Jeffrey more to talk this through like any other case rather than to dwell on the horror of his involvement. At this moment in time, it was irrelevant that this wasn't what she needed.

He asked, 'Where from?'

'I think they were from up North somewhere. Her mother moved down here after what sounded like a nasty divorce.'

'How do you know this?'

'Parents tell me things.' She paused. 'I didn't know Jenny was pregnant. I don't think she's been in for at least six months, maybe more.' Sara put her hand to her chest. 'She was such a sweet kid. I never would have imagined that she'd do something like this.'

He nodded, rubbing his eyes. 'Tessa's not sure she can I.D. anybody from the restroom. Brad's gonna take over one of the yearbooks from the school, see if anybody looks familiar. I want you to look, too.'

'Of course.'

'It was so packed,' he said, obviously meaning the skating rink. 'People left before giving statements. I don't know if we'll be able to track everyone down.'

'Did you get anything?'

He shook his head no. 'You're sure only two people went into the bathroom? Jenny and one other?'

'That's all I saw,' Sara answered, though after tonight she did not know how she could ever be sure of anything again. 'I didn't see her. I suppose if she was in my practice I would have recognized her. I guess.' Sara stopped, trying to remember, but nothing new popped into her head. 'She was tall, maybe wearing a baseball cap.'

He looked up at this. 'You remember the color?'

'It was dark, Jeffrey,' Sara answered, knowing she was letting him down. She understood now why so many witnesses willingly gave false testimony. She felt stupid and useless for not knowing who the other girl was. Her mind tried to compensate for this by throwing out random bits of information that could or could not be real memories.

Sara said, 'I'm not even sure if it was a baseball cap, now that I'm thinking about it. I wasn't paying attention.' She tried to smile. 'I was looking for you.'

He did not smile back. Instead, he said, 'I talked to her mother.'

'What did you say?'

His flippant tone was back. '"I shot your daughter, Mrs. Weaver. Sorry about that."'

Sara chewed her bottom lip. In a larger county, Jeffrey would not have been in charge of notification; he would be off the job pending an investigation. Of course, Grant County was far from large. All the responsibility rested squarely on his shoulders.

'She didn't want the autopsy,' he said. 'I had to explain to her that she didn't really have a choice. She said it was . . .' He paused. 'She said it was killing her twice.'

Sara felt guilt settle into the pit of her stomach.

'She called me a baby killer,' he said. 'I'm a baby killer now.'

Sara shook her head no. 'You didn't have a choice,' she said, knowing this was true. She had made love to this man, shared her life with him. There was no way he had misjudged.

Sara said, 'You followed procedure.'

He gave a derisive laugh.

'Jeff –'

'You think she would have done it?' he asked again.

'I don't think she would have, Sara. I'm thinking back on it, and maybe she would have walked away. Maybe she would have –'

'Look at this,' Sara interrupted, indicating the table. 'She killed her own child, Jeffrey. Do you think she wouldn't have killed the father, too?'

'We'll never know, will we?'

Silence came like a thick cloud. The morgue was in the basement of the hospital, a tiled room with an institutional feel. The compressor on the freezer was the only noise, and it turned off with a loud click that echoed against the walls.

'Was the baby alive?' Jeffrey asked. 'When she was born, was she alive?'

'She wouldn't have survived long without medical help,' Sara said, not answering his question. For some reason, she wanted to protect Jenny.

'Was the baby alive?' he repeated.

'She was very small,' she said. 'I don't think she would have . . .'

Jeffrey walked back to the table. He tucked his hands into his pockets as he stared at the baby. 'I want . . . ,' he began. 'I want to go home. I want you to go home with me.'

'Okay,' she answered, hearing his words but not sure she understood what he wanted.

He said, 'I want to make love to you.'

Sara's eyes must have registered her shock.

'I want to –' He stopped himself midsentence.

Sara stared at him, a sinking feeling in her chest. 'You want to make a baby.'

The look in his eyes told her this had been the last thing on his mind. Sara felt a flush of humiliation. Her heart jumped into her throat, and she could not speak.

He shook his head. 'That's not what I was going to say.'

Sara turned away from him, her cheeks burning. She could not think of words to cover what she had already said.

He said, 'I know you can't –'

'Forget about it.'

'It's just that I –'

She was mad at herself, not Jeffrey, but when she spoke to him, her tone was sharp. 'I said forget about it.'

Jeffrey waited a few beats, obviously looking for the right thing to say. When he finally spoke, his tone was plaintive and sad. 'I want to go back about five hours, okay?' He waited for her to turn around. 'I want to be back in that stupid fucking skating rink with you, and when my pager goes off, I want to throw it in the fucking trash.'

Sara stared at him, not trusting herself to speak.

'That's what I want, Sara,' he repeated. 'I wasn't thinking about the other. What you said –'

She stopped him, holding up her hand. There were footsteps on the stairs, two sets of them. Sara walked into her office, drying her eyes as she went. She tugged a Kleenex out of the box on her desk and blew her nose, then counted to a slow five, bracing herself, swallowing back the humiliation she felt.

When she turned around, detective Lena Adams and Brad Stephens were in the morgue, standing by Jeffrey, who by his look had managed to mask his emotions much as Sara had. All three of them had their hands clasped behind their backs the way cops do when they're at a scene so they won't accidentally contaminate anything. In that moment, Sara hated them all, even Brad Stephens, who was as harmless as a fly.

'Hey, Dr. Linton,' Brad said, taking off his hat as she walked into the room. His face was paler than usual and there were tears in his eyes.

'Will you . . . ?' Sara began, then had to stop. She cleared her throat. 'Will you please go upstairs and get some sheets for me?' she asked. 'Bed sheets. About four of them.' Sara did not need the sheets, but Brad had been one of her patients. She still felt the need to protect him.

Brad gave her a smile, obviously glad to have something to do. 'Yes, ma'am.'

After he had left, Lena asked in a matter-of-fact way, 'Have y'all already done the baby?'

Jeffrey answered, 'Yes,' even though he had not been there. He noticed the chart at the end of the table and picked it up. Sara did not say anything as he took his pen out of his breast pocket and scribbled his signature along the bottom of the autopsy report. Technically, Sara had violated several laws by performing the autopsy without at least one witness.

'Is the girl in the freezer?' Lena asked, walking toward the door. There was a cavalier bounce to her walk, as if what Lena was seeing was a common occurrence. Sara knew Lena had been through a lot recently, but she still felt angry at the other woman's attitude.

'Here?' Lena prompted, her hand on the freezer door.

Sara nodded, not moving. Jeffrey walked over to help Lena, and Sara zipped the bag closed around the baby before she could stop herself. Her heart was pounding like a drum in her chest by the time Lena and Jeffrey rolled the gurney containing Jenny Weaver's body into the room. They both braked the wheels by the table, waiting for Sara to move the bag. Finally, Jeffrey scooped the large black bag into his arms. Sara looked away as he cradled what was obviously the head with his hand. The loose ends of the bag dragged the floor as he walked toward the freezer.

Lena made a point of looking at her watch. Sara wanted to slap her, but instead she walked over to the metal supply cabinet beside the sinks. She opened a sterile pack and slipped on a gown, glancing over her shoulder at the freezer, wondering what was taking Jeffrey so long. Sara was helping Lena move the body onto the table when he finally emerged.

'Here,' he said, taking Lena's place as they maneuvered the body of Jenny Weaver onto the white porcelain table. Weaver was a large girl, and the hoses at the head of the table rattled as they moved her into place.

Sara propped the head up on a black block, trying to think of herself as a coroner rather than the girl's pediatrician. In her ten years as Grant's medical examiner, there had been only four cases where Sara had known the deceased. Jenny Weaver was the first victim who had also been a patient at the clinic.

Sara rolled over a fresh tray with clean instruments, making sure she had everything that she needed. The two hoses at the head of the table were used to evacuate the body during examination. Over this was a large scale for weighing organs. At the foot was a tray for dissecting. The table itself was concave in shape, with high sides to keep matter from spilling over and a pronounced downward slant toward a large brass drain.

Carlos, Sara's assistant at the morgue, had placed a white sheet over Jenny Weaver's body. A medium-sized red dot spread out over the part that covered her throat. Sara had let Carlos take care of Jenny while she worked on the child. He had taken the X rays and prepared Jenny for autopsy while Sara had tried in vain to do something right for the baby. If Carlos was surprised when Sara told him to go home when he was finished with Jenny, he did not say.

Sara folded back the sheet, stopping just above the girl's chest. The wound was far from clean and most of the right side of her neck dangled like pieces of raw meat. Cartilage and bone stood out from the black blood that had clotted around the wound.

Sara walked over to the light box on the wall and turned it on. The light flickered, then showed the X rays Carlos had taken of Jenny Weaver.

She studied the films carefully, at first not understanding what she was seeing. She checked the name on the chart again before calling out her findings. 'You can see here there are faded lines of a fracture to the left humerus, which I would date at less than a year old. It's not a typical fracture, especially for someone who was not athletic, so I'm assuming it came from some kind of abuse.'

'Did you treat her for this?' Jeffrey asked.

'Of course not,' Sara answered. 'I would have reported it. Any doctor would have reported it.'

'Okay,' Jeffrey said, holding up his hands. Her tone must have been sharper than Sara realized, because Lena seemed to be taking a sudden interest in the floor.

Sara turned back to the X ray. 'There's also evidence of trauma around the costal cartilage, which is here in the rib.' She pointed to the chest film. 'Up here, near the sternum, there's bruising that's consistent with a hard push or shove, moving posteriorly. That's to the back.' She let this sink in, wondering if Jenny had seen another doctor for this. A first-year resident would recognize something was not right with this kind of injury.

Sara said, 'I would guess the person who did this was taller than her. It's recent, too.'

Sara popped a new X ray into the light box. She crossed her arms over her chest, studying the film. 'This is the pelvic girdle,' she explained. 'Note the fade line here against the ischium. This would indicate traumatic pressure to the pubis. It's what's commonly referred to as a stress fracture.'

'Stress from what?' Jeffrey asked.

Sara was surprised when Lena provided the answer to Jeffrey.

'She was raped,' Lena said, the same way she might say the girl's eyes were blue. 'Raped hard. Right?'

Sara nodded, and was about to say something else when she heard footsteps on the stairs again. She guessed from the sloppy lope that Brad had returned.

'Here you go,' Brad said, walking backward through the door. He held an armful of sheets, his hat dangling from his hand.

Sara stopped him, asking, 'Did you get pillowcases?'

'Oh,' Brad said, surprised. He shook his head. 'Sorry, no.'

'I think they're on the top floor,' Sara said. 'Could you get at least four?'

'Yes, ma'am,' he answered, setting the sheets down on a table by the door.

Lena crossed her arms as he left. 'He's not twelve,' she said.

Jeffrey spoke to Lena for the first time since she had entered the morgue, giving her an uncharacteristic, 'Shut up.'

Lena colored, but she was silent; also out of character.

'The bruising on her chest couldn't really be treated with anything other than Tylenol,' Sara continued.

'The pelvic fracture could heal on its own. It might explain why she had weight gain recently. It would be hard for her to get around.'

Jeffrey asked, 'You think the boyfriend was abusing her?'

'Someone was,' Sara said, looking over the films again, trying to see if she had missed anything. All the times she had seen Jenny Weaver, Sara had never suspected child abuse. How the child had kept it hidden, and why, Sara did not know. Of course, it wasn't as if Sara ordered X rays for sore throats. Jenny had never taken off her clothes for an examination. Teenage girls were very sensitive about their bodies, and Sara had always slipped her stethoscope under Jenny's shirt to listen to her chest and lungs so the girl would not be embarrassed.

Sara walked over to the table to resume the preliminary examination. Her hands shook slightly as she pulled back the sheet, and Sara was so absorbed in trying to get her hands to stop shaking that she did not notice what she was uncovering.

'Holy shit,' Lena said, giving a low whistle.

Jeffrey did not reprimand her this time, though, and Sara understood why. There were small cuts across the girl's body, specifically on her arms and legs. The wounds were at various stages of healing, but some of them looked as recent as the last few days.

'What happened?' Jeffrey asked. 'Was she trying to kill herself?'

Sara looked at the slices marking the skin. None of them was across the wrist or in places that would be apparent to anyone who was not looking for something specific. This would at least explain why the girl was wearing a long-sleeved shirt in the middle of summer. Thin rows of very deep cuts lined Jenny's left forearm, starting about three inches from the wrist and where the sleeve might have rolled up. Dark scars indicated that the injuries were a common occurrence. The leg cuts were much deeper, and seemed to have a crisscross pattern to them. Sara could guess from the scarring that the deeper cuts radiated from the knee to the thigh. The girl had done this to herself.

'What is this?' Jeffrey asked, though he must have known.

'Cutting,' Lena provided.

'Self-injuring,' Sara corrected her, as if that made it any better. 'I've seen it at the clinic before.'

'Why?' Jeffrey asked. 'Why would someone do this?'

'Stupidity, for the most part,' Sara told him, feeling anger well into her stomach. How many times had she seen this girl? How many signs had Sara missed? 'Sometimes they just want to know what it feels like. Usually they're just acting out, not thinking about the consequences. This, though,' she stopped, staring at the deep cuts along Jenny's left thigh. 'This is something else. She hid them, she didn't want people to know.'

'Why?' Jeffrey repeated. 'Why would she do this?'

'Control,' Lena answered him, and Sara did not like the look she was giving the child. It was almost respectful.

'It's a deep psychosis,' Sara countered. 'Usually bulimics or anorexics do it. It's a form of self-loathing.' She gave Lena a purposeful look. 'Usually something sets it off. Abuse or rape, for instance.'

Lena held her gaze for just a second before looking away.

Sara continued, 'There are other things that can lead to it, too. Substance abuse, mental illness, problems at school or at home.'

Sara walked over to the supply cabinet and took

out a plastic speculum. After slipping on a second pair of gloves, she unwrapped the speculum and clicked it open. Lena cringed slightly at the sound, and Sara was thankful that the detective was capable of showing a little emotion.

Sara walked down to the foot of the body and propped the feet apart. She stopped suddenly, her mind not accepting what her eyes saw. She dropped the speculum on the table.

Lena asked, 'What is it?'

Sara did not answer. She had thought that after tonight nothing could shock her. She had been so wrong.

'What is it?' Lena repeated.

'She hasn't given birth to a child,' Sara answered. 'Any child.'

Jeffrey indicated the unused speculum. 'How can you be sure without completely examining her?'

Sara stared at them both, not sure how to say this. 'Her vagina has been sewn shut,' she finally told them. 'From the rate of healing, I'd say it's been that way for at least six months.'

SUNDAY

SUNDAY

FOUR

Lena ran her tongue along her front teeth as she stared out the car window. She could not get used to the fake feeling of the temporary partials. In three weeks, she would be fitted with four permanent replacements that would screw into her gums like tiny lightbulbs. She could not imagine how that would feel. For now, they served as a constant reminder of what had happened to her four months ago.

She tried to block out the memory as she watched the scenery go by. Grant County was a small town, but not as small as Reece, where Lena and Sibyl, her twin sister, had grown up. Their father had been killed in the line of duty eight months before they were born and their mother had died giving birth to them. The task of raising the girls had fallen to their uncle Hank Norton, an admitted speed freak and alcoholic, who had struggled with both addictions well into the girls' childhood. One sunny afternoon, a drunk Hank had backed his car down the driveway and slammed into Sibyl. Lena had always blamed him for blinding her sister. She would never forgive Hank for his role in the accident, and his response to her hatred was a seemingly insurmountable wall of anger. They had a past, the two of them, that prevented each from reaching out to the other. Even now, with Sibyl dead and Lena just as good as, Lena could not see Hank Norton as anything but a necessary evil in her life.

'Hot outside,' Hank mumbled as he patted the back of his neck with a worn-looking handkerchief. Lena could barely hear him over the roar of the air-conditioning. Hank's old Mercedes sedan was a tank of a car, and everything inside the cab seemed overdone. The seats were too big. There was enough legroom to accommodate a horse. The controls on the dash were large and obvious, their design intended to impress more than elucidate. Still, it was comforting being inside something so solid. Even on the gravel road down from Lena's house, the car seemed to float across the ground.

'Sure is hot,' Hank repeated. The older he got, the more he did this, as if repeating phrases made up for the fact that he didn't have much to say.

'Yeah,' Lena agreed, staring back out the window. She could feel Hank looking at her, probably contemplating small talk. After a few beats, he seemed to give up on this, and turned on the radio instead.

Lena leaned her head back against the seat, closing her eyes. She had agreed to go to church with her uncle one Sunday shortly after she had gotten home from the hospital, and her attendance had turned into a habit over the ensuing months. Lena tagged along more because she was afraid to stay alone in her own home than because she wanted absolution. In her mind, Lena would never need forgiveness for anything ever again. She had paid her dues to God or whomever was keeping track of things four months ago, raped and drugged into a nightmare world of pain and false transcendence.

Hank interrupted her again. 'You doin' okay, baby?'

What a stupid question, Lena thought. What a stupid fucking question.

'Lee?'

'Yes,' she answered, conscious that the word hissed through her temporary teeth.

'Nan called again,' he told her.

'I know,' Lena said. Nan Thomas, Sibyl's lover at the time of her death, had been calling off and on for the last month.

'She's got some of Sibby's stuff,' Hank said, though surely he knew Lena was aware of this. 'She just wants to give it to you.'

'Why doesn't she give it to you?' Lena countered. There was no reason she needed to see that woman, and Hank knew it. Still, he kept forcing the issue.

Hank changed the subject. 'That girl last night,' he began, turning down the radio. 'You were there, huh?'

'Yes,' she said, making the same hissing sound. Lena clenched her jaw, willing herself not to cry. Would she ever talk normally again? Would even the sound of her voice be a constant reminder of what *he* did to her?

He, Lena thought, unable to let her mind use his name. Her hands rested in her lap, and she looked down, staring at the matching scars on the back of her hands. If Hank had not been there, she would have turned them over, looked at the palms where the nails had pierced through as they were hammered into the floor. The same scars were on her feet, midway between her toes and ankles. Two months of physical therapy had returned the normal use of her hands and she could now walk without cringing, but the scars would always be there.

Lena had only a few sharp memories of what had happened to her body while she was abducted. Only the scars and her chart at the hospital told the entire story. All she remembered were the moments when the drugs wore off and *he* came to her, sitting by her on the floor as if they were at Bible camp, telling stories about his childhood and his life as if they were lovers, just getting to know each other.

Lena's mind was filled with the details of his life: his first kiss, his first time making love, his hopes and dreams, his sick obsessions. They came to her now as easily as memories from her own past. Had she told him similar stories about herself? She could not remember, and this scarred her more deeply than the physical aspects of the attack. At times, Lena thought of the scars as inconsequential compared to the intimate conversations she'd had with her abuser. He had manipulated Lena so that she was no longer in control of her own thoughts. He had not just raped her body, but her mind as well.

Even now, his memories constantly mingled with her own, until she was uncertain whether or not something had happened to her or to him. Sibyl, the one person who could settle this, the one person who could give Lena back her life, her childhood, had been taken by him as well.

'Lee?' Hank interrupted her thoughts, holding out a pack of gum. She shook her head no, watching him try to hold the wheel and retrieve a stick of Juicy Fruit. The sleeves of his dress shirt were rolled up, and she could see the track marks lining his pasty white forearms. They were hideous, these scars, and they reminded Lena of Jenny Weaver. Last night, Jeffrey had kept asking why anyone would purposefully cut herself, but Lena understood how pain could be a comfort. About six weeks after being released from the hospital, Lena had accidentally slammed her fingers in the door of her car. Searing hot pain had radiated up her arm, and for the briefest moment,

Lena had caught herself enjoying it, thinking, *This is what it's like to feel again.*

She closed her eyes, clasping her hands in her lap. As usual, her fingers found the scars and she traced the circumference of one, then the other. There had been no pain when it had happened. The drug had convinced her that she was floating on the ocean, that she was safe. Her mind had created an alternate reality from the one her rapist created. When he touched her, Lena's mind had told her it was Greg Mitchell, her old boyfriend, inside of her. Lena's body had responded to Greg, not *him.*

Yet, the few times since then that Lena had been able to sleep long enough to dream, she had dreamed of her rapist touching her, not Greg. It was *his* hands on her breasts. It was *him* inside of her. And when she awakened, startled and scared, it was not Greg that she looked for in her dark, empty room.

Lena clenched her fists when the sickly sweet smell of Hank's chewing gum hit her. Without warning, her stomach pitched.

'Pull over,' she managed, using one hand to cover her mouth, grabbing the door handle with the other. Hank abruptly swerved the car to the side of the road just as Lena lost it. She had only had a cup of coffee for breakfast, but that and more came up quickly. Soon, she was dry heaving, her stomach clenching. Tears came to her eyes from the exertion, and her body shook hard as she tried to hold herself up.

After what seemed like several minutes, the nausea finally passed. Lena wiped her mouth with the back of her hand just as Hank tapped her on the shoulder, offering his handkerchief. The cloth was warm and smelled of his sweat, but she used it anyway.

'Your gum,' she mumbled, grasping the dashboard

as she tried to sit up. 'I don't know why –'

'It's okay,' he answered abruptly. The window sucked down at the press of a button, and he spit out the gum before pulling onto the road again. Hank stared straight ahead, his jaw a straight line.

'I'm sorry,' she said, not knowing why she was apologizing even as she said the words. Hank seemed angry, but she knew his animosity was directed toward himself for not knowing how to help, not at Lena. It was a familiar scene that had played out every day since she had come home from the hospital.

Lena reached around to retrieve her purse from the back seat. There were Pepto Bismol tablets and Altoids in there for this very occasion. She hated her days off from work. When she was on the job, she was too busy to allow the luxury of these episodes. There were reports to fill out, and calls to make. She knew who she was at the station, and riding around with Brad, an assignment she had balked at initially, made her feel competent and safe.

It wasn't that she was throwing herself into her job because being a cop was the only thing keeping her alive. Lena knew better than that. She would feel the same way if she were a cashier at the hardware store or a janitor at the high school. Crime and criminals had as much meaning to her as giving out the correct change would, or getting a stain off the cafeteria floor. What her job gave her these days was structure. She had to show up at eight in the morning. Certain tasks were expected of her. Brad needed direction. At noon, they had lunch, or, rather, Brad did. Lena did not have an appetite lately. Around three, they stopped for coffee at the Donut King over in Madison. They were back at the station by six and Lena's world fell apart until it was time to go back to work the next day. On the rare nights – nights like last night – when Jeffrey allowed her to take overtime, she nearly wept with relief.

Hank asked, 'You okay now?' the accusatory tone still in his voice.

She gave it right back to him. 'Just drop it.'

'Yeah, okay,' he answered, thumping the turning signal down as he stopped behind a line of cars in front of the church. They were both silent as the car inched closer to the parking lot.

Lena looked up at the small white building, resenting it for being there. She had never liked church and had even been thrown out of Sunday school at the age of twelve for ripping out the pages of a Bible. When Hank had confronted her, she had told him she had done it out of boredom, but the truth was that even then Lena had resented rules. She hated being told what to do. She could not follow an authority that had not proven itself to her. The only reason she was good at being a cop was she had a certain degree of autonomy in the field, and everyone had to listen to *her* when she told them to.

'That girl,' Hank said, picking up the conversation as if the last ten minutes had not happened. 'It's a sad thing, what she did.'

'Yeah,' Lena shrugged, not really wanting to think about it.

'People get lost along the way, I guess,' Hank said. 'Don't ask nobody for help until it's too late.' He paused, then, 'Not until it's too late.'

She knew what he was doing, making a comparison between the dead girl and herself. Some bullshit A.A. pamphlet probably had the directions for doing this on the back, right beside a little space where you could fill in your sponsor's name and phone number.

Lena snapped, 'If I was going to kill myself, I would have done it my first day home.'

'I wasn't talking about you,' Hank shot back.

'Bullshit,' she hissed. She waited a beat, then said, 'I thought you were going home soon.'

'I am,' he answered.

'Good,' she told him, and for the moment, she really meant it. Hank had been living with her since she came home from the hospital, and Lena was over having him pry into every part of her life.

'I got a business to run,' he told her, as if the dilapidated bar he owned on the outskirts of Reece was IBM. 'I need to get back to it. I'll leave tonight if you want me to.'

'Fine,' she said, but her heart started pounding at the thought of being alone at night. Lena did not want Hank in her home, but she knew that she would never feel safe if he left. Even during the daytime when she was working and Hank went to check on his bar, she felt an aching fear that he would get into a car accident or just decide not to come back at all, and Lena would have to come home to a dark, empty house. Hank was not just an unwanted house guest. He was her shield.

He told her, 'I got better things I could be doing.'

She was quiet, though in her mind, she repeated her mantra – please don't leave me, please don't leave me. Her throat was closing up with the need to say it out loud.

The car jerked as Hank accelerated, taking a parking space close to the chapel. He slammed the gear into park and the old sedan rocked back and forth several times before it settled.

He glanced at her, and she could tell that he knew he had her. 'You want me to go? Tell me to go, then.

You never had a hard time telling me to leave before.'

She bit her lip hard, wanting to taste blood. Instead of her flesh giving, her front teeth moved, and she put her hand to her mouth, startled by the reminder.

'What? You can't talk now?'

Lena choked a sob, overcome with emotion.

Hank looked away from her, waiting for her to get hold of herself. She knew that he could listen to a room full of strangers whine about wanting needles in their arms or double shots of whiskey, but could not handle Lena's tears. Part of her also knew that he hated Lena for crying. Sibyl had been his baby, the one he had taken care of. Lena was the strong one who didn't need anybody. The role reversal had knocked him on his ass.

'You gotta go to that therapist,' Hank barked at her, still angry. 'Your chief told you that. It's a requirement, and you're not doing it.'

She shook her head side to side in a violent arc, her hand still at her mouth.

'You don't run anymore. You don't work out,' he began, as if this was part of an indictment against her. 'You go to bed at nine and don't get up until late as you can the next morning,' he continued. 'You don't take care of yourself anymore.'

'I take care of myself,' she mumbled.

'You go see a therapist or I'm leaving today, Lee.' He put his hand over hers, forcing her to turn her head. 'I am serious as a fucking heart attack, child.'

Suddenly, his expression changed, and the hard lines around his face softened. He pushed back her hair with his fingers, his touch light against her skin. Hank was trying to be paternal with her, but the soft way he touched her was a sickening reminder of the way *he* had touched her before. The tenderness had been the worst part: the soft strokes, the delicate way he used his tongue and fingers to soothe and stimulate her, the agonizingly slow way he had fucked her, as if he were making love to her instead of raping her.

Lena started to shake. She could not stop herself. Hank moved his hand away quickly, as if he had just realized he was touching something dead. Lena jerked back, her head banging into the window.

'Don't ever do that again,' she warned, but there was only fear in her voice. 'Don't touch me. Don't ever touch me like that. Do you hear me?' She panted, trying to swallow the bile that came up her throat.

'I know,' he said, holding his hand close to her back but not touching her. 'I know that. I'm sorry.'

Lena grabbed for the door handle, missing it several times because her hands were shaking so hard. She stepped out of the car, taking gulps of air into her lungs. The heat enveloped her, and she squeezed her eyes shut, trying not to make the connection between the heat and her dreams of floating on the ocean.

She heard a familiar friendly voice behind her. 'Hey there, Hank,' Dave Fine, the pastor of the church, said.

'Good morning, sir,' Hank returned, his voice kinder than it ever was when he spoke to Lena. She had heard Hank use that tone before, but only with Sibyl. For Lena, there had always been nothing but sharp words of criticism.

Lena concentrated on getting her breathing back under control before she turned around. She could not smile, but she felt the corners of her mouth rise slightly in what must have seemed like a pained grimace to the pastor.

'Good morning, detective,' Dave Fine said, the preacher-compassion in his voice getting under her skin worse than anything Hank had said in the car.

For the last four months, Hank had been pushing Dave Fine on Lena, trying to get her to talk to the preacher. Pastor Fine was also a psychologist, or so he said, and saw patients in the evenings. Lena did not want to talk to the man about the weather, let alone what had happened to her. It wasn't that Fine was the Antichrist, it was that of all the people Lena could possibly talk to, a preacher would be the last one she would pick. It was like Hank had forgotten exactly what had happened to her in that dark room.

She gave him a curt 'Pastor,' walking past him, her purse tight to her chest like an old lady at a rummage sale.

She could feel his eyes on her back, hear Hank make his apologies as she walked away from them. Lena felt a flush of shame for being rude to Fine. It wasn't his fault – he was a nice enough man – but there was really nothing she could say to make them understand.

She quickened her step, her eyes staring straight ahead as she walked toward the church. A crowd of people milling around the entrance parted for her as she took the steps one at a time, forcing herself to move slowly and not run into the church like her body ached to do. Everyone except for Brad Stephens, who grinned at her like a puppy, found something better to do as she ascended the stairs. Matt Hogan, who was Frank Wallace's partner now that Lena had been assigned to patrol, focused on lighting his cigarette as if he were attempting nuclear fusion in the palm of his hand.

Lena kept her chin raised, her eyes averted so that no one would talk to her. Still, she could feel them staring at her, and she knew they would start whispering as soon as they thought she was out of earshot.

The people were the worst part about going to

church. The whole town knew what had happened to her. They knew she had been kidnapped and raped. They had read every detail of the assault in the paper. They had followed her recovery and return home from the hospital the way they followed their soap operas and football games. Lena could not go to the store without someone trying to look at the scars on her hands. She could not walk through a crowded room without someone casting a sad, pathetic look her way. As if they could understand what she had been through. As if they knew what it was like to be strong and invincible one day and completely powerless the next. And the next.

The doors to the church were closed to keep the cold air in and the heat out. Lena reached for the handle just as one of the deacons did, and their hands brushed. She jerked back as if she had touched fire, waiting for the door to open, keeping her eyes cast down. Walking through the foyer and then into the chapel, she stared at the red carpet, the white molding trimming out the bottom of the pews lining the large room, so that no one would think to talk to her.

Inside, the church was simple by Baptist standards, and small considering the size of the town. Most of the older residents attended the Primitive Baptist on Stokes Street, their tithes going with them. Crescent Baptist Church was about thirty years old, and they hosted singles parties and divorce recovery groups and Parents Without Partners get-togethers in the basement of the small chapel. Crescent was not about a vengeful God. Sermons were about forgiveness and love, charity and peace. Pastor Fine would never admonish his congregation for their sins or threaten them with hell and brimstone. This was a place of joy, or so the church bulletin said. Lena was not surprised at all that Hank had chosen it. His A.A. meetings were held in the basement, right beside the parenting class for teens.

Lena took a pew close to the front, knowing Hank would want to be close to the pastor for his usual Sunday dose of forgiveness. Dave Fine's wife and two kids were in front of her, but thankfully they didn't turn around. Lena crossed her legs, smoothing out her pants until she felt the woman down at the other end of the pew staring at her hands. Lena crossed her arms and looked up at the stage. The pulpit sat in the center, large velvet-covered chairs fanning out from it on either side. Behind this was the choir loft, the organ to the side. Its pipes climbed the walls like a vertical rib cage on either side of the baptismal. In the center of it all was Jesus, his arms spread out, his feet crossed one over the other.

Lena made herself look away as Hank slid into the pew beside her. She checked her watch. The nine-thirty service would start soon. It would last an hour, then Sunday school would be another half hour. They would leave around eleven, then go to the Waffle House off Route 2 where Hank would eat lunch and Lena would nurse a cup of coffee. They would be home by noon. Lena would clean the house then work on a couple of reports. At one-thirty, she was expected at the station to go over the Jenny Weaver case. The briefing would take about three hours if she was lucky, then it would be time to come home and get ready for the Sunday potluck and the evening service. After that, there was some kind of choir concert that would last until around nine-thirty. By the time they got home, it would be well past time for Lena to go to bed.

She exhaled slowly as she thought this through, inordinately relieved to know that today, at least, she had things to do. Her hours were spoken for.

'About to start,' Hank whispered. He took a hymnal out of the rack in front of them as the organ music started. He fidgeted with the book, then said, 'Pastor Fine says you can come by tomorrow after work.'

Lena pretended not to hear him, but her mental clock made a note of the appointment; at least it would be something to do. At least in agreeing to see him it would keep Hank in town a little longer.

'Lee?' he tried. Finally, he gave up as the choir started its hymn.

Lena stood with the crowd, Hank's baritone vibrating in her ear as he sang 'Nearer My God to Thee.' Lena did not bother to mouth the words. She traced her tongue along her front teeth, following Hank's finger along the page as he kept his place in the song. Finally, she looked back at the cross. Lena felt a lightness, an eerie kind of peace, staring at the crucifixion. As much as she wanted to deny it, there was something comforting about its familiarity.

FIVE

Sara kept her dark green BMW Z3 in second gear as she drove through downtown Heartsdale. The car had been an impulse buy insofar as any purchase that ran over thirty thousand dollars could be considered impulsive. At the time Sara bought it, the ink was just drying on her divorce papers, and she had wanted something impractical and a little flashy. The Z3 more than fit the bill. Unfortunately, as soon as she drove the thing back from the Macon dealership, Sara realized that a car was not going to make her feel better. As a matter of fact, she had felt conspicuous and silly, especially when her family was through with her. Two years later, Sara still sometimes felt a tinge of embarrassment when she saw the car parked in her driveway.

Billy, one of her two greyhounds, rode in the passenger's seat, his head ducked down because the clearance in the small sports car was too low for him. He licked his lips occasionally, but was quiet for the most part, keeping his eyes closed as the cold air from the vents pushed back his pointy ears. His lips tugged up a bit at the edges, as if he was smiling, enjoying the ride. Sara watched him out of the corner of her eye, wishing life could just once be that simple for her.

Main Street was fairly empty, since none of the shops stayed open on Sunday. Except for the hardware store and the five-and-dime, most of them were closed by noon on Saturday. Sara had been born here, right down the street at the Grant Medical Center back when it was the only hospital in the region. She knew every part of this street like a favorite book.

Sara made a slow turn at the college gates and coasted into her parking space in front of the Heartsdale Children's Clinic. Despite the fact that she had the air on high, the back of her legs stuck to the leather car seat as she opened the door. She braced herself for the heat, but it was still overwhelming. Even Billy paused before jumping out of the car. He looked around the parking lot, probably regretting that he had come along with Sara instead of staying in the cool house with Bob.

Sara used the back of her hand to wipe her forehead. She had thrown on a pair of cutoff jeans, a sleeveless undershirt, and one of Jeffrey's old dress shirts this morning, but nothing could keep the heat and humidity at bay. Rain, when it deigned to come, was about as useless as throwing water on a grease fire. Some days, it was hard for Sara to remember what it was like to be cold.

'Come on,' Sara told the dog, tugging at his retractable leash.

As usual, Billy ignored her. She let the leash out and he showed her his skinny behind as he loped toward the back of the building. There were scars on his hind legs and rear end from where the gates had popped him one too many times at the racetrack. It broke Sara's heart every time she saw them.

Billy took his time doing his business, lazily lifting his leg against the tree closest to the building. The college owned the property behind the clinic, and they kept it heavily forested. There were trails back there that the students jogged along when it was not too hot to breathe. Sara had watched the Savannah news this morning and learned that they were advising people not to go outside in the heat unless they absolutely had to.

Sara checked her key ring and found the one for the back door. By the time she had it open, sweat was trickling down her neck and back. There was a bowl by the door, and she used the outside hose to fill it while Billy scratched his back on the grass.

Inside the clinic was just as hot as out, mostly because Dr. Barney, who had been a better pediatrician than architect, had insisted on lining the south-facing front wall of the building with heat-trapping glass brick. Sara could not imagine what the temperature must be in the waiting room. The back of the building seemed hot enough to boil water.

Sara did not have enough saliva left to whistle. She held the door open, waiting for Billy to amble in. After a long drink of water, he finally came. Sara watched as he stopped in the middle of the hallway, glanced around, then fell onto the floor with a snort. Looking at the lazy animal, it was hard to imagine the years he had spent racing at the track over in Ebro. Sara leaned down to pet him and remove his leash before heading back to her office.

The layout at the clinic was typical of most pediatricians' offices. A long L-shaped hallway lined the length of the building, with three exam rooms on either side. Two exam rooms were at the back of the L, though one of them was used for storage. In the center of the hallway was a nurses' station that served as the central brain of the clinic. There was a computer that held current patient information and a row of floor-to-ceiling filing cabinets where current charts were kept.

There was another chart room behind the waiting room that was filled with information on patients dating back to 1969. One day, they would have to be purged, but Sara did not have that kind of time and she could not bring herself to ask the staff to do something she herself was not prepared to do.

Sara's tennis shoes snicked as she walked across the clean tile floor. She did not bother to turn on the lights. Sara knew this place in the dark, but that was not the only reason she left them off. The flickering of a fluorescent light, the click of brightness as the tubes came to life, would seem intrusive considering the task ahead.

By the time she reached her office across from the nurses' station she had already unbuttoned her overshirt and tied it around her waist. She wasn't wearing a bra, but she did not expect to run into anyone who would care.

Pictures of patients lined her office walls. Initially, a grateful mother had given Sara a school snapshot of a child. Sara had stuck it on the wall, then a day later another photo had come, and she had taped it beside the first. Twelve years had passed since then and now photographs spilled into the hallway and the staff bathroom. Sara could remember them all: their runny noses and earaches, their school crushes and family problems. Brad Stephens's senior picture was somewhere near the shower in the bathroom. The photo of a boy named Jimmy Powell, a patient who just a few months ago had been diagnosed with leukemia, had been moved by Sara's phone so that she could remember him every day. He was in the hospital now, and Sara knew in her gut that within the next few months another patient of hers would be put into the ground.

Jenny Weaver's picture was not on the wall. Her

mother had never brought one in. Sara only had the girl's chart to help reconstruct their history together.

The filing cabinet drawer groaned as Sara yanked it open. The unit was as old as Dr. Barney and just as difficult. No amount of WD-40 would fix it.

'Crap,' Sara hissed as the cabinet tilted forward. The top drawer was full to overflowing, and she had to use her free hand to keep the whole cabinet from falling.

Quickly, Sara ran her fingers along the file tabs, reading off Weaver on her second run through. She pushed the cabinet back, slamming the drawer into the unit. The sound was loud in the small office. Sara was tempted to open it and slam it again, just to make some noise.

She snapped on her desk lamp as she sat, her sweaty legs skidding on the vinyl seat. Probably it would have been wiser to take the chart home. At the very least, it would be more comfortable. Sara did not want comfort, though. She considered it a small penance to sit in the heat and try to find what she had missed over the last three years.

Her wire-rimmed reading glasses were in the breast pocket of her shirt, and Sara felt a moment of panic, thinking she had broken them when she sat down. They were bent, but otherwise fine. She slipped on her glasses, took a deep breath, and opened the chart.

Jenny Weaver had first come to the clinic three years ago. At ten years old, the child's weight had been within normal ranges in relation to her height. Her first ailment had been a persistent sore throat that a round of antibiotics had evidently cured. There was a follow-up notation in the chart, and from what Sara could barely decipher from her own handwriting, Dottie Weaver had been contacted a week later by phone to make sure Jenny was responding to treatment. She had been.

About two years ago, Jenny had started to put on weight. Unfortunately, this was not uncommon these days, especially for girls like Jenny, who had gotten her first menstrual period shortly after her eleventh birthday. Their lives were more sedentary, and fast food was more readily available than it should be. Hormones in meat and dairy products helped the process along. Case studies in some of the journals Sara read were already dealing with ways to treat girls who entered puberty as early as eight years old.

Sara continued reading through Jenny's chart. Shortly after the weight gain began, Jenny had been diagnosed with a urinary tract infection. Three months later, the girl had come in with a yeast infection. According to Sara's notes, there was nothing suspicious about this at the time. In retrospect, Sara questioned her judgment. The infections could have been the beginning of a pattern. She turned to the next page, noting the date. Jenny had come in a year later with another urinary tract infection. A year was a long time, but Sara pulled out a sheet of paper and made notes of the dates, as well as the two other visits Jenny had made after, both for sore throats. Perhaps Jenny's parents shared custody. They could trace the dates to see if they corresponded with visits to her father.

Sara set down her pen, trying to recall what she knew about Jenny Weaver's father. Mothers were more likely to bring their children into the clinic, and as far as Sara could remember she had never met Jenny's father. Some women, especially women who were recently divorced, would volunteer information about their husbands as if their children were not in the room. Sara was always uncomfortable when this happened, and she usually managed to cut it off before it could really start, but some women talked over her, bringing up the kind of personal information that a child should never know about either parent. Dottie Weaver had never done this. She was talkative enough, even chatty, but Dottie had never disparaged her ex-husband at the clinic, even though Sara had gathered from the sporadic way the single mother paid her insurance balance that money was tight.

Sara's glasses slipped up as she rubbed her eyes. She glanced at the clock on the wall. Sunday lunch at her parents' was at eleven, then Jeffrey was expecting her at the station around one-thirty.

Sara shook her head, skipping over any thoughts of Jeffrey. A headache had settled into the base of her neck and the dull throbbing made it difficult to concentrate. She took off her glasses and cleaned them with her shirttail, hoping this might help her see things more clearly.

'Hello?' Sara called, throwing open the door to her parents' house. The cold air inside brought welcome goose bumps to her clammy skin.

'In here,' her mother said from the kitchen.

Sara dropped her briefcase by the door and kicked off her tennis shoes before walking to the back of the house. Billy trotted in front of her, giving Sara a hard look, as if to ask why they had spent all that time in the hot clinic when they could have been here in the air-conditioning. To punctuate his displeasure, he collapsed onto his side halfway down the hallway so that Sara had to step over him to get to the back of the house.

When Sara walked into the kitchen, Cathy was standing at the stove frying chicken. Her mother was still dressed in her church clothes, but had taken off her shoes and pantyhose. A white apron that read DON'T MESS WITH THE CHEF was tied loosely around her waist.

'Hey, Mama,' Sara offered, kissing her cheek. Sara was the tallest person in her family, and she could rest her chin on her mother's head without straining her neck. Tessa had inherited Cathy Linton's petite build and blonde hair. Sara had inherited her pragmatism.

Cathy gave Sara a disapproving look. 'Did you forget to put on a bra this morning?'

Sara felt her face redden as she untied the shirt she was wearing around her waist. She slipped it on over her T-shirt, offering, 'I was in the clinic. I didn't think I'd be there long enough to turn on the air.'

'It's too hot to be frying,' Cathy countered. 'But your father wanted chicken.'

Sara got the lesson on sacrificing things for your family, but answered instead, 'You should have told him to go to Chick's.'

'He doesn't need to eat that trash.'

Sara let this go, sighing much as Billy had. She buttoned the shirt to the top, giving her mother a tight smile as she asked, 'Better?'

Cathy nodded, taking a paper napkin off the counter and wiping her forehead. 'It's not even noon and it's already ninety degrees out.'

'I know,' Sara answered, tucking a foot underneath her as she sat on the kitchen stool. She watched her mother move around the kitchen, glad for the normalcy. Cathy was wearing a linen dress with thin, vertical green stripes. Her blonde hair, which was only slightly streaked with gray, was pulled up behind her head in a loose ponytail, much the same way Sara wore hers.

Cathy blew her nose into the napkin, then threw it in the trash. 'Tell me about last night,' she said, returning to the stove.

Sara shrugged. 'Jeffrey didn't have a choice.'

'I never doubted that. I want to know how you're holding up.'

Sara considered the question. The truth was, she was not holding up well at all.

Cathy seemed to sense this. She slipped a fresh piece of battered chicken into the hot oil and turned to face her daughter. 'I called you last night to check in with you.'

Sara stared at her mother, forcing herself not to look away. 'I was at Jeffrey's.'

'I figured that, but your father drove by his house just to make sure.'

'Daddy did?' Sara asked, surprised. 'Why?'

'We thought you would come here,' Cathy answered. 'When you weren't at home, that was the obvious place to check.'

Sara crossed her arms. 'Don't you think that's a little intrusive?'

'Not nearly as intrusive as childbirth,' Cathy snapped, pointing at Sara with her fork. 'Next time, call.'

After almost forty years, Cathy could still make Sara feel like a child. Sara looked out the window, feeling as if she had been caught doing something wrong.

'Sara?'

Sara mumbled a quiet, 'Yes, ma'am.'

'I worry about you.'

'I know, Mama.'

'Is everything okay?'

Sara felt her color rise again, but for a different reason. 'Where's Tessa?'

'She's not down yet.'

Tessa lived over the garage of their parents' home. Sara's house was just a mile down the road, but that was far enough to give her some sense of independence. Tessa did not seem to mind the closeness. She worked with Eddie, their father, in the family's plumbing business, so it was easier for her to walk down the stairs and report for work every morning. Besides, part of Tessa was still a teenage girl. It had not hit her yet that one day she would want a house of her own. Maybe it never would.

Cathy flipped the chicken, tapping her fork on the edge of the pan. She slipped it into the spoon rest, then turned to Sara, her arms crossed. 'What's going on?'

'Nothing,' Sara answered. 'I mean, other than last night with the girl. And the baby. I guess you heard about the baby.'

'It was all over the church before we even walked through the doors.'

'Well' – Sara shrugged – 'it was very hard.'

'I can't even imagine how you do that job, baby.'

'Sometimes, I can't either.'

Cathy stood, waiting for the rest. 'And?' she prompted.

Sara rubbed the back of her neck. 'At Jeffrey's . . . ,' she began. 'It just didn't work out.'

'Didn't work out?' her mother asked.

'I mean, didn't work out as in . . .' Sara gestured with her hands, encouraging her mother to fill in the rest.

'Oh,' Cathy finally said. 'Physically?'

Sara blushed again, which was answer enough.

'Well, that's not a complete surprise, is it? After what happened?'

'He was so . . .' Sara looked for the right words. 'He was . . . abrupt. I mean, I tried . . .' Again, she left out the details.

'Is this the first time that's happened?'

Sara shrugged. It was the first time it had happened with her, but who knew about Jeffrey's other conquests. 'The part that was awful . . . ,' Sara began, then stopped. 'As long as I've known him, I have never seen him that mad. He was furious. I thought he was going to hit something.'

'I remember once when your father couldn't –'

'Mama,' Sara stopped her. It was hard enough talking to her mother about this without bringing Eddie into the picture. Not to mention that Jeffrey would kill Sara if he knew that she had told anyone his performance had been less than stellar. Jeffrey's sexual prowess was as important to him as his reputation as a good cop.

'You brought it up,' Cathy reminded her, turning back to the chicken. She snatched a paper towel off the roll and lined a plate to put the chicken on.

'Okay,' Sara answered. 'What should I do?'

'Do whatever he wants,' Cathy said. 'Or nothing at all.' She picked up another piece of chicken. 'Are you sure you even want to bother at this point?'

'Meaning what?'

'Meaning, do you want to be with him or not? Maybe that's what it boils down to. You've been dancing around this thing with Jeffrey since the divorce.' She tapped the fork on the pan. 'As your father would say, it's time for you either to shit or get off the pot.'

The front door opened, then banged shut, and Sara heard two thumping noises as Tessa kicked off her shoes.

Tessa yelled, 'Mama?'

'In the kitchen,' Cathy answered. She gave Sara a pointed look. 'You know what I mean?'

'Yes, ma'am.'

Tessa stomped her way down the hall, mumbling, 'Stupid dog,' as she obviously stepped over Billy. The kitchen door bumped open, and Tessa came into the kitchen with an irritated expression on her face. She was wearing an old pink bathrobe with a green T-shirt and a pair of boxer shorts underneath. Her face was pale, and she looked a bit sickly.

Cathy asked, 'Tessie?'

Tessa shook her head as she walked to the refrigerator and opened the freezer door, saying, 'I just need coffee.'

Cathy ignored this, and kissed her on the forehead to take her temperature. 'You feel warm.'

'It's a hundred freaking degrees outside,' Tessa whined, standing as close to the freezer as she could without actually getting in. 'Of course I'm warm.' As if to reinforce this, she flapped her robe open and closed several times to generate some cool air. 'Jesus, I'm moving somewhere where they get real seasons. I swear I am. I don't care how funny they talk or that they don't know how to make grits. There has got to be a better alternative.'

'Is that all that's wrong?' Sara asked, putting her hand on Tessa's forehead. As a doctor, Sara knew this was about as effective a gauge for a fever as Cathy's kiss, but Tessa was her baby sister. She had to do something.

Tessa pulled away. 'I'm premenstrual, I'm hot, and I need chocolate.' She stuck out her chin. 'Do you see this?' she asked, pointing to a large pimple.

'I don't see how we could miss it,' Cathy said, closing the refrigerator door.

Sara laughed, and Tessa popped her on the arm.

'Wonder what Daddy's gonna call it?' Sara teased, slapping her back. When his daughters were teenagers, Eddie had taken great delight in drawing attention to their facial blemishes. Sara still felt a flush of shame when she remembered the time her father had introduced her to one of his friends as his oldest daughter Sara, and Bobo, her new pimple.

Tessa was phrasing a response when the phone rang. She picked it up on the first ring.

Two seconds passed before Tessa hissed a curse and yelled, 'I got it, Dad,' as Eddie obviously picked up the extension upstairs.

Sara smiled, thinking this could have been any Sunday from the last twenty years. All that was missing was their father walking in, making some silly comment about how happy he was to see all three of his girls barefoot and in the kitchen.

Tessa said, 'Hold on,' then put her hand over the mouth of the receiver. She turned to Sara. 'Are you here?'

'Who is it?' Sara asked, but she could guess the answer.

'Who do you think?' Tessa snapped. She did not wait for a response. Instead, she said into the phone, 'Hold on, Jeffrey. Here she is.'

SIX

Ben Walker, Grant County's chief of police before Jeffrey, had kept his office just off the briefing room in the back of the station. Every day, Ben had settled himself behind the large desk that almost filled the entire room, and anyone who wanted to talk to him had to sit on the other side of this mammoth hunk of wood, their knees grazing the desk, their backs firm to the wall. In the mornings, the men – and they were all men then – on the senior squad were called in to hear their assignments for the day, then they left and the chief shut his door. Nobody saw him again until quitting time, when Ben got in his car and drove two blocks up the street to the diner where he ate his supper.

The first thing Jeffrey did when he took over the station was throw out Ben's desk. The oak monstrosity had to be disassembled to get it through the door. Jeffrey made Ben's old office the storage room, and took the small office at the front of the squad room as his own. One quiet weekend, Jeffrey installed a picture window so he could look out on the squad and, more important, so they could see him. There were blinds on the window, but he seldom closed them. Jeffrey made a point of leaving his office door open whenever possible.

He stared out at the empty squad room, wondering what his people would make of Jenny Weaver's shooting. Jeffrey felt an overwhelming sense of guilt for what he had done, even though his mind kept telling him he had not been given a choice. Every time he thought about it Jeffrey felt like he couldn't breathe right, like not enough air was getting to his lungs. He could not let go of the obvious questions in his mind: Had he made the right decision? Would Jenny have really killed that kid in cold blood? Sara seemed to think so. Last night, she had said something about having two dead teenagers today instead of one if Jeffrey had not stopped the girl. Of course, Sara had said a lot of other things last night that had not exactly been a comfort.

Jeffrey pressed his hands together in front of his face, leaning his head against his thumbs as he thought about Sara. Sometimes, she could be too analytical for her own good. One of the sexiest things about Sara was her mouth. Too bad she didn't know when to shut up and use it for something more helpful to Jeffrey than talking.

'Chief?' Frank Wallace knocked on the door.

'Come in,' Jeffrey answered.

'Hot outside,' Frank said, as if to explain why he wasn't wearing a tie. He was dressed in a dark black suit that had a cheap shine to it. The top button of his dress shirt was undone, and Jeffrey could see his yellowed white undershirt underneath. As usual, Frank reeked of cigarette smoke. He had probably been outside, smoking by the back door, giving Jeffrey some time before he came in for their meeting. Why anyone would voluntarily hold a burning cigarette in this kind of heat, Jeffrey would never know.

Frank could have had Ben Walker's job if he had asked. Of course, the old cop was too smart for that. Frank had worked in Grant County his entire career, and he had seen the way the cities were changing. Once, Frank had told Jeffrey that being chief of police was a young man's job, but Jeffrey had thought then as he did now that what Frank meant was it was a foolish man's job. During Jeffrey's first year in Grant, he had figured out that no one in his right mind would sign up for this kind of pressure. By then, it had been too late. He had already met Sara.

'Busy weekend,' Frank said, handing Jeffrey a weekend status report. The file was thicker than usual.

'Yeah.' Jeffrey indicated a chair for the man to sit down.

'Alleged break-in at the cleaners. Marla told you about that one? Then there's a couple or three DUIs, usual shit at the college, drunk and disorderly. Couple of domestic situations, no charges filed.'

Jeffrey listened half-heartedly as Frank ran down the list. It was long, and daunting. There was no telling what a larger city dealt with this weekend if Grant had been hit so hard. Usually, things were much quieter. Of course, the heat brought out violence in people. Jeffrey had known that as long as he had been a cop.

'So . . .' Frank wrapped it up: 'That's about it.'

'Good,' Jeffrey answered, taking the report. He tapped his finger on the papers, then with little fanfare slid Jenny Weaver's file across the desk. It sat there like a white elephant.

Frank gave the file the same skeptical look he would give an astrology report, then reluctantly picked it up and started to read. Frank had been on the job long enough to think he had seen everything. The shocked expression on his face belied this as he examined the photographs Sara had taken.

'Mother of God,' Frank mumbled, reaching into his coat pocket. He pulled out his cigarettes, then, probably remembering where he was, put them back. He closed the file without finishing it.

Jeffrey said, 'She didn't give birth to the child.'

'Yeah.' Frank cleared his throat, crossing his legs uncomfortably. He was fifty-eight years old and had already put in enough time to retire with a nice pension. Why he kept working the job was a mystery. Cases like this must make Frank wonder why he kept showing up every day, too.

'What is this?' Frank asked. 'Good Lord in heaven.'

'Female Genital Mutilation,' Jeffrey told him. 'It's an African or Middle Eastern thing.' He held up his hand, stopping Frank's next question. 'I know what you're thinking. They're Southern Baptist, not Islamic.'

'Where'd she get the idea, then?'

'That's what we're going to find out.'

Frank shook his head, like he was trying to erase the image from his mind.

Jeffrey said, 'Dr. Linton is on her way in to do the briefing,' feeling foolish for using Sara's title even as he said it. Frank played poker with Eddie Linton. He had watched Sara grow up.

'The kid gonna be here, too?' Frank asked, meaning Lena.

'Of course,' Jeffrey answered, meeting him squarely in the eye. Frank frowned, making it obvious that he did not approve.

For everything Frank was – sexist, probably racist, certainly ageist – he cared for Lena. He had a daughter about Lena's age, and from the moment Jeffrey had partnered her with Frank, the old cop had protested. Every week Frank had come in, asking for a change in assignment, and every week Jeffrey had told him to get used to it. Part of the reason the city had brought in Jeffrey, an outsider, was to drag the force out of the Stone Age. Jeffrey had handpicked Lena Adams from the police academy and groomed her from day one to be the first female detective on the squad.

Jeffrey did not know what to do with her now. He had put Lena with Brad Stephens on a temporary basis until her hands healed, hoping the downtime would help her ease back into her job. Just last month she had gotten a clearance from her doctor to return to active duty, but Lena had yet to ask for her old assignment back. For Frank's part, he could not even look her in the eye when she said hello to him. Jeffrey had heard Frank say a million times that women did not belong on the force, and Frank seemed to take Lena's attack as confirmation of this.

Logically, Jeffrey did not agree with Frank's assessment. Women cops were good for the force. Ideally, the makeup of the force should reflect that of the community. Lena had brought a thoughtfulness to the job. She was better with certain types of perpetrators and knew how to handle female victims of crime, something that had been missing in the senior squad prior to her promotion. What's more, having a female detective had encouraged other women to join the ranks. There were fifteen women on patrol now. When Ben Walker had left the force, the only women in its employ had been secretaries. Despite all of this progress, when Jeffrey thought about what Lena had gone through, what had been done to her, he wanted to lock her up in her house and stand outside with a shotgun in case anyone ever tried to hurt her again.

Frank interrupted his thoughts, asking, 'There gonna be some kind of internal investigation on this thing?' He paused, picking at the corner of the case file. 'The Weaver shooting, I mean.'

Jeffrey nodded, sitting back in his chair. 'I talked

to the mayor this morning. I want you to take Brad and Lena's statements. Buddy Conford's the city attorney on this one.'

'He's a public defender,' Frank pointed out.

'Yeah, well, not on this one,' Jeffrey told him. 'There's some concern about the girl's mother. The city has an insurance policy for this kind of thing. Maybe they'll settle it out of court. I dunno.' Jeffrey shrugged. 'She was threatening someone with a gun and all. It's just kind of tricky, you know?'

'Yeah,' Frank answered. 'I know.' He waited a few beats, then asked, 'You okay with this, Chief?'

Jeffrey felt some of his resolve falter. The sinking, lost feeling he had experienced last night with Sara came back, and he felt a heaviness in his chest. He had never shot anyone, let alone killed a little girl. His mind kept playing back the scene with Jenny, picking apart the clock, trying to find the place where his negotiations had gone sour. There had to be something else he could have said or done that would have made her put down that gun. There had to be an alternative.

'Chief?' Frank said. 'For what it's worth, Brad and Lena will back you a hundred percent. You know that, right?'

'Yeah,' Jeffrey answered, not taking comfort in Frank's words because he knew that Brad and Lena would back him even if they did not think what Jeffrey had done was right. There were gray areas in law enforcement, but when it came down to the wire, cops always backed cops. Brad would do this because at some level he worshipped Jeffrey. Lena would do it because she felt she owed Jeffrey something for letting her back on the job.

For Jeffrey, this was hardly a consolation.

Both men were silent. Jeffrey turned his head, looking at the shelves lining the far wall of his office. Shooting trophies were there, awarded for his marksmanship. An old football from when he played for Auburn was on the bottom shelf. Pictures of guys he had worked with on the job in Grant as well as back in Birmingham were alongside a couple of snapshots of Sara he had taken on their honeymoon. He had put these up recently, when they started dating again. Now, he wasn't so sure about wanting the pictures in his office, let alone wanting Sara in his life. Jeffrey still could not get over how distant she had been last night, tensing up when he touched her, telling him what to do. Like he didn't know how to do what he was doing. Like he hadn't done it hundreds of times before with other women who were a hell of a lot more receptive than Sara had been.

Frank turned around in his chair when the half-doors separating the squad room from the reception area clapped open. Sara walked through, her briefcase in one hand. She was dressed in a light blue dress that looked like a long T-shirt. Jeffrey could see she had decided to go with tennis shoes without socks to complete the ensemble. She probably hadn't even shaved her legs.

Both men watched as Sara made her way to the office. Her hair was a mess and Jeffrey wondered if she had even bothered to comb it. Sara had never been the kind of woman who was interested in high fashion and she seldom wore makeup. Sometimes this was sexy, sometimes it made her look sloppy, like she was more interested in being a doctor than being a woman. As she got closer to them, he could see that her glasses were crooked on her face. For some reason, this irritated him more than anything else.

Frank stood when she entered the room, so Jeffrey followed suit.

'Hi,' she said, smiling nervously. Jeffrey was glad she was uncomfortable.

'Hey there,' Frank said, buttoning his jacket.

Sara smiled at Frank, then said, 'I've called Nick Shelton,' referring to Grant County's Georgia Bureau of Investigations field agent. 'I asked him to track any cases involving this kind of mutilation. He said he'd have something Wednesday at the latest.'

When Jeffrey did not address this, Frank supplied, 'Good thinking.'

'And,' Sara continued, 'I called around to the hospitals. Nobody came in last night seeking postlabor treatment. I left the number here at the station in case they get someone in.'

Frank pulled at the collar of his shirt. 'So, you think there's any way the girl could have done this to herself? This circumcision thing?'

'God, no.' Sara seemed to bristle at this. 'And, it's not circumcision,' she told him. 'This is tantamount to castration. Her clitoris and labia minora were completely scraped away, then what was left was sewn together with thread.'

'Oh,' Frank said, obviously uncomfortable with this information.

Sara pursed her lips. 'It's the same as cutting off a man's penis.'

Frank looked uncomfortably from Jeffrey to Sara, then back again.

'Anyway.' Sara gestured to her briefcase. 'I'm ready to start the briefing.'

'That's been postponed,' Jeffrey said, hearing the hard tone to his voice but unable to do anything about it. When he had called to ask Sara to come in early, he had not mentioned why. He told her, 'Dottie Weaver will be here in about fifteen minutes. I want to get her out of here as soon as I can.'

'Oh,' she said, surprised. 'Okay. I guess I can do some paperwork at the clinic. You think a couple of hours will do it?'

He shook his head no. 'I want you to sit in on the interview.'

Sara gave him a careful look. 'I'm not a cop.'

'Lena is,' he told her. 'She'll be leading the interview. I want you there because she knows you.'

She tucked her hand into her hip. 'Lena or Dottie?'

Frank cleared his throat. 'I got some calls to make,' he said, giving Sara a polite nod before leaving the room.

After he was gone, Sara turned to Jeffrey, giving him a questioning look.

He asked, 'Is that a nightgown?'

'What?'

'What you're wearing,' he said, indicating her dress. 'It looks like a nightgown.'

Sara laughed uncomfortably. 'No,' she said, as if he was leaving out some part of the joke.

'You could have worn something more professional,' he said, thinking about what she had worn last night. Her sweat pants and a ratty old T-shirt didn't exactly help the situation. And her legs had felt hairier than his.

He asked, 'Would it kill you to dress up a little bit?'

Sara lowered her voice, the way she did when she got angry. 'Is there some reason you're talking to me like you're my mother?'

He felt a flash of anger that was so intense he knew not to open his mouth and say what wanted to come out.

'Jeff,' Sara said, 'what is going on?'

He walked past her and slammed the door shut. 'Would it kill you to do me this one favor?'

'Favor?' She shook her head, as if he had started talking gibberish.

'Sit in on the interview,' he reminded her. 'With Weaver.'

Sara exhaled sharply. 'What could I possibly say to her?'

'Never mind,' he answered. To give himself something to do, he closed the blinds. 'Just forget about it.'

'Just tell me what you want me to do,' she said, her voice irritatingly reasonable. 'Do you want me to go home and change? Do you want me to leave you alone?'

He turned around, saying, 'I want you to stop breaking my balls, is what I want you to do.'

Sara tucked in her chin. It seemed to be her turn to hold back something she wanted to say.

He raised his eyebrows, prompting her to speak. 'What?' he demanded, knowing he was pushing her, wanting a fight to release some of the anger he felt.

Sara took a deep breath, letting it out slowly. 'I don't understand why you're so angry at me.'

Jeffrey did not answer.

She smoothed down his tie with the back of her fingers, then put her palm to his chest. 'Jeff, please. Just tell me what you want me to do.'

Words failed him. He turned away from her and then, because there was nothing else for him to do, he twisted the wand to open the blinds again. He felt Sara's hand on his shoulder.

She said, 'It's all right.'

'I know that,' he snapped, but he didn't. He felt like his brain was on fire, and every time he blinked all he could see was Jenny Weaver's head jerking back as the bullet cut through her neck.

Sara put her arms around him, then pressed her lips against the back of his neck. 'It's okay,' she whispered against his neck, and he felt the coolness of her breath calming him. She kissed his neck again, holding her lips there for what seemed like a long time. His body started to relax, and Jeffrey wondered why she hadn't done this last night. Then he remembered that she had.

She told him again, 'It's all right.'

He felt calm for the first time that morning, like he could breathe again. It felt so good that for just a second he thought he might do something really stupid, like cry or, worse, tell Sara that he loved her.

He asked, 'You gonna sit in on the interview or not?'

She let her hands drop, and he could tell this was not the reaction she had been hoping for. He looked at her, trying to think of something to say. Nothing came to mind.

Finally, she nodded once, telling him, 'I'll do whatever you want me to do.'

Jeffrey stood in the observation room, watching through the one-way mirror as Sara comforted Dottie Weaver. He had never been able to stay mad at Sara for long, mostly because Sara would not allow it.

Dottie Weaver was a largeish woman with dark brown hair and olive colored skin. Her hair looked long, but she kept it in a neat bun on top of her head. The style was a bit dated, but it seemed to suit her. She had what Jeffrey thought of as an older face, the kind where the person looks the same at ten as she does at forty. Her cheeks were more jowls, and she carried about twenty pounds more on her than she should have. There were deep creases in her forehead above her nose, which gave her a stern look, even when she was crying.

Jeffrey glanced at Lena, who was standing beside him with her arms crossed over her chest. She was watching Sara and Dottie with her usual focused intensity. Here they were, the two most emotionally raw people in the station, responsible for finding out what had happened the night before. Jeffrey knew then that he had asked Sara to do this for selfish reasons. She would act as his sanity.

Jeffrey turned to Lena, telling her, 'I'm using you.'

She did not react, but that was hardly uncommon. Six months ago, Lena Adams would have been rabid for this interview. She would have strutted through the station, flaunting the fact that she had been chosen by the chief. Now, she just nodded.

'Because you're a woman,' he clarified. 'And because of what happened to you.'

She looked at him, and there was an emptiness to her eyes that struck him to his core. Ten years ago, at the training academy in Macon, Jeffrey had watched Lena fly through the obstacle course like a bat out of hell. At five-four and around a hundred twenty pounds, she was the smallest recruit in her group, but she made up for it by sheer force of will. Her tenacity and drive had caught his attention that day. Looking at her now, he wondered if that Lena would ever show herself again.

Lena broke eye contact, staring back at Sara. 'Yeah, I guess she'll feel sorry for me,' she said, her tone flat. It unnerved him the way she did not seem to feel anything. He even preferred her intense anger to the automaton Lena seemed to be lately.

'Go slowly,' he advised, handing her the case file. 'We need as much information as we can get.'

'Anything else?' she asked. They could have been discussing the weather.

Jeffrey told her no and she left without another

word. He turned back to the mirror, waiting for Lena to enter the interview room. When the young detective had returned to her job, Jeffrey had told her she would have to get some kind of therapy to deal with what had happened. As far as he knew, Lena had not. He should ask her about this. Jeffrey knew that. He just did not know how.

The door creaked as Lena opened it. She walked into the room, her hands tucked into the pockets of her dress slacks. She was wearing tan chinos with a dark blue button-down dress shirt. Her shoulder-length brown hair was tucked back neatly behind her ears. At thirty-three years old, she had finally grown into her face. Lena had always been attractive, but in the last couple of years she had developed a woman-liness that was not lost on the senior squad.

Jeffrey looked away, uncomfortable with these thoughts. After what she had been through, it felt wrong for him to be considering Lena this way.

'Mrs. Weaver?' Lena asked. She extended her hand, and Jeffrey cringed along with Dottie Weaver as they both stared at Lena's open palm. The scar in the center was horrible to see. Sara was the only one who did not seem to react.

Lena withdrew her hand, clenching it by her side as if she was embarrassed. 'I'm Detective Lena Adams. I can't tell you how sorry I am for your loss.'

'Thank you,' Dottie managed, her Midwestern twang a sharp contrast to Lena's soft drawl.

Lena sat opposite Sara and Dottie at the table. She clasped her hands in front of her, drawing attention to her scars again. Jeffrey half expected her to take off her shoes and put her feet on the table.

'I'm sorry . . . ,' Dottie began, then stopped. 'I mean, for what happened with you.'

Lena nodded her head once, staring down as if she needed to collect herself. One of the first interrogation tricks Jeffrey had taught the young detective was that silence is a cop's best friend. Normal people do not like silence, and invariably they try to fill it. Most of the time, they do this without letting their brain enter the equation.

'And your sister,' Dottie continued. 'She was a lovely person. I knew her from the science fair. Jenny loved science. She was . . .'

Lena's chest rose and fell as she took a deep breath, but that was all the reaction she gave. 'Sibyl was a teacher,' Lena supplied. 'She loved teaching kids.'

The room was silent again, and Jeffrey found himself staring at Sara. Strands of her dark red hair had fallen loose from her ponytail and were sticking to her neck. Her glasses were no longer crooked on her nose, they were crooked on the top of her head. She was staring at Lena the way she might stare at a snake, trying to decide whether or not it was poisonous.

Lena asked, 'Do we need to contact your husband, Mrs. Weaver?'

'Dottie,' the mother answered. 'I've already told him.'

'Will he be coming down for the funeral?'

Dottie was quiet, and she fidgeted with a thin silver bracelet on her wrist. When she spoke, she directed her words to Sara. 'You cut her open, didn't you?'

Sara opened her mouth as if to respond, but Lena answered the question.

'Yes, ma'am,' Lena said. 'Dr. Linton performed the autopsy. I attended the procedure. We wanted to do everything we could to make sure Jenny was taken care of.'

Dottie stared from Lena to Sara, then back again. Suddenly, she leaned over the table, her shoulders stooped as if she had been punched in the gut. 'She was my only child,' she sobbed. 'She was my baby.'

Sara reached out to touch the grieving woman on the back, but Lena stopped her with a look. She leaned forward herself and took Dottie's hand in her own. Lena told the woman, 'I know what it's like to lose someone. I really do.'

Dottie squeezed Lena's hands. 'I know you do. I know.'

Jeffrey realized he had been holding his breath, waiting for this moment. Lena had broken through.

Lena asked, 'What happened with her father?'

'Oh.' Dottie took a tissue out of her purse. 'You know. We weren't getting along. He wanted to do more with his life. He ended up running away with his secretary.' She turned to Sara. 'You know how men are.'

Jeffrey felt mildly irritated, because she was obviously referring to Jeffrey's infidelities. Such was the nature of a small town.

'He never married her, though,' Dottie finished. 'The secretary.' Her lips curved in a slight, triumphant smile.

'My best friend in high school went through this,' Lena began, making the bridge between her and Dottie Weaver more solid. 'Her father did the same thing to them. He just picked up one day and never looked back. They never saw him again.'

'Oh, no. Samuel wasn't like that,' Dottie provided. 'Not in the beginning, anyway. He saw Jenny once a month until he got transferred to Spokane. That's in Washington.' Lena nodded and Dottie continued. 'I think the last time he saw her was over a year ago.'

'What was his response when you told him last night?'

'He cried,' she said, and tears rolled down her own cheeks. She turned to Sara, perhaps because Sara had known Jenny. 'She was so sweet. She had such a gentle heart.'

Sara nodded, but Jeffrey could tell she was uncomfortable with the way Lena was handling the interview. He wondered what Sara had expected after her physical findings last night.

Dottie blew her nose, and when she spoke her words were more punctuated. 'She just got mixed up in this crowd. And that Patterson boy.'

'Mark Patterson?' Lena asked, referring to the boy Jenny had threatened to kill.

'Yes, Mark.'

'Was she seeing him? Dating him?'

Dottie shrugged. 'I can't tell you. They did things in groups, and Jenny was friends with his sister, Lacey.'

'Lacey?' Sara asked. She seemed to realize she'd interrupted the flow, and nodded for Dottie to continue.

'Jenny and I were so close after her father left, more like friends than mother and daughter. She was my anchor through everything that happened. Maybe I was too close to her. Maybe I should have given her more independence.' Dottie paused again. 'It's just that Mark seemed so harmless. He used to cut our grass in the summer. He did odd jobs around the house to earn extra money.' She laughed without a trace of humor. 'I thought he was a good kid. I thought I could trust him.'

Lena did not let her go on this tangent for long. 'When did Jenny start hanging around with Lacey?'

'About a year ago, I guess. They were all in the church together. I thought it was good, but these kids . . . I don't know. You would think that a church would

85

be a safe place for your child, but . . .' She shook her head. 'I didn't know,' she said. 'I didn't even know she had ever been with a boy, let alone . . .'

Lena gave Sara an almost imperceptible nod. Jeffrey saw Sara brace herself as she prepared to deliver the news. 'Dottie, I did examine Jenny last night.'

Dottie pressed her lips tightly together as she waited.

Lena said, 'Jenny wasn't pregnant. That wasn't her baby in the skating rink.'

The mother stared openly from Sara to Lena, then back again. She seemed too shocked to show anything but disbelief.

Sara clarified. 'Lena's right. She wasn't pregnant, though I can tell you that she was sexually active prior to six months ago.'

Dottie's mouth worked, but no words came. She smiled, finally, interpreting this as good news. 'So, she didn't do it? She didn't hurt the baby?'

Lena answered, 'We don't really know what happened with that yet.' She paused, looking at her hands, this time not for effect. After a few beats, she looked back up at Dottie. When she spoke, her voice was low, her eyes locked on the mother as if Sara were no longer in the room. 'This is just my opinion, ma'am, but from everything I've learned about your daughter, I can't see her doing what she's been accused of.'

The mother's shoulders dropped in obvious relief. She began to cry again, putting a tissue to her nose. 'She was so gentle,' she said. 'There's no way she would ever do this kind of thing.' She turned to Sara for confirmation. 'She was such a good girl.'

Sara nodded again, her smile weak.

'She talked about being a doctor one day,' Dottie

told Sara. 'She said she wanted to help kids just like you do.'

Sara's smile wavered, and Jeffrey could see the guilt flash in her eyes.

Lena cut through the moment, asking, 'Jenny and this group she was with, the Patterson children?'

'Yes, Mark and Lacey.'

'She was still going to church with them? Still active?'

'Until about eight months ago,' Dottie answered. 'She stopped going. I can't tell you why. She just said she didn't want to go anymore.'

'This would have been in January?'

'I suppose.'

'Right after Christmas?'

Dottie nodded. 'Thereabouts.'

'Did anything happen during that time? Maybe a falling out? Did she get angry at anyone? Maybe have a fight with Mark Patterson?'

'No,' Dottie answered firmly. 'As a matter of fact, she went on a youth retreat with the church the week after Christmas. They all went to Gatlinburg to go skiing. I didn't want her out of the house around the holidays, but she had her heart set on it, and she had brought her grades up in school, so . . .' She let her voice trail off.

'So, she was gone a week?'

'Yes, a week, but then I had to go to my sister's in Ohio because she wasn't feeling well.' Dottie pressed her lips together. 'Eunice, my sister, was diagnosed with emphysema a couple of months prior to that. She's doing better now, but it was a really difficult time.'

'Jenny was alone in the house then?'

'Oh, no,' Dottie shook her head. 'Of course not.

She stayed with the Pattersons for three or four days, then I came back.'

'That was normal, for her to stay with the Pattersons?'

'Yes, then it was,' Dottie provided. 'Every weekend Lacey would stay over or Jenny would go to the Pattersons'.'

'You know the Pattersons well?'

'Teddy and Grace?' She nodded. 'Oh, yes, they both go to the church. I'm not too crazy about Teddy,' she said, lowering her voice a little. 'You can see where Mark gets it, I'll tell you that.'

'How's that?'

'He's just kind of . . .' Dottie began, then shrugged. 'I don't know. If you ever meet him, you'll see what I mean.'

'So,' Lena summed it up. 'At Christmas, Jenny was on the church retreat, then she stayed with the Pattersons, then she stopped going to church and stopped talking to the Pattersons?'

'Well,' Dottie seemed to go over this in her mind. 'Yes, I guess so. I mean, it seems that way now. Before, when it was happening, I didn't make a connection.'

'Did you ever suspect your daughter of using drugs?'

'Oh, no, she was adamantly against them,' Dottie answered. 'She didn't even drink caffeine, and just recently she cut out all sugar.'

'For her weight?'

'For her health, she said. She wanted to make her body pure.'

'Pure,' Lena repeated. 'Did that have something to do with the church, do you think?'

'She had stopped going by then,' Dottie reminded her. 'I don't know why she did it. We were driving home from school one day, and she just said it: "I don't

88

want to eat anything with sugar in it anymore. I want my body to be pure."'

'This didn't strike you as odd?'

'At the time, no,' Dottie said. 'I mean, maybe it did, but she had been acting so strange lately. Not strange like you would notice, but strange like she stopped drinking Co-Colas when she got home from school, and she started concentrating more on her homework. It was like she was trying to do better. She was more like her old self.'

'Her old self before she started hanging out with the Patterson children?'

'Yes, I guess you could say that.' Dottie pursed her lips. 'It was very strange, because Lacey was a cheerleader, and very popular, and from the day Jenny walked through the school doors Lacey tortured her.'

Sara asked, 'Tortured her how?'

'Just mean,' Dottie answered. 'Teasing her about her weight. And this was back when she was just a little chubby. Not like she's been lately.'

'You don't think Lacey or Mark ever hit her?'

Dottie seemed surprised. 'Heavens no. I would have called the police.' She patted her eyes with the tissue. 'They just teased her is all. Nothing physical. Like I said, they became friends.'

Lena said, 'Why did that change?'

'I don't really know. Maybe when they all went from the middle school to the senior high. It's a big adjustment. I think Lacey didn't make the cheerleading team, and she kind of dropped in the pecking order. You know how kids are. They want to belong. Now that I think about it, the sugar thing was probably Lacey's idea.'

'Lacey's?' Lena asked.

'Oh, yes. She was always coming up with things for them to do. What kind of clothes they would wear to school, where they would go for the weekend. They spent hours on the telephone talking about it.'

Lena smiled. 'My sister and I used to do the same thing,' she said. Then, 'Was it some kind of religious thing, you think?'

'What's that?' Dottie asked, caught off guard.

'The sugar. The caffeine. It sounds kind of religious.'

'You don't think . . . ?' Dottie stopped herself. 'No, I don't think it's religious. She was very happy with the church. I think it must have been those Patterson children. Mark has some kind of criminal record for stealing things.' She shook her head in a slow arc. 'I didn't know what to do. Should I have told her she couldn't see him? That would have made her want to spend even more time with him.'

'That's generally the case with young girls,' Lena agreed. 'You still go to church, right?'

'Oh, of course,' Dottie answered, nodding her head. 'It's a great consolation to me.'

'Have you made arrangements yet? I guess they'll do the service?'

Dottie sighed. 'I don't know. I just . . .' She stopped, blowing her nose on a tissue. 'I think she liked Preacher Fine. He came by the house to talk to her. So did Brad Stephens. He's the youth minister at the church.'

'That so?' Lena asked.

'Oh, yes, Brad is very active in the community.'

'Did Pastor Fine come by after Jenny stopped going to church?'

'Yes,' she nodded, and she seemed glad to be able to remember something that might be important. 'He came by after she had missed a couple of Sundays.'

'Did you hear what she said to him?'

'No,' Dottie answered. 'They were in the den, and I wanted to give them some privacy.' She seemed to remember something. 'He did call back a week later on the telephone, but she told me to say she wasn't in. That must have been a Saturday, because I was home during the daytime. And I remember that she got a couple more calls that day, and didn't take those, either.'

'Was this odd?'

'Not by then,' she said. 'This must have been around February. I remember I was kind of relieved that she didn't want to talk to Mark anymore.'

'Did she have some kind of argument with him?'

Dottie shrugged. 'All I know is that she hated him. She went from spending most of her time with him to absolutely hating him.'

'Hating him the way a girl hates a guy who won't ask her out?'

Dottie sat back, giving Lena a hard look of appraisal. She finally seemed to realize that this interview was being conducted to establish Jenny's guilt, not clear her name.

Lena repeated her question. 'She hated Mark because he didn't want to go out with her anymore?'

'No,' Dottie snapped, her nasally twang back. 'Of course not.'

'You're certain?'

'He was arrested around that time,' Dottie told her, obviously more comfortable putting Mark in the criminal role. 'For assault. He attacked his sister.'

Jeffrey cursed himself for not having checked this before. He picked up the phone in the interview room and punched Marla's extension.

'Yep?' Marla asked.

'Pull a file for me,' he said, keeping his voice low. 'Mark Patterson.'

'Kid from last night?'

'Yes.'

'Sure thing,' she answered, ringing off.

When Jeffrey turned his attention back to the room, the climate had changed drastically. Dottie Weaver sat in her chair, her jaw set in an angry line.

Lena asked, 'Would you like something to drink?'

'No, thank you.'

'Did you know your daughter's arm was fractured last year?'

Dottie seemed surprised. She asked Sara, 'Did she come see you without me?'

'No,' Sara answered, not elaborating. She seemed angry, but not at Dottie Weaver.

Lena pressed on. 'Was your daughter interested in African or Middle Eastern culture?'

Dottie shook her head, not understanding. 'Of course not. Why? What does that have to do with anything?'

Sara asked, 'Dottie, do you want to take a break?'

Lena shifted in her seat, keeping the questioning up. 'Your daughter also had a stress fracture in her pelvis, Mrs. Weaver. Did you know this?'

Dottie's mouth worked, but she did not answer.

Lena said, 'She was probably raped.' She paused, then without emotion added the word, 'Brutally.'

'I don't . . .' Dottie turned to Sara, then back to Lena. 'I don't understand.'

'What about the scarring on her arms and legs?' Lena demanded. 'What happened there? Why was your daughter cutting herself?'

'Cutting herself?' Dottie demanded. 'What are you talking about?'

'There were cuts all over her body. Self-inflicted, from the looks of them. You want to tell me how she could do this without you knowing?'

'She was secretive,' Dottie countered. 'She covered herself up with her clothes. I never –'

Lena interrupted, 'Did you know that she'd had surgery in the last six months?'

'Surgery?' Dottie repeated. 'What are you talking about?'

'Not surgery,' Sara interrupted, putting her hand on Dottie's arm. She said, 'Dottie, when I examined Jenny –'

Lena opened the case file. She tossed a picture across the table, then another. From his position, Jeffrey could not make out which ones, but he knew by the expression on Dottie's face exactly what the mother was looking at.

'Oh, my God, my baby.' She put her hand to her mouth.

'Lena,' Sara warned, putting her hand over the pictures. She tried to move them away, but Dottie stopped her. They struggled for a few seconds with one of the photos before Sara reluctantly let go.

'W-what?' Dottie stuttered. Her hand shook as she held the photo close to her face.

Lena looked smug as she sat back in her chair, crossing her arms over her chest. She actually turned to the mirror, to Jeffrey, and raised her eyebrows in a sort of triumph.

Sara put her hand to Dottie's back. 'Let me have this,' she said, trying to take away the photo.

'My God, my God,' the woman muttered, sobbing openly. 'My baby. Who did this to my baby?'

Sara shot a look at Lena, and Jeffrey could feel the heat from her stare. Lena shrugged, as if to say, 'What did you expect?'

'Oh, God, oh, God,' Dottie whispered, then stopped abruptly. Her body went limp, and Sara softened the woman's fall as she fainted to the floor.

* * *

Jeffrey stood in the hallway outside the briefing room, talking to Lena.

'We'll need to get to the Patterson boy right away,' Jeffrey told her. 'Sara can do the autopsy briefing by herself.'

Lena looked over his shoulder toward the back door. Sara had walked Dottie to her car to make sure the woman was okay, but not before giving a taut warning to Lena that she would be back.

Jeffrey said, 'Marla is pulling his address right now. There may be something more to his involvement in this. Hopefully, we'll catch his sister at home, too.'

Lena nodded, crossing her arms. 'You want me to take the sister and you can do Mark?'

'Let's see how it goes,' Jeffrey answered. 'I also want to get a look at this preacher.'

Something flickered in Lena's eyes. She said, 'He's at my church. Well, not my church, but it's where Hank goes, and I go along with him sometimes.' She shrugged. 'You know, for something to do. I'm not religious like that or anything.'

'Yeah,' Jeffrey answered, a little startled that she had offered this information. It was as close to chatty as Lena had gotten since her attack. He thought maybe it was doing her some good to be involved in the case, and Jeffrey was pleased with that.

'I'm gonna call Brad in off patrol,' Jeffrey said. 'I want to talk to him as soon as I can and see what he says about Fine.'

'You think Fine's the one who did this to Jenny?'

Jeffrey tucked his hands into his pockets. He could not imagine anyone harming a child, but the fact remained that someone had. 'We need to find out if Fine was on that retreat during Christmas.'

'Maybe I could –' Lena stopped as the back door

was thrown open with a loud bang.

Jeffrey turned just as Sara closed the door. He could tell from the way she walked up the hall that she was angry as hell.

About ten feet away from them, Sara demanded, 'What were you doing in there? How could you do that to her?'

Lena dropped her hands to her side. Jeffrey saw her fists clench as Sara shortened the distance between them.

Lena moved away, so that her back was against the wall. She kept her hands clenched and her voice was strong when she said, 'I was doing my job.'

'Your job?' Sara shot back, getting in Lena's face. Sara had a good six inches on Lena, and she was using them to her advantage. 'Is it your job to torture a woman who's just lost her kid? Is it your job to show her those pictures?' Sara's voice cracked on this last word. 'How could you do that to her, Lena? How could you make those pictures the last memory she'll ever have of her daughter?'

Jeffrey said, 'Sara –' just as Sara leaned in and whispered something in Lena's ear. He could not hear what she had said, but Lena's reaction was immediate. Her shoulders dropped, and she reminded Jeffrey of a kitten that had been picked up by the scruff of its neck.

Sara saw this, and he could see the immediate guilt on her face. She put her hand over her mouth, as if she could keep the words in. 'I'm sorry,' she said to Lena. 'I am so sorry.'

Lena cleared her throat, looking down at the floor. 'It's okay,' she said, though clearly it was not.

Sara must have realized that she was still crowding Lena, because she stepped back. 'Lena, I'm sorry,' she repeated. 'I had no right to say that.'

Lena held up her hand to stop Sara. She took a breath, but did not let it go. Instead, she said, 'I'll be in the car when you want to go.'

The comment was meant for Jeffrey, he realized, and he told Lena, 'Okay. Good.' He fumbled for his keys and held them out to her, but she did not take them. Instead, she extended her hand, palm up, waiting for him to drop them.

'Okay,' Lena said, holding the keys in her fist. She did not look at Jeffrey or Sara again. She stared at the floor, even as she walked down the hallway. Her posture was still slack, and she had an air of being completely defeated about her. Whatever Sara had said to the woman had cut to the bone.

Jeffrey turned to Sara, not understanding what had just happened, or why. He asked, 'What the hell did you just say to her?'

Sara shook her head, putting her hand over her eyes. 'Oh, Jeff,' she said, still shaking her head. 'The wrong thing. The completely wrong thing.'

SEVEN

Lena sat in Jeffrey's Lincoln town car, her body tight as a drum. Her breathing came in pants, and she felt slightly light-headed, as if she might pass out. She was sweating, and not just from being trapped in the hot car. Her whole body felt lit up, as if she had touched a live electrical wire.

'Bitch,' she breathed, thinking of Sara Linton. 'Stupid bitch,' she repeated, as if calling her this would take away what had been said.

Sara's words still echoed in Lena's head: *Now you know what it's like to hurt somebody.*

Hurt, Sara had said, but Lena knew what she had meant. Now you know what it's like to rape somebody.

'Goddamn it!' Lena screamed as loud as she could, trying to replace the sound. She slammed her hand against the dashboard, cursing Sara Linton, cursing this stupid job.

Back in the interrogation room, drilling Dottie Weaver like that, for the first time in forever, Lena had started to feel human again, and Sara had taken that away with one simple sentence.

'Dammit!' Lena screamed again, her voice hoarse from the effort. She wanted to cry, but there were no tears left, just a seething anger. Every muscle in her body was tense, and she felt like she could lift the car up and flip it over if she wanted to.

'Stop it, stop it, stop it,' Lena told herself, trying to calm down. She had to be okay with this when Jeffrey got to the car, because he would tell Sara – he was fucking her, for God's sake – and Lena did not want Sara Linton to know her words had struck so deep.

Lena snorted a laugh at the thought of Sara's lame apology. As if that made a difference. Sara had said exactly what she meant. The only reason she apologized was she felt bad for saying it out loud. On top of being a bitch, she was a coward.

She took another deep breath, trying to get herself together. 'It's okay,' Lena whispered to herself. 'It doesn't matter. Nothing matters.'

After a couple of minutes, Lena felt better. Her heart was not beating so hard, and her stomach seemed to unclench. She kept reminding herself that she was strong, that she had been through worse than this and survived. What Sara Linton thought did not matter in the big scheme of things. What mattered was that Lena could do her job. She had done her job. They had gotten some solid leads to follow in that interview, something that would not have happened if Sara Linton had been in charge.

Lena looked at her watch, then did a double take. She had not realized what time it was. Hank would be wondering what was taking her so long. There was no way she could go to church with him now.

Jeffrey's car had a cell phone mounted into the console, and Lena leaned over, cranking the engine so she could use the phone. She turned on the air conditioner and cracked the window to let some of the heat out of the car. The phone took its time powering up, and she glanced at the station, this time to make sure Jeffrey was not coming out.

Hank picked up on the first ring. 'Hello?'

'It's me,' she said. There was a pause from his end, and she realized what her voice must sound like. There was a rawness to it, and the edge from her confrontation with Sara was still there. Thankfully, Hank did not ask her what was wrong.

She said, 'I'm not going to be able to make it to church.'

'Oh?' he said, but did not go further.

'I've got to do an interview with Jeffrey,' she told him, even though she did not owe Hank Norton an explanation. 'We're going to be a while, probably. You should go without me.' Lena's voice went down on the last part of her sentence as she thought about going home and being by herself.

'Lee?' Hank asked, obviously sensing her fear. 'I can stay here for you if you want. You know, just until you get home.'

'Don't be stupid,' she said, aware that her tone wasn't very convincing. 'I'm not a three year old.'

'You could come after, you know,' Hank said, hesitancy in his voice. 'I mean, to hear the choir sing.'

Lena experienced a sinking feeling as she remembered the concert. It would be dark outside by the time Hank got home. Inside the house would be darker, no matter how many lights Lena turned on.

'I gotta get up early to go check on the bar, anyway,' Hank offered. 'I could come home after the service.'

'Hank,' Lena said, trying not to let on that her heart was about to explode in her chest. 'Listen, go to the fucking concert, okay? I don't need you baby-sitting me all the time. I mean, for fuck's sake.'

Sunlight flashed off the back door as Jeffrey came out of the building. Marla Simms was right behind him, holding a file folder out to the chief.

Hank asked, 'You're sure?'

'Yeah,' she answered before she could think about it. 'Listen, I've gotta go. I'll see you when you get home.'

She hung up the phone before Hank could respond.

'Jesus,' Jeffrey said as soon as he opened the car door. 'Is the air on?' he asked, throwing her the file Marla had handed him.

'Yeah,' Lena mumbled, shifting in her seat as he got in. Without thinking about it, she had moved away from him, as close to the door as she could get. If he noticed this, Jeffrey did not comment.

Jeffrey threw his suit jacket into the back seat. 'I got a call,' he said, obviously preoccupied. 'My mother's had an accident. I've got to go to Alabama tonight.'

'Now?' Lena asked, putting her hand on the door handle, thinking she could call Hank from her car and tell him to wait for her.

'No,' Jeffrey told her, making a point of looking at her hand. 'Tonight.'

'Okay,' she said, keeping her fingers on the handle, as if she was resting them there.

'It's gonna be a pain in the ass to leave in the middle of this. Maybe Mark Patterson can straighten things out.'

'What do you mean, like it was a lover's tiff or something?' Lena asked.

'Maybe he can tell us who the other girls were, who the mother is.'

She nodded, but did not think it was likely.

'I talked to Brad. Fine wasn't on the ski retreat.' Jeffrey frowned. 'I'll call Brad again after we talk to Mark and see if I can push him to remember anything else.' He paused. 'I'm sure he would have said if something bad happened.'

'Yeah,' Lena agreed. Brad was the kind of cop who would turn in his own mother for jaywalking.

'First thing tomorrow, I want you and Brad to talk to Jenny Weaver's teachers and see what kind of kid she was, maybe find out if there was somebody she was hanging around with. Also, talk to the girls who went on the retreat with Jenny and Lacey. They probably all go to the same school.'

'Okay.'

'I can't get out of going to Alabama or I'd do this myself.'

'Sure,' she said, wondering why he kept making excuses. Technically, he was in charge. Besides, it wasn't like there was much Jeffrey could do on the case right now. Unless Mark pointed the finger at someone, they didn't have very much to go on.

He said, 'I also want you to interview Fine as soon as possible.' He looked at his watch. 'Tomorrow morning. Take Frank with you for that one, not Brad.'

She repeated, 'Okay.'

'You said you know him, the preacher,' Jeffrey began, putting the car into reverse. 'You think he's got this in him?'

'This?' Lena said, then remembered why they were here. 'No,' she answered. 'He's not a bad guy. I just don't get along with him is all.'

Jeffrey gave her a look that said she didn't seem to get along with anybody.

Lena offered, 'Actually, I've kind of got an appointment with him tomorrow evening.'

'An appointment?'

Lena looked at the dashboard. 'Like you said before. What you wanted me to do,' she prompted, but he did not pick up on it. 'Talk to somebody,' she supplied.

'Well, maybe you shouldn't be the one to –'

'No,' she insisted. 'I want to do it.' She tried to smile, but it felt fake, even to her. 'It'll surprise him, right? Thinking that I'm there for a session or whatever, but turning it around and asking him about Jenny and the Pattersons.'

Jeffrey frowned as he turned the car out of the parking lot. 'I'm not sure I like that.'

'You always said that the best time to interview somebody is when you catch him off guard,' she reminded him, trying to keep the desperation out of her voice. 'Besides, Hank set it up. It's not like I would talk to him about . . .' Lena looked for a word, but could not find one. 'I wouldn't talk to him, okay? He's a freak. I don't trust him.'

'Why?'

'I just don't,' she said. 'I just have a feeling about him.'

'But you don't think he did this?'

She shrugged, trying to find a way to backpedal. How could she explain to Jeffrey that the main reason she did not like Dave Fine, did not trust him, was that he was a pastor? Jeffrey was being just as stupid about it as Hank. How anyone could not make the connection between Lena's being assaulted by a religious fanatic and her not wanting to talk to a preacher about it was beyond her.

She said, 'I dunno, maybe he's got it in him.'

The lie seemed to swing Jeffrey. 'Okay. But take Frank with you.'

'Sure.'

'This isn't an interrogation. We're just trying to find out if he knows anything. Don't go in there and piss him off for no good reason.'

'I know.'

'And set something else up,' he said. 'Something

with somebody else.' He paused. 'That was a condition, Lena. The only reason I let you come back so early was because you promised you would talk to somebody about what happened.'

'Yeah,' she nodded. 'I'll set something up with somebody else, first thing.'

He stared at her, as if he could figure her out just from looking.

She tried to sound casual as she changed the subject, asking, 'She okay? Your mom, I mean.'

'Yeah,' he answered. 'Are you all right?'

She tried not to sound glib. 'I'm fine.'

'That thing with Sara –'

'I'm fine,' she reassured him, using a tone that would have shut up Hank in two seconds flat.

Jeffrey, of course, was not Hank Norton. He persisted. 'You're sure?'

'Yeah.' Then, to prove it, she asked, 'What was that thing in the interview? Dr. Linton sounded surprised when the mother mentioned Lacey Patterson.'

'She was a patient of Sara's at the clinic,' Jeffrey told her. Then, almost to himself, he said, 'You know how Sara feels about her kids.'

Lena didn't, and she looked down at the file, not answering him. Mark Patterson's name was on the tab, and she flipped it open to see what he had been up to. The top sheet had his vitals on it, including his address. 'They live in Morningside?' she asked, referring to a shady part of Madison.

'I'm thinking it's that trailer park. The one with the green awning over the sign?'

'The Kudzu Arms,' Lena supplied. She and Brad had been called out to the Kudzu on several occasions over the course of the last few months. The hotter the weather, the hotter the tempers.

'Anyway,' Jeffrey said, moving things along. 'What's he got on his sheet?'

Lena thumbed through the pages. 'Two B and Es when he was ten, both of them at the Kudzu Arms. Most recently, he beat up his sister pretty bad. His father called us out, we got there, they wouldn't press charges.' She stopped reading, providing, '"We" means Deacon and Percy,' she supplied, referring to two beat cops. 'They pulled this one, not me and Brad.'

Jeffrey scratched his chin, seeming to think this through. 'I don't even remember when it happened.'

'Just after Thanksgiving,' Lena told him. 'Then, around Christmas time, Deacon and Percy were called back. It was the father again, and he asked for them specifically.' She skimmed the report Deacon had written. 'This time, charges were filed. They took him down to the pokey for a couple of days, Mark was supposed to take some anger management classes in exchange for time served.' She snorted a laugh. 'Buddy Conford was his lawyer.'

'Buddy's not that bad,' Jeffrey said.

Lena closed the file, giving him an incredulous look. 'He's a whore. He puts addicts and murderers back on the streets.'

'He's doing his job, just like we are.'

'His job screws our job,' Lena insisted.

Jeffrey shook his head. 'He's gonna be talking to you about the Weaver situation,' he told her. 'The shooting.'

Lena laughed again. 'He's working for Dottie Weaver?'

'The city,' he told her. 'I guess he's doing it as a favor to the mayor.' Jeffrey shrugged. 'Anyway, work it out with him. Tell him what happened.'

'It was a clean shot,' Lena told him, because if there

was one truth in her life right now, it was that Jeffrey had taken the only option given to him. She said, 'Brad will say the same thing.'

Jeffrey was quiet, and he seemed to drop the subject, but after a few minutes he pulled the car over to the side of the road. Lena felt a sense of déjà vu, and her stomach lurched as she thought about being in the car with Hank that morning, and how she had embarrassed herself. There was no question in her mind now that Lena would not have the same problem with Jeffrey. She could be stronger around Jeffrey because he did not see her the way that Hank did. Hank still thought of Lena as a teenage girl because that was the only way he had ever really known her.

Lena waited as Jeffrey put the car in park and turned toward her. She felt the hair on the back of her neck rise, and thought she might be in trouble or something.

'Between you and me . . . ,' Jeffrey said, then stopped. He waited until she looked him in the eye and repeated himself. 'Between you and me,' he said.

'Yeah,' Lena nodded, not liking the serious tone in his voice. Her stomach sank in her gut as she realized he was going to say something about Sara.

He surprised her, saying instead, 'The shot.'

She nodded for him to continue.

'With Weaver,' he said, as if he needed to narrow it down. She could see how upset he was. For the first time, she understood what it meant to read someone like a book. She saw the kind of pain in his eyes that she would never expect to see in Jeffrey Tolliver.

'Tell me the truth,' he said, a begging quality to his voice. 'You were there. You saw what happened.'

'I did,' she agreed, feeling a startling need coming off of him.

'Tell me,' he said, begging more openly this time. Lena felt a kind of rush from his desperation. Jeffrey needed something from her. Jeffrey Tolliver, who had seen her naked, nailed down to the floor, bruised and bleeding, needed something from Lena.

She let the moment linger, savoring the power more than anything else. 'Yeah,' she finally said, though with little conviction.

He continued to stare, and she could see the doubt in his eyes. For a moment, she thought he might even tear up.

'It was a clean shot,' she told him. He kept staring straight at her, as if he could see into her. Lena knew that her tone wasn't confident, and that he had picked up on this. She knew, also, that she had not made it clear that she trusted his judgment. Her response had been purposefully ambiguous. Lena had no idea why she had done this, but she felt the thrill of it for a long while, even as Jeffrey put the car back into gear and drove down the road.

Grant County was made up of three cities: Heartsdale, Madison, and Avondale. Like Avondale, Madison was poorer than Heartsdale, and there were plenty of trailer parks around because it was cheap housing. This did not necessarily mean that the people occupying the trailers were cheap. There were some better parks with community centers and swimming pools and neighborhood watches, just as there were some that festered with domestic violence and drunken brawls. The Kudzu Arms fell into this second category. It was about as far from a neighborhood as a place could get without falling off the map. Trailers in various states of dilapidation fanned out from a single dirt road. Some of the residents had tried to plant gardens to no avail.

Even without the drought, which had put all of Georgia on water restrictions, the heat would have killed the flowers. The heat was enough to kill people. The plants did not have a chance.

'Depressing,' Jeffrey noted, tapping his fingers on the steering wheel. It was a nervous habit she had never seen in him, and Lena felt the guilt come back like a strong undertow, pulling her the wrong way. She should have been more adamant about the shooting. She should have looked him right in the eye and told him the truth, that killing the teenager was the only thing he could have done. Lena could not think how to make it better. A thousand adamant yeses would never erase her initial reticence and the impact it had made. What had she been thinking?

Jeffrey asked, 'What's the address?'

Lena flipped the file open, tracing her finger to the address. 'Three-ten,' she said, looking up at the trailers. 'These are all twos.'

'Yeah,' Jeffrey agreed. He looked over his shoulder across the road from the park. 'There it is.'

Lena turned as he backed out of the park. A large mobile home, she guessed a doublewide, was on the other side of the road. Unlike the ones in the park across from it, this trailer looked more like a house. There was something like landscaping in the front yard, and a cinder block foundation covered the bottom portion. Someone had painted the concrete blocks black to offset the white trailer, and a large covered deck served as a front porch. To the side was a carport, and beside this was a large diesel semi.

'He's a truck driver?' Jeffrey asked.

Lena thumbed down to the proper space on the form. 'Long hauler,' she told him. 'Probably owns his own rig.'

'Looks like he makes some money from it.'

'I think you can if you own your own truck,' Lena told him, still skimming Mark Patterson's file. 'Oh, wait,' she said. 'Patterson owns the Kudzu, too. He put it up as collateral when he bailed out Mark.'

Jeffrey parked in front of the Patterson trailer. 'Sure doesn't take good care of it. The park, I mean.'

'No,' Lena answered, looking back across the road. The Patterson house was a stark contrast to the desolate-looking Kudzu Arms across the street. She wondered what this said about the father, that he would take such pride in his own home, yet let the people living less than thirty yards away live in such squalor. Not that it was Patterson's responsibility to help people out, but Lena would have thought the man would try to pick himself some nicer neighbors, especially with two kids in the house.

'Teddy,' Lena told Jeffrey. 'That's the father's name.'

'Marla pulled his sheet back at the station,' Jeffrey told her. 'He's got a couple of assaults on him, but they go back about ten years. He did some time on one of them.'

'Apple doesn't fall far from the tree.'

A large man stepped from the trailer as Jeffrey and Lena got out of the car. Lena guessed this was Teddy Patterson, and she felt a momentary flash of panic because he was such a physically large man. Taller than Jeffrey by a couple of inches and at least thirty pounds heavier, Patterson looked as if he could pick up both of them in one hand and toss them across the road.

Lena felt angry that she even took note of his size. Before, Lena had felt like she could take on anybody. She was a strong woman, muscular from working out in the gym, and she had always been able to push herself to do whatever she wanted to do. Now, she had lost that feeling, and the sight of Patterson gave her a slight chill, even though he wasn't doing anything more threatening than wiping his hands on a dirty dish towel.

'You lost?' Patterson asked. He had that look about him that all cops learned to recognize: Teddy Patterson was a con, right down to the jailhouse tattoos clawing up his arms like chicken scratches. Lena and Jeffrey exchanged glances, which did not seem to be lost on Patterson.

'Mr. Patterson?' Jeffrey asked, taking out his badge. 'Jeffrey Tolliver, Grant Police.'

'I know who you are,' Patterson shot back, tucking the dish towel into his pocket. Lena could see it was soiled with what looked like grease. She also took note of the fact that Patterson had not bothered to acknowledge her.

Lena opened her mouth to speak, to let him know that she was there, but nothing came out. The thought of him training his animosity on her brought a cold sweat.

'This is detective Lena Adams,' Jeffrey said. If he noticed her fear, he did not seem to register it. 'We're here to talk to Mark about what happened last night.'

'Alright,' Patterson said, running the words together like most people in Madison did, so that it came out more as 'Ahte.'

Patterson turned his back to them and walked toward the house. He stood in the doorway as Jeffrey passed, crowding him on purpose, and Lena could see that the man was a lot taller than she had thought from the car. Lena was not sure, but Patterson seemed to narrow the space between his stomach and the door jamb as Lena passed through. She turned slightly so that she would not be forced to touch him, but even then Lena could tell from the smile on his face that he knew she was feeling intimidated. She hated that she was so transparent.

'Have a seat,' Patterson offered, indicating the couch. Neither Jeffrey nor Lena took him up on this. Patterson's arms were crossed over his barrel chest, and Lena noticed that his head was about three inches from the low ceiling. The room was large, but Patterson filled the space with his presence.

Lena looked around the trailer, trying to behave like a cop instead of a scared little girl. The place was orderly and clean, certainly not what she would have guessed if she had met Teddy Patterson in a bar somewhere. The room they stood in was long, a kitchen at one end, with a hallway to what she assumed was the rest of the trailer, then the room they stood in, which had a medium-sized fireplace and a big-screen television. A floral scent was in the air, probably from one of those plug-in air fresheners. The living room seemed feminine, too, the walls painted a light pink, the couch and two chairs covered in a light blue with a matching pink stripe. A quilt was over the couch, the pattern complementing the decor. On the coffee table, a bowl of fresh cut flowers was surrounded by women's magazines. There were some nice framed prints on the walls, and the furniture looked new. The carpet, too, was freshly vacuumed. Lena could see Patterson's footprints indenting the pile where he had walked.

'We just need to talk to Mark about what happened last night,' Jeffrey told Patterson as Lena continued her survey of the room. She stopped midturn, seeing a picture of Jesus hanging over the fireplace. His pierced and bleeding hands were open in the classic 'let's be pals' Jesus pose. Jeffrey seemed to notice the painting at the same time, too, because he was staring at Lena when she made herself look away. He raised his eyebrows, as if to ask if she was all right. Lena could feel rather than see Patterson assessing this exchange. Of course he had heard about what had happened to Lena. She could only imagine what kind of pleasure Patterson was getting out of reviewing the details of her assault in his mind. The hold this gave Patterson over Lena was suffocating, and she made herself look the man right in the eye. He held her gaze for just a second, then glanced down at her hands.

She knew exactly what he was looking for, and Lena was fighting the urge to tuck her hands into her pockets when a small woman with a ravaged look about her walked up the hallway, asking, 'Teddy? Did you get my pills?'

She stopped when she saw Jeffrey and Lena, putting her hand to her neck. 'What's this about?'

'Police,' Patterson said, looking away quickly. Something like guilt flashed in his eyes, as if his wife might guess what he had been thinking about Lena a few seconds before.

'Well,' she said, a wry look on her face. 'Tell me something I don't know.'

She was a small woman, probably no taller than Lena's own five-foot-four. Her dark blonde hair was thin, her scalp showing through in places. She looked almost emaciated, like pictures Lena had seen in history books of Holocaust survivors. There was strength to her, though, and Lena imagined this was the woman who was responsible for keeping the trailer so neat and organized. Underneath her sickly appearance, she had the stance of a person who knew how to take care of things.

'I knew you were coming,' the woman said, 'so I know I shouldn't feel surprised.' Her hand stayed at her neck, nervously playing with a charm on her necklace. Lena guessed from the Jesus on the wall that it was a cross.

'Mrs. Patterson?' Jeffrey asked.

'Grace,' she told him, holding out her hand. Jeffrey shook it, and Lena took the opportunity to let herself study Teddy Patterson. He watched his wife and Jeffrey with a slack expression on his face. His shoulders stooped somewhat when his wife was in the room, and he did not seem so threatening in her presence.

'We want to talk to Mark,' Jeffrey told the woman. 'Is he around?'

Grace Patterson gave her husband a worried look.

Patterson told his wife, 'Why don't you sit down, hon?' Then, as if he needed to explain this to Jeffrey, he said, 'She's been sick lately.'

'I'm sorry to hear that,' Jeffrey said. He sat down by Grace on the couch and nodded to Lena, indicating that she should sit as well. Lena hesitated, but did as she was directed, sitting in one of the chairs.

The light coming through the window hit Grace Patterson just right, and Lena could see how pale she was. There were dark circles under her eyes, and her lips were an unnatural shade of pinkish-blue. Lena realized the woman matched the living room perfectly.

Grace spoke. 'I appreciate your not interrogating Mark last night, Chief Tolliver. He was very upset.'

Jeffrey said, 'It's understandable that he would need some time to recover from what happened.'

Teddy Patterson snorted at this. Lena was not surprised. Men like Teddy Patterson did not think that people needed to recover from things. He was actually more like Lena in that regard. You dealt with it and you got over it. Or at least you tried and did not whine about it.

'Is his sister around?' Jeffrey asked. 'We'd like to talk to her, too.'

'Lacey?' Grace said, putting her hand to her necklace again. 'She's at her grandmother's right now. We thought it would be best.'

Jeffrey asked, 'Where was she last night?'

'Here,' Grace answered. 'She was taking care of me.' She swallowed, looking down at her hands in her lap. 'I don't usually ask her to stay with me, but I had a very bad night, and Teddy had to work.' She gave him a weak smile. 'Sometimes the pain gets to be too much for me. I like having my children around.'

'But Mark wasn't here?' Jeffrey said, even though that much was obvious.

Her face clouded. 'No, he wasn't. He's been a bit difficult to control lately.'

'He smacked up his sister a while back,' Patterson told them. 'I guess you got that on his sheet. He's a real shit, that boy. Nothing good coming from him.'

Grace did not make a sound, but her disapproval traveled through the room.

'Sorry,' Patterson apologized. He actually looked contrite. Lena wondered at the hold Grace had over her husband. In the space of a few short minutes, she had subdued the man.

Patterson said, 'I'll go fetch Mark,' and left the room.

Lena caught herself running her tongue along the back of her teeth again. For some reason, she could not speak. There were questions to ask, and Lena knew that Jeffrey wanted them to come from Lena, but she was too preoccupied to focus. Her goal was to get out of this trailer and away from Teddy Patterson as quickly as possible. The truth was that even with his wife sitting three feet away, and Jeffrey right beside her, Lena felt scared. More than that, she felt threatened.

Lena tried to take her mind off the claustrophobia she was feeling. She stared off into the kitchen, which was roomy but not large. Strawberry wallpaper lined the walls, and there was even a clock with a strawberry on it over the kitchen table.

Grace cleared her throat. 'Mark has had a bad time lately,' she said, picking up where she had left off. 'He's been in and out of trouble at school.'

'I'm sorry to hear that, Mrs. Patterson,' Jeffrey said. He sat up on the couch, probably to establish a sense of rapport. 'How about Lacey?'

'Lacey has never been in trouble a day in her life,' Grace told him. 'And that's the God's truth. That child is an angel.'

Jeffrey smiled, and Lena could guess what he was thinking. Usually the angels were the ones who committed the most heinous crimes. 'Is she dating any boys?'

'She's thirteen,' Grace told him, as if that answered it. 'We don't even let boys call the house.'

'She couldn't have been seeing anyone on the side?'

'I don't see how,' Grace answered. 'She's home from school every day when she's supposed to be. Whenever she goes out, it's always with a group of her girlfriends and she always comes back in time for her curfew.'

Lena could sense Jeffrey trying to catch her eye, but she ignored him.

He asked, 'What time is her curfew?'

'School nights we don't let her go out, of course. Fridays and Saturdays, nine o'clock.'

'Does she ever sleep over with anybody?'

Grace looked as if she had just realized that Jeffrey's interest in Lacey was more calculated than she had originally thought. The look was similar to the one Dottie Weaver had given Lena just hours before, but there was far more menace in Grace Patterson than there had been in Dottie Weaver.

She demanded, 'Why are you asking so many questions about my daughter? It was Mark that little girl pointed the gun at.'

Jeffrey said, 'Dottie told us that Lacey and Jenny were friends.'

'Well . . . ,' she began, the hesitancy still there as she obviously tried to think a step ahead of Jeffrey's questions. Finally, she said, 'Yes, they were friends. Then something happened and they stopped hanging around each other.' She shrugged. 'I guess it's been a few months since that happened. We haven't seen Jenny around for a while, and I know Lacey hasn't gone over to her house.'

'Did she tell you why?'

'I assumed it was some silly little disagreement.'

'But you didn't ask her?'

Grace shrugged. 'She's my daughter, Chief Tolliver, not my best friend. Little girls have their secrets. You can ask your ex-wife about that.'

He nodded at this. 'Sara said Lacey's a great kid. Very smart.'

'She is,' Grace agreed, and she seemed pleased to have her daughter complimented. 'But, it's not my place to pry if she's not ready to talk about it.'

'Maybe she wouldn't mind talking with someone else about it?'

'Meaning?'

'Do you mind if I talk to her?'

Grace gave him another sharp look. 'She's a minor. If you don't have cause, you can't talk to her without my permission. Is that right?'

'We don't want to talk to her as a suspect, Mrs. Patterson. We just want to get some idea of what state of mind Jenny Weaver was in. We don't really need your permission for that.'

'But I've just told you that Lacey hasn't seen Jenny for a while – probably since Christmas. She wouldn't have any idea about this.' Grace gave a polite but humorless smile. 'I do not want my daughter interrogated, Chief Tolliver.' She paused. 'By you or by Dr. Linton.'

'She's not suspected of any wrongdoing.'

'I want to keep it that way,' she said. 'Do I need to call the school and tell them that she is not to talk to anyone without either her father or me in the room?'

Jeffrey paused, probably thinking that she knew a hell of a lot more about the law than they had initially suspected. Schools were very friendly with law enforcement, and since administrators served in loco parentis while the kids were on campus, they could allow interviews.

Jeffrey said, 'That's not necessary.'

'Do I have your word on that?'

Jeffrey gave a quick nod. 'All right,' he said, and Lena could hear the disappointment in his voice.

'We'd still like to talk to her,' Jeffrey said. 'You're more than welcome to sit in on an interview.'

'I'll have to talk to Teddy about that,' she told him. 'But we can both imagine what he'll say.' She gave a slight almost-smile, ending the hostility. 'You know about daddies and their little girls.'

Jeffrey sighed, and nodded again. Lena knew that Teddy Patterson was more likely to slip on his wife's

Sunday best than to let his daughter talk to a cop. Cons learned to distrust the police early on, and despite the fact that he had been out of prison for a good while, Teddy still seemed to be practicing this.

To his credit, Jeffrey did not completely give up. He asked, 'She hasn't been sick lately, has she?'

'Lacey?' Grace asked, obviously surprised. 'No, of course not. Ask Dr. Linton if you like.' She put her hand to her chest self-consciously. 'I'm the only one in the family who's ever been ill.'

'She was going to church? Lacey was?'

'Yes,' Grace told them. She smiled again, and Lena could see that her teeth were slightly gray. 'Mark was, too. For a while, anyway.' She paused, looking at the fireplace. Lena thought she was looking at the painting, but then she noticed there were pictures of the family on the mantel. They were the kinds of snapshots every family had, kids and parents at the beach, at an amusement park, out camping in the woods. The Grace Patterson in these photos was a little heavier and not so sunken-looking. The kids looked younger, too. The boy, who must have been Mark, looked around ten or eleven years old, his sister around eight. They seemed like a happy family. Even Teddy Patterson smiled for the camera in the few shots that showed him.

'So,' Jeffrey prompted, 'they went to the Baptist?'

'Crescent Baptist,' Grace answered, her voice animated for the first time. 'Mark seemed very happy there for a while. Like some of his nervous energy was being directed, finally. He even started doing better in school.'

'And then?'

'And then . . .' She shook her head slowly, her shoulders slumped. 'I don't know. Around Christmas, he started to get bad again.'

'Christmas this past year?' Jeffrey asked.

'Yes,' she said. 'I really don't know what happened, but the anger was back. He seemed so . . .' Again, she let her voice trail off. 'We tried to get him into counseling, but he wouldn't show up. We couldn't make him go, though' – she looked down the hallway, as if to check to see if they were alone – 'his father tried. Teddy thinks that people should be like him. Boys, that is. Or men, I should say. He has strong ideas about what's acceptable.'

'There was a church retreat at Christmastime. Did Mark go on that?'

'No,' she shook her head. 'This was around the time he started to act up. He was grounded, and his father wouldn't let him go.'

'Lacey went?'

'Yes,' she smiled. 'She'd never been skiing before. She had a wonderful time.'

They fell silent, and Grace Patterson picked at some nonexistent lint on her dress. Obviously, she had more to say.

'I'm very sick,' she said, her voice low. 'My doctors don't hold out much hope for me.'

'I'm sorry to hear that,' Jeffrey said, and he truly seemed to be.

'Breast cancer,' Grace said, putting her hand to her chest. Lena noticed for the first time that the woman's chest was almost completely flat under her blouse. 'Lacey will be fine. She always lands on her feet. I don't like to think what will happen to Mark when I'm gone. For all his posturing, he's a gentle boy.'

'I'm sure he'll be okay,' Jeffrey assured her, though even to Lena he did not seem confident. Short of a miracle, boys like Mark did not turn themselves around.

Grace picked up on the deception. She gave a small, knowing chuckle. 'Oh, I'm no fool, Chief Tolliver, but I thank you all the same.'

Teddy Patterson's footsteps were heavy in the hallway, and the trailer shifted slightly from his weight as he entered the room. His son was behind him, a stark contrast to the father. Patterson grabbed the boy's arm and pulled him into the room.

Lena's first impression of Mark Patterson was that he was incredibly handsome. Last night, she had not taken much notice of him because so much had been going on. In the trailer, she took her time assessing him. Mark's dark blond hair matched his mother's, but it was more full, and slightly shorter. His eyelashes were longer than any she had ever seen on a man, and his eyes were a piercing blue. Like most sixteen-year-old boys, he had the beginnings of a goatee on his chin and the semblance of a mustache over his full lips.

As Lena watched, he tucked his hair behind his ears with his fingers. She could not help but think there was something erotic in the gesture. There was also something about the way he walked and held his shoulders that gave him a certain sensuality. His faded jeans rested a little below his thin hips, and the tight white T-shirt he wore rode up a little, showing off the definition in his abs.

Despite all of this, there was a sexlessness to him. Mark Patterson was a sixteen-year-old child on the verge of becoming a man. He was boyish in that androgynous way that was now popular with teenagers. When Lena was in high school, boys had done everything possible to make themselves appear more masculine. Today, they were more comfortable with blurring the roles.

'Here he is,' Patterson barked, pushing Mark farther into the room. The man seemed angry, even more so than before, and his hands were in tight fists like he wanted nothing more than to pummel his son. For some reason, Teddy Patterson reminded Lena of Hank. The gruff way he had pushed Mark and the nasty tone of his voice could have come from Hank twenty years ago.

'We'll go for a drive,' Patterson told his wife. 'Get your pills from the pharmacy.'

'Teddy,' Grace said, the word catching in her throat. Lena wondered, too, why a man with Teddy Patterson's innate distrust of the police would leave his only son alone with them. By law, Teddy could be in on the interview. He was effectively hanging his son out to dry.

Jeffrey obviously wanted to capitalize on this. 'Mr. Patterson,' he began. 'Do you mind if we schedule an appointment with Mark tomorrow to get a blood sample from him?'

Patterson's eyebrow went up, but he nodded. 'Just tell him when and he'll be there.'

Grace said, 'Teddy.'

'Let's go,' Patterson ordered his wife. 'The pharmacy closes soon.'

If Grace Patterson had power over her husband, she had learned when not to use it. She stood, offering her hand first to Jeffrey, then to Lena. Grace had not even talked to Lena the entire time, but the woman kept Lena's hand in hers for longer than just a polite good-bye.

'Take care,' she told Lena.

Grace Patterson stopped in front of her son before she followed her husband out the door, giving him a kiss on the cheek. She was a couple of inches shorter than he was, and she had to rise up on her toes to do this.

'Good-bye,' Grace told him, patting his shoulder.

Mark watched her leave, touching his fingers to his cheek where his mother had kissed him. He looked at his fingers, as if he might see the kiss on them.

'Mark?' Jeffrey asked, getting the boy's attention.

'Sir?' he said, drawing out the word. His body was too loose to stand still, and he swayed a bit.

Jeffrey asked, 'You stoned?'

'Yes, sir,' he answered, putting his hand on the back of a chair to steady himself. Lena saw a large gold class ring on his finger. The red stone caught the light, and she guessed there was an initial underneath.

Mark asked, 'You wanna take me to jail?'

'No,' Jeffrey told him. 'I want to talk to you about what happened last night.'

'What happened last night,' he mimicked, his words slurring together. 'I wanna thank you for shooting the right person.'

Jeffrey took out his notebook, flipping it open to a blank page. As Lena watched, he took out his pen and wrote Mark's name at the top of the page, asking, 'You think I did?'

Mark smiled lazily. He walked around the chair and sat down, blowing air out between his lips as he did. There was something sexual even in this movement, and rather than being repulsed, as Lena thought she would have been, she was intrigued. She had never met a grown man who seemed so comfortable with himself, let alone a teenage boy.

Jeffrey started out with a hard question. 'Were you the father of that baby last night?'

Mark raised his eyebrow the same way his father had. 'Nope,' he said, his lips smacking on the word.

Jeffrey tried a different avenue, asking, 'Was your sister with you last night?'

'Naw, man,' Mark answered. 'My mom, you know. She's not doing too well. Lace stayed home with her.' He shrugged. 'She don't ask often, you know? My mom likes to leave us out of the fact that she's fucking dying.'

He swallowed visibly, turning his head to the side, looking out the window. He seemed to compose himself, because when he looked back at Jeffrey, the smile was there, teasing at his lips. There was something more to this kid than his looks. A shadow seemed to be hanging over him, and not just because of what happened last night. He had about him the air of being damaged, something Lena could relate to. He seemed fragile, but slightly dangerous at the same time. Not that he was threatening like his father. If anything, Mark Patterson seemed to be a danger only to himself.

Lena found her voice for the first time since they had gotten to the trailer. 'You like your sister?' she asked.

'She's a saint,' Mark said, twisting the ring on his finger. 'Daddy's little girl.'

'Has she been feeling okay lately?' Lena asked. 'She hasn't been sick or anything, right?'

Mark stared openly at Lena. There was nothing hostile about the stare. He seemed curious about her and nothing more. He said, 'She seemed fine this morning. You'd have to ask her.'

Lena tried, 'Why was Jenny Weaver so mad at you?'

He raised his shoulders, held them there for a while, then let them drop. Lena watched as he lifted up his shirt and absently started to stroke his flat stomach. 'You know, lots of girls get mad at me.'

Jeffrey asked, 'Were you involved with her?'

'What, in a relationship?' He shook his head slowly side to side. 'Nah. I mean, I did her a couple of times, but it was nothing serious.' He held up his hand to stop the next question. 'This was when I was fifteen, officer.'

Lena told him, 'There has to be at least a five-year age difference for statutory rape.'

Jeffrey shifted on the couch, obviously not pleased that Lena had given Mark this information. He could have used this threat for leverage. Now he had to find something else.

Jeffrey asked, 'When was the last time you had sex with her?'

'I dunno,' Mark said, still stroking his belly. There was a small tattoo on the webbing between his thumb and forefinger. Lena could make out a black heart with an inverted white heart in the center of it. Mark had obviously done this himself, because the symbol looked as rudimentary as his father's jailhouse ball-point ink tattoos.

Lena prompted, 'You had sex with her a lot?'

Mark shrugged. 'Often enough,' he said, still stroking his stomach. He started picking at the trail of hair between his navel and his pubis, giving Lena a sly look. She glanced at Jeffrey, wondering what he was making of this. Jeffrey was not looking, though. Instead, he was copying the tattoo into his notebook.

'Well,' Jeffrey began, blacking in the heart. 'Take a guess.'

'Maybe a year or so ago?' Mark offered. 'She wanted it, man. She begged me.'

Jeffrey finished the drawing, looking up. 'This isn't about nailing you for rape, Mark. I don't care if you've been banging goats in the backyard. You know what this is about.'

'It's about her wanting to kill me,' he said. 'And why.'

'Right,' Lena said. 'We just want to get to the bottom of this, Mark. This is about Jenny, and why she would do what she did.'

Mark gave Lena a lazy smile. 'Gosh, detective, you sure are pretty.'

Lena felt embarrassed, and wondered what signals she had given the boy. Certainly, sex was the last thing on her mind, and she wasn't sure that she thought Mark Patterson was so much attractive as perfect. There was a cinema-idol quality to his appearance. He seemed too good looking to be true. She was showing the same interest in him as she would a beautiful painting or an exquisite sculpture.

'You're pretty handsome yourself, Mark,' she countered, making her words sharp. Teddy Patterson might be able to fuck with her, but she would be damned if his precocious boy would. 'Which is why I'm puzzled about Jenny. She wasn't exactly homecoming queen material. Couldn't you get any better than that?'

Her words hit him exactly where she had intended them to, in his ego.

'Trust me, detective, I've had a *lot* better than that.'

'Yeah?' she asked. 'What, you banged her out of the goodness of your heart?'

'I let her suck me off sometimes,' he said, his fingers moving lower down his belly, his eyes on Lena as he obviously tried to gauge her reaction to him touching himself. His interest gave Lena some insight into the boy. She imagined that someone so attractive was used to trading on his looks. No wonder his father, a man who had the physical presence of a freight train, was so disgusted by his son.

Suddenly, she felt sorry for him. Lena shifted on the

couch, feeling a bit unsettled. She had spent such a long time feeling sorry for herself that for a moment she did not know what to do with this new emotion.

Mark said, 'She had this thing she did with her tongue, like a lollipop. No teeth. It was great.'

Lena felt her heart rate accelerate, willing herself not to react to his words. Probably the boy had no idea who she was or what had happened to her.

She could sense Jeffrey about to step in, so she said the first thing that came to her mind to keep him from interfering. 'So, you let her give you blow jobs?' she said, trying to be flippant. Still, she kept her tongue firmly against the back of her teeth as she waited for his answer.

A smile broke out on his lips, and he stared at her, his piercing blue eyes sparkling with humor. 'Yeah.'

'Here? In this house?'

Mark gave a light chuckle. 'Right down the hall.'

'With your mama in the house?'

He stopped, seeming more afraid than angry. 'Don't bring my mama into this.'

Lena smiled. 'We have to, Mark, because that's where you've tripped yourself up. You wouldn't do that kind of thing in your mother's house.'

He twisted his lips to the side, obviously thinking this through. 'Maybe we did it in her house. Maybe we did it in the car.'

'So, you went out with Jenny? Dated her?'

'Shit no,' he countered. 'I took her places with my sister.' He shrugged, and thankfully his hand stopped. 'The mall, the movies. Different places.'

'This is when you let her do you? On these trips?'

He shrugged, meaning yes.

'And your sister was where? In the front seat?'

He paled slightly. Mark seemed to transition back

and forth from a child to a teenager to a man. If someone had asked her how old Mark Patterson was, she
would have guessed anywhere between ten and twenty.

Lena cleared her throat, then asked, 'Where was
Lacey when you were letting Jenny do you, Mark?'

Mark stared at the flower arrangement on the coffee
table. He was very quiet for what seemed like a long
time. Finally, he told them, 'We met at the church,
alright?' He said alright the same way his father did,
running the words together.

'You were having sex with her in church,' Lena said,
not a question.

'The basement,' he told them. 'They don't check
the windows. We sneaked out, okay?'

'That sounds pretty elaborate,' Lena said.

'What does that mean?'

Lena thought about how to phrase her answer. 'It's
not opportune, Mark. You know what that means?'

'I'm not stupid.'

'Taking her to the mall, maybe running her and
your sister to the store,' Lena paused, making sure she
had his attention. 'Those things sound like opportune
times to me. She was there, you were there, it just kind
of happened.'

'Right,' he said. 'That's how it was.'

'But the church,' Lena countered. 'The church seems
more deliberate. These were not sudden opportunities. These were planned meetings.'

Mark nodded, then stopped himself. He said, 'So?'

'So,' Lena picked up again, 'if your relationship was
casual, why were you arranging these late night meetings?'

Mark turned his head slightly, looking out the
window. He was obviously trying to come up with an
answer to the question, but unable to.

Lena said, 'She's dead, Mark.'

'I know that,' he whispered, his eyes flickering toward Jeffrey, then back to the floor. 'I saw it happen.'

'Is this how you want to talk about her, like she was a whore?' Lena asked him. 'Do you really want to tear her down like that?'

Mark's throat bobbed as he swallowed. After a couple of minutes, he mumbled something she could not understand.

'What?' Lena asked.

'She wasn't bad,' he said, looking at her out of the corner of his eye. A tear slid down his cheek, and he turned his gaze back toward the window. 'Okay?'

Lena nodded. 'Okay.'

'She listened to me,' he began, his voice so low she had to strain to hear him. 'She was smart, you know? She read and things, and she helped me with school, some.'

Lena sat back on the couch, waiting for him to continue.

'People think things about me,' he said, his tone more childish. 'They think I'm a certain way, but maybe I'm not. Maybe there's more to me than that. Maybe I'm a human being.'

'Of course you are,' Lena told him, thinking that she probably understood Mark more than he thought. Every time she walked out in public, Lena felt like the person she really was had been erased. All she was now was the girl who had been raped. Sometimes, Lena wondered if she would not have been better off if she had died. At least then people would see her as tragic rather than as some kind of victim.

Mark rubbed his fingers along his goatee, pulling Lena back into the interview. He said, 'There's things I did, okay? That maybe I didn't want to do and maybe she didn't want to do . . .' He shook his head, his eyes closed tightly. 'Things she did . . .' His voice trailed off. 'I know she was fat, okay? But she was more than that.'

'What was she, Mark?'

He tapped his fingers on the arm of the chair. When he spoke, he seemed more sure of himself, back under control. 'She listened to me. You know, about my mom.' He gave a humorless laugh. 'Like when my mom told us she didn't want fucking chemo this time, that she was just gonna let herself die. Jenny understood that.' He found a thread on the arm of the chair and picked at it until it pulled. Mark's concentration was so focused on the string that Lena wondered if he had forgotten she and Jeffrey were there.

Lena let herself look at Jeffrey. He was sitting back on the couch, too. Both of them stared at Mark, waiting for him to finish.

'She tutored me in school, some,' he said, twisting his ring. 'She was younger than me, but she knew how to do things. She liked to read.' He smiled, as if a distant memory had come back. He used the back of his hand to wipe under his nose. 'She started hanging out with Lacey. I guess they had a lot in common. She was so nice to me.' He shook his head, as if to clear it. 'I just liked her because she was nice to me.' His lips trembled. 'When Mama got sick . . .' he started. Again he was quiet. 'We thought she'd beat it, you know? And then it was back, and she was in and out of the hospital, and sick all the time. So sick she couldn't even walk sometimes. So sick Daddy had to help her stand up to take a shower, even.' He paused, then, 'And then she said she wasn't gonna do it anymore, couldn't take the chemo, couldn't take the being sick. Said we didn't need to see her like that, but how does she want us to see her, man? Dead?'

Mark put his hands over his eyes. 'Jenny was just there, you know? She was there for me, not anybody else . . .' He paused. 'She was so sweet, and she was interested in me, and talking to me, and she understood what I was going through, right? She wasn't about being a cheerleader or wearing my damn class ring. She was all about being there for me.' He dropped his hands, staring at Lena. 'It wasn't about Lacey, or about Dad. She thought I was good. She thought I was worth something.' He dropped his head into his hands, obviously crying.

Lena became conscious of the clock on the wall. Its tick was loud, popping in her ears. Jeffrey was completely still beside her. He had a way of making himself seem part of the scenery, letting her take the lead in things. This was the old Lena and Jeffrey. This was Lena who knew how to do her job, Lena who was in charge of things. She took a deep breath, pulling her shoulders up, letting the air fill her lungs. In this moment, in this room right now, she was herself again. For the first time in months, she was Lena again.

She let a full minute pass before asking Mark, 'Tell me what happened.'

He shook his head. 'It's so wrong,' he said. 'It all just went so wrong.' He leaned forward, his chest almost to his knees, his face contorted in pain as if someone had kicked him. He covered his face with his hands and started to sob again.

Before she knew what she was doing, Lena was down on her knees beside the boy, holding one of his hands. She put her hand on his back, trying to comfort him. 'It's okay,' she told him, hushing him.

'I love her,' he whispered. 'Even after what she did, I still love her.'

'I know you do,' Lena told him, rubbing his back.

'She was so mad at me,' Mark said, still sobbing. Lena pulled a Kleenex out of the box and gave it to him. He blew his nose, then whispered, 'I told her we had to stop.'

'Why did you have to stop?' Lena whispered back.

'I never thought she needed me, you know? I thought she was stronger than me. Stronger than everybody.' His voice caught. 'And she wasn't.'

Lena stroked the back of his neck, trying to soothe him. 'What happened, Mark? Why did she end up hating you?'

'You think she hates me?' he asked, his eyes searching hers. 'You really think she hates me?'

'No, Mark,' Lena said, pushing his hair back out of his face. He had switched to present tense, something people often did when they could not accept that a loved one had died. Lena had found herself doing the same thing with her sister. 'Of course she doesn't hate you.'

'I told her I wouldn't do it anymore.'

'Do what?'

He shook his head no. 'It's all so pointless,' he said, still shaking his head.

'What's pointless?' Lena asked, trying to make him look up at her. He did, and for a shocking moment, she thought he might try to kiss her. Quickly, she moved back on her heels, catching herself on the arm of the chair so she wouldn't fall. Mark must have seen the shock in her expression because he turned away from her, taking another tissue. Mark looked at Jeffrey as he blew his nose. Lena looked at neither of them. All she could think was that she had somehow crossed a line, but what that line was and where it had been drawn she could not figure.

Mark spoke to Jeffrey, and his voice had more authority to it. The kid who had broken down moments ago was gone. The surly teenager was back. 'What else?'

'Jenny liked to study?' Jeffrey asked.

Mark shrugged.

Lena said, 'Was she interested in other cultures, other religions?'

'What the fuck for?' Mark countered angrily. 'It's not like we're ever gonna get out of this fucking town.'

'That's a no, then?' Lena asked.

Mark pursed his lips, almost as if he was going to blow a kiss, then said, 'Nope.'

Jeffrey crossed his arms over his chest, taking back over. 'Around Christmas, you stopped being friends with Jenny. Why?'

'Got tired of her,' he shrugged.

'Who else did Jenny hang around with?'

'Me,' Mark said. 'Lacey. That was it.'

'She didn't have other friends?'

'No,' Mark answered. 'And we weren't really even her friends.' He laughed lightly. 'She was all alone, I guess. Isn't that sad, Chief Tolliver?'

Jeffrey stared at Mark, not answering.

'If you don't have any more questions,' Mark began, 'I'd like you to go now.'

'Do you know Dr. Linton?' Jeffrey asked.

He shrugged. 'Sure.'

'I want you at the children's clinic tomorrow by ten o'clock to give that blood sample.' Jeffrey pointed his finger at Mark. 'Don't make me come looking for you.'

Mark stood, wiping his palms on his pants. 'Yeah, whatever.' He looked down at Lena, who was still on the floor. She was at his crotch level, and he smiled, more like a sneer, when he noticed this.

Mark raised one eyebrow at her, his lips slightly parted in the same sly smile he had given her before, then left the room.

MONDAY

MONDAY

EIGHT

Around six o'clock in the morning, Jeffrey rolled out of bed and fell onto the floor. He sat up, groaning at the pain in his head as he tried to remember where he was. The trip to Sylacauga had taken him six long hours last night, and he had tumbled into the twin bed without even bothering to take off his clothes. His dress shirt was wrinkled, the sleeves pushed up well past his elbows. His pants were creased in four different places.

Jeffrey yawned as he looked around his boyhood room. His mother had not changed a thing since he had left for Auburn over twenty years ago. A poster of a cherry-red 1967 Mustang convertible with a white top was on the back of the door. Six pairs of worn-out sneakers were on the floor of the closet. His football jersey from Sylacauga High was tacked to the wall over the bed. A box of cassette tapes was stacked high under the room's only window.

He lifted the mattress and saw a stack of *Playboy*s that he had started stockpiling at the age of fourteen. A much-loved copy of Penthouse, purloined from the local store down the street, was still on the top. Jeffrey sat back on his heels, thumbing through the magazine. There had been a time in his life when he had known every page of the Penthouse by heart, from the cartoons to the articles to the lovely ladies in provocative poses that had been the focus of his sexual fantasies for months on end.

'Jesus,' he sighed, thinking some of the women were probably old enough to be grandmothers now. Christ, some of them were probably eligible for social security.

Jeffrey groaned as he slid the mattress back into place, trying not to push the magazines out on the other side. He wondered if his mother had ever found his stash. Wondered, too, what she must have thought of it. Knowing May Tolliver, she had ignored them, or made up an excuse that allowed her to block out the fact that her son had enough pornography under his mattress to wallpaper the entire house. His mother was good at not seeing things she did not want to see, but then most mothers were.

Jeffrey thought about Dottie Weaver, and how she had missed all the signs with her daughter. He put his hand to his stomach, thinking about Jenny Weaver standing in the parking lot at Skatie's. The image was like a Polaroid etched into his eyelids, and he could see the little girl standing there, the gun in her hand trained on Mark Patterson. Mark was more defined in Jeffrey's memory now, and he could pick out details about the boy: the way he stood with his arms out to his sides, the way his knees bent a little as he stared at Jenny. The whole time, Mark had never really looked at Jeffrey. Even after Jeffrey had shot her, Mark had stood there, staring down at the ground where she lay.

Jeffrey rubbed his eyes, trying to push out this image. He let his gaze travel back to the Mustang, taking it in the way he had every morning of his teenage life. The car had represented so much to him when he was growing up, chief among these things being freedom. As a teenager, he had sometimes sat in bed, his eyes closed, imagining getting in that car and taking off across country. Jeffrey had wanted so much to get away, to leave Sylacauga and his mother's house, to be something other than his father's son.

Jimmy Tolliver had been a petty thief in every sense of the term. He never stole big, which was a point in his favor, because he always got caught. Jeffrey's mother liked to say that Jimmy couldn't break wind in a crowded building without getting caught. He just had that look of guilt about him, and he liked to talk. Jimmy's mouth was his biggest downfall; he couldn't stand not taking credit for the jobs he pulled. Jimmy Tolliver was the only person who was surprised when he had ended up dying in prison, serving out a life term for armed robbery.

By the time he was ten years old, Jeffrey knew practically every man on the Sylacauga police force by name, because at some time or another, one or all of them had come to the house, looking for Jimmy. To their credit, the patrol cops knew Jeffrey, too, and they always made a point of taking him aside whenever they saw him. At the time, being singled out by the police had annoyed Jeffrey. He had considered it harassment. Now, as a policeman himself, Jeffrey knew the cops had been taking time with him as insurance. They did not want to waste their time chasing down another Tolliver for stealing lawn mowers and weed whackers out of his neighbors' yards.

Jeffrey owed these cops a lot, not least of all his career. Watching the fear in his father's eyes that last time the cops had come to the house and slapped the cuffs on Jimmy, Jeffrey had known then and there that he wanted to be a cop. Jimmy Tolliver had been a drunk, and a mean one at that. To the town, he was a bumbling crook and a sloppy drunk, to Jeffrey and his mother, he was a violent asshole who terrified his family.

Jeffrey stretched his hands up to the ceiling, his palms flat against the warm wood. As he padded to the bathroom, he noticed that even his socks were wrinkled. The heel had slid around sometime during the night. Jeffrey was balancing on one foot, trying to twist it back, when he heard his cell phone ringing in the other room.

'Dammit,' he cursed, bumping his shoulder into the wall as he turned the corner to his room. The house seemed so much smaller now than it had when he was growing up.

He picked up the phone on the fourth ring, just before the voice mail came on. 'Hello?'

'Jeff?' Sara asked, a bit of concern in her voice.

He let it linger in his ear before saying, 'Hey, babe.'

She laughed at the name. 'Less than ten hours in Alabama and you're calling me "babe"?' She waited a beat. 'Are you alone?'

He felt irritated, because he knew part of her was not joking. 'Of course I'm alone,' he shot back. 'Jesus Christ, Sara.'

'I meant your mother,' she told him, though he could tell from her lack of conviction that she was covering.

He let it pass. 'No, they kept her overnight in the hospital.' He sat on the bed, trying to get his sock to twist back into place. 'She fell down somehow. Broke her foot.'

'Did she fall at home?' Sara asked, something more than curiosity in her tone. He knew what she was getting at, and it was the same reason Jeffrey had come to Alabama himself in the middle of a case instead of just making a phone call. He wanted to see if his mother's drinking was finally getting out of hand. May Tolliver had always been what was politely called a functional alcoholic. If she had crossed the line into hopeless drunk, Jeffrey would have to do something. He had no idea what this would be, but knew instinctively that it would not be easy.

Jeffrey tried to redirect her interest. 'I talked with the doctor. I haven't really seen her to find out what happened.' He waited for her to get the message. 'I'll see her today, see what's going on.'

'She'll probably be on crutches,' Sara told him. He could hear a tapping noise, and assumed she was at her office. He looked at his watch, wondering why she was there so early, but then he remembered the time change. Sara was an hour ahead of him.

'Ms. Harris across the street will look in on her,' Jeffrey volunteered, knowing that Jean Harris would do whatever she could to help a neighbor. She worked as a dietician at the local hospital, and had often waved Jeffrey over after school to make sure he had a hot meal. Sitting at the table with her three lovely daughters had been a bit more enticing than Ms. Harris's chicken pot pie, but Jeffrey had appreciated both at the time.

Sara said, 'You need to tell her to be very careful not to mix her pain meds with alcohol. Or tell her doctor that. Okay?'

He looked at his sock, realizing it was still backward. He twisted it the other way, asking, 'Is that why you called?'

'I got your message about Mark Patterson. What am I pulling a sample for?'

'Paternity,' he told her, not liking the image the word brought to his mind.

Sara was silent, then asked, 'Are you sure?'

'No,' he told her. 'Not at all. I just thought I should look at everything I could.'

'How'd you get a court order so fast?'

'No order. His father's sending him in voluntarily.'

She was still incredulous. 'Without a lawyer?'

Jeffrey sighed. 'Sara, I left all of this on your machine last night. Is something going on?'

'No,' she answered in a softer tone. Then, 'Yes, actually.'

He waited. 'Yeah?'

'I wanted to make sure you were all right.'

Sarcasm came, because that was all he could muster in light of her question. 'Other than waking up knowing I killed a thirteen-year-old little girl, I guess I'm just peachy.'

She was quiet, and he let the silence continue, not knowing what to say to her. Sara had not called him in a long time, not even for county-related matters. In the past, she had faxed him documents on cases, or sent Carlos, her assistant, over with sensitive information. Since the divorce, personal calls were out of the question, and even when they had started back kind of dating, Jeffrey had always been the one to pick up the phone.

'Jeff?' Sara asked.

'I was just thinking,' he said, then, to change the subject, he asked, 'Tell me a little bit more about Lacey.'

'I told you yesterday. She's a good kid,' Sara said, and he could hear something off in her tone. He knew she was feeling responsible for Jenny Weaver, but there was nothing he could do about it.

Sara continued, 'She's bright, funny. Just like Jenny in a lot of ways.'

'Were you close to her?'

'As close as you can be to a kid you only see a few times a year.' Sara paused, then said, 'Yeah. Some of them you connect with. I connected with Lacey. I think she has a little crush on me.'

'That's weird,' he said.

'Not really,' Sara told him. 'Lots of kids get crushes on adults. It's not a sexual thing, they just want to impress them, to make them laugh.'

'I'm still not following.'

'They get to be a certain age and their parents can't be cool anymore. Some kids, not all of them, can transfer their feelings onto another adult. It's perfectly natural. They just want someone to look up to, and at that point in their lives it can't be their parents.'

'So, she looked up to you?'

'It felt that way,' Sara said, and he could hear the sadness in her voice.

'You think she would've told you if something was going on?'

'Who knows?' Sara replied. 'Something happens to them when they get into middle school. They get a lot more quiet.'

'That's what Grace Patterson said. That they keep secrets.'

'That's true,' Sara agreed. 'I just chalked up the change to puberty. All those hormones, all those new feelings. They've got a lot to think about, and the only thing they're certain of is that adults have no way of understanding what they're going through.'

'Still,' Jeffrey countered, 'don't you think she would've talked to you if something was wrong?'

'I'd like to think so, but the truth is, she'd have to have her mother drive her here. I can't kick the mother out of the room without causing some suspicion.'

'You think Grace would have been reluctant to leave y'all alone?'

'I think she would've been worried. She's a good mother. She takes an interest in her kids and what they're doing.'

'That's what Brad said.'

'What does Brad have to do with this?' Sara asked.

'He's the youth minister at Crescent Baptist.'

'Oh, that's right,' Sara said, making the connection. 'He must've been on the retreat.'

'Yeah,' Jeffrey told her. 'There were eight kids from the church: three boys, five girls.'

'That doesn't sound like a lot of kids.'

'It's a small church,' Jeffrey reminded her. 'Plus, skiing is expensive. Not a lot of people have that kind of money to begin with, especially around the holidays.'

'That's true,' she agreed. 'But it was just Brad chaperoning?'

'The church secretary was supposed to help out with the girls, but she got sick at the last minute.'

'Have you talked to her?'

'She had some kind of stroke. She was only fifty-eight years old,' he said, thinking that when he had been a kid, fifty-eight had seemed ancient. 'She moved down to Florida so her kids could take care of her.'

'So, what did Brad say about Jenny and Lacey?'

'Nothing specific. He said Lacey and Jenny pretty much stayed by themselves while the rest of the kids were off skiing and having fun.'

'That's not uncommon for girls that age. They tend to form tight little groups.'

'Yeah,' Jeffrey sighed, feeling yesterday's frustrations settling into his gut. 'Brad went over to Jenny's house when she stopped coming to church. She pretty much burst into tears the minute she saw him and wouldn't talk.'

'What'd he do?'

'Left with his hat in his hands. He asked Dave Fine to check in on her, but Dave got the same treatment.'

'Did you talk to Dave about it?'

'Briefly. He was about to go into a therapy session.' Jeffrey felt a flash of guilt, thinking about Lena. He should not have allowed her to use her therapy appointment to interview Fine. Jeffrey had given in too easily because it was convenient.

'Jeffrey?' Sara said, her tone indicating she had asked him a question and was waiting for an answer.

'Yeah, sorry,' Jeffrey apologized.

'What did Fine say?'

'The same as Brad. He offered to come in tomorrow and talk some more, but neither one of them seem like they're going to be much help.' Jeffrey rubbed his eyes, trying to think of any straw he could grasp. 'What about Mark Patterson?' he finally asked. 'Does he seem kind of weird to you?'

'Weird how?'

'Weird like . . .' Jeffrey tried to find the words. He did not really want to go into the Patterson interview with Sara, mostly because of what had happened with Lena. There had been something between her and the boy, something that set his teeth on edge. They both worked off each other somehow. 'Weird like I don't know.'

Sara laughed. 'I don't think I can answer that.'

'Sexual,' he said, because that was a good word to describe Mark Patterson. 'He seemed really sexual.'

'Well,' Sara began, and he could hear the confusion in her voice. 'He's a good-looking kid. I imagine he's been sexually active for a very long time.'

'He just turned sixteen.'

'Jeffrey,' Sara said, as if she were talking to an idiot. 'I've got ten-year-old girls who haven't even started their periods asking me about birth control.'

'Jesus,' he sighed. 'It's way too early in the morning to hear that kind of thing.'

'Welcome to my world,' she told him.

'Yeah.' He stared at the jersey on his wall, trying to remember what it had felt like to be Mark Patterson's age and have the world in the palm of his hand. Though Mark Patterson did not seem to feel that way.

Jeffrey did not like this helpless feeling. He should be back in Grant, trying to figure this out. At the very least, he should be keeping an eye on Lena. For a while Jeffrey had felt she was on the edge, but not until yesterday did he realize that she was closer to falling than keeping herself balanced.

'Jeff?' Sara asked. 'What's wrong?'

'I'm worried about Lena,' he told her, and the words felt familiar to him. He had been worried about Lena since he hired her ten years ago. First, he was worried that she was so aggressive on patrol, taking every collar like her life depended on it. Then, he had worried that she put herself in danger too often as a detective, pushing suspects to their breaking point, pushing herself to her own breaking point. And now he worried that she was about to lose it. There was no question in his mind that she would explode soon. It was just a matter of when. With a start, he realized this had been his fear from the beginning: When would Lena finally break in two?

'I think you should be worried about her,' Sara said. 'Why won't you take her off active duty?'

'Because it would kill her,' he answered, and he

144

knew this was true. Lena needed her job like other people needed air.

'Is there something else?'

Jeffrey thought about the conversation he'd had with Lena in the car. She had not been exactly sure of herself when she told him the shot was clean. 'I, uh,' he began, not knowing how to say this. 'When I talked to Lena yesterday . . . ,' he said.

'Yeah?'

'She didn't seem too sure about what had happened.'

'About the shooting?' Sara demanded, obviously irritated. 'What exactly did she say?'

'It wasn't what she said so much as how she said it.'

Sara mumbled something that sounded like a curse. 'She's just playing with you to get back at me.'

'Lena's not like that.'

'Of course she is,' Sara shot back. 'She's always been like that.'

Jeffrey shook his head, not accepting this. 'I think she's just not sure.'

Sara mumbled a curse under her breath. 'That's just great.'

'Sara,' Jeffrey said, trying to calm her down. 'Don't say anything to her, okay? It'll only make it worse.'

'Why would I say anything to her?'

'Sara . . .' He rubbed sleep from his eyes, thinking he did not want to talk about this now. 'Listen, I was just fixin' to go to the hospital –'

'This really ticks me off.'

'I know that,' he said. 'You've made it clear.'

'I just –'

'Sara,' he interrupted. 'I really need to go.'

'Actually,' she said, moderating her tone, 'I was calling for a reason, if you've got a minute?'

'Sure,' he managed, feeling a sense of trepidation. 'What's up?'

He heard her take a deep breath, as if she were about to jump off a cliff. 'I was wondering if you'll be back tonight.'

'Late, probably.'

'Well, then, how about tomorrow night?'

'If I come back tonight, I won't have to come back tomorrow night.'

'Are you being dense on purpose?'

He played back their conversation in his mind, smiling when he realized that Sara was trying to ask him over. Jeffrey wondered if she had ever done something like this in her life.

He said, 'I've never been very bright.'

'No,' she agreed, but she was laughing.

'So?'

'So . . . ,' Sara began, then she sighed. He heard her mumble, 'Oh, this is so stupid.'

'What's that?'

'I said,' she started again, then stopped. 'I'm not doing anything tomorrow night.'

Jeffrey rubbed his whiskers, feeling the grin on his face. He wondered if there had ever been a time in this room when he had felt happier. Maybe the day he got the call from Auburn, saying he could go to college for free in exchange for getting the shit beaten out of him on the football field every Saturday.

He said, 'Hey, me neither.'

'So . . .' Sara was obviously hoping he would fill things in for her. Jeffrey sat back down on the bed, thinking hell would freeze over before he helped her out.

'Come over to my house,' she finally said. 'Around seven or so, okay?'

'Why?'

He could hear her chair squeak as she sat back. Jeffrey imagined she probably had her hand over her eyes.

'God, you are not going to make this easy, are you?'

'Why should I?'

'I want to see you,' she told him. 'Come at seven. I'll make supper.'

'Wait a minute –'

She obviously anticipated his problem with this. Sara was not exactly a good cook. She offered, 'I'll order something from Alfredo's.'

Jeffrey smiled again. 'I'll see you at seven.'

As a boy, Jeffrey had done his share of stupid things. His two best friends from elementary school to high school had lived down the street from him, and between Jerry Long, a boy with a curiosity about fireworks, and Bobby Blankenship, a boy who liked to hear things explode, they had managed to risk their lives any number of times before puberty took hold and girls became more important than blowing things up.

At the age of eleven, the three had discovered the pleasure of exploding bottle rockets in a steel drum behind Jeffrey's house. By the time they were twelve, the drum was as dented and pockmarked as Bobby 'Spot' Blankenship's face. By the time they were thirteen, Jerry Long had been given the name 'Possum' because, when the drum had finally exploded, a piece of shrapnel had nearly sliced off the top of his head, and he had lain in Jeffrey's backyard like a possum until Jean Harris had called an ambulance to take him to the hospital, and the police to scare the bejesus out of Jeffrey and Spot.

Jeffrey had not earned his nickname until later, when he had started to notice girls and, more important, they had started to notice him. Like Possum and Spot, he was on the football team, and they were pretty popular in school because the team was winning that year. Jeffrey was the first of the trio to kiss a girl, the first to get to second base, and the first to finally lose his virginity. For these accomplishments, he was given the nickname 'Slick.'

The first time Jeffrey had taken Sara to Sylacauga, he had been so nervous that his hands would not stop sweating. They had just started dating, and Jeffrey had been under the impression that Sara was a little too socially elevated for Possum and Spot, and more than likely for ol' Slick as well. Sylacauga was the epitome of a small Southern town. Unlike Heartsdale, there was no college up the street, and no professors in town to add some diversity to the mix. Most of the people who lived here worked in some kind of industry, whether it was for the textile mill or the marble quarry. Jeffrey was not saying they were all backward, inbred hicks, but they were not the kind of people he thought Sara would be comfortable hanging around.

Sara wasn't just what the locals would call 'book learned,' but a medical doctor, and her family might have been blue collar, but Eddie Linton was the kind of man who knew how to manage a dollar. The family owned property up and down the lake, and even had some rental units in Florida. On top of that, Sara was sharp, and not just about books. She had a cutting wit, and wasn't the kind of woman who would have his slippers and a hot meal waiting for him when he got home from work. If anything, Sara would expect Jeffrey to have these things ready for her.

About six miles from the Tolliver house, there was

a general store called Cat's that Jeffrey and everyone else had frequented growing up. It was the kind of place where you could buy milk, tobacco, gasoline, and bait. The floor was made from hand-hewn lumber and there were enough gashes and scars in it to trip you up if you did not watch where you were walking. The ceiling was low, and yellowed from nicotine and water stains. Freezers packed with ice and Coca-Colas lined the entranceway, and a large Moon Pie display was up by the cash register. The gas pumps outside dinged with every gallon pumped.

While Jeffrey was at Auburn, Cat had passed away, and Possum, who worked at the store, had taken over for Cat's widow. Six years later, Possum had bought out the widow Cat, and changed the name to 'Possum's Cat's.' When Sara had first seen the sign over the dilapidated building, she had been delighted, and made reference to the Eliot poem. Jeffrey had fought the urge to crawl under the car and hide, but Sara had laughed when she found out the truth. As a matter of fact, she had enjoyed herself that weekend, and by the second day there, Sara was lying out by the pool with Possum and his wife, laughing at stories about Jeffrey's errant youth.

Now, Jeffrey could smile at the memory, though at the time he had been slightly annoyed to be the butt of their jokes. Sara was the first woman who had made fun of him like that, and, truth be told, that was probably the point at which she had hooked him. His mother liked to say that he liked a challenge.

Jeffrey was thinking about this, thinking that Sara Linton was, if anything, a challenge, as he turned into the parking lot of Possum's Cat's. The place had changed a lot since Cat had owned it, and even more since the last time Jeffrey had been in town. The only thing that remained the same was the big Auburn University emblem over the door. Alabama was a state divided by its two universities, Auburn and Alabama, and there was only one important question every native asked the other: 'Who are you for?' Jeffrey had seen fights break out when someone gave the wrong answer in the wrong part of town.

A day care was to the right of the store, a new addition since the last time Jeffrey had visited. On the left was Madam Bell's, which was run by Possum's wife, Darnell. Like Cat, Madam Bell had passed a long time ago. Jeffrey thought that Nell ran the place just to give her something to do while the kids were at school. He had dated Nell off and on in high school until Possum had gotten serious about her. Jeffrey could not imagine that same restless girl being happy with this kind of life, but stranger things had happened. Besides, Nell had been three months pregnant the week they all graduated from school. It wasn't like she had been given a lot of choices.

So he wouldn't take up one of the spaces in front of the store, Jeffrey let the car idle outside Bell's, Lynyrd Skynyrd's 'Sweet Home Alabama' playing softly on the car's speakers. He had found the tape in the box under the window in his room, and experienced a bit of nostalgia when the first chords of what was one of his favorite songs reached his ears. It was odd how you could love something so much, but forget about it when it wasn't right under your nose. He felt that way about this town, and his friends here. Being around Possum and Nell again would be like nothing had changed in the last twenty years. Jeffrey did not know how he felt about that.

What he did know was that seeing his mother in the hospital ten minutes ago had made him want to get back to Grant as fast as he could. There was something suffocating about the way she held on to him when she hugged him, and the way she let her voice trail off, saying things by leaving them unsaid. May Tolliver had never been a happy woman, and part of Jeffrey thought his father had been such a bumbling crook so that he would get caught and taken off to jail, where his miserable wife could not nag him every day about what a disappointment he was. Like Jimmy, May was a mean drunk, and though she had never raised her hand to Jeffrey, she could cut him in two with her words faster than anyone he had ever met. Thankfully, she still seemed to be functioning, even with enough alcohol in her to fuel a tractor for sixty miles. If May could be believed, a feral cat from under the neighbor's house had startled her and she had fallen down the steps. Since Jeffrey had heard some cats over there this morning, he had to give his mother the benefit of the doubt. He did not want to admit to anyone, let alone to himself, how grateful he was that his mother did not need further intervention.

Jeffrey stepped out of the car, his foot sliding a little on the gravel drive. He had changed into jeans and a polo shirt back at his mother's house, and he felt odd being clothed so casually in the middle of the week. He had even considered wearing his dress shoes, but had changed his mind when he caught a glance of himself in the mirror. He slipped on his sunglasses, looking around as he walked toward Madam Bell's.

The fortune-teller's building was more like a shack, and the screen door groaned when Jeffrey opened it. He knocked on the front door, stepping into the small front parlor. The place looked just as it had when he was a boy. Spot had once dared Jeffrey to go in and have his palm read by Madam Bell. He had not liked what she had to say, and never stepped foot back in the place again.

Jeffrey craned his head around the door, looking into the shack's only other room. Nell sat at a table with a deck of tarot cards in front of her. The television was on low, or maybe the air conditioner in the window was drowning out the sound. She was knitting something as she watched her show, her body leaning forward as if to make sure she caught every word.

Jeffrey said, 'Boo.'

'Oh, my God.' Nell jumped, dropping her knitting. She stood from the table, patting her palm against her chest. 'Slick, you 'bout scared me half to death.'

'Don't let that happen twice,' he laughed, pulling her into a hug. She was a small woman, but nice and curvy through the hips. He stepped back to get a good look at her. Nell had not changed much since high school. Her black hair was the same, if not a little gray, straight and long enough to reach her waist, but pulled back in a ponytail, probably to fight the heat.

'You been over to Possum's?' she asked, sitting back down at the table. 'What're you doing here? Is it about your mama?'

Jeffrey smiled, sitting across from her. Nell had always talked a hundred miles an hour. 'No and yes.'

'She was drunk,' Nell said in her usual abrupt way. Her candor was one of the reasons Jeffrey had stopped dating her. She called things the way she saw them, and at eighteen Jeffrey had hardly been introspective.

Nell said, 'Her liquor bills 'bout kept us afloat last winter.'

'I know,' Jeffrey answered, crossing his arms. He had paid his mother's utility bills for some time now just to keep her in liquor. It was pointless to argue with the old woman about it, and at least this way he knew she would stay at home and drink instead of going out to do something about it.

He said, 'I just came from the hospital. They gave her a shot of vodka while I was standing there.'

Nell picked up the cards and started to shuffle them. 'Old biddy'd go into the DTs if they didn't.'

Jeffrey shrugged. The doctor had said the same thing in the hospital.

'What're you lookin' at?' Nell asked him, and Jeffrey smiled, realizing that he had been staring at her. What he had been thinking was that it was easier to talk to Nell about his mother's alcoholism than it was to talk to Sara about it. He could not begin to understand why this was. Maybe it was because Nell had grown up with it. With Sara, Jeffrey tended to get embarrassed, then ashamed, then finally angry.

'How is it you get prettier every time I come see you?' he teased her.

'Slick, Slick, Slick,' Nell said, clucking her tongue. She laid a couple of cards face up on the table, asking, 'So, why'd Sara divorce you?'

Jeffrey startled, asking, 'You see that in the cards?'

She smiled mischievously. 'Christmas cards. Sara's had "Linton" on the return address.' She put another card down on the table. 'What'd you do, cheat on her?'

He indicated the cards. 'Why don't you tell me?'

She nodded, laying down a couple more. 'I'd guess you cheated on her and got caught.'

'What?'

Nell laughed. 'Just 'cause she don't talk to you don't mean she don't talk to me.'

He shook his head, not understanding.

'We've got a phone, too, puppy,' she told him. 'I talk to Sara every now and then, just to catch up.'

'Well, then you must know I've been seeing her again,' he said, aware he was sounding like the cocky old Slick he had been, but unable to stop it. 'What do your cards say about that?'

She turned a couple more over and studied them for a few seconds, a frown tugging her lips down. Finally, she scooped the cards back into a deck. 'These stupid things don't tell you nothing anyway,' she mumbled. 'Let's get over to Possum's. I'm sure he'll be glad to see you.'

She held her hand out to him, and he hesitated, wondering if he should push her on the reading. Not that Jeffrey believed Nell had the gift, or that anyone did for that matter, but it set his teeth on edge that she would not at least make something up so that he would feel better.

'Come on,' she said, tugging at his sleeve.

He acquiesced, letting her lead him out of the shack and back into the unrelenting Alabama heat. There were no trees in the gravel parking lot, and Jeffrey could feel the sun baking the top of his head as they crossed toward the gas station.

Nell looped her hand through his arm, saying, 'I like Sara.'

'I do, too,' he told her.

'I mean, I really like her, Jeffrey.'

He stopped, because she seldom called him 'Jeffrey.'

She said, 'If she's giving you another chance, don't fuck it up.'

'I don't plan to.'

'I mean it, Slick,' she said, tugging him toward the store. 'She's too good for you, and God knows she's too smart.' She waited at the door so he could open it. 'Just don't fuck it up.'

'Your faith in me is inspiring.'

'I just don't want Little Jeffrey messing things up for you again.'

'"Little?"' he repeated, opening the door. 'Your memory giving out on you?'

Jeffrey could tell she was going to answer him, but Possum's booming voice drowned out everything.

'That Slick?' Possum yelled as if Jeffrey had just gone out for a walk instead of been away for years. Jeffrey watched as the other man edged over the counter. His belly got in the way, but he landed on his feet despite the laws of physics.

'Damn,' Jeffrey told him, rubbing the other man's large gut. 'Nell, why didn't you tell me you got another one on the way?'

Possum laughed good naturedly, rubbing his belly. 'We're gonna call it Bud if it's a boy, Dewars if it's a girl.' He put his arm around Jeffrey, leading him into the store. 'How you been, boy?'

Without thinking, Jeffrey delivered his standard response. 'I ain't been a boy since I was your size.'

Possum laughed, throwing back his head. 'Wish we had Spot around. How long you gonna be in town?'

'Not long,' Jeffrey told him. 'I'm actually on my way out.' He turned around to see that Nell had left them alone.

'Good woman,' Possum said.

'I can't believe she's still with you.'

'I take away her keys at night before I go to sleep,' he told Jeffrey, giving him a wink. 'Wanna beer?'

Jeffrey looked at the clock on the wall. 'I usually don't drink until at least noon.'

'Oh, right, right, right,' he answered. 'How about a Co-Cola?' He scooped a couple out of an ice chest without waiting for a response.

'Hot out,' Jeffrey said.

'Yep,' Possum agreed, popping the bottles open on the side of the chest. 'I guess you dropped by to ask me to keep an eye on your mama.'

'I've got a case back home,' he said, and it felt good that home meant Grant now. 'If you don't mind.'

'Shit,' he waved this off, handing Jeffrey a Coke. 'Don't worry about that. She's still just right down the street.'

'Thanks,' Jeffrey said. He watched as Possum took a bag of peanuts off the rack and ripped it open with his teeth. He offered some to Jeffrey, but Jeffrey shook his head no.

'Damn shame her falling,' Possum said, funneling some peanuts into the open neck of his Coke bottle. 'Been real hot lately. Guess she just got dizzy in this heat.'

Jeffrey took a swig of Coke. Possum was doing what he had always done, and that was covering for May Tolliver. Jerry Long didn't just get his nickname from playing dead that day in Jeffrey's backyard. If there was one thing Possum was good at, it was ignoring what was right in front of his face.

The heavy baseline from a rap song shook the front windows, and Jeffrey turned around in time to see a large burgundy colored pickup truck pull into a space in front of the store. Rap music blared, a cacophony of missed beats, before the engine was cut and a surly-looking teenager got out of the cab and walked into the store.

He was dressed in a shirt that matched the color of his truck, with the words ROLL TIDE emblazoned in white over a rampaging elephant. His hair was what got Jeffrey's immediate attention, though. It was corn rowed with little crimson colored barrettes at the end, and they snapped against each other as he walked.

The boy was wearing black-and-gray camouflage pants that were cut off at the knee, but his socks and sneakers were colored the Crimson Tide. Jeffrey realized with a start that the kid was dressed head to toe in the colors of Alabama University.

'Hey, Dad,' the boy said, meaning Possum.

Jeffrey exchanged a look with his friend, then turned back to the boy. 'Jared?' he asked, certain this could not be Possum and Nell's sweet little kid. He looked like a motorcycle thug dressed for an Alabama gang.

'Hey, Uncle Slick,' Jared mumbled, shuffling his feet across the floor. He walked right past Jeffrey and his father and into the room behind the counter.

'Man,' Jeffrey said. 'That has got to be embarrassing.'

Possum nodded. 'We're hoping he changes his mind.' Possum shrugged. 'He likes animals. Everybody knows Auburn's got a better vet school than Alabama.'

Jeffrey kept his teeth clamped so he would not laugh.

'I'll be back,' Possum said, going after the boy. 'Help yourself to anything you want.'

Jeffrey finished his Coke in one swallow, then walked to the back of the store to see what kind of bait Possum had stocked. There were wire-meshed cages with crickets chirping up a storm as well as a large plastic barrel filled with wet dirt that probably had a thousand or so worms in it. A small tank of minnows was over the cricket stands, with a net and some buckets in which to transport the bait. Sara liked to fish, and Jeffrey thought about getting her some worms before he considered what a hassle it would be, taking live bait back in his car. He would probably have to stop outside of Atlanta for something to eat, and it wasn't like Jeffrey could leave the worms to fry in the heat of his car. Besides, there were plenty of bait stands in Grant.

He dropped the empty Coke bottle into a box that looked like it was used for recycling and glanced out the window at the day-care center beside the store. Obviously, it was time for recess, and kids were running around, screaming their heads off. Jeffrey wondered if Jenny Weaver had ever felt that free. He could not imagine the overweight girl running around for any reason. She seemed more like the type to sit in the shade reading a book, waiting for the bell to ring so she could go back to class, where she felt more comfortable.

'You work here?' someone asked.

Jeffrey turned around, startled. A thirtyish-looking man was standing behind him at the bait display. He was what Jeffrey always thought of as a typical redneck: skinny and soft-looking with razor burns from shaving too close. His arms seemed to be well-developed, probably from working construction. A cigarette dangled from his lips.

'No,' Jeffrey said, feeling a little embarrassed to be caught staring so aimlessly out the window. 'I was looking at the kids.'

'Yeah,' the man said, taking a step toward Jeffrey. 'They're usually out this time of day.'

'You got one over there?' Jeffrey asked.

The man gave him a strange look, as if to assess him. His hand went to his mouth, and he rubbed his chin thoughtfully. With a start, Jeffrey noticed a tattoo on the webbing between the man's thumb and index finger. It was the same tattoo Mark Patterson had on his hand.

Jeffrey turned away, trying to think this through.

He stared out the window, and he could make out the man's partial reflection in the glass.

'Nice tattoo,' Jeffrey said.

The man's voice was a low, conspiratorial whisper. 'You got one?'

Jeffrey kept his lips pressed together, shaking his head no.

'Why not?' the man asked.

Jeffrey said, 'Work,' trying to keep his tone even. He had a bad feeling about this, like part of his mind was working something out, but not sharing it with him.

'Not many people know what it means,' the man said, fisting his hand. He looked at the tattoo on the webbing, a slight smile at his lips.

'I've seen it on a kid,' Jeffrey told him. 'Not like them,' he nodded toward the day care. 'Older.'

The man's smile broke out wider. 'You like 'em older?'

Jeffrey looked back over the man's shoulder to see where Possum was.

'He won't come back for a while,' the man assured him. 'That boy of his gets hisself into trouble most every day.'

'Yeah?'

'Yeah,' the man said.

Jeffrey turned back to the window, looking at the children running around the yard in a different light. They no longer seemed young and carefree. They seemed vulnerable and in jeopardy.

The man took a step toward Jeffrey and used the hand with the tattoo to point out the window. 'See that one there?' he asked. 'Little one with the book?'

Jeffrey followed the man's direction and found a little girl sitting under the tree in the middle of the yard. She was reading a book, much the way Jeffrey had imagined Jenny Weaver would.

The man said, 'That one's mine.'

Jeffrey felt the hair on the back of his neck rise. The way the man said the words made it clear he was not referring to the girl as his daughter. There was something proprietary to his tone, and under that, something unmistakably sexual.

The man said, 'You can't tell from this far, but up close, she's got herself the prettiest little mouth.'

Jeffrey turned around slowly, trying to hide his disgust. He said, 'Why don't we go somewhere else where we can talk about this?'

The man's eyes narrowed. 'What's wrong with here?'

'Here makes me nervous,' Jeffrey said, making himself smile.

The man stared at him for a long while, then gave an almost imperceptible nod. 'Yeah, okay,' he said, and he started walking toward the door, tossing a look over his shoulder about every five feet to make sure Jeffrey was still there.

Behind the building, the man started to turn, but Jeffrey kicked him in the back of his knees so that he fell to the ground.

'Oh, Jesus,' the man said, pulling himself into a ball.

'Shut up,' Jeffrey ordered, raising his foot. He kicked the man in the thigh hard enough to let him know there was no use trying to stand.

The man just stayed there, curled into a ball, waiting for Jeffrey to beat him. There was something at once pathetic and disgusting about his behavior, as if he understood why someone might want to do this, and was accepting his punishment.

Jeffrey looked around, making sure no one could see him. He wanted to do this man some serious harm for threatening the child, but part of his resolve was lost when faced with the pathetic, whimpering lump lying on the ground in front of him. It was one thing to kick the shit out of somebody who fought back, quite another to harm what was basically a defenseless man.

'Stand up,' Jeffrey said.

The man looked out between his crossed arms, trying to gauge if this was a trick. When Jeffrey took a step back, the man slowly uncurled himself and stood. Dust kicked up around them, and Jeffrey coughed to clear his throat.

'What do you want?' the man asked, taking a pack of cigarettes out of his shirt pocket. They were crushed, and the one he put in his mouth bent at an angle. His hands shook as he tried to light the tip.

Jeffrey fought the urge to slap the cigarette out of his mouth. 'What's that tattoo for?'

The man shrugged, some surliness slipping into his posture.

Jeffrey asked, 'Is that for some kind of club you're in?'

'Yeah, the freak club,' the man said. 'The club that likes little girls. That what you're going after?'

'So, other people have this?'

'I dunno,' he said. 'I don't got no names, if that's what you want. It's from the Internet. We're all anonymous.'

Jeffrey hissed a sigh. Among other things, the Internet fed child molesters and pedophiles, linking them together to share stories, fantasies, and sometimes children. Jeffrey had taken a law enforcement class on this very thing. There had been some spectacular busts in recent history, but even the FBI could not work fast enough to track down these people.

'What does it stand for?' Jeffrey asked.

The man gave him a hard look. 'What the fuck you think it stands for?'

'Tell me,' Jeffrey said through clenched teeth, 'unless you want to be back on that ground trying to figure out why your intestines are coming out of your asshole.'

The man nodded, taking a drag on the cigarette. He blew smoke out through his mouth and nose in a slow stream.

'The heart,' the man began, pointing to his hand. 'The big heart is black.'

Jeffrey nodded.

'But, inside, there's this little heart, right?' The man looked at the tattoo with something like love in his eyes. 'The little heart is white. It's pure.'

'Pure?' Jeffrey asked, remembering that word from somewhere. 'What do you mean, pure?'

'Like a child is pure, man.' He allowed a smile. 'The white heart makes just a little part of the black heart pure, you know? It's love, man. It's nothing but love.'

Jeffrey tried to do something with his hands other than beat the man into the ground. He held out his palm, saying, 'Give me your wallet.'

The man did not hesitate to do as he was told, nor did he protest when Jeffrey took a small spiral note-book out of his pocket and recorded the information.

'Here,' Jeffrey said, throwing the wallet so hard at the man that it popped off his chest before he could catch it. 'I've got your name now, and your address. You ever come back in this store again, or even think about hanging around that day care, my friend in there will beat the shit out of you.' Jeffrey waited a beat. 'You understand me?'

'Yes, sir,' the man said, his eyes on the ground.

'What's this Web site?' he asked.

The man kept staring at the ground. Jeffrey started to take a step toward him, but the man backed up, holding up his hands.

'It's a girl-lovers newsgroup,' he said. 'It moves around sometimes. You gotta search for it.'

Jeffrey wrote down the phrase, though he was familiar with it from the class.

The man took another drag on his cigarette, holding the smoke in for a second. He finally let it go, asking, 'That all?'

'That kid,' Jeffrey began, trying to keep his composure. 'You ever hurt that kid . . .'

The man said, 'I've never even been with one, okay? I just like looking.' He kicked at a rock with his shoe. 'They're just so sweet, you know? I mean, how could you hurt something that was so sweet?'

Without thinking, Jeffrey slammed his fist into the man's mouth. A tooth went flying, followed by a stream of blood. The man dropped to the ground again, prepared to take a beating.

Jeffrey walked back to the store, a sickening feeling washing over him.

NINE

Robert E. Lee High School was what locals called a 'super school.' This meant that the building was designed to house about fifteen hundred students from the three cities comprising Grant County. As it was, the school was still not large enough, and temporary classrooms – what other people called trailers – were in the back of the building, taking over the baseball field. Grades nine through twelve were offered here, while two middle schools served as feeders for Lee. There were four assistant principals and one principal, George Clay, a man who from all accounts spent most of his time behind his desk pushing paperwork for the governor's innovative new education program – a plan that made sure teachers spent more time filling out forms and attending certification classes than actually teaching kids.

Brad fiddled with his hat as they walked down the hallway, his police-issue sneakers thumping against the floor. Without thinking, Lena had started to count his steps as they walked up the locker-lined corridor. The place was institutional in its ambiguity, with its bright-white tile floor and muted cement-block walls. To match the school's colors, the lockers were painted a dark red, the walls a darker gray. There were posters cheering the Rebels to victory on every available blank space, but this served more to clutter than to encourage. Bulletin boards urged students to say no to drugs, cigarettes, and sex.

'It seems so small,' Brad said, his voice a hushed whisper.

Lena did not roll her eyes at this, though it was hard. Since they had talked to George Clay, Brad had been acting like a high school freshman instead of a cop. Brad even looked the part, with his round face and wispy blond hair that seemed to fall into his eyes every three seconds.

'This is Miss Mac's room,' he said, indicating a closed door. He glanced through the window as they passed by. 'She taught me English,' he said, pushing back his hair.

'Hmm,' Lena answered, not looking.

All the doors on the hall were closed between classes, and all of them were locked. Like most rural schools, Lee had taken precautions against intruders. Teachers walked the hallways, and there were two officers, what Jeffrey called 'deputy dogs,' in the front office in case anything bad went down. As a patrolman, Lena had been called to the school more than her share of times to arrest drug dealers and brawlers. In her experience, perps picked up from school were a hell of a lot harder to deal with than their adult counterparts. Habitual juvenile offenders knew the laws governing their arrests better than most cops, and there was no fear in them anymore.

'Things have changed so much,' Brad said, echoing her thoughts. 'I don't know how the teachers do it.'

'The same way we do,' Lena snapped, wanting to cut off the conversation. She had never liked school and was not comfortable being here. Actually, since her interrogation of Mark Patterson, Lena had felt off. She was experiencing an odd mixture of self-assurance from being able to connect with the kid and an unsettling feeling that she had connected too closely. Worst of all, Jeffrey seemed to have picked up on this, too.

'Here we go,' Brad said, stopping in front of Jenny Weaver's locker. He pulled a sheet of paper out of his pocket and started to unfold it, saying, 'The combination is –' as Lena hooked her thumb under the latch and popped the locker open.

'How'd you do that?' Brad asked.

'Only geeks use the combinations.'

Brad blushed, but covered for it by taking things out of Jenny Weaver's locker. 'Three textbooks,' he said, handing them to Lena so she could thumb through the pages. 'A notebook,' he continued. 'Two pencils and a pack of gum.'

Lena peered into the narrow cabinet, thinking that Jenny Weaver was a lot neater than she had been. There weren't even pictures taped on to the inside. 'That's all?' she asked, even though she could see for herself.

'That's all,' Brad answered, going through the books Lena had already checked.

Lena opened the notebook, which had a puppy on the cover. There were six colored tabs, one for each period, dividing the paper into sections. Almost every page was filled, but as far as she could tell there were only class notes. Jenny Weaver had not even doodled on the edges.

'She must've been a good student,' Lena said.

'She was thirteen and in the ninth grade.'

'Is that unusual?'

'Just means she skipped a grade,' Brad told her, stacking the books back in the locker the way they had found them. He checked the packet of gum to make sure it was just gum. 'She sure was neat.'

'Yeah,' Lena agreed, handing Brad the notebook. She waited while he thumbed through it, looking for something she might have missed.

'She wrote real neat,' Brad said in a sad voice.

'What'd you think of her on the retreat?'

Brad pushed his hair out of his eyes. 'She was quiet. I hate to say that I barely noticed her, but the girls pretty much kept to themselves. Mrs. Gray was supposed to be there to help out with them, but she got sick at the last minute. I didn't want to disappoint everybody, and the deposits were nonrefundable . . .' He shook his head. 'The boys were a handful. I had to spend most of my time looking after them.'

'What about Jenny and Lacey?'

'Well . . .' Brad's forehead wrinkled as he thought. 'They didn't do much, is the thing. The other kids skied and had fun. Jenny and Lacey kind of kept to themselves. They had their own room and I only really saw them around supper time.'

'How'd they act?'

'Kind of like they had their own language. They'd look at me and giggle, you know, like girls do.' He shifted uncomfortably, and Lena could see exactly why the girls had giggled. Brad probably knew as much about teenage girls as a goat did.

'They didn't act strange?'

'Stranger than giggling for no reason?'

'Brad . . . ,' Lena said. She stopped herself before she told him why the girls were laughing at him. Telling him they probably thought he was a dork would only make him pout, and Lena did not want to deal with that for the rest of the day.

He stared at her openly, waiting for her to finish.

'Just . . . ,' Lena began, then stopped again. 'Did it seem like Jenny was sick?'

'That's what the chief asked,' Brad said, and it seemed like he felt this was a compliment to Lena. 'He asked a lot of questions about Jenny and how she looked, who she was hanging around with.'

Lena closed the locker and indicated that they should continue walking. 'So?'

'She didn't look sick to me,' he said. 'I mean, like I told you, they kept to themselves. They didn't seem to like the other kids. Honestly, I don't know why they went. They're not exactly part of that group.'

'Meaning what?'

He shrugged. 'Popular, I guess. I mean, Lacey could've been. She's real cute, like a cheerleader.' He shook his head, as if he was still trying to figure it out. 'Jenny definitely wasn't popular. I didn't catch anyone being mean to her – I would'a done something about that – but they didn't go out of their way to be nice to her, either.'

'Weren't you supposed to be chaperoning them?'

He took this as it was meant, and immediately became defensive. 'I watched them as best I could, but it was just me there, and the boys were getting into a lot more trouble than the girls.'

Lena bit her tongue, wondering how someone as dense as Brad had gotten on the force.

'Here we go,' Brad said, stopping in front of the library. He held the door open for Lena, something Brad's mama had taught him to do from an early age. Working with Frank, then Jeffrey, Lena was so used to men opening doors for her that she barely noticed it anymore.

The library was cool, yet friendly. Student projects were tacked up on the walls, and row after row of bookshelves were packed almost to overflowing. About twenty computer stations – another education initiative funded by Georgia's lottery – sat empty, their monitors dark because the school's electrical system was not equipped to handle the extra load. There was a second-level balcony with an open railing lining the back wall, and for just a moment Lena imagined that some kid had probably sat up in that second level, thinking about how easy it would be to open fire on his classmates.

Brad was staring at her, an expectant look on his face. 'That's them,' he said, indicating three girls and three boys sitting by the librarian's desk. Lena knew instantly what Brad had been talking about. These were the popular kids. There was something about the way they sat there, talking and laughing with each other. They were an attractive bunch, dressed in the latest fashions and with that casual air of entitlement that kids have who are worshipped by their peers.

'Let's get this over with,' Lena told him, walking purposefully toward the table. She stood there for several seconds, but none of the kids acknowledged she was there. Lena gave Brad a wary look, then cleared her throat. When that didn't work, she rapped her knuckles on the table. The group started to quiet down, but two of the girls finished their conversation before looking up.

Lena said, 'I'm detective Adams, this is Officer Stephens.'

Two of the girls giggled as if they knew the best secret in the world. Lena was reminded of one of the many reasons she did not like kids, especially girls this age. There was nothing more vicious than a teenage girl. Maybe it was because boys were more capable of settling an argument with their fists, but girls at this age were much more conniving and torturous than anyone wanted to believe.

One of the giggling girls smacked her gum while the other said, 'We know Brad.'

Lena tried not to be hostile as Brad introduced the kids. 'Heather, Brittany, and Shanna,' he said, pointing them out. Then, indicating the boys, who were slouching so far into their chairs their butts were nearly touching the ground, 'Carson, Rory, and Cooper.' Lena wondered when parents had stopped giving their kids normal names. Probably around the time they stopped teaching them manners.

'Okay,' Lena began, sitting opposite them. 'Let's wrap this up quickly so y'all can go back to class.'

'Why are we here?' Brittany demanded, her tone as hostile as her posture.

'You were on the ski retreat with Officer Stephens,' Lena told them. 'Jenny Weaver was there. You know what happened to her Saturday?'

'Yeah,' Shanna said, smacking her gum. 'Y'all shot her.'

Lena took a deep breath and let it go. As shitty as she had been at this age, Lena would never have talked to a cop like this. She said, 'We're just asking some routine questions about her, trying to figure out why she did what she did.'

One of the boys spoke. Lena couldn't remember his name, but it was hardly relevant as they all looked alike. 'Does my father know you're talking to me?'

'What's your name?' Lena asked.

'Carson.'

'Carson,' she repeated, returning the belligerent stare he gave her. His eyes were bloodshot, the pupils dilated.

'What?' he said, finally breaking the stare. He crossed his arms, looking around the room as if he was bored.

'One of your classmates is dead,' Lena reminded him. 'Are you not interested in helping us find out why?'

'The "why" is because you shot her,' Carson answered, picking up his backpack. 'Can I go now?'

'Sure,' Lena told him. 'Why don't we get Dr. Clay to take a look in your bookbag?'

Carson smirked. 'You don't have probable cause.'

'No,' Lena agreed. 'But Dr. Clay doesn't need it.'

Carson knew she was right. He dropped the bag onto the floor. 'What do you want to know?'

Lena exhaled slowly. 'Tell me about Jenny Weaver.'

He waved his hand. 'I didn't know her, okay? She was on the retreat and all, but she and Lacey didn't really socialize.'

The other boys nodded. One of them said, 'They didn't like to party.'

Lena assumed that by 'party' he meant get high. From what little she knew about Jenny Weaver, this was not surprising.

'She was younger than us,' Carson added. 'We don't hang around with babies.'

Lena turned to the girls. 'What about y'all?'

Brittany started first. Her posture was as poor as the others', and her backbone seemed pliable, molding her into the back of the chair like Silly Putty. She sounded just how Lena had imagined she would: whiny and put-upon. There was something wrong with a society that let children talk to adults this way.

Brittany said, 'Jenny was weird.'

Lena tried to stir them up, asking, 'I thought y'all were friends.'

'We most certainly weren't,' Shanna toned in. 'I for one couldn't stand her.'

She said this as if she was proud of the fact.

'That so?' Lena asked.

Shanna's bravura dropped down a notch when she saw Lena was taking her seriously. She was considerably less confident when she said, 'We weren't friends.'

'None of us was really,' Heather said, and she seemed to be the logical one. She had uncrossed her arms, and Lena thought that, of the six, she was the only one who seemed to show any regret. Actually, Heather reminded Lena a little of herself at that age, on the periphery of things, more interested in sports than school gossip.

Heather said, 'Jenny was quiet most of the time. Even back in middle school.'

'You all went to the same school?'

They all nodded.

Heather indicated the other girls. 'All of us live near her. We rode the bus together for a while.'

Lena asked, 'But you weren't friends?'

'She didn't really have a lot of friends.' Heather was quiet for a few beats, then said, 'When she first moved into the neighborhood, I tried to talk to her and all, but she liked to stay home and read a lot. I invited her to hang out a couple of times, but she didn't want to, then I just stopped trying.'

'No one liked her,' Brittany provided. 'She was a real – what do you call it? – introvert.'

Shanna laughed, covering her mouth with her hand. 'Yeah, right,' she said.

Lena pointed out, 'She was friends with Lacey Patterson.'

The girls exchanged a look.

'What?' Lena asked.

They shrugged in unison. The boys were either comatose or not interested.

Lena sighed, sitting back in her chair. 'We'll sit here

all night until you tell me what I need to know.'

They seemed to believe her, even though Lena wanted nothing more than to leave this school.

Brittany spoke first. 'Lacey was only friends with her because of Mark.'

'Mark Patterson, Lacey's brother?'

'Okay,' Shanna said, holding out her hand palm up, her voice excited, as if she'd just been cracked by Lena's tough interrogation and was now giddy to tell them all they needed to know. 'She was a whore.'

'Shanna,' Heather gawked.

'You know it's true,' Shanna countered. 'She slept around, and not just with Mark.'

Brad stirred in his seat, looking as uncomfortable as Lena had ever seen him, which was saying a lot.

'Who did she sleep with?' Lena asked, looking at the boys. None of them would meet her eye.

'I don't know for sure, other than Mark,' Shanna said, as if she were talking with one of her girlfriends over the lunch table. 'But there were all kinds of rumors that she'd blow guys —'

'*Jeesh*,' Heather interrupted. 'She's dead, okay? Why do you have to say all this?'

'Because it's the truth!' Shanna countered, her voice high and excited.

Heather seemed angry. 'It was just rumors. Nobody knows if they were true or not.'

Lena asked, 'What were the rumors?'

Shanna was more than happy to supply this. 'She was having sex with some of the guys behind the gym after fifth period.'

'Intercourse or blow jobs?' Lena asked, still watching the guys.

Shanna shrugged, giving Heather a sideways glance. 'I wasn't there.'

'Heather was?'

'Heather doesn't like boys,' Shanna provided.

'Shut up!' Heather ordered, alarmed.

Lena wondered if she looked just as shocked as Brad. It was like having their very own Jerry Springer show right here in the school library.

'Okay,' Lena said, holding up her hands, trying to rein this in. 'What proof do you have that Jenny was sleeping around?'

The girls were silent, looking back and forth at each other.

'Nothing, right?' Lena asked. 'You can't tell me any of the boys she was with?'

Carson stirred in his chair, but he didn't volunteer anything.

'Mark,' Shanna said, shrugging. 'But Mark was with, like, everybody.'

'No kidding,' Brittany muttered, with something like regret in her tone.

Lena sighed, rubbing the bridge of her nose. She was getting the kind of headache that would probably last for the rest of the day. 'Okay, then who started the rumor?'

They all shrugged. This seemed to be the universal teenage response to any question. Lena wondered if they would later have rotator cuff problems.

'Pansy Davis told me,' said Shanna.

'She told me she slept with Ron Wilson Thursday night,' Brittany countered, 'And you know Ron was at Frank's house that night.'

'Frank said he sneaked out!' Shanna squealed.

'Stop, stop,' Lena said, holding up her hands. It was like being nibbled to death by ducks. 'None of y'all remembers where you heard the rumor?'

'It was just a known thing,' Heather told Lena. 'I

mean, I don't remember who told me, but Jenny just acted weird, okay? She would go off with boys she didn't know. Boys, like, in twelfth grade.'

'And you don't know their names?'

Heather shook her head. 'They're seniors.'

'Not popular seniors?' Lena asked.

'Some of them were skanky,' Brittany provided. 'Not seniors I would know. Not popular, okay? Sort of like Jenny.'

'Did she ride the bus home with them?'

'They had cars,' Heather said. 'Seniors are allowed to drive.'

'Do you remember any of the cars?'

Heather shook her head no, but Brittany snapped her fingers. 'There's one I remember.' She turned to Shanna. 'Do you remember that cool black Thunderbird?'

'A new one or an old one?' Lena asked.

'The older kind that's really big in the back,' Shanna said. 'It was really loud, like something was wrong with the engine or something.'

'Did the driver go to this school?'

They exchanged glances again. 'Maybe,' Brittany said.

'I don't think so,' Shanna added.

Heather shrugged. 'I don't pay attention to cars. It doesn't sound familiar.'

Lena looked at the boys. 'Do any of y'all recognize the car?'

They all shrugged or shook their heads.

Lena tried another line of questioning. 'Do y'all have any idea why Jenny wanted to kill Mark?'

The girls were silent, then Brittany finally said, 'We've all wanted to at least once.'

Lena sat back, crossing her arms. She stared at the boys, guessing why they were being silent. 'Okay,' she said, and they all started to stand, but she stopped them. 'Carson, Cory, Roper –'

'Rory and Cooper,' Brad corrected.

'Right,' Lena said. 'Whatever. You guys stay. The girls can leave.' She turned to Brad. 'Why don't you get their phone numbers and addresses?'

Brad nodded. He knew she was getting rid of him, but didn't seem to mind.

Lena sat at the table across from the boys, silent until they started to squirm in their chairs.

'Well?' she said.

Carson spoke first. 'Yeah, she was doing it.'

The other boys nodded.

'All of you slept with her?'

They did not answer.

'Blow jobs? Hand jobs?' Lena asked.

'Sex,' Carson clarified.

Lena felt her cheeks flush, but not from embarrassment. 'When was this?'

'Mark brought her over to my house one time. We were all partying.'

'I thought you said Jenny didn't party.'

'No, she didn't,' Carson said. 'Not usually, but Mark told her to have something to take the edge off.' He snorted a laugh. 'She did whatever Mark told her to do.'

'So,' Lena said, trying to get all of this straight, 'it was Mark, Jenny, and you three?'

They all nodded.

Carson said, 'She got a little drunk and started coming on to us.'

Lena pressed her lips together so she would not say anything.

'Mark said she'd do anything we wanted.'

One of the boys smiled. 'She sure did.'

'You all had sex with her?' Lena asked.

Carson shrugged, smirking. 'She was pretty drunk.'

Lena looked down at the table, trying to compose herself. 'So, she got drunk and you all had sex with her, Mark included?'

'Mark just watched,' one of the boys said. 'She let us do anything we wanted.' His anger sparked like a brush fire. 'She was a whore, okay? Why do you even care?'

Lena was startled by the hatred in his voice, as if it was Jenny's fault entirely that they had done this. She asked, 'What was your name?'

He looked down, mumbling, 'Rory.'

'All right, Rory,' Lena said. 'Did she have sex with any of you on the retreat?'

'Fuck no.' Carson crossed his arms angrily. 'That was the thing. Why the fuck else would we go on that stupid retreat?'

'You were having sex with her then?' Lena asked.

'No,' he said, still angry. 'She wouldn't go near us. She was fine at the party. Couldn't get enough of it.' He grabbed himself, as if Lena needed the visual aid. 'But over Christmas she was tight as a drum. Wouldn't even talk to us.' His lip curled. 'The bitch.'

Lena bit her tongue.

'She was a cock tease,' Carson said. 'She would've fucked a dog if Mark asked her to, but on the retreat it was like she was better than us.'

'What do you think changed this?' Lena asked.

He shrugged. 'Who the fuck cares?'

'Did you approach her on the retreat, or did she just ignore you?'

His lip curled. 'It was this way, all right? We offered her a little something to help her relax, told her we all wanted to party, and she froze up.'

'Exactly,' Rory said. 'It was like we weren't good enough for her all the sudden.'

'Hell, yeah,' Carson agreed. 'She was pretending like it didn't happen, and I said to her, "Hey, you know what you did, you whore."'

'Should've offered her money for it,' Rory suggested. 'Should've offered Mark money for it.'

'Right,' Lena mumbled, trying to remember the third boy's name. He had been very quiet during all of this, not hostile like the others. 'Cooper?' she guessed. He looked up, and she asked, 'Did you ever wonder why a thirteen-year-old girl would do something like that in the first place?'

'She liked it,' Cooper suggested, shrugging like they all shrugged. 'I mean, why else would she do it?' He looked up at his friends and his whole demeanor changed. He was more adamant and just as hateful as his friends when he insisted, 'She was a whore and she liked it.'

'Yeah,' Rory said, his tone filled with spite. 'I mean, you could tell she liked it.'

Lena suggested, 'Even though she was drunk?'

They didn't answer her.

'How could you tell she liked it?'

'Hell, man,' Rory said, 'who knows? Her face was buried in the couch the whole time.'

'Dude,' Carson laughed, holding up his hand for a high-five.

Lightning fast, Lena reached out and grabbed his hand. She was holding on to his wrist tight enough to feel the bones, and he grimaced from the pain.

She said, 'You think she enjoyed it, huh?'

'Hey,' Carson said, looking around the room for help. 'Come on, we were just having fun.'

'Fun?' Lena asked, jerking his arm like she might

rip it out of the socket. 'Where I come from, we call that rape, you little shit.' She let go of him because there was nothing else she could do short of taking out her gun and pistol-whipping him, which was tempting in light of the smirk that returned to his face when he sat back in his chair.

The bell rang for class changes, and Lena had to force herself not to jump at the loud sound. The boys had a Pavlovian response, gathering their bookbags, not waiting for Lena to release them.

She told them, 'Give Officer Stephens your phone numbers and addresses in case we have any questions.' She made sure she had their attention. 'I'm going to make sure every cop at the station knows your name.'

'Yeah,' Rory said. 'Whatever.'

They started to shuffle away, but Carson stayed, asking, 'You gonna tell Dr. Clay to search me or what?'

'I'm going to do every possible thing I can to make sure you're in jail before you're old enough to vote.'

'Shit,' he groaned, shuffling off.

Lena stood, wanting to get away from the table where she had heard their vile talk. She walked over to the computer area and rested her hand on the top of a monitor, feeling a cold sweat break out all over her body. It sickened her to know that boys this young were already learning to think this way about women. Lena could imagine *him* feeling the same way at that age, like girls were expendable. They all liked it. They were all whores.

'Lena?' Brad said, pulling her out of her thoughts. She looked back at the table and saw a couple of older women and one man taking their seats. 'Jenny's teachers,' Brad told her.

Lena put her hand to her chest, feeling claustrophobic. Brad was standing too close, and the room felt like it was getting smaller. 'Why don't you start?' Lena suggested, thinking she needed to get out of here to catch her breath. She walked toward the doors, but he stopped her.

'By myself?' he asked, standing too close to her again. She could smell his aftershave, and something that smelled like a strong breath mint. She could not lose it here. Lena knew if she got sick in front of Brad she wouldn't be able to go back to work again.

She indicated her cell phone as she took another step back. 'I'll call back to the station and check on things there, maybe see if we can find out who owns a black Thunderbird in the area.'

'I bet the principal would know,' Brad suggested, stepping forward. 'They keep logs on that, right? You can't park here unless you've got a parking pass.'

'Good thinking,' Lena said, taking another step back, aware that if she didn't get her breathing under control she would hyperventilate. 'I'll check that out while you interview them. Be sure to ask about what the girls said.'

He gave her a funny look. 'Are you okay?'

'Yeah,' she said. Suddenly, the room felt hot and unbearable, and she could feel her shirt starting to cling to her back. 'Just get preliminary stuff, an impression of what she was like. I'll be back as soon as I make some calls.'

He gave her a quick nod, his jaw tightening. 'All right,' he said, and she could tell he wanted to ask her again if she was okay.

She walked quickly into the hall, taking a deep breath to calm herself. She was still sweating, and took off her jacket. A kid jogged by. He slowed when he saw Lena's gun in her shoulder holster.

Lena slipped the jacket back on and leaned her head

against the wall. She closed her eyes until the nausea passed. After a few deep breaths she felt better, if not a hundred percent.

Lena flipped open her cell phone to give herself something to do. She dialed the station and talked to Marla about the car, glad that Frank wasn't in. It was still hard for Lena to talk to Frank, and part of her felt that he blamed Lena for what had happened. That same part of her agreed with him. She had been so stupid.

Even though she was standing less than a hundred yards from the front office, Lena called the principal and asked him about the black car. He went through his records while she waited on the phone and gave her the answer she had assumed all along: No one in the school had registered a car fitting that description. Lena thanked the principal, then hung up, thinking it felt good to get some things done instead of just treading water. The more time that passed on this case, the more they seemed to be moving away from solving it. She should talk to Mark again and see what his reaction was to this latest information. Jeffrey probably wouldn't let her near Mark again after what happened last time.

Lena opened the phone again and dialed her voice mail at home. The first message was from the video store in town, telling her that her tapes were late. The second was from Nan Thomas, Sibyl's lover.

'Lena,' Nan said, her low voice an irritated grumble. 'I've still got this stuff, Sibby's stuff. If you want it, let me know. I don't . . .' She stopped, then, 'It's just . . .'

Lena looked at her watch, wondering how much Nan's stuttering was costing her.

'I'll be at Suddy's tonight around eight,' Nan said.

'I'll have the boxes in my car if you want them. Meet me there if you . . . Otherwise, well . . .' Again, she stopped.

Lena fast forwarded, skipping the rest of the message. Suddy's was a gay bar on the outskirts of Heartsdale. There was no way in hell she was going to meet her sister's lover in a gay bar.

Lena's heart dropped into her stomach when she heard the next message. Hank said, 'Lee, Barry's sick. I gotta cover here tonight, maybe tomorrow.'

She closed her eyes, leaning her back against the wall as Hank explained that it would be easier for him to stay in Reece because there was a beer delivery tomorrow morning. She felt panicked again, then angry, because he had taken the coward's way out, leaving the message instead of calling her cell phone to explain.

Lena walked over to the other side of the hallway, looking out the window. There was an atrium in the middle of the school, and across the way she could see the cafeteria staff setting up the tables. She was so absorbed in their movements that she missed part of the last message. She rewound it and listened again.

'This is Pastor Fine, Lena,' the message began. 'I apologize, but I'll have to cancel our appointment this evening. One of our parishioners has taken ill. I need to be with the family right now.'

Lena snapped the phone closed as he asked for her to return his call so they could reschedule. She would let Jeffrey deal with that. She was not in the habit of letting herself think too far ahead, but the meeting with Fine had been something she had settled her mind on as something to do tonight. In a flash, she saw herself going back to her empty house, being alone. Panic enveloped her.

She put her hand to her chest, feeling her heart pounding against her rib cage. She was sweating, she noticed, and the back of her knees felt hot and sticky. She wanted to hear Hank's message again, to see if there was a nuance in his voice she had missed. Maybe he had left an opening. Maybe he was playing some kind of game to make her say that she wanted him there.

The final bell rang, a loud, piercing tone that vibrated in Lena's ears. She looked around the empty hallway, forgetting for a moment exactly where she was and why. As if out of a dream, she saw the image of a woman walking toward her. Lena's eyes felt like they blurred for a moment, then with a start she realized that she was in Jenny Weaver's school, and that Dottie Weaver was walking down the hall toward her.

'Shit,' Lena mumbled, looking down at her cell phone, willing it to ring. She flipped it open like she might make a call, but it was too late. Dottie Weaver was less than ten feet away holding a heavy-looking textbook in her hands.

Weaver stopped in the hallway, her mouth an angry straight line. Her eyes were bloodshot, like she had been crying for the last year. Red splotches were all over her face.

'Mrs. Weaver,' Lena said, flipping her phone closed.

Dottie shook her head, like she was too angry to say anything.

'We're just talking to some classmates and teachers to see if they can shed any light on –'

'Why can't you just leave her alone?' Dottie begged. 'Why can't you just let her rest in peace?'

'I'm sorry,' Lena told the woman, and she meant it.

'She was my baby.'

'I know that,' Lena answered, looking down at her phone.

'You're here raking her name over the coals, trying to make her out to be a bad person.'

'That's not my goal.'

'Liar!' Dottie screamed, throwing the book at Lena. Lena dropped her phone to catch it, but missed. The spine slammed into her stomach and she winced as it dropped to the floor.

'Mrs. Weaver,' Lena began, stooping to retrieve the textbook.

'The school wanted her book back,' Dottie said, her bottom lip trembling. 'Take it. Take it and tell them all they can go to hell.'

Lena tried to close the book without damaging the pages. She picked up her phone, which didn't seem to be broken.

Dottie dabbed her eyes with some tissue, then blew her nose. She did not leave, though, which Lena could not understand until she spoke again.

'Jenny loved this school,' the mother said, wrapping her arms around her stomach as if it brought her pain to speak. 'She loved being here.'

Lena thought now was as good a time as any to get this out of the way. 'Was she seeing anybody, Mrs. Weaver?'

Dottie shook her head. 'A psychiatrist?' she asked.

'A boy,' Lena clarified. 'Was she seeing any boys?'

'No,' Dottie snapped. 'Of course not. She was just a child.'

Lena nodded, feeling an encroaching dread. 'Some of the girls said she was.'

'Which girls?' Dottie asked, looking around as if they might be there.

'Just girls,' Lena answered. 'Friends from school.'

'She didn't have friends,' Dottie told her, narrowing her eyes, sensing some kind of trick. 'What are they saying about my daughter?'

Lena tried to think of a way to say it. 'That she . . .'

'That she what?' Dottie demanded.

Lena said, 'That she saw a lot of boys. That she was with a lot of boys.'

The slap came suddenly, and stung so much that after a few seconds the right side of Lena's face went numb. Before Lena could think to respond, let alone react, she was looking at the back of Dottie Weaver as the woman left the school.

The library door bumped open, and Brad stood there, holding the door for the group of teachers he had been interviewing. They looked tired, and a bit irritated, but this was pretty normal from Lena's recollection of teachers around lunchtime. One of them looked at Lena, and she could tell from the way the woman assessed her that she sensed something was wrong. The teacher raised an eyebrow as if to invite conversation, but Lena was too shocked to speak.

'Lena?' Brad prompted. She nodded that she was okay, wondering if her face was red where Dottie had slapped her.

Brad introduced all of the teachers, whose names Lena promptly forgot. He said, 'They know about the rumor.'

Lena blinked, not understanding.

'The rumor about Jenny,' Brad clarified. 'They said they had heard it.'

'None of us believed it,' one of the teachers said, her voice indicating that she had resigned herself a long time ago to the fact that there were things that went on in the school that no teacher would ever know about.

'She was a good student,' another teacher said. 'Very quiet, turned her work in on time. Her mother was involved.'

The other teachers nodded, and Lena duplicated the gesture, still too shocked to offer anything of consequence.

'Thank you for your time,' Brad said, moving things along. He shook hands with each of them in turn, and to the last one they gave him an encouraging look.

'I'm sorry we couldn't help more,' one said.

Another told him, 'If we think of anything, we'll call you.'

The woman who had looked at Lena was last, and she told Brad, 'You did an excellent job, Bradley. I'm very impressed.'

Brad beamed. 'Thank you, ma'am,' he said, tucking his head down like a happy puppy. He waited until the teachers were gone before asking Lena, 'Whose book?'

'Jenny Weaver's,' Lena provided, thumbing through the pages to see if any notes were tucked in. It was empty, just like the others.

'How'd you get it?'

Lena could not answer him. 'Here,' she said, handing him the book. 'Take it to the front office, then meet me in the car.'

The parking lot of Suddy's was pretty empty, even at eight o'clock. If Sibyl and Nan's life had been any indication, probably most of the lesbians in town were at home, watching sitcoms. Not that Sibyl could watch them, she was blind, but she liked to listen sometimes, and Nan would narrate what was happening.

Lena crossed her arms, thinking about Sibyl, and

how she had looked the last time Lena had seen her; not the time in the morgue, but the day before she had died. As usual, Sibyl had been full of energy, and laughing at something that had happened in one of her classes. Above everything, Sibyl loved teaching, and she had taken great joy from being in front of a classroom. Maybe that was why Lena had had such a negative reaction to being at the school today.

Before she could stop herself, Lena got out of the car. Suddy's was nice by most bar standards. Compared to the Hut, Hank's bar over in Reece, it was a palace. Outside, the decor was spare, probably because a place like this would not want to draw attention to itself. Other than a Budweiser sign with a neon rainbow flag incorporated into the logo, the building was pretty nondescript.

The interior was more festive, but the lights were down low, making the room a little too intimate for Lena. Something soft played on the jukebox, and a spinning mirrored ball did a slow turn over what looked like the dance floor. Lena had always been uncomfortable with this side of Sibyl, and never understood how someone who was so pretty, who was so outgoing and energetic, could choose this kind of life for herself. Sibyl had always wanted children, always wanted to be taken care of and loved. Lena would not have predicted this kind of life for her sister in a million years.

When Sibyl had first come out to Lena fifteen years ago, Lena's response had been an emphatic, 'No, you're not.' Even after Sibyl moved in with Nan, Lena had still let herself believe that Sibyl was not gay. It sounded trite to say, but Lena could not help thinking in the back of her mind that it was just a phase, and that one day Sibyl would laugh about her confusion and settle

down and have children. Being Sibyl's twin complicated matters, because Lena had always felt that a
piece of herself was in Sibyl, and a piece of Sibyl
was in Lena. It was unsettling to think that Lena
might somewhere in her psyche share Sibyl's sexual
leanings.

Lena dismissed this as she walked across the room.
Two women at a corner table ignored her completely,
seeming more intent upon pushing their tongues down
each other's throat than seeing who had walked
through the door. The bartender was reading a newspaper when Lena approached her, and she looked up,
doing a startled double take.

The woman said, 'You must be her sister.'

Lena sat a couple of stools down from her. 'I'm
meeting someone here.'

The woman closed the paper. She walked over and
offered Lena her hand. 'I'm Judy,' she said.

Lena stared at the hand, then reluctantly shook it.
The woman was tall, with long dark hair and a heart-
shaped face. Her eyes were an intense hazel, which
Lena noticed because the woman would not stop
staring at her.

'Beer, please,' Lena said, then, 'Make it a Jim Beam
instead.'

Judy paused, then walked over to the liquor display
behind the bar. 'Sibyl never drank,' she said, as if by
extension this meant that Lena, her twin, would not
drink.

Lena pointed out, 'She didn't fuck men, either.'

Judy conceded the point. 'Jim Beam?'

'Yeah,' Lena answered, trying to sound bored as she
took some money out of her front pocket. She had
changed into jeans and a T-shirt at home before
coming here, a decision she now regretted. She prob-

ably looked gayer than the women in the corner to these people.

Judy said, 'She liked cranberry juice, though.'

'Could you make that a double?' Lena asked, tossing a twenty-dollar bill onto the bar.

Judy glanced at her before filling the order. 'We all really miss her.'

'I'm sure you do,' Lena told her, aware that she sounded glib. She stared at the dark liquid in her glass, remembering that the last time she had anything to drink was the night Sibyl had died. Lena did not like alcohol, because she hated the feeling of being out of control. Not that she had control of anything lately, anyway.

Lena looked at the clock over the bar. It was five till eight.

Judy asked, 'Who you meeting here?'

Lena knocked the drink back in one swallow. 'Jim Beam,' she said, tapping the glass.

Judy gave her another look, but retrieved the bottle from the shelf.

To discourage conversation, Lena turned on the stool, looking out on the dance floor. A lone woman stood there, her eyes closed as she swayed to the beat. There was something familiar about her, but the light was bad, and Lena's memory did not want to work. Still, Lena watched her, wondering at the self-absorbed way the woman danced, as if no one else were in the room. As if nothing else mattered.

The song changed, and Lena recognized the tune before the lyrics to Beck's 'Debra' came from the speakers. Mark Patterson popped into her mind again. There was something sensual and disturbing about the way the dancer moved that reminded her of the young man. She watched the dancer, wondering again what the hell had been going on with Jenny Weaver. What was Mark's hold over her? What was it about him that would make a thirteen-year-old kid prostitute herself? It did not make sense.

Lena wondered if this was the way Mark Patterson would dance, though she could not imagine the kid doing something so audacious as standing in the middle of an empty dance floor. The thought surprised her, because Lena was not aware that she had put herself in a position to make assumptions about Mark's personality. She knew so very little about him, yet somehow, her subconscious had assigned him certain traits.

Lena turned back around to break the spell. Judy was reading her paper, having left Lena's drink and her change on the bar. Lena was thinking about what to leave for a tip when she noticed her reflection in the mirror. For just a moment, she startled, and Lena imagined she looked much as Judy had when Lena had first walked into the room. In a split second, Sibyl was there, and Lena felt her heart jump at the sight.

Suddenly, shouting came from outside, and a crowd of people walked into the bar. They were laughing and raucous, all dressed in matching softball uniforms. The pants were black with white stripes up the sides, the shirts white with the word BUSHWHACKERS across the chest.

'Jesus Christ,' Lena groaned, getting the reference. She stood up as she recognized Nan Thomas in the center of the group. The mousy librarian had a neon-pink athletic strap around her glasses and the front of her shirt was streaked with dirt as if she had slid across home plate. Unlike some of the others in the group, Nan showed no sign of mistaking Lena for her sister. As a matter of fact, she frowned.

Someone patted Lena on the back, and she turned around, surprised to see Hare Earnshaw standing beside her. He was dressed in jeans and a Bushwhacker T-shirt as well as a hat with a large B on it.

'How's it going, Lena?' Hare asked.

Maybe it was the alcohol, but Lena blurted out a surprised, 'You're gay?' to him before she could stop herself. Hare was a doctor in town. Lena had actually seen him a couple of years ago for a cold that would not go away.

Hare laughed at her surprise. 'I play on the team,' he said, indicating his shirt. Then, he leaned closer, giving her a coy wink. 'I'm the catcher.'

Lena backed up right into Nan. There were people everywhere, though they seemed to be involved in their own conversations about the game they had just played. Lena pulled at the neck of her shirt, feeling claustrophobic. She moved away from the group, toward the front door.

'Lee?' Nan said, then corrected herself before Lena could, saying, 'Lena.'

'I told you not to call me that,' Lena said, crossing her arms.

'I know,' Nan held her hands up, palms out. 'I'm sorry. It's just that Sibby always called you that.'

Lena stopped her. 'Can we get the stuff, please? I need to get home.' Her voice went down on the word 'home' as she thought about the empty house. Hank had not answered the phone when she called the Hut looking for him. The bastard was obviously ignoring her. It was so typical of him to leave her when she needed him most.

'It's out in the parking lot,' Nan said, holding the door open for Lena. Lena stopped, waiting for Nan to go first. It was one thing to let Brad Stephens hold a door open for her; Lena would be damned if she would let some woman do it.

Nan talked as they walked out to the parking lot. 'I tried to keep it the same way she had it,' she said, a forced lightness to her voice. 'You know how Sibby liked to keep things orderly.'

'She had to,' Lena shot back, thinking it was obvious that a blind person would have a system to things so that they would not be lost.

If Nan noticed Lena's biting tone, she ignored it.

'Here,' Nan said, stopping in front of a white Toyota Camry. The driver's side window was down, and she reached in, popping the trunk.

'You should keep your doors locked,' Lena told her.

'Why?' Nan asked, and she really seemed to be puzzled.

'You've got your car parked in front of a gay bar. I would think you might want to be a little more careful.'

Nan tucked her hands into her waist. 'Sibyl was killed in a diner in broad daylight. Do you really think locking my car door is going to protect me?'

She had a point, but Lena was not going to give it to her. 'I wasn't saying you could get killed. Someone might vandalize the car or something.'

'Well . . .' Nan shrugged, and for just a moment, she seemed exactly like Sibyl. Not that Nan was in any way similar to Sibyl in appearance, it was just her 'whatever happens will happen' attitude.

'These are some of her tapes,' Nan said, handing Lena a box that was about eighteen inches square. 'She labeled them in braille, but most of them have their own titles.'

Lena took the box, surprised at how heavy it was.

'These are some photographs,' Nan said, stacking

another box on top of the first. 'I don't know why she had them.'

'I asked her to keep them for me,' Lena provided, remembering the day she had brought the box of pictures to Sibyl. Greg Mitchell, Lena's last boyfriend, had just left her, and Lena did not want the photographs she had of him in the house.

'I'll get this one,' Nan offered, picking up the last box. It was bigger than the other two, and she rested it on her knee to close the trunk. 'This is just a bunch of stuff she had in the closet. A couple of awards from high school, a track ribbon I guess is yours.'

Lena nodded, walking to her Celica.

'I found a picture of you two at the beach,' Nan said, laughing. 'Sibyl's got a sunburn. She looks miserable.'

Because she was in front of Nan, Lena allowed a smile. She remembered the day, how Sibyl had insisted on staying outside even though Hank had warned her it was too hot. Sibyl's black glasses had shaded her eyes, and when she took them off, the only part of her face that was not beet red was where the glasses had been. She looked like a raccoon for days after.

'. . . stop by Saturday to pick them up,' Nan was saying.

'What?' Lena asked.

'I said that you can stop by Saturday to go through the other stuff. I'm donating her computer and equipment to the school for the blind over in Augusta.'

'What other stuff?' Lena asked, thinking Nan meant to throw away Sibyl's things.

'Just some papers,' Nan told her, setting the box down at her feet. 'School stuff, mostly. Her dissertation, a couple of essays. That kind of thing.'

'You're just going to throw them away?' Lena demanded.

'Give them away. They're not really valuable,' Nan said, as if she were talking to a child.

'They were valuable to Sibyl,' Lena countered, aware she was close to yelling. 'How can you even think about giving them away?'

Nan looked down at the ground, then back at Lena. The patronizing tone was still there. 'I told you that you're more than welcome to have them if you like. They're in braille. It's not like you can read them.'

Lena snorted a laugh, setting the boxes on the ground. 'Some lover you were.'

'What the hell do you mean by that?'

'Obviously, it meant something to her or she wouldn't have kept it,' Lena said. 'But go ahead and give it away.'

'Excuse me,' Nan said, indicating the boxes. 'How many times did I have to call you and beg you to take this stuff?'

'That's different,' Lena said, digging in her pocket for her keys.

'Why?' Nan shot back. 'Because you were in the hospital?'

Lena glanced back at the bar. 'Lower your voice.'

'Don't tell me what to do,' Nan said, her tone louder. 'You don't get to question me about whether or not I loved your sister. Do you get that?'

'I wasn't questioning you,' Lena answered, wondering how this had escalated so quickly. She could not even remember what had started this, but Nan was obviously pissed.

'The hell you weren't,' Nan barked. 'You think you're the only one around here who loved Sibyl? I shared my life with her.' Nan lowered her voice. 'I shared my bed with her.'

Lena winced. 'I know that.'

'Do you?' Nan said. 'Because I'll tell you what, Lena, I am sick and tired of the way you treat me, as if I'm some sort of pariah.'

'Hey,' Lena stopped her. 'I'm not the one playing softball for Suddy's.'

'I don't know how she put up with this,' Nan mumbled, almost to herself.

'Put up with what?'

'Your misogynistic cop bullshit, for one.'

'Misogynistic?' Lena repeated. 'You're calling me misogynistic?'

'And homophobic,' Nan added.

'Homophobic?'

'Are you a parrot now?'

Lena felt her nostrils flare. 'Don't fuck with me, Nan. You don't know how.'

Nan didn't seem to catch the warning. 'Why don't you go back into that bar and meet some of your sister's friends, Lee? Why don't you talk to the people who really knew her and cared about her?'

'You sound like Hank,' Lena told her. 'Oh, I see,' she said, putting the pieces together. 'You've been talking to Hank about me.'

Nan pressed her lips together. 'We're worried about you.'

'That so?' Lena laughed. 'Great, my speed freak uncle and my dead sister's dyke girlfriend are worried about me.'

'Yes,' Nan said, standing her ground. 'We are.'

'This is so fucking stupid,' Lena said, trying to laugh it off. She slipped the key into the lock, opening the trunk.

'You wanna know what's stupid?' Nan said. 'What's stupid is me giving a crap about what you do. What's stupid is my caring about the fact that you're throwing your life away.'

'Nobody asked you to look after me, Nan.'

'No,' Nan agreed. 'But it's what Sibyl would have wanted.' Her tone was more moderate now. 'If Sibyl were here right now, she would be saying the same thing.'

Lena swallowed hard, trying not to let Nan's words get to her, mostly because they rang true. Sibyl was the only person who had ever really been able to get to Lena.

Nan said, 'She would be saying that you need to deal with this. She would be worried about you.'

Lena stared at the jack in the trunk of the car because it was the only thing she could focus on.

Nan said, 'You're so angry.'

Lena laughed again, but the sound was hollow even to her. 'I think I have pretty damn good reason to be.'

'Why? Because your sister was killed? Because you were raped?'

Lena reached out, holding on to the trunk of her car. If only it were that easy, Lena thought. She was not simply mourning the death of Sibyl, she was also mourning the death of herself. Lena did not know who she was anymore, or why she even got up in the morning. Everything Lena had been before the rape had been taken away from her. She no longer knew herself.

Nan spoke again, and when she did, she said his name. Lena watched Nan's lips forming the word, saw his name travel through the space between them like an airborne poison.

'Lee,' Nan said, 'don't let him ruin your life.'

Lena kept her grip on the car, certain her knees would buckle if she let go.

Nan used his name again, then said, 'You've got to deal with it, Lena. You've got to deal with it now, or you'll never be able to move on.'

Lena hissed, 'Fuck off, Nan.'

Nan stepped forward, like she might put her hand on Lena's shoulder.

'Get the fuck away from me,' Lena warned.

Nan gave a long sigh, giving up. She turned and walked back to the bar without giving Lena a second glance.

Lena sat in the empty parking lot of the Grant Piggly Wiggly, sipping cheap whiskey straight from the bottle. She was past the harsh taste, and her throat was so numb from the alcohol that she could barely feel it going down. There was another bottle in the seat beside her, and she would probably go through that one, too, before the night was over. All Lena wanted to do was stay in her car in this empty parking lot and try to figure out what was happening in her life. Nan was right to some degree. Lena had to get over this, but that did not mean talking to some idiot like Dave Fine. What Lena needed to do was get her shit together and stop obsessing about stupid things. She just needed to get on with her life. She needed, Lena supposed, a night of self-pity, where she finally went through the motions of grieving and letting things go.

She listened to snippets of Sibyl's tapes, popping them one by one into the cassette player to see what was on them. She should label them, but she could not find a pen. Besides, it seemed wrong to write on Sibyl's things, even though Sibyl would not have minded. There were a few tapes that were already labeled, most of them Atlanta singers: Melanie Hammet, Indigo Girls, a couple more names Lena did not recognize. She ejected the last tape, which had been some kind of compilation of classical music on one side and old Pretenders tunes on the other, and tossed it in with the others.

Lena reached around to the back seat and pulled at the last box. It was heavier than the others, and when she finally managed to get it to the front, pictures spilled onto the seat beside her. Most of the photos were of Greg Mitchell and Lena at various stages in their relationship. There were some beach pictures, of course, as well as snapshots from the time they went to Chattanooga to see the aquarium. Lena blinked away tears, trying to remember what it had been like that day, standing in line to see the exhibit, the breeze coming off the Tennessee River so strong that Greg had stood behind her to keep her warm. She had loved the way her body felt when he put his arms around her waist, rested his chin on her shoulder. It was the only time in her life she could remember ever being truly content. Then, the line had moved, and Greg had stepped back, and said something about the weather, or a story on the news, and Lena had purposefully picked a fight with him for no reason whatsoever.

Lena thumbed through another stack of pictures, sipping the alcohol with deliberate care. She was beyond drunk now, but not beyond caring. Looking at the photos, she wondered how there had ever been a time when she wanted a man's company, or felt like being alone with one, let alone intimate. For all Lena had said when Greg left her, she had still wanted him back.

Lena found the picture Nan had told her about.

Sibyl did look miserable, but she was still smiling for the camera. They were both about seven in the photograph. At that age, they had looked almost identical, though one of Sibyl's front teeth was missing because she had tripped and knocked it out on the front porch. The tooth that grew in to replace it was snaggled, but it gave Sibyl's mouth some character. At least, that's what Hank had told her.

Lena smiled as she spotted a stack of pictures bound together with a rubber band. Hank had given her an instant camera for her fifteenth birthday, and Lena had used two boxes of film in one day, taking pictures of everything she could think of. Later, she had done her own editing, splicing some of the images together. There was one picture in particular she remembered, and Lena thumbed through the stack until she found it. Using a razor blade, she had made a kisscut over the image, scoring just the surface of the photograph but not cutting all the way through to the back, and excised Hank from the scene. Bonnie, their golden lab, had been glued in his place.

'Bonnie,' Lena breathed, aware that she was crying openly now. This was one of the reasons Lena did not drink alcohol. The dog had been dead for ten years and here she was, crying over him like it was just yesterday.

Lena got out of the car, taking the bottles of liquor with her. She wanted to get them out of the car because she knew she would end up passed out if they stayed there. As she walked, she realized that she was closer to this than she had thought in the car. Her feet felt like they did not belong to her, and she tripped several times over nothing in particular. The store had been closed for hours, but she still checked the windows to make sure no one saw her stumbling across the parking lot. Lena pressed her palm against the side of the building as she walked around it, holding both bottles with her free hand. When she got to the back of the store and let go of the wall, she tumbled, her knees giving out from under her. Somehow, she caught herself with one hand and kept from falling, face first, onto the asphalt.

'Shit,' she cursed, seeing rather than feeling the cut on her palm. Lena stood, more determined now than ever to throw away the alcohol. She would sleep some of it off in her car and drive home when she could see straight.

Reeling back, she tossed the near empty bottle into the Dumpster. It made a rewarding crash as it broke against the metal wall inside the steel chamber. Lena picked up the other bottle and tossed it in. A couple of thunks later, and the bottle had not broken. She contemplated for just a moment going into the Dumpster and retrieving the bottle, but stopped herself before she did.

There was a stand of trees behind the building, and Lena walked over, her feet still feeling as if they were asleep. She bent over and made herself vomit. The alcohol was bitter coming up, and the taste made her sicker than she would have thought possible. By the end, she was on her knees, dry heaving, much as she had been in the car with Hank.

Hank, Lena thought, making herself stand. She was so angry with him that she thought just for a moment about driving into Reece, to the Hut, and confronting him. He had said four months ago that he would stay with Lena as long as she needed him. Where the hell was he now? Probably at some damn A.A. meeting talking about how worried he was about his niece, talking about how much he wanted to support her instead of actually being here and supporting her.

The Celica turned over with a rewarding purr, and Lena gassed the car, thinking just for a moment about letting off on the brake and smashing into the front windows of the Piggly Wiggly. The impulse was surprising, but not completely unexpected. A sense of worthlessness was taking over, and Lena was not fighting it. Even after throwing up the alcohol, her brain was still buzzing, and it was as if her barriers had been broken down, and her mind was letting her think about things that she did not really want to think about.

She was thinking about *him*.

The drive home was dicey, Lena crossing the yellow line more often than not. She nearly ran into the shed behind her house, the brakes squealing on the drive as she slammed them on at the last minute. She sat in the car, looking at the dark house. Hank had not even bothered to turn on the back porch light.

Lena reached over and unlocked the glove box. She pulled out her service revolver and chambered a round. The clicking sound from the bolt action was solid in her ears, and for some reason Lena found herself looking at the gun in a different light. She stared at the black metal casing, even sniffed the grip. Before she knew it, she had put the muzzle in her mouth, her finger resting on the trigger.

Lena had seen a girl do this before. The woman had put the gun right into her mouth and almost without hesitation pulled the trigger because she had seen this as the only way to get the memories out of her brain. The aftershock of the single shot to the head still reverberated to Lena, and what she remembered most of all from that day was that parts of the woman's brain and skull had actually dug into the Sheetrock on the wall behind her.

Lena sat in the car, breathing slowly, feeling the cold metal against her lips. She pressed her tongue against the barrel as she considered the situation. Who would find her? Would Hank come home early? Brad, she thought, because Brad was supposed to pick her up for work in the morning. What would he think, seeing Lena like this? What would that do to Brad to see Lena in her car with the back of her head blown out? Was he strong enough to handle it? Could Brad Stephens go on with his life, with his job, after finding Lena like that?

'No,' Lena said. She ejected the clip and kicked out the chambered round, then locked all of it back in the glove box.

She got out of the car quickly, jogging up the stairs to the back porch. Her hands were steady as she unlocked the door and turned on the kitchen light. Lena walked through the house, turning on all the lights as she went. She took the steps upstairs two at a time, turning on more lights. By the time she was finished, the house was completely lit up.

Of course, with the lights on, anyone could look through the windows and see her. Lena reversed her steps, turning off the lights as she ran down the stairs. She could have pulled the curtains and closed the blinds, but there was something rewarding about moving, getting her heart pumping. She had not been to the gym in months, but her muscles remembered the movements.

When she had left the hospital, the doctors had given Lena enough pain medication to kill a horse. It was as if they wanted to give her as much medication as humanly possible to numb her. They had probably thought it would be easier on her to be medicated than to consider what had happened to her. The hospital shrink they had made Lena talk to even offered to give her Xanax.

Lena ran back upstairs and opened the medicine cabinet in her bathroom. Alongside the usual things were a half bottle of Darvocet and a full bottle of Flexeril. The Darvocet was for pain, but the Flexeril was a heavy-duty muscle relaxer that had knocked Lena on her ass the first time she had taken it. She had stopped taking them because at the time it was more important for her to stay alert than not to feel the pain.

Lena read the labels on the bottles, looking past the warnings to take the medications with food and not operate heavy machinery. There were at least twenty Darvocet and twice as many Flexeril. She turned on the faucet, letting the cold water run for a while. Her hand was perfectly steady as she took the cup out of its holder and filled it nearly to the brim.

'So,' Lena mumbled, looking at the clear water, thinking she should say something important or poignant about her life. There was no one to hear her words, though, so it seemed silly to be talking to herself at this point. She had never really believed in God, so it wasn't as if Lena expected to meet up with Sibyl in the great hereafter. There would be no streets of gold for her to walk on. Not that Lena was well-versed in religious doctrine, but she was pretty sure that anyone who committed suicide, no matter what the religion, was pretty fucked as far as heaven was concerned.

Lena sat down on the toilet, considering this. For just a brief moment, she wondered whether or not she was still drunk. Certainly, she would not be contemplating such an act if she were sober. Would she?

Lena looked around the bathroom, which had never

been her favorite room in the house. The tiles were orange with white grout, a popular color scheme when the house had been built in the seventies, but now was tacky. She had tried to compensate for the color by adding other colors: a dark-blue bathmat by the tub, a dark-green cover for the box of Kleenex on the back of the toilet. The towels tied the colors together, but not in a pleasing way. Nothing had helped the room. It seemed appropriate, then, that she would die here.

Lena opened the bottles and spread the pills out on the vanity. The Darvocet were large, but the Flexeril were more like little breath mints. Moving them around with her index finger, she alternated the big pills with the little pills, then moved them all back into their own separate piles. She sipped some of the water as she did this, and realized that to some degree she was playing.

'Okay,' Lena said. 'This one is for Sibby.' She opened her mouth and popped in one of the Darvocets.

'To Hank,' she said, chasing it with a Flexeril. Then, because they were small, she popped two more Flexeril, followed by two Darvocet. She did not swallow yet, though. Lena wanted to take them all at the same time, and there was one more person she felt the need to recognize.

Her mouth was so full that when she said his name, the sound was muffled.

'These are for you,' she mumbled, scooping the remaining Flexeril into the palm of her hand. 'These are for you, you fucking bastard.'

She shoved the handful into her mouth, tilting back her head. She stopped midtilt, staring at Hank in the doorway. They were both quiet, their eyes locked on to each other's. He stood there with his arms crossed, his lips a firm line.

'Do it,' he finally said.

Lena sat there on the toilet, holding the pills in her mouth. Some of them had started to break down, and she could taste an acrid, powdery paste forming at the back of her mouth.

'I won't call an ambulance, if that's what you're thinking.' He gave a tight shrug. 'Go ahead and do it if that's what you want to do.'

Lena felt her tongue going numb.

'You scared?' Hank asked. 'Too scared to pull the trigger, too scared to swallow the pills?'

Her eyes watered from the taste in her mouth, but she still did not swallow. Lena felt frozen. How long had he been watching her? Was this some kind of test she had failed?

'Go on!' Hank yelled, his voice so loud that it echoed against the tiles.

Lena's mouth opened, and she started to spit out the pills into her hand but Hank stopped her. He crossed the small bathroom in two steps and clamped his hands around her head, one over her mouth, the other behind her so that she could not pull away. Lena dug her nails into his flesh, trying to pull his hand from her mouth, but he was too strong for her. She fell forward off the toilet, onto her knees, but he moved down with her, keeping her head locked between his hands.

'Swallow them,' Hank ordered, his voice gravelly and low. 'That's what you want to do, swallow them!'

She started to shake her head back and forth, trying to tell him no, that she did not want to do this, that she could not do this. Some of the pills started to slide down her throat, and she constricted the muscles in her neck to stop them. Her heart was beating so hard that she thought it might explode.

'No?' Hank demanded. 'No?'

Lena kept shaking her head, digging at his hand to release her. He finally let go, and she fell back against the tub, her head popping against the edge.

Hank threw open the toilet lid and half grabbed, half dragged her toward it. He pushed her head down into the bowl and she finally opened her mouth, gagging, spitting the pills out. Retching sounds echoed back at her until her mouth was empty. She used her fingers to clean around her gums and then used her nails, scraping at her tongue to get the taste out.

Hank stood, and when she looked up at him she could tell that he was pissed as hell.

'You bastard,' she hissed, wiping her mouth with the back of her hand.

His foot moved, and she thought he was going to kick her. Lena curled, anticipating the blow, but it did not come.

'Get cleaned up,' Hank ordered. With an open palm, he swept the remaining pills off the basin and onto the floor. 'Clean up this shit.'

Lena moved to do as she was told, walking on her hands and knees, collecting the Darvocet.

Hank leaned against the wall, his arms crossed over his chest. His voice was softer now, and she looked up at him, surprised to see that there were tears in his eyes. 'If you ever do that again . . . ,' he began, then looked away. He put his hand over his mouth as if to fight back the words. 'You're all I got, baby.'

Lena was crying now, too. She said, 'I know, Hank.'

'Don't . . . ,' he began.

Lena asked, 'Don't what?'

He slid down the wall, sitting on the floor with his hands to his side. He stared at her openly, his eyes searching hers for something. 'Don't leave me,' he whispered, his words hanging in the air above them like a dark cloud.

The distance between them was only a few feet, but to Lena it felt like an endless chasm. She could reach out to him. She could thank him. She could promise him that she would never try this again.

She could have done any or all of those things, but what Lena ended up doing was picking up the pills off the floor one by one and throwing them into the toilet.

TUESDAY

THURSDAY

TEN

'Hold on, Sam,' Sara coaxed, struggling to hold a wriggling two year old in her lap so that she could listen to his chest.

'Be still for Dr. Linton, Sammy,' his mother said in a singsong voice.

'Sara?' Elliott Felteau, who worked at the clinic for Sara, poked his head into the room. She had hired Elliott right out of his residency to help her out, but so far Sara had spent most of her time holding his hand. It was a trade-off, because an older doctor would have insisted on some kind of partnership, and Sara was not about to relinquish her control. She had worked too hard to get to where she was to start listening to someone else's opinions.

'Sorry,' Elliott apologized to the mother, then said to Sara, 'Did you tell Tara Collins that Pat could play football this weekend? She needs a medical release before the school will let him back on the team.'

Sara stood, taking Sam with her. His legs wrapped around Sara's waist, and she scooted him up on her hip as she lowered her voice, asking Elliott, 'Why is this question coming from you?'

'She called and asked for me,' he told her. 'Said she didn't want to bug you.'

Sara tried to unclench Sam's fist as he tugged her

hair. 'No, he can't play this weekend,' she whispered. 'I told her that on Friday.'

'It's just an exhibition game.'

'He has a concussion,' Sara countered, the tone of her voice a warning to Elliot.

'Hmm,' Elliott said, backing out of the room. 'I guess she thought I'd be an easier target.'

Sara took a deep, calming breath, then turned back around. 'Sorry about that,' she said, sitting down in the chair. Thankfully, Sam had stopped fidgeting, and she was able to listen to his chest.

'Pat Collins is their star quarterback,' the mother said. 'You're not going to let him play?'

Sara avoided the question. 'His lungs seem clear,' she told the woman. 'Make sure he finishes his antibiotics, though.'

She started to hand the child back to his mother, but stopped. Sara lifted up Sam's shirt and checked his chest, then his back.

'Is something wrong?'

Sara shook her head no. 'He's fine,' she told the woman, and the boy was. There was no reason to suspect abuse. Of course, Sara had thought the same thing with Jenny Weaver.

Sara walked to the pocket door and slid it open. Molly Stoddard, her nurse, was at the nurses' station writing out a lab request. Sara waited until she was finished, then dictated Sam's directions.

'Make sure I follow up,' Sara told her.

Molly nodded, still writing. 'You doing all right today?'

Sara thought about it, and decided that no, she was not doing all right. She was actually pretty on edge, and had been since her confrontation with Lena yesterday afternoon. She felt guilty, and ashamed of herself for letting her temper get the better of her. Lena had been doing her job, no matter what Sara thought about it. It was unprofessional to question the young detective, especially in front of Jeffrey. On top of that, what Sara had said was not only inexcusable, it was just plain mean. Sara was not the kind of person who liked to be mean. It was not in her nature to attack, and the more Sara thought about it, the more she believed that she *had* attacked Lena. Of all people, Sara should have known better.

'Hello?' Molly prompted. 'Sara?'

'Yes?' Sara said, then, 'Oh, I'm sorry. I'm just . . .' She nodded toward her office so that they could get out of the hallway.

Molly let Sara go first, then slid the door closed behind her. Molly Stoddard was a compact woman with what could be called a handsome face. In great contrast to Sara, the nurse was always neatly dressed, her white uniform starched to within an inch of its life. The only jewelry Molly wore was a thin silver necklace that she kept tucked into the collar of her uniform. The smartest thing Sara had ever done was hire Molly as her nurse, but some days Sara felt tempted to snatch off the woman's hat and ruffle her hair, or accidentally spill ink on her perfect uniform.

'You've got about five minutes before your next appointment,' Molly told her. 'What's wrong?'

Sara leaned her back against the wall, tucking her hands into her white lab coat. 'Did we miss something?' she said, then amended, 'Did *I* miss something?'

'Weaver?' Molly asked, though Sara could tell from her reaction that the other woman knew. 'I've been asking myself that same question, and the answer is I don't know.'

'Who would do that?' Sara asked, then realized Molly had no idea what she was talking about. The physical findings from the autopsy were hardly public, and even though Sara trusted Molly, she did not feel like she was in a position to share the details. Molly probably would not want to hear them.

'Kids are hard to explain,' Molly provided.

'I feel responsible,' Sara told the nurse. 'I feel like I should have been there for her. Or paid more attention.'

'We see thirty to forty kids a day, six days a week.'

'You make it sound like an assembly line.'

Molly shrugged. 'Maybe it is,' she said. 'We do what we can do. We take care of them, we give them their medicine, we listen to their problems. What else is there?'

'Treat 'em and street 'em,' Sara mumbled, remembering the phrase from her E.R. days.

Molly said, 'It's what we do.'

'I didn't come back here to work like this,' Sara said. 'I wanted to make a difference.'

'And you do, Sara,' Molly assured her. She stepped closer, putting her hand on Sara's arm. 'Listen, honey, I know what you're going through, and I'm telling you that I see you here every day, putting your heart and soul into this job.' She waited a beat. 'You're forgetting what Dr. Barney was like. Now, there was an assembly line.'

'He was always good to me,' Sara countered.

'Because he liked you,' Molly said. 'And for every kid he liked, there were ten he couldn't stand, and toward the end he passed the ones he hated on to you.'

Sara shook her head, not accepting this. 'He didn't do that.'

'Sara,' Molly insisted, 'ask Nelly. She's been here longer than I have.'

'So, that's my standard? That I'm better than Dr. Barney?'

'Your standard is you treat all the kids the same. You don't play favorites.' Molly indicated the pictures on the wall. 'How many kids did Dr. Barney have on his walls?'

Sara shrugged, though she knew the answer to that. None.

'You're being too hard on yourself,' Molly said. 'And it's not going to accomplish anything.'

'I just want to be more careful from now on,' Sara told her. 'Maybe we can cut the schedule so I can spend more time with each patient.'

Molly snorted a laugh. 'We barely have enough time in the day to see the appointments we have now. Between that and the morgue –'

Sara stopped her. 'Maybe I should quit the morgue.'

'Maybe you should hire another doctor?' Molly suggested.

Sara tapped her head against the wall, thinking. 'I don't know.'

The door shook as someone knocked on it.

'If that's Elliott . . . ,' Sara began, but it was not. Nelly, the office manager at the clinic since before Sara was born, slid open the door.

'Nick Shelton's on the phone,' Nelly said. 'Want me to take a message?'

Sara shook her head. 'I'll take it,' she answered, then waited for Molly to leave before picking up the phone.

'Hello, sunshine,' Nick said, his south Georgia drawl clear across the line.

Sara allowed a smile. 'Hey, Nick.'

'I wish I had time to flirt,' he told her. 'But I gotta meeting in about ten seconds. Real quick, though,' he began, and she could hear him shuffling papers. 'Nothing current came up on female castration, at least, not in the United States. But I'm sure you're not surprised to hear that.'

'No,' Sara agreed. Something so volatile would have certainly ended up in the press.

'A few years ago in France, a woman was tried for performing over fifty procedures. I think she was originally from Africa.'

Sara shook her head, wondering how a woman could do this to a child.

Nick said, 'Hey, what do you already know about this?'

'Infibulation falls under the general heading of F.G.M.,' she said, using the acronym for Female Genital Mutilation. 'It's sometimes practiced in the Middle East and parts of Africa. It's tied somehow to religion.'

'Well, about as much as suicide missions are tied to religion,' Nick corrected. 'You can make a religious justification for just about anything these days.'

Sara made a noise of agreement.

'Mostly, it's a custom passed down from village to village. The more uneducated the group, the more likely they are to do it. There isn't a real good religious argument to justify it, but the men over there like the idea of making sure their women don't stray.'

'So they make it impossible for them to enjoy sex. Perfect solution. If this was happening to men over there, Africa and the rest of the Middle East would be an empty crater.'

Nick was silent, and Sara felt guilty for painting him with the same brush. 'I'm sorry, Nick. It's just –'

'You don't have to explain it to me, Sara,' he offered in a soft tone.

She waited a beat, then asked, 'What else?'

'Well,' he began, and she could hear him shuffling through his notes. 'After the procedure, they usually bind the legs together to promote healing.' He paused as if to catch his breath. 'In a lot of cases, they sew them shut, you know, like your girl was, and leave an opening for her time of the month.'

'I read about that,' Sara confirmed. She also knew that women in the village who weren't mutilated were not considered marriage material.

'The thread you pulled from the area looks common. I've sent samples to the lab, but they're pretty certain you can find it in any Kmart.' He made a thinking noise. 'You think whoever did this has some kind of medical experience?'

'Are you looking at the photographs?'

'Yep,' he answered. 'Looks kind of elementary, but not half-assed.'

'I agree,' she told him, thinking that whoever had sewn the girl up was probably good with a needle and thread.

'I read this statistic,' he said. 'A lot of the girls die from shock. They don't exactly anesthetize them, if you know what I mean. Most times they use a piece of broken glass to perform the procedure.'

Sara shuddered, but tried to maintain her composure. 'Any idea why someone would do this here?'

'You mean someone who's not part of an immigrant population?' he asked, but didn't let her answer. 'Over there they do it to make sure a girl stays pure. Usually, the husband opens her up on their wedding night.'

'Purity,' Sara said, focusing on the word. Jenny Weaver had used it with her mother.

Nick asked, 'Was she a virgin?'

'No,' Sara answered. 'Judging from the size of the vaginal orifice as compared to the urinary meatus, she was sexually active well before the castration. Probably with a number of partners.'

'You check her for any STDs?'

'Yes,' Sara said. 'She came back negative.'

'Well, it was worth a shot.'

'Anything else?'

Nick was quiet for a few beats, then asked, 'You talking to Jeffrey this week?'

Sara felt a bit embarrassed, but said, 'Yes.'

'Tell him that drawing he sent didn't come up on our computers. We faxed it up to the FBI for a run-through, but you know they'll take their time.'

'What's the drawing?' Sara asked.

'Some tattoo. I dunno. He said it was on the webbing between the thumb and pointer finger.'

'I'll tell him.'

'Over dinner?'

Sara laughed. 'What are you getting at, Nick?'

'If you're not busy, I'm gonna be down in your neck of the woods this weekend.'

Sara smiled. Nick had asked her out several times before, mostly as a courtesy. He was about six inches shorter than Sara and wore more gold jewelry than any man ought to be allowed. She doubted very seriously that he thought he had a chance in hell with her, but Nick was the kind of man who liked to leave no stone unturned.

She told him, 'I guess I'm seeing Jeffrey again.'

'You guess?'

'I mean,' she paused. 'Yes, we're dating again.'

He took the refusal good-naturedly, as usual. 'Can't blame an old boy for trying.'

After they said their good-byes, Sara stayed in her

chair, thinking about what Nick had told her. There had to be some connection between Jenny's desire for purity and the castration. She was missing something, probably something very obvious. What would make a girl feel unclean, Sara wondered. Unfortunately, the only thing she could come up with was sex. Jenny Weaver had certainly been active. Maybe the guilt from her sexual promiscuity had been too much for Jenny to bear.

Also, there was the greater question of who had performed the mutilation on Jenny. It wasn't as if the girl could do it to herself. She would pass out from the shock or the pain before it was completed. There had to be another person involved, someone who could do the cutting and sewing. Perhaps Jenny had drunk until she passed out, or bought pain killers or muscle relaxers from someone at the school. A veritable pharmacy existed at the high school. Anyone with the right money could practically stock an operating room.

Nelly slid open the door, saying, 'The Patterson kid is here.' Then added, 'Without the mother,' in a hushed whisper.

Sara glanced at her watch. Mark was supposed to have been in yesterday morning. His dropping by today would throw her whole schedule out of whack. 'Put him in six,' she said. 'Tell him he'll have to wait.'

'Him?' Nelly asked. 'It's Lacey, the girl.'

Sara sat up in her chair. 'Did she say why she's here?'

'Just that she's not feeling well,' Nelly answered, then whispered again, 'She doesn't look well, if you ask me.'

Sara whispered, 'Why are you whispering?'

Nelly allowed a smile, walking into the office. She closed the door, saying, 'She's acting strange. She's not with her mother.'

Sara felt the hair on the back of her neck rise. 'How long has she been waiting?'

'Not long,' Nelly answered. 'Put her in six?'

Sara nodded, a sinking feeling in her stomach. She picked up the phone to dial Jeffrey's number, then changed her mind. Lacey had come to the clinic because she trusted Sara, and Sara would not betray that confidence. At the very least, the girl needed help. Whatever laws she had broken could be dealt with after Sara made sure she was okay.

Exam six was in the back of the building, at the end of the L-shaped hallway. Normally, it was reserved for very sick children or used as a waiting room for parents while Sara talked to their kids about sex, or birth control, or whatever things they felt they needed to talk to their pediatrician about in private. Sara supposed Molly had stuck Lacey back here to win the girl's trust. Kids did not just show up at the clinic without their parents, even the ones who could drive themselves.

Molly was waiting by the closed exam room door when Sara turned the corner.

She handed Lacey Patterson's chart to Sara outside the exam room, saying, 'I'll be in two if you need me.'

Sara flipped open the chart to review her notes from Lacey's last visit, even though Sara had looked at the chart just a few days ago. Two months ago, the girl had presented with what appeared to be strep throat. Sara had started her on antibiotics, pending the lab results. Sara thumbed through the chart, but the pink sheet the lab usually sent was not in there. She was about to find Molly when she noticed a noise coming from behind the exam door.

'Lacey?' Sara asked, sliding back the door. 'Are you —' She stopped midsentence, thinking that the last time she had seen someone so pale was in the morgue. The girl was sitting in the chair by the exam table, her arms wrapped across her stomach. Despite the weather she was wearing a neon-yellow raincoat. She was doubled over, her arms wrapped around her stomach as if in pain.

Sara put her hand on the girl's back, surprised at how clammy it felt through the coat.

Lacey's teeth were chattering, but she managed to say, 'I need to talk to you.'

'Come here,' Sara said, helping her stand. 'Let's get you on the table.'

Lacey hesitated, and Sara lifted her up onto the exam table.

'I don't . . . ,' Lacey began, but she was shaking too hard to continue. Sara put her hand to the girl's forehead, wondering if Lacey was shaking from fear or from fever. As hot as it was outside, Sara could not tell the difference.

'Let's get this coat off,' Sara suggested, but Lacey would not unwrap her arms from her waist.

'What happened?' Sara asked, trying to keep her voice steady. There was an electric charge in the room, as if something really bad had happened.

Lacey tilted forward, and Sara caught her before she fell off the table.

'I'm so sleepy,' she said.

'Sit up for me a minute,' Sara told her. She raised her voice, calling into the hallway, 'Molly?'

'I'm not feeling well,' the girl said.

Sara held her hands against Lacey's thin shoulders. 'Where do you hurt?'

She opened her mouth to speak, vomiting all over Sara. Of course this had happened to Sara before, and she stepped back, but not in time to keep from getting splattered.

After her sickness subsided, Lacey murmured, 'I'm sorry.'

'It's okay, sweetie,' Sara told her.

'My stomach hurts.'

'You're okay,' Sara told her. Holding Lacey up with one hand, she stretched toward the paper towel dispenser and gave the girl some cloths.

'I feel sick.'

Sara raised her voice again, this time louder than before. 'Molly?' she called, knowing that it was futile. Exam two was on the other side of the building.

'Lie back,' Sara told Lacey. 'If you get sick, turn to the side.'

'Don't leave me!' the girl cried, holding on to Sara's hand. 'Please, Dr. Linton, I gotta talk to you. I gotta tell you what happened.'

Sara could guess what happened, but there were more important things right now than hearing the girl's confession.

'I gotta tell you,' the girl repeated.

'About the baby?' Sara guessed. She could tell from Lacey's expression that her guess was right. Sara felt stupid for not having figured it out before. She said, 'I know, sweetie. I know. Just lie down and I'll be right back.'

The girl's body tensed. 'How do you know?'

'Lie down,' Sara told her. Thinking this would soothe her, Sara offered, 'I'll go call your mom.'

Lacey bolted upright. 'You can't tell my mom.'

'Don't worry about that now.'

'You can't tell her,' Lacey insisted, tears streaming down her face. 'She's sick. She's real sick.'

Sara did not understand what the girl meant, but she soothed her anyway. 'It's going to be okay.'

'Promise me you won't tell her.'

Sara said, 'Honey, we'll worry about that later.'

'No!' she yelled, gripping Sara's arm. 'You can't tell my mom. Please. Please don't tell her.'

'Stay right here,' Sara ordered. 'I'll be right back.'

She did not wait for an answer. Sara stepped into the hallway, slipping off her soiled lab coat as she walked toward the nurses' station.

Nelly asked, 'What happened?'

'Call an ambulance,' Sara said, tossing her coat into the dirty linen bin. She leaned back, looking around the corner to make sure Lacey had not left the room. 'Get Molly in six right now, and then call Frank over at the police station.'

'Oh, my,' Nelly mumbled, picking up the phone.

Elliot came out of one of the exam rooms. 'Hey, Sara?' he asked. 'I've got a six year old with —'

'Not now,' Sara told him, holding up her hand. With a glance down the hallway, she went into her office and dialed Jeffrey's cell phone. She let it ring four times before hanging up. Next, she dialed the station.

Marla Simms answered. 'Grant County Police Station. How may I help you?'

'Marla,' Sara said. 'Find Jeffrey, send him over to the clinic right now.'

A banging noise echoed up the hallway, and Sara mumbled a curse as she recognized the sound of the back door popping open.

Marla said, 'Sara?'

Sara slammed down the phone and ran out into the hallway, prepared to chase after Lacey. What she saw stopped her cold. Mark Patterson stood at the end of the hall, every muscle in his body tensed. There was a cut across his abdomen that stained his blue shirt to a dark purple, and his jeans were torn at the knee as if he had skidded across asphalt.

'Lacey?' he screamed, sliding open the first door he came to.

Sara heard a shocked gasp from the mother of the patient in the room, followed by the wails of a frightened child.

'Sara?' Nelly asked. She was standing at the nurses' station with the telephone in her hand.

Sara said, 'Call the station. Tell them to send whoever they can.'

'Lacey?' Mark repeated, his voice vibrating through the hallway. Thankfully, he had not noticed the tail end of the hall and the two exam rooms off to the side.

He came closer, and Sara could see that his clothes were stained and dirty-looking. Flecks of white paint covered everything. His hair looked greasy and was uncombed, as if he had not bathed in a while. Sara had seen Mark many times over the last decade, but she had never seen him looking so unclean.

'Goddamn it!' Mark screamed, throwing his hands into the air. 'Where's my fucking sister?'

A couple of doors behind Sara slid open, and she turned, signaling for the parents to stay inside.

Molly stood beside Sara, holding a chart to her chest. It was the first time Sara had ever seen the nurse shocked by anything that happened in the clinic.

'Mark,' Sara said, putting some authority into her tone. 'What are you doing here?'

'Where's Lacey?' he said, slamming his hand into the next door. The panel shook on its slider, and Sara could hear a child screaming behind it.

Nelly's voice was muffled as she talked to someone on the phone. Sara could not make out the conversation, but she hoped to God they were sending somebody.

'Mark,' Sara began, trying to keep her voice calm. 'Stop this. She's not here.'

'The hell she's not,' he countered, taking a step toward her. 'Where is that little cunt?' He slammed his hand against the door again, punching an impression into the wood. Nelly screamed and ducked behind the counter.

'Where is she?' he demanded.

Sara purposefully made what she hoped was a nervous glance toward her office. Mark picked up on it immediately.

'Aha,' he said. 'She in there?'

'No,' Sara told him.

He smiled, stepping closer to her. Sara could see that his pupils were as small as pinpricks, and guessed that whatever he was on was not about to dissipate any time soon. Up close, he seemed to be giving off an odor. Sara was not certain, but the smell reminded her of chemicals.

She asked, 'What are you on, Mark?'

'I'm about to be on my fucking sister if she doesn't keep her fucking mouth shut.'

'She's not here,' Sara told him.

'Lace?' Mark said, craning his head around the office door. 'You better get the fuck out here right now.'

Sara caught movement out of the corner of her eye. She knew from the neon-yellow blur that it was Lacey, trying to make her way out the back door. A cold sweat chilled Sara as she calculated how long it would take for Lacey to make it to the exit. She stared at Mark, willing Lacey to hurry, but the girl was not moving. She was standing stock still as if someone had pinned her to the wall.

'She in there?' Mark asked.

'No,' Sara said, looking over his shoulder. 'She's behind you.'

Lacey's hand went to her mouth as if to stop herself from screaming.

'Right,' Mark said, giving Sara a scathing look.

'I want you out of here right now, Mark. You're trespassing,'

He ignored her, walking into the office. Sara followed him at a distance, trying to be casual about the fact that she was trapping him in the room. She prayed that Marla had gotten hold of someone, even if it was Brad Stephens.

'Lacey?' Mark said, his voice softer, but in a more menacing way than before. He walked around the desk. 'It's only gonna be worse if you don't come out now.'

Sara crossed her arms. 'What's purity, Mark?'

Mark looked under the desk, cursing when he found it empty. He kicked it, moving the steel desk across the floor a couple of inches.

'Did you make Jenny feel dirty? Is that why she wanted to make herself pure?'

'Get out of my way,' he ordered, walking toward Sara. She put her hand on the door, blocking his exit.

'Get out of the way.'

'What's purity?'

He looked like he might answer, but Sara realized too late he was just trying to throw her off guard. The next thing she knew, she was being pushed back, and hard. She fell into the hall, whacking her head on the floor.

'Sara!' Molly said, running around to help her.

'I'm okay,' Sara managed, trying to sit up. She looked down the hallway and saw that Lacey was still there about the same time that Mark did.

'Run!' Sara told her. Lacey hesitated, but finally seemed to understand she needed to get out of here. She ran to the door and slammed it open.

'Bitch,' Mark yelled, taking after her.

Without thinking, Sara reached out and grabbed at Mark's foot. He tried to yank it away, but she caught the leg of his pants in her fist.

'Stop it,' Sara said, trying to hold on.

He reached down, hitting at her hand with his fist. When this did not work, he punched at her face. Sara saw the glint of the red stone in his ring before the first blow caught her on the forehead, and she was so surprised that she let go.

'Oh, my God,' Molly breathed, putting her hand to her mouth.

'Crap,' Sara hissed, touching her forehead. Mark's ring had caught her right at the temple. She looked at the blood on her fingers, but then thought of Lacey and made herself stand.

Molly began, 'Maybe you should –'

Sara took off after Mark and Lacey, shouting, 'Where the hell is Jeffrey?' over her shoulder.

Sara stopped outside the back door, trying to get her bearings. The sun was beating down, and Sara shielded her eyes as she tried to spot Lacey in the trees behind the building.

'Did they go around front?' Molly asked, jogging toward the side of the clinic. Sara followed her, bumping into the nurse as she turned the corner.

Molly was pointing to the road. 'There she is.'

They both took off at the same time, but Sara's stride was longer, and she soon left Molly behind. The road in front of the clinic was hardly a busy thoroughfare, but at lunchtime the professors and students left campus to come into town. Sara watched as Lacey ran into the street, Mark right behind her, screaming at the top of his lungs.

Somehow, they both made it across the road. Lacey ran toward the lake, but Sara watched as another figure, a blur, really, came from the side and tackled Mark to the ground. By the time Sara and Molly crossed the street, Lena Adams was straddling Mark's back like a rodeo rider as she jerked his arms behind him and cuffed his wrists.

'Oh, shit,' Lena said, looking up the street.

Lacey was too far away for Sara to recognize her by any other means than the bright yellow raincoat. Sara stood helpless, watching as an old black car stopped beside the girl. The passenger-side door swung open and an arm reached out, grabbing Lacey around the waist and pulling her inside the car.

Sara touched the bandage on her forehead as she got out of the car. Molly had sewn in two sutures, then canceled the rest of Sara's appointments so that she could have some downtime in order to recover from the ordeal at the clinic. Sara's head hurt, and she was hot and irritable. She might as well have stayed at the clinic and seen patients, but Molly had not really given her a choice. Maybe the nurse was right. Every time Sara thought about what had happened at the clinic, she felt as if a band were being tightened around her chest. Knowing another one of her kids was in jeopardy and that there was absolutely nothing she could do made Sara want to put her head on her mother's shoulder and cry.

'Mama?' Sara called, kicking off her shoes as she closed the front door behind her. There was no answer, and Sara walked back to the kitchen, asking, 'Mama?' again.

There was still no answer, and Sara felt her heart sink. She filled a glass with water and finished it all in several gulps, then wiped her mouth with the back of her hand.

Sara flopped onto the kitchen stool and picked up the phone, dialing Jeffrey's number. Lena had taken Mark off to the station before Sara had thought to ask her where he was.

'Tolliver,' he answered, and she could tell from the hollow echo of his voice that he was in his car.

'Where are you?' she asked.

'I got caught up in Alabama for a while,' he told her. 'I talked to Lena. She told me about Lacey. You didn't get a look at who was in the car?'

'No,' Sara answered. 'Did you talk to her parents?'

'Frank's with them now. They don't know anybody who drives a car like that.'

'What has Mark said?'

'He won't talk to anybody,' Jeffrey told her. 'Not even Lena.'

'Who would want to kidnap her?'

'I don't know,' Jeffrey said. 'We've put out an A.P.B. all over the state. I want to talk to Mark and see if we can find anything out.'

'I feel like we're missing something big here,' she said. 'Something right under our noses.'

'Yeah.' He was quiet, and she could hear the engine rev in his car as he accelerated. He said, 'Tell me what happened today. Beginning to end.'

Sara took a deep breath, then told him. The part Jeffrey seemed to focus on most was Mark hitting her, probably because it was the only thing he knew he could take care of.

'What did he hit you with?' he asked, his tone sharp.

'His ring,' she said, then amended, 'His fist, really,

but his ring did most of the damage. He wasn't really hitting hard. He just wanted me to turn him loose.' She put her fingers to the bandage. 'It's not bad.'

'Lena wrote him up on assault?'

'Probably,' Sara answered, letting him know he should drop it.

He got the hint. 'Did it look like Lacey knew the people in the car?'

'It was so far away, Jeffrey. I don't know. I wouldn't have even known it was her except for the bright-yellow coat she was wearing.'

'Lena knew the car. Some of the kids from school had seen Jenny Weaver get into it.'

Sara played with the cord of the phone as he told her what Lena had learned at the high school. When he was finished, all she could say was, 'That doesn't sound like the Jenny I knew.'

'I'm beginning to think nobody really knew her.'

She said what had been nagging in the back of her mind all along. 'Do you think Mark and Lacey are the parents?' she asked. 'I mean, I know that's why you wanted the sample on Mark, but it never occurred to me that . . .'

'I know,' he said. She could tell from the quick way he answered her that Jeffrey had been thinking about this for a while. 'I think it's possible.'

She asked, 'What was your reading on Teddy Patterson?'

'Possible there, too.'

'I doubt he'll submit to a test without an order.'

'You got that right.'

Sara sighed, wondering how all of this fit together. 'Maybe Jenny found out and was jealous?'

'Could be,' he said, and she could tell he was concentrating on something else.

'Jeff . . . ,' Sara began, not knowing how to broach the subject without making him angry. 'Mark was cut across his abdomen. It wasn't bad, but I think some-one probably tried to hurt him.'

'Good.'

'No,' she stopped him. 'He's a kid. Promise me you won't forget that.'

'A kid who may have raped his sister and pimped out her friend,' he said. 'A kid who punched you in the face.'

'Forget about me,' Sara told him. 'I mean it, Jeffrey. Don't make it about me.'

He said something under his breath.

'Jeff?'

He asked, 'You didn't get any more information out of her?'

'She seemed disoriented, and terrified.'

'Do you think she's seriously ill?'

'I don't know if it's fear or shock or if she's recovering from giving birth. I didn't get to spend much time with her. I . . .'

'What?'

'I feel responsible for not looking out for her. She was in my clinic. If I'd been able to keep her there —'

'She ran away, Sara. You did what you could do.'

She pressed her lips together. 'I wish that made me feel better.'

'I wish it did, too,' he said. 'I wish I could tell you how to get rid of the guilt, because I sure as hell don't know.'

Sara felt tears well into her eyes. She put her hand to her mouth so that Jeffrey could not hear her cry.

'Sara?'

She cleared her throat, wiping under her eyes with

her free hand. She sniffed, because her nose was running. 'Yes?'

Jeffrey said, 'Was there anything else Lacey said? Maybe something about Mark, why he was after her?'

Sara bristled, because asking her the same questions over again wouldn't get them any closer to finding Lacey Patterson. 'Stop questioning me. I've had a bad enough day without getting the third degree from you.'

He was silent, and she could hear the engine accelerate again.

Sara closed her eyes and leaned her head back against the wall, waiting for him to speak.

'I just . . .' He stopped, then, 'I gotta tell you, the idea of somebody hurting you really pisses me off.'

She laughed. 'Me, too.'

'Are you all right?' he asked again.

'Yeah,' she said, though she was feeling very unsettled. The clinic had always been a safe place for Sara, and she did not like the fact that her work at the morgue had somehow seeped into her private practice. She felt vulnerable, and she did not like that.

'Nick called,' she told Jeffrey, then explained to him what Nick had said.

'Purity?' Jeffrey repeated. 'That's what Jenny said.'

'Right,' Sara agreed. 'I think it all goes back to sex. She wanted to be clean again, right?'

'Right.'

'So what made her feel unclean?'

'Banging all those guys at the party might have done it.'

'She was drunk,' Sara reminded him, feeling anger stirring deep inside of her.

'They say she wasn't too drunk to know what she was doing.'

'Of course they said that. What else would they say, that they raped her?'

He cleared his throat. 'That's a point.'

'Why else would she do what she did?' Sara demanded. 'Jenny wasn't like that. She was just a little girl, for Christ's sake.'

Jeffrey's tone was indulgent. 'We don't know exactly what happened, Sara. We probably never will.'

Sara changed the subject, knowing she could not have a logical conversation with him about this right now. 'Nick sent that tattoo to the FBI. Nothing kicked out on their database.'

'That's actually what held me up,' Jeffrey told her. 'I'll tell you about it tonight.'

'No,' she said. 'Tell me about it tomorrow.'

He was silent, then, 'I thought you wanted to see me tonight?'

'Yes,' Sara assured him. 'I do, but not to talk business.' She waited a few beats. 'I need to not think about this tonight. Okay?'

'Okay,' he agreed. 'As long as I still get to see you.'

'If you can stand it,' she said, trying to make light of it. 'I've got a big green Band-Aid on my head.'

'Does it hurt?'

'Mmm,' she mumbled, looking out the window. She saw her mother walking up the steps to Tessa's garage apartment.

'Sara?'

Sara turned back to the conversation. 'I'm counting on you to help me take my mind off of it.'

He laughed at this, and seemed pleased. 'I've got to talk to Mark and do a quick briefing with evening patrol about looking for Lacey. Not that there's much any of us can do tonight. I'll be there as soon as I can, okay?'

'You think it'll be late?'

'Probably,' he said. 'You want me to let you sleep?'

'No,' she told him. 'Wake me.'

She could almost hear him smiling. 'I'll see you then.'

'Okay,' she answered, then hung up the phone.

Sara got another glass of water before going outside. The pavement was hot as white coals against her bare feet, and she tiptoed the last couple of yards to get to the stairs.

Tessa's apartment was large, with two bedrooms and two baths. She had painted the walls in primary colors and accented these with comfortable chairs and a roomy couch that tended to make the occupant want to take a long nap. Sara had often slept over at Tessa's, especially after the divorce, because she felt safer at the time being here than being in her own home.

'Tessie?' Sara called, trying not to let the screen door slam behind her. Cathy had left the wooden door wide open, which seemed odd since the air was on.

Tessa's voice seemed strained. 'Just a minute.'

Sara walked back to her sister's bedroom, wondering what was going on. 'Tess?' she said, stopping in the doorway.

Tessa was holding a tissue to her nose, and she did not look up when Sara came into the room. Cathy was beside her, arms crossed over her chest.

'What happened?' Sara asked at the same time Cathy did.

'What?' they both said.

Sara pointed to her sister. 'What's wrong with you? Why are you crying?'

Cathy walked over to Sara and put her hand to Sara's head. 'Did you hurt yourself?'

'It's a long story,' Sara said, waving away her mother's hand. 'Tessie, what's wrong?'

Tessa shook her head no, and Sara found herself suddenly feeling dizzy. She sat on the bed, asking, 'Is it Daddy?'

Cathy frowned. 'Don't be silly. He's healthy as a horse.'

Sara put her hand to her chest and let out a puff of air. 'Then, what's the matter?'

Tessa walked over to her dresser and picked up a long piece of white plastic. Sara recognized the pregnancy test stick before her sister handed it to her.

Sara could not think what to say, so she said, 'You're supposed to do these early in the morning.'

'I did,' Tessa answered. 'Then I did it again at lunch, and then again just now.'

'All positive,' Cathy said. Then, 'I guess we can take her into the city next weekend.'

'Into the city?' Sara asked, wondering why they would need to go to Atlanta. She figured it out soon enough, and shook her head no, not accepting this. 'You're going to get an abortion?'

Tessa took back the test stick. 'I don't really have a choice.'

'That's not true,' Sara snapped, standing. 'Of course you have a choice.'

'Sara,' Cathy chided.

'Mother,' Sara began, then, 'Jesus Christ, Tess, you're thirty-three years old, you make a great living, you've got Devon so in love with you he can't see straight.'

'What does that have to do with anything?' Tessa asked.

'It has everything to do with it,' Sara told her.

'I'm not ready.'

Sara felt so shocked that for a moment she could not speak. Finally, she asked, 'Do you know what they do, Tessa? Do you know what the procedure entails? Do you know how they –?'

Tessa stopped her. 'I know what an abortion is.'

'How could you even think –?'

'Think what?' Tessa snapped. 'Think that I'm not ready to have a baby? I can think that pretty easily, Sara. I'm not ready.'

'Nobody's ever ready,' Sara countered, trying not to yell. 'How can you be so selfish?'

'Selfish?' Tessa asked, incredulous.

'All you're thinking about is yourself.'

'I am not,' Tessa shot back.

Sara put her hand over her eyes, not believing she was having this conversation. She dropped her hand, asking, 'Do you know what they'll do? Do you know what will happen to the baby?'

Tessa turned away. 'It's not even a baby yet.'

Sara grabbed her sister's arm and turned her back around. 'Look at me.'

'Why? So you can try to talk me out of this?' Tessa asked. 'This is my choice, Sara.'

'What about Devon?' Sara asked. 'What does he have to say?'

Tessa pursed her lips. 'It's not his decision.'

Sara knew what Tessa meant, but asked anyway, 'What, you're not sure he's the father?'

'Sara,' Cathy warned.

Sara kept her back to her mother. 'Is he?'

'Of course he is,' Tessa said, indignant.

Sara stared at her sister, trying to find something to say that would stop this. When she opened her mouth to speak, what came out surprised them all. She said, 'I'll raise it.'

Tessa shook her head no. 'I couldn't do that.'

'Why?'

'Sara,' Tessa said, as if she was being obtuse on purpose. 'I couldn't let you raise my child.'

Sara tucked her hands into her hips, trying to keep her anger down. 'That's just about the most immature thing I've ever heard you say. What, if you can't have it, no one will?'

Tessa's mouth opened and closed. 'When did you become so self-righteous? I happen to remember a time when you were pretty pro-abortion.'

Sara felt her cheeks turn red. She was very conscious that her mother was in the room. 'Stop it.'

'Oh, you don't want to tell Mama about the time you thought Steve Mann had knocked you up?'

Cathy kept silent, but Sara could feel that her mother was hurt. Cathy had always made it clear that her daughters could come to her with anything. And, except for this one time, Sara always had.

Sara tried to explain to her mother. 'It was a false alarm. I was studying for finals. I was stressed out. My period was late.'

Cathy held up her hand, telling Sara to stop.

'I was a teenager,' Sara added, her voice weak. 'My whole life was ahead of me.'

Tessa said, 'And the first thing you did was call the women's center in Atlanta to see how fast they could get rid of it.'

Sara shook her head, knowing this was not true. The first thing she had done was burst into tears and tear up her acceptance letter from Emory. 'That's not how it happened.'

Tessa was not finished, and her next remark cut to the bone. 'This is so easy for you because you know you'll never get pregnant.'

'Tessa,' Cathy hissed, but it was too late. The damage was done.

Sara's mouth formed an O but the word would not come out. She felt as if she had been slapped.

Cathy started to say something, but it was Sara's turn to hold up her hand.

'I can't do this right now,' she said, because she could not. Sara could not ever remember a time when Tessa had hurt her so much, and she felt as if she had lost her best friend.

Without another word, Sara left Tessa's apartment, letting the screen door slam closed behind her.

ELEVEN

Marla handed Jeffrey a stack of pink messages before he even had time to take off his jacket. He felt as if he had been gone for three months instead of twenty-four hours.

'This one's important,' Marla said, pointing to one of the slips. 'And this one, too.' She kept going until she had identified all but one of the messages as important. Jeffrey glanced at the unimportant one. There was a man's name he did not recognize, followed by a one–eight hundred number.

'What's this about?'

Marla frowned as she obviously tried to remember. 'Either vinyl siding or coffee service. I forget which one.' She shrugged apologetically. 'He said he'd call back.'

Jeffrey balled up the message and tossed it into the trash, asking, 'Is Lena around?'

'I'll fetch her,' Marla said, backing out of the office.

Jeffrey sat at his desk and the first thing he saw was a missing poster of Lacey Patterson. She was a thin, boyish-looking girl with blonde hair like her mother. The photo was a school picture with an American flag in the background and a globe of the world in front. Her height and weight were under the photo, along with where she was last seen and a number people could call. The flyer had been faxed out to all the precincts in the area and put into the national database that tracked missing children. It would take time for the Georgia Bureau of Investigation to put together a packet to send to law enforcement all around the Southeast. If today was like every other day in America, Lacey Patterson's name had been keyed in along with a hundred other newly missing or abducted children.

Jeffrey picked up the phone and dialed Nick Shelton's number. When Nick answered, Jeffrey was somewhat surprised. The field agent was seldom at his desk.

'Nick? Jeffrey Tolliver.'

'Hey, Chief,' Nick said, his twangy good-old-boy drawl a bit jarring to Jeffrey's ears. Considering Jeffrey had spent the last twenty-four hours in central Alabama, this said a lot.

Jeffrey asked, 'You riding a desk today?'

'Somebody's gotta take care of all this paperwork,' Nick told him. 'No word yet on your missing girl?'

'No,' Jeffrey told him. 'Anything on the state-wide alert?'

'Not a peep,' Nick said. 'It'd help if you had a license plate on that car.'

'It was too far away for anyone to see it.'

Nick sighed. 'Well, I sent it over to the computer lab. Who knows how long it'll take for them to get somebody on it? It's not top priority until something happens one way or the other.'

'I know,' Jeffrey said. There would need to be a break in the case, some kind of clue to follow or angle to work, before the big guns could be called in. Right now, all they could do was stand around with their hands in their pockets.

Jeffrey asked, 'There's no way to move her up on

this? Jesus, Nick. Sara and Lena saw the kid being snatched.'

'You know how many kids have gone missing in the last twelve hours?'

'Still —'

'Hey, now.' Nick lowered his voice. 'I made it my business to talk to this old boy used to work in child crimes. He's gonna make a couple of phone calls and see if they can put some kind of priority on it.'

'Thanks, Nick.'

'Meanwhile, it won't hurt to have some of your boys follow up on those faxes you sent around.'

Jeffrey made a note of this, thinking Nick was right. So much trash came through the fax machines at the office that sometimes it took hours before somebody could sort through it.

Nick asked, 'Any chance this is just a do-gooder, snatching her up to keep her safe?'

'Hell, Nick,' Jeffrey said. 'I don't know.'

'None of your primaries drives a black Thunderbird?'

'No,' Jeffrey said. They'd checked the vehicles of everyone even remotely involved in the case, then spread it out to include all of Grant. No one in the county had an old Ford Thunderbird registered to him.

'In the meantime,' Nick said, 'what can I do ya for?'

'Purity,' Jeffrey said. 'Tell me what that means in relation to pedophiles.'

'No idea,' Nick said. 'I can beep it through the computers and let you know.'

'I'd appreciate that.'

'Your lady was on the phone with me earlier talking about purity,' Nick told him. 'That castration case, right?'

'Right,' Jeffrey said.

'Well, I'll tell you,' Nick began, 'this castration has a religious angle to it most times. They do it to make sure the girl stays a virgin.'

'We know she wasn't that.'

'Hell, no,' Nick agreed. 'From what I heard, she'd been around the block more than a time or two.'

Jeffrey tried to let this slide off his back, but Nick's characterization of the child was a little harsh even for him. Law enforcement people tended to be as tough as they could about this kind of thing, and Jeffrey was no exception. Had he not killed the little girl in question, Jeffrey might have laughed. As it was, he could only say, 'I've got a name for you to run through the computer.'

'Shoot,' Nick said.

'Arthur Prynne,' Jeffrey said, then spelled out the name of the man he had almost beaten that morning behind Possum's store.

Nick mumbled something, obviously writing down the name. 'What is that, Polish, or something?'

'I've got no idea,' Jeffrey said. 'He's got a tattoo like the one I sent you.'

'What am I looking for?'

'He was cruising a day-care center when I happened upon him.'

'Can't really arrest him for that,' Nick said, though they both knew this was obvious.

'He's got a computer at home. Probably hooks up with other pedophiles that way,' Jeffrey said. 'Said he was a girl-lover.'

'Man,' Nick sighed. 'I really hate that phrase.'

'We could do a search here at the station, but to tell you the truth, Nick, I don't think any of us knows how to find that kind of thing.'

'Feds have got a whole squad on it. Having a name makes it a priority. Maybe they can squeeze this guy and get him to flip?'

'Very possible,' Jeffrey said. 'He didn't have much of a spine when I interviewed him. I can see him turning in some of his friends to save his hide.'

'Interviewed him, huh?' Nick chuckled. 'He know you were a cop at the time?'

Jeffrey smiled. Nick was a lot of things, but he was not stupid. 'Let's say we had a conversation and leave it at that.'

Nick laughed again. 'How fast you want me to do this?'

'Really fast,' Jeffrey said, not wanting the responsibility if Prynne turned out to be less innocent than he seemed.

'I'll put it through to the Alabama boys, pronto,' Nick said. Then, 'We just caught something over in Augusta that might interest you.'

'What's that?'

'Augusta cops busted this guy at his hotel on coke distribution. They kind of stumbled across a bunch of magazines that weren't exactly legal.'

'Pornography?' Jeffrey guessed.

'Kiddy porn,' Nick confirmed. 'There was some freaky shit.'

'In Augusta?' Jeffrey asked, surprised that he did not know about this. Augusta was pretty close to Grant, and they tended to swap information with the cops there just to keep everyone in the loop.

'We're sitting on it,' Nick said. 'Trying to pull down the big guys.'

'The perp's turning state's evidence?' Jeffrey asked.

'Flipped faster than a two-dollar whore,' Nick told him. 'And, before you ask, he doesn't know anything about a black Thunderbird or a missing little girl.'

'You sure?'

'Sure as two fists can be.'

Jeffrey frowned, though he was hardly in a position to feel superior. 'Thanks for checking.'

'No offense, Chief, but you better hope she's not with one of these guys. They trade kids like you and me used to trade baseball cards.'

'I know that,' Jeffrey said, but the truth was, he didn't want to. Thinking about Lacey Patterson being trapped with someone like Prynne made Jeffrey sick.

'Anyway,' Nick sighed, 'there's supposed to be a delivery tonight or tomorrow. Evidently, Augusta is the distribution point for the Southeast.'

'I can't believe they're still printing that shit when you can get it for free on the Internet.'

'You can trace through the Internet if you know what you're doing,' Nick reminded him. 'You want me to give you a holler when it's going down?'

'You've got my cell number, right?'

'Yep,' Nick said. 'You think this Prynne freak is active?'

'No,' Jeffrey said, because his impression had been that Arthur Prynne was the kind of pedophile who was content to look at pictures and not act on his fantasies. 'I don't know how long that'll last, though.'

Nick asked, 'He gonna be expecting a knock on his door?'

'I think he has been all his life,' Jeffrey said, looking up to see Lena standing in the doorway. 'I've gotta go, Nick. Call me back when you get something on that bust, okay?'

'Will do, Chief.'

They hung up, and Jeffrey motioned Lena in, surprised by the way she looked. Her eyes were bloodshot, the way people tend to get when they've been crying for long periods of time. Her nose was red and there were dark circles under her eyes.

'Wanna talk about it?' Jeffrey asked, indicating one of the chairs across from his desk.

She gave him a puzzled look, like she didn't understand. She asked, 'Any word on Lacey?'

'Nothing,' he said. 'Have you set up that appointment we talked about?'

Lena bit her lower lip. 'I didn't have time.'

'Make time,' he told her.

'Yes, sir.'

Jeffrey sat back in his chair, staring at her for a few beats. He said, 'Tell me what happened when you snatched up Mark. Did he say anything?'

'He's being real tight-lipped all the sudden,' she told him. 'He won't say anything.'

'He lawyer up?'

'Buddy Conford,' Lena told him. 'Won't that be a conflict of interest?'

Jeffrey considered this. Buddy was the lawyer representing the county if and when Dottie Weaver brought a case against Jeffrey. He asked, 'Does Buddy know there's a connection between Mark and what happened with Jenny Weaver?'

'He knows Mark's the one Jenny wanted to shoot. Everybody knows that.'

'I mean,' Jeffrey said, 'does he know we suspect Mark of being the father of the child?'

Lena's eyebrows went up. 'Do we?'

'Tell me why he wouldn't be.'

'There could be another boy,' she suggested.

'With the mother around?'

'She's been sick a lot,' Lena said, shrugging. 'I get a vibe from the father. He likes to push people around.'

'I'll give you that,' Jeffrey said, because Patterson had made a sport out of pushing Lena around in the trailer the other day. Jeffrey had been torn between stepping in and seeing if Lena could take care of it herself.

Lena said, 'Maybe he molested Mark, and so Mark molested his sister? Kind of like a cause and effect?'

'That's not how pedophiles work,' Jeffrey said.

'I don't follow.'

'Not all pedophiles were abused as children. You can't make that assumption.'

'We're talking theory here, right?' Lena asked. 'I mean, it could have happened that way. I don't see Patterson being into boys, though.'

'The vibe again?'

'Yeah,' Lena nodded. 'I don't get that vibe.'

'What about Mark?' Jeffrey asked, remembering how Lena had behaved when they first interviewed the kid. 'What kind of vibe do you get off of him?'

Lena had the grace to look down. 'Well,' she began, 'he's hypersexual.'

'Go on.'

'He really seems to work off his appearance, his sexuality.' She looked back up. 'I think he probably doesn't know how to communicate any other way.'

'That tattoo,' Jeffrey began. 'I found a guy in Alabama who had the same one.'

'The hearts?'

'He was watching a day care,' Jeffrey said, feeling the same disgust he had felt at Possum's store. 'Looking at the kids there.'

'Little kids?' Lena asked. 'He's a child molester?'

'More like a pedophile,' Jeffrey corrected. Sara had given him a lesson on the difference between these two a long time ago during another case, and he told Lena about it now. 'Child molesters tend to hate children, and don't want to be around them except to abuse them. Pedophiles think they're doing the kid some good. They think they love them.'

'Uh-huh,' Lena said, skeptical.

'Pedophilia is considered a mental illness.'

'So was homosexuality until the early sixties. I still don't see the difference.'

Jeffrey knew that Lena's sister had been gay, so he was surprised to hear her say this. 'I suppose the big difference would be that adult-to-adult sexual contact is healthy. Children aren't prepared for that kind of thing.' She did not respond, so he continued, 'With a child-adult relationship, the balance of power is always going to be on the adult's side. It's not a level playing field. The adult is always going to be the one in control of the kid.'

Lena gave him an incredulous look. 'It sounds like you're justifying it.'

'I'm not doing that at all,' Jeffrey said, feeling prickly at her accusation. 'I'm just telling you what the mindset is.'

'The mindset is pretty fucking perverted.'

'I agree with that,' Jeffrey told her. 'But you can't let your disgust color how you approach this, Lena. If Mark has that tattoo because he's a pedophile or a child molester, you can't let him know that you disapprove. He'll never open up to you.' Then, because he had taught her this before, he added, 'You know that.'

'Well,' Lena said. 'Which one do you think he is? He's barely older than Lacey.'

'Three years at least.'

'That's not a huge difference.'

'Maybe from thirty to thirty-three it's not, but with

kids, that's a pretty big jump when you think about it. That's the difference between being a child and being a young adult.'

She was silent, obviously thinking this through.

Jeffrey said, 'Look at it this way: A pedophile is more comfortable around children because he's scared of adult relationships. Adults scare him.'

'What about Jenny? How did she get sewn up like that? What's the story?'

'That I don't know,' Jeffrey said. 'Maybe Mark will give it up?'

'He's not talking,' Lena told him. 'Frank was in with him, and he just stared off into space.'

'Is he high?'

She shook her head no. 'He was before, but it's worn off by now.'

'Is he looking for a fix?'

'He seems okay,' she said. 'He's not twitching, if that's what you're getting at.'

'What about his physical state? Sara said he looked like someone had worked him over.'

'Yeah,' Lena said. She took some Polaroids out of her breast pocket. 'We took some pictures to document it. Dr. Linton said the cut on his belly looks like it was done with a sharp knife. It wasn't deep enough for stitches, though. He's got a bruise coming out on his eye.'

Jeffrey looked at the pictures one by one. Mark stared at the camera with a dead look in his eyes. There was one shot where he had his shirt off, and there were grass stains on the waist of his jeans as well as superficial scrapes on his lower abdomen.

'We didn't do any of this?' Jeffrey asked, just to make certain.

'Of course not,' Lena said, which was odd, because he had asked her this question on other cases and gotten a straightforward answer with none of the attitude. As if to get a jab in, she said, 'Ask your girlfriend. She saw him before I did.'

'Someone chased him?' Jeffrey asked, moving along. 'Or was he chasing someone else?'

'One or the other,' she said. 'Defensive wounds on his arms, too.'

Jeffrey thought about Arthur Prynne, and how he had covered himself with his arms to keep Jeffrey from hitting his face.

Lena said, 'We bagged his clothes. I think Dr. Linton's gonna run the blood on his shirt for the DNA match.'

'Did you ask him about his sister?'

'If he cares, he's not showing it. Like I said, he's not talking about anything.'

Jeffrey's phone beeped, and he pressed the intercom button.

Marla said, 'Pastor Fine is here to see Mark.'

Jeffrey and Lena exchanged a look. 'In what capacity?'

'He says the parents asked him to act as proxy during your interview.' Marla lowered her voice. 'Buddy Conford is here with him.'

'Thanks,' Jeffrey said, pressing the button again. He sat back in his chair, staring at Lena.

She finally asked, 'What?'

'You've got this connection with Mark. I don't know what it is, but you need to be careful in there.'

'I don't have a connection with him,' Lena said, obviously uncomfortable with the thought.

'Maybe he's transferring some emotions on to you because his mother's sick.'

Lena gave a half-assed shrug. 'Whatever,' she said. 'Can we just get this over with?'

* * *

Buddy Conford had lived a hell of a life. At seventeen, he had lost his right leg from the knee down in a car accident. Later, he lost his left eye to cancer and a kidney to a dissatisfied client with a gun. These losses seemed to have made Buddy stronger rather than weaker. He could fight like a dog with a bone when he put his mind to it. On the other side of that, Buddy was a logical man, and, unlike most lawyers, he was able to recognize right from wrong. He had helped Jeffrey on more than one occasion. Jeffrey approached Mark Patterson's interview hoping this would be such an occasion.

'Chief,' Dave Fine said, 'I wanted to thank you for letting me be present during this. Mark's mother has taken a turn for the worse, and they wanted me to be here in their stead.'

Jeffrey nodded, trying not to point out that he did not really have a choice. Whatever crimes he had committed, Mark was technically still a child. It would be up to the courts to change that designation, if it ever came to that.

Fine asked, 'Is there any word on his sister?'

'No,' Jeffrey said, staring at Mark, trying to figure out what was going on with the sixteen year old. He looked horrible, and the bruise on his eye was turning blacker by the minute. His lip was cut down the center and his eyes were as bloodshot at Lena's. The orange prison jumpsuit they had given him made the boy look even more pale than he already was. He seemed smaller, too, somehow reduced by his circumstances. His shoulders slouched and he looked slight, even compared to Buddy Conford, who was not exactly tall.

'Mark?' Jeffrey asked.

Mark's lips moved silently, and he kept his gaze on

the table, as if he did not want to look up and recognize the situation he was in. There was something pathetic about the boy that made Jeffrey feel something like compassion. Sara was right. No matter what Mark had done, he was still just a kid.

Buddy shuffled through Mark's paperwork. 'What are the charges here, Chief?'

'Assault,' Jeffrey told him, still staring at Mark. 'He hit Sara in the face.'

Buddy frowned at his client. 'Sara Linton?' he asked, surprise making his voice go up. Buddy had grown up in Grant, and like most natives he considered Sara sort of sacred for the work she did at the clinic.

A jangling noise came from under the table. Mark was handcuffed, and Jeffrey guessed the sound was the cuffs bouncing up and down on his thigh. Jeffrey had heard this sound before in several interviews.

'In front of about ten witnesses,' Jeffrey said, talking over the noise. 'He was also threatening his sister with bodily harm.'

'Uh-huh,' Buddy said, stacking the papers. 'He get those bruises on his face before or after he was arrested?'

Lena snapped, 'Before,' with a silent but understood, '. . . *you idiot.*'

Buddy gave her a chastising look. 'Witnesses back that up?'

'We took photos,' Jeffrey said, pulling the Polaroids Lena had given him out of a folder. He slid them across the table to Buddy. Mark flinched a bit at the movement, and again Jeffrey was struck at how fragile the boy seemed.

Buddy thumbed through them, not looking at Mark until he was finished. 'Who did this to him?' he asked Jeffrey.

'You tell us,' Jeffrey said.

Mark kept staring down, the cuffs jangling like a metronome.

Buddy slid the photos back to Jeffrey. 'Don't look like he wants to talk.'

Lena said, 'What's going on, Mark?'

Mark looked up, seemingly surprised that Lena was speaking to him. The noise stopped, and he appeared frozen in time, waiting for Lena to say more.

Lena's voice was softer than Jeffrey had ever heard it, and it felt like Lena and Mark were the only two people in the room when she said, 'Tell me what's wrong, Mark.'

He continued to stare, and his breathing became more pronounced.

'Who hit you?' she asked, using the same concerned tone. She reached across the table to him, and Mark lifted his hands so that she could touch him. A small sob escaped from his lips when her hand covered his.

Buddy shot Jeffrey a look, and Jeffrey shook his head once, willing the lawyer to stay silent. Dave Fine was silent without prompting, staring at Mark and Lena's hands.

Lena used her thumb to smooth Mark's tattoo. Jeffrey did not need to look at the other men in the room to know that they were a bit uncomfortable with the gesture. The air seemed charged with something unspeakable.

Lena said, 'What's going on, Mark? Tell me.'

Tears came to his eyes. 'You've got to find Lacey.'

'We will,' Lena told him.

'You've got to find her before something bad happens to her.'

'What will happen to her, Mark?'

He shook his head, sobbing, 'It's too late. No one can help her now.'

'Do you know who could have taken her? Did you recognize the car?'

He shook his head again. 'I want to see my mama.'

Lena swallowed visibly, and Jeffrey could see that Mark's frailty was getting to her, too.

'I just want to see my mama,' Mark repeated, his voice soft.

Dave Fine reached out to the boy, and Mark jerked away so hard that Buddy had to hold his chair to keep Mark from toppling over.

'Don't touch me!' Mark screamed, standing.

Lena stood, too, and half ran around to the other side of the table. She tried to touch Mark's arm, but he jumped away, nearly slamming into the wall. He backed into the corner of the room, putting his head into the angle of the walls. Lena put her hand on his shoulder, whispering something to him.

'Mark,' Dave Fine said, holding up his hands. 'Settle down, son.'

'Why aren't you with my mother?' Mark demanded. 'Where's your fucking God when my mother's dying?'

'I'll see her later tonight,' Fine said, his voice shaking. 'She wanted me to be here for you.'

'Who was there for Lacey?' Mark demanded. 'Who was there when some freak snatched her off the street?'

Fine looked down, and Jeffrey guessed the man was feeling the same guilt they all did about Lacey Patterson.

'I don't need you,' Mark screamed. 'Mama does. She needs you, and you're here with me like you can do something.'

'Mark –'

'Go help my mother!' Mark screamed.

Fine opened his mouth to say something, then seemed to change his mind.

Mark shook his head, looking away. Lena put her hands on his shoulders and led him back to his chair.

Buddy rapped his knuckles on the table to get Jeffrey's attention, then indicated the door.

Jeffrey stood, indicating that Fine should stand as well. The preacher hesitated, then did as he was told, following Buddy out into the hallway.

'Goddamn,' Buddy said, then apologized. 'Sorry, Preacher.'

Fine nodded, tucking his hands into his pockets. He looked through the small window in the door, watching Lena talk to Mark. He mumbled, 'I'll pray for his soul.'

Buddy leaned heavily onto his crutch, asking Jeffrey, 'What the hell is going on here, Chief?'

Jeffrey did not know how to answer. He asked, 'Dave, can you make any sense of this?'

'Me?' Fine asked, surprised. 'I have no idea. The last time I saw Mark, he seemed okay. Upset about his mama, but okay.'

'When was this?' Jeffrey asked.

'The other night at the hospital. I was praying with Grace.'

Jeffrey said, 'What happened between you and Jenny Weaver?'

'Jenny Weaver?' Fine asked, genuinely puzzled.

Jeffrey reminded him, 'You said you dropped by a couple of times to see her around Christmas.'

'Oh, right,' Fine agreed. 'Brad asked me to see her. She had stopped coming to church and he was worried something was wrong.'

'Was there?'

'Yes. At least I think so,' Fine answered, frowning.

'She wouldn't talk to me. None of them would talk to me about anything.'

'None of them meaning who?' Jeffrey asked.

Fine indicated the door. 'Mark and Lacey. I talked to Grace about it, but she couldn't do anything with them at that point. Put it down to teenage rebellion, I guess.' He shook his head sadly. 'A lot of kids drop out of church at that age, but they usually come back when they get older. Grace was worried, though, so I talked to him.'

'What did he say?' Jeffrey asked.

Fine colored. 'Let's just say he used some words I wouldn't want his mama to hear and leave it at that.'

Jeffrey nodded, letting it go. He had heard Mark enough times to know what the boy was capable of. He asked, 'What about Grace? How is she doing?'

'She's very sick. I don't think she'll make it to the weekend.'

Jeffrey thought about Mark wanting to see his mother. 'It's that bad?' he asked.

'Yes,' Fine answered. 'There's nothing more that they can do for her at this point except try to make her comfortable.' He glanced back through the window. 'I don't know what this family is going to do without her. It's tearing them apart.'

'You weren't on the youth retreat last Christmas, is that right?'

Fine shook his head. 'I stayed here. I'm not really involved in the retreats; that's more the youth minister's job. Brad Stephens.'

'I've talked to him already.'

'He's a fine young man,' Fine told them. 'I hoped he'd serve as an example for some of the boys.'

Jeffrey said, 'You counseled Mark some in the past, is that right?'

'A bit,' Fine answered. 'He didn't really open up. I can look over my notes and let you know if anything came up.'

'Do that,' Jeffrey told the pastor. 'Where will you be tomorrow morning?'

'I suppose at the hospital,' Fine told him, glancing at his watch. 'As a matter of fact, I'd like to get back over there tonight, unless you have any more questions for me.'

'You can go,' Jeffrey said. 'I'll be at the hospital around ten tomorrow morning. Have your notes.'

'I'm sorry I haven't been much help,' Fine apologized. He shook Jeffrey's hand, then Buddy's, before leaving.

Buddy watched the preacher go, then turned back to Jeffrey. 'I don't much like whatever is going on between your detective and my client.'

Jeffrey thought about feigning ignorance, but decided they were past that. 'I'll put him on suicide watch tonight.'

Buddy didn't buy it. 'You still haven't addressed my concern.'

Jeffrey looked back into the room. Lena had managed to get Mark to sit down, and she rubbed his back as he cried.

Jeffrey said, 'This is connected somehow to the Weaver shooting.'

'Aw, shit,' Buddy cursed, stamping the floor with his crutch. 'Thanks a lot for telling me that, Chief.'

'I wasn't sure,' Jeffrey lied. 'You know he's the kid Weaver wanted to shoot.'

'This seemed like a simple assault.'

'It is,' Jeffrey said. 'I mean, it was.'

'Wanna speak English with me here?'

Jeffrey looked back into the room. Lena still had her hand on Mark's back, comforting him.

'Honestly, Buddy, I've got no idea what's going on.'

'Start from the beginning.'

Jeffrey tucked his hands into his pockets. 'The baby we found at the skating rink,' he said, and Buddy nodded. 'We think Mark is the father.'

Buddy kept nodding. 'Makes sense.'

'We think his sister might be the mother.'

'One that's been taken?'

Jeffrey nodded. His gut clenched as he thought about Lacey Patterson and what might be happening to her.

Buddy said, 'I thought Weaver was the mother.'

'No,' Jeffrey said. 'Sara did the autopsy. Jenny wasn't the mother.' He left out what else Sara had found.

'I still haven't heard from Dottie Weaver,' Buddy told him. 'The mayor's sweating like a whore in church.'

'She'll probably wait until the funeral's over,' Jeffrey said, wondering when the funeral would be held. He doubted seriously that Sara would be invited, and she had not mentioned anything about it.

'I need to get your deposition in the next day or so, regardless,' Buddy ordered. 'We need to get it down on paper while it's fresh in your mind.'

'I don't think it'll ever not be fresh in my mind, Buddy,' Jeffrey said, thinking that he would carry Jenny Weaver's death around with him for the rest of his life.

'What else is going on here?' Buddy asked. 'Don't hold back on me.'

Jeffrey tucked his hands into his pockets. 'Mark has this tattoo on his hand.'

'The heart thing?' Buddy asked.

'Yeah,' Jeffrey confirmed. 'It's a symbol for something.'

'Kiddy porn,' Buddy supplied, much to Jeffrey's shock.

'How do you know that?'

'I've got another client who has the same tattoo,' Buddy said. 'Some guy a couple of weeks ago over in Augusta. I took the case as a favor to a friend.'

'What was the case?'

Buddy glanced around, obviously debating whether or not to answer the question.

Jeffrey pointed out, 'I've been more than forthcoming here, Buddy.'

Buddy agreed. 'Yeah, okay,' he said. 'He got nailed for coke. Not a lot, but enough to push distribution. He had some information to make the charge go away.'

'I've heard this already,' Jeffrey said. 'He's a distributor, right? For the porn?'

Buddy nodded.

'And he turned state's evidence to keep his ass out of jail.'

'Bingo,' Buddy said. 'How'd you hear about it?'

'The usual way,' Jeffrey said, not wanting to give any more information.

'What usual way?' Buddy asked.

Jeffrey tried to divert him. 'Where's your leg?' he said, indicating the empty space below Buddy's right knee.

'Shit,' Buddy sighed. 'My girlfriend took it. Won't give it back.'

'What'd you do?'

'That's a cop for you,' Buddy said, leaning on his crutch. 'Always blame the victim.'

Jeffrey laughed. 'You want me to talk to her?'

Buddy furrowed his eyebrows. 'I'll handle it,' he said. 'You gonna answer my question about how you know?'

'Nope,' Jeffrey said. He looked back into the room.

Mark had his head on the table, and Lena sat beside him, holding his hand.

Jeffrey opened the door. 'Lena,' he said, indicating she should come out into the hall.

Lena opened her mouth, probably to ask him to let her stay, but seemed to think better of it. She stood, not looking at Mark, not touching him, and walked out of the room.

'What did he say?' Jeffrey asked her.

'Nothing,' Lena answered. 'He wants to go to the hospital and see his mother.'

'Go home,' Jeffrey told her, and without waiting for her to acknowledge him, he stepped back into the room with Buddy right behind him.

'Mark,' Jeffrey began, sitting in the chair Lena had vacated. 'We know about the tattoo.'

Mark kept his head down. The table shook as he cried.

'We know what it means.'

Buddy leaned against the table on the other side of Mark. 'Son, it's in your best interest to tell us what's going on here.'

Jeffrey said, 'Mark, do you have any idea who might have taken your sister?' When there was no answer, he tried, 'Mark, we think some bad people have got her. Some people who might hurt her. You need to help us here.'

Still, he did not answer.

'Mark,' Jeffrey tried again. 'Dr. Linton said Lacey seemed sick when she saw her.'

Mark sat up, wiping his eyes with his hands. He stared straight ahead at the wall, his body rocking back and forth.

Jeffrey asked, 'Was Lacey pregnant? Was that the baby in the skating rink?'

Mark kept rocking back and forth, almost like he was being hypnotized by the wall.

Jeffrey asked, 'Were you the father of that baby, Mark?'

Mark continued to stare. Jeffrey waved his hand in front of the boy's eyes, but Mark did not move.

'Mark?' Jeffrey asked, then louder, 'Mark?'

Mark did not flinch.

'Mark?' Jeffrey repeated, snapping his fingers.

Buddy put his hand on Mark's shoulder, but the boy did not acknowledge him. Buddy said, 'I think we should get him a doctor.'

'Sara can —'

'No,' Buddy interrupted. 'I think he's seen enough of Sara for one day.'

It was ten o'clock by the time Jeffrey left the station. Nearly two hours of his time had been spent calling around the state, making sure other police departments had gotten the flyer on Lacey and knew to be on the lookout for the black Thunderbird. A lot of the cops he spoke with wanted to give him details on open cases they were working. While Jeffrey didn't think he could help some of them, he made all the right noises, hoping the cops on the other end didn't feel like he was giving them lip service. It was more likely some patrol car in Griffin would run across the black Thunderbird than it was for Jeffrey to find a missing wide-screen television that had been stolen out of a police sergeant's mother's house, but he wrote down and repeated back the serial number anyway.

Despite what he had told Nick, Jeffrey wanted to see what he could find on the Internet on his own. With Brad's help, they had found thousands of sites under the general heading of 'girl-lovers.' Brad's face had turned completely white by the third site they visited, and Jeffrey had dismissed the young patrolman and tried to navigate the Web on his own.

Even with Jeffrey's rudimentary knowledge of the Internet, he was able to find links to site after site containing images of children posed in various compromising positions. By the time he signed off, Jeffrey had felt the need to take a shower just to clean some of the images from his mind. Sara was right. Maybe some distance from the case would give him some perspective. As it stood, Jeffrey did not know where to look next.

Jeffrey tried not to think about what he had seen on the computer as he drove to Sara's house. He had called Sara before he'd left the station to tell her there was still no word on Lacey and that he was on his way over if she still wanted to see him. Thankfully, she did. He pulled into the driveway, noticing that she had left the lights on for him. When he got out of the car he could hear a soft, jazzy song playing in the house. Sara must have been looking out for him, because she opened the door before he had a chance to knock. Everything that had been troubling him for the last few days left his mind when he saw her standing there.

'Hi,' Sara said, a sly smile at her lips.

Jeffrey was speechless, and all he could do was look at her. Sara's hair was down around her shoulders, the curls softer than usual. She was wearing a silky black dress that wrapped around her body, showing her curves to their best advantage. A long slit up the side showed a hint of leg. She was wearing high heels, and they flexed her calf in a way that made him want to lick it.

She took his hand and led him inside. Jeffrey

stopped her in the hallway, and pulled her close to him. The high heels added about three inches to her height, and Sara leaned her hand on his shoulder while she slipped off the shoes so that she would be back at eye level.

'Better?' she asked. When he did not answer, she leaned in, brushing her lips across his. He kept his eyes open as long as he could, watching her kiss him. Her mouth was sweet, and he tasted wine and a bit of chocolate on her tongue.

Jeffrey closed the door behind him still watching her. He could not remember a time when she had looked more beautiful, even with the Band-Aid on her forehead.

She said, 'I don't want to talk about my day, or your day, or what's going on.'

All he could do was nod.

Sara leaned her arm against the wall, giving him a quizzical look. 'Cat got your tongue?'

Jeffrey put his hand to his chest, trying to articulate how he felt. 'Sometimes,' he began, 'I forget how beautiful you are, and then I see you . . .' He let his voice trail off, trying to find the right words. 'It just takes my breath away.'

She raised an eyebrow, as if to ask if he was feeding her some kind of line or not.

'I love you, Sara,' he said, taking a step closer to her. 'I love you so much.'

She seemed to be fighting a smile, and he loved her even more for that. As long as Jeffrey had known her, Sara had never been able to take a compliment.

She said, 'I guess this means you like the dress.'

'I'd like it even better on the floor.'

She stood away from the wall, and he watched as she reached behind her and did something with her hands. She wasn't wearing anything under the dress, so when it fell to the floor she stood completely nude in front of him.

Jeffrey drank her in, craving her in a way that frightened him. He went down on his knees and kissed her until she could not stand anymore.

WEDNESDAY

TWELVE

Lena dreamed that she heard a hammer pounding against a nail. When she rolled over in bed, she half expected to see her hand being pinned to the floor, but what she saw instead was Hank, tapping out the hinges to her bedroom door.

Lena sat up in bed, yelling, 'What the fuck?'

'I told you things were gonna change,' Hank said, still tapping at the pin holding the hinge together.

'Jesus Christ,' Lena said, putting her hands to her ears, trying to block out the hammering sound. She looked at the clock on the dresser. 'It's not even six o'clock,' she yelled. 'I don't even have to be at work until nine today.'

'Gives us plenty of time,' Hank said, sliding the pin from the hinge.

'You're taking off my door?' Lena demanded, pulling the sheet to her chest even though she was wearing a heavy sweatshirt and matching pants. 'Who the hell do you think you are?'

Hank ignored her as he started working on the top hinge.

'Stop it,' Lena ordered, getting out of bed and taking the sheet with her.

Hank kept tapping, still ignoring her.

He said, 'Things are changing, starting today.'

'What things?'

He reached into his back pocket and pulled out a folded piece of notebook paper. 'Here,' he said, handing it to her.

Lena unfolded the paper, but her eyes could not focus on the words. She was reminded of when she was a teenager, and Hank had not approved of a boy Lena was seeing. His solution then had been to nail her bedroom windows shut so that she would not be able to sneak out anymore at night. She had pointed out this was a fire hazard, and Hank had countered that he would rather see her burned alive than hooked up with that trash she was seeing.

Lena tried to take the hammer from him, but he was too strong.

She said, 'I'm not a baby, goddamn it.'

'You're my baby,' Hank said, jerking the hammer back. He tapped out the last pin and the door dropped to the floor. 'I held you in these hands,' he said, dropping the hammer to show her his hands. 'I walked with you at night when you wouldn't stop crying, I made sure you had your lunch when you went to school, and I loaned you the money to make the down payment on this house.'

'I paid you back every goddamn penny.'

'This here's the interest,' he said, wrapping his hands around the edges of the door. He lifted it with a heavy groan.

Lena watched, incredulous, as he carried the door out into the hallway.

'Why are you doing this?' she whined. 'Hank, stop it.'

'No more secrets in this house,' he mumbled, straining to set the door against the wall. He turned to her, saying, 'I'm laying down the law here, child.'

'I'm not doing any of this,' she said, throwing the list at him.

'The hell you say,' he countered, catching the paper before it hit the floor. 'You're gonna do every goddamn thing on this list every day, or I'll have a talk with your boss. How's that?'

'Don't threaten me,' she said, following him back into the bedroom.

'You take it as a threat if you want,' Hank said, yanking open one of the drawers in her bureau. He rummaged through her underwear, then slammed the drawer closed and opened the next one.

'What are you doing?'

'Here,' he said, pulling out a pair of running shorts and a T-shirt. 'Put these on and be downstairs in five minutes.'

Lena looked at him, and she noticed for the first time that Hank was not dressed in his usual jeans and loud Hawaiian shirt. He was wearing a white T-shirt with a beer advertisement on it and a pair of shorts that looked so new they still had the creases in them from being folded in the package. Brand new sneakers were on his feet, white socks pulled up to just under his knees. His legs were so white that she had to blink several times to see where his legs stopped and the socks began.

'Downstairs for what?' she asked, crossing her arms.

'We're going running.'

'You're going to go running with me?' she asked, not believing this. Hank was about as out of shape as a geriatric in a wheelchair. He did not even like walking to the mailbox.

'Five minutes,' he said, leaving the room.

'Bastard,' Lena fumed, contemplating whether or not to go after him. She was so mad she couldn't see straight, but still, she took off her pants and slid on the shorts.

'Fucking prick,' she mumbled, slipping on the shirt.

She had no choice, and that was what was pissing her off. If Hank told Jeffrey half of the stuff he knew about Lena's behavior, Lena would be out on her ass so fast her head would spin.

Lena allowed herself a glance at the list. It started off with 'exercise every day,' and ended with 'eat normal meals for breakfast, lunch, and supper.'

From deep inside somewhere, she pulled up every curse word, every expletive, she had ever heard in her ten years as a cop and directed them all toward Hank. She finished with '. . . fucking motherfucker,' then grabbed her sneakers and went downstairs.

Lena sat in Jeffrey's office, staring at the clock on his wall. He was ten minutes late, which had never happened as long as Lena could remember. She should probably be glad he wasn't here yet, because Lena needed to sit in order to recover from her morning run with Hank. He was a tough old man, and she had found herself being outpaced by him from their first step outside. Lena had to admit that some of her dogged determination must have come from her uncle, because he seemed to be like Lena: Once he got something in his head that he was going to do, nothing would stop him. Even when Lena had lagged behind, her lungs about to explode, her stomach churning from all the amino acids her muscles were giving up, he had simply jogged in place, his jaw set in an angry line, waiting for her to get over it and get moving.

'Hey,' Jeffrey said, rushing into the office. His tie was loose around his neck and he carried his jacket over his arm.

'Hey,' Lena said, standing.

He motioned for her to sit down. 'Sorry I'm late,' he said. 'Traffic.'

'Where?' Lena asked, because the only traffic in town was around the school, and then only at certain times.

Jeffrey did not answer her. He sat at his desk, buttoning his collar with one hand. Lena was not certain, but she could have sworn she saw a red mark on his neck.

She asked, 'No word on Lacey yet?'

'No,' he told her, tying his tie. 'I talked to Dave Fine on my way in. He's got the notes from his sessions with Mark.'

'He's just going to hand them over?' Lena asked, and not for the first time she was glad she had not talked to the pastor about her problems.

'Yeah,' Jeffrey said, smoothing down his tie. 'I was surprised, too.'

Lena crossed her arms, staring at her boss. There was something different about him. She just couldn't place it.

'He's going to meet me at the hospital at ten,' Jeffrey said, then looked at his watch. 'I'm already late.'

'I thought you wanted me to go with you?' Lena asked.

'I want you to get Brad and take Mark to his house,' Jeffrey told her. 'Get him some clean clothes, let him take a shower, whatever he needs to do, then take him to the hospital.'

'Why?'

'His mother took a bad turn last night,' Jeffrey said. 'Fine thinks she'll probably be gone this morning.' He tapped his fingers on his desk. 'No matter what he did, I'm not going to keep that boy from seeing his mama one last time before she dies.'

Lena was touched by this, but she tried not to let on.

Jeffrey jabbed a finger at her, as if in warning. 'I mean it about Brad, Lena. You're not to be with Mark alone. Do you understand me?'

She thought to protest, but he was right. She did not want to be alone with Mark Patterson. There was something about him that was too raw. Perhaps she identified with him too much.

'Lena?' Jeffrey prompted.

She cleared her throat, then answered, 'Yes, sir.'

As usual, Brad drove through town at exactly the speed limit. Lena tried to suppress her impatience at the same time she tried to ignore Mark sitting in the back seat. Without looking, she knew that Mark was staring at her. Both she and Jeffrey had agreed that it would be best to let his father deal with telling the boy his mother would probably be dead before the end of the day, but sitting there in the car with Mark less than two feet behind her, Lena felt like she was doing something wrong. Even with the safety guard between the front and back seats, she felt like Mark might come through the fence and grab her, demanding to know what was going on.

For Mark's part, whatever medication the doctor had given him last night seemed to work. He was back to his usual surly self, standing too close to Lena when she cuffed him, making a suggestive noise as she led him to the car. Lena wondered what had brought the change. Mark had seemed nearly catatonic the day before.

'It sure is hot out,' Brad said, taking a left off of Main Street.

'I know,' Lena agreed, wanting to keep up the small talk. 'It's hotter now than it was last year.'

'That's the truth,' Brad answered. 'I remember when

I was little, it didn't seem like it ever got this hot.'

'Me, neither,' Lena said.

'Didn't even have an air conditioner until I was twelve.'

'We got ours when I was fifteen,' she told him, allowing a smile at the memory. Lena and Sibyl had stood in front of the little unit until their faces had felt like they were frozen in place.

'We used to beg my daddy to turn the hose on out in the yard,' Brad said, giving a little laugh. 'I remember once when my cousin Bennie came over –'

Mark kicked at the guard between the seats, saying, 'Shut the fuck up.'

Brad slammed on the brakes and turned around. 'You do that again and we're gonna have to have us a talk.'

Lena had never heard Brad threaten anyone, and she was surprised to see that he had it in him. For the first time, she let herself see that Brad actually didn't seem to like Mark Patterson.

'Chill, John Boy,' Mark said.

Lena let herself glance back at Mark, and he licked his tongue out suggestively. She turned back around, staring out the front window, trying not to let him know that he had gotten to her.

The car lurched a bit as it moved forward, and Brad was quiet for the rest of the trip. Lena directed him toward the Patterson trailer by pointing with her finger instead of giving him verbal directions. She tried to let herself think that Mark was not in the back seat, but every few minutes she would remember, and it was almost like she could feel his breath on her neck.

'This is it,' Lena said, indicating the trailer. She was out of the car before Brad had come to a complete stop. Her thigh muscles protested as she moved, and she cursed Hank again for making her run that morning.

Brad opened the back door, saying, 'You gonna behave now?'

Mark took his time getting out of the car. When he stood, he was several inches shorter than Brad. He said something to the young patrolman that Lena could not hear. Whatever it was, it served to embarrass Brad, because his face turned completely red.

'Watch your mouth,' Brad said, but there was no real threat to his tone, only what could be called shock. Brad grabbed the handcuffs around Mark's wrists and pulled him toward the trailer.

At the front door, Lena pulled Mark's keys out of her pocket. They had confiscated his things when he was arrested. She guessed that a key to the door would be on the ring.

'It's the third one,' Mark said. 'The one with the green rim.' He smiled at Brad suggestively. 'Rim, rimming, rim.'

Brad's jaw worked, and he stared at the door as if he could open it with his mind.

Lena found the key and turned it in the lock. A breeze of cold air came from the trailer when she opened the door.

Mark stood in the doorway for just a second, his eyes closed, inhaling the scent of lilacs that greeted them.

'Come on,' Brad said, pushing the boy inside.

Lena shot Brad a questioning look, wondering what had gotten into him. Brad was usually the most docile person in the world.

'Take the cuffs off him,' Lena said.

Brad shook his head no. 'We shouldn't do that.'

Lena crossed her arms. 'How's he supposed to bathe and get dressed with cuffs on?'

Mark gave Brad a wink. 'You could stay with me, officer. Help scrub my back.'

Before Lena knew what she was doing, she popped Mark on the back of the head. 'Stop that,' she told him, angry that he was making Brad so uncomfortable. She told Brad, 'Why don't you watch the back of the trailer in case he tries to sneak out?'

Brad seemed relieved by this suggestion, and left without another word.

'What did you say to him?' she demanded.

'Just offered to help him relieve some of that stress he seems to have.'

'Jesus Christ,' Lena breathed. 'Why would you do that to him?'

'Why not?' Mark shrugged.

Lena took out her handcuff key and motioned him over. He put the cuffs tight to his crotch so she would have to touch him to work the key.

'Hands out, Mark,' Lena ordered.

He sighed dramatically, but did as he was told. 'You like being chained up?' he asked.

'I'll give you ten minutes in the shower,' she told him, releasing the cuffs. 'If I have to come in after you, I won't be nice about it.'

'Mmm . . . ,' Mark said, drawing out the sound. 'Sounds tasty.'

Lena clipped the handcuffs onto the back of her belt. 'Ten minutes,' she said, wondering if this was how Hank had felt this morning, ordering her around. She walked over to the couch and picked up a magazine before sitting down. Mark stood in the kitchen, watching her for what seemed like a full minute before he went back to his room. A couple of minutes later, she heard water running in the shower. Lena closed the magazine, feeling an overwhelming sense of relief.

She stood from the couch, holding on to the mantel as she stretched out her quads. Her legs hurting this much after what a year ago would have amounted to a light run was beginning to piss her off. She was stronger than this. There was no way she could be so out of shape.

Lena picked up a framed photograph of Mark and Lacey standing in front of a nondescript roller coaster. Both children were smiling, and Mark's arm was thrown around Lacey's shoulders. In turn, she had her hand around his waist. They looked about three years younger than they were now. They looked happy.

'That was at Six Flags,' Mark said.

Lena tried not to show he had startled her. Mark was standing about three feet away from her, wearing nothing but a towel around his waist.

'Get dressed,' she said.

He pressed his lips together in a lazy smile, and she felt like an idiot for not checking his room first for contraband.

'What are you on?' she asked him.

'Cloud nine,' he smiled, dropping onto the couch.

'Mark,' Lena said, 'get up. Get dressed.'

He stared at her, his lips slightly parted.

She asked, 'What?'

He kept staring for just a second more, then asked, 'What did it feel like?'

'What did what feel like?'

He looked down at her hands, and she crossed her arms so that he could not see the scars. She shook her head. 'No.'

'My dad told me what happened.'

'I'm sure he took great pleasure in it.'

Mark frowned. 'He didn't, actually. Teddy doesn't get off on that kind of thing.' He must have noticed Lena's surprise, because he said, 'Old Ted's a straight arrow, now. Very vanilla.'

Lena turned back to the photograph. 'Go get dressed, Mark. We don't have time for this.'

'You tell me your secrets and I'll tell you mine.'

Lena laughed. 'You watch too many movies.'

'I'm serious.'

'I don't think so, Mark.'

She heard a lighter click several times, and turned around to see Mark lighting a joint.

'Put that out,' she told him.

He inhaled deeply, not obeying.

He said, 'Don't you want to know what happened?'

'I want you to get dressed so that you can go see your mother.'

He smiled, making himself comfortable on the couch. 'I really thought you were going to pull that trigger the other night.'

Without thinking, Lena sat at the opposite end of the couch. 'You were watching me?' she asked, not feeling violated so much as caught.

He nodded, taking a long hit off the joint.

'Where were you?'

'By the shed,' he told her. 'I thought you were going to run right over it.'

Lena felt a flush of shame.

'That man was beside the house. I thought he saw me, but he was watching you.' Mark blew on the tip of the joint. 'He's your father?'

'Uncle,' she told him.

Mark took another hit on the joint, holding in the smoke for a few beats. He exhaled slowly, then asked, 'How'd it feel, holding that gun in your mouth?'

'Wrong,' she said, trying to recover. 'That's why I didn't do it.'

'No. Being raped,' he said. 'How'd it feel?'

Lena looked around the room, wondering why she was having this conversation with this kid.

'Bad,' she said, then shrugged. 'Just . . . not good.'

He choked on a laugh. 'I guess so.'

'No,' Lena said, then, wanting to get back in charge of the conversation, she said, 'Why don't you tell me what happened, Mark?'

'Have you had sex yet?'

She didn't like the way he said 'yet' as if it was something inevitable. 'That's not really any of your business,' she told him, amazed that she was able to talk about it so casually. For the first time in a while, Lena felt in control of herself and her emotions. She felt strong, and capable of handling this kid. In light of the fact that just a day ago she had tried to kill herself, this came as somewhat of a shock to her.

Lena said, 'Tell me what's going on.'

'My mom's gonna die,' he said. 'You know that, don't you?'

'Yes,' she told him, looking down at her hands because she did not want him to read the truth in her face. 'Is that what you want to talk about, your mom?'

He did not respond.

'Mark,' Lena said. 'Do you know where your sister is?'

He stared at her, his eyes watering. She was struck again by how much of a child he still was.

He said, 'We're a lot alike, you know?'

'In what way?'

'In here,' he said, putting his hand over his chest. 'How did it feel being raped?'

She shook her head, not letting him distract her.

'How are we alike, Mark? Has somebody hurt you?'

Something flashed in his eyes, and for just a moment she could see that he was in a tremendous amount of pain. Lena's heart went out to him, and she felt something akin to a maternal urge to take care of Mark Patterson, even if she could not completely take care of herself.

She asked, 'Who hurt you, Mark?'

He propped his foot up on the coffee table. 'Why are you a cop?'

'Because I want to help people,' she told him, though that was no longer entirely true. 'Let me help you. Tell me what happened.'

He shook his head over this. 'How did it feel?' he asked again. 'When you were being raped. What did that feel like?'

'Tell me why you want to know and I'll tell you.'

He sucked on the joint, finishing it. He looked around for somewhere to put the butt, and Lena slid a plate across the coffee table for him.

He sat up, putting his elbows on his knees. 'I wonder sometimes why people do things.'

'I do, too,' she said. 'For instance, why would Jenny want to kill you?'

He waved this off. 'She wasn't going to kill me.'

'Is that why you pissed yourself?'

He laughed. 'Hindsight is twenty-twenty.'

'Why'd she do it, Mark?'

'She thought she could stop it.'

'Stop what?'

'Stop me?' he asked, as if Lena might actually know the answer.

'Stop you from what?' She waited for him to answer, and when he didn't she tried, 'Tell me about that party with Carson and the other boys.'

He scowled. 'Carson's a pussy.'

'Why'd you make Jenny sleep with them?'

'I didn't make her do shit,' he spat out. 'She wanted to do that. She was trying to make me jealous, showing me it didn't mean anything.'

'Didn't hurt you got her drunk, either.'

'Yeah, well,' he said, waving her off.

'What did Jenny think she could stop, Mark?' Lena asked. 'That night at Skatie's. What did she think she could stop?'

Mark twisted his lips to the side, as if he might tell her, then seemed to change his mind. He asked, 'You think you'll find my sister?'

'Do you know where she is?'

He looked down, and she wondered if he knew where Lacey was or if he was feeling guilty for not knowing.

Lena sat back, her arms crossed, waiting for him to say what he needed to say.

'I feel like sometimes I'm not even real,' he said. 'Like maybe I'm in the room, and maybe I'm breathing the air, but nobody really sees me.' He rubbed his eyes. 'Then I think maybe if I'm not really here, that I need to be someplace else. Like, maybe I should just go ahead and pull the trigger, you know?'

Lena nodded, because she did know.

'What made you stop?' he asked her. 'Why didn't you pull the trigger?'

She told him the truth about the gun, but not about the pills. 'I thought about my partner finding me in the morning, and I couldn't do that to him.'

'Do you believe in God?'

'I'm not sure,' she answered. 'Do you?'

He shook his head no.

'Is that why you stopped going to church?'

He looked at her, angry. 'Don't be a cop with me.'

'I am a cop, Mark.' Lena kept her tone even, not matching his anger. She reached out and put her hand on his arm. 'I want to know what happened. Why did Jenny want to kill you?'

He sighed, slouching against the pillows. 'She was such a sweet kid,' he said. 'I really cared about her.'

'I know you did.'

'Do you?' he asked. 'I mean, do you really understand what it means to care about somebody?'

Lena thought of Sibyl when she said, 'Yes, I do.'

'Not me,' he said. 'I mean, before Jenny. I just didn't know what it meant to care like that.'

'You love your mother.'

He laughed, a hollow sound that vibrated in his chest. 'She's going to die soon, isn't she?'

Lena pressed her lips together.

'I feel it,' he said, putting his hand over his heart. 'I felt it this morning, somehow, like she wasn't going to last much longer, like she wanted to let go.' He started to cry. 'It's this connection, you know? Like, I can feel what she feels.' He turned to her suddenly, a bit of desperation in his tone. 'Did you know when your sister died?'

'Yes,' Lena lied. At the time, she had been on her way back from Macon and had no idea that something bad had happened. 'I could feel it here,' she said, putting her hand to her chest.

'Then you know,' he said. 'You know what that emptiness feels like.'

Lena nodded, not saying more.

Mark looked away, then closed his eyes. She studied his profile, his sharp nose and squared jaw. Tears rolled down his cheeks and fell onto his chest.

'The first time,' Mark began, his voice low, 'I guess it was at Thanksgiving.'

Lena kept her mouth closed, letting him take his time.

'Lacey and Jenny were down the hall in Lacey's room, and I wanted to borrow one of her CDs.' He sighed, his chest rising and falling with the sound. 'She started yelling at me, all mad and shit. I dunno. I guess Mama heard her yelling and came in and told us to stop.'

Lena felt her heart rate accelerate, and said a small prayer to whoever was listening that Brad would not pick now to come back into the trailer. She tried to do the math and figure out how much time had passed since he left, but since she dared not look at her watch, Lena wasn't sure.

'Lacey turned up the radio in her room really loud,' he said. 'Mama let her. It's always been like that. She was always the favorite.' He shook his head. 'Lacey's sweet underneath, you know? Maybe she's spoiled, but she's sweet underneath. She has a good heart, just like Mama.'

Lena waited, counting to twenty-five before Mark started speaking again.

'She came into my room a little later,' he said. 'I guess she knew I was still pissed off. Wanted to smooth things over. She was always like that, trying to make peace. I guess that's why so many people liked her, because she was good like that.' A slight smile came to his lips, but he kept his eyes closed. 'She just put her hand around the back of my neck, and then we started kissing for some reason. I mean, just kissing real deep for a long time.'

Lena tried to remember what Jeffrey had said about not letting her personal feelings ruin a confession, but the thought of Mark Patterson kissing his baby sister made her stomach roll. She wanted to say something, to stop him so that she would not go through the rest of her life knowing this story, but she knew that she could not.

'I don't know how the rest of it happened,' Mark said. 'You know, we were kissing, and then she started rubbing me, and it felt so good.' He looked at her, asking for her approval. 'I know it was wrong, okay? It just felt so good. I didn't want to stop.'

Lena nodded, trying to control her expression. She doubted very seriously that Lacey Patterson had seduced her brother. Saying the victim had 'asked for it' was a common theme among sexual predators.

'I can tell you don't understand,' he said. 'But you don't know what it's like. My dad is so fucking hard on me.' He slammed his fist into his leg. 'He just never lets up on me. Ever.'

'I know,' Lena told him, reaching out, making herself touch his arm. 'I understand that part, Mark. I really do.'

His expression softened, and he said, 'I didn't make her do it.'

'I believe you.'

'She came on to me first,' he said. 'She was the one who came into my room. She was the one who started kissing me, who started touching me.'

Lena nodded because that was all that she could do.

'She was so wet for me. I just . . .' He shook his head, squeezing his eyes shut, as if to bring back the memory. 'It felt so right being inside of her. And she wanted me. I could tell she wanted me. The way she put her hand on the back of my neck, and pulled me closer to her, deeper.'

Lena swallowed back bile.

'Touching her and being with her and inside of her,' Mark said. 'I just felt complete, you know? Like things were finally right.' He put his hand over his eyes. 'She was so good at it. I mean, where did she learn to be so damn good at it?'

He seemed to want an honest answer, but Lena could not give him one.

'I mean, I look at my dad,' he said, shaking his head. 'It's not like he knows anything.'

Lena spoke without thinking. 'Your dad was sleeping with her, too?'

'Well, duh,' he said, as if she were stupid.

Lena put her hand to her stomach, thinking about poor Lacey Patterson, and what hell she must have been through.

She said, 'Tell me about Jenny.'

Mark gave a humorless laugh. 'Yeah, Jenny,' he said. 'I had been with her a couple of times before, like I told you.' He paused. 'She was sweet. She was all those things I told you.'

'She seemed like a good friend.'

'Yeah, well,' he said, a bit of derision slipping into his tone. 'She was a good friend until she caught us.'

'Is that why she pointed the gun at you?'

'I guess part of it was that,' he said. 'Then, you know, maybe she just wanted it to stop. She said that a lot, that she just wanted it to stop.'

'Was she jealous?'

He nodded slowly. 'It hurt her to see it.'

'She saw you together?'

He nodded again, the same slow movement. 'We were in my bed, and she and Lacey came home from school.'

Lena felt her heart stop midbeat. She opened her mouth to ask for a clarification, then closed it. She did not want to know. If she could have moved her body, she would have run from the room, covering her ears so that she could not hear any more. She couldn't move, though, and she sat motionless on the couch, watching Mark the way she would watch a car wreck.

'We were together, you know? I guess this was around Christmastime, right before they went on that stupid retreat.' He threw his hand into the air. 'Mama let me stay home from school. We had the whole day together.' He smiled. 'She lit some candles, and we took a long bath, and then we made love.'

Lena was aware that she had stopped breathing.

'I guess we lost track of time,' Mark said, giving a pitiful laugh. 'Lacey and Jenny walked right into my room, and that was it.'

Lena put her hand to her mouth to keep herself from speaking.

'Jenny loved my mom. I mean, it was complicated. Maybe it's better that Jenny's not around to watch Mama die. I think that would've killed her.'

'Right,' Lena managed.

'I know what you think, but she loved me, man. It felt so good to know that she loved me. It was like Lacey was always the favorite, but then she came to me, and I was the one. I was the one she loved most.' Mark started to cry again. Before Lena knew what was happening, he had buried his face in her neck.

Lena forced the word, 'Mark,' out of her mouth, trying to push him away from her.

'Don't,' he whispered, and his wet lips against her flesh made her want to vomit.

'Mark, no,' she said. When he didn't move, Lena pushed him away as hard as she could. 'Get away from me!' she yelled.

From the way he was looking at her, she imagined that every ounce of disgust she was feeling was written all over her face.

'Mark –'

'Bitch,' he said, standing. 'You fucking bitch!'

'Mark –'

The door popped open, and Brad stood there, his hand on the butt of his gun. Lena motioned him back as Mark stepped toward her.

Mark said, 'I thought you would understand.'

'I do,' she told him, feeling panicked. 'I do understand, Mark.'

'Fucking bitch,' he hissed. 'You don't understand shit.'

'Mark –'

He closed the distance between them in two steps, grabbing her hand and holding it up between them. 'I thought you understood,' he said, and she knew he meant her scars. 'I thought you knew because you'd been there, man. You know what it's like. I know you do. You just won't fucking admit it because you're a coward.'

Lena opened her mouth, but could not speak.

'Hey,' Brad said, taking Mark's arm.

'Get away from me, faggot,' Mark screamed, yanking his arm out of Brad's grasp. He pointed an accusatory finger at Lena, saying through clenched teeth, 'You tricked me. You're all alike, goddamn it. She was right. You're all so weak. You never do the right thing.'

Lena cleared her throat, trying, 'Mark –'

Mark walked toward the hallway, his footsteps so heavy that the trailer shook.

'What the heck was that about?' Brad asked, his hand still resting on his gun.

Lena shook her head, unable to speak for just a moment.

'Are you okay?' Brad asked, going to the couch. He put his hand on her arm and she did not pull away.

'I can't believe . . .' Lena began, not knowing exactly what to say.

Brad sat beside her, taking her hand. 'Lena?' he asked, patting her hand. 'Talk to me.'

She shook her head, taking back her hand. 'He's just a kid,' she said.

'A nasty kid,' Brad told her. 'Sometimes I wonder how they can get that way. When I was his age, I barely even knew what sex was. I thought a good time on a date was getting a kiss at the end.'

Lena nodded, zoning out as he talked about his idyllic teen years.

'I just wonder,' Brad said. 'What makes them like that? What's changed?'

'Their parents,' Lena said, but she knew that wasn't right. She pushed her hair back behind her ear, trying to suppress the shock she was still feeling. She looked at her watch, wondering if she should go get Mark. He had been gone a while.

'What did he mean?' Brad asked. 'Wasn't that the same stuff Jenny was saying before?'

Lena finally managed to focus on the conversation. 'Before when?' she asked.

'In the parking lot,' Brad said. 'You know, when she said adults never do the right thing.'

'Oh, Jesus,' Lena breathed, feeling all the air going out of her lungs. She jumped up from the couch and started off down the hall, Brad close behind her.

'Mark?' she yelled, knocking on the only closed door. She tried the handle, but it was locked.

'Dammit,' Lena hissed, jamming her shoulder against the door. It would not budge. She motioned to Brad. 'Kick it in.'

He braced himself against the other side of the hall and punched his foot into the door. Unfortunately, the door was hollow at the center, and Brad's foot stuck in the splintered wood. He used Lena for leverage, pulling his foot out of the hole. She leaned down, looking into the room, trying to find Mark through the narrow opening.

'Oh, God,' Lena gasped, stepping back to kick at the hole Brad had made. He joined in, and between them they managed to enlarge the opening enough for Lena to slip through. The splintered wood tore at her arms and face, but she barely noticed the pain as she tried to get into the room.

'Mark,' she said, her voice high with panic. 'Hold on, Mark. Hold on.'

Brad pushed her from behind, and she fell into the room. Mark had hanged himself from a rod mounted high in the closet. The ceiling of the trailer was not high, and his feet dragged the ground. Still, the belt around his neck seemed to be doing the trick. His face was blue, his tongue protruding slightly. She grabbed his legs, holding him up to take some of the stress off his neck.

'Goddamn it, Brad,' she cursed. 'Get in here.'

Brad finally managed to bust the door open wide enough to squeeze through, and he used his pocket knife to cut the belt while Lena held Mark's legs. It took forever for the knife to cut through the thick leather, and Lena felt her arms start to shake from holding Mark up for so long.

'No, no, no,' Lena cried until Mark fell to the ground. She put her ear to his chest, trying to make out a heartbeat. A few seconds passed, then she finally heard a telltale thump, followed by another stronger one.

'Is he okay?' Brad asked, loosening the belt from Mark's neck.

Lena nodded, pulling a blanket off the bed. She wrapped it around Mark's body, saying, 'Call an ambulance.'

THIRTEEN

'Sara?' Molly asked, then repeated, 'Sara?'

'Hmm?' Sara said. Molly, Candy Nelson, and her three children were all staring at her expectantly.

Sara shook her head a little, saying, 'Sorry,' before she went back to the examination. She had been worrying about Lacey Patterson, wondering what was happening to her.

'Breathe deeply,' Sara told Danny Nelson.

'I've been breathing deeply for the last ten minutes,' Danny complained.

'Hush up,' his mama said.

Sara could feel Molly staring at her, but kept the focus on Danny. 'That's good,' she told him. 'Put your shirt back on and I'll talk to your mother.'

Candy Nelson followed her out into the hallway.

Sara said, 'I want to send him to a specialist.'

The mother put her hand to her heart, as if Sara had just told her Danny only had a couple of months to live.

'It's nothing to be nervous about,' she assured her. 'I just want you to get his ears checked by someone who knows more about them than I do.'

'Are you certain he's okay?'

'I'm certain,' Sara said, then, 'Molly, could you write a referral for Matt DeAndrea over in Avondale?'

Molly nodded, and Sara walked into her office,

dropping her stethoscope on the desk. She sat down in her chair, trying not to sigh. She found herself thinking about Jeffrey. Every part of her body felt alive, if not slightly bruised. Her back was killing her, but that wasn't surprising, considering they had not made it out of the hallway until around three that morning.

'So,' Molly said, interrupting Sara's thoughts. 'I guess this means we're taking Jeffrey's calls now?'

Sara blushed. 'Is it that obvious?'

'Let's just say an ad in the *Grant Observer* would be more subtle.'

Sara narrowed her eyes at the nurse.

'That's your last patient,' Molly told her, smiling. 'Are you going to the morgue?'

Sara opened her mouth to respond, but a banging noise echoed up the hallway, followed by a curse. Sara rolled her eyes at Molly, and trotted up the hall toward the bathroom. Thanks to a six year old with a keen interest in flushing his Matchbox collection down the toilet, the waste pipe had backed up. Sara had actually debated whether or not to call her father, knowing that Tessa would be working with him today. She did not have the proper tools to fix the toilet, however, and since she had taken yesterday afternoon off, she did not have the time to do the job. Besides, her father would have been very hurt if she had not called him to come to her rescue.

'Daddy,' Sara whispered, shutting the bathroom door behind her. 'This is a children's clinic. You can't cuss like that around here.'

He shot her a look over his shoulder. 'I cussed around you girls all the time and you turned out okay.'

'Dad . . . ,' Sara tried again.

'That's right,' he said. 'I'm your father.'

She gave up, sitting on the edge of the tub. As a child, Sara had often watched her father work, and Eddie had put on quite a show for Sara and Tessa, banging pipes, dancing around with a wrench in one hand and a plunger in the other. He wanted to teach his girls to be good with their hands, and comfortable with their abilities. Sara often thought that he had been somewhat disappointed that Sara had not joined the family business when she got out of college, and chose instead to go to medical school. He had picked up the part of her tuition that the scholarships did not pay for, and made sure she had money to live on, but in his heart Sara knew Eddie would have been perfectly happy to have her back living at home, snaking drains and welding pipes alongside him. Some days, Sara was tempted. She certainly would be working fewer hours as a plumber.

Eddie cleared his throat and began, 'The old West, right?'

Sara smiled, knowing he was about to tell one of his jokes. 'All right.'

'This sheriff goes into a saloon and says, "I'm lookin' for a cowboy wearing a brown paper vest and brown paper pants.' He waited a beat, making sure Sara was listening. 'The bartender says, "What's he wanted for?" And the sheriff says, "Rustling."'

Sara laughed despite herself.

Eddie returned to the job at hand, shoving a toilet auger down the bowl. The spindle beside him turned slowly, letting out the flexible metal snake with a pointed tip on the end that would hopefully clear the blockage.

He asked, 'What'd this kid flush down again?'

'Matchbox car,' Sara said. 'At least, that's what we think.'

'Little bastard,' Eddie mumbled, and Sara just shook her head, knowing it was useless to try to censor him. She had learned that lesson nearly thirty years ago at a particularly embarrassing parent-teacher conference. Instead, Sara leaned her elbows on her knees and watched him work. Eddie Linton was not what anyone would call a snappy dresser, even when he tried. He was wearing a Culture Club T-shirt from a concert he had taken Sara and Tessa to when they were in high school. His green shorts were so old that they had strings hanging down. She leaned over and pulled at one.

'Hey,' he said.

'You should let me get the scissors,' she offered.

'Don't you have patients to see?'

'This is my morgue day,' she told him. Even though there was a stack of paperwork waiting for her at the morgue, Sara did not want to deal with it. As a matter of fact, she would be perfectly content to sit here all day with her father. At least until Jeffrey got off work.

Eddie looked at her over his shoulder. 'What are you so happy about?'

'Having you here,' she said, rubbing his back.

'Yeah, right,' he mumbled, shoving the snake in harder. 'This is a pain in the ass. You should charge that kid for my time.'

'I'll see what his insurance company says.'

Eddie sat back on his heels. 'Your sister's in the van.'

Sara did not respond.

He gave her a serious look. 'When I was in the war, I watched men die.'

Sara barked a laugh. 'You fixed toilets at Fort Gillem, Daddy. You never even left Georgia.'

'Well . . .' He waved this off. 'There was that corporal from Connecticut who couldn't handle his grits.'

Eddie crossed his arms and gave her a serious look. 'Anyway, what I mean is, life is too short.'

'Yes,' Sara agreed. She saw evidence of that at the morgue on an almost weekly basis.

'Too short to be mad at your sister.'

'Ah,' Sara said, getting it. 'Did she tell you what we're arguing about?'

'Do you girls ever tell me anything?' he grumbled.

'It's complicated,' Sara told him.

'I bet it's not,' Eddie countered, pulling the snake out of the toilet, hand over hand. 'I bet it's real simple.' He rolled the metal snake around a spindle, telling her, 'Go get me the power auger.'

'I have to get to work,' she said.

'Right after you get the auger,' he told her, handing her the coiled snake.

Sara hesitated, then took it. 'I'm not doing this because you told me to.'

He held up his hands. 'You haven't done anything I've told you to do since 1979.'

She stuck out her tongue at him before leaving the room. Sara took the back door and walked around the clinic so that the patients in the waiting room would not see her. Technically, she was off-duty, but there was always someone who knew her, and Sara did not want to be stopped.

Eddie's work van was backed into a parking space beside Sara's car. LINTON AND DAUGHTERS was painted on the side panels. A drawing of a commode with a roll of pink toilet tissue on the back of the tank served as the logo. As Sara drew near, she could see Tessa sitting behind the wheel, the windows rolled up and the engine on. She had probably been waiting out here for at least thirty minutes.

Sara yanked the passenger's side door open. Tessa

did not look up. Obviously, she had seen Sara approach.

'Hey,' Sara called over the roar of the air-conditioning, tossing the auger into the back of the van. She got into the van and slammed the door behind her.

Tessa gave a reluctant, 'Hey,' back, then, 'Did they find that kid?'

'Not yet.' Sara leaned her back against the door so that she was facing her sister. She slipped off her clogs and hooked her toes onto the edge of Tessa's seat.

'That's my side,' Tessa told her, a phrase that had been oft repeated when they took car rides as children.

'So,' Sara said, prodding Tessa's leg with her big toe. 'What're you gonna do?'

'Stop it,' Tessa slapped at her feet. 'I'm mad at you.'

'I'm mad at you,' Sara told her.

Tessa turned back around, resting her hands on the steering wheel. 'I'm sorry I said what I said.' She paused. 'About not having children.'

Sara let some time pass. 'I'm sorry I asked if Devon's the father.'

'Well . . .' – Tessa shrugged – 'he is, if you were really wondering.'

'I wasn't,' she said, though part of her had been.

Tessa turned, leaning her back against the door so she could face Sara. She pulled her feet up under her and the two sisters stared at each other, neither saying anything.

Sara broke the silence. 'If you want to do this . . . ,' she began, trying to sound like she meant it. 'If you really need to do this . . . I'll support you. You know that.'

Tessa asked her, 'Where did all that come from?'

'I just . . .' Sara began, looking for a way to explain her feelings. 'I've just seen so many kids hurt this week, and I . . .' She let her voice trail off. 'How I feel about this doesn't matter, Tessie. It's your decision.'

'I know that.'

'I know it's your choice,' Sara repeated. 'I know that you're not doing this lightly –'

'It's not that,' Tessa stopped her.

'What is it, then?'

Tessa looked out the window, and was silent. After a while, she said, 'I'm just really, really scared.'

'Tessie.' Sara reached out, taking her sister's hand. 'What are you scared of?'

'It's Mom and Dad,' she said, and she started to cry. 'What if I'm not as good as they are? What if I'm a horrible mother?'

'You won't be,' Sara assured her, stroking Tessa's hair back.

'You were right before,' Tessa told her. 'I *am* selfish. I *do* only think of myself.'

'I didn't mean that.'

'Yes, you did. I know you did, because it's true.' Tessa wiped her eyes with the back of her hand. 'I know I'm selfish, Sara. I know I'm immature.' She laughed with some irony. 'I'm thirty-three years old and I still live with my parents.'

'Not in the same house.'

Tessa laughed, even as she cried. 'Oh, God, please, don't stick up for me.'

Sara laughed, too. 'Tess, you're such a good person. You love kids.'

'I know I do. It's just different thinking about having them around twenty-four hours a day.' She shook her head. 'What if I do something horrible? What if I drop him, or what if it's a girl and I end up dressing her up like that Ramsey kid?'

'Then we'll have you committed.'

'I'm serious,' Tessa whined, but she laughed as well. 'What if I don't know how to do it right?'

'Mama and Daddy will be there to help,' Sara reminded her. 'I will, too.' She let that sink in, then amended, 'If that's what you decide to do, I mean. If you want to keep it.'

Tessa leaned forward. 'You would be a great mother, Sara.'

Sara pressed her lips together, not wanting to cry.

'I just don't know what to do.'

Sara took a deep breath, then let it go. 'You don't have to decide right now,' she said. 'You could wait a couple of days, just to see how you feel once the shock has worn off.'

'Yeah.'

'I do think you should tell Devon. He has a right to know.'

Tessa nodded slowly. 'I know he does,' she said. 'Maybe I didn't want to tell him because I know what he'll say.' She gave a wry smile. 'He'll get exactly what he wants.'

'You don't have to marry him.'

'Oh, and give Dad a heart attack, living in sin?'

'I seriously doubt he'd have a heart attack.' Sara smiled. 'He might take you over his knee . . .'

'Yeah, well.' Tessa took a tissue from the center console. She blew her nose in three short bursts, the way she had done since she was a baby. 'Maybe somebody should take me over his knee.'

Sara squeezed her hand. 'You make this decision, Tess. Whatever you decide, I'm with you.'

'Thank you,' Tessa mumbled, wiping her nose with another tissue. She sat back against the window again, and took a long look at Sara. After a few beats, a smile broke out on her face.

Sara asked, 'What?'

'You look so obvious.'

'So obvious what?'

Tessa kept smiling. 'So obviously fucked.'

Sara laughed, and the sound echoed in the van.

'Was it good?' Tessa asked.

Sara glanced out the window, feeling a bit mischievous. 'Which time?'

'You slut,' Tessa screamed, throwing the used tissue.

'Hey.' Sara deflected the tissue with her hand.

'Don't go all big sister on me,' Tessa warned. 'Tell me what happened.'

Sara felt a blush creeping up her neck. 'No way.'

'What changed your mind?' she asked. 'I mean, last I heard, you didn't even want to date him.'

'Mama,' Sara answered. 'She told me to make up my mind.'

'And?'

'We've just been doing this stupid back-and-forth thing for so long.' Sara paused, thinking about how to phrase it. 'I have to give it another try. I either have to get him out of my system and go on, or keep him in my system and live with it.'

Tessa asked, 'Was it good?'

'It was nice to feel something new,' she said, thinking about the night before. 'It was nice to stop feeling guilty for a while.' As an afterthought, she added, 'And scared.'

'Over that missing girl?'

'Over everything,' Sara said, not going into details. She made it a point not to talk about her work at the morgue with her family. This protected Sara as much as it protected them. There had to be a part of her life that wasn't overshadowed by death and violence. 'It was nice to . . .'

'Have a screaming orgasm?'

Sara clicked her tongue, smiling. 'It was pretty spectacular.' She shook her head, because that wasn't right. 'It was amazing. Totally –'

'Oh, shit.' Tessa sat up, wiping her eyes. 'Dad's coming.'

Sara sat up, too, though she did not know why. It was not as if Eddie could send her to her room for sitting in the parking lot too long.

'Where's that auger?' he demanded, throwing open Sara's door. 'What're you two talking about in here?' When he did not get an answer, he said, 'Do you know how much gas you're wasting, sitting here with the engine running?'

Sara laughed, and he popped her on the leg, asking, 'What would your mama say if she saw that look on your face?'

Tessa answered, 'Probably, "It's about damn time."'

They started giggling, and Eddie gave them both a sharp look before slamming the door closed and walking away.

The morgue was housed in the basement of the Grant Medical Center, and no matter how hot it got outside, it was always cool in the tiled subterranean rooms. Sara felt bumps come out on her skin as she walked back to her office.

'Hey, Dr. Linton,' Carlos said in his soft, heavily accented voice. He was dressed in his usual green scrubs, and held a clipboard at an angle against his thick waist. Sara had hired Carlos six years ago, right out of high school. He was short for his age, and wore his hair cut in a bilevel, which did not do much for his round face. Carlos was efficient, though, and he never complained about having to do what amounted to shit work, literal and figurative. Sara could trust him in the morgue to take care of things and keep his mouth shut.

Sara managed a smile for him. 'What's up?'

He handed her his clipboard, saying, 'That Weaver kid is still here. What do you want me to do with her?'

Sara felt her heart sink as she thought of the baby. Dottie Weaver had no reason to claim the child since Sara had told her it was not Jenny's. Something about that fragile little girl sitting in the freezer broke Sara's heart.

'Dr. Linton?' Carlos asked.

'I'm sorry,' Sara apologized. 'What did you say?'

'I asked what you wanted to do with the bodies.'

Sara shook her head at the plural, thinking she had missed something. She looked down at the chart and saw that Jenny Weaver's name was at the top. Sara thumbed through the paperwork, noting that she had released the body on Sunday. There was no accompanying form from the funeral home to verify that she had been picked up.

'She's still here?' Sara asked.

Carlos nodded, tucking a hand into his hip.

'We haven't gotten a call from Brock?' she asked, referring to the funeral director in town.

'No, ma'am,' he said.

Sara glanced back at the paperwork, as if that could offer an explanation. 'We haven't heard from the mother?'

'We haven't heard from anybody.'

'Let me make some phone calls,' she told him, walking into her office.

Sara knew the number to Brock's Funeral Home by heart, and she dialed it into the phone, watching Carlos through the window. He was mopping the floor in slow, deliberate strokes, his back to her.

The phone was picked up on the first ring. 'Brock's Funeral Home.'

'Brock,' Sara said, recognizing the man's voice. Dan Brock was Sara's age, and they had gone to school together from kindergarten on.

'Sara Linton,' Brock said, genuine pleasure in his voice. 'How you?'

'I'm great, Brock,' she answered. 'I hate to cut right down to business, but have you gotten a call on a Jennifer Weaver?'

'The one what was shot last weekend?' he asked. 'Sure haven't. Gotta say, I was expecting that call.'

'Why is that?'

'Well, Dottie goes to my church,' he told her. 'I just assumed she'd call on me.'

'Do you know her well?'

'Well enough to say hi to,' he answered. 'Plus, that little Jenny was a peach. She was in the children's choir for a while. Sang like an angel.'

Sara nodded, remembering that Brock directed the children's choir in his spare time. 'Sara?' Brock prompted.

'Sorry,' Sara told him, thinking she was too easily distracted lately. 'Thanks for the information.'

'It hasn't been in the paper, either.'

'What's that?'

'The obituaries,' Brock said, giving a self-deprecating chuckle. 'Tools of the trade. We like to see who's doing who, if you know what I mean.'

'And there's been no mention?'

'Nary a peep,' he told her. 'Maybe they sent her up North? I think that's where her daddy is.'

'Still, it would've been in the paper, right?' Sara asked, playing dumb. Brock was generally discreet because of the business he was in, but she did not want to start rumors.

'Maybe,' he said. 'Or the church bulletin at least. I haven't seen it there, either.' He paused, then said, 'Heck, Sara, you know how some people are about death. They just don't want to admit it happened, especially with a kid involved. Maybe she handled it quietly just so she could get through it, you know?'

'You're right,' Sara told him. 'Anyway, thanks for the information.'

'I hear Grace Patterson doesn't have much longer,' he said, and she imagined business was slow if he was being so chatty. 'That's gonna be a hard one.'

'You know her, too?'

'She helped me with the choir before she took sick this last time. Wonderful woman.'

'I've heard that.'

'From what I've gathered, she's just eat up with the cancer,' he said. 'Those are always the hard ones.' His voice had dropped, and he seemed genuinely upset. 'Well, hell, Sara, you know what I'm talking about.'

Sara did, and she understood his grief. She couldn't imagine having to do Dan Brock's job. He probably felt the same way about hers.

'Guess there's no word on the little girl yet?' he asked.

'No,' Sara said. 'Not that I know of.'

'Jeffrey's a good man,' he told her. 'If anyone can find her, it's him.'

Sara wanted to believe this, but with everything she had learned about the case lately, she wasn't too sure.

Brock lightened his tone. 'You take care now,' he said. 'Best to your mama and them.'

Sara wished him the same and hung up the phone. She pressed the button for a new line and called Jeffrey.

FOURTEEN

Lena tried not to make it too obvious that she was listening to Jeffrey's telephone conversation with Sara Linton. This was incredibly difficult to do, as they were both in the front seat of Jeffrey's car. Lena looked out the window, feigning a casualness she did not feel. Part of her was still struck by what had happened with Mark only hours before. Only time would tell if he would make it. Oxygen had been cut off to his brain for some time, and until he woke up from the coma, there was no way to predict how much damage had been done.

Lena glanced at Jeffrey as he told Sara what Mark had said about his relationship with Grace Patterson. Whatever Sara said in response was brief and to the point, because Jeffrey agreed with her immediately.

'I'll see you tonight,' Jeffrey said, then replaced the phone in the cradle. He started in on Lena immediately. 'I told you not to be alone with Mark,' he said.

'I know,' Lena responded, and started to tell him again why she had let Brad leave the trailer. He stopped her, holding up his hand.

'I'm only going to say this once, Lena,' Jeffrey began, and it seemed like he had been wanting to say this for a while. 'You're not the boss here.'

'I know that.'

'Don't interrupt me,' he ordered, cutting his eyes at her. 'I've been doing this job a hell of a lot longer than you, and I tell you to do things a certain way because I know what I'm doing.'

She opened her mouth to agree, but then thought better of it.

'Being a detective gives you some autonomy, but at the end of the day you take your orders from me.' He looked at her, as if anticipating she'd argue. 'If I can't trust you to follow simple orders, why should I keep you working for me?'

Obviously, it was her turn to speak, but she couldn't come up with anything to say.

'I want you to think about this, Lena. I know you like your job and I know you're good at it when you decide to be, but after what happened . . .' He shook his head, as if that wasn't right. 'Even before what happened. You've got a problem taking orders, and that makes you more dangerous to me than the crooks.'

Lena felt the sting from his words and rushed to defend herself. 'Mark wouldn't have confided in me if Brad had been there.'

'He might not have tried to take his life, either,' Jeffrey said. He was quiet, staring out at the road as he drove. He sighed, then said, 'That wasn't fair.'

Lena was silent.

'Mark probably would've found a way to do something like this. He's a very troubled kid. It wasn't your fault.'

She nodded, not knowing whether what he was saying was true or not. At least he was trying to comfort her, which is a hell of a lot more than she had done with him when they had talked about his shooting Jenny Weaver.

'And it's not just Mark. Have you made an appointment with a therapist yet?'

She shook her head.

Jeffrey said, 'Lena, I hate to say this now, but there never seems to be a good time.' He paused, as if making sure to word this carefully. 'You need to think about whether or not you want to be a cop anymore.'

She nodded, biting the tip of her tongue so that she wouldn't start crying. How could she not be a cop? If she wasn't a police detective, what was she? Certainly not a sister; barely a woman. Lena wasn't even sure some days if she was a human being.

'You're a good cop,' he said.

She nodded again, resting her head against her hand, staring out the side window so he wouldn't see her face. Her throat felt like it was closing up as she strained not to cry. She hated herself for being so weak, and the thought of breaking down in front of Jeffrey was enough to keep her from sobbing like a girl.

'We'll talk when this case is over,' Jeffrey told her, and his voice was reassuring, but it didn't help. 'I want to help you, Lena, but I can't help you if you don't want to be helped.'

It sounded like Hank's A.A. bullshit, and Lena had had enough of that to last her a lifetime. She cleared her throat and said, 'Okay,' still staring out the window.

Jeffrey was silent as he drove, and she didn't speak again until she noticed that he had missed the turnoff heading back into town and the station.

'Where are we going?' she asked.

'Dottie Weaver's house,' he said. 'She hasn't picked up the body at the morgue.'

'It's been a while,' Lena said, surreptitiously wiping her eyes with the back of her hand. 'Do you think something's wrong with her?'

'I don't know,' Jeffrey told her, his jaw working.

'Do you think she's done something?' Lena asked. 'Like Mark?'

He gave her a curt nod, and she did not push it.

Jeffrey pointed up the road, saying, 'Randolph Street is up here, right?'

'Yes,' Lena confirmed, and Jeffrey took the turn onto Randolph. The driveways were few and far between, most of the houses set back from the road and resting on three to four acres each. They were in an older section of Grant, built back before people started throwing cheap houses on top of each other. Jeffrey braked the car in front of a gray mailbox that was open in the front, mail stacked so tight someone would have to use a crowbar to get it out.

'This is it,' he said. He backed up the car and turned into a tree-lined driveway. If he noticed the four copies of the *Grant Observer* wrapped in plastic bags at the head of the drive, he did not say.

The Weaver home was farther back from the road than Lena would have guessed, and a few seconds passed before a small ranch house came into view. A second level had been added at some point, and the bottom of the house did not really match the top.

'Do you see a car?' Jeffrey asked, stopping in front of an open carport.

Lena looked around, wondering why he had asked a question with such an obvious answer. 'No.'

They both got out of the car, and Lena walked around the perimeter of the house, checking every window on the first floor. Either the curtains or the blinds were drawn on each one, and she could not see inside. There was a double door leading to what was probably the basement, but it was locked tight. The small windows around the foundation had been painted black from the inside.

As she circled back around the house, she could hear Jeffrey knocking on the front door, calling, 'Mrs. Weaver?'

Lena stood at the bottom of the porch steps, wiping the sweat off her forehead with the back of her arm. 'I couldn't see anything. All the curtains are drawn.' She told him about the basement and the blackened windows.

Jeffrey glanced around the yard, and she could sense how anxious he was. Dottie Weaver had not bothered to get her newspapers or mail for a while. She was divorced and her daughter had just been killed. Maybe she had felt there wasn't a lot to go on living for.

Jeffrey asked, 'Did you check the windows?'

'They're all locked tight,' she reported.

'Even that broken one?'

Lena got his meaning. As law officers, they needed a damn good reason to go into Weaver's house without a warrant. A bad feeling was not good enough to go on. A broken window was.

She asked, 'You mean the broken one in the basement?'

He gave her a curt nod.

'What if an alarm goes off?'

'Then we'll call the police,' he said, walking down the steps.

Lena would have broken the window herself, but she appreciated that Jeffrey was trying to keep her out of this gray area of the law as much as he could. She leaned against the porch railing, waiting for the sound of broken glass. It came about a minute later, and then several more minutes passed with nothing further from Jeffrey. She was about to go around to the back of the house when she heard his footsteps inside.

He stood in the doorway, one hand on the knob, the other holding a bright yellow raincoat.

'Lacey's?' Lena asked, taking the coat. It was small enough for a child, but the label in the back took away all doubt. Someone had sewn the child's name onto it in case it was lost.

'Jesus,' Lena mumbled, then looked back up at Jeffrey. He shook his head no, meaning he had not found her in the house.

He stepped aside so that she could walk in. Heat enveloped her, and the house felt hotter inside than it was outside. The first room was large, and probably was used as a living room. It was hard to tell, though, because all the furniture was gone. Even the carpet had been pulled up from the floor, and the tacking around the perimeter stood out like teeth.

'What the . . . ?' Lena said, walking through the room. She noticed that Jeffrey had his weapon drawn, the muzzle pointed toward the floor. Lena followed suit, kicking herself for being so stupid. She had been so shocked to see Lacey's coat and the state of the house that she had forgotten that someone might still be in the house. With all the noise they had made outside, whoever might be inside was certainly aware there was company.

Jeffrey nodded for her to follow him into the kitchen, which was in the same state as the main room. All the cabinet doors were open, showing empty shelves. Lena walked through the dining room, a den, and a small office, all of them empty, all of them missing carpeting.

The house had a bad feeling to it, and she let herself think what Jeffrey had probably thought when he had found the yellow raincoat. Lacey had been here. She could still be here. At least, her body could.

'Smell that?' Jeffrey whispered.

Lena sniffed the air, and realized that she had been smelling fresh paint with something sharper underneath. 'Bleach,' she whispered back. 'Something else I can't place.'

'Those pictures of Mark you took when you arrested him,' Jeffrey began. 'He had paint on his clothes, right?'

Lena nodded, turning around in the room. She looked around the corner, finding the stairs. 'Have you been up yet?' she asked, just as a tapping noise came from upstairs.

They both raised their weapons at the same time, and Lena took point before Jeffrey could. She walked sideways up the stairs, keeping her gun directed up toward the ceiling. She tested her foot on each stair, noting that they, too, had been stripped. Every muscle in her body tensed as adrenaline pumped through her system.

At the top of the stairs, Lena paused before looking down a long hallway. A wall was to her left, a small window that she had not noticed from the outside mounted up high. It was cracked open, and Lena saw some leaves and debris on the floor. Black curtains hung from a rod with weights sewn into the bottom edges. The paint under the window was marked where the weights had hit it, and fresh white paint lined the edge of the material. Lena pointed this out to Jeffrey, thinking it might have caused the noise they heard, and Jeffrey shrugged, as if to say maybe, maybe not.

Lean started to go down the hall, but Jeffrey walked ahead of her, peering into the open doorway of each room. She followed, seeing that the bathroom and two bedrooms had been cleaned out just like the downstairs. She wondered if Jeffrey's gut clenched each time he looked into a room, thinking Lacey Patterson might be in there. Lena had an eerie reminder of this morning with Mark as Jeffrey stopped in front of the only closed door at the end of the hall.

He stood in front of the door, both hands cupping his gun. For some reason, he wasn't moving, and Lena thought to take over, but something about the look on his face stopped her. Was he scared of what he would find? Lena knew she was.

He leaned toward the door, like he heard something. She mouthed, 'What?'

He shook his head, as if to tell her to give him a minute to think. Lena stood beside him, her shoulder to the wall by the door, sweating as she waited for him to make a decision. She hoped he would not wait too long, because stopping to think was taking away some of her resolve.

Finally, he motioned her back behind him, then even farther back. He kept waving her down the hall, then into the stairway. When she was standing on the stair second from the top, her neck craned so she could look around the corner, he seemed satisfied. Lena braced herself for action as he raised his foot and kicked in the door. A flash of light came a split-second later, and somehow the door blew back, pushing Jeffrey down the hallway. A roar came a couple of beats later, and Lena ducked into the stairs as a ball of fire flashed up the hallway.

'Jesus,' she whispered, covering herself with her arms as she knelt on the stairs. Lena waited for the heat to envelop her, or flames to eat her alive, but nothing happened. She stood from her crouch and peered around the corner into the hallway. Jeffrey was underneath the door, but he was moving. The top of the door was charred to a crisp. There were black soot marks along the walls, but there was no fire. The heat must have been so intense that it burned itself out.

She heard a crackling to her left and turned quickly. The black curtains were on fire. Lena took off her jacket and beat them until they fell from the rod. She stamped the last embers out on the floor just as Jeffrey pushed the door off of him.

'What the hell happened?' he demanded, touching his face and body, probably to see if he had been burned. He seemed okay from what Lena could tell. Somehow, the door had protected him from the blast.

'I have no idea,' she said, dropping her coat and walking over to help him stand.

'I thought I smelled something outside the door,' he told her, leaning heavily on her shoulder. 'What the hell was that?'

She asked, 'What did you smell?'

'Gasoline, I guess. I wasn't sure. It was hard to tell with the paint.' He brushed his slacks off, but there was really no point. They both looked at his shoes. The soles had melted from the heat.

'Dammit,' he muttered. 'I just bought these last week.'

Lena stared at him, wondering if he had hit his head.

'Are you all right?' he asked, brushing something off her shoulder.

'I'm fine,' she told him, and she was, but only because Jeffrey had made her stand in the stairwell.

'Is that out?' he asked, pointing to the window. The heat from the blast had knocked out the panes and busted the sash. There were dark gashes in the wall where the curtains had ignited.

'I think so,' Lena said, brushing back her hair. Dust

fell out, and she guessed the ends might have been burned.

Jeffrey walked down the hall, stopping just outside the doorway of the room. He was being careful, looking for a second device. Finally, he stepped into the room and turned around. 'There was a trigger over the door,' he said, his hand over his chest. Lena wondered just for a second how he could be thinking so clearly. He could have easily been killed by the blast.

Jeffrey pointed over the jamb, saying, 'There's a wire here that goes . . .' He followed something with his eyes, turning slowly around the room. 'Here.'

Lena peeked in to see what he was talking about. Three cans of gasoline were stacked in the corner. On top of them was a scorched bath towel and something that looked like it had been a clock radio at one time. The plastic was blown apart, and wires spewed out. The walls and ceiling were scorched and the plastic slats of the blinds in the window looked melted together, but remarkably nothing had ignited.

Lena looked at the device, wondering who could have built something so rudimentary. The metal cans were sealed tight, and the clock had not even been connected to them, as far as she could tell. She touched the towel, then sniffed it. Whoever had arranged the bomb had not even doused the towel in gasoline to help it ignite.

She said, 'This was stupid.'

'Yeah,' Jeffrey agreed. 'What exploded, though?'

'I have no idea,' she said, looking around the room. For the first time, she noticed that this was the only room in the house that was still furnished. Carpet was on the floor, and posters of boy bands were stuck on the wall. There was a little-girl feel to the room, with its once pink walls, white wicker furniture, and shelves full of stuffed animals. A full-sized bed with a pink blanket over it was against the wall opposite the door. The material was stiff-looking, as if it had been saturated at one point, then air-dried in the heat. Lena touched the blanket, then sniffed her fingers.

She said, 'Gasoline.'

Jeffrey was looking around the room, too. 'Everything looks like it was soaked in gas,' he said. 'The windows are locked tight. Maybe the fumes built up, and when the door triggered the clock, the fumes caught fire?' Jeffrey looked down the hallway. 'Fire needs oxygen to burn. Maybe the open window at the end of the hall sucked it out?'

'It sure looked that way from where I was standing,' Lena told him. 'The bomb guys can figure that out.'

'Right,' he said, and pulled his cell phone out of his breast pocket. He made two calls, one to Frank at the station to get the bomb squad moving, the other to Nick Shelton at the Georgia Bureau of Investigation. He requested that a crime scene team come out to the house and search it with a fine-tooth comb.

'We've got some time before they show up,' Jeffrey said, closing the phone.

'Great,' Lena mumbled, thinking between the heat and the odor in the house, they might asphyxiate before reinforcements came.

'Why didn't she strip this room, too?' Jeffrey asked.

Lena shrugged. 'Maybe it was too hard for her to come in here after Jenny died.'

'I guess,' he mumbled, wiping something out of his eyes. 'But why go to the trouble to strip the house if they thought the bomb would burn it down?'

'Arson inspectors can find just about anything,' Lena told him. 'You can watch the Discovery channel and know that.'

'It's like she hated her,' Jeffrey said, not letting it go. 'I can understand not stripping the room, but this . . .' – he indicated the gas tanks – 'this doesn't make sense.'

Lena thought about Mark, and how he might have purposefully rigged the bomb not to explode.

'Who would do this?' he asked. 'Grace? Dottie? Was it Mark? None of this makes any sense.'

To give herself something to do, she looked around the room. A set of cat figurines was on the dresser alongside some makeup that could only belong to a little girl.

'Maybe she didn't want to be reminded of Jenny?' Lena suggested, and even as she said the words, she got a bad taste in her mouth. 'The bomb would have taken out everything.'

'Maybe Dottie was abducted,' Jeffrey guessed.

'By whom?' Lena asked. 'That doesn't jibe. And if she was, how did Lacey's coat get in here? Are you saying that whoever snatched Lacey came after Dottie, too? Then took the time to strip and clean the house?'

Jeffrey asked, 'You think Dottie planted the bomb?'

Lena shrugged, even though she was sure in her heart that Mark had planted the bomb. The paint on his clothes, the chemical smell on his body, all pointed to him at the very least being in this house during the last few days. There was no telling what he had been doing.

Jeffrey was obviously thinking the same things as Lena. He said, 'Mark had paint on his clothes. We can have the lab check it against the paint on the walls.'

'It looked fresh,' Lena reluctantly provided.

'Why would Dottie Weaver strip the house this way? Why would she leave without at least burying her daughter?'

Lena wondered again if he'd hit his head. He was

repeating the same questions over and over again, as if she might suddenly come up with the answer. She was about to ask him if he wanted to sit down when he turned around and looked at the bed in the middle of the room as if it might start talking to him. After a couple of moments of this, he took his foot and kicked the mattress over.

'What's that?' Lena asked, but she could see well enough for herself. About twenty cheap-looking magazines had been stowed between the mattress and the boxspring. All of them had children on the covers doing the kinds of things that children should never be made to do. They all had the same title, too, *Child-Lovers,* in a fancy script with a familiar heart drawing inserted where the 'o' in lover should be.

Lena put her hand on the wall, trying to steady herself.

'You okay?' Jeffrey asked, cupping her elbow as if she might faint.

'The design.'

'It's the same one Mark has on his hand,' he said, pushing through the stack of magazines. He mumbled, 'I used to hide shit under my bed, too.'

'Why would Mark do that?' Lena asked, not able to move past this point. 'Why would he put that on his hand?'

Jeffrey turned back to the bed. 'Maybe it's his way of saying he likes younger girls. Maybe that's how those guys operate so they know each other,' he suggested, picking up one of the magazines. He leafed through it, then picked up another. His jaw worked as he stopped on a particular page.

'What?' Lena asked, looking over his shoulder. A picture of Mark, probably taken a few years ago, served as the centerfold.

Lena picked up a magazine and skimmed through it until she found another picture of Mark. Jenny was in this one, and they were doing something Lena could not describe. Worse, in the back pages there were photos of Mark with older men and some women. The adults' faces were not shown, but Mark was revealed from head to toe. His expression was pained, and it brought tears to Lena's eyes to see him compromised like this. Seeing what Mark had done and what he had obviously been made to do hurt Lena more than she wanted to admit. She finally understood why he had wanted to know what it felt like for her to be raped. He wanted to compare notes.

Jeffrey examined the magazines, his jaw clenched so tight she had trouble understanding him when he spoke. 'These aren't exactly sophisticated. I guess a small press could handle it.'

'Probably,' she agreed.

'Christ,' Jeffrey hissed, scowling at the magazine he was holding. 'This guy has on his wedding ring.' The disgust in his voice would have peeled paint off the walls. 'That's Jenny,' he said.

Lena looked at the photograph. Jenny Weaver was pictured, a man's hand firm on the back of her neck as he guided her down. The gold of the man's wedding ring caught the light, and Lena wondered if that was part of the thrill for the perverts who looked at these pictures, thinking that the guy was married and having sex with little girls.

She said, 'That's disgusting.'

'Here's the same ring in another one,' Jeffrey said, but he didn't show her the photo. He continued to flip the pages. 'And another one.'

Lena asked, 'Are you sure it's the same –?'

'Fucking pervert,' Jeffrey yelled, then twisted the

magazine in his hands and threw it against the wall. 'What the fuck is happening here?' he screamed. She could see a vein in his neck throbbing. 'How many kids were involved in this thing?'

Lena tucked her hands into her pockets, letting him get it out.

Jeffrey turned, looking out the window at the back-yard. His voice was softer, but she could still hear the anger when he asked, 'Do you recognize any of the other kids?'

Lena picked up a magazine, but he stopped her. 'I don't want you looking at this shit,' he said. 'We'll get Nick's people on it.' He put his hand to his forehead, like a bad headache was about to strike. 'How many kids are involved in this thing?' he repeated. 'How many Grant kids were wrapped up in this?'

She didn't have the answer, but he knew that.

He flipped open his phone again. 'I'm going to get Nick here to look at this,' he said. 'I want you to go to the hospital and try to get something out of Grace Patterson.'

She shook her head, not understanding.

'She's connected to Mark *and* Jenny. She has to know something,' he told her. 'I'd do it myself, but I'd probably rip her fucking throat out.' She saw his grip tighten around the phone. 'Voice mail.' He waited a couple of beats, then said, 'Nick, Jeff Tolliver. I need you to call me as soon as possible. We've got some-thing new on the Lacey Patterson case.' He ended the call, saying to Lena, 'There's no way this isn't a prior-ity now.'

Lena nodded, thinking she had never seen him this angry, not even at her.

He dialed another number into the phone. While he was waiting for someone to answer, he instructed Lena,

'I want you to confront Grace on what you know. I want you to tell her exactly what Mark told you, and I want you to find out what the fuck has been going on.'

'Do you think she'll tell me anything?'

'Her daughter is missing,' he reminded her. 'We found her coat here.'

Lena looked down at her hands. 'Considering what she was doing to Mark, do you think she cares?'

He flipped the phone closed again, looking her in the eye. 'Tell you the truth, Lena, I don't know what the hell to think about anybody involved in this case.'

He was about to open his phone again when it rang. Before he answered it, he gave Lena his keys and nodded toward the door, telling her, 'Go.'

THURSDAY

THURSDAY

FIFTEEN

Jeffrey felt like he had been blown across a hallway with a wooden door plastered to his body. His arms ached, and his knees felt like they would never bend right again. Working at the Weaver house had taken the rest of the day, but when he had called Sara at one in the morning, she had not hesitated to ask him over. Part of him was nervous about the way they had picked up so easily again. He kept waiting for the other shoe to drop, for Sara to say that she could not go through with this. Another part of him was just so damn happy to be back in her life that he wanted to enjoy every minute of it as much as he could. Even sitting in the tub with her, talking about what was probably one of the most horrible cases he had ever worked, he felt at home.

He watched Sara across the tub as she sipped her wine, obviously letting what he had just told her sink in. Jeffrey had forgotten how great the claw-footed tub in her master bathroom was. Six feet long with a center-mounted faucet, it was perfect for two people. They had spent half their marriage in this tub.

Sara rested her glass on her knee. 'Where is Lena now?'

'The hospital,' Jeffrey told her. 'Patterson's still holding on.'

'She saying anything?'

'Grace?' Jeffrey asked. Sara nodded, and he said, 'She's pretty lucid, but she's got one of those morphine pumps for the pain.'

'Breast cancer is an incredibly painful way to die.'

'Good,' he said, leaning over the tub to pick up his glass of wine. With his parents' shining example, Jeffrey had never taken to alcohol, but after today he needed something to take the edge off. Before he started talking to Sara, he had felt like his mind was spinning, not able to concentrate on one thing at a time like he needed to do. There were so many pieces to the case floating around, and so many questions that had yet to be answered. Somehow, the alcohol was giving him focus.

Sara asked, 'Do you really think Grace Patterson will give a deathbed confession?'

'Not really, but you never know . . .' He paused, measuring his words. 'Lena's got this thing about Mark.'

'What kind of thing?'

'She kept insisting that he was raped.'

'He was,' Sara pointed out. 'Are you saying he willingly posed for those magazines, that he seduced his mother?'

'Of course not,' he said, and he was glad she had made that point. 'What I'm really worried about right now is Lena.'

'She's doing the best she can,' Sara told him. 'Give her some time.'

'I just can't take that kind of chance with her, Sara.' He rubbed his eyes, still smelling gasoline on his hands even though he had scrubbed himself thoroughly with soap.

He said, 'She's too close to the edge. I don't want

to be the one standing there watching when she finally goes over. I don't think I could live with myself.'

'It's going to take time for her to get past what happened,' Sara said in a measured tone. 'If she ever does at all.'

'She won't even talk to anybody about it.'

'You can't force her to do it,' Sara countered. 'She'll talk about it when she's ready to.'

He stared into his glass, not responding.

'So,' Sara said, obviously realizing he wanted to move on. 'Let's change the subject.'

'Okay.'

She summarized what they knew, ticking the points off on her fingers. 'Mark and Jenny were posing for the magazines at Dottie's house. Grace Patterson was involved with her son.'

'Right.'

'What about Teddy Patterson?'

'He could be the link here,' Jeffrey said. 'He's a truck driver. Maybe he picks up the magazines and takes them across the country.'

'Where is he now?'

'Either at the hospital or at his trailer. Frank's been tailing him.' Jeffrey took a healthy drink from his glass. 'He doesn't seem too concerned that one of his kids might be brain dead and the other has been kidnapped.'

'What's he doing?'

'Staying by his wife, mostly.'

'Maybe he's focusing on one thing at a time?' Sara suggested. 'His wife's dying, he's with her. That's something immediate he can do instead of just sitting around feeling helpless.'

'Trust me, he's not the kind of guy to feel helpless.'

'You think he'll do something?'

'I think he'll leave town as soon as his wife is dead,' he told her. 'I talked to Nick Shelton. We're thinking Teddy's going to be the contact for his collar over in Augusta.'

'The guy Nick arrested who had the child pornography?'

He nodded, debating whether or not to tell Sara the rest, then deciding he should be open with her. 'The meeting is being scheduled for tomorrow at noon.'

'What meeting?' she asked, and he could see the concern in her eyes.

'Nick's guy, this porn distributor, got a call from a pay phone. A man's voice was on the other end.' He paused, trying to gauge Sara's reaction. 'I didn't recognize the voice, but they're meeting at the hotel over in Augusta to drop off the magazines.'

'And I take it you're going to be there?'

'Yeah,' he said. 'I take it you've got a problem with that?'

She sighed. 'I remember when we were married how I would cringe every time the phone rang and I didn't know exactly where you were.'

He drank some wine, letting this sink in. 'You never told me that before.'

'I know I didn't,' she said, then changed the subject again. 'So, how does this work? Dottie and Grace do the magazines, Teddy Patterson delivers them, then Nick's guy distributes them around here?'

'Pretty much,' Jeffrey confirmed. 'We think Patterson probably makes stops all around the Southeast. Nick is going to pull his records from the Department of Transportation as soon as we bust him.'

'Why not before?'

'Who knows who'd tip him off?' Jeffrey pointed out.

'Besides, Frank's glued to Teddy. It's not like he's going to be able to get away with anything.'

'Why arrest Patterson now? Why not follow him on his route and pick up all the distributors?'

'Nick says they have a phone network. If one of them doesn't call the next with the okay, then they close shop. It's very sophisticated.'

'I don't suppose anyone knows anything about where Lacey might be?'

'You don't suppose right.'

'How long has the GBI been working on this pornography ring?'

'Years,' Jeffrey said. 'They just needed to know who was bringing them in.'

'Is this where Dottie comes in?'

Jeffrey shrugged, because nothing was clear at this point. 'I don't like to think about that woman having some kind of network. It means she's got a safe place to go and hide. It means she's connected to all kinds of people all over the world who are invested in helping her because she keeps supplying them with their sick porn.' He felt his anger swelling again, and took a deep breath to calm himself. When that didn't work, he settled on drinking some more wine.

'You know they swap kids,' Sara said, her tone measured. 'Lacey could be in Canada or Germany by now.' She paused, then continued, 'Or, Dottie could be abusing Lacey herself. Dottie could be keeping her somewhere, doing God knows what.' Sara's voice went up on this last part as the threat seemed to hit her.

Jeffrey rubbed his eyes, like he could wipe this away. 'How could a woman, a mother, do that kind of thing to a child?'

'In my experience,' Sara began, 'women who abuse children are much more sadistic than men. I think it's because they know they can get away with it. They know no one will believe they're capable of hurting children.' She added, 'It's especially bad when it's a boy who is being abused. Let's take the incest out of it for a minute. A boy having sex with a woman twice his age is patted on the back. A girl doing the same thing is considered a victim. There's a big disparity there.'

Jeffrey said, 'I never even suspected his mother.'

'Why would you? There was no reason to.'

'I didn't have a problem with Teddy Patterson as a suspect.'

Sara sat back in the tub and let him talk.

Jeffrey told her, 'The crime scene techs are still at Weaver's house, but preliminary results show printer's ink in the basement.'

'For magazines?' Sara asked. 'I thought they needed a big press.'

'They're not exactly slick,' Jeffrey said. He drank more wine. 'All the articles are about how to meet the right kid.'

Sara pressed her lips together.

'I'll tell you what, Sara, I wish to God I hadn't seen any of it.'

She stroked his leg with her foot. 'Have you found the carpeting from the house?'

'Brad and Frank are going to check the dump at daybreak. Based on what they sampled from the floor, the carpets are coated in fluids.'

'Body fluids?' she asked. 'They soaked through?'

He nodded, not liking how that sounded, either. 'There's also a room in the basement that looks like it was used as a darkroom.' He rested his glass on the rim of the tub. 'My guess is they used the house to take the pictures, and printed up the magazines there.'

'An explosion would have destroyed all of that evidence.'

'Yeah,' he agreed. 'I still can't figure out why she didn't strip Jenny's room.'

'She didn't really need anything from Jenny's room, did she?'

'I guess not,' he agreed.

'Did you find any evidence in the room?'

'Nothing. The gasoline might have covered semen traces. I don't know how that works.'

'But there was nothing obvious?'

'Nothing,' he said. 'None of the pictures was taken in there. Maybe it was the only room in the house that was clean.' He rubbed his eyes, feeling incredibly tired. 'I can't believe this was going on in town and nobody knew about it.'

Sara picked up the bottle of wine and filled his glass. 'Do you remember what she said to me?' she asked. 'She asked if I had cut Jenny open. Do you think she meant the castration?'

Jeffrey thought about this for a second. 'She could have.'

'I keep playing that interview back in my mind, and when I get to that point, I see how Dottie changed. You know what I'm talking about? She was almost relieved.'

'I guess,' Jeffrey said, though he could not remember. The interview seemed like a lifetime away.

Sara said, 'I called the hospital. Mark still hasn't regained consciousness.'

'Do they have a prognosis?'

'It's hard to tell with ABIs,' she said, then, 'anoxic brain injuries.' He nodded, and she continued, 'There's a lot of swelling in his brain. They won't know how much damage was done until the swelling goes down.

The longer it takes, the worse it will be.'

'Does he have a chance of being normal?'

She shook her head. 'No.' She paused, as if to let this sink in. 'He'll never be the same again. That is, if he wakes up. There's going to be some damage.'

'He just seemed like this punk kid.'

Sara finished the wine and set her glass on the floor. 'You think Teddy Patterson beat him up before he came to the clinic?'

Jeffrey had forgotten that detail. 'I guess it's possible. What about Lacey, though? Why was Mark chasing after her?'

'She could have been threatening to tell.'

'We didn't find any pictures of Lacey. Wouldn't Teddy Patterson handle something like that anyway?'

'Possibly,' she said. 'Maybe he was in the black Thunderbird.'

'He was probably at the hospital,' Jeffrey pointed out. 'I'll have Frank check, but I'm pretty sure.'

'If Lacey is the mother of that baby, who do you think the father is?'

'I don't know,' he answered, because none of it really made any sense. Jeffrey put his hand over his eyes, trying to understand this. Lately, it seemed like every case he dealt with had some kind of weird twist to it that took a part of him with it. He longed for a simple money-motive or jealous threat gone wrong. He figured that he could take just about anything but knowing a child was in jeopardy.

Sara must have sensed his anguish. She slid toward him, and Jeffrey moved over so that she could put her head on his chest.

'You still smell smoky,' she told him.

'Explosions can do that.'

She ran her fingers along his chest, but it seemed

like she was doing this more to make sure he was really there than to arouse anything in him. She curled a piece of his hair around her finger, saying, 'I want you to be careful tomorrow.'

'I'm always careful.'

Sara sat up a little so that she could look him in the eye. 'More careful than usual,' she said. 'For me, okay?'

'Okay,' he nodded, pushing her hair back behind her ear. 'What's going on with us?' he asked.

'I dunno,' she said.

'It feels good, whatever it is.'

She smiled, touching her fingers to his lips. 'Yeah.'

He opened his mouth to say more, but his cell phone rang, spoiling the moment.

'It's two in the morning,' Jeffrey said, as if this made any difference. The phone was on the closed toilet lid, and Sara picked it up and handed it to him. 'Maybe it's Nick?'

He checked the caller I.D. 'It's the station.'

Paul Jennings was a tall, barrel-chested man with a dark beard accentuating his round face. His white dress shirt was wrinkled, as were his brown polyester pants. But for the expectant expression on his face, Jeffrey thought he looked like a high school math teacher.

'Thank you for coming in,' he said. 'I was going to wait to call you, but I couldn't sleep. I had this feeling.'

'It's all right,' Jeffrey said, leading the man into his office.

'I know this is a shot in the dark. I just had this feeling,' he repeated. 'I took the first flight they had.'

'I apologize for not returning your call,' Jeffrey told

him. 'My secretary thought you were trying to sell me something.'

Paul told him, 'I work for a vinyl supply company up in Newark. I guess I should have made it clear why I was calling.' He paused. 'I've been looking for my daughter for so long, and I've been disappointed so many times.' He held his hands up in a shrug. 'Part of me couldn't believe they might be here, after all this time.'

'I understand,' Jeffrey told him, though he really had no idea what kind of pain this man had suffered over the last ten years. 'Would you like some coffee?'

'No, no,' Paul said, taking the seat Jeffrey indicated.

'We've got a fresh pot in the back,' Jeffrey offered, walking around to the opposite side of the desk. He knew who this man was, and what he had to be told. Jeffrey wanted to keep some distance between them. He needed space.

'This is a picture of Wendy when she was three,' Paul said, showing Jeffrey a photograph of a happy-looking child. Though it was taken several years ago, Jeffrey was still able to tell that the girl in the photograph had grown up to be Jenny Weaver.

'Was this just before she disappeared?' Jeffrey asked, sliding the photo back across his desk.

The man nodded, showing Jeffrey another picture. 'Wanda took her shortly after that.'

Jeffrey studied the next photograph, though he knew from first glance that Wanda Jennings was the person he knew as Dottie Weaver. He slid this back across, and watched as Paul stacked them together, putting the picture of Dottie Weaver on the bottom so he would not have to look at her while they talked.

Jeffrey asked, 'Can you tell me when it was your wife and daughter disappeared?'

Paul shifted in his chair. 'We were living in Canada while I went to graduate school,' he said. 'Vinyl siding wasn't how I planned to spend my professional career. But when Wendy was taken from me . . .' He paused, a sad smile on his lips. 'Wanda was working as a nurse at the hospital. I guess she was there about five months when the allegations started.'

'What kind of allegations?'

'She worked in the maternity ward,' Paul said. 'There were rumors that something wasn't right. That something was going on.' He took a deep breath. 'I didn't listen to them, of course. We had been married for three years by then. I loved my wife. I would never have thought she was capable of . . . And women don't really do that kind of thing, do they?'

Jeffrey was silent. They both knew the answer to that.

'So,' Paul began. 'She was put on administrative leave while they investigated the charges. Babies can't really tell you what happens to them, but there were rumors of some physical findings. I still didn't believe what people were saying, until one day there was a knock on the door. Two cops wanted to talk to me.'

'Where was your wife?'

'She was out doing the shopping. I suppose they were watching the house, because they knocked on the door ten minutes after she left.'

Jeffrey nodded for him to continue.

'They told me about the physical evidence,' he said. 'They had photographs and . . .' He stopped. 'It was graphic.'

'You don't have to tell me what they found,' Jeffrey told him, and Paul seemed relieved.

'They wanted to check Wendy to see if she had been . . .' He paused. 'I still could not accept that Wanda had done these things, let alone that she would ever harm our daughter. Wanda is very good at making people think she's trustworthy.'

'Yeah,' Jeffrey agreed, because he had seen that first-hand.

'When Wanda got back from the store, I confronted her with what they had said. We argued. Somehow, she convinced me that the police were wrong, that it was another woman at the hospital. A nurse I had met a couple of times and, honestly, did not like.'

'People like your wife can be pretty persuasive.'

'Yes,' Paul said. 'A week went by, and it was still in the news. The police actually did investigate this other woman.' Tears came to his eyes. 'We believe what we want to believe, don't we?'

Jeffrey nodded.

'I suppose it was three weeks later that the police came back. They had a warrant this time, and wanted to search the house.' Paul looked at the picture of his child, resting his hand beside it. 'They had talked to her the day before. It was an official interview. I guess they had finally found enough evidence to do some-thing.' He looked back at Jeffrey. 'They came very early, about six in the morning. I was still asleep.' He gave a humorless laugh. 'I had stayed up late study-ing for a final. How something like that could have seemed important to me . . .'

'We all cope in different ways.'

'Yes, well,' he said, obviously not accepting this. 'They were gone. Wanda had taken Wendy sometime during the night. I never saw or heard from them again.'

'What brought you here?'

'A friend of mine called me,' he said. 'He runs credit checks for us at work, for the siding, and I had asked him a while back to keep an eye out for their social security numbers. About a week ago, Wendy's came up on a Visa application. The address was a post office box in your town.'

Jeffrey nodded, thinking that Dottie Weaver, or whatever the hell her name was, had probably thought it was safe to use her daughter's identity after all of this time. She would have gotten away with it if Paul Jennings had not been so vigilant.

'Do you have the address?' Jeffrey asked, feeling hope for the first time. Dottie obviously wanted that credit card. She would have to come back for it.

Paul Jennings handed him a slip of paper. Jeffrey thought he recognized the address as that of the Mailing Post over in Madison. He copied it down and handed back the paper, hoping they might use this to trace Dottie and maybe find Lacey Patterson.

'I just had to come down and see for myself,' Paul said, tucking the page back into his pocket. 'To see if she was here.'

Paul waited for Jeffrey to speak, but Jeffrey could not think how to tell the man what had happened to his daughter. What's more, Jeffrey was not sure how he could admit to this man, who had been searching for so many years, that the person who had killed Wendy Jennings was sitting across the desk from him.

'Is she here?' Paul repeated, a hopeful tone to his voice that cut Jeffrey in two.

'I don't know how to say this, Paul, but Wanda has disappeared and Wendy's dead.'

Jeffrey did not know what he had been expecting the other man to do, but the look Paul Jennings gave him was surprising. For a split second, he seemed almost relieved to finally know for a fact where his daughter was, then it seemed to hit him that after all of this time, all of his searching, she was dead. His face fell, and he covered his eyes with his hands for a moment as he started to cry.

'I'm so sorry,' Jeffrey told him.

Paul's voice shook as he asked, 'When?'

'Last Saturday,' Jeffrey said, then explained to Paul exactly what had happened, leaving out the fact that his daughter had been mutilated. Through the entire story, Paul shook his head, as if he could not accept what he was hearing. When Jeffrey revealed his own involvement in Jenny's death, the father's mouth dropped open.

'I didn't . . .' Jeffrey stopped, because he had been about to say that he did not have a choice. He wasn't so sure about that. Maybe there had been another choice. Maybe Jenny Weaver had not had it in her to pull the trigger. Maybe Jenny Weaver would be alive today.

The two men stared at each other over Jeffrey's desk, neither of them really knowing what to say. Paul's eyes were glazed like he was too shocked by what he had heard to go on.

'With her mother,' Paul finally said, 'I expected the worst.' He pointed to the pictures on Jeffrey's desk. 'That's how I think of her, Mr. Tolliver. I think of my little girl. I don't think of what Wanda did to her, the kind of horrible life she must have lived.' He stopped, choking on a sob. 'I think of my happy little girl.'

'That's best,' Jeffrey said, picking up on the man's grief. Tears came to his eyes, and when Paul saw this, he seemed to lose his reserve.

'Oh, God,' the man said, putting his hand over his mouth. His body shook as he sobbed. 'My poor little girl. My baby. My baby.' He rocked back and forth to soothe himself.

334

'Paul,' Jeffrey said, his voice thick with his own grief. He reached across the desk to pat the man's arm, but Paul Jennings took Jeffrey's hand in his own. Jeffrey had never held another man's hand before, and it felt odd to be doing so now. Though, if it helped Paul Jennings through his grief, it was the least he could do.

Paul tightened his grip on Jeffrey's hand. 'She was such a sweet girl.'

'I know she was,' Jeffrey agreed, squeezing back. 'My wife, Sara, saw her.' Jeffrey realized suddenly that he had mis-spoken. 'I mean my ex-wife. She's a pediatrician. Sara.'

He looked up, hope in his eyes. 'She saw Wendy?'

'Yes,' Jeffrey told him. 'Sara said she was a bright girl. Very intelligent, very sweet. She had a caring heart.'

'Was she healthy?'

Jeffrey lied on purpose this time. There was no reason to tell this father what his daughter had been through. 'Yes,' he said. 'She was very healthy.'

Paul released Jeffrey's hand and picked up the photograph of his daughter. 'She was always sweet, even as a baby. You can just tell with some kids. She had such a good heart.'

Jeffrey took out his handkerchief and blew his nose. At the last minute he realized he should have offered it to Paul.

'I'm sorry,' Jeffrey said.

'I don't blame you,' Paul told him. 'I blame her. I blame Wanda. She took my child. She did those horrible things to her.' He cleared his throat and wiped his nose with his hand. 'She put all of this into motion by being the kind of person she is.' He locked eyes with Jeffrey. 'I don't blame you,' he repeated, his tone vehement. 'Don't live with that guilt, Mr. Tolliver. I've lived with guilt my entire life. What if I had never married her? What if I had listened to the rumors? What if I had let the police check my little girl to see if her mother . . . ?' He put his hand to his mouth, and again his body shook as he cried.

Jeffrey felt himself tearing up again, and tried to collect himself. All he could think of was Lacey Patterson's school picture on the flier in his desk drawer. He thought about what Jenny had been through, and what Mark still had ahead of him if he managed to pull out of the coma. He thought of Sara, too, and what she must be going through, the guilt she had to be feeling because these were her kids. Hell, they were Jeffrey's kids, too. Maybe because they didn't have any of their own they felt responsible for the whole town. And look at what Jeffrey had let happen. How many children had been hurt because Jeffrey had been blind to the evil going on in his own backyard?

'You did your job,' Paul told Jeffrey, as if reading his mind. 'You did what you had to do to protect that boy.'

Jeffrey had not helped the girl he knew as Jenny Weaver. He had not rescued Mark or Lacey Patterson. He had not protected anyone but Dottie Weaver, who had sat in this very station house and spoon-fed them her lies.

Paul said, 'So much came out after she left town.' He looked down at his hands. 'She did some baby-sitting on the weekends. Those children were abused, too.'

Jeffrey sat up, trying not to let his own grief overshadow Paul's. He asked, 'Was a warrant ever issued?'

'No,' he said, then gave an ironic smile. 'A couple

of days later, they issued a warrant to arrest the other woman, but she had left town, too.'

Jeffrey felt the hair on the back of his neck rise as he thought about Lacey Patterson. 'What was her name?'

'Markson,' Paul said, wiping his nose again. 'Grace Markson.'

SIXTEEN

Lena sat beside Grace Patterson's bed, listening to the slow beeps of the heart monitor beside her. The blind was drawn on the window overlooking the hospital parking lot, but there wasn't much to see at this hour, anyway. Teddy Patterson sat across the bed from Lena in a tall recliner, his head leaned back, his mouth open as he snored, seeming not to have a care in the world. He had laughed in Lena's face when she suggested Grace had anything to do with what had happened to their children. Patterson was a con, and he had an innate distrust of cops. Of course, if he was involved in this thing up to his eyeballs, he wasn't likely to come clean and tell Lena where his daughter was being held. Teddy had actually demanded Lena leave, but for some reason Grace had requested she be allowed to stay. He had grumbled, but acquiesced. Patterson's wife had her nails dug so deep into his balls he didn't take a shit without getting her permission first. Grace seemed to be the center of Teddy's life and the longer Lena was in the same room with him, the clearer it was to her that Teddy didn't give a shit for either of his children.

Lena looked at Grace Patterson, watching her sleep, wondering at the power the woman seemed to have over her family. She had refused to be put on a ventilator, but a mask gave her oxygen to help her breathe. Pillows were propped around and under her body to keep her comfortable, but there was no mistaking that the woman was dying an extraordinarily painful death. In the few days since Lena had seen her, Grace Patterson had declined rapidly. Maybe it was being in the hospital that had done it to her, but Grace looked as much on her deathbed as she was. Her skin was sallow, her cheeks sunken. Her eyes were rheumy and constantly wept what on a normal person would have been tears.

Lena shifted in her chair, trying to get into a more comfortable position. Her tailbone felt as if it had been beaten with a bat, and her hands and feet were aching like they had after the attack. She had figured out an hour before that this was because she kept clenching her fists and curling her toes. Her body was tight with tension, and just being in the room with the Pattersons made her stomach clench like the rest of her body. She wanted to throttle them both, to remind them that every second ticking by could mean something horrible for Lacey.

Maybe they were being quiet because Lena was in the room. Teddy wasn't exactly acting the part of the grieving husband, as far as Lena could tell. He had watched television while his wife slept, laughing at sitcoms, then narrating for no one in particular the events unfolding during an action movie.

'He's gonna whup his ass,' Teddy would tell them. Or, 'Give that brother something to think about.'

Teddy had fallen asleep during the news and seemed to be a heavy sleeper. Even when the nurse had come in to check Grace's stats, he had not stirred.

All this left Lena with was time to stare at Grace Patterson and think about what had happened in the last few days. Mark was at a different hospital than his mother because the ambulance crew had taken him to the closest emergency room. There was no telling what was going to happen to him, but none of his doctors seemed to think he would ever recover from what he had done to himself.

Lena thought about Mark, who was just like any other boy, just wanting love, wanting his mother's attention, and taking it any way he could. She also remembered herself at that age, and how fucked up she had been. Everything had been so emotional, and she had been desperate for anyone but Hank's approval. She had defined herself by what a small handful of outcasts at school thought of her, and used how she looked to get what in retrospect could only be called the wrong kind of attention.

Lena was fifteen when she first started sleeping with Russ Fleming, and while her body had been ready for the physical side of the relationship, emotionally, she had been a wreck. Russ was twenty-two, something Hank had a really big problem with, but Lena had thought she loved him, and Russ had played her like a pro. Anything he wanted, she gave him. He was a moody asshole, and Lena reacted to him like a thermometer, trying to soothe him one minute and seduce him the next. Her days were constant ups and downs, depending on how Russ was treating her, and if she wasn't crying in her room, she was sitting on the front porch, hands between her knees as she nervously waited for him to show up. She had been so young and so stupid, and Russ had given her what she thought was love.

Looking back now, Lena knew that he was just a paranoid pothead, getting his rocks off screwing a teenage girl, but at the time Lena had thought he was the best thing that had ever happened to her. It was amazing how stupid kids could be, and how desperate they were for love and attention. Mark must have been such an easy target for his mother. He must have felt like an open wound, convinced that only his mother could heal him. And now everything that he had survived had made him want to die. Lena understood the dichotomy all too well.

Grace took a sharp breath, waking up. Her eyes slowly opened. She stared for a while at the ceiling, as if her brain was trying to work out where she was and what was happening. Lena wanted to remind her, to tell her that she was dying, but Grace seemed to make that connection on her own.

The stiff pillowcase crackled as Grace turned her head toward Lena. Her eyes traveled down as far as they could go, past the blood pressure monitor on her arm to the I.V., which she followed to the self-administering morphine pump beside the bed. Lena had had one of these when she was in the hospital. The patient could control the release of morphine by pressing a button attached to the pump. The machine wouldn't let you kill yourself by holding the button down, but it did give the patient some sense of control over her own pain management.

Without being aware of what she was doing, Lena reached over and took the button away from Grace before the woman could press it. Lena had not been alone with Grace since she'd gotten here. Teddy seemed a sound enough sleeper for her to take advantage of the moment.

'Looking for this?' Lena whispered, holding up the device.

Grace's eyes flashed, then darted toward Teddy.

'You want to wake him up so he can hear what I

have to say?' Lena asked, still keeping her voice low. 'I talked to Mark, Grace. You want Teddy to know just how much you love your little boy?'

She swallowed, but that was all.

'You can talk,' Lena said. She had heard Grace ask for ice chips only a few hours before. 'I know you can talk.'

Slowly, Grace reached up to the mask covering her nose and mouth. She pulled it to the side, panting with the effort. 'Give . . . ,' she said. 'Pump . . .'

Lena tested the weight of the button in her hand. It had felt so much heavier when she had used it for her own pain relief.

She asked, 'Hurts, huh?'

Grace nodded, her face contorted in pain.

'You want to trade?' Lena asked, wagging the device like a piece of candy.

Grace had the audacity to smile, and something in her eyes seemed to say that she had underestimated Lena.

'Yeah?' Lena prompted. 'Tell me where Lacey is and I'll let you drug yourself to hell and back.'

Grace still smiled, but there was a hardness to her eyes now. She turned her head away from Lena to stare back up at the ceiling. Lena could see that the woman's hand shook as she placed it over her chest. The doctor had ordered more powerful narcotics on standby. Why Grace had not called for them earlier was a mystery. It wasn't as if the woman had a chance of getting out of this bed.

Lena said, 'I know you want it, Grace. I know you need it.'

Grace turned back to her. She inhaled sharply, then breathed out a labored, 'No.'

Lena stood, clenching her fist around the device.

She still kept her voice down so as not to wake Teddy. 'I know you raped Mark.'

Grace's smile widened, as if this was a fond memory. She closed her eyes, and Lena was under the impression she was recalling a shared moment with her son.

'Tell me about Jenny Weaver,' Lena hissed. 'What did you do to her?'

'She was . . . ,' Grace began, still staring at the ceiling, tears streaming from her eyes. The tears were part of her medical condition, a sign of the physical pain she was in, not an indication that she felt any grief.

The mask was still pushed to the side, and Grace put her hand on it to move it back, but not before saying, 'Such . . . a . . . sweet . . .'

Her voice trailed off, and Lena stood there, waiting for her to finish the sentence. When nothing came, she prompted, 'Sweet what?'

Grace gave an almost angelic smile behind the mask. 'Sweet . . . fuck.'

'You bitch,' Lena whispered, grabbing the pillow at Grace's side. She moved the mask off the woman's face and pressed the pillow down over her. Grace did not struggle under Lena, who was keeping her eye on Teddy as she tried to smother his wife. Grace's legs twitched slightly, and Lena stopped – made herself stop – pulling back the pillow. She fumbled, putting the mask back onto Grace's face, making sure she got the oxygen. What seemed like minutes but could have only been seconds passed before Grace opened her eyes again. She seemed surprised, then angry. Lena knew that killing her would have been a mercy. Grace Patterson only had a few hours at most left in this world. Lena would not hasten them.

Grace was panting angrily as she glared at Lena. Her mouth worked, and she whispered, 'Coward.'

Mark had called Lena this before, and maybe it was true, but not for the reason Grace was thinking.

Lena countered, 'Not as cowardly as raping a child.'

Grace shook her head, either denying that Mark was a child or that what she had done to him was rape.

'He tried to kill himself,' Lena told her. 'Did you know that?'

She could tell from Grace's reaction that she did not.

'Hanged himself in his closet, right after he told me you'd fucked him,' she clarified. 'He didn't want to live anymore, knowing what you'd done to him.'

Grace stared back at the ceiling. The tears still came, but Lena could not tell if they were from grief or pain.

'He's in a coma. Probably won't wake up.'

Grace whispered something, but Lena could not make out what she was saying. Lena leaned down, putting her ear close to the woman's mouth, her hand on the side of the bed. Without warning, Grace reached out, grabbing Lena's hand. The woman was weak from the labor of dying, and Lena was able to pull her hand away, but not before she felt Grace's thumb brush across the scar on Lena's hand. The touch was tender, almost sexual, and Lena could see the charge Grace got out of it.

'You sick bitch,' Lena said, rubbing her hand as if she could wipe off the sensation. 'You're going to rot in hell.'

It seemed to take all of her energy, but the mother said in one smooth line, 'I'll see you there.'

Lena backed away until she was standing against the wall, feeling an eerie sense of déjà vu. Mark and Jenny had said almost the exact same thing to each other the night Jenny had died.

Lena stood there for a moment, watching Grace Patterson, then checking on Teddy. He was still sound asleep. She checked her watch. There were three more hours until sunrise, when the nurse would be back to check on Grace. Lena clipped the morphine button to the railing, well out of Grace's reach. She sat down in the chair, ignoring her own shaking hands as she waited for Grace Patterson to die.

SEVENTEEN

Jeffrey was sweating under his bulletproof vest. The August heat combined with the weight of the Teflon vest would have felled an elephant by now. He had lost enough water from sweating to make the back of his throat feel like it had been rubbed with sandpaper.

'Good times,' Nick said, using his handkerchief to wipe the back of his neck.

Jeffrey bit back a cutting remark, asking instead, 'What time is it?'

Nick checked his watch. 'Ten after,' he said. 'Don't sweat it, Chief. Criminals got their own sense of time.'

'Yeah,' Joe Stewart piped up. He was Nick's perp who had flipped, and from the way he was acting, Jeffrey imagined Nick had let the man do a little blow to keep the edge off. He was as wired as a Las Vegas street corner.

Jeffrey said, 'You're sure you don't know anything about a missing girl?'

'How young is she?' Joe licked his lips. 'You gotta picture of her?'

'Sit down,' Nick ordered, kicking at Joe's shins with his pointy cowboy boots. Nick had gone all out for the part of a pedophile, and was wearing a pressed black shirt tucked into the tightest pair of blue jeans Jeffrey had ever seen on a man. Nick had even taken off his gold necklace and trimmed his beard for the occasion. Jeffrey imagined Nick lived for this kind of action. Truthfully, so did every cop Jeffrey knew, including himself.

'I tole you to sit,' Nick reminded Joe.

Joe slumped on the bed, scratching his arms as he mumbled something under his breath. He was a skinny kid, probably in his late twenties. Pimples littered his face like spots on a dog, and he had picked at some of them, bringing blood.

Jeffrey looked at Nick. 'Did you have to get him pumped up like this?'

'You want him pissing in his pants?' Nick asked.

'Wouldn't be much of a difference,' Jeffrey pointed out. Joe smelled almost as bad as the musty thirty-dollar-a-night hotel room they were standing in.

Jeffrey asked, 'Are you sure the air conditioner isn't working?'

'We turn it on, we won't be able to pick up the audio,' Nick reminded him. 'Settle down, Chief. It'll be over soon.'

'What about Atlanta?' Jeffrey asked.

Nick's eyes darted to Joe. The post office box in Grant that Dottie had used for the credit card was a dummy drop. A forwarding address had been given so that all mail sent to Grant would automatically be forwarded on to a different post office box in Atlanta. Jeffrey had asked Nick to set up a surveillance, hoping Dottie would show up.

'It's in place,' Nick told him. 'As soon as I know something, you'll know something.'

Jeffrey's phone vibrated at his side, and he clipped it off his belt. 'Yeah?'

'Hey,' Frank said. 'Patterson's been in his trailer since his wife died this morning.'

Jeffrey felt the tension drain from his body. Maybe

347

Patterson had canceled the meeting. 'Are you sure?'

'Of course I'm sure,' Frank bristled. 'He didn't even go to the hospital to see his kid.'

'All right,' Jeffrey said. He snapped the phone shut and reported the news to Nick.

'Maybe we'll be seeing Dottie?' Nick suggested. 'Patterson's no fool. He knows he's being watched.'

As if on cue, two knocks came at the door, followed by a pause, then another knock.

Jeffrey slipped into the bathroom, leaving the door slightly open so as not to draw attention to it. He grimaced at the smell in the tiny room, which probably had not been ventilated since the Nixon administration.

Joe said, 'Hey, man,' and the door squeaked open.

'Who's this?' a man asked. Jeffrey strained to place the voice. The only thing he was certain of was that it did not belong to Dottie Weaver.

'Friend of mine,' Joe said. 'He likes little girls.'

'Little, little girls,' Nick chimed in. 'Know what I mean, hoss?'

'Let's just get this over with,' the man said in a terse voice. 'I got the van pulled up on the side of the building. Let's go.'

Jeffrey waited until they had left the room before walking out of the bathroom. He kept playing the man's voice in his mind, trying to place it, but no epiphany came. What did come was more sweat, and Jeffrey loosened the belt on his vest, wishing he hadn't worn it. Sara had asked him to, though, and he had told her that he would. Maybe if she had considered that he might pass out from heat exhaustion, she would not have insisted.

The door was too dirty to lean against, so Jeffrey just stood beside it, sweating his ass off, waiting for Nick to give him the all-clear. To make the case stick, they had to get delivery, and that meant making sure the truck outside was filled with magazines.

To pass the time, Jeffrey counted to a slow one hundred in his head. He was around sixty-five when he heard Nick yelling, 'Get down! Get down!'

Jeffrey pushed the door open, his weapon drawn. Nick had already taken down the suspect, and a lanky looking man in a black suit was facedown on the ground with his hands on the back of his head.

'Don't move, you perverted motherfucker,' Nick told him, frisking for weapons. 'Am I gonna find anything that'll cut me?' he asked.

The man mumbled something, and Nick kicked him. 'Am I?' he repeated.

A firm 'No' came this time.

There were three other GBI agents covering the perp, so Jeffrey tucked his gun back into his holster as he walked toward the scene.

Nick was still so pumped full of adrenaline from the arrest that when he spoke to Jeffrey he was still yelling. 'This your man?' he asked. 'This the scumbag motherfucker?'

Jeffrey could tell from the back that it wasn't Teddy Patterson, never mind the fact that Teddy would have had to have been Superman to get from Grant to Augusta this fast.

'Turn him over,' Jeffrey said, resting his hand on the butt of his gun.

Nick grabbed the guy by his cuffed hands and yanked him around so hard that Jeffrey thought he heard the man's shoulder popping.

'Hold on,' the man yelled. He gave Nick a dirty look, and started to give one to Jeffrey before recognition came. All the color drained from the man's face, and his lips parted slightly in surprise.

Jeffrey imagined he looked just as shocked.

Nick asked, 'I guess you know him?'

Jeffrey couldn't find his voice. He cleared his throat a couple of times before he could tell Nick, 'His name is Dave Fine.'

EIGHTEEN

Brock's Funeral Home was housed in one of the oldest houses in Grant. The man who had been in charge of the railroad maintenance depot had built the Victorian castle, complete with turrets, before his bosses in Atlanta thought to question where he was getting all the money to build such a prestigious home. John Brock had purchased the house at auction for a ridiculously low sum and started a funeral home out of the first floor and basement shortly after. The family lived above the business, and Dan Brock had suffered endless taunts from other kids, starting when the bus picked him up in front of the house every morning and only ending at the end of the day when he was dropped off. Brock had learned to fight back at an early age, and threatened to touch them all with his dead-man hands if they did not leave him alone. All of them but Sara, that is. She had never been part of the boisterous crowd, and spent most of the ride studying for class. Dan usually shared a seat with Sara on the bus, because everyone else was too scared he would give them cooties.

Inside the funeral home, the first floor of the house was decorated with rich velvet curtains and heavy green carpeting. Chandeliers dating back to the early 1900s hung at opposite ends of the long hall that divided the house. Long benches were against the wall, interspersed with tables containing boxes of Kleenex and trays with water pitchers and fresh glasses. Two large viewing rooms were at the front of the hall, with a smaller one in back, opposite the casket showroom. The house's original kitchen served as an office. Sara stood outside the heavy oak door in front of the office, giving it two soft knocks. When no one answered, she opened the door and peered in. Audra Brock, Dan's mother, had her head down on the desk. Sara listened quietly, picking out the older woman's muffled snores. A plate of half-finished barbecue was by Audra's arm, and Sara assumed the old woman was taking an after-lunch nap.

Sara had attended many viewings at Brock's, and she was familiar enough with the layout to find her way to the basement, where the embalming room was. She held on to the railing lining the narrow stairway, stepping carefully on the bare wooden steps. A long time ago Sara had slipped on these stairs and it had taken her bruised tailbone three weeks to heal.

At the bottom of the steps, she took a left, going past the casket storage room and into a large open space that served as the embalming area. A pump had been turned on, and Sara could feel the noise vibrating through the walls. Dan Brock sat by the body of Grace Patterson, reading a newspaper as the embalming machine removed her blood and replaced it with chemicals.

Sara said, 'Dan,' to get his attention.

Brock jumped, dropping his newspaper. 'Oh, me,' he laughed. 'I thought that came from her.'

'I know the feeling,' she told him, because despite the fact that she had worked for the county going on ten years, Sara still got spooked sometimes late at night when she was alone in the morgue.

He stood from the chair and offered her his hand. 'To what do I owe this pleasure, Dr. Linton?'

Sara took his hand, wrapping it in both of her own. 'I've got a really strange request,' she began. 'And you may throw me out for asking.'

He cocked his head, giving her a puzzled look. 'I can't imagine anything you could say that would make me do that, Sara.'

'Well,' she said, still holding onto his hand. 'Let me ask you, then you can decide.'

The clinic was humming with activity when Sara opened the back door. She walked to the nurses' station, and without even saying hello asked Nelly, 'Has Jeffrey called?'

Nelly gave a tight smile. 'And how was your lunch, Dr. Linton?'

'I had to postpone,' Sara told her, leaving out why. Nelly had made it clear that she wasn't exactly comfortable with the work Sara did at the morgue.

Sara asked, 'Has he called?'

Nelly shook her head. 'I did hear something about Dottie Weaver, though.'

Sara raised an eyebrow. 'What, exactly?'

Nelly lowered her voice. 'Deanie Phillips lives next door to her,' she said. 'She heard a loud boom yesterday and walked over to see what was happening.'

'What was happening?'

'Well,' Nelly said, leaning her elbows on the counter. 'According to Deanie, she heard some of the cops talking about Dottie being involved in something to do with Lacey Patterson's disappearance.'

Sara tried not to groan. Despite the fact that she had lived in Grant almost all of her life, Sara was still amazed at how fast gossip got around town. 'Don't believe everything you hear,' Sara told Nelly, though the fact that the gossip was closer to the truth than not was a little startling. There was no telling what the town would do when they found out that Dottie Weaver was really Wanda Jennings. Sara was having a hard time reconciling that fact herself, not to mention that her exam at the funeral home pointed to the fact that Grace Patterson had recently given birth to a child.

'Yes, ma'am,' Nelly said, a coy smile at her lips. She could read Sara almost as well as Cathy Linton could.

'Anyone call while I was out?'

'You've got three achy-grumpies,' Nelly said, handing her the messages.

Sara glanced through them, asking, 'When's my next appointment?'

'The Jordans in about five minutes,' Nelly said. 'They're scheduled for one-thirty, but you know Gillian's always late.'

Sara looked at her watch, wondering why Jeffrey had not called. Surely it didn't take as long as an hour to process Teddy Patterson, especially considering it was still technically Nick's case. For just a second, she thought about calling him, but then reconsidered. Jeffrey probably would not appreciate her checking up on him, even if she had a good reason.

'I'm gonna grab a Coke,' she told Nelly. 'I'll be right back.'

Sara looked at her watch again as she walked down the hallway. She did the math in her head, thinking Jeffrey should not take longer than an hour to get back to Grant.

She walked into exam room seven and flipped on the lights. Over the past ten years, they had used this room for storage, and it looked like it. Rows of shelves ran the length of the room like bookshelves in a library. Sara could not even remember half the things that were in here.

She opened the refrigerator and let out a curse when she saw that all the Diet Cokes were gone. 'Elliot,' she muttered, because he was always stealing things from the fridge. She opened the freezer and was not too surprised to see that her Dove Bars and a couple of frozen dinners were gone. Well, not technically gone. With his usual sensitivity, Elliot had thought to leave the empty boxes and wrappers in the freezer.

'I'm gonna kill him,' she said, slamming the fridge shut.

Sara walked up the hallway, feeling all the anger that had been welling up for the last week coming to a head. She stopped herself outside her office, thinking it wasn't fair to Elliot to let him take the brunt of this, even if he was a Dove-Bar-stealing ferret.

'Give me a minute,' she said, holding up her hand to Nelly, who was approaching with an armful of charts.

Sara walked into her office and slid the door closed behind her. She looked around the small room, taking in all the pictures stuck on the wall, until she got to Lacey Patterson's. The photo had been taken a few years ago, and the girl's hair was shorter than Sara remembered. Compared to the school picture in the missing-person flier, Lacey could be a different girl. That was the thing with children at this age – in couple of years, there was no telling what she would look like. She could put on weight or lose weight. Her hair might get darker or lighter. Her cheekbones might become pronounced, her jaw softer. Dottie Weaver, or whoever she was, had this huge advantage going for her: Lacey would grow up. Of course, after a certain amount of time, this would become a liability for someone in the business of exploiting young children. What would happen to Lacey when she was too old for the game? Would she end up like her mother, abusing other children? Would she find a way to get out from Dottie's clutches?

'Dr. Linton?' Nelly knocked on the door. 'Chief's on line four.'

Sara leaned over her desk, snatching up the phone. 'Jeff?' she asked, aware of the hope in her voice.

'We haven't found her,' he said, sounding defeated.

Sara tried to hide her disappointment. The more time that passed the less likely they would be to find the girl. 'I'm just glad you're okay,' she said. 'Did Teddy come without a fight?'

'It wasn't Teddy,' he said, then told her who it was.

Sara was sure she had heard wrong. 'The preacher?'

'I'll call you later, okay?'

'Yeah,' she said, hanging up the phone.

Sara looked around the office. She found pictures of Dave Fine's two kids to the left of Lacey's, then let her eyes travel over the others: girls who had been in the church choir Dave helped out with, or who had been coached by him on the softball team. There was no telling how many kids Dave Fine had been trusted with, and no telling how many kids there were whose trust he had betrayed.

NINETEEN

Dave Fine had asked for a Bible, and the preacher rested his right hand on top of the book as he stared blankly at Nick Shelton. He seemed almost perplexed as to why he was here.

'I love children,' Fine said. 'I've always loved children.'

Nick leaned back in his chair, balancing it on the back legs. 'Sure you do, Preacher.'

Jeffrey kept his mouth closed, because Dave Fine was Nick's collar. His fists were itching to do some real damage to the preacher, and there was a buzzing in the back of Jeffrey's mind, telling him that Dottie was still out there, doing God only knows what to Lacey Patterson, and the asshole pervert across the table from him was one of the people who had helped her get away.

'Well,' Nick said, holding his arms out in a big shrug. 'Tell me your story.'

Fine stared at the Bible, as if he felt he could get strength from the book. His hands were sweating, and Jeffrey could see a darker streak on the black cover where perspiration had rubbed off his palm.

'I've worked at the church for going on fifteen years,' Fine said. 'I grew up in Grant. I was baptized in that very chapel.'

Nick bounced the chair slightly, waiting him out.

'I married my wife there,' he continued. 'I baptized my two little boys there.'

Silence filled the room, and Jeffrey let himself look at Dave Fine. He was the type of man who served as a living example of the phrase 'pillar of his community.' Fine volunteered with the seniors' program down at the Y, delivering meals to the elderly every weekend. His children played softball on the peewee league, and Fine coached the girls' team.

Jeffrey loosened his collar, thinking about all the young girls Fine came in contact with on a daily basis. His fists clenched again.

'I never touched any of them,' Fine said, as if he could read Jeffrey's mind. 'I know it's wrong. I know that.' He ran his thumb along the spine of the Bible. 'I prayed for strength, and God gave it to me.'

Nick crossed his arms, and Jeffrey could sense that this was getting to the other man. Nick wasn't overtly religious, but Jeffrey knew that he attended church every Sunday. One of the clunky gold charms around his neck was a cross with a diamond embedded at the center.

'I never touched my children,' Fine insisted. 'I never hurt my boys.'

Nick said, 'You understand we can't take your word for that.'

Fine seemed shocked that someone would not trust him. 'I would never touch my sons,' he said. 'I would never do that.'

'We know you're not into little boys,' Nick told him. 'But, you gotta understand, Preacher, we gotta check it out.'

Fine stared at the Bible. 'I would never have acted on my feelings if she hadn't approached me.'

'Dottie Weaver?' Nick clarified.

'Jenny was such a sweet child. She had a light in her. A true light that God put there.' Fine's lips curved up in a smile. 'She sang like an angel. She really did. You could hear God coming through her voice.'

'Yeah,' Nick said. 'I bet you could.'

Fine gave him a sharp look, as if he deserved more respect than this. The man seemed not to realize that he was in a police station, about to be sent to jail for a long time.

Jeffrey said, 'How did Dottie approach you?'

Fine seemed relieved that Jeffrey was taking over. 'She didn't exactly approach me so much as lure me,' he said. 'Adam never thought to eat of the forbidden fruit until Eve tempted him.'

Nick said, 'Seems to me Adam's snake had something to do with that.'

Fine frowned. 'It wasn't like that. It was never about sex for me.'

'But, you did have sex with her,' Nick said.

Fine chewed his lip. 'Not at first,' he said. 'I just wanted to spend some time with her.' He paused, and took a deep breath. 'Dottie let me take her to the movies, and sometimes we would go into Macon to get her some clothes.' He looked up at Jeffrey and Nick, obviously needing their approval. 'Her father had abandoned her,' he told them. 'I was just trying to fill in, to make her feel loved and wanted.'

Nick was silent, but Jeffrey could see the muscles in his arms tense.

'I just wanted to nurture her, to give her some guidance.'

'Did you?' Nick asked, not bothering to hide his hostility.

'I know what you're thinking, and it's not like that, it's not like that at all.'

Jeffrey tried to remain calm, asking, 'What's it like?'

'It's like . . .' – Fine made a wide gesture with his

hands – 'it's about love. It's about listening to children, and trying to understand their wants and their needs.'

'Did she want sex from you?' Nick asked.

Fine dropped his hands. 'I never would have touched her that way. I was content just to have her company.'

Jeffrey asked, 'What changed that?'

'Dottie.' He spit the word out of his mouth as if it was poison. 'I had always thought about it, always. Not with Jenny, but with other girls. Some girls that I saw just around town.' He blinked his eyes several times, and Jeffrey was struck by how easily these men cried for themselves. They never seemed to cry for the children they hurt.

Fine said, 'But I've always been content with my fantasies. That's always been enough for me.' His voice rose. 'I'm a happily married man,' he told them. 'I love my wife and my sons.'

'Sure you do,' Nick said, the flippant tone back.

Fine shook his head. 'You don't understand.'

Jeffrey leaned over the table. 'Explain it to me, Dave. I want to understand.'

'She was such a smart girl, and so well-spoken.' He picked up the Bible. 'She read the Book with me. We prayed. We understood each other.'

Jeffrey glanced at the Bible. While at some level Jeffrey had always believed in the presence of good and evil, he had never really attached a biblical significance to it. Seeing Dave Fine's hand on the Bible, hearing his tale of seducing Jenny Weaver through prayer, struck him as the highest form of blasphemy.

Nick said, 'Okay, you prayed with her. What happened to change that?'

Fine set the book back on the table. 'Dottie changed that,' he said. 'She called me in the middle of the night.'

'When was this?'

'Around Thanksgiving,' he said. 'This past Thanksgiving.'

'Then what?' Jeffrey asked, thinking the bastard was probably lying.

'I went to her house, because she said that Jenny wasn't doing well. She said she was upset, and that she needed to talk to me.' His eyes filled with tears again. 'I was her friend. I couldn't ignore a plea for help.'

Jeffrey nodded for him to continue, trying to block the image that came to his mind of Sara pointing out the pelvic fracture in Jenny Weaver's X ray. The girl had been brutally raped. Dave Fine could have been the man who did it.

Dave cleared his throat. 'I had never really been inside the house before. Jenny always waited for me on the front steps.' He wiped his eyes with the back of his hand. 'When I got there, Dottie led me upstairs. Upstairs to Jenny's room.'

Fine fell silent, and neither Jeffrey nor Nick prompted him to continue. After what seemed like a long while, he picked back up where he had left off.

'We did things,' he said, his voice low. 'I'm ashamed to say that we did things.'

'*You* did things,' Jeffrey told him, wanting to make that point.

'Yes,' Fine agreed. 'I did things.'

'Did the acts only take place in Jenny's room?' Jeffrey asked, thinking that this would explain why Dottie would risk not stripping Jenny's room. The only evidence they found would point back to Dave Fine.

'Yes.' He swallowed hard. 'Only in her room.'

The men were silent as Fine seemed to get his thoughts together. He was certainly good at painting himself as a helpless victim. A thirteen-year-old girl might have bought his act, but the more excuses Fine made for his actions, the more Jeffrey wanted to kill him.

Finally, Fine said, 'Dottie took pictures. I didn't know until later.' He gave a humorless chuckle. 'She brought them to the church the next day, and threatened to expose me if I didn't do what she said.'

'What did she want you to do?'

'Make those deliveries,' he said. 'I used the church van.' He put his hand over his mouth. 'God forgive me, I used the church van.'

Jeffrey crossed his arms, willing himself to calm down. Nick Shelton was so angry there was almost a heat coming off of him. How this sick fuck could cry for himself was beyond him. Dave Fine felt sorrier for himself than he did for the kid he raped.

Jeffrey asked, 'Where's Dottie now?'

'I have no idea,' Fine said, tapping his palm on the Bible for emphasis. 'That's the God's truth.'

'When did you see her last?' Jeffrey asked, knowing he could not trust the answer.

'Monday. She had Mark at the house. They stripped everything. They painted the walls, they moved the printing press.'

'Where did they move it to?'

'I don't know,' he said, and he seemed to be telling the truth. 'They put it in a truck, an unmarked truck.'

'And then?'

'She told me that I still had to make this last delivery or she would send the pictures to the police station.'

'What about Lacey Patterson?'

Jeffrey wasn't sure whether or not something registered in Fine's eyes. The man said, 'I have no idea.

Dottie wouldn't tell me something like that. I wasn't involved in that end of things. I only did what she said to protect my family. Our lives.'

Jeffrey crossed his arms, asking, 'When did you get the magazines?'

'That night,' he answered. 'I put them in the basement of the church until this morning.'

'You already knew about the meeting in Augusta?'

'No,' he shook his head, vehement. 'She called me last night. It sounded like she was on a cell phone.'

'You said the last time you saw her was Monday,' Jeffrey reminded him.

'It was the last time,' Fine countered. 'You said the last time I saw her, not the last time I spoke with her.'

Jeffrey let this pass. 'What did she say?'

'She told me about the hotel, when to meet Joe, what the code word was for the next pickup.' Fine paused. 'She said she was still around, watching me.'

'Do you believe that?' Nick asked. 'You think she's still in town?'

Fine shrugged. 'She's capable of anything,' he said.

'Capable of what, for instance?' Jeffrey asked. When Fine did not answer, he asked, 'What do you think she's going to do to Lacey Patterson?'

Fine looked away. 'I don't know what she does. I was only involved with Jenny.'

Jeffrey stared at the other man, trying to understand him. Fine was so good at justifying his actions, he could probably pass a lie detector test. Jeffrey seriously doubted the man even believed what he had done to Jenny Weaver was wrong.

Fine volunteered, 'I know Dottie needs money. She told me she had to wait around for the next payoff.' His voice rose as he tried to defend himself. 'I was being blackmailed. I had no choice.'

Jeffrey ignored the excuse, instead thinking about Dottie's post office box in Atlanta. Dottie had no way of knowing that they knew about the drop. She would think she was safe. They might have a chance of catching her before she had time to rape another kid, or sell off Lacey Patterson.

'So,' Nick said. 'You packed the magazines in the church van this morning and toddled on over to Augusta?'

'I had a bad feeling about it,' he said, picking at the pages of the Bible. 'I guess I wanted to get caught. I couldn't go on with this hanging over me.'

Jeffrey said, 'Mark felt the same way.'

Fine snorted. 'Mark,' he said, as if he were talking about the devil himself.

Nick exchanged a glance with Jeffrey.

'You know why Jenny wanted to shoot him?' Fine asked them, a slight grimace on his face. 'Because he was going to end up doing the same thing.'

'Doing what?'

'He enjoyed it,' Fine told them. 'Mark didn't have any qualms about what he was doing.'

'And you did?' Nick shot back.

Fine ignored the question.

'You're saying Mark liked posing for the pictures?' Jeffrey asked, and in his mind he saw Mark's pained expression in the magazines they had found. This was not the face of a kid who was enjoying himself.

'He didn't just like it. He wanted to do it.' Fine tapped his finger on the table. 'If you ask me, it was just a matter of time before he started in on his sister. Jenny knew that. As cruel as that family was to her, she knew what Mark had become. She knew he would end up abusing Lacey.' He sniffed, as if holding back tears. 'Jenny was trying to protect Lacey from that animal.'

'You have proof of this?' Jeffrey demanded.

'Grace had him in the game since he was six,' Fine told them. 'It was only a matter of time. Jenny knew this.'

'You have no way of knowing what Mark would've ended up doing,' Jeffrey said. 'If every kid who was raped by some freak like you grew up to molest children –'

Fine interrupted him. 'You don't know Mark very well, Chief Tolliver. Trust me, he would've been hurting kids, just like his mother.' He shook his head, giving a snort. 'He learned from the master.'

Jeffrey countered, 'He was just a kid himself.'

Fine held up his finger, as if he was making a good point. 'He was a grown man. He could've stopped.'

Nick barked, 'So could you.'

The comment cut, and Fine showed it by looking down at the Bible, his lips pursed in a classic pout, like he had been falsely accused.

The room was quiet as they all seemed to take a deep breath.

Jeffrey tried to keep his tone even, asking, 'Did you tell Jenny your theory about Mark? Is that why she wanted to shoot him?'

Fine stared at the Bible.

Jeffrey took his silence as a confirmation. 'What else did Dottie have you do?'

'Just the deliveries.'

'No, before that.'

'She made me come over when she was taking the pictures,' he said. 'I didn't want to, but she held my life in her hands.' He held out his hands to illustrate the point. 'If those pictures ever got out,' he said, 'it would have ruined me. My wife, my children . . .' Tears welled into his eyes. 'I have responsibilities.'

'You posed for more pictures?' Jeffrey asked, wondering at anyone who could be so stupid. Or, maybe he wasn't stupid, maybe he enjoyed it.

Fine nodded. 'I didn't want to. She . . .' – he looked for the right word – 'she liked to humiliate people. She got something out of that.'

'How did she humiliate you?'

'She knew I didn't like boys, and she made me do things.'

'Things with Mark Patterson?'

He gave a tight nod, and for the first time, he actually showed shame. 'What Jenny and I had was . . . special. I know you don't understand that, but there was something between us. Something that bonded us.' He put his hand over his eyes. 'She was my first. I loved her so much.'

Jeffrey cut him off. 'Shut up about that part of it, Dave, or I swear to God I'll beat the ever loving shit out of you.'

Fine looked up, and he seemed hurt that they did not understand.

Jeffrey said, 'Why did you stop? With Jenny, I mean. What stopped the sexual contact?'

'She rejected me,' he told them, tears welling into his eyes. 'She said she didn't want anything more to do with me.' He sniffed loudly. 'After the pictures . . . I don't know. It was as if Dottie was proving something to Jenny, my showing up that night.'

'Proving you were all alike,' Jeffrey provided, thinking this was just the kind of thing a woman like Dottie Weaver would do.

'That's not true,' Fine insisted. 'I loved Jenny. I cared about her deeply.'

'That's why you tried to visit her after the church retreat?'

366

'She looked sick,' Fine told them. 'I didn't know what was wrong with her and Dottie wouldn't let me near her. I even posed for more of her pictures just to get into the house, just to see if Jenny was all right, but Grace kept her at the trailer when I was there.'

Jeffrey clenched his teeth together knowing Fine had willingly gone to Dottie's so he could molest more children. The fact that Fine truly believed he loved Jenny Weaver was just as obvious as the fact that there was something seriously wrong with his mind.

Nick asked, 'What about Grace Patterson? What was her involvement in this?'

Fine scowled at the name. 'She was worse than Dottie. She was disgusting.'

'How so?'

'The things she came up with,' he said, his voice coarse. 'May she rot in hell for her sins.'

Jeffrey did not point out the obvious. 'Dottie and Grace were together on this?'

He nodded. 'Grace directed most of the photo shoots. Dottie took care of the business end of things.' He waited a beat. 'All the poses were Grace's idea. She liked to get in on them, touch some of the children. The more sadistic it could be the better.'

'Dottie never did this, too?'

'She knew how to make the ones that looked real. The romantic ones. Dottie worked the softer stuff and Grace worked the hard core.' He licked his lips nervously, as if by default the women were more guilty than he was. 'They knew each other from way back.'

'They told you this?'

'No,' he said. 'Jenny did. Jenny said that she and her mother moved around a lot. Wherever they went, Grace would visit them at least once a month.'

Jeffrey asked, 'What about Teddy Patterson?'

Fine shook his head. 'He would have killed us all if he had known.'

Nick showed his surprise. 'He didn't know?'

'Of course not,' Fine snapped. 'We never did anything unless he was out of town on business. He drove a truck.'

Nick sounded as skeptical as Jeffrey felt. 'He never delivered any of the magazines?'

'Grace kept him out of it,' Fine said. 'He wasn't that kind of man.'

'What kind of man is that?' Nick asked.

Fine stared at the Bible again. 'A man like me, I guess. A man who would be with children.'

'A man who would hurt children,' Nick corrected.

'I didn't hurt her.'

'You didn't?' Jeffrey asked, leaning across the table. 'You wanna tell me how a thirteen-year-old girl gets a pelvic fracture?'

'There were other men she was with,' Fine countered, yet he did not seem surprised by the information.

'Other men who weren't gentle like you?' Jeffrey goaded.

'It wasn't like that.'

'Really?' Jeffrey said, incredulous. 'How big are you, Dave? You want me to look up in Jenny's autopsy records how much smaller she is than you?'

Fine cleared his throat, but he did not answer. He took the Bible off the table and held it to his chest. Jeffrey stared at the man, thinking there was something he was missing. He saw it then – the wedding ring on Dave's left hand. His mind flashed on the image he had seen earlier in the magazine: the hand firmly behind Jenny Weaver's head, pushing her down so that she gagged on him.

368

'You son of a bitch,' Jeffrey said, lunging across the table. His knee caught the edge, but he didn't care as his hands wrapped around the Bible.

'Jeffrey,' Nick yelled, halfheartedly trying to pull Jeffrey back.

Jeffrey let the anger take hold of him, saying, 'You sick son of a bitch,' as he ripped the Bible from the preacher's hands. Fine had been holding on so tightly that he fell back in his chair. 'I saw the pictures, asshole. I saw what you did to her. I saw how you raped her.'

Jeffrey stood, looking at him over the table. 'You don't deserve this,' he said, indicating the Book. 'What you did to those kids . . . what you did to her . . .'

'It was just Jenny,' Fine insisted, sitting up.

Jeffrey started to go around the table, then stopped himself, thinking Fine wasn't worth it.

Fine repeated, 'It was just Jenny.'

'You left your fucking wedding ring on in those pictures,' Jeffrey told him, putting the Bible down. 'I saw it in at least ten different pictures with ten different kids.' He walked around the table, groaning at the pain in his knee. 'You fucking idiot.'

'You can't talk to me that way,' Fine snapped.

Jeffrey grabbed his arm, yanking him up off the floor. 'You'd better be glad I'm talking and not beating the shit out of you.'

'This is police brutality,' Fine said, brushing off his pants. 'I want a lawyer.'

Jeffrey said, 'Buddy Conford wouldn't touch you with a ten-foot pole.'

'I've got someone else,' Dave said, tucking his shirt into his pants. 'Someone from Atlanta.'

Nick provided, 'Someone who defends perverts like him all the time. Probably takes his fee in pictures.'

Fine smiled, and for the first time, he appeared to be on the outside what he was on the inside. 'Or little girls.'

Jeffrey felt his shoulders tighten, and the animal desire to rip Fine's throat out was only quelled by the possibility that Fine knew more than he was saying.

'You're going to jail,' Jeffrey told the preacher. 'You know what they do to people like you in jail?'

'Right,' Fine said. 'I watch television. I know you're just talking crap.'

'Crap?' Nick said. 'You mean that bloody stuff you're gonna find in your underwear every morning?'

Fine had the gall to look smug. 'I don't think I'm going to jail.'

Nick asked; 'What makes you think that?'

'I've got a bargaining chip,' Fine said, smiling.

'What bargaining chip,' Jeffrey shot back, trying not to sound eager. If Fine thought he had power here he would never tell them what he knew.

'Let's just wait for my lawyer to get here,' Fine said, holding out his hands to be cuffed. 'I don't have anything to say without my lawyer.'

'Think about that in general lockup,' Jeffrey said, pulling out his handcuffs.

'Goodness me,' Nick breathed. 'General lockup.'

'What's that?' Fine asked, something close to panic in his voice.

Jeffrey tightened the cuffs on Fine's wrists. 'Just jail.'

'Funny thing about jail, though,' Nick began. 'Lots of fellas in there had someone just like you in their lives when they were growing up.'

Fine turned around. 'What does that mean?'

Jeffrey smiled, turning Fine toward the door. 'Means while you're waiting for your fancy lawyer to drive here all the way from Atlanta, you'll have plenty of time to explain to your fellow inmates how it's all about love.'

'Wait a minute.' Fine stood where he was, even as Jeffrey tried to push him. 'I'll have my own cell,' he said as if he was certain this would happen.

'No you won't, you sick fuck,' Jeffrey said, pushing him so hard that Nick had to catch him before he fell.

'It's the law,' Fine insisted. 'You can't put me in with other inmates.'

'I can do whatever I want,' Jeffrey told him.

'Wait a minute,' Fine repeated, his voice shrill and panicked. 'You can't do that.'

'Why not?' Jeffrey asked, grabbing the preacher by the collar and forcing him out of the room.

'No,' Fine said, reaching for the door but missing. His fingernails trailed across the wood as he grabbed for anything to hold on to.

'You got something to tell me, Dave?' Jeffrey asked, pushing him down the hall.

'Help me,' Fine said, reaching for a patrolman who happened to be coming out of the bathroom. The cop looked at Fine, then Jeffrey, then walked on as if he hadn't seen anything.

'Move,' Jeffrey said, still holding him up by his collar.

'Somebody help me!' Fine screamed, bending his knees until he was on the floor. Jeffrey still dragged him down the hallway by his shirt collar.

'Help!' Fine screamed.

'Help you like you helped Jenny?' Nick asked, walking beside him. 'Help you like you're helping Lacey?'

'I don't know where she is!' Fine screamed, putting his hands on the floor to give more resistance.

371

Jeffrey saw Marla stick her head around the corner. She looked at Fine, then turned back around.

'Help me!' Fine cried, his voice hoarse from the effort. 'Oh, Lord, please help me.'

Jeffrey's hand was cramping. He let go, and Fine dropped to the floor, sobbing. 'Oh, Lord, please deliver me from these men,' he prayed.

Nick bent down in front of him. 'The Lord helps those who help themselves,' he suggested.

'But you can keep on praying, Dave,' Jeffrey told him. 'You can pray the papers don't print how you died from having your asshole ripped open.'

Nick put his hand on Fine's shoulder. 'Hate to have your wife and kids read about that, Dave. It's a bad way to have to go.'

Fine looked up, tears streaming down his face. 'Okay,' he said. 'Okay, okay.'

'Okay what?' Jeffrey asked.

'Okay,' he repeated. 'I might know where she is.'

Jeffrey drove while Nick sat in the back seat alongside Fine. Behind them, an unmarked car with four GBI officers drove at a safe distance.

'You better not be fucking with us, Dave,' Jeffrey said, making a right turn to circle the block for the third time.

'I told you I'm not sure what the address is,' Fine insisted. 'Dottie only took me here once.'

'What'd she take you here for?' Nick asked.

'Nothing,' he mumbled, looking out the window.

Jeffrey looked at him in the rearview mirror. 'This better not be just you postponing the inevitable.'

'I'm not, okay?' Fine snapped. 'I told you this was where she did some business.'

'What kind of business?' Jeffrey asked.

Fine looked like he wasn't going to answer, but for some reason he did. Jeffrey liked to think it was guilt that made Fine tell them things, but he had been a cop long enough to know it was plain and simple stupidity.

Fine said, 'This guy, he keeps kids here sometimes.'

'You sure it's just him alone there?' Jeffrey asked.

'Yes,' Fine insisted. 'It's mostly used as a safe house.'

'Safe for who?' Nick asked.

'Who do you think?' Fine snapped. 'He keeps pictures mostly, but a couple of times I saw some kids and a couple of cameras.'

'And out of the goodness of your heart you reported him to the police,' Nick suggested.

Fine stared out the window, probably feeling sorry for himself. They had spent an hour driving to Macon, then another two hours driving around different subdivisions looking for this house that Dave Fine said he would recognize only by sight. Jeffrey looked in the rearview mirror, wondering how much longer they had before somebody called the Macon cops about two suspicious-looking cars in the neighborhood.

They were on tricky ground here. Technically, the Georgia Bureau of Investigation had jurisdiction over the state, but as a courtesy, they should have notified the Macon Police Department that they were conducting surveillance on their turf. As Jeffrey and Nick weren't even sure Dave Fine had ever been here, let alone whether or not Lacey Patterson was being held in Macon, there wasn't much they could tell the Macon Police Department. They couldn't get a warrant without a street address, but Nick was counting on imminent jeopardy to cut through that red tape. They could always say later that they saw something suspicious in the house. With a child involved, and time being of the essence, neither one of them was worried about getting slapped on the wrist for this.

'Turn here,' Fine said. 'Left up here. This street looks familiar.'

Jeffrey did as he was told, thinking it was pointless because they'd already been down this road.

'Then up here on the right,' Fine told him, excitement in his voice.

Jeffrey took the right, going down a new street. He exchanged a look with Nick.

'There it is,' Fine told them. 'It's the one on the right with the gate.'

Jeffrey didn't slow the car, but he had enough time to see that all the windows had the blinds drawn. The outside security lights were also on even though it was the middle of the day. The gate had a large padlock on it. Whether or not this was to keep people out or keep them in remained to be seen.

Jeffrey stopped the car at the end of the street and waited for the other car to catch up with them. He could hear cars from the interstate, which was less than thirty feet from where they had parked. Jeffrey guessed the people who lived around here got used to the noise, but right now, every car was like fingernails against a blackboard.

Agent Wallace got out of the car, leaving two men and one woman inside. He adjusted his belt, even though he was wearing a shoulder harness. He was a beefy young guy who worked out enough to make the material around the short sleeves of his shirt look about ready to break. His cheeks were so close-shaven that Jeffrey could almost make out the razor marks.

'That the house, with the gate?' he asked, taking off his sunglasses.

'That's what our guy says,' Jeffrey told him.

Wallace looked back at the car, meeting Dave Fine's glare. He spit on the road, crossing his arms across his broad chest. 'Motherless piece of shit,' he mumbled.

Nick had been on the other side of the car, calling the Macon Police Department. 'He's not happy,' Nick said.

'Didn't think he would be,' Jeffrey answered, knowing that if someone from the GBI had called Jeffrey to say an operation was going down in Grant that Jeffrey knew nothing about, he'd be pissed, too.

Nick said, 'It'll take 'em a while to get their heads out of their asses and get over here.'

'Did you tell them the house?'

Nick smiled. 'Hell, I couldn't even remember the street.'

Jeffrey laughed, glad he was here instead of back at the Macon Police Department.

Nick opened the back door and grabbed Dave Fine's hands. Before the preacher could protest, Nick had cuffed him to the strap over the door. 'That'll hold him.'

Fine said, 'You can't leave me here.'

'If I were you,' Nick said, 'I'd relish this time alone.'

Fine colored. 'You said I'd get my own cell back at the station.'

'Yeah,' Jeffrey agreed. 'That's the station, though. I've got no control over what happens to you in prison.'

Nick chuckled, knocking on the hood of the car. 'Don't worry, Davey boy. I'm sure you'll meet yourself some quality folk in prison.'

'You can't do that,' Fine insisted.

Nick smiled. 'Don't worry there, preacher. Near about all of 'em already found God. You can pray with them till your heart's content.'

Fine shot Jeffrey a panicked look. 'You promised!'

'I promised about my jail, Dave,' Jeffrey reminded him. 'I've got no control over what happens in the big jail. That's up to you and the state.'

'You said we'd work out a deal.'

Jeffrey said, 'A deal for reduced sentence, but you're still going to jail.'

Fine started to say more, but Nick slammed the door in the man's face.

'Pussy,' Nick said.

'He will be to somebody,' Jeffrey agreed, using the remote to lock the car doors.

'Goddamn,' Nick said, his eyes lighting up as he checked his revolver. 'Can't believe I'm getting to do this twice in one day.'

'We'll take junior, here.' Jeffrey indicated Wallace, who looked about ready to jump out of his skin. Jeffrey probably looked the same way. There was enough adrenaline in his blood to give a lesser man a heart attack.

Nick bounced on the balls of his feet as he walked toward the other car and told the three agents inside they were in charge of the back.

'Let's give 'em a couple, three minutes head start,' Nick said, checking his watch. Time could either stand still or fly during a situation like this.

Nick looked back at the car, where Dave Fine was pouting. He said, 'I wouldn't leave a dog trapped in that car in this heat.'

'Me, neither,' Jeffrey said, making no move to roll down the windows.

They were quiet, staring out at the busy interstate while they waited for Nick's signal.

Finally, Nick looked at his watch and said, 'Let's go.'

Jeffrey tucked his gun into his shoulder holster as they walked. He had worn his ankle holster as well. Normally, Jeffrey would feel uncomfortable armed this way, but for the moment he felt ready for anything the small house might have to offer.

Trees and high shrubs had obscured a lot of the house from the street. Up close, Jeffrey could see it was mostly brick with vinyl siding on the trim and overhangs. The gutters were painted a bright white to match the trim. The house was small, probably two bedrooms with one bath and a kitchen–living room combination. There were houses like this all over Grant, built cheap just after the war, meant to be starter homes for returning veterans. Cement blocks served as the foundation with vents to let the house breathe.

'No basement,' Nick said.

Jeffrey nodded, pointing to the roofline. There did not appear to be a second story, either, but someone could definitely hide in the attic.

Wallace went first, easily scaling the five-foot-tall chain-link fence from the side that was most concealed by the shrubs. Nick had a little more difficulty, and groaned quietly as he lost his footing on the other side, his butt hitting the ground. Jeffrey followed them, wondering why his knee was giving him trouble, then remembering how he had hurt it lunging for Fine.

When they were all safe on the other side, Nick took a small walkie-talkie out of his pocket and said, 'We're inside the perimeter.'

There was a faint 'Check,' as the others got into position.

Jeffrey took out his gun indicating they should head toward the front door. As they got closer, they could hear soft music coming from the house. Jeffrey recognized a boy group, but couldn't put a name to them.

Wallace stopped at the front door, his gun held up beside his head. He counted off to three then kicked at the door.

Nothing happened.

'Shit,' Wallace cursed, shaking his leg out. For just a moment, Jeffrey considered that they might have the wrong house. Then he thought about the fact that someone could be waiting behind that locked front door with a double-barreled shotgun, ready to blow off their heads. He thought of Sara for a split second, and how she said she worried about him, then he thought about Lacey Patterson and pushed everything else from his mind.

Jeffrey indicated to Wallace that they would kick together this time. He counted off to three, and this time the door didn't hold.

'Police!' Nick yelled, storming in after them. There was no man standing inside with a shotgun. Instead there was a young girl wearing a short pink T-shirt and matching underwear. She could have just woken up from a nap.

Jeffrey pointed his gun up to the ceiling. He was about to ask her if she was okay when the little girl pointed silently down a hallway.

Jeffrey took off his jacket and put it around the girl while Nick and Wallace checked the other side of the house. He ushered her to the front porch, telling her to wait for him inside the front of the gate. He wanted to say something to her, to put his arm around her and tell her that she was okay now, but there was something so vacant about the child he could not bring himself to do it. She seemed beyond any kind of comfort.

Nick and Wallace came back, shaking their heads that no one was in the other side of the house. Nick tilted his chin up, indicating he would go first down the hall. Jeffrey was eerily reminded of Dottie Weaver's house as they walked in. The setup was similar, but the feeling was different. A dirty strip of carpeting muffled the sound of their feet on the hardwood floor. There were framed pictures of children's art on the wall.

Ahead, Nick flattened himself against the wall beside a closed door. This was where the music was coming from, and Jeffrey could make out the chorus now, 'I love you, love you, my sweet baby.'

Nick reached down and opened the door, crouching in the entrance in one swift motion. Something unreadable passed on his face, and he stood, walking into the room with his gun still drawn. Jeffrey followed him, seeing a king-size bed with mirrors all around it. The sheets were messed up, as if there had been recent activity, and there was a smell in the room that Jeffrey did not want to put a name to. The stereo was propped up on the box it came in, sickly sweet music still pouring out from the speakers. Two video cameras on tripods were pointed at the bed, the mirrors on the walls reflecting the scene back to Jeffrey. He stood there, wanting nothing more than to get out of this room, as Nick checked under the bed, then opened the door to one of the closets.

Wallace made a noise to get their attention then nodded down the hallway. Jeffrey backed outside the room as Nick checked the last closet, then followed.

Wallace put his mouth close to Jeffrey's ear and whispered, 'I saw a boy go in there,' indicating a closed door on the opposite side of the hall.

Nick pointed to a cord hanging down from the ceiling where the retractable stairs to the attic were. The cord wasn't moving, but that was no guarantee no one was up there.

Jeffrey passed the bathroom, which was small and dirty. Toys were stacked on the counter and in the empty tub. There was no shower curtain or closet in there, but some cabinets were built into the wall along the hallway. Jeffrey opened the first cabinet, but all it contained were the items you would expect: towels, wash rags, some diapers. The diapers got to him for some reason, and for the first time that day, he lost what little hope he had that they would find Lacey Patterson alive.

Nick put his hand on Jeffrey's shoulder, and Jeffrey got the feeling he was thinking the same thing.

There was one last room in the small house, and Jeffrey took the lead this time, pressing himself to the closed door just as Nick had. He threw the door open, crouching around the corner with his gun drawn, but the room appeared empty.

Three twin beds were shoved into the corner, dirty-looking sheets bunched up on them. There were no frames or box springs, just the mattresses flat on the floor. Sheets were nailed tightly to the windows like canvas over a frame. There was only one closet in the room, and Jeffrey walked over to it, expecting to see the worst behind it. He stood to the side and opened it, only to find shelves packed tight with boxes. Red numbers labeled the boxes, and Jeffrey pulled one of them out, frowning when he saw it was full of pictures. He looked at the other boxes and realized the numbers were probably the age of the kids in the pictures. The top row contained a few that were labeled '0–1.'

He remembered the boy Wallace had seen, and bent down on one knee. A couple of boxes on the bottom of the closet looked crooked, and Jeffrey pulled them out. He leaned down and saw a frightened little boy, not more than six years old, with his head between his knees. The boy saw Jeffrey, then reached out to pull the boxes back around him. He was so frightened that the boxes shook from his touch.

Jeffrey stood, thinking he would see the fear in that kid's eyes for as long as he lived. He wanted to pull the boy out from his hiding place and tell him that it was over, but Jeffrey wasn't sure that it was. The adult or adults who had done this were still in this house somewhere. It was better to leave the kid where he was safe rather than put him in more danger.

Jeffrey heard Nick's boots on the floor and turned to see him walking out the door. He watched as Nick lowered the attic stairs, the springs squeaking loud enough to vibrate in Jeffrey's ears. He unfolded the steps, which made a hollow thunking noise against the floor. Nick took out a mini flashlight, holding it between his teeth as he used one hand to climb the stairs and held his service revolver in the other. Jeffrey held his breath as Nick poked his head into the attic space. After a quick look around, Nick shook his head, taking the flashlight out of his mouth.

'Empty,' Nick said. He took the radio out of his pocket and asked, 'Did anyone come out the back?'

Crackling came, then a woman's voice said, 'That's a negative, sir. We've got the back and the sides.'

Nick sighed heavily, disappointment coming off him like sweat. 'Let Robbins stay back there. I need you and Peters inside to help us do another check.'

'You think we missed anything?' Wallace asked.

'Hell, I don't know,' Nick said. He picked up the stairs to fold them back up, but his hand slipped, and the stairs thunked to the ground again. He started to try again, but Jeffrey stopped him, pointing to the floor.

Nick shook his head, but then he seemed to play it

back in his mind and realized what Jeffrey had. The stairs hadn't sounded right when they hit the floor. Nick finally nodded, and he leaned down, pointing to a line of dirt where the rug had been raised then dropped back down.

Jeffrey pulled the stairs up and tucked them back into the attic. He holstered his gun and picked up the carpet. There was an outline of a trap door underneath it, about three feet square with a small, hinged pull in the center. Jeffrey indicated for Wallace to stand on the back side of the door, straddling the sides, and open it. Nick and Jeffrey stood on the other side, their guns drawn.

Time moved slowly, and Jeffrey could hear the stupid song that had been playing since they'd come in switch to another equally drippy ballad as the trap door creaked open. He could feel sweat dripping down his face, and tasted blood in his mouth as he bit the inside of his lip. Then the door was open, and about three feet down he saw a very scared-looking Lacey Patterson lying curled up on the ground under the house. She was filthy, and her hair had been cut close to her scalp. There was a bruise on her forehead, and her eyes were barely open. She had either been drugged or beaten or both.

'Holy Jesus,' Wallace muttered.

Jeffrey got down on his stomach so that he could see her better, asking, 'Lacey?'

The child did not respond, though at this distance, he could see there was something white at the corners of her mouth.

'Lacey?' he tried again, putting his gun beside him on the floor so he could reach in and touch her forehead. She felt clammy and there was something gritty on her skin.

Jeffrey told Wallace, 'Hold my feet,' as he reached into the hole. He managed to hook his hands under her arms and get a good grip on her. Wallace kept him from sliding in as Jeffrey started to pull Lacey out. She was small, but her body was deadweight. He asked Nick for help, and between the three of them they managed to get her out of the hole.

'You're okay,' Nick said, setting her down on the floor inside the bedroom.

Jeffrey sat back on his heels, wiping the dust from his forehead. The crawl space was filthy, red Georgia clay like powder from the heat.

Suddenly, there was a scratching noise from underneath the house as if someone was moving. Without thinking, Jeffrey dove into the hole, catching himself with his hands so he wouldn't fall on his face. It was dark under the house, low-hanging pipes giving it the appearance of a maze. Jeffrey blinked several times, trying to acclimate himself, when a flash of light came from the far end of the house.

'Nick!' he yelled, taking off, using his elbows and feet to propel himself through the small space. From above, he heard footsteps running through the house, and prayed Nick's man in the back would act quickly.

Up ahead, he saw a pair of feet slipping through a narrow vent opening. Jeffrey followed as fast as he could, banging his head on a gas line. He kept going toward the light, turning at the last minute and using his feet to kick at the hole. The mortar was weak in the old house, and bricks flew out from the force. Jeffrey turned back around, pushing himself through the opening, feeling intense pain as his pants tore on the jagged brick.

'Stop!' Robbins screamed. He was just a kid, his feet out wide, his gun in front of him, pointing at the figure running toward him.

Jeffrey knew what was going to happen and it did. The runner smacked right into Robbins, who dropped his gun. Jeffrey stood, unable to move as he recognized the runner.

'Dottie!' Jeffrey yelled.

Dottie stood, their eyes locking. She raised her hands like she meant to surrender, then took off running toward the backyard. Jeffrey knelt, pulling out his ankle gun in one swift movement as he lined up to take the shot. He stopped as Dottie jumped the fence and ran into the neighbor's backyard, which was full of kids playing on a swing set.

Jeffrey took off after her, pumping his arms as he ran. He hurdled the fence without breaking stride, running around kids like an obstacle course. He saw Dottie run into the house, slamming the door behind her. Jeffrey took the steps two at a time, busting the door open with his shoulder, breaking into the hallway and nearly smacking into a line of kids. The first one barely came up to Jeffrey's waist, and he sidestepped to miss the boy, slamming full force into the wall. His arm felt like it was on fire, and Jeffrey dropped his gun.

'Sir?' a young woman asked. She was probably around twenty, and her dark brown hair was pulled back into a ponytail. She looked terrified.

Jeffrey sat up, pressing his fingers into his arm to see if he had broken anything. He realized he was panting from running. There were at least ten kids around, all of them looking at Jeffrey with the same fear in their eyes as the young woman had. His heart stopped as he realized he was in a day-care center. All of these kids, so close to Dottie; he could not fathom the implications.

'Sir?' the woman repeated, pulling some of the kids close to her.

Jeffrey pulled his badge out of his back pocket, showing it to her. He tried to catch his breath so he could speak. 'Where . . . ?' he began. 'The woman . . . ?'

'Wendy?' the girl asked. 'Wendy James?'

Jeffrey shook his head, thinking she did not understand.

'She just left,' the girl told him. 'She ran through the house and –'

Jeffrey jumped up, scattering the kids as he retrieved his gun. He ran out the open front door, into the yard and to the street. He could see a car ahead, taking a right to merge onto the busy interstate. It could have been white or tan or gray. It could have been a four door or a coupe or a hatchback. He did not know what kind of car it was. All he knew was that it was gone.

TWENTY

Jeffrey walked around to the dock behind Sara's house. The moon was high above the trees, and a breeze was coming in off the lake. Jeffrey stood in the grass, watching Sara, feeling some of the stress start to drain out of him. She sat in one of the two deck chairs on the dock, her legs crossed at the ankle in front of her. In the moonlight, Jeffrey could see she was staring out at the rocks in the water. The greyhounds were with her and she rested her hand on Bob's head. She was wearing a pair of shorts and one of his old shirts. Jeffrey stared at her, thinking that she looked even better now than she did the night before.

She turned in her chair when she heard his footsteps on the dock. Billy and Bob kept their heads down, staring out at the water.

'Don't let them scare you,' Sara teased.

'They're so ferocious,' Jeffrey said. He went on one knee to pet Bob on the head. The dog rolled over, kicking his left leg into the air as Jeffrey scratched his belly.

Sara put her hand on Jeffrey's shoulder. 'How's Lacey?'

He sighed. 'Better. The sleeping pills are wearing off, but she's still groggy.'

'Did they find anything?'

'There was no evidence of recent abuse,' Jeffrey said.

'Just recent?'

He nodded. 'There were signs that something happened before.'

Sara seemed to sense he did not want to give specifics right now. She asked, 'What did her father say?'

Jeffrey kept scratching Bob's belly, enjoying the simple pleasure. 'He said he's glad to have her back.'

'Does he have a problem with me talking to her tomorrow?'

'Not last I checked,' Jeffrey said. 'He still thinks it was all Dottie.'

She stroked his hair back behind his ear. 'Have they identified the kids yet?'

'They're running the fingerprints now. Who knows what will come up? One of them sounded Canadian. This boy . . .' He let his voice trail off, not sure he could tell Sara what they found in that house. It was like a cancer, rotting his brain every time he thought about it.

'What about the day care behind the house?'

'She had just started working there,' Jeffrey said. 'Maybe a week or so. All the kids are being checked out, but they're thinking she didn't have time.'

Sara asked the question that had kept him up at night: 'Do you think you'll ever find Dottie?'

'We're hoping she doesn't know we picked up on Jenny's social security number,' he said, giving Billy equal time behind the ears and on his belly. 'She's picked up mail there before, according to one of the workers. She's been renting the box about a year now. Mail from two other boxes has been forwarded there.'

Sara pressed her lips together. 'Sounds like she knows what she's doing.'

'We're coordinating with the credit card company.

They're mailing it out tomorrow. It should be in the box in a couple of days.' He shrugged. 'From there, we just sit and wait. She shouldn't take long to get it. I'm sure she needs the money to set up shop, wherever she is.'

'You think that's what she's doing?'

He gave her a sad smile. 'The guy at the post office says there's another card from a different company in the box right now.'

'What's with all the cooperation?' Sara asked. She knew better than anyone that people were reluctant to assist the police these days. 'Didn't they ask for a subpoena?'

'No,' Jeffrey told her. 'It's amazing how helpful people are when you tell them that children are involved.'

'So,' Sara began. 'What next?

'We're going to have to coordinate with the school, find out how many kids were involved in this thing.'

'I want to check every file at the clinic.'

'Will Molly help you?'

Sara nodded. 'I already talked with her. We need to be careful about this. The hard part is going to be dealing with the hysterics whose kids never had contact with Dave Fine or Dottie or Grace.'

'You think people will do that?'

'Yes,' Sara answered. 'You can't blame them, but we're going to have to find a way to screen out the real cases from the bogus ones. We're lucky in a way that this was happening to older kids who can talk about what happened.'

'They didn't look that old in the pictures.'

'The FBI will have someone assign ages to the kids. They'll use the Tanner scale. There are certain markers that tell you how old a kid is.'

'I hate that there's even such a thing.'

'Do you want me to go to the school with you?'

Jeffrey sighed, thinking about how hard the next few days were going to be. Of course, it wasn't her job to talk to Lacey Patterson, either. He said, 'I know you don't have to, Sara, but do you mind?'

'No,' she told him. 'Of course not.'

'What I want to know is why do the kids protect these people?' Jeffrey asked, because that was the one thing that he could not understand. 'Why didn't Lacey or Jenny talk to one of their teachers, or go to you?'

'It's hard for them,' Sara explained. 'Their parents are all they have, all they know. It's not like they can move out and get jobs. A lot of times parents convince them that it's normal, or that they don't have an alternative.'

'Like Stockholm syndrome,' he said. 'Where the victim falls in love with the abductor.'

'That's a good analogy,' Sara told him. 'Their parents set up this pattern where they abuse them, then buy them ice cream. Or they guilt them into doing what they want, or trick them. Kids don't know that it's not supposed to be that way.' Sara sighed. 'And the fact is, the kids love their parents. They want to please them. They don't want to get their parents in trouble. They want the behavior to stop, but they don't want to lose their mother and father.' She paused. 'There's a real dependency there. The parents cause the pain, but they're also the ones who take it away.'

She continued, 'I've also been thinking about the baby.'

He didn't look at her, but said, 'Yeah?'

'Grace's baby was a girl. Maybe Jenny thought she was protecting the baby. Maybe that's why she helped Grace get rid of the baby.'

He thought it over, thinking that Jenny was so afraid of Grace she would've done anything to avoid her wrath. Jeffrey finally said, 'It's possible.'

'I really think that's why she did it,' Sara said with conviction. 'I think Grace made her help kill the baby and Jenny was so upset all she could think to do was kill Mark, the father.' She sounded so sure of herself that Jeffrey looked up at her. He could see how this was eating her up inside as much as it was him.

Jeffrey stood and stretched his arms up to the sky. He did not want to think about this anymore. He did not want to know that there were other kids like Jenny and Mark out there, being abused by their parents. He did not want to think about Dottie Weaver holding on to Lacey Patterson so she could exploit the child. Something had to give. Jeffrey did not think he could go on knowing that Dottie Weaver was out there doing whatever she wanted to children. He did not want to think about her preying on another small town somewhere.

He said, 'It's almost cool out here.'

'Isn't the breeze nice? I'd forgotten what it was like.'

'It doesn't bother you to be out here in the dark?'

'Why would it?' she asked.

He looked at her. 'Sometimes I think you're the strongest person I know.'

She smiled, indicating that he should sit beside her.

He sat in the chair with a groan. Jeffrey had not realized until that moment just how tired he was. He leaned his head back, looking up at the night sky. Clouds obscured the stars, and it looked like August was releasing its stranglehold on the thermometer. Fall would come soon, and the leaves would drop from the trees and the air would turn colder and Jenny Weaver would still be dead.

Jeffrey asked, 'Did you release the body?'

'Yes,' she answered.

'What about the baby?'

'I talked to Brock. He's donating the service. There's a plot in the Roanoke Cemetery.'

'I'll pay for it.'

'I already took care of it,' she said. 'Will you go to the service with me?'

'Yeah,' he answered, feeling it was the least he could do.

'Paul Jennings said to tell you to remember what he said.'

Jeffrey was silent.

'What did he say?'

'That I shouldn't blame myself for what happened,' he told her. 'That I shouldn't make myself live with that guilt.'

She reached over and squeezed his arm. 'He's right.'

'He said I should blame Dottie.'

'Maybe you should.'

'Dave Fine blames Dottie, too.'

'It's not the same thing,' she told him, sitting up in her chair. 'Jeffrey, look at me . . .' She waited until he did. 'You did what you had to do.'

'I stopped Jenny from killing Mark so that he could turn and hang himself,' Jeffrey told her. 'He still hasn't regained consciousness. He might never.'

'And that's your fault?' she asked him. 'I never knew you were so powerful, Jeffrey.' She listed things out: 'You made Jenny Weaver point a gun at Mark, you made Mark hang himself. Did you bring Dottie here, too? Did you make her abduct Lacey? Did you make Dottie work with Grace Patterson at that hospital? Did you make her do those things she did to children?'

'I'm not saying that.'

'But you are,' she insisted. 'If you want to blame somebody, blame me.'

He shook his head, saying, 'No.'

'I saw all of them,' Sara pointed out. 'I saw Mark and Lacey practically from the time they were born. Jenny was a patient of mine. Is it my fault?'

'Of course it's not.'

'Then how is it yours?'

Jeffery leaned his head on his hand, not wanting Sara to see how upset he was. 'You didn't pull the trigger,' he said. 'You didn't kill her.'

Sara got out of her chair and knelt in front of him. She took his hands in hers and said, 'You know how I told you I worry about you when I don't know where you are and the phone rings?'

He nodded.

'I worry because I know you,' she said, squeezing his hands for emphasis. 'I know what kind of cop you are, and what kind of man you are.'

'What kind of man am I?' he asked,

Her voice took on a softer tone. 'The kind of man who wouldn't hesitate to be the one to kick in that door instead of Lena. The kind of man who risks his life every day to make sure that other people are safe. I love that about you,' she insisted. 'I love that you're strong, and that you think things through, and that you don't just react.' Sara put her hand to his cheek. 'I love that you're gentle, and that you worry about Lena, and that you feel responsible for everything that happens in town.'

He started to speak, but she pressed her finger to his lips so that he would not interrupt her. 'I love you because you know how to comfort me and how to drive me crazy, and how to make my dad want to beat you to a pulp.' She lowered her voice. 'I love how you touch me, and how safe I feel when I'm with you.' She kissed his hands. 'You're a good man, Jeffrey,' she told him. 'Listen to Paul Jennings. Listen to me. You did the right thing.' She held his hands to her lips and kissed his fingers.

She said, 'It's okay to question yourself, Jeffrey. You did that, and now you have to move on.'

He looked out at the rocks jutting from the lake, and wondered if there would ever be a day in his life when he did not think of Jenny Weaver, and the role he had played in her death.

Sara told him, 'You're a good man, Jeffrey.'

He did not believe her. Maybe if he still didn't feel pain in his knee from jumping Dave Fine, or remember how good it felt to kick Arthur Prynne in the gut, it would be easier. Maybe if he didn't still see that set of frightened eyes from the back of the closet in Macon.

'Jeffrey,' Sara repeated. 'You're a good man.'

'I know,' he lied.

'Know it in here,' she told him, pressing her fingers to his chest.

Jeffrey brushed Sara's hair back behind her ear, and all he could think to say was, 'You're so beautiful.'

Sara rolled her eyes at the compliment. 'Is that all you've got to say?'

He offered, 'Why don't we go inside, and I'll answer you in greater detail?'

Sara leaned back on her hands, a smile playing at her lips. 'Why do we have to go inside?'

FRIDAY

TWENTY-ONE

Lena gritted her teeth, pounding her feet into the pavement. She could hear Hank's heavy footsteps behind her, his cheap Wal-Mart sneakers popping against the ground like a stick on an oil drum.

'That all you got?' he asked, pulling ahead of her. She let him take the lead for a while, watching him from behind. The sun did not agree with him, and rather than tanning, his pasty skin had taken on a reddish tone. The track marks on his forearms stood in a burgundy relief against this, and the back of his neck was as red as fire.

His breathing was more like a wheeze, but he held his own against her as she sped up to run beside him. His yellowish-gray hair was pasted to his head with sweat, and the turkey giblet hanging down from his neck bounced with each step he took. Still, Lena couldn't help but think he wasn't in bad shape for an old man. She had certainly seen worse.

'This way,' he said.

Lena followed him as he took a sharp turn off the road, and jogged along a path through the woods. The soft ground underfoot brought some relief to her aching knees, and her thighs started to feel like they might not ignite from the heat in her muscles as her second wind kicked in. Before, this was what she had lived for: the intense pain, then overcoming it. Pushing herself past the physical through sheer force of will, making herself finish the course. Her body felt strong and powerful, invincible, like she could do anything she wanted. Like she was the old Lena again.

She knew in the back of her mind where he was going, but she was still surprised when they reached the cemetery. They jogged through the rows of stones, both of them keeping their eyes straight ahead, not stopping until they got to Sibyl's marker.

Lena put her hand on top of the gravestone, using it to steady herself as she stretched her legs. The black marble stone was cool to the touch, and it felt good against her hand. Touching it was like touching part of Sibyl.

Hank stood beside her, lifting his T-shirt to wipe the sweat out of his eyes.

'Jesus, Hank,' Lena said, shielding her eyes from the glare off his white belly. There were track marks there, too, but she did not comment on them.

'It's a warm day,' Hank said. 'I think the heat's about to break, though. Don't you?'

Lena took a minute to realize that he was talking to her and not Sibyl. 'Yeah,' she mumbled.

Hank continued to talk about the weather, and Lena stood there, trying not to show how awkward she felt.

She looked at Sibyl's gravestone. Hank had taken care of the arrangements, and chosen the words on the stone. Above the dates, chiseled into the stone, were the words SIBYL MARIE ADAMS, NIECE, SISTER, FRIEND. Lena was surprised he had not put 'lover' for Nan's benefit. That would have been just like him.

'Look at this,' Hank mumbled, bending down in front of the stone. Someone had placed a small vase with a single white rose at the base, and it was starting to wilt in the morning heat. 'Isn't this pretty?'

'Yeah,' Lena said, but she could tell from the star-tled look Hank gave her that he had been talking to Sibyl.

He said, 'I bet Nan left this for her. Sibby always liked roses.'

Lena was silent. Nan had probably left the flower here that morning. She must have always done this early in the morning, because Lena had never run into her. Not that Lena made a habit out of visiting Sibyl's grave. At first, she had been incapable of making the trip because it was difficult to walk, let alone sit in the car for the ride from the house. Then, she had been embarrassed, thinking that Sibyl knew what had happened, that Lena had somehow been changed, compromised. Lately, it just felt eerie, visiting her dead sister. And the way Hank talked to Sibyl, as if she were still there, made Lena feel uncomfortable.

Hank said, 'White looks pretty against the black, don't you think?'

'Yeah.'

They both stood there, Lena with her arms crossed, Hank with his hands in his pockets, staring at the stone. The single rose did look pretty against the black marble. Lena had never understood people sending flowers to a funeral home, but she finally realized that the flowers were something for the living to enjoy, a reminder that there was still life in the world, that people could go on.

Hank turned to her, waiting for her attention. 'I guess I'm going back to Reece,' he said. 'Maybe tomor-row.'

Lena nodded, swallowing past the lump in her throat. 'Yeah,' she said, 'that's probably a good idea.' She had not told him that Jeffrey had given her an ultimatum: either take the time to get some help, or don't bother coming back at all. Partly, she had kept this secret because she did not want Hank to make the choice for her. He would easily take her back to Reece, give her a job in his bar, so that she could live her life under his watchful eye. That wouldn't really work, though, because one day Hank would be gone. He was an old man. He would not be there forever, and then what would Lena do?

For some reason, the thought that one day Hank would be dead brought tears to her eyes. She looked away from him, trying to gain her composure. Silently, he took his handkerchief out of his back pocket and handed it to her. The cloth was wet from his sweat, and hot, but she used it to blow her nose with anyway.

'I can postpone it,' he offered.

'No,' she said. 'It's probably better.'

'I'll sell the bar,' he offered. 'I can find a job here.' He added, 'You could come with me, back home.'

She shook her head no, feeling the tears coming again. There was no way to tell Hank that she wasn't upset about his leaving so much as about knowing that one day he would be dead. It was all too morbid, and what she really wanted from him, needed from him, was to know that she could always pick up the phone and he would be there. That was all Lena had ever wanted from Hank. That was actually the one thing he had always given her.

Hank cleared his throat and said, 'You've always been the strong one, Lee.'

She laughed, because she had never felt so weak and helpless in her life.

'With Sibby, I knew I had to be there, had to hold her hand every step of the way.' He paused, staring back at the tent from the recent funeral. 'With you, it was harder. You didn't want me. Need me.'

'I don't know if that's true.'

'Hell, yes, it is,' he countered. 'You always did everything on your own. Skipped college, joined the police academy, moved here, didn't tell me about it until after it was all done.'

Lena felt there was something she should say, but could not think what.

'Anyway,' he said, taking back the handkerchief. She watched as he folded it. 'I guess I'll take off tomorrow.'

'Okay,' she nodded, turning back to Sibyl's grave.

'They'll probably need you here for a while, anyway,' Hank said. 'What with that girl being found. I'm sure there's a lot more kids around here who went through the same thing. Those people don't tend to be as isolated as you'd think.'

'No,' Lena agreed. 'They don't.'

'Good that girl's back, though,' Hank added. 'That your chief found her.'

'Yes,' Lena said, but she wondered about that. What kind of things had been done to Lacey Patterson in that house? What memories would she carry with her for the rest of her life? Would she even be able to carry them, or would she take the easy way out, like her brother? Lena knew from her own experience that the lure of not having to think about the things that happened was seductive. Even after all she had been through, she was not sure that tomorrow she might decide that it wasn't worth it to keep on going.

Hank said, 'I'm sorry about pushing Preacher Fine on you. I guess it's hard to see something like that.'

Lena took the apology in stride. 'Brad's a cop and he didn't see it either,' she told him, though if Hank knew Brad, he would know that wasn't much of a consolation.

Hank tucked the handkerchief back into his pocket. He dropped his hands to his sides, the back of his hand brushing against hers for just a moment. Like Lena, he was sweaty, and she could feel the heat coming off his skin.

After a while, he said, 'You know if you need me you can call me, right? You know I'll be there.'

Lena smiled, and she really felt it this time. 'Yeah, Hank,' she said. 'I know.'

Lena walked through the hospice, trying to breathe through her mouth so that the smell didn't overwhelm her. The building had a certain odor that reminded her of piss and alcohol. It kind of reminded her of Hank's bar.

She jabbed at the button on the elevator, feeling claustrophobic as it slowly climbed to the third floor. Her neck felt gritty, and she used her hand to wipe it. After her run with Hank, she had taken a long shower, but she was already sweating again from the heat.

Lena sighed with relief as the doors opened and the smell of urine did not assault her nostrils. Most of the residents on Mark's floor were catheterized and somewhat sterile compared to their more active counterparts on the lower floors. The stench was controlled because of this.

She stepped into the hall, looking out the window across from the elevator. The clouds were dark and fluffy, filled with rain that seemed on the verge of falling. She was reminded of the morning Grace Patterson had died, and how she had stood behind Teddy Patterson while he slept, watching the sun come up and relishing the thought that the monster lying in the bed would never be able to feel the sun on her face again. Lena never questioned herself about making sure Grace did not go peacefully. She knew she had done the right thing. There was no doubt in her mind.

'Can I help you?' a woman asked as she walked in front of the nurses' station.

'I'm looking for Mark Patterson's room,' Lena told her.

'Oh,' the woman said, obviously surprised. 'He hasn't had any visitors.'

Lena could have guessed that Teddy Patterson would not want to see his son, but she still felt surprised.

Even though Lena knew the answer, she had to ask, 'Has he regained consciousness?'

The woman shook her head, saying, 'No,' as she pointed down the hallway. 'Three-ten,' she told Lena. 'Right, then left, across from the linen storage.'

Lena thanked her and followed the directions. She traced her fingers along the railing lining the hall as she walked, purposely taking her time. There was no reason for Lena to see Mark. She wasn't working the case. Hell, she wasn't even sure if she was a cop anymore.

Even though Mark was not about to tell her to come in, Lena knocked on the door marked 310. She waited outside, then pushed the door open. The lights were out, and no one had opened the blinds to let the sun in. Mark lay in bed, tubes running in and out of him, looking paler than she had ever seen him. Machines beat softly in the background, and a bag filled with urine hung off the railing around the bed. The room was stark and institutional. There were no flowers on the bed table, and the single chair pushed against the wall had not been used. The television was off, the dark screen looking almost sinister.

'Let's let some light in,' Lena said, not knowing

what else to do. She twisted the wand on the blinds and the slats opened, pouring in light. She turned back to Mark, and adjusted the blinds so that he wasn't getting the full force of the sun.

There was a tube in his mouth helping him breathe, and saliva had built up around it. Lena went into the bathroom and wet a washcloth with warm water. At the bed, she wiped Mark's mouth. Then, because she had appreciated this when she was in the hospital, she folded the cloth and ran it along his face and neck, then along his arms. Next, she got some lotion out of the unopened patient-care kit in the stand beside the bed. She warmed it in her hands before rubbing it on his arms and neck, then patting some on his face. Lena wasn't sure, but his skin seemed to have more color to it when she was finished.

'Looks like they're treating you okay here,' Lena said, though she didn't think that was necessarily true. 'I, uh . . . ,' Lena began, then stopped. She looked at the door, feeling foolish for talking to Mark when he obviously could not hear her, thinking this was about as stupid as Hank talking to Sibyl's grave.

Despite this, she took his hand. 'Lacey's okay,' she told him. 'Well, she's back. They found her over in Macon and she's . . .'

Lena looked around the room not knowing how to do this.

'They're watching the post office,' she told him. 'The chief thinks Dottie will show up soon.' Lena took a deep breath and held it awhile before exhaling. 'We'll catch her, Mark. She won't get away with this.'

She was silent, listening to the in and out of his breath as the machine pushed air into his lungs. Of course Mark did not respond to her, and again she felt foolish. Why did Hank do this with Sibyl? What did it accomplish, telling her things? It was like talking to the wind. It was really just talking to yourself.

Lena laughed, realizing that of course this was why Hank did it. Talking to someone who could not answer you, who could not voice concern or disapproval or anger or hatred, was the ultimate freedom. You could say anything you wanted without fear of repercussion.

'I'm not sure I'm going to be a cop anymore,' she told Mark, feeling a little giddy as she spoke the words aloud. Her mind had been playing around with this thought for a while, like a marble spinning through a maze in a child's game, but she had not let herself accept the possibility until just this moment.

'I've got to talk to my boss in a couple of days.' She paused, looking at the tattoo on Mark's hand. She wondered briefly what she could do to have the tattoo removed. There were procedures that could take them off. She had seen them advertised on television.

'I don't know what I'm going to tell Jeffrey,' Lena said, still feeling silly. 'I talked to Hank, and I know I could move back to Reece with him.' She stopped. 'I don't know, though. I don't know if I can go back.'

Lena noticed that his blanket had come undone, and she walked around the bed to tuck it back in. She smoothed the material with her hand, saying, 'Anyway, I don't want to leave Sibyl here alone. I know she's got Nan to look after her, but still . . .'

Lena walked around the room, trying to think of what to say. The sound of her voice in the room was making her self-conscious, but it felt better to say these things, to speak the words that had been jumbled up in her head for so long.

The chair screeched across the floor as she moved it to the bed. She sat, and took Mark's hand again. 'I wanted to say,' she began, but could not go on. She

405

finally forced herself to speak. 'I wanted to say that I'm sorry for the way I reacted when you told me what happened . . .' She paused, as if waiting for a response, then clarified, 'About you and your mom.'

Lena looked at his face, wondering if he could hear any of this.

She said, 'I wanted to let you know that I understand. I mean, I understand as much as I can.' She shook her head. 'I mean . . . ,' she began, then stopped again. 'I know what it took, Mark. I know what it took for you to tell me your secret.' She paused, trying to remember to breathe. 'You were right when you said I'd been through the same thing, that I knew what you were talking about.'

She looked at him again, and still he was mute. His chest rose and fell with the pump that forced him to breathe. The heart monitor beeped with his heart.

'I didn't think this would be so hard,' she whispered. 'I thought I was being strong . . .' She stopped again. 'You were right, though. I was a coward. I *am* a coward.'

Lena took a deep breath, holding it in until she thought her lungs might burst. She felt the room closing in on her, and suddenly, she was back in that dark place, splayed to the floor, with *him* somewhere in the house, ignoring her. The worst part was when the drugs started to wear off, and she realized where she was and what was being done to her, and that she was powerless. She would feel a pressure in her chest, as if someone had carved her out and filled her with a liquid-black loneliness. When she got to this place, this stripped-down, empty place, the light under the door became her salvation, and she would find herself wanting to see him, wanting to hear his voice, no matter what the cost.

'I was so scared,' she told Mark. 'I didn't know where I was, or how much time had passed, or what was going on.'

She felt her throat tighten as the memory overwhelmed her. 'He nailed me down to the floor,' she told him, though surely Mark knew this. 'He nailed me down, and I couldn't move away. I didn't have a choice. There was nothing I could do except wait, and let him do to me what he did.'

Lena's breath came in pants, and she could feel herself going back to that room again, feeling trapped and helpless. 'The drugs . . . ,' she said, then stopped herself. Mark had obviously used drugs to dull his pain, too. Only, Lena had not been given a choice about what she would take, or when.

'He gave me these drugs,' she said. 'They made me feel . . .' She tried to find words. 'Free,' she said. 'Like I was floating, like I was above everything. And Greg, my boyfriend – ex-boyfriend – was there.' She stopped again, thinking about the Greg from her drugged dreams, not the Greg she had actually known. In her dreams, Greg was much more sure of himself, more in control of their lovemaking. He pushed her in her dreams, pushed her to the edge where she did not know the difference between pain and pleasure, and did not *want* to know. All she wanted when she was in this state was to have him inside of her, to have him touching her, and filling her up from the inside, pushing deeper into her, until she thought she might explode. Then, when he took her to this point, the release was almost ethereal. She had never known such pleasure in her life as her body opened up to him completely.

She told Mark, 'Greg was never like that. I knew that. I knew that in my mind.' She squeezed Mark's hand. 'I knew it somewhere, and I didn't care. I just wanted to be with him. I wanted to feel him.'

She put her hand to her mouth, but there was no turning back now. 'Then, the drugs would wear off,' she said, feeling like she was describing something that had happened to someone else. 'And I would start to feel things. I would start to realize what was going on, who I really was.' She swallowed hard. 'What I had done with him.' Lena felt her stomach turn in disgust. 'The noises I had made,' she whispered, remembering them now, how she had talked back to him, how she had pleaded with him the way she would plead with a lover.

Her hand dropped to her chest, and she could feel her heart pounding. 'And then I would cry,' she said, tears streaming down her face. 'I would cry, because I was so disgusted with myself, and then I would cry because I felt so alone.' She wiped her eyes with the back of her hand. 'I would cry because I didn't want to be alone, didn't want to know what had happened.'

'And when he came to me . . . ,' she whispered. 'When he came back into the room, and I wasn't alone anymore . . .'

Lena had to stop, because she was going to hyperventilate if she did not get her breathing under control. She looked at Mark's hand, rubbing her fingers across the tattoo.

Mark's confession came back to Lena in a flood, and she could hear now what she could not let herself hear in that trailer. He had talked about the crime against him like a lover recalling a particularly passionate moment. As Lena played his words in her head over and over again, she finally knew why he had branded himself with the tattoo. She knew the guilt Mark carried around with him like an anvil tied to his heart. Part of him would always be his mother's son. Part of him would always be back in that trailer, listening to a CD, when his mother came into his room and raped him. Part of him would always remember how good it felt, if only for the moment, to be inside of her, to fuck her. No matter where he went or what he did, Mark would carry that brand inside of him. The tattoo only made it so that other people could see. The tattoo was Mark's way of telling people that he did not belong to them, that he would always belong to his mother. What she had done had marked him inside the way no needle and ink could ever mark his skin.

For the rest of his life, maybe even right now, trapped in his body as he was, Mark would carry with him the knowledge that he had enjoyed it. Just for that moment in time, he had been his mother's favorite, he had experienced what he thought of as love for maybe the first time in his life. In her sick, twisted way, Grace Patterson had made her son feel wanted, and he had loved her back for it, even as he had hated her for doing something so wrong.

The room was silent but for the machines and the blood pounding in Lena's ears. She heard a high-pitched whining noise, but knew it was only in her head. She wanted to stand up, to let go of Mark, to leave him in this bed to die because he would do that with or without her.

Still, she had come this far. There was no one stopping her, no one questioning the insanity of her revelations. There was just Lena in the room, and if Mark was there, if he was really there with her, hearing what she was saying, then he was probably the only other person in the world who could understand what she was saying.

'I was so lonely when he left me there,' Lena began,

her voice a hoarse whisper as she made herself go back to that horrible place. She clenched her teeth, not sure she could go on. It was this part that killed her every time, the reason she would never go into therapy or tell anyone what had really happened in that room four months ago.

'When he came back – back into the room – and I wasn't alone anymore . . .' Lena stopped, choking on a sob. She could not say this. She could not make herself admit this to anyone, not even Mark, not even this lifeless shell who wasn't even Mark anymore. She was not strong enough. She could not overcome this.

'Shit,' Lena cried, trying to keep herself from breaking down. Her body shook, and soon she was wracked with sobbing. If Mark could still feel things, he would be able to feel her hands shaking, sense the fear that held her body like a steel trap. He would understand the pain that touched her deep inside the way no one ever would be able to again. No pills would take this away. Even a bullet passing through her brain would not push out the knowledge, and Lena knew that even if she did manage to do it, to pull that trigger or take all of those pills, her last thoughts would still be of *him*.

'No,' Lena said, shaking her head violently side to side. 'No, no, no,' she insisted, thinking about what Nan had said, knowing what Sibyl would say if she were here.

'Be strong,' Lena said, speaking for Sibyl. 'Be stronger than this.'

Lena thought of Hank, too, sitting on the floor in her bathroom, weeping openly, just as she wept now.

'When he came back into the room with me,' Lena began, forcing herself to speak, pushing herself to say *his* name. 'When he came back to me,' she repeated, 'part of me was relieved.' She stopped, knowing that was still not right. She could tell Mark this, because Mark understood. He knew what it was like to be so empty that you took whatever people gave you. She knew the loneliness of being locked in a pitch-black room with nothing to do but wait. She knew that there came a point when your mind told you everything was wrong, but your body betrayed you anyway, reaching out for whatever comfort was offered.

She swallowed, starting again. 'When he came back into the room,' she began, 'part of me was . . . happy.'

TWENTY-TWO

Sara sat on the floor across from Lacey Patterson in the back room of the children's clinic. Just a few days ago, Lacey had come here seeking help. Now she was back, having gone through unspeakable things, and all Sara could do was wait for the girl to talk.

'Dottie just left you at Wayne's house?' Sara asked.

'Yeah,' Lacey said, looking down at her shoes. She had asked to sit on the floor for some reason, and Sara had obliged, wanting to make the girl as comfortable as possible. She did not want Sara close, and so they had decided Sara would sit a foot away with her back against the closed door. Lacey sat in the middle of the room.

Lacey said, 'The pills made me sleepy.'

'And you don't remember anything that went on until you woke up in the hospital?'

She nodded, then started to bite her fingernails. Time passed, and the little girl was down to the cuticle on her thumb, and working on her pinky finger when Sara reached out and stopped her.

'You'll hurt yourself,' Sara said, then realized from Lacey's expression how silly the warning was.

Lacey chewed at her cuticle, asking, 'Is Mark going to be okay?'

'I don't know, sweetie.'

Lacey teared up, but she did not cry. 'I didn't mean to hurt him,' she said.

'How did you hurt him?'

'He was coming after me again, and I just grabbed the knife.'

'You're the one who cut him?'

She nodded, chewing another nail. 'They were at Dottie's, taking things out of the house and painting. I was hiding, but Mark found me.' I kicked him in the head with my foot.' She took her fingers out of her mouth. 'Mark didn't want me to come here to see you. I wanted to say goodbye, and then I was so scared I got sick. I'm sorry.'

'That's okay,' Sara assured her. 'So you came here and then Mark showed up? And then you ran and Dottie picked you up in the black car?'

Lacey nodded, but she still would not say who had been driving the car. She asked, 'You don't think that's why he tried to kill himself, do you? Because I hit him?'

'No,' Sara assured her. 'I think that Mark had a lot of other problems that led him to think that was his only choice.'

'Can I see him?' she asked in a small voice.

'If you want to.'

'I want to.'

Sara sat back, watching the girl chew her fingers. Lacey's hair had been cut almost in a buzz cut. Dottie had probably planned to disguise her as a boy until she could sell her off to the highest bidder.

'Is my daddy coming back soon?' Lacey asked.

'Do you want to see him?'

'He didn't know,' she said, as if she could read Sara's mind. 'I knew about Mark and Mama, but Daddy didn't know.'

'Are you sure?'

She nodded. 'If he found out, he would've killed Mark.'

'How about you, honey?' Sara asked. 'Did Mark ever touch you?'

She looked away.

'Lacey?'

She shook her head vehemently, but Sara did not believe her. She was still torn on the subject of Mark Patterson. On the one hand, he had been a victim, and on the other, he had obviously been an abuser.

Lacey said, 'Mark was nice to me.'

Sara let this pass. 'Did Dottie ever make you sit for pictures?'

'No,' she said. 'Mark and Jenny did, though. They got their pictures taken, and sometimes they were in movies. I saw them doing it.'

'But you never did?'

Lacey put her hand back in her mouth. 'Mark said if he ever caught me doing any of that he would tell Daddy.'

'Mark didn't want you to do it?'

'I wanted to,' she countered, taking on a petulant child's tone. 'Jenny was doing it, and she went to a party and did it with lots of boys.'

'Do you think Jenny enjoyed doing that?'

'I tried it once, and Mark found out.' She dropped her hand into her lap. 'That's when he hit me.'

Sara let this sink in. She had never even dreamed that Mark was trying to protect his sister.

'This was when Mark got arrested, right?'

Lacey seemed surprised that Sara knew this. 'Yeah.'

'But he didn't tell your father?'

'I told him if he did that I would tell about him and Mama.'

She said 'him and Mama' in a singsong way, as if the phrase had been practiced over and over. Sara imagined that Lacey had used this as a threat on more than one occasion. She was still a child at heart, and most children would do anything they could to get their way.

'I didn't like it anyway,' Lacey said. 'I told him I wouldn't do it anymore. I didn't like it.' She frowned. 'Dottie was mean when she was like that. Not like she was when we were playing.'

'You played with her?'

'She would baby-sit us sometimes.' Lacey smiled. 'She had this game we would play, where we would get all dressed up, and she would take us to the movies and let us stay dressed up.'

'That sounds nice.'

'She wasn't like that all the time, though.' Lacey started to pick at a scab on her leg. 'She was mean sometimes. I didn't like her then.'

'I don't blame you,' Sara told her. 'Was she the one who talked about purity?'

Lacey jerked her head up. 'Where did you hear that?'

Sara decided to lie. 'Mark told me.'

Lacey shook her head. 'He wouldn't have told you about that.'

'Are you sure?'

She shrugged, but Sara could see that she wasn't. 'Dottie got mad at Jenny because she said she was obsessed with it.'

'Obsessed with what?'

'What they do to little girls over there,' she mumbled. 'Jenny had this report in school last year about Africa, and different tribes. She said that the women were lucky because they belonged to people. To their daddies, or their husbands, and as long as they did right they were safe.'

'Do you believe that, Lacey?'

She ignored Sara's question. 'Dottie was mad. Jenny wouldn't drop it. Even when Mama came over and told her to stop.' She turned her head to the side. 'Mama can usually make people do things that maybe they don't want to do. She's good at that.'

Sara took a deep breath, trying to get her head around what the child was revealing. She asked, 'So your mom and Dottie told Jenny to stop talking about the mutilation?'

'They were worried she'd get in trouble at school. They had to move before because of it. A guidance counselor came to the house. Dottie said he was gonna call the police because of what Jenny said.'

'About girls being cut like that?' Sara asked, wondering at a girl obsessed with self-mutilation.

'Jenny said women over there didn't have to worry about stuff . . .' She paused, then, 'Like, sex stuff. And like what Dottie was doing. They don't have that over there, because children are sacred. Girls are protected.'

'Why would Dottie cut her, Lacey?'

'She didn't,' Lacey said. 'After the Christmas trip, Jenny decided to do it to herself.'

Sara shook her head, not accepting this. 'There's no way she could have done that to herself, sweetie.'

'But she did,' Lacey insisted. 'She used a razor, only she started screaming, and Dottie ran upstairs and started screaming, too.'

'You were in the house?'

'I was downstairs with Mama because it was payday.'

Sara knew she should not have been surprised that these women had a regular payday, but it made sense that they ran their sick little publication like a business. They had been doing this for at least thirteen years, and knew what they were doing.

'Jenny yelled so loud, like she was dying,' Lacey said. 'And then Mama came back downstairs and told me what Jenny had done to herself.'

Sara nodded for her to continue, because that was all she could do.

'They couldn't take her to the hospital, so Mama said the best thing they could do was finish what she started . . .' Lacey paused. 'So, they did.'

'Did they anesthetize her?' Sara asked.

'Mama gave her some of her pills so she wouldn't get an infection.'

'That's not what I meant,' Sara told her. 'Did they knock her out before they finished cutting her? Or make her go to sleep so she wouldn't feel it?'

'I think she fell asleep on her own when they started,' Lacey provided. 'At least, she stopped screaming after a while.'

Sara chewed her bottom lip, trying to think of a response. She asked, 'What made Jenny do that to herself?'

'Carson and Rory were making fun of her when we went skiing, like she would go with them, and she wouldn't.'

'Go with them, meaning sex?'

She nodded. 'She said she wouldn't, that they weren't clean, and they got mad at her and called her a whore, and she didn't know why, but when Cooper told her that she had before, this time she went over to their house with Mark.' She shrugged. 'Mark put something in her drink to make her act funny and not remember.'

'Do you know what it was?'

'Something that makes you feel really bad the next day,' Lacey answered. 'She got sick to her stomach and had to stay home from school for two days, and Dottie said she had the flu.'

Rohypnol, Sara thought. The date rape drug.

Lacey continued, 'She did what she did, you know.

Mark says that drugs just make you do the things you want to do anyway.'

'That's not true,' Sara told her. 'Especially with the drug he probably gave her.'

Lacey shrugged as if it didn't matter. 'She liked Cooper Barrett anyway.'

'Was he on the ski retreat?' Sara asked.

'Him and Rory and Carson,' she said. 'They slipped notes under the door at the hotel, and when we got up one morning, there was a sign over the room number that said some mean things.' She looked up at Sara. 'I guess they were the ones who stole stuff out of her locker at school.'

'What kinds of stuff?'

'Pictures and things. They tore them up, so she had to stop keeping stuff in there except for books.'

'I guess that upset her a lot.'

Lacey shrugged, but Sara could tell it had bothered her.

'Why did Mark do that to her, do you think?' Sara asked. 'Did Dottie ask him to take her to the party?'

Lacey nodded, and Sara put her hand to her stomach, thinking about Mark pimping out Jenny Weaver to recruit more kids for Dottie.

'Jenny was upset about them bothering her,' Lacey said. 'And Dottie told Jenny just to go with them again and that would make them stop, but Jenny didn't want to. She said she wanted to be pure.'

'So, that's what made her cut herself between the legs?' Sara asked.

Lacey said, 'She started it, but Dottie had to finish it.'

Lacey returned to the scab, and Sara watched as she picked it until it started to bleed.

Sara took a tissue out of her pocket and dabbed

the blood off the girl's leg. She asked, 'Did you ever see what Dottie did to Jenny that night?'

Again, she shook her head. 'I wasn't allowed to talk to her anymore.'

'Why?'

'Because Mama told me not to,' she said, looking back down at the scab as she picked it. 'Mama told me if I talked to Jenny, then she would let Dottie do me the same way.' She indicated her lap. 'Down there.'

'Was your mother mad at Jenny, too?'

With her head down, Lacey's voice was muffled. Sara had to strain to hear her say, 'Mama said Mark had been with Jenny, and that wasn't right. It made Jenny crazy, and that's why she did that to herself.' She paused. 'Children should only be with adults, because adults know what they're doing, and kids don't.'

'Are you sure your daddy didn't know about this?'

She shook her head again, her lips pressed together in a straight line. 'He would've killed Mark.'

'Don't you think he would have been mad at your mother, too?' Sara decided to push her a little further. 'Don't you think he would have been upset that your mother was pregnant?'

Lacey's head jerked up. 'How did you know?'

'I know a lot of things,' Sara told the girl.

'It was Mark's fault she got pregnant,' Lacey said, and again, Sara was struck by the practiced tone. Obviously, this was something the child had been taught. 'Mama told Daddy she couldn't be with him when she got sick again. That's how she knew it was Mark's.'

Again, Sara took a deep breath. She doubted very seriously whether or not they would ever know who the real father of that baby was.

'Last Saturday,' Sara began. 'What happened?

'Mama went up to Skatie's to find Mark, and she got sick.'

'Sick how?' Sara asked.

Lacey looked back down at her leg. 'She drove us up there, looking for Mark, and she got real sick and had to go to the bathroom.'

Sara tried to remember how tall Grace Patterson was. She was a small woman, and Tessa could have easily mistaken her for a teenage girl.

Sara asked, 'Did you go with her into the bathroom?'

Lacey nodded.

'And then did Jenny come?'

'She saw us go in.'

'What happened then?'

Lacey gave a long sigh. 'The baby came out from between her legs, and there was a lot of blood . . .' She paused, still not looking up at Sara. 'Mama said it was sick from the cancer medicine she took, and they had to take care of it.'

Sara swallowed hard.

'She told me to go wait in the car while she and Jenny took care of it.'

'Why did she make Jenny stay?'

'To punish her. It was Jenny's fault all of this happened. If she hadn't been with Mark to begin with, then Mama wouldn't have had to do what she did.'

Sara leaned her head against the door, trying to think of something to say. She was amazed at the power Grace Patterson and Dottie Weaver had over these children. That Sara had been in their presence and not noticed how horrible they were was something for which she would never forgive herself.

Lacey made sure she had Sara's attention, then told her, 'Mama told Jenny if she didn't stay and help, then she'd tell you what Jenny had been doing.'

'Me?' Sara asked, unable to hide her shock.

'Jenny wanted to be a doctor for kids like you are,' the girl said. 'She didn't think you'd help her if you knew she was having sex with all those people.' The practiced tone came back to her voice as she said, '"If you don't do this, I'm gonna tell Dr. Linton what a whore you are."'

Sara felt horrified her name had been used to threaten a child. 'That's not true,' Sara told her vehemently. 'That's not true at all.'

Lacey shrugged as if it didn't matter.

Sara wanted to shake her. 'I would have done everything I could to help her, Lacey. Just like I'll do whatever I can to help you.'

'I don't need help now,' Lacey said, her tone implying that it was too late.

Sara was so angry that tears welled into her eyes. She had autopsied the baby. She knew exactly what Grace and Jenny had done to the poor creature. To think Jenny complied in the mutilation for fear of being exposed to Sara made bile rise into her throat.

'Mama said that a lot,' Lacey told her. 'Jenny wanted you to think she was a good person.'

Sara put her hand to her throat. 'She was a good person.'

Lacey looked down at the floor. 'Whatever.'

'What happened to Jenny was horrible. It wasn't her fault.'

Again, Lacey shrugged.

'Sweetheart,' Sara said, trying to sound reassuring. She reached for Lacey's hand, but the girl pulled away.

Sara let a minute pass before asking, 'Why do you think Jenny threatened to kill Mark?'

Lacey shrugged, but Sara could tell she knew the answer.

'Do you think she wanted it to stop?'

She shrugged.

'Do you think this was the only way she thought she could stop it, by pointing that gun at Mark? By ending up in . . .' Sara stopped, feeling a heavy weight settle on her chest. Jenny had known that she would end up on a table in the morgue. Making Jeffrey pull that trigger was her way of forcing Sara to see what was happening to her.

Lacey looked up, her face completely devoid of emotion. 'Jenny knew better than that,' she said. 'She knew it could never be stopped.'

Sara reached for a response, more afraid than anything that what the girl said was true. 'We'll catch Dottie before she does this again, Lacey. I promise we'll do everything we can to stop her.'

'Yeah, well . . .' She shrugged, as if Sara had just told her an impossible fantasy. She asked, 'Is my daddy gonna be here soon? I wanna go home.'

'Lacey,' Sara began, not knowing what else to say.

The girl looked up, tears in her eyes. The past few days had aged her. She no longer looked like a carefree little girl with nothing more to worry about than whether or not she would make the cheerleading squad. The people who had abused her were gone, but she would always carry around what they did to her in her heart. Looking at her, Sara had never felt so helpless in her life. She wanted to do something, to help, but she knew it was much too late for that. She also knew that there were more kids like Lacey out there, more children who had fallen victim to Dottie Weaver – and many more who still could.

Lacey wiped her nose with the back of her hand, sniffing loudly. She managed a smile for Sara, repeating, 'Is my daddy gonna be here soon? I wanna go home.'

SUNDAY

ONE WEEK LATER

TWENTY-THREE

Tessa flopped into the chair opposite Sara at the dining room table. 'Am I going to be throwing up like this for the rest of my life?'

'I hope not,' Sara mumbled, not really paying attention. She was reading through a chart, trying to make sense of her own handwriting. 'What does this say?' she asked, sliding the chart across to Tessa.

Tessa studied the scribble. 'Permanent apples?' she guessed.

'That's what I got, too,' Sara mumbled, taking back the file. She stared at the words, willing them to make sense.

Tessa reached into Sara's briefcase and took out a magazine.

'That's a journal,' Sara told her.

'I may not be a doctor, but I *do* know how to read,' Tessa shot back, flipping through the pages. After a couple of beats, she closed it, saying, 'There aren't any pictures.'

'There're some in the back,' Sara told her, reaching across the table to show her sister a close-up of a very red, very enlarged appendix. She flipped the page to the companion shot, which showed the organ dissected in all of its bleeding glory.

'Oh, Jesus,' Tessa groaned, clamping her hand over her mouth as she stood from the table. She nearly knocked Cathy over as she ran out of the room.

Cathy asked, 'What's wrong with her?' as she put a plate of deviled eggs on the table.

'Dunno,' Sara said, staring at the chart. 'Oh,' she said, finally figuring it out. 'Palpated appendix.'

Cathy frowned. 'Do you have to do that at the dining room table?'

Sara stacked the charts together. 'Not anymore,' she said. 'That was the last one.'

Cathy sat across from her, taking a sip of Sara's iced tea. 'How's that going?' she asked, indicating the charts.

'Slowly,' Sara told her. 'But better than I thought. I mean, better for Grant. She kept a low profile here.'

'As your father would say, don't shit where you eat.'

'Exactly,' Sara answered, her smile feeling tight across her face.

'Speaking of which,' Cathy said, 'I heard Dave Fine is going to trial.'

Sara nodded. 'He thinks he can stay out of jail.'

'I think jail might be the only safe place for him,' Cathy said, taking another sip of tea. 'Did you talk to Lacey's father about her helping out at the clinic after school?'

Sara nodded, tucking the charts into her briefcase. 'He's going to think about it.'

'I don't imagine he'll stick around town long,' Cathy said, giving Sara a careful look. 'No matter what he's saying, people think he knew.'

Sara shrugged, not comfortable talking about this with her mother.

Cathy said, 'I heard his tires got slashed outside the Piggly Wiggly the other day.'

Sara studied her mother, trying to figure out what she was getting at.

'I just don't want you to get hurt,' Cathy finally

said. 'I don't want to see you get close to this girl, then have her father take her away.'

Sara busied herself arranging her briefcase. Jeffrey had said the same thing to her the other night.

'You know,' Cathy began, 'you could always adopt a child.'

Sara felt a tight smile on her face. She took off her glasses and set them on the table. 'I, uh . . .' She stopped, giving a humorless laugh. It was so much more complicated than that.

Cathy waited for Sara to speak.

'I really don't want to talk about that right now, Mama.'

Cathy reached over and took Sara's hands in hers. 'I'm here when you want to.'

'I know.'

Tessa walked back into the room and popped Sara on the back of the head, muttering, 'Bitch.'

Sara laughed, and Tessa stuck out her tongue.

Cathy raised an eyebrow as she stood from the table, but did not comment. She asked Tessa, 'You feeling okay, baby?'

'Yes, Mama,' Tessa answered, but she did not look it. Sara felt a flash of guilt for showing her the photograph.

'You sure?' Sara asked.

'Oh, I'm just peachy,' Tessa snapped back. 'My hair is oily, my skin feels scritchy, my pants are too tight.' She stopped on this, tugging at the legs of her shorts. 'They keep crawling up my crotch.'

'Nature abhors a vacuum,' Sara told her, laughing.

'Sara,' Cathy warned, but she was laughing as she walked back into the kitchen.

Tessa sat down again, taking one of the deviled eggs. 'Where's Jeffrey? He's half an hour late.'

'I don't know,' Sara said, watching her sister suck down the egg. 'I thought you were sick to your stomach.'

'I was,' Tessa said, taking another egg. 'Now . . . not so much.'

Sara started to say something, then stopped when she heard a car pull up in the driveway. 'That's Jeffrey,' she said, standing up from the table so quickly that her chair fell back. She caught it before it hit the ground, and gave Tessa a nasty look, hoping to cut off the comment her sister obviously wanted to make.

Sara purposefully took her time walking to the front door. Jeffrey was about to knock when she opened the door. She leaned in to kiss him, but stopped when she saw the expression on his face. 'What is it?'

He held up a videotape as his answer.

She shook her head, asking, 'What?'

'Let's go into the den,' he said, leading the way down the stairs. She could tell from the way Jeffrey held his shoulders as he walked that he was angry. His posture was rigid, his jaw set in a firm line.

Sara sat on the couch, watching Jeffrey put the tape in the VCR. He took a seat beside her, working the remote control until the picture came up. Sara recognized the black-and-white format as a surveillance tape.

'The post office in Atlanta,' she said.

Jeffrey leaned back on the couch, and Sara pressed herself against him as they watched the tape. The scene was pretty ordinary, a room full of post office boxes with a table in the center of it. Jeffrey fast-forwarded the tape, playing it when a slim-looking young man came into the frame.

'He could be Mark Patterson,' Sara whispered, watching the kid walk to the back of the room. As he came closer to the camera, the similarity between the boy and Mark was amazing. They had the same lanky build and insolent look about them. The way his clothes hung on his body conveyed the same androgynous sexuality.

Jeffrey said, 'He looks just like him.'

On screen, the boy had a suspicious walk as he crossed the room. He stopped, furtively looking around before opening a box. His back was to the camera, blocking the view, as he took out the contents of the box, looked around again, then shoved the envelopes into the waist of his pants. He tucked his shirt in as he walked toward the exit and past the camera.

Jeffrey paused the tape, freezing the image of the boy on the screen.

'She sent someone else,' Sara guessed.

'He walked out into the parking lot, got into a black Thunderbird, and drove to a local mall,' Jeffrey said. 'No one showed up to meet him. He waited a couple of hours, then used a pay phone.'

'To call whom?'

'Nick traced the number to a cell phone. No one answered it.'

'What about the kid?'

'David Ross, a.k.a. Ross Davis,' he told her. 'Nick ran his prints. He was abducted ten years ago from his home in broad daylight. Missing, presumed dead.'

Sara felt her heart sink in her chest. 'Ten years?'

'Yeah,' Jeffrey said, anger in his tone. 'He was playing outside with his older brother. Dottie came up in her car. They think it was Dottie. Wanda. Whoever the fuck she is. It was a woman. Ross Davis went with her and never came home.'

Sara put her hand to her heart. 'His poor parents.'

'He's not their kid anymore, Sara. He's just like Mark. He won't talk. Nick grilled him for six hours, and the kid wouldn't say a word. Wouldn't even acknowledge that he knew Dottie. He just said he was there picking up some of his mail.'

'Did he have a tattoo like Mark?'

Jeffrey shook his head.

'How old is he?'

'Seventeen.'

'He was taken when he was seven?' she asked.

'He's legally an adult now,' Jeffrey said, and there was such an air of defeat to him that Sara took his hand in hers.

She asked, 'Did you notify his parents?'

'Nick did,' Jeffrey said. 'He couldn't hold the kid, though. It's not illegal to check a post office box, and the car is legally registered to him.'

'Nick put a tail on him, right?' Sara asked. 'At least he can tell the parents where he is.'

Jeffrey nodded, his eyes on the frozen image of the boy. 'Watch,' he said, pointing the remote at the VCR again. He pressed play, and the boy left.

The tape showed the empty room for the next few seconds. Sara was about to ask what she was supposed to be looking for when another figure came on screen. A woman wearing a baseball cap and glasses walked purposefully into the camera's range. She went directly to the back of the room and opened the same box the boy had just checked minutes ago. She took out a couple of envelopes, then tucked them into her purse. When she turned, Sara gasped, even though she should not have been surprised.

'Is that Dottie Weaver?' Sara asked, but she knew that it was. There was no mistaking the woman on screen for anyone else. Then, as if she knew that they would one day be watching her, Dottie lifted up her sunglasses, stared right into the camera, and raised her middle finger at them.

Jeffrey paused the tape.

'Where was everybody?' Sara demanded, sitting up on the edge of the couch. 'Where was the tail?'

'They followed the boy,' Jeffrey told her. 'Nick found a bunch of junk mail on him. The credit cards were left in the box.'

'She can't possibly use them,' Sara countered, still incredulous. 'As soon as the numbers come up in the computer, they'll know where she is.'

'She knows that,' Jeffrey assured her. 'She gave you and Lena all those clues when you interviewed her. It's all a game. She's just fucking with us.'

'Why?'

'Because she can,' he said caustically. 'God damn her.'

Sara put her hand on his shoulder. 'Jeff.' She tried to help, pointing out, 'Dave Fine will never get out of jail. Lacey is home. Grace is dead.'

'Don't comfort me, Sara,' he said, his voice tight in his throat. 'Please.'

She dropped her hand, and he leaned forward, putting his elbows on his knees, his head in his hands.

Jeffrey said, 'She's out there, Sara. She's out there doing this again.'

'Someone will catch her,' Sara told him, but she wasn't sure of this herself. Jeffrey must have sensed the hesitancy in her tone, because he turned to look at her. There was so much pain in his eyes that Sara had to look away.

Sara stared instead at the television, at Dottie Weaver telling them in no uncertain terms that she was not only free from the law, she was free to do whatever she wanted to children like Mark and Lacey Patterson. She was probably doing it right now.

'How could this happen?' Sara asked, but there was no answer to the question. She thought of Lacey, and what the child had been through, and the things that Lacey had experienced but was still incapable of talking about. The thirteen-year-old girl had been through more pain and suffering than anyone should be expected to bear, yet she was still getting up for school in the mornings, going to church with her father on Sundays, as if she were still a child, and not aged by circumstance.

Jeffrey sat back on the couch, taking Sara's hand in his, holding it too tight. They sat like that, neither of them talking, both of them incapable of expressing how they felt, until Cathy stood at the top of the stairs and called them up for dinner.

ACKNOWLEDGMENTS

First thanks as always goes to my agent, Victoria Sanders. It would take three people to fill her shoes. Meaghan Dowling, my editor at Morrow, gave me focus and spot-on advice. Kate Elton at Century was great help as well. The marketing and publicity people at Morrow and Century have been fabulous. Juliette Shapland is worth her weight in Tim Tams.

Medical information again came from Michael A. Rolnick, M.D., and Carol Barbier Rolnick. Captain Jo Ann Cain fielded procedural questions. Ric Brandt offered firearms advice. Melissa Cary told me how to snake a drain. Jatha Slaughter answered my drug questions with honesty and aplomb. Fellow authors Jane Haddam, Keith Snyder, Ellen Conford, and Eileen Moushey were there for moral support. Writer Sal Towse walked with me across the Golden Gate Bridge, an experience I will never forget. Laura 'Slim' Lippman was a good sounding board. Any mistakes I've made are entirely her own.

My daddy has been a constant support throughout my life and I feel lucky to have him. Judy Jordan is a cherished friend. As for D.A. – whatever our souls are made of, yours and mine are the same.

I will always owe a debt of gratitude to Billie Bennett Ward, my ninth-grade English teacher. I am just one of the few people I know who owe their careers if not their lives to a teacher. They should all be praised for the good they do.

Lastly, thanks to the little scamps who go over the posted thirty-minute time limit at my local Y; I have conjured many a violent murder waiting in line for a treadmill.